At the dawn of time, two ancient adversaries battled for control of Earth. One man rose to stand at humanity's side. A soldier whose name we still remember today...

Angelic Special Forces Colonel Mikhail Mannuki'ili awakens, mortally wounded, in his crashed ship. The woman who saves his life has abilities which seem familiar, but with no memory of his past, he can't remember why! With his ship destroyed and a shattered wing, he has no choice but to integrate into her village.

Ninsianna's people have prophecies of a winged champion, a Sword of the Gods who will defend her people against an Evil One. Mikhail insists he's no demi-god, but her dark premonitions and his uncanny ability to kill say otherwise. Even without the technology destroyed along with his ship, the sword he carries is a weapon of mass destruction to a people who still throw sticks and stones. When young women start to disappear, Mikhail must organize her people to fight back.

Evil whispers to a sullen Prince. A dying species seeks to avoid extinction. Two emperors, entrenched in their ancient ideologies, cannot see the larger threat. As intrigues roil the heavens, a tiny Mesopotamian town becomes ground-zero for this fantasy fiction retelling of mankind's most epic story about the battle between good and evil, the clash of empires and ideologies, and the greatest superhero to ever walk the Earth. The Archangel Mikhail.

Omnibus Edition Contains:
—Sword of the Gods
—No Place for Fallen Angels
—Forbidden Fruit

Praise for Sword of the Gods:
"This novel was a fantastic read. I loved the blending of hard-core sci-fi and fantasy genres. It is notoriously difficult to merge the two. The author does this seamlessly however. I also enjoyed the hidden history aspect. What if heaven, angels, & early human history faded to legend and then myth..." –Reader review

"Eric Van Daniken [Chariots of the Gods] meets Star Wars! ... Action packed, romance, humor - it's a fun book to read. And hard to put down..." –Reader review

"Such a clever take on the many angelic and demonic archetype[s] ... Truly original and hard to stop reading..." –Reader review

"Really well written. Great character development. It will have you stirring on the edge of your seat wondering what the gods will be up to next..." –Reader review

"You can't put the book down, it is that good. Just when you think you have figured out the outcome of certain characters, whoops here comes a twist and eye opener..." –Reader review

"I love how Anna brings an alternate universe with enough supporting story to be plausible ... The sex scenes were handled tastefully and the fighting handled with ample gore..." –Reader review

"The Chosen One pops between ancient Mesopotamia and an intergalactic empire. The details of life in the fertile crescent are so well drawn that I felt like I was there..." –Reader review

"It is rare in science fiction to find compelling love relationships like this. This book walks the line between science and fantasy, populated as it is with creatures of legend and powerful shamans. But everything is explained in an internally consistent, scientifically-plausible framework. The non-humans were extremely-well characterized, their gestures matching their physiology. I learned what it feels like to have wings. If you want to soar..." –Reader review

"Interesting how good and evil battle in different times and galaxies and planets. Everything is nicely connected right along with a beautiful love story between two races..." –Reader review

"When a winged man falls from the sky, what do you do? If you are Ninsianna, first you ask the goddess, "Can I keep him?" Then, you stitch him up and fix him breakfast..." –Reader review

"Much better than 90% of current science fiction .... would be epic as a cable series or movie trilogy..." –Reader review

Sword of the Gods:
The Chosen One

by
Anna Erishkigal

Sword of the Gods saga
Book 1

SERAPHIM PRESS
Cape Cod, MA

Copyright 2012, 2020 by Anna Erishkigal
All Rights Reserved

Sword of the Gods: The Chosen One (second edition). Copyright © 2012, 2020 by Anna Erishkigal. All rights reserved. No part of this book may be reproduced in any form or by any electronic or mechanical means, including information storage and retrieval systems, without permission in writing from the publisher, except by a reviewer, who may quote brief passages in a review.

This is a work of adult fiction. All of the characters and events portrayed in this novel are products of the authors' imagination or used fictitiously.

Published by Seraphim Press, Cape Cod, Massachusetts, USA.

SERAPHIM PRESS

Cape Cod, MA

www.seraphim-press.com

Paperback Edition:
ISBN-13: 978-1-949763-46-1
ISBN-10: 1-949763-46-3

Electronic Edition:
eISBN-13: 978-0-9854896-0-1
eISBN-10: 0-9854896-0-X

Cover art: Copyright © 2015 by Anna Erishkigal / Seraphim Press using self-created art, self-taken photographs, and licensed images from 123rf.com, Dreamstime and DepositPhotos. All rights reserved. No part of this cover art may be reproduced in any form or by any electronic or mechanical means, including information storage and retrieval systems, without permission in writing from the artist.

Table of Contents

Book I: Sword of the Gods

Book II: No Place for Fallen Angels

Book III: Forbidden Fruit

HELPFUL STUFF located at the end of the book:
-- The Chess Pieces (cast of characters)
-- List of Species

Prelude to the Second Edition

When I wrote "*The Chosen One*" back in the late 2000's, it was the best book that I could write at the time, and I am still proud of my first-born "baby" as evidenced by the strong sales and positive reviews. But then two things happened: 1) two publishing companies expressed an interest in translating my series into other languages, but I would have to "break them apart into shorter novels" to be financially viable; and 2) I started taking screenwriting classes and had to write the first episode for a proposed television show.

In both instances, I refused to give my readers (or potential viewers) anything less than my best work, so I poured a decade's worth of additional writing experience into breaking apart my book so that each translated sub-book still told a complete story, while also weaving in some of the really cool stuff that came out of my proposed "Sword of the Gods" television series (yeah, it's just a dream, but I'd love to see the Archangel Mikhail on the big screen).

For several years now, the translated editions have reflected this *rewritten* version of The Chosen One. *Sword of the Gods, No Place for Fallen Angels,* and *Forbidden Fruit* have found avid fans in more than a dozen languages. But as for my *English* language original, I have struggled what to do about the book. While the story-arc and characters that were in the original book have not materially changed, the newer version reflects what I'm capable of writing in 2020. So I finally put the question to some of my earliest fans who, over time, have become trusted friends.

"Release it," they said. *"We like the old version, but this is so much better…"*

I hope you like it. It's not often you get a chance to do something you love -- twice.

Dedication

I dedicate this book to all the brave men and women who serve in the armed forces. To you I dedicate the biggest, baddest superhero to ever walk the earth. The Archangel Michael. A soldier ... like you.

You are the wind beneath our wings.

Thank you!

A note about time...

All times in this novel occur chronologically or concurrently unless specifically stated otherwise (i.e., *three hours ago*, or *the present time*). Because the story is told through the point of view of different characters, sometimes there may be a minor time-overlap to get the reader caught up, but all times should otherwise be treated as sequential.

Both the Galactic Alliance and the Sata'anic Empire compute time from the day the Eternal Emperor ascended to the Alliance throne and signed the current Galactic Agreement which divides the Milky Way between the two empires (i.e., 152,000+ years). A.E. stands for *'After Emperors.'* The decimal point after the year is the month, i.e., 02=February. All Galactic Standard dates run concurrently with time as it occurs on Earth unless specifically noted otherwise.

152,323.02 = February 2, 3390 B.C.

A note about language...

The ancient Sumerian language died out in 2,000 B.C. While scholars can translate ancient cuneiform words and guess at the grammar by looking to proto-Indo-European isolate languages such as Lithuanian, we don't know what it sounded like. Unlike the ancient Egyptian language, which the Coptic Christian church fortuitously preserved in some of their prayers, the last known spoken 'high mass' in ancient Sumerian was held around 1,000 B.C.

Rather than risk having this entire series sound like a lame rendition of Shakespeare, I have chosen to have the characters speak in plain language.

Book I:
Sword of the Gods

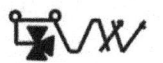

SHE shall send a winged Champion
A demi-god fair and just,
A Sword of the Gods to defend the people,
And raise armies from the dust.

—Song of the Sword

Prologue

Ascended Realms
Emperor Shay'tan

SHAY'TAN

The two old gods bent over the sparkling silver galaxy which spun in space, contemplating their next move. So they had done since time immemorial, god and the devil, two ancient adversaries locked forever in a game of chess.

The larger of the two deities, an enormous red dragon, moved a black pawn into the path of a white rook.

"You're out of pawns!" Shay'tan rumbled.

"Court pieces are worth more than pawns!" His white-robed adversary easily overtook it. "They can outmaneuver them."

"Ahh…." Shay'tan's snout transformed into a predatory grin. "You don't have enough respect for your pawns. No matter how powerful your court pieces—" he moved a second black pawn to overtake the rook "—you will never have enough of them. Especially if you keep throwing them away on trivial moves."

He dropped the unfortunate rook into his growing pile of conquests which lay scattered around his throne like broken toys. The Eternal Emperor Hashem feigned an indignant expression.

"I'm using superior pieces to employ a superior strategy!" he said. "Really, Shay'tan. You think too short-term to grasp the subtleties!"

"Winning is about the numbers!" Shay'tan laughed. "He, who has the most chess pieces, wins."

The Emperor's bushy eyebrows bunched together in concentration. He scrutinized a black rook orbiting a planet deep in the uncharted territories.

"What are you up to, you old devil?"

Shay'tan feigned his most innocent smirk, his long red tail twitching like a cat stalking a mouse. Hashem picked up a white knight and considered his next move. Shay'tan's grin disappeared as he recognized which chess piece his opponent intended to bring into play. His leathery wings jutted outward as Hashem moved the white knight towards his greatest prize.

"White knight to Zulu Sector three…"

"Oh no you don't!"

Shay'tan grabbed his black rook and slammed it down onto the galaxy, knocking the white knight out of the sky.

The room convulsed.

The ceiling disappeared into a canopy of blinding white light.

"Shay'tan!" a woman shrieked. "You were supposed to wait your turn!"

A vague golden shape became visible in the heavens, looming over them as though they, themselves were chess pieces on a much larger board. With a twist of her wrist, She-Who-Is stripped them of their foreknowledge and cast them back into the galaxy to see how their manipulations played out in the galactic empires they both ruled.

Chapter 1

*When men began to increase in number on the earth
And daughters were born to them,
The sons of God saw that the daughters of men were beautiful,
And they married any of them they chose. [...]
The Nephilim were on the earth in those days—
And also afterward—when the sons of God
Went to the daughters of men
And had children by them.
They were the heroes of old, men of renown.*

--Genesis 1-6

February – 3,390 BC

Pain.

Metal pierced his flesh in a gyrating, burning, shrieking ball of sparks. He gurgled in agony as a steel rod impaled his chest, pinning him to the deck of his ship like a butterfly. Blood welled in his lungs, burning and gagging. Its sweet, coppery stench filled the air; the scent of his own impending death.

He tried to remember his name; but there were no memories, only the sensation of falling.

'So this is it? The end...'

A single tear escaped as the ship hit the atmosphere and began to burn; the sting of salt as it passed over a cut oddly sharp even through the heat and pain of his other injuries. *Alone.* He had always known that he would die alone.

The ship shrieked a warning.

He closed his eyes and prayed to pass quietly into the void, to feel his life slip from his body so his pain would end. But even close to death, the part that remembered who he was whispered:

Fight!

Survive!

Live another day.

He clenched his fist around the small, dark figurine he always kept next to his heart. He would complete the mission. He would smite those who had done this; even though he had no recollection of who he fought or what he was fighting for.

Long after he should have passed from this world, he continued to fight for each and every breath.

Chapter 2

February – 3,390 BC
Earth: 12 hours earlier

NINSIANNA

The desert which lay between the two great rivers was an inhospitable place, even during the rainy season. There was little cover here. Only rubble and the occasional desiccated clump of brush, the skeletal remains of long-dead streams, and the distant mountain which their enemies claimed was the sacred abode of their god.

Ninsianna, whose name meant *She-who-serves-the-goddess,* crouched behind a pile of rocks, her heart pounding as three kilt-clad warriors moved dangerously close to where she hid, gathering dried bits of brush to build a fire.

"Why would she come this way?" Tirdard asked.

"She wanted to get away from *him*." Dadbeh said.

"Don't let *him* hear you say that," Firouz said. "He fancies himself in love with her."

"I should hope so!" Tirdard said. "They're supposed to marry at the summer solstice."

"Not if he can't catch her," Firouz said.

"If you ask *me*," Dadbeh snorted, "she ran off with another man."

Ninsianna clamped her hand over her mouth to quell her urge to shout: *'Can't you understand I just don't want to marry him?'* She'd voiced that protest, vociferously, many times, but nobody cared about the wishes of a woman.

'Just think what fine sons you'll have?' Papa had scoffed at her hesitation. *'She-Who-Is looks favorably upon this union. He's the son of a chief. Think what prestige it will bring to merge our two houses together?'*

Well she didn't *want* to be anybody's brood goat! Not for the village. Not even for She-Who-Is!

The conversation cut off as Jamin strode back into the campsite carrying a dead gazelle slung over his muscular shoulders. He was a beautiful man, with a swarthy complexion, a fine straight nose, and the blackest eyes she'd ever seen. Around his neck, he wore a necklace made of lion's teeth, a lion he had killed using nothing but a knife. Every woman in the village swooned at his sexual prowess.

Every woman except for *her*...

She was the only prey he'd never been able to lure into his bed!

His best friend, Siamek, a tall, competent man, set down their obsidian-tipped[1] spears and Jamin's cape.

"You see any sign of her?" Firouz asked.

"Just footprints—" Jamin pointed north-east "—a few thousand cubits *that* way."

"Why would she head straight towards our enemies?" Firouz asked. "Doesn't she realize the Halifians[2] will take her in-hand?"[3]

"Because she's a *woman*," Jamin laughed. "The gods only know what flutters through her pretty head."

Ninsianna picked up a stone, resisting the urge to throw it at the arrogant son-of-a-Chief's head. If not for her 'mental faculties,' he'd be dead right now!

"That's what you get for chasing after the shaman's daughter," Firouz said.

"We all warned you," Siamek said. "Ninsianna is fickle."

Dadbeh laughed.

"Oh, Jamin!" I want you!" The small man spoke in a high, falsetto voice. He turned his head, pretending to be his other self. "No I don't!" He turned it back. "Yes, I do!" He turned back again. "No, I don't!"

Tirdard clamped his hand over his mouth, trying not to laugh.

"The whole while—" Firouz joined in, thrusting out his hips in a woman's walk "—spinning her father's magic."

"Shazam!" Dadbeh wiggled his fingers. "Jamin falls under her spell."

"Fallen?" Jamin snorted. "Hardly. My father favors the match." He stared at the rock where Ninsianna hid. "Typical woman! Too foolish to know her own mind."

He kneeled next to the dead gazelle, took out his water skin and sprinkled a few drops of water onto its head.

"Thank you, brother," he murmured, "for the gift of your life."

The wind picked up and answered in a voice only Ninsianna could hear.

'You're welcome, favored son...'

He sliced into its belly with an obsidian blade, expertly separating the inner organs from the entrails they would leave for the hyenas to eat.

Siamek crouched down next to him and pointed at the scar in Jamin's belly.

---

[1] *Obsidian;* a naturally-occurring volcanic glass, suitable for knapping into spears, knives, and other sharp tools.

[2] *Halifians:* a nomadic tribe who roamed Mesopotamia until the Ubaid tribe displaced them by planting fields. Also called *Halaf.*

[3] *In-hand:* take her as a concubine.

"You looked like that gazelle when I carried you back with your guts hanging out from the auroch[4] hunt—" he spoke low so the other men couldn't hear him. "If she hadn't stitched you back together, you'd be dead. Perhaps you mistook her ministrations for love?"

Behind the rock, Ninsianna held her breath.

Please? Make him listen?

Jamin stabbed his knife into the dead gazelle.

"Which is why we need to bring her back!" he said. "Assur[5] needs its apprentice healer."

He dislocated a leg and handed Siamek the meat. His black eyes bore into his second-in-command.

Siamek nodded. He *never* contradicted Jamin in front of the other men, but they'd been friends long enough that he often spoke up in private. Siamek strode over and placed the meat into the fire.

Jamin stood and faced the distant mountain, his expression vulnerable as the sun raced towards the horizon.

"Where are you?" he murmured.

He placed his leather-wrapped foot on the rock Ninsianna hid behind, studying the horizon, and fastened his cape using an elaborately carved bone pin.

Ninsianna crouched like a prey animal, hidden among the rocks. The wind shifted. Smoke wafted in her direction, carrying with it the luscious scent of roasting meat, spiced with wild garlic and a bit of desert *ajwain*[6] herb. Her stomach growled, reminding her she'd had nothing but *bastirma;* dried, salted meat, for the last three days.

Where would she live? A woman without a village?

No other tribe would dare take her in.

The wind whispered:

'*Will it really be so bad? To be the wife of a future chief?*'

She gripped her hem, torn with indecision. She'd always resisted him, the seduction and the gifts; the way he'd always sought her out like a lion stalking prey. But after he'd gotten injured, a whole, new vulnerable side of Jamin had emerged. Each day, as she'd gone to change his bandages, he would tell her stories about all the places he had traveled, the people he had met, and the wild and beautiful things he had seen.

He'd promised, if she became his wife, she would travel with him.

She'd finally told him "yes."

But then he'd recovered and gone back to being—him!

---

[4] *Auroch:* an extremely aggressive wild prehistoric cow.

[5] *Assur:* a Sumerian city-state located along the Tigris River, later capital of the Assyrian Empire.

[6] *Ajwain:* a wild herb in the same family as caraway seeds.

He'd been in a terrible temper, when she'd broken off their engagement. Maybe, if she explained she'd been frightened? Perhaps he had learned his lesson?

All she had to do was stand up and say, *'here I am.'*

"Hey, Jamin?" Firouz called out. "What are you going to do with her once we catch her?"

"Put her over my knee and spank her," Jamin said, "like her father should have done long ago."

The warriors laughed.

Ninsianna's doubts froze within her chest. Typical man! Say one thing to woo a woman, another thing entirely to impress his friends. She'd been taken in by him once. She would *not* have her better judgment compromised a second time!

She waited until they all sat down to eat and then, very carefully, began to crawl backwards. A tiny pebble skittered and hit another one.

Crack!

Ninsianna froze.

All five warriors looked in her direction. Her heart pounded. She pressed her body into the ground.

Please don't see me!

If they stood up, she'd be exposed.

She whispered the prayer her father used whenever they needed to start a fire and the wood was damp, picturing the solstice fire they lit twice a year. The fire flared up in a great, gusty puff of flame, causing the meat to sizzle and catch on fire. The men scrambled to contain it before the meat turned into charcoal.

Thank you, Mother!

She waited until they sat back down to eat, and then crept backward until she reached a *wadi*,[7] a dry desert stream that only carried water after the most torrential rain. At the bottom lay a dark, moist hole where Dadbeh and Firouz had dug for water. Here, in the desert, water evaporated quickly. Not only had the hole already dried up, but the soil bore a sick, malodorous air.

That sense of *seeing* she'd inherited from her father warned of evil spirits. Anyone who drank this water would be gripped with belly pain and explosive diarrhea.

Ninsianna giggled. Maybe *that* would deter Jamin and his men?

She hurried west, away from Ubaid[8] territory, away from Assur, away from her parents who spoke of obligation and duty. Here in the desert, a

---

[7] *Wadi:* the dry streambed of a seasonal stream.

[8] *Ubaid:* the first tribe to practice large-scale agriculture and build cities along the Tigris and Euphrates Rivers in Mesopotamia.

single traveler might pass unnoticed, but a band of warriors would arouse the attention of their enemies.

Not even Jamin dared risk a war with the fierce Halifian tribe!

The sun dipped behind the mountain which the Ubaid called 'Hyena's Teeth.' The Halifian tribe considered the mountain sacred. If Jamin got caught there, they would draw him off in battle for certain.

The *wadi* grew dark as the land slipped into darkness, but that sense of *knowing* she'd inherited from her shaman father illuminated her path. Every living thing gave off a faint spirit-light, from the smallest blade of grass to the scorpions which skittered among the rocks. Her father claimed women were not supposed to *see*, but she could sense far more than he believed.

She tripped on a rock.

With a cry, she found herself face-down on the ground. Hyperventilating, she picked herself back up and dusted the ochre yellow dust out of her dress. She needed to find shelter. This far into the desert, there was barely any spirit-light.

Oh! How she *hated* the dark!

She squeezed a sip out of her goatskin bladder, now flaccid and limp. If she didn't find water soon, she'd have no choice but to return to the river.

She closed her eyes and raised her palms to the sky.

Great Mother? I am thirsty…

Just to her left, the soil glowed with a faint hint of life. Subterranean water? If she hadn't fallen, she probably would have missed it.

She followed the side-wadi straight towards the sacred mountain. A faint, earthy scent carried in the wind. Ninsianna stopped and sniffed.

Water?

She rushed towards a rock so big the *wadi* had been forced to route around it. Trickling down from a crack, a tiny spring seeped life-giving water.

"Thank you, Mother!" She scooped up a handful and offered her first drink to the earth before dipping her hand into the tiny pool which gathered at its base. It was cold and sweet, with none of the murky stench which indicated evil spirits.

She pulled a wool blanket out of her leather satchel. Out here in the desert, a man could die from heat sickness during the day, and then freeze to death at night, but lighting a fire was the surest way to draw unwanted attention. She leaned against the rock, contemplating her sorry predicament.

Betrothed! To a man she did not love!

The night grew frigid. Ninsianna began to shiver. A pack of hyenas moved closer with their disquieting, laughing bark. She dug out her obsidian blade and clutched it to her chest. A snake slithered out of its burrow and hissed. Out in the desert, an animal gave its death scream.

"Mother?" Her voice warbled. "I know you favor Jamin, but he has a terrible temper. Couldn't you make him fall in love with somebody else?"

What would make the goddess spurn her favorite son? She stared up at the stars.

Shazam! Ninsianna performed her father's magic...

Well she hadn't. Not really. Well, maybe just a little... She'd been stuck caring for him, and he'd been such an insufferable bore.

What if?

"Maybe I could perform a love ritual for him?"

Ninsianna giggled as she rummaged through her satchel for the sacred relics she'd stolen from her father. A sack of bones to divine the future. Dried parrotia[9] to symbolize the spirit. A piece of lapis[10] to symbolize the Earth. Her hand trembled as she touched the last item; a small, clay flask containing a tincture of belladonna berries and poppy pods. *He* claimed, if a woman drank the potion, she'd become lost in the dreamtime. But without it, not even Papa could hear messages from the gods.

"Why should men dictate the fate of women when a *goddess* created all that is?"

She pried the stopper out of the flask and gave it a wary sniff. It wasn't like she could make the situation any worse. Pinching her nose, she gagged down the entire bottle.

Ugh! It tasted like goat urine!

She clamped her hand over her mouth to keep the vile substance down.

A sound like roaring water grew inside her ears. She crawled to the sacred spring and gulped down handfuls of water, trying to force the taste out of her mouth, but the roaring grew louder as the world around her spun. She curled up into a ball, clenching her stomach. Why, oh why, had she performed forbidden magic?

At last the noise began to grow quiet. No. Not silent. Thoughts flowed around her like a gentle river of information. She held her palms up to the heavens and began to chant a prayer:

> O Great Mother!
> You have the power to alter fate.
> At your benevolent hands,
> An ill event becomes good.
> At your right is Justice,
> At your left is Goodness.
> To you, I turn to make entreaty.

---

[9] *Parrotia:* Persian ironwood, a small, deciduous tree in the witch hazel family; used for its anti-bacterial properties and to promote wound-healing.

[10] *Lapis lazuli:* a deep blue, semi-precious stone.

As she chanted, the spirit light which flowed through every living creature began to glow brighter. Gerbils[11] spoke. Scorpions clicked out messages. Even the dung-beetles had something important to say. She picked up her obsidian blade and sliced the black volcanic glass through her palm.

She squeezed three drops of blood onto the small, clay flask; she picked it up and held it up to the sky.

"O Great Mother!" she shouted. "Find Jamin a mate strong-willed enough to put him back into his place? And bring *me* somebody powerful enough to make him back off!"

Out in the desert, a pack of jackals howled, but this time they didn't sound threatening. It felt as though she'd become one with the pack.

A paralyzing numbness crept into her limbs. The chirp-chirp-chirp of insects took on the eerie percussion of a shamanic rattle. Grass and shrubbery glowed brilliantly bright, ringed with phosphorescent green. Slender threads of spirit-light stretched between everything she saw, revealing it was all connected. Even the rocks glowed with a soporific, sleepy light, very much alive.

Up in the heavens, the stars spun in a slow, graceful dance. Tears streamed down her cheeks as they sang a wordless song.

Sister! Join us…

She reached up to touch them.

"So beautiful," she whispered. "When can I join you?"

Time and space became meaningless as images floated towards her on the vast, wide river; a white-robed man seated upon a throne. Behind him rose a magnificent tree out of a lush, green garden, surrounded by a city with three golden suns. In and out of the city, strange creatures traversed between the stars in strange, enclosed sky canoes.

The song changed.

A terrifying darkness slithered towards the center.

'Mother! Help us!' the stars cried out.

The wind picked up.

'Ninsianna…' She-Who-Is whispered. *'I need your help.'*

The goddess drew her eyes to a silver sky canoe. A man battled the cancer which blotted out the stars, beautiful and deadly, unlike any man she'd ever seen. A flash of lightning smote the sky canoe. It tumbled through the heavens, towards a round, blue stone she understood to be her home.

'Will you help him?' She-Who-Is asked.

---

[11] *Gerbil:* a small rodent.

A thrill of excitement rippled through Ninsianna's body.

Would she get to see the heavens?

"Yes, Great Mother," she swore eagerly. "I will help him."

The wind grew brisker, picking up her hair and casting its' cold breath onto her skin. In the eastern sky, a shooting star illuminated the desert as it hurtled out of the heavens. It grew closer and closer, so large it dominated the horizon.

"Mother?"

The star bore down on her, a terrible, burning, hellish object.

It grew larger and larger.

A high-pitched whine split the air.

"Ack!"

The earth shuddered as the fireball passed directly overhead. She threw herself down onto the ground.

WHAM!!!

The shooting star slammed into the earth. A pillar of flame shot straight into the air, mushrooming outwards and covering her with rocks and debris. Rocks the size of fists rained down like hail from an angry god. Her heart beat so fast, she feared it might leap right out of her chest.

Ninsianna covered her head and screamed.

Gradually the rocks turned into dust. Ninsianna stood up and faced the bright, red glow. Was she in heaven, or a strange, fiery hell dimension?

'Go,' She-Who-Is whispered, *'and do as we agreed.'*

Ninsianna picked up her satchel and headed towards the mysterious, glowing object. She reached a place where a landslide blocked off the *wadi*. Just beyond, the stream backed up to form an oasis. Two paths of fire stretched across a bowl-shaped valley towards a glowing shape embedded in the foot of the sacred mountain.

The first ray of light shot above the horizon.

'Here,' She-Who-Is whispered. *'Here you shall teach our champion to become mortal.'*

Chapter 3

February 3,390 BC

Sparks crackled in the smoke, giving everything an unearthly, hellish appearance. The rod scraped through his chest, threatening to drown him in his own blood. Gasping like a fish, he panted small, painful breaths, trying to get enough oxygen into his brain to clear the fog. He couldn't remember his name, but if he didn't extricate himself from this wreckage, he was a dead man!

Crepuscular rays of golden sunlight burst down through a crack in the ceiling, illuminating a beautiful, dark-haired spirit. Light reflected off her skin as she kneeled next to him, wearing the form of a creature of legend.

The source race?

A sense of awe flit into his mind and was gone before he had time to contemplate what 'source race' meant.

"O-kim-oldugunu yardim etmek icin beni buraya gonderdi ise," the spirit said. "Ben sana zarar demek."

The hand which touched his cheek and sympathetic look in her golden eyes was understood. There was no surviving such a wound. The spirit had come to guide him into the dreamtime.

An overwhelming sense of relief flooded his body.

Not alone.

Despite his pain, he smiled as he placed his fate into the spirit's hands.

Chapter 4

February - 3,390 BC
Earth: Crash site

NINSIANNA

What at first appeared to be a burning rock, transformed into a spearhead the closer she got to the fallen star. Even half-buried, she recognized the sky canoe she'd seen in her vision. It glowed bright red like a bed of coals, but the vessel itself did not burn except for smoke which billowed from one of its two chimneys. While she could not find a discernable doorway, a massive crack split the vessel from the ground all the way up to the ceiling right where it disappeared into a landslide.

'Hurry!' She-Who-Is whispered.

Ninsianna squeezed through the crack into a room filled with smoke. The only light came from hundreds of sparks which spat out of spiderwebs dangling from the ceiling. The rising sun shot through the crack, illuminating a bloody man who lay buried beneath a pile of rubble. Through his chest, he'd been impaled with a spear.

"No!"

Sharp edges tore at her hands and knees as she scrambled towards the dying man. A copper stench filled her nostrils, the scent of impending death.

The man reached for her. Blood poured out of his mouth and nose.

"An rás fhoinse?"[12] he said.

She placed one hand onto the man's pale cheek, praying he didn't see her terror. Their eyes met in the murky light, a frightened, dying creature and a stranger. His expression turned grateful.

"Neo-aonar?"[13]

His eyes fluttered shut.

Ninsianna pressed her fingers against his throat. *Please don't die!* Sobs wracked her lungs when a faint heartbeat fluttered against her fingertips.

'Here—' a whisper of intuition drew her attention to the spear which pinned him to the floor *'—attend to the most deadly object first.'*

He wore a peculiar garment fastened to his chest, neither a cape nor a robe. She used her obsidian knife to slice the fabric away from the spear.

---

[12] *"An rás fhoinse?"* The source race?

[13] *"Neo-aonar?"* Not alone.

Once removed, he'd bleed out in a matter of heartbeats, so she had to work fast.

Rummaging through her satchel, she pulled out a bone needle and a bundle of hair plucked from the tail of a wild horse. She'd helped Mama tend to many terrible wounds, including Jamin's, but never had she treated so grievous an injury without the benefit of her mother's guiding hand.

She rinsed her hands with water from the goatskin, and then planted her feet on either side of his torso. She sang the song Mama sang whenever she needed strength, usually when an entire band of warriors came in injured from a skirmish.

> She gathers the divine powers,
> She announces the sacred rites.
> She works with intricate skill,
> As she ministers the injured.

She pictured white light flowing from the top of her head all the way down into her fingers, and then into her feet rooted deeply in the ground. It was forbidden for a woman to use magic for anything but healing, but she'd spied on Papa whenever the shamans came together and talked. It flowed around her, an exhilarating tingle, like water pouring into an urn until the power wouldn't rise any further.

She gripped both fists around the shaft and yanked.

"Hiyah!!!"

The man groaned, but the spear would not release.

She pulled harder, praying and chanting, until the energy grew so powerful her body began to hum. She pulled so hard his torso lifted right up off the floor. The spear made a horrible sucking sound as it slid from his chest.

Ninsianna dropped to her knees, still chanting:

> She takes the bandages and wipes them;
> She treats the bandages with embrocation,[14]
> She mops up the blood and suppuration,[15]
> And places a warm hand on the horrid wound.

That river of information she'd seen in the vision flowed around her now, more clear and powerful than the tentative spells she'd cast away from her father's disapproving eyes.

The man's breath became more labored. Just left of his heart, the flesh sank into his ribcage where the shaft had shattered several ribs. She pressed

---

[14] *Embrocation:* a liniment or ointment.
[15] *Suppuration:* an infection, pus.

two fingers into the hole until she hit a hollow cavity. Her heart sank. The shaft had pierced a lung.

She ran her fingers inside his chest, gauging the extent of the damage. Something pulsated against her fingertips. Ninsianna paused, awestruck as the man's heart fluttered through the delicate lung tissue.

"O Great Mother!" she said, awed "—not even Mama has ever touched a still-beating heart."

Was this what it felt like to be a goddess?

She picked up the bone needle she'd threaded moments before. This wasn't the first time she'd stitched a punctured lung, though in both cases, the patient had died. She stitched in and out of the tender flesh, tuning into that whisper of information which told her what to do. Pulling the flesh shut like a goatskin pampootie,[16] she cut the thread, and then moved on to sew the outer layer of muscle and skin.

As she stitched, she continued to sing:

> She gathers up the divine powers,
> She takes his life into her hands.
> She attaches them to the great garment,
> While speaking favorable words.
>
> She tests the surgical lancet;
> As she sharpens her scalpel.
> She makes perfect the divine powers of medicine,
> She places them into my hands.

The stranger reopened his eyes.

He watched her stitch, his expression strangely calm given the fact her fingers were buried deep inside his chest.

"An bhfuil tú spiorad, teacht a chur mé go harm an réimse an aisling?"[17] he said.

"Don't be afraid. She-Who-Is sent me here to help you."

Since both hands were bloody, she kissed his cheek, hoping he would understand the gesture of comfort. She tied off the thread. He spoke in a language she felt she should recognize.

"Ní raibh mé riamh eagla bás, ach go bás ina n-aonar," he said. *"Tá áthas orm tú ag teacht a thabhairt dom ar an aistear."*[18]

---

[16] *Pampooties:* crude leather shoes.

[17] "Are you a spirit, come to guide me into the dreamtime?"

[18] "I have always feared to die alone. I am glad you have come to help me make this journey."

Chills tingled throughout her body. But each word he spoke came with a terrible, wheezing sound.

"I think the shaft came out the other side." She pointed at her own back. "I have to roll you over. Okay?"

She made a rolling gesture with her hands so he'd understand.

The man nodded, *"Is ea."*[19]

She tried to push him sideways, but a heavy cabinet had come down on top of his legs. She tried to lift the wreckage, but her feet kept slipping on the slippery, bloody floor. She wedged a piece of debris underneath the cabinet. If he could pull his own legs out, maybe she could roll him to see what had happened in the back?

She crawled back next to him. Her hand came down in a pile of bloody feathers.

"What is this?" She tugged at the feathers. "Some kind of cape?"

The 'cape' flapped upward, scattering debris.

"Ack!"

Ninsianna skittered backwards.

A dark shape rose up in the darkened sky canoe. Vaguely wedge-shaped, hundreds of spear-like tips jutted out of the edge as it flapped. It settled back upon the floor, trembling. She stared with disbelief at the enormous brown feathers which had come to rest against her foot.

"You have wings?"

She touched the bloodied feathers and traced them to their origin beneath his back. She stared up at the ceiling.

"You sent me to save a living god?"

The man's brows knit together in confusion, as though he wished to figure out why she wished to hurt him. She glanced at the handful of dark feathers she'd just ripped out of his living flesh.

"Oh! Sorry!"

She touched his cheek to convey she hadn't meant to cause him any pain. His skin felt cold, the pallor of death. With her enhanced vision, she could see his spirit light float halfway between the world of the living and the dead. With each gasp for breath, his spirit-light grew dimmer.

She touched the place where his legs disappeared beneath the heavy wreckage.

"You're too heavy for me to roll all by myself—" she moved her hands to communicate what he needed to do "—I will pull—" she mimicked pulling with both hands "—but you must pull out your own legs. Okay?"

The stranger nodded. *"Is ea."*

---

[19] *"Is ea."* Yes.

She kneeled behind his head and threaded her forearms through his armpits.

"Pull!"

Ninsianna pulled with every ounce of her strength. The man moved his legs just far enough to free them before he lost consciousness. She rolled him onto his side.

Protruding from his back, a pair of enormous, muscular brown wings lay trapped beneath the debris. The wing which had flapped upward appeared to be intact, but the other wing bent backwards at an ominous angle.

"When you sent me a vision of a man with wings," she spoke to the goddess, "I had no idea you were being literal!"

She stitched the exit wound where the shaft had come out the other side, and then moved on to attend to the next most critical injury, his broken wing.

Once, when she'd been little, Mama had saved a hawk. Raptors were sacred to the Ubaid, favorable omens. Papa claimed raptors were the eyes of She-Who-Is. She felt along the bones hidden beneath the feathers. Just below the knee joint, a slender bone had snapped and punctured though his skin.

"It's a good thing you're not awake," she said, "or I don't think you'd let me do this."

She slid the delicate bone back beneath his skin and winced as she ground the bone into place. Lying next to her, the spear she'd just ripped from his chest would make a respectable splint. Now all she needed was some rope. Where, in this temple, would a man keep rope?

Dozens of colorful spiderwebs dangled from the ceiling like roots inside a cave, no doubt dislodged when the sky canoe had slammed into the valley wall. She ripped down several long, colorful strands. While thinner than a rope, the peculiar threads bent and held their shape. She wrapped them around the spear and his broken wing.

What next? Mother! The man is bloody and broken!

His left wrist bent at an unnatural angle. *This* injury was at least familiar. She braced her feet against his side to gain leverage and rammed his elbow between her knees, yanking until his wrist made a cracking noise.

"Mama would do a better job—" she chattered to keep his spirit light from trying to escape his body "—but it's a two-day run back to my village. If I leave you alone, the death-sleep will take you."

At last she had done all she could. Either he would live, or choose to pass into the dreamtime. All she could do was encourage him to stay.

The man's flesh felt pale and clammy; his heart beat unevenly and far too light. To fend off the death-sleep, she needed to keep him warm. She grabbed the blanket she'd brought with her in her satchel and covered him.

The man shivered.

She curled against his side to share her warmth.

Exhausted, she fell fast asleep.

Chapter 5

義

Galactic Standard Date: 152,323.02 AE
Earth Orbit: SRN 'Jamaran'
Lieutenant Kasib

LT. KASIB

The *SRN Jamaran*[20] orbited the blue resource planet which Shay'tan (a thousand blessings upon his name) had sent this battle cruiser to secure. Sata'anic Royal Navy Lieutenant Kasib stared at ship's communications console, a no-frills black and white flatscreen just like the others which ringed the command center, flicking the air with his long, forked tongue as he scanned the reports scrolling in from the planet's surface.

In the commander's chair behind him, shaped remarkably like the pedestal of a black rook, General Hudhafah's sharp dorsal ridge[21] reared in irritation.

"Any word on that Angelic[22] scout ship?" he hissed.

Kasib eyed the reports with his gold-green serpentine eyes.

"We can detect no energy signatures emanating from the planet, Sir," Kasib said. "It appears to have broken up during reentry."

"And what about the wreckage?"

Kasib tasted the air for pheromones[23] indicating General Hudhafah's level of irritation. Like all low-ranking males who served in Shay'tan's armies, he was hyper-alert to the slightest reddening of his commanding officer's dewlap.

"It broke up here."

He pointed at a part of the map, a narrow sea fed by two great rivers in the middle of a desolate swath of ochre yellow desert.

"Calculate the most likely crash area and find the wreckage." General Hudhafah bared his fangs. "The last thing we want is the Alliance knowing what we've found."

---

[20] *SRN Jamaran:* a Sata'anic battlecruiser. SRN stands for *'Sata'anic Royal Navy.'*

[21] *Dorsal ridge:* the sharp fin which runs up a lizard's back, neck, and head.

[22] *Angelic:* a genetically engineered species of half-human, half-aquatic mammal super-soldiers bred to be the Eternal Emperor's air force.

[23] *Pheromones:* secreted hormones that trigger a social response in members of the same species.

Chapter 6

February - 3,390 BC
Earth: Crash site

Pain ... but duller than before. Hadn't a spirit come to guide him into the dreamtime? He found her soft, warm form nestled into his side, her cheek resting on his bicep as her chest rose and fell in the gentle rhythm of a peaceful, *mortal* sleep. He took a deep breath and realized he was still alive.

"Are you my mate?"

He touched the long, dark tresses which had fallen across the woman's face and fished a strand out of her lush, pink lips. The woman had kissed him as he'd stood at the entrance to the void.

If this was the dreamtime, it sure hurt like Hades.

He lifted his arm and studied the splint she'd fashioned with debris and bits of wire. Moving his legs to reassure himself he still possessed them, he turned his head to examine his broken wing. Would he ever be able to fly again? That depended upon this planet's gravity.

Information flitted through his mind. There was something urgent about this planet, but the image departed as fleetingly as it had appeared.

Who was he? What was his name? All he knew was that this woman had taken heroic measures to save his life and now she slept curled up beside him in a manner that felt both alien, and also heart-yearningly familiar. Something about her scent tugged at an instinct, deep within his loins.

Maybe she *was* a spirit? If this was death, it wasn't half bad.

Curling his good wing so as not to wake her, he pulled her closer, wrapping the limb around her like a blanket before allowing himself to drift back to sleep.

*

"O-kim-hayatini bagislamasi icin uygun gordum."[24]

He awoke to find the woman kneeling at his side. Her hands accentuated her words as she poured droplets from a water skin onto a rough cloth and dabbed blood off of his skin. He watched her work, fascinated by her wavy dark hair, olive skin, and unusual tawny beige eyes.

Urgency clawed at his belly with drunken glee.

"Who are you?" he asked.

The woman smiled and said something unintelligible.

---

[24] "Thank you, goddess, for saving his life."

Every nuance of her behavior gnawed at his subconscious. Her shapeless beige dress was little more than a length of cloth belted around her waist and thrown over one shoulder to cover the lush fullness of her breasts. The fabric appeared crude, as were the implements she used to tend his wounds; the tools of a stone-age culture.

By gods! How had she saved his life?

"Who?" He crossed his hands palms-up in the sign of asking a question. "Are you?" He pointed to her chest.

"Nin-si-anna." She held her palms up. "Who. Are. You?" She repeated, word for word.

He wracked his brain, but his mind remained frustratingly blank. Ninsianna repeated the question. How could he explain to someone who didn't speak his language that he couldn't remember who he was?

"I don't know."

"Ninsianna—" she pointed to her own chest. "Idonno—" she pointed at him.

"No—" he shook his head. "I don't remember."

"Ninsianna—" the woman pointed to her chest. "Idonremember," she pointed at him.

"No! I don't know who I am! I don't remember!"

He hit his forehead to emphasize it wasn't working. A stab of pain shot into his skull. He closed his eyes until the vertigo subsided.

The woman frowned until it dawned on her what he was trying to say. She touched his head, the place where it hurt the worst. Underneath his hair, a terrible lump attested he'd hit his head.

Ninsianna resumed her ministrations, dabbing dried blood from his scalp. Every now and again, she paused to pat his wings as though she'd never seen such limbs before. He suspected she explained his injuries to him, but he couldn't understand a single word.

He avoided wincing, not wishing to see her expression of dismay every time he flinched. When she got to his chest wound, she pointed at a pair of silver, hexagonal tags strung around his neck with a sturdy chain.

Pulling the chain from beneath his shirt, he read the information etched into the dog tags in boxy cuneiform.[25]

Colonel Mikhail Mannuki'ili
352d SOG
Angelic Air Force
Second Galactic Alliance

---

[25] *Galactic cuneiform:* the "official business" alphabet of the Galactic Alliance. The inhabitants of Mesopotamia adopted a simplified "pictographic" version of this writing.

Although the information failed to jog any personal recollection, he understood what it meant. The only reason a soldier wore dog tags was so his fellow soldiers could identify his body for burial. While he couldn't *remember* anything, it meant he was part of something bigger.

"I'm a soldier," he said. "A soldier in the Galactic Alliance."

He pointed at Ninsianna.

"You are Ninsianna."

He pointed at his own chest.

"I am Mikhail."

Ninsianna smiled.

"Mikhail?"

"Yes."

She repeated his name several times, and then held out her primitive water skin and pressed it against his lips.

"Icki," she said. The rest was unintelligible except for the word at the end. "Okay?"

Drink, maybe?

"Oh-kay," he repeated.

He gulped down the water until it was empty.

Ninsianna pointed at a crack which split the hull. She tucked the blanket up to his neck and communicated, using her hands, that she wished for him to sleep.

"Oh-kay," he said, uncertain. Was she going to fetch more water?

Ninsianna slipped out of the crack.

As he lay there, it occurred to him just how very vulnerable he was.

Chapter 7

February - 3,390 BC
Earth: Crash site

NINSIANNA

The stream tumbled down from the mountain into the bowl-shaped oasis, a small island of paradise in the middle of the desert, with a thick strip of vegetation which grew on either side of the stream. Unlike the barren desert, it smelled rich and filled with life.

No wonder the Halifian tribe considered this area sacred!

Ninsianna whirled in a dance, formulating clever things to say to her newest patient using nothing but sign language.

"Free! I am free!"

And not only that, a creature of heaven was now forever in her debt!

Her gait turned into a girlish skip as a small shadow fell across her path. An enormous golden eagle swooped into the stream which widened into a pond behind the rock fall which blocked it.

"An omen!"

The eagle dove beneath the surface, its wings splashing water as it came up carrying a nice, fat fish. She laughed as it carried its squirming dinner up into the sky.

She wracked her memory for what little she knew about amnesia. Mama had spoken of such after a warrior suffered a blow to the head. Usually a few hours would pass and then the memories would return, although Mikhail (she said his name several times and decided she liked the way it rolled across her tongue) appeared to be unusually lucid for someone who couldn't remember his own name. Perhaps he'd misunderstood her question? Or was he withholding information? It didn't matter. Either way, She-Who-Is had answered her prayer.

She reached the brook, swollen with late winter rain which tumbled down from the sacred mountain, and refilled her water skin. Her reflection shone back at her, smeared with Mikhail's blood.

He wouldn't carry her into the heavens if she looked ugly, would he?

She waded into the water and sat down in the spot where the eagle had snatched the fish. It was just deep enough to sink up to her neck. She scrubbed the blood from her hands, and then her body, and then ducked beneath the surface to get her head wet. She stood back up, singing a song of freedom as she ran her fingers through her hair to wash out the dried, clumped blood.

> Man comes from the sky,
> He's going to carry me up into the heavens.
> Take me away from here!
> Away from the machinations of men.

All of a sudden, the birds fell silent. She flipped back her sopping wet hair. At the edge of the oasis stood Jamin and the warriors, leaning over their spears.

A tremor gripped her lower gut.

"Ninsianna!" Jamin beckoned. "I've come to take you home."

Ninsianna stood defiantly.

"Home?" she said. "I don't have a home, remember? You ran to your father like a spoiled brat and made him declare I either marry you, or be banished from the village." She gestured at the oasis. "As you can see, I choose banishment. Now go away!"

The warriors gaped at the silver sky canoe which still streamed smoke from one of the ruined chimneys, though at least it no longer glowed red with fire.

"It's an evil omen," Jamin said. "The gods have cast this object down from the heavens."

"And what would *you* know of the gods? Oh he who swore on the goddess he would take me to Nineveh?[26] And then, when his friends laughed, cared more for his own prestige than his future bride!"

Jamin flinched.

"You don't understand. My father—"

"Didn't want you to be seen as taking orders from a woman!" she shrieked. "So instead, you broke your promise. So *I* have broken off our engagement!"

She luxuriated in Jamin's wounded expression as she turned her back on him and crossed her arms. Jamin made a sound like a duck that was having its neck wrung.

The warriors laughed.

"We warned you this would happen!" Firouz said.

"The women in Immanu's house have *always* worn the kilts," Dadbeh said.

"Ninsianna's just angry you won't let her boss you around," Tirdard said.

---

[26] *Nineveh*: a Mesopotamian city-state located at the juncture of the Tigris and Khosr Rivers.

Jamin's cheek twitched as he glanced down at his luxurious four-layered kilt, demarcating him as a person of prestige.

"Perhaps that's why you find her so attractive?" Firouz teased. "You wish *her* to assume your chiefly duties?"

Dadbeh held his hand out by his groin.

"Oh! Jamin—" Dadbeh said in a high falsetto voice. "Empty out the chamber pots, and then I wish you to service me with your tongue."

"Oh, Ninsianna—" Firouz sidled up to him with a false bass voice "—I am your slave!"

He pretended to lick Dadbeh's hand.

"Oh! Oh! Oo-oh!" Dadbeh groaned with fake pleasure. "Don't stop! Oh! Jamin! Next you shall kiss my toes!"

Tirdard bent over, holding his sides as he laughed.

Jamin's eyes grew black with fury. He pointed at Ninsianna.

"You will come away from this accursed fallen star!"

She jutted out her chin.

"No I won't!"

"Oh, yes you will!"

The water splashed around him as he waded into the oasis, as though the water itself wished to flee. Ninsianna ran for the opposite shore, her heart racing as Jamin caught up with her. He grabbed her by the arm.

"Let me go!"

"Your father sent me to—"

"No!" She kicked and slapped him. "You are NOT my chief! And I *will not* marry you!"

The warriors laughed.

Jamin grabbed her by the hair.

"You *will* treat me with respect!"

"I will n—"

Her shriek was cut short as he shoved her face beneath the water. With a panicked shriek, Ninsianna fought to break his grip, but he kept his fingers wrapped securely in her hair. With an ungentle yank, he pulled her back above the surface.

"Do you yield?"

"No!" she sputtered. "I'd rather marry a goat!"

The warriors taunted him.

"Do you need help wrangling that she-goat?" Siamek laughed.

"No," Jamin said. "There's nothing wrong a good beating won't cure."

Ninsianna's blood boiled. How *dare* he treat her with such disrespect? Not only was she the daughter of a shaman, but she was Lugalbanda's granddaughter! A warrior-shaman so powerful he'd stopped the hearts of their enemies!

She pictured all the terrible things she wanted to do to him. The things they'd whispered her grandfather could do, things Mama forbade of her father. The energy she'd felt earlier when she'd pulled the spear from Mikhail's chest surged through her body. Forming a fist, she hit Jamin as hard as she could.

"I'd rather die!" she shrieked.

As she hit him, she pictured hitting him with a rock.

Jamin's head snapped back.

"You, bi—" Jamin shouted.

The rest of what he said cut off as he shoved her face beneath the water again.

Water rushed up into her nose. She kicked and hit with all of her might, but Jamin was more than twice her weight and had her by the hair. With a yank, he pulled her back above the surface.

"Do you yield?"

"Never!" she gasped for breath.

She landed her heel in his testicles.

"Ow!" Jamin doubled over.

The warriors laughed.

"Hey, Jamin," Firouz said. "I think you met your match!"

Jamin's spirit-light turned a furious shade of crimson.

"I will teach you some respect, woman!"

He shoved her head beneath the water, and this time he held her, until it felt as though her lungs might explode. Her limbs grew weak as her body used up its breath. Her heartbeat pounded in her ears. The world grew dark and far away.

'Mother? Help me...' she prayed. *'I'm not strong enough to fight him on my own...'*

Suddenly Jamin loosened his grip. She popped back above the surface, gasping for precious air. All five men stared at the sky canoe. Walking towards them, Mikhail came with his one good wing outstretched, the other dragging uselessly behind him.

"Winged demon!" they all shrieked.

The warriors lifted up their spears.

Down the front of Mikhail's shirt, his blood had dried into a dark brown stain.

"He is my protector," she shouted, hoping to panic them before they noticed how badly injured he was. "Run, before he smites you!"

Mikhail held up some kind of stick. Solid black. Larger than a knife. A bolt of blue lightning shot out of the end like a fireball. Rocks exploded near the warrior's feet, tossing them backwards as though they'd just been rammed by a herd of aurochs. Smoke and a scent like a thunderstorm drifted in the wind. With a shout, the warriors ran away.

Jamin grabbed her and shoved her behind his back. He eyed the spear he'd left on the banks of the stream, no doubt calculating his best chance to regain the high ground.

Mikhail gestured towards them with the strange, black firestick.

"*Lig di dul*," he growled.

A second bolt of lightning landed perilously close to Jamin's side. A burst of water geysered up into the air, and then showered down, jolting them with an unpleasant sensation as though they'd both been stung by a hive of bees. Jamin yelped, but he did not let go of her.

"Get behind me," Jamin said. "I'll protect you."

Mikhail pointed the firestick at Jamin's chest.

"Ninsianna, *teacht anseo!*"[27] He gestured for her to come to shore.

"Over my dead body!" Jamin shouted.

He broadened his stance to appear as threatening as a man could possibly appear whilst standing waist deep in water with no weapon and nowhere to run.

The two alpha-predators stared one another down, both of them eager to claim *her* to be their prize. A thrill of excitement rippled through Ninsianna's body. Which combatant would win? Mikhail had the high ground, but he was also badly injured, while Jamin was in top physical form. She needed to distract him before he realized the dark coloring of Mikhail's shirt was blood.

Forming a fist, she punched Jamin in the face.

She broke free.

Splashing water, she skittered up the banks of the stream. Beads of cold sweat glittered above blue lips as Mikhail swayed, barely able to stand with his injuries. If he lost consciousness, Jamin would surely kill him. She ran into his arms and snaked her arms around his waist as though she embraced her lover.

"Hang on," she whispered.

Using every ounce of healing energy she'd ever possessed, she called upon it now and fed it through her hands. A warm, pleasant tingle rippled through her body. Mikhail stopped swaying.

Jamin looked from her to Mikhail, his black eyes filled with dismay, and then hatred as he jumped to the conclusion Ninsianna *intended* for him to jump to.

"You said that you loved me?"

---

[27] "*Teacht anseo*": come here.

The chief's son stepped towards her, his hand outstretched like a common beggar. Ninsianna lifted her chin and hugged Mikhail in a universal, feminine symbol of *mine*.

"I *never* said I loved you," Ninsianna hissed. "I told you I would marry you because you promised to treat me like an equal! But then you reneged, so I found somebody *better!*"

Jamin stiffened.

Mikhail's firestick hummed next to her ear, higher and higher pitched, like a pack of jackals working itself up into a killing frenzy. He held it out, a shrieking, angry raptor about to go in for the kill.

"Téigh ar!" Mikhail growled. *"Faigh an ifreann as anseo!"*

"You'll regret this!" Jamin said.

He bolted out of the stream and grabbed his spear. Without looking back, he stalked off in the same direction as his compatriots, his expression so dark it gave her chills.

As soon as Jamin climbed up out of the valley, Mikhail collapsed, dragging her down with him. Wiggling to extricate herself from his enormous wings, she spat out a mouthful of black-brown feathers.

She looked at the landslide where Jamin had just disappeared. She *should* feel something. Maybe regret? But she felt nothing. Only relief that their engagement was at an end.

She kneeled on the ground next to her patient. The ground was hard and rocky, so she wiggled her lap beneath his head.

"It's okay," she whispered. "Jamin is gone."

She touched the base of his throat. Although deathly pale, a steady throb greeted her sensitive fingertips. With a sigh, she shut her eyes as the energy she'd felt earlier abandoned her, leaving her as tired and weak as a newborn lamb.

Out here in the daylight, she studied his magnificent, twenty-cubit wings, brownish-black, with sable stripes which grew paler the closer you got to his skin. She ran her fingers through his feathers, relishing the contrast between the long, stiff primary feathers and the soft, downy under feathers.

Wings! The goddess had sent her a man with wings!

She ran her fingers through hair the color of roasted hazelnuts, a sharp contrast to his flesh which was as pale and creamy as goat's milk. Her fingers memorized each exquisite detail. His chiseled features were not those of the Ubaid, but the flint warriors shaped to adorn their spears: sharp, beautiful and deadly. She ran her fingers over his muscular chest and relished each striation, the body of a warrior in peak condition.

Her very own demi-god!

"Thank you for sending a champion to rescue me," she prayed.

She closed her eyes and focused the healing light of She-Who-Is through her hands to speed his recovery, raising the forbidden magic with the sing-song voice of a shaman. Her hands tingled; warmer, even, than when she had prayed to heal the Chief's son.

Oh, thank the goddess! She-Who-Is had answered her prayers!

The birds began to sing again. A frog croaked. Locusts buzzed. The eagle returned and snatched another fish. As it carried its dinner up to the sky, she raised her face up to the sun.

"Can I keep him? I'd *really* like to keep him."

She touched his black-brown wings and frowned.

"But what would a creature of heaven want with *me*?"

Chapter 8

But you said in your heart,
I'll ascend to heaven;
I'll raise my throne above the stars of God,
And I'll sit on the mount of assembly
In the recesses of the north.
I'll ascend above the heights of the clouds;
I'll make myself like the Most High.

Isaiah 14:13-14

Galactic Standard Date: 152,323.02 AE
Haven-3: Alliance Hall of Parliament
Prime Minister Lucifer

LUCIFER

Haven-3 was the third planet in an artificially crafted solar system of one natural sun and two smaller artificial ones so the sun never set in the Alliance capital. Fairy tale spires twisted gracefully towards the sky, sleek, modern buildings of glass and steel and composite plastic so strong, not even an earthquake could shake them from their pillars. From her spaceport, traffic ebbed and flowed to every planet and solar system in the galaxy. At its center stood a massive building, round, so that no delegate ever sat closer to the empty throne than any other.

A tall, serpentine creature which vaguely resembled a dragon ascended the steps, leaning heavily upon his cane. The Speaker of the Commons was a Mu'aqqibat[28] dragon, not a *real* dragon, like Shay'tan was, but one of the species which preceded the formation of the Alliance. He stopped in front of the podium and fished out his spectacles before taking out his gavel.

"The Prime Minister will now address Parliament," he said in a formal voice.

Lucifer ascended the central platform, his niveous white wings draped artfully behind his back like the Eternal Emperor's mantle. Balcony after balcony cascaded upwards towards the dome; each delegate representing a homeworld in an empire which spanned almost half the galaxy. The delegates were as varied as the worlds they represented: mammals,

---

[28] *Mu'aqqibat dragon:* an ancient species of wise serpent, similar in appearance to a Chinese dragon.

insectoids, amphibians and other life forms. Each species had a homeworld where they'd evolved naturally under the protection of the Eternal Emperor until they'd achieved a level of sentience sufficient to earn membership in the Galactic Alliance. Each species had a voice to assert their rights; every species except for one...

His...

The delegates chattered, cutting deals as elected officials were wont to do.

"Didn't we already vote on this deal?" a delegate asked.

The Emperor vetoed it," the delegate next to him replied. "Stabbed his own son in the back."

"I'm not about to override the Eternal Emperor!" the first one said.

"Why not?" the second delegate said. "The sonofabitch abandoned us for two hundred years, and *now* he shows up and wants to be our god?"

Lucifer pressed his lips together, waiting for the General Assembly to quiet down.

The cacophony continued; a feeding frenzy of back-room deals; this vote for that one; cast your vote for this pet project and I'll release your bill from committee. Lucifer closed his eyes and focused on the flow of self-interest which, due to the gift of empathy bestowed upon him by a half-Seraphim mother, allowed him to visualize the delegate's desires.

Enhanced Angelic senses registered the sybaritic tickle of expensive aftershave, aged brandy, and the lingering scent of *todóg*.[29] The acoustics were such that the slightest whisper carried across the chamber. His eerie platinum eyes scanned the coliseum; perceptive, cynical, reflective as he put a name to the strongest of those desires and noted the places he might bring persuasion to bear. At last he signaled the Speaker to begin the show.

"In the name of the Eternal Emperor—" the tall, serpent-like Speaker pounded his gavel "—I hereby call this joint session of Parliament to order!"

The delegates stared down from their lofty balconies. Once already he'd passed this measure by the slenderest of margins. It had ignited such a firestorm that the Eternal Emperor *himself* had intervened to slap it down with a rare imperial veto.

Determination stiffened Lucifer's spine as he ruffled his snow white feathers. He turned his good side towards the cameras which broadcast these proceedings to every television network in the Alliance.

"Today I come to you not as the adopted son of the Eternal Emperor," Lucifer said, "a man who by virtue of an accident of fortune had a voice bestowed upon him because my father appointed *me* to represent your interests—" he lowered his wings into a gesture of humility "—but as an

---

[29] *Todóg:* cigars.

Angelic, a species whose only purpose is to lay down our lives to protect *you*, the naturally evolved races."

He moved to position himself before an enormous, golden Leonid[30] and an even burlier bay Centauri[31] who he'd appointed to stand guard just at the edge of the stage. He turned back to face the cameras which panned like greedy vulture's beaks to follow him, cognizant of the fact their refractive lenses would make it appear the two hybrids stood directly behind him.

"For as long as the Alliance has existed—" Lucifer spoke into the cameras "—the Emperor has relied upon the stick of military might to keep the Sata'an Empire in check."

He gestured towards the lion-man and half-horse-human hybrid.

"To achieve this end, he created four species of genetically engineered super-soldiers: the Angelic Air Force, Leonid Multi-Purpose Fighters, the Centauri Cavalry, and the Merfolk Navy."[32]

He made eye contact with the delegates he'd tagged earlier as impressionable, the ones who stared down from their lofty perches like the ascended beings who forever dabbled in the affairs of mortals. Sunlight streamed down from the atrium like an omen from She-Who-Is, creating a brilliant golden halo around his white-blonde hair and framing the perfection of his too-symmetrical features, reminding the delegates he was the adopted son of their emperor and god.

"For 150,000 years, our military superiority has kept an uneasy balance between the Sata'anic Empire and our own Galactic Alliance," he continued. "But now a new threat has dawned against our Alliance. Not the external threat of Shay'tan, but one of our own making."

He paused to make eye contact with a delegate to his left, and then to his right, before turning back to face the cameras. He lowered his voice as if he revealed a secret, just low enough to force the delegates to all lean forward to hear.

"The armies that defend us, ladies and gentlemen, are a dying species."

A gasp rippled through the assembly, to hear him speak their shame before the cameras, making it official, making their weakness *real*. The perpetual cacophony of self-interest began anew:

"My constituents were angry I voted to outsource our jobs."

"Who cares if the hybrids die?"

"What does that have to do with -me-?"

---

[30] *Leonids:* a genetically engineered species of half-human, half-lion super-soldiers bred to be the Eternal Emperor's multi-purpose fighters (marines).

[31] *Centauri:* a genetically engineered species of half-human, half-horse super-soldiers bred to be the Eternal Emperor's cavalry.

[32] *Merfolk:* a genetically engineered species of half-human, half-aquatic mammal super-soldiers bred to be the Eternal Emperor's navy.

A feisty young Spiderid[33] Lord stood up, a freshman delegate who had not yet learned that when there were cameras present, it was always prudent to exercise restraint.

"YOUR race is dying!" the Spiderid shouted. "Our race is doing just fine!" He turned to the delegates on either side of him as they chortled back a snigger. "So tell Shay'tan he can take his trade deal and shove it up his scaly tail!"

The discord grew chaotic as Parliament twittered like magpies coveting a shiny golden trinket. Such forthrightness on the record was a political blunder, but the freshman lord voiced a sentiment which many not-so-secretly shared.

Lucifer's silver eyes bored into the Spiderid's compound ones as he brought both hands to his heart and allowed his expression to soften.

"Yes," Lucifer said gently. "*My* race is dying. My race, that protected *your* race until it evolved enough to join this Alliance, is dying."

He drew his hand into a fist and stared at it, as though he were making a decision. In the pause, the cameras shifted, zooming inwards, zooming outwards, placing the dispute between himself and the sentiment the Spiderid lord had dared voice into the public eye of a centillion television viewers.

"My race, which kicked Shay'tan off of *your* planet when he tried to annex it, and you came running to *us* for help, is DYING!"

He raised his voice into a shout as he shook his fist at the mouthy Spiderid lord.

"And now that millennia of constant warfare has reduced our numbers *so low* that we now have more pieces of equipment than hybrids in existence to *man* that equipment, my race is coming to *your* race to beg for help so we don't all go extinct!"

He slammed his fist onto the podium, his eerie silver eyes flashing in fury. The Spiderid delegate squirmed in his seat while the others who only moments before sniggered now glared at the young lord, publicly distancing themselves from the foolish upstart. Lucifer gave the mouthy Spiderid a smile that did not reach his eyes.

"It is *good* that the Spiderid species is thriving," Lucifer said. "It means the hybrids didn't sacrifice their lives in vain."

He stared up at the delegates perched upon their balconies like vultures.

"When the Emperor created us," he said, "he declared our sole purpose was to serve the naturally evolved species. We were denied Alliance citizenship because you feared we might abuse the genetic enhancements he grafted onto our DNA."

---

[33] *Spiderid:* a naturally evolved species of gigantic, sentient spiders.

He gestured towards an empty seat, left ceremonially empty to commemorate a planet no longer with the Alliance.

"Once upon a time, the source race which spawned our species still walked among us. Because they saw us as their children, they made sure we hybrids didn't languish without a voice."

"But then, 74,000 years ago, an asteroid hit Nibiru.[34] And just like that—" he snapped his fingers "—all of humanity was destroyed."

He gave his deceased progenitors a moment of silence.

"When humans went extinct, they took with them the closest thing we hybrids had to a homeworld. They took away our voice. And they took with them the genetic diversity we needed to survive."

He spread his arms in the T-like posture of a victim strapped to a Tokoloshe[35] feeding pole. His wings drooped as though they were too heavy for him to lift. He bowed his head, a martyr offering himself as a sacrifice for the greater good.

"As the Alliance expanded, the galaxy looked to *us* to police their problems. So you took our species *off* of your homeworlds and put us into ships in space. "Then you declared hybrids have to serve 500 years in the military, not just 20 like the volunteers, because if we don't get killed in battle, we can live that long."

His voice rose in anger.

"But it didn't end there!" he shouted. "When hybrid birthrates dropped even further, you pulled our females off of your planets and made *them* start fighting, as well!"

He whirled to face the ancient races that had been in existence longer than there had been an Alliance, his wings flared like a raptor. Their base of power depended upon maintaining a slave army.

"And then six hundred years ago you told us it was forbidden to form relations for any reason except to begat offspring to perpetuate the glory of the Alliance!" he shouted. "Or even sire offspring with the same partner twice! Because we've become so inbred that genetic diversity is now an issue!"

He flapped his wings. His beautiful, white wings that meant his species could never have a voice because those wings had not evolved naturally onto his back.

"All because the genetic modifications the Emperor gave us to maintain these—" he yanked out a snowy white feather "—these wings. And the other genetic modifications which enslave our species to serve the rest of you are a *recessive gene!*"

---

[34] *Nibiru:* mythological homeworld of the gods, the Annunaki.

[35] *Tokoloshe:* an aggressive, bear-like species which is infamous for their cruelty and preference for eating their food while still alive, including other sentient creatures.

He threw the feather into the air. A ray of sunlight caught it from the atrium above as though She-Who-Is herself wished to say, *'see!'* The feather floated down in silence. Only the shuffling of feet and an occasional cough broke the silence in the great hall as the feather hit the ground.

"These improvements—" Lucifer flapped his wings "—require so much selective breeding to maintain that we've INBRED OURSELVES INTO EXTINCTION!"

He stepped over to an Electrophori[36] delegate and stared down the conservative religious leader from an ancient world of sentient eels which loathed all hybrids as 'manufactured abominations.'

"*You* can get married?" Lucifer shouted at him. "But *we* can't? Because you need us to make lots of babies who have *these* for your enemies to shoot at without the inconvenience of voting rights?"

Lucifer flapped his wings again. The wind they made blew the delegate's paperwork off of his desk.

"What are we? Animals you breed for slaughter?"

A blue jolt of electricity lit up that section of the chamber as the Electrophori's deadly tail sparked with fanatical indignation. The delegates on either side of the eel hissed at him in disapproval. Several delegates whispered 'hypocrite' just loud enough to be picked up by the cameras.

Lucifer slammed his fist down upon the railing. "Even Shay'tan doesn't do that to his own citizens!"

He whirled to face the cameras.

"And now…" Lucifer's voice choked up as a lump rose into his throat. "Now, the moment a hybrid baby is born, before his umbilical cord is even cut, a representative from the Emperor's youth training academy is there to whisk him away from his mother, whether or not she agrees."

Tears rolled down his cheeks.

"Babies. We indoctrinate babies less than a minute old to defend you because we can't afford to have their parents take a few years off to raise their offspring."

His white wings drooped, trembling with emotion. He turned, eyes shut, away from the cameras and tried to quell the raw emotion which threatened to overtake him. The hall was so quiet you could have heard a pin-feather drop. He coughed and rubbed his cheek, determined not to let them see him weep. His legislative aide rushed out with a glass of water. Lucifer gulped down the liquid and composed his features back into the mask of a professional politician.

"We give all these great speeches about free will—" Lucifer's voice sounded weary "—but from the moment a hybrid takes their first breath, we

---

[36] *Electrophori:* a tall, slender species that can generate an electrical charge to "shock" its enemies like an electric eel.

brainwash them into believing their only purpose is to die supporting the Emperor. And now we can't even give you that anymore, for our species has lost the ability to reproduce."

Total silence reigned in Parliament. A nervous cough broke the air. Lucifer made eye contact with key delegates from the old block that would otherwise oppose him and watched them squirm. Money. It all came down to money. He'd just laid out a moral justification the younger delegates could take back to their constituents and justify voting for the override. Now he needed to spell things out in terms the older delegates cared about.

"Only consider this question, ladies and gentlemen," he said. "If the hybrids die out and are no longer here to protect you, then who will? Who will protect the Alliance when all of the hybrids are gone?"

He let the question hang before them like a bad odor before reciting a famous Alliance slogan.

"As the hybrid races that defend us go, so shall the Alliance."

In the back of his subconscious, his inner voice whispered:

'Guilt. Guilt. Guilt.'

'Fear.'

'Just like a well-crafted television commercial.'

He could practically *hear* violins playing in the background as that small, sarcastic voice which had whispered to his subconscious for as long as he could remember whispered to ram this veto override through Parliament and overrule his immortal father's objections. It was time to end the stranglehold the eternal bickering between the two ascended emperor-gods had upon the citizens of *both* empires. It whispered to save his species. It whispered to save *himself*.

"Never-ending war is not the answer." Lucifer held out his hand. "I am here to offer a better way to achieve peace."

He lifted his wings from their dejected slump. His demeanor shifted from sorrowful repentant to television preacher peddling absolution to a circus-tent full of sinners. He'd pointed out the ugly reality. Now it was time to sell redemption.

"Over the past decade—" Lucifer's wings gave a hopeful flutter "— border skirmishes in certain sectors are down. The Sata'an Empire has left those sectors alone, not because we patrol them with warships, but because those planets trade with the Sata'an Empire."

Lucifer paced, looking each delegate in the eye. He was selling a solution to an ugly problem that nobody wanted to face. He was a contact team sports coach cheering on his team. He spoke quickly so the opposition wouldn't interrupt him.

"If the Alliance expanded this partnership, everyone would win. We win, the manufacturers win, and the Empire wins. Win-win-win.

Everybody's happy. Everybody's rich. And nobody will go to war because their economies are too closely tied to risk upsetting the fruit cart."

The Spiderid who had interrupted him earlier heckled him from his balcony. "That's the rhetoric Shay'tan gave the 51-Pegasi-4 colony! And look what it got them. Shay'tan slaughtered the whole planet!!! *And* the entire race of Seraphim Angelics along with it!"

Lucifer's white wings shuddered with anger and loss. *The Seraphim…* He hid the emotion behind the mask he had built to hide his true self from the world.

"That was 25 years ago." Lucifer spoke solemnly. "It was not Shay'tan's doing. Hashem himself verified it was pirates acting on their own accord."

"So claims Shay'tan!!!" the Spiderid lord rebutted. "An eyewitness reported soldiers wearing Sata'anic uniforms invaded the planet. Not a disorganized band of pirates."

That small, sarcastic voice whispered into his mind:

'He is drunk with power at the thought of snatching the vote. You must treat him like the child he is…'

"So said one frightened 9-year-old boy!"

Lucifer turned his back on the Spiderid and appealed, instead, to the ancient races who were so close to genetic perfection that they identified more closely than any species with his father.

The Mu'aqqibat delegate hit his staff against the floor. Old money. Power. The block of ancient races immediately grew silent. The power brokers would not allow a silly upstart to steal the show. The ripple of silence which moved through the great assembly was unspoken, but it was complete. Lucifer had spelled out the tragedy in terms they cared about … money and power. They would allow him to finish his speech.

"Shay'tan is willing to give peaceful trading companies access to sell products his people need. All he asks in return is that we do the same." He paused to let his words sink in. "Fair is square."

The notion of fundamental fairness was one of the basic underpinnings of Alliance society.

That inner voice whispered:

'They don't -really- care about fairness. Spell it out in the only terms they'll understand. What it will cost them if they -don't- vote for this trade deal…'

"It's either that," Lucifer swept his wings upwards like a raptor swooping in for the kill and gestured towards the cameras as though he was the *Devourer of Children*, "or we need to figure out whose children we'll draft into the military to defend us. Because at the rate the hybrids are dying out, within ten years there won't be enough of us left to defend you anymore."

He pointed at the ancient races.

"It takes six naturally evolved humanoids to fill the shoes of a single hybrid, and those species all have voting rights. So compute *those* numbers when you figure out how much it will cost to reject Shay'tan's peace offering. It's trade agreements or the draft. Your choice."

Lucifer waited until the delegates who'd been blocking his trade proposal made eye contact. The Mu'aqqibat dragon took his staff and thumped it solidly upon the floor. He had won them over.

"I hereby make a motion for Parliament to expand the existing Free Trade agreement to all Alliance territories," Lucifer said. "I move said motion to an immediate vote…"

The young Spiderid lord leaped up.

"Shay'tan conquers newer sentient planets and conscripts their citizens to be his labor force so he can undersell us," the Spiderid shouted. "It's little more than slavery!"

That small sarcastic voice whispered:

'It's convenient how they call what Shay'tan does slavery, but overlook the 500 years of forced military service required of hybrids.'

"What Shay'tan does within the confines of his own empire is irrelevant," Lucifer said aloud. "We are ratifying a trade deal, not submitting to Sata'anic Rule."

The other delegates began to waffle. With his *gift,* Lucifer could hear the delegate's thoughts.

"I'm up for re-election."

"Unemployment is up to 17%."

"Why should I support him when his own father voted against him?"

Lucifer's wings drooped.

'You're losing them,' his inner voice whispered. *'Promise them something they can bring back to their constituents and say they did the right thing…'*

Lucifer watched the energy in the room shift away from him. As much as he hated his own inner cynic, it was always right.

"It will give our besieged hybrid military a chance to replenish their ranks!" he shouted.

He could *feel* the moment the energy shifted back, but his victory rang hollow because death in battle was not the problem, but pure inability to reproduce. But fewer wasted lives would buy the hybrids time, and time was what he desperately sought.

The Spiderid lord shouted a losing challenge.

"If you open Alliance markets to unfettered trade, money will flow into Shay'tan's coffers. He will use it to build up his military. Our industry will be decimated and our standard of living will be reduced to poverty."

"Oh, shut up!" several delegates hissed at him. "Do you think we want *our* kids to be Hashem's cannon fodder?"

"Shay'tan won't *have* to defeat us in battle," the Spiderid shouted. "This resolution will allow him to simply bankrupt and buy us!"

Lucifer interrupted before things could get out of hand.

"We have a choice," Lucifer shouted. "Are we going to tell our hybrid soldiers we don't *care* if they go extinct so long as they continue to protect us while doing it? Or will we take charge of this situation and say NO MORE WAR!!!"

He swung his arms upward and gestured towards the cameras the way his immortal father did whenever he summoned lightening.

"Who wants to vote for peace?"

"Ay!!!" the delegates cheered.

"Any opposed?" the Speaker of the Commons asked.

"Nay!" The young Spiderid Lord's voice rang alone.

He was not the only delegate who opposed the measure, just the only one naive enough not to simply abstain.

"The Aye's have it!" the Speaker of the Commons shouted, banging on his podium with his gavel. "The free trade agreement passes!"

Lucifer bowed, thanking the legislators as they filed out past him, including delegates who had concerns they wanted addressed. He could *feel* the positive energy flowing off of the crowd, making his head buzz with power. *This* was what his father had trained him to do from birth, creating the position of Prime Minister and putting him in charge of the day-to-day politics of running the Alliance. Lucifer snorted with disgust. Hashem wouldn't deign to muddy his godlike consciousness dealing with the lesser affairs of mortals!

The mouthy Spiderid pushed his way through the crowd.

"I need to speak to you!" he said.

That inner voice whispered:

'Get rid of him. If you don't, he'll keep raising his point until people listen.'

Lucifer feigned friendliness.

"What can I do for you?"

He honed his gift to *listen* to what wasn't being said beneath the young Spiderid's voice. Images leaped into his mind. Concerned constituents. Impoverished families.

Lucifer formed an image, and then clapped the young Lord on the back.

"Make an appointment with my Chief of Staff," Lucifer said. "We'll see what we can do about filing an addendum."

Power flowed through his voice, into the gullible young Spiderid Lord's mind.

'The Prime Minister is taking me seriously. If I work with him, he'll elevate me to a position of power.'

The young Spiderid Lord's palps spread wide in a pleased grin.

"Yes, Sir! I'll have a proposal on your desk tomorrow morning."

A dirty-winged Angelic appeared at his side. Average height, with dishwater blue eyes and unremarkable wings, everything about Chief of Staff Zepar communicated obsequiousness except for the cruel sneer which sometimes graced his lips.

"Sire?" Zepar said.

Lucifer stared at the doorway, eager to escape.

"If you'll excuse me," he said to the young Spiderid, "I'll let you and Zepar discuss the particulars."

He forced his way past the cameras, smiling and waving to the cheering throngs. As soon as he got into the chapel, he leaned back against the wall and shut his eyes.

'See? I told you we could do it.'

"Oh! Shut up," he whispered to the small, sarcastic voice. "All we need is time."

He stared up at the statue of the Eternal Emperor which stood behind the empty throne which was theoretically occupied whenever Parliament needed a tie-breaker, but in reality had only been occupied *once* in the last 225 years, two weeks ago when the Emperor had appeared to veto his earlier trade deal.

"Try and veto *that*, father," Lucifer said.

His words rang hollow. Trade deals weren't going to *fix* his species' problem. He needed his father to *be* a father and start caring about the workings of his empire.

His Angelic Chief of Staff followed him into the room. Zepar glanced nervously at the statue of the Eternal Emperor which overlooked them.

"Sire," Zepar asked. "Shall I ask the Party to cut off all funding to that little Spiderid pain in the ass before the next election?"

"Do it," Lucifer sighed. "And see what dirt you can dig up on him, even if you have to make it up. I want negative reports leaked to the media by nightfall."

"Yes, Sire," Zepar clasped his hands together. "Consider it done. Now … your next appointment is at 3:00 p.m. A cadet right out of the academy…"

Chapter 9

February - 3,390 BC
Earth: Crash site
Colonel Mikhail Mannuki'ili

MIKHAIL

The pleasant tingle of fingertips caressing his cheek sank deep into his subconscious, along with the hypnotic sound of Ninsianna's voice. Gods, it hurt to breathe! He couldn't remember what it felt like *not* to hurt. But so long as it hurt, he knew he was still alive.

Mikhail opened his eyes.

The harsh, golden sun had shifted to sit upon the western rim of the valley. Lengthy shadows indicated he'd been unconscious for quite some time. The scent of fresh-crushed leaves wafted up from the wound in his chest. Medicinal herbs? Yet more proof that this was the source race.

Source race. Source race?

The thought flitted through his mind and left before he could grab hold of it. What in Hades did *that* mean? He had the urgent feeling he was supposed to communicate that piece of information to *somebody*, but he couldn't remember who, or why it was so important!

He looked up into the face which stared at him upside down.

"Hello?" He searched her unusual tawny-beige eyes.

She murmured something which could be hello, or thank you, or I want to smash your skull in with a rock, but by her smile, it appeared to be gratitude.

"Who was that?" he asked, knowing she couldn't understand him.

"Who?" She pointed in the direction her assailant had run away. "Who? Jamin."

Her nose wrinkled up as she gave him a sheepish grin. A disgruntled former boyfriend, perhaps?

"Who—" he pointed in the direction the man had disappeared "—Jamin?"

Ninsianna nodded. "Jamin."

Mikhail studied the way her entire body became animated when she spoke. She appeared to share the same underlying non-verbal body language as his species. Not wanting to make any assumptions, he nodded and said "*sua*, and then shook his head side to side and said "*aon*." He did this several more times until she understood he meant yes and no.

"Yes, *sua*, Jamin!" She pinched her nose as if blocking out a bad smell, and then she laughed, a delightful, musical sound.

Pleasant warmth tingled throughout his body; wherever she touched him, he could feel a lessening of pain.

"Let's get back to the ship?"

He attempted to sit up and groaned.

"Up," she said in her own language, pointing up.

She helped him to his feet, laughing with delight as she experimented with the unfamiliar words. He flared his good wing for balance. She propped herself beneath his armpit, a doll-like crutch, wrapping one arm around his waist to stabilize him as she turned him to face his ship.

A sick feeling settled into the pit of his stomach. Not that he could *remember* what his ship was supposed to look like, but it lay semi-buried against the valley wall, partially covered in rubble from a landslide. The nose cone disappeared completely into rocks, the back bent at a funny angle, causing the crack, and a long, dark weapons blast had burned off the name of his ship in the same shot which had taken out one of the engines.

"I suppose that belongs to me?"

He glanced down at Ninsianna, who viewed the wrecked ship with eager, child-like eyes.

"Who else would it belong to? The question is—" he looked up "—who shot me down?"

Chapter 10

Galactic Standard Date: 152,323.02 AE
Earth Orbit: SRN 'Jamaran'
Lieutenant Kasib

LT. KASIB

Dozens of viewing screens surrounded the *SRN Jamaran's* bridge. Most displayed grainy black-and-white footage, some of it body cameras carried by Sata'anic soldiers, while other screens displayed bug-eye views from three suborbital drones. Lieutenant Kasib placed his clawed hand on the joystick and piloted one of the drones to circle a primitive mud-brick village surrounded by cultivated fields.

In the command chair behind him, General Hudhafah leaned forward, his gold-green eyes aglow with excitement.

"Is that...?"

"Grain, Sir," Kasib hissed with excitement. "You can *see* the seed heads ripening."

He piloted the drone to skim the meter-high grass. Cereal grain! Millions of light-years from the nearest known colony!

General Hudhafah's sharp dorsal ridge reared into a thoughtful, not threatening, crown.

"What's the status of the away parties?" he asked.

"Both report extensive stores of minerals, Sir." Kasib tapped one of the screens to pull up the latest report. "Cobalt. Iron. Pristine stores of uranium. Almost limitless water. And extensive flora and fauna."

Hudhafah's tail twisted around the edge of his commander's chair, thoughtful, calculating, aggressive, brilliant...

"And what about the grain?"

Kasib understood what the General did not voice in the presence of the lower ranking men. *How low are our supplies?*

Kasib dared make direct eye contact with his esteemed commanding officer, one of Shay'tan's most decorated, and highly-ranked generals.

"It appears the planet is fully habitable, Sir."

The other crewmen, lizards and other Sata'anic species, all stopped pretending not to listen and leaned inward, waiting to hear what the general had to say.

Hudhafah glanced at the first image the away party had radioed back. A wingless Angelic male. The broadcast had caused the Angelic to blow his cover when he'd increased power to spy on their scans. On any *other* planet, natural radio wave static would have masked his equipment, but out here in Zulu sector, there was little subspace interference and the planet had *no* advanced technology. Since then, the away teams had discovered thousands of the creatures, scattered across the planet in primitive tents, huts, and even villages. The Alliance would come for this planet, for sure.

The question was, could they hold it this far from the Sata'anic Empire?

This far from their supply chain.

This far from the next-nearest habitable world?

"Sir?" Kasib asked. They were all just *waiting* for the order.

General Hudhafah's dewlap reddened into a deep, dignified burgundy.

"Set up a Forward Operating Base," he said gruffly. "Someplace *warm*. And near productive fields."

"Yes, Sir!"

With a genuflection to his forehead, Kasib pushed the talk button. A thrill of pride rippled through his body as the P.A. system hummed. Hudhafah was giving this honor to *him*. A low-ranking nobody! He poured every ounce of veritas he possessed into his voice.

"Attention all crew," he spoke clearly and crisply. "General Hudhafah has ordered annexation. I repeat. Begin Earth annexation. We shall civilize this planet for the glory of our god."

He genuflected again.

"Shay'tan be praised."

Throughout the ship, the metal echoed with cheers. There would be glory, and plunder, and honor for certain! This was the kind of expedition every soldier dreamed of.

Metallic *thunks* resonated through the ship as the docking clamps which kept the smaller troop carriers attached during hyperspace disengaged. The display screens captured two dozen smaller, boxy shapes detach themselves from the *Jamaran's* hull and race towards the earth.

It now belonged to the Sata'anic Empire.

Chapter 11

February – 3,390 BC
Earth: Assur

JAMIN

A shooting star darted across the pre-dawn sky, illuminating the empty desert.

"Keep moving!" Jamin ordered.

The men continued jogging as the star shot overhead.

"How many does that make?" Firouz asked.

"Twenty-two," Siamek said.

"Where do you think they're all going?"

Jamin glanced over his shoulder, waiting to see if *this* star would crash, but it disappeared over the western horizon. They'd seen many shooting stars the last several hours, but none came down in the desert, at least not close enough for them to see the sky erupt in fire again.

"I have a bad feeling about this—" Siamek huffed through heavy breath. "Never have we seen so many all at once."

Jamin sped up, forcing the men to match his pace.

A stitch in his side begged for mercy, but he forced his trembling muscles to keep moving. All that mattered was the frantic pace of his heart. The sun finished rising and moved towards its apex, mercilessly beating down on them, but he refused to let his men rest.

At last Assur rose out of the desert, a gleaming, golden fortress with houses built with the outer walls all joined together. They were made of mud-brick, mortared smooth to deny the enemy a foothold, with windows and doorways all facing inward. It would take four men, standing one on top of the other, to reach the rooftops. Rooftops patrolled by men wielding atlatls[37] and spears.

Not that it would matter to an enemy with wings...

"Faster!" he ordered.

The warriors tightened into a tight-knit group, heartened by the sight of home. He'd made them run through the night with very little rest. The *elite* warriors...

The winged demon had defeated the best warriors this village had!

---

[37] *Atlatl:* a "throwing stick." It increases the velocity of a lightweight, slender spear.

They approached the outer gate, a ten cubit tall monstrosity built of the hardest cedar, a man's-foot thick, with two massive tree-trunks anchoring the gates into the adjacent houses. No army had ever breached the walls of Assur. Not since Lugalbanda had performed great magic to make their walls impenetrable.

Ninsianna's grandfather…

And now she was under control of the enemy.

"Ho! Jamin!" the sentries called down. "I see Ninsianna gave you the slip?"

Disembodied anger boiled up into his veins.

"She's been kidnapped!" he snapped. "Raise the alarm! Order the warriors to assemble."

The swarthy-skinned sentry lifted a ram's horn to his lips and blew a deep, throaty warning. *Beware. Beware. Beware.* It reverberated through the village, into the pounded earth streets. Villagers toppled out of their houses, anxious to see who had raised the alarm.

"Step aside," Siamek shouted. "We make our way to the chief!"

"Did you see them?" An old woman pointed upward. "Did you the stars falling from the heavens?"

Jamin's chest heaved as they wound through the concentric inner rings to reach the central square. Siamek and the other warriors bent forward, holding their sides from the killer pace he had set, but Jamin held himself erect, gasping to control his breath. As their future chief, it was *his* job to lead them into battle.

His father, Chief Kiyan, stepped out their front doorway, wearing the five-fringed kilt which marked him as their *chief*. Behind him came Immanu, Ninsianna's father, wearing full ceremonial attire, no doubt summoned to interpret the omens.

"What seems to be the problem, young *Muhafiz*?"[38] Immanu asked.

A lump rose in his throat as he pointed the way they had come.

"A winged demon has come to take our women!"

---

[38] *Muhafiz:* literally "guardian." A title usually given to a chief's eldest son, military leader and presumed heir.

Chapter 12

February – 3,390 BC
Earth: Crash site
Colonel Mikhail Mannuki'ili

MIKHAIL

A small, dark-winged Angelic stares across the chess board, his blue eyes sullen because he doesn't understand the game. An anxious tick counts out the seconds. He doesn't speak. But then, he never does.

"Tá sé do bhogadh,[39] Gabriel," I say.

The boy picks up his black bishop and makes an L-shaped move to capture my white queen.

"Ní sin an dóigh go bhfuil píosa ceaptha a bhogadh!" I chide him. That's not the proper move!

The boy stands up, his expression dark. With a chubby arm, he sweeps the chess pieces off the board. The pieces tinkle onto the floor, the seconds counted out by the too-slow clock.

A knock interrupts my rebuke. The door explodes inward. Backlit by the sun stands the largest lizard I have ever seen.

He raises his arm and points at the chess board.

In his hand, he carries a sword…

*

Mikhail bolted upright and swung at the phantasm, but already the dream had faded, leaving him with nothing but the sword in his hand and the memory of a pair of sullen blue eyes staring across the chess board, gripping his white queen. His chest heaved as he fought a sense of rage and loss.

"Not real, not real, not real, not real…" he gasped.

Pain stabbed into his lung, reminding him he was supposed to be dead.

He took long, deep, shuddering breaths, fighting the urge to kill someone, to hunt them down and destroy them. The emotion sat like rotted meat, screaming at him to *do something*. But the memory had already sunk back into his subconscious, a foul creature lurking beneath rancid, swampy water.

He glanced at the fair creature which lay, asleep, in the bunk across from him. Wingless. Female. Swarthy complexion. Lush, pink lips. And a

---

[39] *"Tá sé do bhogadh."* It's your turn.

matching pink nipple which had escaped from the blanket she'd slid beneath last night, utterly naked except for a loincloth, leaving him gaping like an idiot.

Her chest rose and fell in a peaceful sleep, oblivious to his distress.

Oblivious to the tightening in his loins.

"Not real," he whispered.

He wasn't sure whether he meant the nightmare, or the sleeping woman.

He stared at the weapon which had found its way into his hand. Long and slender, it had materialized right out of the nightmare, a primitive weapon on a modern spaceship. He had no memory of it, other than the hilt felt familiar, but he knew it was his. It felt *good* there. Powerful. Insurance against the boogieman.

Ninsianna murmured something in her sleep. He closed his eyes and tried to remember a life before her, but his memory started, and ended, with his first image of her, a benevolent spirit stepping out of a golden ray of sunlight.

He sheathed the sword before he terrorized her more than he already had by firing his pulse pistol at her boyfriend. *He* might not have a past, but she obviously did. It was angry, and jealous, and he was certain they hadn't heard the last of the black-eyed man she called Jamin.

The room spun as he kicked off the blanket and slid to the edge of his bed, wincing when his broken wing banged against the empty upper bunk. The splint forced his wing into an awkward angle, making it difficult to maneuver in the tight confines of his ship. When she'd re-splinted it last night, he'd almost passed out from the pain.

Ninsianna rolled towards him, causing the blanket to slide completely off her breast. His crotch tightened. *She* didn't have inhibitions against nudity, but *he* obviously did, because every time she came near him, it felt as though a thousand bells and alarms all went off at once.

"You'd think I've never seen a naked woman before?"

Not that he could remember. He couldn't remember anything. Not even his own name. For all he knew, he'd stolen the dog tags from some poor, slain soldier's body and was nothing but a thief?

"No," he whispered. In his gut, he knew that wasn't true.

He took shallow breaths until the sense of vertigo subsided, unable to fully inflate his lung. The only reason he hadn't bled out was because the accursed ceiling strut had stemmed the flow of blood until she'd pulled it out, and then she'd had the wherewithal to stitch him back together, quick.

Across the aisle, Ninsianna's pink lips curved up into a smile. His *own* lip twitched upward, an awkward gesture, unfamiliar, as though he'd never done it before. He suppressed the emotion. There. That felt more natural. Watch. Don't react. Observe without making it obvious he studied her.

Who was she? Why had she saved him? And why did it feel like he'd just won the mother of all galactic wagers?

Every ounce of training, and he knew he must have training by virtue of the *Colonel* stamped onto his dog tags, warned him to exercise caution in the face of the unknown.

That tightening in his crotch grew more urgent, almost frantic. Maybe it *wasn't* arousal? When was the last time he'd visited the latrine, anyways?

He glanced at his wrist-computer, partially buried beneath the sleek, composite splint he'd found in his first responder kit.

Two days?

He'd been asleep for two whole days since Ninsianna had half-carried him back into his ship? No wonder it felt like his bladder might explode.

He heaved himself up, careful not to knock into Ninsianna with his splinted wing. A sense of vertigo threatened to topple him, but he gripped the edge of the bunk and ordered his feet to carry him forward.

Move, soldier! Onward, march! That's an order Colonel Nobody!

The amount of effort necessary to keep one foot moving in front of the other shoved all thought of memory loss out of his under-oxygenated brain. He stumbled into the galley kitchen, dimly lit by a couple of tiny LED lights, and navigated through debris cast out during the crash. Deep within his bones he *knew* he would never tolerate anything this disorganized. While he couldn't *remember* his ship, his body *knew* exactly where everything should be, especially the latrine.

He urinated in the hopper without thinking about it or even wondering where, in the room, it would be. When he touched the handle, the substance disappeared, but the biomatter recycling system failed to give a reassuring hum.

He stared into the mirror.

The face which stared back at him was neither familiar, nor unfamiliar. It didn't feel alien, but it didn't feel like anything which belonged to him, either. Only his eyes. Those were similar to the boy in the nightmare.

"Who are you?" he asked.

The man in the mirror's lips moved at the same time that his did.

He reached out and traced his features. Dark brown hair, cropped into a short cut. Chalk white skin, mostly due to blood loss. High cheekbones. A straight nose. No beard, not even a shadow of one, unlike the men who'd attacked Ninsianna.

Dried blood clung to his skin despite Ninsianna's attempts to wash it off. More blood seeped into the clean shirt he'd changed into last night—no— three nights ago. His broken wing had solidified into an ugly, brown clump that smelled like a slaughterhouse.

"You're out of uniform, soldier," he told the man in the mirror.

"Yes, Sir," the man in the mirror answered back. "I'll get cleaned up, Sir. Just as soon as I remember where my uniforms are stored."

His hands found the faucet without any thought or fumbling, but when he turned the handle, nothing happened.

He stared down at the sink with dismay. Hadn't it worked last night?

Three nights ago, he corrected himself.

Had it really been that long?

He stared mournfully at the sonic shower. For all he knew, his species never took a bath, but from the way he cringed every time the stiff, bloody fabric brushed against his leg, he suspected he tended to be fastidious in his grooming. He could almost *feel* the water biting into his skin, soothing away his pain.

"No problem—" said the man in the mirror. "As soon as you can walk without stumbling face-first into the dirt, go outside and bathe in that stream."

In the cupboard he found a spare uniform. Olive drab cargo pants. A matching shirt. Clean underwear. Socks. All impeccably clean and folded to fit in a compact space.

He took it out and placed it on the sink.

"So what else can you tell me, soldier?" he asked the man in the mirror.

The man in the mirror stared back, his blue eyes worried.

He stripped off his shirt and stared at the gaping hole in his chest. Red and angry, it sank past two shattered ribs which would probably never heal. Primitive black thread pulled the hole together like the mouth of a purse. The skin had begun to fuse at a rate he suspected was far faster than normal.

At least he'd stopped coughing up blood.

He pressed his fingers against the savaged flesh, past the ribcage, into parts of his body no mortal creature was meant to touch. The flesh pulsated rhythmically against his fingertips. It was a good heart. Strong, despite its brush with death. Whatever the reason, he'd been given a second chance.

A chance to *do something*.

It screamed at him with every heartbeat.

Complete the mission. Complete the mission. Complete the mission…

It might help if he could remember what the mission had been?

One by one he transferred the rank pins over to his clean shirt. A pair of silver wings which said *'Protect and Serve.'* A golden leaf which he *knew* meant *'Colonel'* even though he had no memory of ever leading men. And the final pin, a circle around a tree which said *'Second Galactic Alliance,'* along with the inscription, *'In light, there is order, and in order there is life.'*

He fondled the tree. It *meant* something. He knew it. While he couldn't *remember* it, deep within his gut an emotion whispered *'this is something you will serve with your dying breath.'*

Gingerly, he undid the modern wrist brace he'd used to replace the splint. While less swollen than three days ago, the flesh had turned an ominous shade of black and purple. He pressed against the bone and was rewarded with a mind-shattering stab of pain.

"Yup. It's broken."

He pulled his clean shirt over the broken arm, rolled up the sleeve, and then slid the composite brace back over his wrist. A scar testified he'd broken that wrist before.

He pulled tight the straps, and then fished out some analgesics out of the medical kit. He swallowed them without water since the faucet wasn't working.

If only he had a proper brace for his broken wing?

The limb reared up behind him as far as the knee-joint, and then it stuck out stiffly to his wingtip, five meters of feathers trapped uselessly in a primitive brace. His long, brown primary feathers jutted helter-skelter. Yeah, they'd grow back. But in the meantime, the broken feathers would destabilize him.

He picked up a feather-brush and preened each feather, straightening the vanes which weren't outright broken, and picked out the dried blood. A sensation of dread settled into his gut. Did Ninsianna know what she was doing? To splint a limb which she, herself, did not possess? What if he wasn't able to fly again? He had no way to ask her. Right now, their vocabulary was limited to perhaps three dozen words.

"Computer?" he asked. "Analyze her language?"

The AI remained silent.

Did the ship even *have* an AI?

Of course it did. One didn't fly across the heavens without some form of advanced computing.

He set a goal. *Fix the computer.* It would tell him who he was, and in the meantime, it would keep his mind occupied with something other than his distressing *lack* of thought.

The dried, bloody cargo pants scraped against his lower body like a harsh, iron suit. The new pair felt soft and crisp, worn before, but not too often. He finished transferring over the rest of his equipment: gun belt, survival knife, pulse pistol.

He held up the weapon he'd fired, purely by instinct, at Ninsianna's unwelcome 'friends.' The power indicator light blinked like an angry red eye.

He was low on ammunition…

He felt for a spare power cartridge, but his side pouch was empty.

"Computer," he said. "Inventory the ship."

The computer's silence was almost as terrifying as the gaping emptiness within his own mind. He'd been shot down on this planet and had no idea who his enemy was. Had he sent a distress beacon? How would he defend himself if that Jamin fellow came back?

Without his memory, how long could he survive?

He finished buttoning up his uniform and stared at the stranger in the mirror. There was something missing. While he couldn't remember it, he *knew* by the way his hand kept creeping up to touch his chest. Something which belonged inside his pocket wasn't there.

What?

His mind remained frustratingly, maddeningly blank.

He fished through the bloody shirt he'd just pulled off his body, but the pockets were empty, as were his pants. Nor had it fallen upon the floor, whatever *it* was.

"Maybe it's not important?"

His empty hand said otherwise.

He stared at his reflection, making faces, until the man in the mirror settled into an unreadable expression he knew, deep down in his gut, was his natural way of relating to the world.

His wrist computer beeped. He stared at the display screen.

GST - 152,323.02 - 05:00 - Light Emerging

Oh-five-hundred? Time for a soldier to get up. Light emerging? Wherever he had come from, it must now be sunrise.

The digital display changed from 05:00 to 05:01. That small change of time, only a single minute, instilled terror in a way his injuries had failed to do.

Three days since he'd crashed? And nobody had come looking for him?

Did anybody even care that he was gone?

Chapter 13

Galactic Standard Date: 152,323 AE
Command Carrier: 'Light Emerging'
Border between Zulu and Tango sector
Colonel Raphael Israfa

RAPHAEL

Smaller and sleeker than other command carriers[40] in the Angelic Air Force, the *Light Emerging* belonged to the 42nd Intelligence Division, and Colonel Raphael Israfa was her commander. Built for stealth and deep-space intelligence gathering, it was *his* job to figure out what the old dragon was up to, or that's the excuse Supreme Commander-General Jophiel had given when she'd assigned him command of this ship and banished him into the uncharted territories.

"Where did Mikhail's distress call originate from?" Raphael asked his second-in-command, a two-and-a-half meter-tall Mantoid[41] by the name of Major Glicki.

"All we received was a truncated data burst." Glicki touched her voice modulation box which helped her enunciate non-insectoid sounds. "I didn't receive enough data to triangulate his position, Sir."

Raphael flared his buff-gold wings. When Mikhail had gone to ground two weeks ago, he'd been running black-ops. With dual hyperdrives geared to push a ship seven times that size, he could be anywhere in the galaxy right now. *Anywhere!*

"According to his last check-in—" Glicki tilted her heart-shaped green head "—he was tracking a suspicious Sata'anic merchant vessel, Algol-class, somewhere up into the Orion-Cygnus spur."[42]

Raphael rose and paced over to the vast, spinning hologram of the galaxy which blinked at them in varied, multi-colored lights. Each light represented a red giant, brown dwarf, or other stellar body; all teeming with planets, all teeming with moons and asteroids where a ship could go down and never be heard from again.

"Damantia!" Raphael ruffled his reddish-gold under-feathers. "Even if we launch an armada, it will take a hundred years to search that spiral arm. Orion-Cygnus is almost completely uncharted!"

---

[40] *Command carrier:* an Alliance military spaceship, equivalent to an aircraft carrier.
[41] *Mantoid:* a sentient, six-limbed insectoid species which resembles a praying mantis.
[42] *Orion-Cygnus spur:* the arm of the Milky Way galaxy where Earth is located.

"Two hundred twenty-seven years, Sir." Glicki tapped her command module as she calculated the odds. "Based upon the number of known stars multiplied by the likely percentage we *don't* know about in an area this size. That's how long I estimate it would take to search all habitable planets, not including asteroids and moons."

Glicki met his gaze.

"Unless he rigs a homing beacon, Sir, we shall never find him."

Raphael's golden eyebrows came together in worry. They were due back in Tango Sector next week. How long would the Emperor let him dither in the middle of nowhere?

"Play the distress call again?"

Glicki slid her prayer-like tibia across the console which served as the *Light Emerging's* nerve center. With the click of an armored fingertip, she boosted the audio signal, ran it through a series of data sequencers to enhance the quality, and then replayed it loudly enough for the entire bridge to hear.

<< *Raphael ... I've been hit! Shay'tan has found the godsdamned Holy Grail!!! This planet is crawling with enough Sata'an to...* >>

An explosion cut off the message, and then it went to static.

"I'm afraid that's all we received, Sir," Glicki said. "I boosted the signal and traced the source as best as I could."

Raphael's wings drooped.

"Do you think he survived?"

Glicki enlarged the hologram to focus on the likely search area, silently running calculations to narrow it down to where a scout ship could travel in the amount of time since Mikhail had relayed his last position. Large swaths of the sector displayed nothing but spotty static. She tilted her green head as the *Light Emerging's* long-range sensors pulled up the most obvious stellar bodies and filled in some of the gaps, but the tags which marked those stars were all labeled 'unexplored.'

"Shay'tan's too cheap to terraform an entire planet—" she fluttered her soft, gossamer under-wings. "If it's crawling with Sata'an, we can assume the world is habitable."

He was *her* friend, as well...

"What do you think he meant by Holy Grail?" Raphael asked.

"It could mean almost anything," Glicki said. "If Shay'tan sends in another ship, maybe we can tail them?"

"Nobody is as good at stalking prey as Mikhail," Raphael said. "That's why Jophiel sent him in to investigate."

"He was trained by the Cherubim."[43] Glicki glanced at the lower-ranking officers. "If he could survive..."

She didn't finish the sentence because the information was classified, but Raphael knew what she referred to.

"Anybody who could survive *that* could survive anything," he agreed.

He tucked his wings against his back and settled into his commander's chair, a seat which felt too large despite the eight months he'd sat in it, wishing he was someplace else. He patted the arm as if the *Light Emerging* had heard him.

"That's not true," he whispered. "It's what I had to give up that has my feathers ruffled."

He picked up a portable flatscreen and pulled up Mikhail's service record, one he hadn't had access to until he'd been given command of this ship. He scrolled through images of him and Mikhail going through Basic Training together, *him* goofy looking and inexperienced next to the stoic Seraphim he'd befriended on a dare.

He glanced at Glicki. *She* was the one who'd dared him to approach the dark-winged candidate who'd been dumped into their Basic Training class and try out his fledgling intelligence gathering skills. Nobody dared bunk with the Cherubim-trained novitiate who slept with a sword. Nobody wanted to train with him. Nobody wanted to fight him. They were all scared shitless of the icy young Seraphim who fought without any emotion whatsoever.

The last living Seraphim...

The last of his species...

He never laughed.

He never smiled.

He never warmed up to anybody.

Or that's what people *thought*. Raphael knew otherwise.

Jophiel had ordered him to let Mikhail run black-ops wherever he wished, no questions asked, and gave him just enough information to understand *why*.

It was true...

Mikhail had been *on* 51-Pegasi-4 when the planet had been attacked. Not off-world, like the unclassified portion of his service record implied.

"What happened?" Raphael had once asked.

Mikhail had stared right through him, his expression oddly empty.

"The Emperor said I must never try to remember."

"The base commander ordered you?"

"No," he'd said. "The Eternal Emperor gave me that order himself."

---

[43] *Cherubim*: fierce protectors of the Eternal Emperor.

Raphael stared at the blurry picture of the nine-year-old boy a battalion of Leonids had found, defending his mother's body with a Sata'anic sword.

He'd *seen* that look…

That dark look of fury.

He'd caught glimpses of it, right before Mikhail would withdraw into an icy shell and refuse to speak to anybody for days.

He flipped through the flatscreen to a gruesome image of an autopsy.

According to the forensics report, he'd pulled the sword from his dying mother's body and used it to kill three Sata'anic defectors despite never having used such a weapon before, and then he survived an airstrike. His entire family was burned beyond recognition, but somehow Mikhail, and his mother's body, remained unburned.

Buried alive? For four days? In a burnt house? Clinging to his dead mother's body?

Cold tingled through Raphael's feathers. He hadn't *dared* broach the subject, that Jophiel had divulged his best friend's deepest wound. But he now understood why Mikhail kept that sword at his side. Always. A silent, chilling reminder of a past he refused to discuss.

"Sir?" Glicki interrupted his musings. "Would you like me to send out a bulletin that we are looking for suspicious shipping activity into this sector? If Shay'tan has a base out here, at some point he'll need to resupply?"

"Do it," Raphael said. "And put in a report to Supreme Commander-General Jophiel. We need extra time to organize a search and rescue."

Chapter 14

February – 3,390 BC
Earth: Crash site

NINSIANNA

The bunk across from her was empty when Ninsianna shoved off the covers. He'd finally woken up? Mikhail had terrified her, tossing and turning through two whole sunrises and sunsets, crying out in his sleep. Whatever evil had cast him down from the heavens, it still pursued him, even in his dreams.

She bent to pick up a molted feather and brushed it against her cheek.

Wings!

The goddess had sent her a man with wings!

Maybe, today, he would take her to see the stars?

She left the bed reluctantly, so soft it carried her body like she was floating in the Hiddekel River,[44] with its warm, soft blankets and luxurious pillow, so different than the straw-stuffed sleeping pallet she slept on back in Assur.

She wound her shawl-dress back around her body and belted it into place, flipping the end over her back and into her belt to cover her breasts. What should one wear to visit the dwellings of the gods? The land she'd seen in the vision gleamed more mightily than even Nineveh, but the god seated upon his throne had worn a plain, white robe not so very different than hers.

She adjusted the cloth to appear more goddess-like. She touched the discolored linen with dismay.

"Some impression you'll make," she muttered, "with your shawl-dress all dirty and wrinkled."

She stared at the cupboard he'd pulled a clean chest-garment out of two nights ago, after he'd chased off Jamin. She hadn't dared snoop while he'd lain there, tossing and turning, but now that he'd exited the room?

She crept over to the cupboard and glanced surreptitiously out the door. Outside, she could hear him moving about, mumbling beneath his breath in the front most room, the one with all the damage.

---

[44] *Hiddekel River:* ancient name for the Tigris River in modern-day Iraq.

With a mischievous smile, she tore open up the cupboard. Inside, a small magic lamp sat upon the ceiling. She pressed the sigil he'd taught her would summon a miniature sun and began to rummage through it like an eager gerbil digging for grubs.

She fondled the five identical shirts, each draped on a curved piece of vine he called a hanger. Folded neatly beneath them were six identical pairs of kilts, well, not kilts, they covered his legs. It was a pity, really, to cover such fine, muscular legs, but who was she to question the attire of a demigod? She caressed the fabric between her thumb and forefinger as she made a tally. Unlike the coarse, woolen Ubaid kilts, these 'pants' were dyed the color of a date palm branch.

Six outfits! Plus the shirt she'd cut off of him to save his life. She owned two outfits, while even the Chief possessed only five! Mikhail must be fabulously wealthy.

At the bottom of the cupboard sat a pair of the sturdy animal hide foot coverings he called 'boots.' Ninsianna peeked out the door to make sure he was still busy, and then lifted one to her nose. It had a peculiar odor, neither tanned hide nor dirty foot, but the same sterile scent she affiliated with the sky canoe.

Gosh! He had big feet. She stuck her own foot into the boot and dangled it off her ankle. She could fit *two* of her feet into his shoes at once!

Next she rummaged through the smaller garments. Six pairs of tube-like foot coverings, and some peculiar garments, bright white. Stretchy. With an even stretchier band which ran along the largest hole. She pulled it over her head, but the two holes on either side were so big they wouldn't keep her head warm. What were they?

She wiggled her finger through a little double-layered flap. It came out the other side. Wiggle. Wiggle. Wiggle. Just like a wiggle worm.

"What are these, Great Mother?"

Whatever they were, he owned six of them, just like the pants and foot coverings. She held them up and peeked through the holes. Perhaps they were some kind of brace to support his wings?

She placed them neatly back onto the shelf. Hidden behind them lay a small, black box, delicately interlay with sacred symbols. She pulled it out, chewing on her lip as she turned it over in her sensitive healer's hands. This box was different than everything else in the sky canoe; warm and wooden, the kind of box someone might carve to place upon their altar. She traced the symbols, unable to decipher them. She glanced back to make sure Mikhail was still in the other room, and then opened the lid.

It was empty.

Ninsianna wrinkled her nose in disappointment. She shut the lid and shoved it back into his cupboard.

Not finding anything of further interest, she visited the room with the magic chamber pot, and then moved into the galley. Yesterday she'd found cups, platters, and eating implements and put them back into their cupboards, but found nothing that looked like a cooking crock, storage baskets, or food. She was all out of dried *bastirma* meat. She would have to hunt her own.

Her stomach growled.

"How can a man cross the stars and not provision his sky canoe with food?"

She'd gone out yesterday to dig for roots, but this was enemy territory, and Mikhail's sky canoe had lit up the entire sky.

Would the Halifians come down into this valley?

"Don't worry," she reassured herself. "Now that he's awake, his firestick will summon lightning."

She chewed her lip, pondering how aloof the winged one had treated her when she'd settled him into bed. While polite and thankful, he showed no emotion whatsoever, not even when she'd disrobed for sleep. He certainly didn't treat her the way the Ubaid men always had. Normally, when the women disrobed to swim, the men gathered around.

"Do you think he finds me unattractive?" She furrowed her brow with worry. This was the first time she'd ever been interested in a man who had no interest in *her*.

Would he take her into the heavens if he thought her ugly?

She worked silently, rummaging through the galley, searching for something to cook the man breakfast. Within her culture, a woman was only as valuable as her ability to cook his food and bear him children. What were the females of his species like?

Did they even *have* women?

She closed her eyes, hoping for a stronger answer, but while sometimes it felt like She-Who-Is stood at her side, most of the time, the goddess half-listened the way a mother might let her offspring chatter.

She finished tidying up the galley, and then moved into the ruined room Mikhail called the bridge. While debris still lay helter-skelter, he'd cleared a path to a wall dominated by a large, shiny black square. Laid out carefully on the altar in front of it were a variety of sacred implements. A two-handled scepter? Small, silver cloths. And a sacred knife, some kind of tiny spear? Over the altar, he'd rigged a string of magic suns. He sat on an elaborate stool with thick padding and a short back, his magnificent dark wings shielding him from her view.

He lowered his good wing and met her gaze.

"Good night," he enunciated clearly, the last thing she'd said before he'd fallen unconscious.

Ninsianna froze, her heart beating in her ears. The man who faced her this morning was clear-eyed and conscious, not the wounded creature she'd woken up several times to force him to drink some water.

Should she bow and pray? Or lift her hands in ablution? Maybe she should do both? How was one supposed to treat a demigod?

"G-g-good ... morning," she stuttered.

The man tilted his head.

"G-g-good morning," he enunciated meticulously.

"No, uhm—" she gave him a sheepish expression "—it's just good morning. Not, uhm…"

Her hands flew towards her mouth. Whenever she was nervous, sometimes she giggled. A vacuous, girlish gesture she'd always despised.

Mikhail watched her, studying her carefully, missing nothing. Thankfully he didn't mimic her giggle, which meant he *knew* she acted like an idiot.

Her heartbeat thumped, screaming how very awkward she must appear, an eighteen summer girl too frightened to talk to a powerful man.

How would Mama act?

Mama would act confident, whether or not she felt it.

She gave Mikhail the same healer's smile she'd given Jamin after Papa had ordered her to go to the Chief's house and change his bandages.

"It's just good morning—" she forced her voice not to warble. "Good morning. As in, the sun has risen." She arm-gestured the sunrise, and then pointed at the golden sunlight which streamed through the crack in his roof. "Morning."

"Morning," he nodded. "*Maidin*. Yes—" he pointed at the sun. "Good morning. Yes?"

"Yes." She smiled to accentuate he was correct.

"Yes, good morning." He stared at her, as though waiting for her to do something amazing. Or maybe he was just waiting for her to cook him breakfast? What did demigods eat, anyways?

"I, uhm—"

She gestured for the crack she'd been using as a doorway.

"Why don't I fetch some water?"

"Water." He held up one of the containers she'd used to fetch water yesterday from the stream. *"Deoch.* Drink?"

"Yes," she said. "Water. *Deoch.* Drink."

Mikhail shook his head.

"No water. You—" he pointed at the crack "—you no go—" He struggled for a word. "You no go *taobh amuigh.*"

He flared his wings.

Outside? Yes. He wasn't afraid of Jamin? Was he?

"He wouldn't dare come back," Ninsianna scoffed. "If he does, you'll hit him with lightning!"

She pointed at the deadly black weapon strapped to his hip.

Mikhail's expression remained unreadable as he held out one of the silver packets he'd placed on the altar. It rustled as he reached inside and pulled out two small, white squares. He held them out in the palm of his hand.

"You eat?"

He picked one up and held it up to his mouth, and then gestured for her to take the other the way one might lure a skittish cat.

Ninsianna stared with disbelief.

Mikhail had made her breakfast?

Awareness tingled through her body as she stepped toward the winged man who towered over her, even seated. She forced a smile as she touched the small, white rectangle. A pleasant tingle warmed her fingers as she took the heavenly food from his hand.

Her head swam with emotion, images, and *feelings*.

Fear. Worry. Doubt. His face said nothing. But his lowered wings said something different. Mikhail felt every bit as anxious as *she* did.

"Eat?" he said.

"Okay," she said breathlessly.

She put the heavenly ambrosia into her mouth.

Her teeth crunched on the hard, square biscuit. It didn't *taste* like food from heaven. In fact, it rather reminded her of Mama's cooking.

Mikhail gave her an apologetic look.

"Food *briste*," he said.

Briste. Briste? Hadn't he used that word to describe his sky canoe?

"Broken?" she guessed.

"Yes," he said. "Food broken."

Broken? How could food be broken?

She forced a smile as she choked the substance down. Crunchy clumps of rock scraped down her throat. But he'd cooked it for her. Or fetched it, perhaps? Because now that she stood next to him, she could see he'd set out *two* silver packages onto the altar, perhaps to bless the meal?

Mikhail nodded approvingly.

"You stay *taobh istigh*?" He gestured at his altar. "Help Mikhail? Yes?"

She stared at the wall he'd decorated with hundreds of colorful spiderwebs. No. Not decorated. Taken apart. She leaned forward, fascinated by a box beneath the shiny, reflective square, filled with a tangle of peculiar looking objects.

"What is this?" she asked.

"Computer." He tapped his temple. "Help Mikhail *cuimhneamh*."[45]

"Cuimhneamh?"

"Yes. *Cuimhneamh*." He made a gesture as though something flew out of his forehead. "No *cuimhneah*. No…"

Behind his unearthly blue eyes, she caught a glimmer of fear.

A faint sheen of sweat glistened on his too-pale skin. He might *look* neatly dressed, but his ghastly pale complexion warned he was still dangerously low on blood. For all his size, his strength, his magnificent wings, just three days ago, he'd tumbled out of the heavens to suffer a mortal wound.

"Let me look at your head." She touched her own head, and then pointed at his.

He bent his neck as though he bowed to *her*. A creature of heaven, even fallen, still filled with far more grace than any mortal man.

Her hands tingled as she touched his short-cropped hair and felt along the skin to gauge the extent of his injuries. One wing twitched as she touched the place she'd given him seven stitches, but though she sensed it hurt, the man did not make a sound.

Ninsianna stepped back.

Mikhail met her gaze. His eyes reminded her of the desert sky.

"You hit your head pretty hard—" she banged her own head for emphasis "—but I don't think it's permanent."

"Mikhail be okay?"

His face remained stoic, but by the way his feathers rustled, his memory loss terrified him.

"Yes," she gave him a reassuring smile. "Everything be okay in two—" she held up two fingers, then made the same gesture she'd made earlier to mimic the sunrise "—maybe three days?"

"Okay."

He turned back to worship his god.

"Computer," he said, *"cad é an t-ordú deiridh a thug mé tú roimh an timpiste?"*[46]

His god didn't answer him. With a sigh, he picked up a small, ceremonial spear and stabbed it into the nest of spiderwebs.

"Computer broken," he explained. "Mikhail *shocrú*."

"Heal?"

His forehead furrowed, as though he knew that wasn't the right word.

"*Shocrú*. Yes. Mikhail heal computer."

How did one heal a god?

---

[45] *Cuimhneamh*: remember.
[46] "Computer, what was the final order I gave before the crash?"

He did that thing that all men do when they are chewing on a problem, disappeared into his work and completely ignored her.

She picked up the small, silver packet he'd taken the food out of.

"I'll just, uhm, clean up."

She backed away.

Mikhail gave her a distracted nod, but already he'd forgotten her. She slid the silver packet into her leather pouch. She would make her *own* altar to She-Who-Is.

She wrung her hands, not sure what to do next. She'd learned the hard way, after pushing Jamin too hard, that men pushed back if a woman got too bossy. The *last* thing she wanted was to be left behind like Jamin had done after she'd begun to make demands. So what *did* women do where Mikhail came from? She doubted they just stood around, looking pretty.

How could she make herself indispensable?

Her eyes fell upon the place she'd found him impaled through the chest. While she knew little about sky canoes which flew between the heavens, even she could see he'd have to clean up this mess before he could take her anywhere.

She glanced at the heavenly creature who prayed furiously to his god, Compyoota, stabbing the sacrificial knife into his god's altar, uttering prayers to give him back his memories.

She picked up a large square which had fallen from the ceiling. She dragged it over to rest against the wall, and then picked up the next one. Mikhail looked up, his expression curious.

"Thank you," he enunciated meticulously.

It was as close as she'd ever seen him come to a smile.

She dug into the pile, sorting ceiling mats, the odd spears, and other types of debris by type until she could see the floor. She stared down at the enormous, red-brown stain.

"How can any creature lose that much blood and live?" She'd seen entire herds sacrificed for a feast that had bled out less than he had.

'Great Mother?' she prayed. *'What should I do next?'*

A male voice floated through the crack.

"Nin-si-anna!"

The hair rose on her neck. No! Not *him!*

Mikhail lurched to his feet.

"Nin-si-anna," the voice called out again. "It's Papa. I know you're in there."

Mikhail pulled his firestick and aimed it at the doorway.

"No!"

She leaped in front of the crack, her arms flailing.

"It's just my father!"

The hum which preceded a bolt of blue lightning shrieked higher and higher pitched. His good wing flailed as he fought to keep his balance, but the hand which held the firestick did not waver.

"*Céim ar leataobh,*"[47] he said.

Ninsianna held up her hands, trembling.

"It's okay," her voice warbled. "It's good. Papa is good."

Thank the goddess her father had the sense to not step into the sky canoe!

Mikhail's skin turned clammy as the blood drained out of his face. From the way he hyperventilated, he fought off passing out.

"It's okay?" his voice lilted upward.

Can I trust you? She understood what he really meant.

"It's okay."

She put down her hands.

She took a deep breath and forced herself to stand straight, as though she were the most confident woman in the world.

"It's okay. Papa good."

Feathers flew as he half-sat, half-crashed back into his seat like a tired old woman. He fought to stay conscious. A bright red stain blossomed outward on his clean shirt, salty and copper, so pungent she could almost *taste* it.

She glanced between her patient and her father. Mikhail needed attention, but if her father stepped through the crack, Mikhail would hit him with a bolt of lightning.

"I'll go get him—" she gestured. "Papa good. You stay here."

She bolted towards doorway before Mikhail could tell her *no*.

She held her hands up, ready to deflect any arms that tried to grab her, but none came. There was only her father. His face appeared red and covered with sweat, his grey-streaked hair helter-skelter above worried, tawny-beige eyes. He stared at the shiny silver sky canoe, owl-eyed.

"Why have you come?" She positioned herself in the crack, ready to dart back inside.

"Jamin said you'd been kidnapped."

"Kidnapped? The only fool who tried to kidnap me was *him!*"

She jabbed a finger at her father, her body shaking with fury. Behind her, the high-pitched whine of the firestick warned that Mikhail sat, prepared to defend her.

"Ninsianna, be reasonable," Papa said.

"Reasonable?" she shrieked. "The bastard tried to drown me in that pond!"

---

[47] "*Céim ar leataobh.*" Step aside.

She scanned the steep walls which surrounded the oasis, positive Jamin sneaked around somewhere behind her. She could almost *feel* him. At least a dozen pair of eyes. Papa hadn't found his way out here alone.

"He was just worried." Papa soothed her. "He said a demon put you under some kind of enchantment."

"The only enchantment was *you*, trying to force me to marry your best friend's son!" Ninsianna snapped. "Did you think I wouldn't notice the sigils you kept putting underneath my pillow, trying to make me predisposed to him in my dreams?"

"It's a perfect match."

"Not if I don't want him!"

She looked up at the cliff which had collapsed onto the sky canoe.

"Do you hear that, Jamin?" she shouted at the top of her lungs. "I don't *want* you! So take your warriors and go away!"

A pebble tumbled down the cliff, clinking and bouncing, betraying the warriors' presence. Ninsianna pointed upward.

"Tell them to back off, or I'll let Mikhail kill them."

Papa glanced up, not sure whether to perpetuate the ruse. Ninsianna backed fully inside the crack. Behind her, the rustle of feathers warned Mikhail was prepared to fight, whether or not he was in any shape to actually do so.

The last thing she wanted was her beloved, if misguided, father, and the man who had fallen from the heavens, getting into a fight to the death over her.

Now Jamin? That was a different story…

"I'm going back inside now," Ninsianna said, "before he punishes you with his magic. He doesn't speak Ubaid. All he knows is Jamin attacked me right in front of his sky canoe."

"Is it true?" Papa's expression grew eager. "The warriors said he looks Angelic."

Ninsianna hesitated.

"An Angelic?"

"Yes."

That was what Mikhail called himself, part of the symbols on the talisman which helped him remember his name. Jamin didn't know that, so how did Papa?

"Maybe," she evaded. "We haven't really discussed it."

Papa raised an eyebrow.

"You've been here three days. What *have* you been doing?"

She snorted with disgust. She *knew* what Jamin thought she'd been up to with the beautiful, winged man. She wasn't about to reveal Mikhail was too weak to stand, much less make amorous advances. With his firestick, he didn't *need* to stand as long as she wasn't stupid enough to step out of lightning range.

"I'm going inside now—" she backed into the shadows "—and *you* are going to live with your decision to tell your only child it was *your* way, or banishment! As you can see—" she bowed mockingly "—I have found a more *respectful* tribe."

"Ninsianna! Wait!" Her father lurched forward. "Let me see him?"

"So you can betray him?"

"No," Papa said. "I just wish to talk to him."

"Why?"

"We have legends about a time the winged ones shall return."

Ninsianna's eyebrows furrowed with suspicion.

"Why have you never told such tales before?"

"Please? You must show him to me." Papa glanced up the cliff behind the ship. "Before Jamin does something rash."

Ninsianna stared at her father's spirit-light. Her Papa, who she loved more than anybody in the world. The father who'd always indulged her. The patriarch who'd betrayed her when he'd refused to let her back out of an arranged marriage.

Papa wouldn't leave until he'd done what he'd come here to do. With Jamin to back him up, the only way to resolve this peacefully was to let him see.

"Fine," she said. "But first let me tell him you're coming. He's not sure who he can trust."

Ninsianna ducked back inside the sky canoe. Mikhail had regained his composure, or more likely it was fake, but Papa didn't know that.

"It's just Papa," she smiled. "He wishes to come and meet you."

Mikhail gave her an unreadable stare. He wasn't buying it. The man was perceptive enough to read her body language.

She made an exaggerated gesture as though inviting somebody into your house.

"Papa? Meet?"

She stood between Mikhail and the firestick. Her heart pounded as she prayed he understood.

"Oh-kay," he said.

"Okay!" she smiled too brightly.

He laid his firestick flat upon his thigh, but from the way he kept his hand over it, he remained ready to smite his enemies.

Backing up, she led her father inside the sky canoe. Mikhail flared his wings like a raptor about to pounce, one magnificently curved, and the other stiff and straight because of the splint.

"Great Goddess be praised!" Papa exclaimed. "It is true!"

He threw himself to his knees and bowed his face all the way down to the floor.

Papa began to sing…

…in the *same* language spoken by Mikhail…

Chapter 15

February – 3,390 BC
Earth: Crash site
Colonel Mikhail Mannuki'ili

MIKHAIL

She skittered out the crack they'd been using as a doorway.

"Wait!" He lurched to his feet, but tilted off-balance. His splinted wrist came down on the console. Pain stabbed into his damaged lung. Darkness enveloped his field of vision. He broke out into a cold sweat as Ninsianna's voice grew far away.

He sat back down before he passed out. Right onto his awkwardly splinted wing.

A pair of voices drifted through the cracked hull. A man, that much was certain. But while her voice rose sharply with anger, the man's voice remained measured and calm.

Ninsianna stepped back in and made an exaggerated gesture to communicate she'd invited the unknown man to step inside.

Mikhail laid the pulse rifle on his thigh, his hand over the handle, ready to fire even from his lap.

Ninsianna led in a middle age man wearing a multi-fringed kilt and a colorful, woven cape which left his chest exposed. Around his neck, he wore an elaborate necklace made of beads and animal claws. Where Ninsianna was beautiful, the man she led was homely, tall and muscular, with a great, big bulbous nose and swarthy skin pock-marked with scars. His eyes, however, were a different story. He possessed the exact same intelligent, tawny beige eyes as Ninsianna.

"Mikhail?" Ninsianna put her arm around the man's shoulders. "*Bu Papa.*"

Mikhail scrutinized the man. The two seemed to share genetic characteristics. He flared his wings, ready, if necessary, to pounce.

The man dropped to his knees and bowed his face all the way down to the floor.

"*Buyuk tanrica! Bu dogru!*" the man exclaimed.

He began to recite in a sing-song fashion a poem, sung not in *their* language, but in *his*.

In Ki's most sorrowful, desperate hour,
When all was lost to blight,
She sang her Song of Creation,
And enticed Darkness to protect the Light.

Primordial Light, the architect,
Ki's daughter, She-Who-Is,
Spun the darkness of He-Who's-Not,
To create life, All-That-Is

But then one day, the sickness returned.
Moloch. Enemy of Ki.
The Evil One. The ex-husband spurned.
Collapse. Entropy.

He spread his evil, throughout the worlds,
Undoing all in his path.
Devouring his own children,
To make Ki feel his wrath.

But He-Who's-Not, the Guardian.
Lord Chaos. The Dark Lord.
Sang the Song of Destruction,
To protect the Light he adored.

She-Who-Is wept bitter tears,
To see her playthings broken,
The Dark Lord couldn't bear her grief,
And offered his mate a token.

To keep the balance so he could protect her,
They would play a game of chess.
She-Who-Is would create new pieces.
He-Who's-Not would reclaim the rest.

But both must remain ever-vigilant,
Against Moloch's eventual return,
He sends forth Agents to pave the way,
To escape the hell whence he burns.

> When Moloch gains a foothold,
> And desires to be fed,
> She-Who-Is shall appoint a Chosen One
> To warn of Moloch's spread.
>
> SHE shall send a winged Champion
> A demi-god fair and just,
> A Sword of the Gods to defend the people,
> And raise armies from the dust.
>
> As Moloch corrupts Agents to do his work,
> So shall Ki appoint Watchmen to do hers,
> From the ashes of despair,
> When all appears lost,
> Hidden Agents shall choose to serve HER.
>
> True love will inspire the Other One,
> To pierce her heart upon a thorn,
> And bring back hope where there is none.
> For agape can access Ki's Song.
>
> When all the players have made their moves,
> And the Morning Star shines bright,
> He shall light the way through the darkest hour,
> And restore the path of Light...
>
> And if these measures should someday fail,
> And Ki's protections fall,
> The Dark Lord shall seize his vessel,
> And protect the Light by destroying them all.

Mikhail's feathers rustled as recognition tingled through his body. The song tugged at his subconscious like an ancient lullaby, one he'd heard many times. Ninsianna waited, her face filled with expectation as the man she called 'Papa' pressed his head back onto the floor and waited for an answer.

Mikhail formed his next words carefully. Not in *his* language. But an ancient dialect of his language so old and melodious it appeared to be a bridge between his language and hers.

"*An féidir leat tuiscint a fháil dom?*" Mikhail enunciated carefully. Can you understand me?

The man listened intently, and then nodded.

"*Roinnt.*"

"*Cár fhoghlaim tú a labhairt mo theanga?*" Where did you learn to speak my language? He leaned forward, anxious to hear what the man had to say.

"*Tá sé tugtha síos trí na glúine a lán.*" It has been passed down through many generations. "The highest level shamans are taught these songs so they can help the winged ones once they return."

"How many of you are there?"

As he spoke, the words flowed easier, as though, at some point he had studied this ancient dialect and perhaps even spoken it, the way one might study an epic historical text or recite a liturgical prayer in grammar school.

"Only a few of us remember the oldest songs," the man said.

A cleric? No. The man had the sturdy build of someone who did more than simply study arcana. But a shock of chestnut hair, peppered with the same color titanium steel as the exterior of his ship, jutted helter-skelter, as though he ran his fingers through it often in thought. The man's eyes niggled at his subconscious, but he couldn't pull up the memory about what he found familiar.

"What is your name?"

"I am called Immanu," the man said. "I am shaman of my village."

"Who is Ninsianna to you?"

"My daughter," he said. "When she didn't come home, I was worried."

Ninsianna stood next to him and placed one hand upon his broken wing. Was she protecting him? Or hiding behind him for protection?

"*Baba? Lutfen cevirin?*" she said.

Immanu conversed with his daughter in their native language, and then translated so Mikhail could understand.

"I told Ninsianna you've been sent by She-Who-Is to protect us." Immanu gestured at his daughter. "I've come to take her home."

Ninsianna darted behind his back, burying herself in his wing.

"*Biliyorum!*" she hissed. "*Ben sana soylemeyi denedim nedir.*"

Common sense said he shouldn't interfere. But another part of him, the part that wanted to protect her because he *owed* her, was all too conscious of the hand which gripped his shoulder.

"What if Ninsianna doesn't *want* to go home?"

Immanu's eyebrows lifted with surprise.

"But I'm her father?"

"Shouldn't she be allowed to make her own choices?"

"But she's a woman," Immanu said.

"A *woman*," Mikhail said. "Not a child."

Ninsianna's tawny-beige eyes pleaded *please don't send me home.*

A lump rose in Mikhail's throat. If she went, he'd have nothing, not even the memory he'd woken up with of a beautiful woman, surrounded by the light. But it was selfish to keep her if it created problems once she went home.

He fingered the pulse pistol in his lap.

"If I make her go," Mikhail said, "what guarantee do I have her boyfriend won't abuse her?"

Immanu's bushy eyebrows reared in surprise.

"Abuse?"

"Yes," he growled. "When I intervened, that black-eyed bastard was trying to drown her."

Ninsianna jabbed a finger at her father and let loose a string of words he understood, without understanding the language, had to be the equivalent of *'see, I was telling you the truth!'*

Immanu's face fell. His shoulders slumped.

"Oh, great winged one," he said. "You have my apologies. That is not the story I was told."

"You doubt me?" Mikhail growled.

"No," Immanu said. "I find your story all too credible."

The same dark rage which had woken him up from a nightmare surged through his body.

"Then why in Hades would you force your daughter to marry such a man!"

Ninsianna raised her chin, confident, defiant.

Immanu bowed his head.

"I only wished to secure the best possible marriage," he said softly. "She's my only child. Please don't take her away."

The pulse rifle hummed softly in Mikhail's lap. Immanu had no idea he could barely stand up. He'd sat here, this entire time, with his hand covering the place the blood had seeped through the bandages. He could see how the shaman might misconstrue his intentions.

He removed his hand, allowing Immanu to see his weakness.

"Ninsianna saved my life," Mikhail said. "Whatever she wishes, that is what I shall do."

Immanu's eyes grew wide as he recognized he was injured.

"But you're a demigod?" he said. "The legends say no mortal weapon can harm you."

"I'm a *soldier*," Mikhail said. "I have terrifying weapons. But I am badly injured, and I find myself in need of continued care."

Immanu stepped towards him, his hand outstretched. Mikhail yanked the pulse pistol up from his lap.

"I wouldn't," he warned.

The pulse rifle hummed a gleeful, ominous sound.

Immanu threw himself back onto the floor. Jamin, it appeared, had told him what happened when a pulse rifle hit the ground in front of you. Just wait until he saw what a direct hit did, on full power, not the lowest setting.

"You misunderstand!" Immanu's voice trembled. "I only wish to check for evil spirits."

"Your daughter already did that."

"But she's a woman."

"A woman with an uncanny knowledge of medicine," Mikhail said.

"I mean no harm," Immanu said. "I only wish to help."

"I don't know you," Mikhail said. "Ninsianna, on the other hand, has more than earned my trust."

Ninsianna spoke, no doubt telling her father about her exploits. Her hands moved as she recreated how she'd found him and stitched him back up. Her father's eyes wrinkled in an expression of pride.

"She gets it from her mother," he said. "She's even more talented than Ninsianna."

Mikhail held his breath as Ninsianna continued speaking, praying the shaman wished to avoid an altercation. When she grew bored with him, she would likely go home on her own.

The shaman's brow furrowed, deep in thought.

"I don't know if she is the Chosen One whom you seek," Immanu said at last. "I will not tell you something unless I know it to be true."

"A Chosen One?" Mikhail said. "You expect me to believe in this song?"

"How else did you get here?" Immanu asked.

"I—"

Mikhail stared past the shaman at his ruined ship. Yes, he'd gotten shot down here. But while his subconscious screeched *'You have to complete the mission!'* it did not resonate with anything in the song.

"Ninsianna claims the goddess sent her a vision of your sky canoe just before you fell from the sky," Immanu said. "She claims the goddess sent her to save your life. She claims..."

The shaman glanced at his daughter apprehensively.

"She claims a terrible sickness threatens to devour the stars."

Mikhail raised an eyebrow. His gut instinct said this 'vision' was little more than a primitive culture's understanding of his technology, but without his memories, he needed these people if he was to survive.

"Although you may have legends about my people visiting your planet in your past—" Mikhail said "—I do not think I'm your sword of the gods."

Immanu translated his words back to Ninsianna. She leaned forward and whispered in his ear.

"Say Papa up, *suas, le de thoil?*" she said, half in his language, half in hers. "Papa, up? Yes?"

Her breath warmed his ear, oddly intimate. Especially with her standing in his vulnerable spot, between his wings and his back. He resisted the urge to curl that wing around her or grip the hand which clung to his shoulder.

"Get up, Sir," Mikhail said. "I don't *like* being bowed down to."

Immanu scrambled back to his feet.

"Perhaps she could stay for a few days? Until I can fetch her mother." His face turned sheepish. "My wife is frantic. Even if you say no, there's no way you'll keep her away."

Mikhail looked from Ninsianna to her father. Not that he doubted Ninsianna's medical training, but if her mother was more experienced, it couldn't hurt to get a second opinion?

"How many days?" he asked.

"Five," Immanu said. "It's a two day journey each way, with a day in between to gather supplies."

"It's only been three days since I crashed."

"Jamin *ran* for help," Immanu said. "The rest of us aren't so vigorous."

Mikhail nodded. He'd gathered that much by how eager the black-eyed man had been to fight. Jamin appeared to be a formidable opponent. In peak shape, he could easily beat him, but in his current condition?

"What guarantees do I have he won't attack?"

Immanu gave him a sheepish look.

"None," he said. "As we speak, he's preparing a raid."

Mikhail grabbed his pulse pistol and held it out.

"You betray me?"

"No!" Immanu trembled. "He thinks you're holding my daughter prisoner. There is nothing on heaven or earth that will stop him from rescuing her."

"Rescue?"

"Yes," Immanu said. "That is what he believes."

Mikhail lowered his voice to a low, threatening rumble.

"If he steps inside, I will kill him."

"That would be most unfortunate," Immanu said. "His father is our chief. If you harm him, it will make things difficult for everybody."

"Then make him understand."

"There is no reasoning with Jamin," Immanu said. "I shall have to convince his father he misunderstood. In the meantime—" he glanced at his daughter "—if she wants to stay, you'd better keep her away from *him*."

Chapter 16

February – 3,390 BC
Earth: Assur

JAMIN

The Ubaid called this mountain *'Hyena's Teeth'* after the rugged ridge which rose up, like incisors, out of the desert floor. It wasn't nearly as impressive as the mountains to their north and east, but the desert-dwelling Halifian tribe believed it to be the abode of their god.

Jamin tossed his cape over one shoulder and signaled the warriors to be *quiet*. The winged demon wasn't the only enemy they had to contend with. For longer than he'd been alive, the people of the river, and the people of the desert, had been at war. His men fanned out, their ranks now swollen to a dozen, to find another way down.

"I never realized this mountain had an oasis," Jamin said. "We've chased them out here, many times, after a raid."

"They've always repelled us before we've gotten this close," Kiaresh said, his father's man from the older generation of warriors. "It is said their shaykh,[48] Marwan, shares the location of their oases with no one."

"I can see why," Jamin said to the older man. "Look at the acacia[49] trees? I'll bet this oasis has water until the summer solstice."

He scanned the valley, the vegetation, the depth of the water. Lush green hazelnut shrubs grew partially under water, while the more deeply rooted acacia trees grew just around the edge. Along the valley wall, nothing grew at all. To his trained eye, he could see where the winter rains flooded the natural dam, and then receded down to nothing in the summer.

Ninsianna's father finished climbing down the landslide, the only way down into the oasis, alone and vulnerable.

"Lure him out," Jamin said. "And I'll fill the bastard with spears."

The shaman made his way across the valley.

Jamin hurried along the rim until he stood directly over the spot where the shooting star lay, half-buried in rubble. For a winged creature, the steep valley wall wouldn't be an obstacle, but for a mortal man, it meant he had to climb down a cliff, utterly exposed.

Jamin peeked over the edge.

---

[48] *Shaykh:* sheikh.
[49] *Acacia:* a shrubby tree which is drought tolerant.

"What do you see?" Siamek asked.

Jamin stared down at the object which had fallen from the sky. It didn't *look* like a fallen star. In fact, it didn't resemble anything he'd ever seen, neither natural, nor shaped by mortal hands. Polished grey, almost silver in the sunlight, it was shaped like the head of a spear with a pair of wing-like cylinders near the tail. Here and there, spear-like objects jutted out of it, and other fathomless shapes. Where it disappeared into the rocks, the back buckled like a piece of folded cloth.

"It looks broken," Jamin said.

"How can you tell?" Siamek asked.

"I just *know*." Jamin pointed. "See the way it cracked open, like a broken egg?"

Kiaresh crept beside them to look down as well.

"Is that it?" the older warrior asked.

"Yeah," Jamin said. "You ever see anything like that?"

"No," Kiaresh said. "Not even in the old days, when your grandfather used to send us to battle the Uruk."[50]

"It looks like magic," Siamek said.

"No," Jamin shook his head. "I looked into the bastard's eyes. He didn't summon magic the way Immanu does when he called down the lightning. The firestick is some kind of weapon, like a talisman?"

"I'd sure like a weapon like that," Siamek said.

"So would I," Jamin said. "And I intend to take it."

Let nobody say that Jamin, son of Kiyan of Assur was a coward. The winged demon had startled him. Or more precisely, the bolt of lightning had.

You left because Ninsianna didn't want you...

"Shut up!" he hissed at his own mocking inner voice.

He'd replayed the scenario, many times, in his own mind between here and Assur. Ninsianna in the water, her nipples erect. Her lips against hers when she'd finally told him, yes, she would marry him. Ninsianna, seated at the edge of his bed, the sunlight gathered around her as she'd laid her hands upon his broken body and, with a whispered prayer, caused his pain to go away.

His heart beat faster. He *had* to get her back. The winged demon must have put her under some kind of enchantment. It was all a trick, a petty conjuration like Immanu did to amuse children during one of the Akitu festivals.[51]

He examined the cliff directly above the sky canoe. It curved inward, making it impossible to scale the valley wall.

---

[50] *Uruk:* an ancient Sumerian tribe who founded Babylon.
[51] *Akitu festival:* a harvest and/or sowing festival.

"Now what?" Siamek whispered.

"We wait," Jamin said.

"What if he flies up here to get us?"

"I am counting on it," Jamin said. "Once he's in the air, he'll be more vulnerable."

He and the others hefted their spears, waiting for the winged demon to walk out so they could finish him off.

"C'mon, c'mon, c'mon," Jamin muttered.

His future father-in-law walked across the valley.

"Ninsianna?" Immanu called. "Ninsianna, I know you're in there."

A sound behind them caused the others to look up.

Dadbeh shrieked. "Halifians!"

Jamin leaped to his feet.

"Don't hurt him!" Dadbeh pleaded. The small man held out his spear as a dozen dark-robed men appeared out of the rocks. In front of them they drove two of their men, both with knives held to their throats. They forced Firouz and Tirdard to kneel.

"You were supposed to stand sentry!" Jamin hissed.

"They appeared out of nowhere." Firouz's brown eyes glittered with fear.

More Halifians appeared, perhaps thirty total, all wearing the brown robes of the people of the desert. The biggest enemy gestured at Jamin.

"I take it you're their chief?" the man spoke in heavily accented Ubaid.

"Yes." He stood proudly. "I am Jamin, son of Kiyan of Assur."

"Good." Halifian teeth glittered in a predatory grin. "Then we shall earn a hefty ransom from your father, little chief."

"Not if we kill you," Jamin growled.

"You will find that hard to do," the Halifian laughed, "caught between a cliff and your enemy." He held up an intricately carved spear, carved with gazelles. "One thrust of this, and we won't *have* to kill you. The fall will do it for us."

Jamin held up his spear, ready to throw it at the leader. The Halifians held out *their* weapons; knives, slings, spears, and deadly-looking clubs embedded with spear-shards. They backed up until they stood against the cliff edge.

The enemy fanned out to cut off their escape. Ninsianna's voice floated upward, arguing with her father who had no idea that a *new* enemy had just appeared.

Thank the goddess she is safe…

But no sign of the winged demon.

'Where are you?' he silently cursed. Right now he could use a diversion.

"Perhaps we could reach an arrangement?" he said out loud. "We meant no disrespect."

"You should have thought of that before you traversed our land."

"We came to *retrieve* something." Jamin gestured at the valley below. "A winged demon has stolen one of our women. We're here to rescue her."

Ninsianna's voice wafted upwards.

"I don't want him!" she shouted. "Do you hear that, Jamin? I don't *want* you! So take your warriors and go away!"

The Halifian leader snickered.

"It appears somebody has stolen the little chieftain's spear!"

He grabbed his crotch. His fellow mercenaries laughed along with him.

Rage punched through Jamin's entire body.

"He *does* exist," Jamin hissed. "Just look down, and you will see."

Immanu disappeared into the ship.

"What's he doing?" Siamek asked.

"Well?" the Halifian leader asked. "Where is this winged demon?"

"He's a *coward*," Jamin nearly spat. "He sent a woman to answer the door."

The Halifian leader guffawed. The mercenaries chattered in the Halifian language. Jamin understood enough to comprehend what they said.

"Back me up," he whispered to Siamek. "I'll go for the leader, you go for the man to his right. Kiaresh?"

"Yes," the older warrior spoke low.

"You go for the one who's holding Firouz."

"There's too many," Kiaresh said. "Your father would rather pay the ransom."

"They plan to take Ninsianna!" he hissed. "I will not let them sully my future bride!"

He reached for the blade he kept tucked into his belt. He knew how to deal with a pack of hyenas. Once you took down the pack leader, the remaining dogs would usually scatter.

The man who stood next to the Halifian leader, with unusual hazel-green eyes, caught the movement as Jamin adjusted his cape to free his knife-hand. His forehead furrowed in confusion.

"Where did you get that?" The man touched his *own* shoulder.

"Get what?" Jamin asked casually.

"That?" he pointed at Jamin's shoulder. "Where did you get that pin?"

Jamin glanced down at the pin which fastened his cape. Carved from bone, it bore the head of a gazelle with a shaft carved with leaves.

"An old man gave it to me—" he switched into speaking the Halifian language. "What of it?"

"That pin belonged to my mother," the man said. "I haven't seen it for fifteen years."

Jamin froze. He'd never told *anyone* about the old man. Especially not his father. The Chief would never understand.

"It was a gift," Jamin said. "From an old man whose goats needed water. He said, if I let them drink from a certain spot each summer, no Halifian would touch me so long as I wore this pin."

The hazel-eyed man and the Halifian leader gave each other a look. They conversed in Halifian.

"He'll bring a hefty ransom."

"You know the law."

"That was fifteen years ago," the Halifian leader said. "How do you know your father wants this *now?*"

"The old lion is only as good as his word," the green-eyed man said. "Would you be like him? Or would you be like that dog, Dirar?"

"One of these days, Dirar will get what is coming," the Halifian leader said. "He thinks I don't see he covets my title, and my wife."

"And will you act like him? Or will you be like our fathers?"

"She was *your* mother."

"But the promise was made by Marwan."

A cold chill settled into Jamin's spine, blended with hope. The old man he'd made a deal with was Marwan, the Halifian shaykh? He'd made a treaty, over the objections of his father?

The two men barked orders at the other Halifians. They hauled Firouz and Tirdard to their feet and shoved them towards them.

"Get them out of here," the Halifian leader said. "*They* don't have a pin. If they come back, we will have no mercy."

Down in the valley, Immanu came out of the broken shooting star. He looked up at the cliffs.

"Jamin!" Immanu shouted. "You have a lot to answer for!"

Behind Immanu, Ninsianna stepped out, along with the winged demon. The demon flared his black-brown wings.

"Ai-Iyah be!" the Halifians gasped. "He speaks the truth!"

The mercenaries all kneeled and pressed their foreheads into the ground, chanting and praying. Jamin gestured for his *own* men to back away, before the Halifian leader changed his mind.

Siamek and the others glanced from Jamin to the Halifians.

"What's going on?" he whispered.

"The Halifians have decided to let us go."

"Why?"

Jamin stared down at the winged demon that stood with his arm thrown over Ninsianna's shoulders, one wing curled around her as if he owned her. A sense of betrayal stabbed him in the gut.

"Because the enemy of our enemy is our friend."

Chapter 17

義

Galactic Standard Date: 152,323.02 AE
Sata'an Forward Operating Base: Earth
Lieutenant Kasib

LT. KASIB

He'd chosen the village for its central location, convenient to the sea and surrounded by fertile fields. A wall of mountains reared up to their east, capturing the rain and returning the precious moisture via a network of naturally occurring streams. Most importantly of all, the climate was *warm*. Pleasantly hot, but not so dry they'd need to draw upon the moisture stored in their tails.

Exactly the kind of weather General Hudhafah preferred…

Lieutenant Kasib checked his flatscreen, scrolling through reports and a map of the village's terrain. All around him, lizard-men and other Sata'anic soldiers moved in frenetic activity, erecting tents, unrolling spools of barbed wire, and most important, finding a secure place to store their ammunition and supplies.

"Unpack it over there."

He shook his claws at the boar-faced skullcracker[52] who wrestled a portable military shelter off the shuttle, still compactly folded inside its box. The burly Catoplebas[53] paused to glance at Kasib's map.

"A hundred meters from the temple?"

"Yes, Private," Kasib said. "We must assert Shay'tan's dominance over the symbols of their gods." He glanced at the *danger* sticker emblazoned on the edge of the crate. "Make it two hundred. In case there's ever a misfire."

The Catoplebas saluted.

"Sir, yes sir, Lieutenant."

Today, at least, the skullcrackers were too busy to give him any guff. He hurried off to oversee the supplies coming off the next shuttle, a boxy grey troop carrier carrying an important payload. As the General's Chief Acquisitions Officer, accounting for all of these supplies fell to *him*. They had to get them unloaded before the *Jamaran* made its next orbital pass so the shuttles didn't waste precious fuel chasing the battlecruiser around the planet.

---

[52] *Skullcracker:* an ordinary soldier, equivalent to a "jarhead" or "grunt."
[53] *Catoplebas:* a pugnacious, boar-like race that was absorbed by the Sata'anic Empire.

His headset crackled with the Air Traffic Controller's voice. He popped one of the earbuds into his earhole.

"Net Control, this is Kasib."

"The General's shuttle has just navigated reentry," the ATC said.

A blend of fear, and excitement, rippled down to Kasib's tail.

"Estimated time to arrival?"

"Twenty minutes, Sir."

"Let me know when it's five," Kasib said. "CAO out."

He flicked his long, forked tongue to taste the air, pausing to relish the scent of fresh cut grass. The first thing he'd done was make sure their intelligence was correct, that this planet possessed grain fields. Their cultivation was primitive, the seed heads smaller and far less productive than Sata'anic grain, but the soil here was fertile and the native population accustomed to working in the fields. As soon as they got word back to Emperor Shay'tan—

Kasib touched his claws to his forehead, his snout and his heart.

"May peace be upon him," he muttered.

—their beneficent emperor and god would transform this backwater into a productive member of the Sata'anic Empire.

The Air Traffic Controller's voice crackled.

"Sir, the General is five minutes out."

"Got it," Kasib said. "Make the announcement. Order the men to assemble."

A quartet of loudspeakers, hastily erected on a tree, blared in a hissing voice: "Attention all crew! Attention all crew! Report to the airfield for inspection."

With a cheerful shout, Sata'anic lizards, boar-like Catoplebas, and blue-skinned Marid,[54] along with a sprinkling of other species which comprised Shay'tan's armies, all rushed to the newly leveled airfield in a masculine show of who could get there first. The men laughed and elbowed each other out of line. They grew silent as a whistling roar came out of the east and gave a pulse cannon-like explosion as the shuttle dropped out of supersonic speed.

"Line it up!" Kasib shouted.

The men snapped into crisp attention, their hands held down along their sides, their tails, if they had tails, or other appendages if they didn't, tucked tightly along the left side of their bodies. Kasib lowered his clear inner eyelids to keep out the dust as the shuttle hovered overhead, and then settled gently upon the ground, a perfect landing.

---

[54] *Marid* and *Free-Marid:* a blue-skinned, humanoid race. The *Marid* homeworld was annexed by the Sata'anic Empire, but several remote colonies, the *Free-Marid,* remain self-governing.

The hydraulics whined as the back of the troop carrier split open and lowered a ramp to the ground. An enormous lizard appeared, almost as burly as General Hudhafah, with a deep russet dewlap and a battle-scarred green and beige striped hide.

"Attention!" Master-Sergeant Dahaka barked the order.

The men clacked their heels together and all shouted "Sir!"

He marched down the ramp. Directly behind him walked General Hudhafah, his arms held loosely at his side, relaxed to an untrained eye, but Kasib's gold-green eyes picked up how readily the general could pull his knife, his pulse-rifle, or simply block a punch. The General moved to stand in front of the assembled men.

His gold-green eyes scanned the men, and then the forward operating base behind them.

"It's a start," he growled, for growling was Hudhafah's natural tone of voice. He turned to Kasib. "Where's Headquarters?"

"It's there, Sir." Kasib gestured towards a moderate stone building. "That's their temple. I've set your office up in the former sanctuary."

Hudhafah moved towards it, his thick tail twitching behind him, a fifth fighting limb. Unlike Kasib, he had to duck to get beneath the lintel, but it was tall enough inside to stand. Kasib led him through a small outer chamber, the one he intended to turn into an administrative office, into what had once been this village's holiest shrine. A simple stone goddess anointed the altar. He'd shoved it against the wall, beneath a framed print of Emperor Shay'tan, to make room for General Hudhafah's desk

The big red dragon smiled down upon the plump, naked woman, now subservient to their god, wrapped in a strip of cloth so that only her eyes peeked out. In a vase in front of her, he'd placed a small bouquet of still-immature grain from the nearby field.

General Hudhafah paused in front of the altar. An unreadable expression passed between him and Master-Sergeant Dahaka.

"That's a nice touch, Kasib," the General said.

"Thank you, Sir," Kasib beamed. "I thought it best to ask for a blessing immediately, in case the Emperor is too busy to respond to our request for supplies."

A low grumble came out of Hudhafah's chest. Not a displeased sound, but not a happy one, either. He moved towards a slit in the stone wall which served as a window and stared out at the still-unspooling base.

"Those houses are too close," Hudhafah said. "I want a thousand meter perimeter from the nearest asset."

"The local population is peaceful."

"I want them bulldozed," Hudhafah said. "Set up a double line of razor wire until we can build a fence."

Kasib nervously flitted out his tongue.

"I promised the village elders there would be no disruption, Sir."

General Hudhafah bared his fangs.

"The Alliance will come for them," Hudhafah said. "The minute they find out these people exist, they will come for them, and nothing on Hades will stop it, not even Shay'tan."

"If we ask," Sergeant Dahaka said, "he will send us reinforcements."

Hudhafah snorted.

"Reinforcements against a ghost?"

"It's an urban legend," Dahaka said. "A well-trained Special Forces unit. Not a single man."

Kasib looked from one man to another, perplexed.

"S-sir?"

Hudhafah's tail twitched in a thoughtful manner.

"Whenever we think we have a planet all sewn up, somebody sneaks in and throws a pulse grenade into the works." He pointed at the line of houses. "When I was stationed on 627-Draconis-6, we had a grain factory. The entire annexation depended on getting that processing plant going. The day we fired it up, somebody snuck in past seven layers of security, dropped a pulse grenade as Shay'tan was making a speech, and got out again without a single man seeing him."

Kasib tasted the air. Both the General, and Dahaka, emitted pheromones of stress.

"Was it the Cherubim?" Kasib's voice warbled.

"Angelic," Hudhafah said. "We found a dead guard clutching a single dark brown feather." He sighed. "We *think* he got in by working his way through some houses we foolishly decided to leave standing too close to the factory."

Kasib bowed his head and whispered

"Excuse my impudence, Sir," Kasib said. "I will tell the humans we have to tear down their homes."

Hudhafah's pupils narrowed into slits. He gestured at Sergeant Dahaka.

"Give the kid something to soften the blow."

"Sir." The burly Sergeant slid his rucksack off his shoulders and undid the flap. Kasib's eyes grew wide as he recognized the bag was filled with treasure.

"Here, give them this," Dahaka handed him a gold *daric*.[55] "Tell them Shay'tan wishes for them to build *better* homes, away from all the noise. And tell the rest of them, if they ever see or hear of a man with wings, that they're to tell us immediately, and we will give that person an entire bag."

---

[55] *Daric:* gold coin.

"Yes, Sir." Kasib gave the Master-Sergeant a crisp salute. Even though he technically outranked him, Shay'tan only gave honors to the *real* heroes of the Empire, the front-line skullcrackers, and not clever little lizards such as himself.

General Hudhafah picked up the report he'd placed upon his desk, the latest satellite download from the *SRN Jamaran*.

"Did you locate the wreckage from that scout ship?" he asked.

"No, Sir," Kasib said. "We think it broke apart on reentry."

"Find me a body," Hudhafah said. "I need to know that Angelic is dead."

Chapter 18

The evil demons who beset mankind,
Dim-me and Dim-mea who enter by night,
Namtar and Asag who will not leave a man alone,
Stand before the man. He is robbed of sleep.

—A sir-gida to Ninisina

February – 3,390 BC
Earth: Crash site

NINSIANNA

She was back in the vision, only this time when the sickness came, she danced among them. The stars cried out as the Evil One devoured them alive.

"No! *Máthair!*"[56] A man's voice cried out in terror.

Ninsianna sat upright, still clutching her covers.

"Ná gortaítear sí! Le do thoil!"[57]

The shadows moved, just like they had in the dream.

"Great Mother!" she squeaked. "Protect me from the dark!"

She'd always hated the dark, the way it crept around her whenever the sun went down and good friends left, leaving her all alone. So long as there was light, she always felt secure. So long as she had friends...

Mikhail cried out: *"Cá bhfuil Gabriel?"*[58]

He flailed at the phantasm, whimpering as he struck at the darkness. The faint blue outline of his spirit light appeared to wrestle a darkness which came from within.

She pulled her covers up to her chest.

"Mikhail?" she whispered.

She'd watched him suffer the last four nights, but tonight was worse. It seemed as though the more he fought to regain his memories, the more it empowered the demons.

'Ninsianna? Help him?' She-Who-Is whispered. *'You have to bind his memories.'*

"Only a shaman can banish a demon."

'You are far more powerful than a shaman.'

"Now I *know* I'm imagining things."

She watched him fight against the dream-demon, the man who had fallen from the heavens, rendered helpless in the face of things which raged

---

[56] *Máthair:* mother.
[57] "Don't hurt her, please."
[58] "Where is Gabriel?"

within. If she sang a song to banish the demons, would she succeed? Or would she become possessed, like her father had always warned?

Maybe Papa could banish the demon? He'd gone back to Assur to secure an invitation from the Chief.

No…

If she brought Mikhail to Assur, he would never take her to see the stars. She had to keep him *here*. Near his god, Compyoota, until he remembered how to make the sky canoe fly again.

Mikhail's spirit light grew dim as it battled the dark.

"*Máthair?*" he called plantitively. "*Ní féidir liom a bhraitheann tú níos mó.*"[59]

Ninsianna's heart caught in her throat. She clutched her blanket to her chest and stepped across the narrow aisle to touch his shoulder.

"Mikhail, wake up!"

Darkness curled around her fingers. A single tendril reached up to touch her forehead.

Fear. Grief.

Blood. Burnt bodies. Smoke.

Terrifying darkness…

Ninsianna shrieked.

Mikhail shot bolt upright, his lungs heaving as he keened a wordless cry. He crushed her to his chest, so hard she feared he might break her ribs. She fought to escape, but he clutched her tighter like a drowning man gripping at a log.

"*Ach aisling, ach aisling, ach aisling…*"[60] he chanted.

His heart pounded so fast she feared it would leap out of his broken ribs.

"Mikhail," her voice trembled. "It was just a nightmare."

Gradually he realized she wasn't part of the dream.

Mikhail stiffened.

"Sorry," he enunciated clearly. "Bad…"

"Dream," she finished.

"Yes. Bad dream."

He looked away, embarrassed, no doubt because she'd seen him vulnerable. His cold, pale skin glistened in the dim light, drenched with sweat. He didn't push her away, but he might as well have when he released his arms and left her sitting there, almost naked on the bed.

Ninsianna realized her blanket had slipped down.

"I'll just, uhm…" She bent to grab the blanket. "I have to use the magic chamber pot."

She bolted out of there before he could order her to *go home*.

---

[59] "Mother, I can't feel you."
[60] *Ach aisling:* not real.

Chapter 19

February – 3,390 BC
Earth: Crash site
Colonel Mikhail Mannuki'ili

MIKHAIL

For three days he'd worked on the computer, and still the AI sat there, every bit as useless as *he* was. Darned technology! How was he supposed to fix it when he couldn't remember anything?

He had a mission. He could *feel* that mission in his bones. It whispered like a heartbeat, *'tell somebody, tell somebody, tell somebody!'* But the mission itself was nothing but an errant emotion. No memories. No clues. No *idea* what he was supposed to tell. Just an uneasy feeling he'd left something important undone.

He closed his eyes and put his head down into his hand, trying to remember *something* about his past. A mother? A father? Loved ones? Sisters and brothers? A commanding officer? Maybe a mate? He couldn't remember anything, just an empty ache that was probably just his chest wound. He needed the computer to tell him who he was and why he was here.

He tried to *think* about how to fix the computer, but no matter how hard he tried, the schematics remained elusive. But when he picked up the screwdriver and stuck it into the mess of wires, he *knew* what to do, even though he couldn't *remember* where it was supposed to go.

He picked up some thin-nosed pliers and coaxed the wire into one of the many terminals which sat empty. By trial and error, he would figure it out, eventually, so long as he tried not to *think* about it. It was just a matter of time.

Ninsianna slipped back in the crack they used as a door. There was something about the woman which made him feel lighter, as if the sun had risen in his lonely world.

An image popped into his mind. Ninsianna. Naked. Plastered to his chest.

It was just a dream…

Thank the gods he hadn't grabbed his sword. Not only might he have stabbed her, but the *last* thing he wanted was to feed into her father's delusion he was some kind of savior. He was nothing but a soldier. A soldier who couldn't remember his own name.

"I asked you to stay inside," he said.

Ninsianna smiled brightly and held up her water skin, still dripping wet.

"*Deoch*," she said in his language.

"Yes, *deoch*," he said. "But what will you do if your friend comes back? I'm not certain this Chief of yours will be able to knock some sense into his head."

Ninsianna went into the galley to search for a cup, and then poured him some water, gesturing as though he was a child.

"*Deoch*," she repeated. Drink, you stubborn ball of feathers.

His hand tingled as he took the cup from her fingers.

"*Cupán*," he said. "Cup. Drink."

Ninsianna's lush, pink lips curved up into a winsome smile.

"Yes. *Cupán*. *Deoch*. Drink. You drink water from cup?"

She practically *glowed*, tempting him with the chalice. His entire body vibrated with hyper-awareness, a primitive urge to shove his nose into her neck and inhale.

You promised her father you would not take her with you.

As soon as he got the computer working, he would signal for help, and then he'd go away, leaving Ninsianna and her jealous boyfriend behind.

He took a small sip, and then put the cup onto the workstation next to him. Ninsianna bit her lip, her thick, brown eyebrows coming together in an expression of bewilderment.

"*Deoch?* Yes?" she said.

"No. I'm trying to conserve resources."

He pointed at the angry red light which blinked on his pulse pistol, warning it was almost out of plasma. Until he got his engines fixed, he had no way to recharge it. He was in no condition to go hand-to-hand with her jilted lover.

Ninsianna tilted her head, unable to comprehend. She picked up the cup and held it back out to him.

"*Deoch*!" Drink.

Her lips moved into a stern '*do as I say or else*' expression. She stood there with her hand on her hip until he drank it down. As he did, he watched her through a veiled expression. Every facial gesture fascinated him; from the way her voice rose and fell with emotion, to the way her entire body placed him in an agitated state of excitement.

You'd think he'd never been attracted to a woman before?

Was he attracted to her?

Probably. Why else did he feel an overwhelming urge to take to the sky and shout with glee every time she came near him?

He stared at the bare expanse of back between her shoulder blades. He wanted to ask '*what happened to your wings?*' but with the ship's computer down, he couldn't power it up to answer his *own* questions, such as *'who am I and how did I get here,'* much less order it to analyze Ninsianna's speech patterns and create an algorithm so he could ask stupid questions.

Ninsianna frowned as she noticed his intense gaze.

"*Go raibh maith agat,*" he said in his own language. "Thank you."

She repeated the phrase to memorize the words, and then repeated it in her own language, pairing it with the other words he'd taught her to create primitive, but intelligible phrases. Mikhail memorized the alien language. Without a working translator, they had no choice but to communicate the old-fashioned way.

She pointed at his chest, now covered with a clean shirt. She pressed one finger against her lips, and then touched, hesitantly, the silver wings on his chest-pocket.

"Those are my wings," he said.

Her lips pursed in concentration.

"Wings?"

She pointed at his *real* wings, and then at the silver pin.

"Yes, wings."

How could he explain the feeling of pride he got whenever he touched the pin? Although he couldn't remember receiving it, it *meant* something, dammit! It meant he belonged to something. Even if he couldn't remember what that something was.

Ninsianna reached into the pouch she kept belted to her waist. One by one, she pulled out several objects and placed them, carefully, on the counter in front of the dead computer. Several flowers. A pebble. She placed them in a circle around his screwdriver.

The last object was a stick, carved to fashion a crude, winged doll.

Terror, love, *panic*, hit him all at once. He grabbed the dolly. The sensation grew larger, more powerful, *and frantic*. Large, prescient eyes stared back at him out of a too-large head, attached to a fragile wooden body. A sob reared up into his throat.

"Where did you get this?"

Ninsianna stared at him wide-eyed.

"*Damantia!* Answer me!"

Her expression turned to fear.

"I f-f-find..." She pointed at the place she'd piled all the debris.

Emotion moved beneath the surface. Just like in the nightmare. Awful, *terrifying* feelings. And an overwhelming sense of loss.

—*A field full of grape leaves.*

—*Mikhail. Come and find me...*

He tried to pull up the memory, but it was lost to him, forever.

Ninsianna backed away, her expression fearful.

He realized how he must look. Twice her size, lording over her with a ten meter wingspan. He put the doll into his chest-pocket, where he *knew* it belonged.

"Ninsianna?" he said softly. *"Le de thoil.* I am sorry. Doll make me remember—" he tapped his forehead "—something."

"Mikhail not—" she struggled for the word.

"Angry," he said.

"Mikhail not angry?"

"No. Just—" he struggled for a suitable substitute for 'surprised.'

Her expression remained dubious.

"Here—" he gestured at the trinkets she'd laid out on his countertop. "Tell me, what these for?"

He feigned a curious expression. If there was one thing Ninsianna enjoyed more than bossing him around, it was telling him stories about her father and his magic. Not that he *understood* her. Nine-tenths of what she said remained gibberish. But it made her happy. And it made *him* look less like a heartless jerk.

She picked up each object and pointed to a different quadrant of his ship. And then she pointed at his computer, chattering as she raised her hands up into the air. She began to sing another of her songs, this one more primitive and guttural than the one she sang whenever she changed his bandages. He stared at her, transfixed, as though she'd suddenly become brighter.

She picked up his screwdriver and held it into the air.

"Ah, Buyuk Bilgisayar!" she said. *"Mikhail'in duasina cevap verin."*

She jabbed the screwdriver into the computer. Sparks flew. Ten thousand volts of electricity threw her backwards. She lay there, twitching. The bridge filled with the stench of burning hair.

"Ninsianna!"

He stumbled onto the floor and yanked the screwdriver out of her hand. Her mouth moved like a gasping fish as she twitched. He clutched her to his chest.

A voice erupted from the loudspeaker.

<< *Raphael … I've been hit! Shay'tan has found the godsdamned Holy Grail!!! This planet is crawling with enough Sata'an to…* >>

A thrill of recognition went through his body as he recognized his own voice. The message cut off.

"Computer!" he cried out. "Answer me! What was my last mission?"

The message repeated. Bits of smoke and sparks flew out of the central processing unit, and then it stopped, leaving him with nothing but the stench of burnt wires.

"Damantia!"

The AI was now every bit as dead as before.

Ninsianna, on the other hand…

"What were you thinking?" he shook her. "Don't you know electricity can kill you?"

Ninsianna opened up her eyes and smiled.

"Computer answer, yes?"

Her tawny-beige eyes glittered golden. His sense of fury wilted beneath their light. She was like the sun, and he the poor, fallen creature she'd come to save.

"I think you broke it worse," he grumbled.

She gave him a victorious grin.

"Computer answer Mikhail!"

He glanced at the smoldering central processing unit. Now it was *really* broken, leaving him with more questions than answers.

Who was Raphael? And what in Hades was the 'Holy Grail?'

Chapter 20

For in the resurrection they neither marry,
Nor are given in marriage,
But are as the angels of God in heaven.

Matthew 22:30

Galactic Standard Date: 152,323.02
Command Carrier: 'Light Emerging'
Colonel Raphael Israfa

RAPHAEL

"Colonel Israfa," Major Glicki called down, "we have a hail from the *Eternal Light*. Supreme Commander-General Jophiel will initiate a subspace wormhole in ten minutes."

"Thank you," Raphael said. "Send it right through."

He glanced in the mirror and straightened out his uniform, fussily tucking a few stray golden feathers so his wings appeared glossy and smooth. M-Theory enabled them to communicate with somebody on the opposite side of the galaxy, but micro-wormholes required an ungodly amount of power, so today's conversation would be brief. He rehearsed in the mirror his most formal expression:

"Supreme Commander-General…"

That didn't feel right.

"*Damantia*, Jophiel!"

That would get him court-martialed for sure.

He gave the mirror a wistful expression.

"Jophie, please…"

His throat closed up. He gave his reflection a wistful smile, an expression he'd been wearing a *lot* lately, and not simply because his best friend had gone missing.

The monitor beeped at precisely the appointed time.

He made a panicked grab for the photograph he kept prominently displayed on his desk and shoved it into a drawer just as Major Glicki sent the hail through.

"Colonel Israfa—" Supreme Commander-General Jophiel's ethereally beautiful face appeared on the monitor. "What have you discovered?"

"He was scouting reports of a Sata'anic incursion when his ship was hit. We can take that alone as an indicator the intelligence has some basis."

Jophiel's expression remained cool and impartial.

"You have thirty days, but I can't justify the resources to hunt down a single man any longer than that. Not even for Colonel Mannuki'ili."

Raphael frowned, and then he grinned as she shifted uncomfortably in her seat. The bulge in her midsection was so large it was impossible to hide, even in the head-and-shoulders only video transmission.

"Jophie—" Raphael's expression grew tender "—how fares our son?"

"He fares well." Jophiel said. "It won't be much longer."

An iron fist gripped Raphael's heart. She was beautiful under any circumstances, but when she let the icy mask of a general slip, Jophiel took his breath away. Wavy white-blond hair, cerulean blue eyes, porcelain skin and snow-white wings, if ever the Eternal Emperor were to point to a single specimen of his genetic tinkering and say, *'this is perfection,'* it would be Jophiel.

"I want to be there with you!" He made a pathetic plea. "Let me come to you when our son makes his appearance?"

Her face composed back into the controlled mask of a general. "You know the law. You're needed *there*."

She abruptly ended the transmission.

Raphael's wings drooped. He wasn't supposed to *care* that marriage was illegal and sexual relations forbidden for any purpose other than to replenish the Emperor's ranks. They were artificial life forms, created solely to perpetuate the glory of the Alliance, but *damantia*! He *was* disappointed!

He fished the photograph of him escorting her to a state dinner at the Emperor's palace out of his drawer and placed it back upon his desk. He'd never understood why she'd brought him out so publicly before selecting him to sire this child, but an ambitious reporter had captured her expression as he'd offered her his hand instead of allowing her to march into the banquet as was the custom. She wore a smile like the heroine on the cover of a Mantoid romance novel.

Silly romantic notions!

Jophiel had made it clear she only entered into a five day union to fill the Emperor's ranks, but for one so icy and distant, she'd thawed considerably during her heat cycle. He'd pulled out all the stops, not to just contribute the necessary genetic matter, which was all that was expected of him, but to imprint himself upon her very soul. Jophiel appeared to respond right up until the test had come back positive. A successful mating!

She'd instantly banished him to the remotest sector of the galaxy, giving him command of the *Light Emerging* as a consolation prize, and had not had any in-person contact with him since. A command carrier was a high honor for a mere Colonel, but he would have much rather have had *her*.

"Major Glicki," Raphael called up to his second-in-command. "You get off shift in half an hour, right?"

"Yes, Sir."

"Who's up there on the bridge to take over?"

"Lieutenant T'trk should be here in twenty minutes."

"Good," Raphael said. "Meet me in the officer's lounge in forty-five. And bring the good stuff."

"That bad, huh?"

"Yeah."

Chapter 21

Galactic Standard Date: 152,323.02
Haven-3
Prime Minister Lucifer

LUCIFER

The outer Alliance Parliament was a large circular building, filled with offices and temporary housing in the upper floors. Depending on his schedule, sometimes Lucifer spent more time in *this* office than his *real* one. He paused, one hand on the door knob to the chamber where these particular types of 'appointments' were kept.

"What's her name and who is she stationed under?"

"Hemaniel—" his Chief of Staff Zepar rattled off the particulars. "She is under the command of Colonel Gavreel on the battle cruiser *Emperor's Eye*."

"Is this her first mating attempt?"

"She is fresh out of the academy." Zepar peered at his flatscreen. "She claims to be a virgin, although we don't verify the veracity of the pre-mating questionnaire. All we care about is that she is coming into heat."

"The Emperor has them all so brainwashed they can only form relations to bear offspring that she probably *is* a virgin." Lucifer flicked his wings with irritation. "It will take extra time to break her in. How long do I have?"

"I scheduled one hour." Zepar said. "You'll need to use your gift to get her to perform within the allotted time. You have an important meeting with the Ministry of Defense at 4:30 and you need time to get cleaned up beforehand."

A senior Ramidreju[61] delegate walked out of an adjacent chamber with his arm around his wife's shoulders, the disheveled nature of their pelts indicating they'd taken advantage of the temporary sleeping quarters to have a little 'appointment' of their own. The wife smiled up at her husband, chattering about their latest litter of kitts. A feeling of jealousy clenched at Lucifer's gut.

"Just once I would like to have enough time to get to know some of these females instead of these constant, meaningless fucks." Lucifer gave a bitter sigh. "If you ask me, *that's* why our species is dying out."

"You know that's forbidden, Sire," Zepar reminded him. "You're the Emperor's adopted son. You *must* produce an heir."

---

[61] *Ramidreju:* a sentient, mink-like species with luxurious fur.

"Like I care what my father forbids?" Lucifer closed his eyes and pressed his forehead against the door, allowing the coolness of real wood to sink into his skin. With his genetic enhancements, his hearing was far better than most naturally evolved creatures. He could hear the anxious rustle of feathers from behind the door as the nervous female paced.

"You know the consequences of forming an emotional attachment during sexual relations," Zepar warned. "You're one quarter Seraphim. The Emperor has refused to disclose whether or not you inherited their defective genome."

That small, sarcastic inner voice that was always irritatingly *right*, parroted his Chief of Staff's warning.

'It will kill you. Just like it did your mother...'

Seraphim! Lucifer's wings trembled with the anger and sorrow that very word inspired. With a genome spliced together from two monogamous species, full-blooded Seraphim Angelics took one mate, for life, a genetic defect which resulted in losing *two* Angelic super-soldiers every time *one* of them died in battle.

Long before he'd been born, the Emperor had segregated out the worst offenders and banished them to their own planet, far from the Alliance so they would stop muddying up the gene pool of his armies. Since then, Hashem had done everything in his power to eradicate the troublesome gene so he would stop losing mated pairs.

Only Lucifer knew it was the *real* reason for the law against fraternization for any purpose other than to fill the ranks. Despite the Emperor's best efforts, Hashem had only been able to *weaken* the instinct to bond, not eliminate it. A bonded hybrid was reluctant to take any action which would result in not only its own death, but also the death of its mate, rendering his armies useless the moment they got married.

He glanced down the hallway towards the disappearing back of his Ramidreju colleague and sighed.

"Remember what happened to your mother," Zepar said. "It didn't matter that she had not seen your biological father in fifteen years. She bonded with him when she conceived you, and when he died, it killed her."

"This isn't fun anymore," Lucifer sighed. "Maybe it's time I admitted it just wasn't meant to be and adopted a child? Like the Emperor did when he adopted *me*?"

"The Emperor's edict was bequeathed upon a *bloodline*," Zepar said. "If the child is not of your loins, the charter becomes null and void."

Lucifer's wings settled into a weary arc. What had at first been an exciting perquisite of the job had turned into a never-ending chore. Zepar scheduled appointment after appointment with Angelic females who were only too willing to throw away one of their precious biennial heat cycles on a futile attempt to bear the Eternal Emperor's adopted son an heir.

"Can't we just pick one out of the academy and bribe somebody to say the kid is mine," Lucifer half-joked.

"The stability of the Alliance depends upon your producing an heir." Zepar gave him an unsympathetic look. "Do you want the Emperor to revoke Parliament's charter upon your death?"

"No," Lucifer sighed.

"Our species is dying," Zepar said. "Your genetic profile is too unique to simply throw away. The Emperor himself has decreed that you *must* keep trying."

'And you –do– so enjoy the conquest. You know you do...'

A sultry image of an Angelic female, her back arched in ecstasy as she cried out his name, danced through his mind. Lucifer squirmed as blood rushed to a certain part of his anatomy. As much as sexual conquest had long ago lost its luster, he had a reputation to uphold.

"Lucifer, we've had this talk before." Zepar put a fatherly hand upon his shoulder. "Sometimes it's necessary to sacrifice a little personal happiness to obtain the greater good. Like it or not, you're a symbol of the vitality of our great Alliance."

'Are you so selfish that you would abandon your species to die out?'

"Of course." Lucifer's wings trembled. "You're right. I must ensure the survival of my species." He curled his wing around his crotch so Zepar wouldn't see him 'adjust' himself. "What was her name again?"

"Hemaniel," Zepar said. "And you've just wasted ten minutes of your hour. You don't have time to break her in naturally."

"Knock five minutes before I need to be out of here for the post-sex niceties."

He resumed the fake persona he assumed for the rest of the world, the charismatic leader who could give everybody their heart's desire. As soon as his wings cleared the door, he flared them like a raptor swooping in for the kill, a pose female Angelics found irresistible.

"Prime Minister Lucifer," Hemaniel stammered. "It's an honor."

The pretty blonde clutched her chest, her eyes wide with awe at the privilege of being this close to the Eternal Emperor's adopted son. She looked out of place in the lushly furnished temporary sleeping quarters, the rich burgundy and black décor clashing with her sandy blonde wings.

Lucifer inhaled the subtle pheromones of an Angelic coming into heat. His olfactory nerves relished the scent of lutropin, a heady drug to a species bordering on extinction. He reached out to tuck an errant strand of golden hair behind her ear, a level of familiarity few Angelics ever exchanged.

"Have you ever attempted a mating before?"

"N-n-no."

Lucifer cleared his mind so that he see could her subconscious longings; telepathy gifted not from his adopted father, who had inadvertently bred the ability out of his armies in an effort to eradicate the pesky bonding gene, but from his half-Seraphim mother. Images of a Mantoid soap opera, a certain actor she had a crush on, came into his mind. Lucifer adjusted his posture, his voice, his demeanor to mimic the archetype of her ideal lover.

"It can be quite pleasurable—" he drew close, moderating his voice to the husky pitch her archetype possessed "—if you allow me to make it so." He didn't touch her, but formed an image of himself kissing her neck and projected it into her mind.

"I've only been told—"

She shuddered as he followed through on the projection by exhaling upon her neck. He didn't touch her, but goose bumps of anticipation appeared upon her flesh.

"What have you been told?" he whispered into her ear, his body inches from hers as he encircled her in his wings. He projected an image of taking her into his arms without actually making physical contact. Over the years, he'd discovered that *anticipation* of being touched was often more erotic than the reality of it. "What do you fantasize about when you touch yourself?"

"I have always wanted…" she said, embarrassed.

"Then do it." His voice was a leonine purr as he projected an image into her mind of unbuttoning his shirt and admiring the taut muscles that rippled beneath. "I'm here to make your wildest fantasies come true."

Her hand trembled as she fumbled each button out of its buttonhole, helped along with the images he imprinted into her subconscious. Two hundred and twenty-five years of non-stop practice had honed his ability to seduce others down to an art form, the 'power of persuasion' Zepar jokingly called his gift.

"Touch me," he whispered. "I like to be touched."

Closing his eyes, he soaked up the feel of her touch, tentative and filled with awe. Touch. The gift hybrids were forbidden to give one another for any purpose other than to create offspring. It was *he* who trembled now, his need to be touched far greater than others of his species because he'd been raised in a home, by a half-Seraphim mother. Asherah had refused send him to one of the Emperor's youth training academies as was done to every other hybrid child to condition that yearning right out of them.

He reached tentatively into her mind, hoping that *this* one would see him. Not that he made it easy! The Emperor's abandonment after his mother had died had taught him to be wary. If you let people inside, they would thank you by tearing out your heart. The one time he'd ever foolishly let down his guard, the female had spurned him after the test had come back negative, refusing to answer his three beautifully hand-written missives!

He projected the same thought he had asked of every woman he had ever fucked, the same heartfelt yearning which only a true mate would answer.

'Can you feel me? Can you look into my eyes and see my soul?'

He saw Hemaniel's thoughts as clearly as though he were inside a movie. His cheek twitched with disappointment. It was not *him* she saw, but the archetype of the movie star she'd spent half her adolescence worshipping. They didn't ever see *him*, or if they did, it wasn't the *real* him, but one of the bullshit publicity stunts Zepar filmed depicting him doing something 'manly' such as riding a land-dragon shirtless through the tundra with a miniature pterodactyl on his wrist to hunt.

"Is this okay?" Hemaniel's hands slid down to touch his slacks. In her fantasy, *she* was the aggressor.

Words from the movie came into his mind; words he sensed that if spoken aloud, would transform her into a bold temptress.

"Your touch is like the rain upon my flesh." He whispered the poetic words she longed to hear. He touched the underside of her chin to look into her eyes before kissing her. It was not *him* Hemaniel saw as he slid his hand up to cup her breast, but the actor of her dreams. "Touch me, Hemaniel. I want to feel what it's like to bathe in your touch."

She trembled as he expertly slid the pretty dress she'd worn for today's appointment down from her shoulder, bending to nip the base of her throat and leave his mark. He could *taste* the lutropin. The scent of fertility was so strong it made him dizzy with the urge to mate. But not for the brainwashing instilled from birth, unattached hybrid males would become aggressive and fight one another. His wings flapped involuntarily, slapping against her smaller beige ones as that small, aggressive voice which lurked in his subconscious egged him on, whispering that this time the union would bear fruit.

"Touch me," his voice filled with hunger. "Touch me, please. I need to be touched."

That small, vicious voice teased him for the yearning no amount of conditioning had been able to eradicate from his psyche, the need to have somebody touch him; not because they needed something from him, but because they loved him. The images his gift enabled him to see within her mind showed Hemaniel did not touch *him*, but the actor who he showed her.

'See! It's not -you- she wants!' his inner voice taunted *'but prestige you can bring to her if she bears your child. She is only after your position of power...'*

His touch grew rougher as he sensed this was what she wanted. Their wings knocked the pictures off the wall as he allowed her to get the better of him and shove him down upon the bed. Yes! This one desired to be the aggressor, a different flavor than the endless stream of females Zepar lined up for him to fuck.

Feathers flew as he used his gift to urge her to take him forcibly. For all the propaganda about Angelics being icy and unemotional, the fact was, if not for the conditioning they received from birth to subdue their animal half, hybrids would be rutting in the streets like beasts every time a female came into heat.

Projecting image after image into her mind, when she finally pinned his shoulders to the bed and impaled herself upon his cock, she was so aroused that she barely felt the pain of her hymen tearing. He withheld his seed until he heard her cry out with pleasure, helped along by his projections into her mind.

Release caused his eyes to roll back into his head, giving him just for a moment that feeling of oneness with the universe he'd yearned to feel ever since his mother had used her Song to heal him as a little boy. He heard it now, but the Song reached into emptiness, finding nothing, for how could you bond with someone who didn't *feel* you?

No sooner had Hemaniel collapsed, panting, on top of him, when the knock came upon the door.

"Sir?" Zepar shouted. "It's time for your next meeting."

They were out of time.

"Thank you," he murmured as he gathered his clothing and gave her a kiss goodbye. "You will let me know if things were successful?"

The female nodded, her hand moving to touch the womb they both prayed he'd been able to fill. The 'Holy Grail.' A productive womb, guaranteeing the survival of their species.

He gave her a wistful smile, knowing in his heart the answer would be the same. The chalice would remain empty because *he* had never been able to fill it. But these trysts were not without *some* benefit beyond the momentary release he felt each time he spilled his seed. So deeply had he imprinted the subconscious connection between her deepest desire and *him* that she would fantasize about their union for the rest of her life. Every male who came after him would fall short. With the mere whisper of another tryst, if he ever needed anything, she would deliver.

Lucifer had long ago learned the secret to getting what he wanted. Figure out people's most secret desire. Encourage them to fantasize about it. And then give it to them.

Chapter 22

Galactic Standard Date: 152,323.02
Command Carrier: 'Light Emerging'
Colonel Raphael Israfa

RAPHAEL

The officer's lounge was where high-ranking members of the *Light Emerging* met to eat, play board games, and yes, get stinking drunk, away from the gossiping eyes of the enlisted men. Like most Alliance warships, the lounge was sparely, but tastefully decorated. A group of white-winged Angelics playing cards cleared Raphael's preferred table in front of the window which overlooked the launch bay.

A tall, slender Mantoid private came to take his order.

"Would you like some supper, Colonel?" she asked.

"Just *coinneac*,"[62] he said. "One bottle, two glasses?"

"Yes, Sir."

The private left to get his drink. He stared out the window. A long, silver arrow of a ship glided into the flight hanger. Before it even set down, an orange-jacketed flight-crew, nearly all of them Mantoids, scurried out to refuel it so it could go right back out to man the search grid. Every ship under his command was out searching for Mikhail, the last living full-blooded Seraphim; a man who had chosen to remain celibate rather than subject himself to the same heartbreak *he* experienced right now.

The private came back balancing a tray. She set the *coinneac* down on the table, along with the two glasses and a bowl full of *brioscaí*.[63]

"Will Major Glicki be joining you?" she asked.

"In twenty minutes."

Her mandibles parted in a knowing grin.

"Just signal when you need more glasses."

The six-limbed waitress moved off to wait upon the lower-ranking officers, most of them Angelic, even though Mantoids now made up the bulk of the Angelic Air Force. This was his reward for giving Jophiel five days of pleasure, to sit at this window and stare down at his ships, dozens of surveillance vessels; the most sophisticated reconnaissance equipment in the Alliance.

---

[62] *Coinneac:* whiskey.
[63] *Brioscaí:* crackers.

He sucked down the *coinneac*, but it was the usual watered-down *cac*.[64] Angelics had a woefully low tolerance to alcohol, so their stock liquor was little more than fruit juice.

"C'mon, Glicki?" He rubbed the ache in his chest. "Where's the good stuff?"

The officers in the table next to him all laid wagers. Gambling was illegal, but he overlooked it so long as the gamblers avoided the exchange of Galactic Credits. The men laughed as they came up with horrible duties for the losers, from cleaning out the latrines to who would get stuck crawling down into the antimatter induction port the next time space junk got sucked into one of the hyperdrives.

"Sir? Would you like to lay a wager?" a mid-level officer asked.

"What's the bet?"

"Which pilot will find Mikhail?"

Raphael glanced down at the scout ship being refueled below.

"I lay one shore leave on LE-27," he said. "Anywhere in the galaxy."

The men prattled with excitement. Here at the edge of civilization, shore leaves were few and far between. Not because there was extra work, but because there were so few places to *go*. He took another drink, trying to drown out the inner voice which pleaded for him to take his *own* shore leave, right to Supreme Commander-General Jophiel's command carrier.

Glicki limped in, two and a quarter meters of naturally armored fighting machine. She'd earned her oak leaf after she'd survived a near-fatal injury helping Mikhail seriously mess up Shay'tan's best-laid plans. The leg pained her—not even a Mantoid exoskeleton was a match for a Sata'anic pulse rifle—but she never complained. Intelligence work was intelligence work, she said, whether creeping through the underbrush, or using her skill to mentor a new generation of intelligence officers.

She sat down across from him and plunked a bottle onto the center of the table.

"Special issue," she said. "Straight from Aunt Hrr'll's distillery."

"Give my regards to your Aunt."

"You're lucky she likes you," she laughed. "This bottle is worth an emperor's ransom."

The half-meter high bottle glowed phosphorescent, brilliant bright green, with a swirl of vapors kept trapped beneath the cork. Commercially produced *choledzeretsa*[65] was heavily taxed, but most Mantoids operated their own stills to keep their kin suitably sloshed. Which was difficult, since Mantoids could drink every other species in the universe under the table.

---

[64] *Cac*: crap.

[65] *Choledzeretsa*: (lit. intoxicating liquor) a mildly hallucinogenic liquor brewed by the Mantoids. Illegal, but the prohibition is widely flaunted.

Raphael finished his *coinneac* and clunked his empty glass in front of her.

"You're already drunk," she said.

"Not nearly drunk enough."

She refilled his glass with the potent green liquor.

"Bottoms up," she said.

Raphael sucked it down.

One of the junior officers in the table next to them called out: "Hey, Major Glicki? We're taking bets on Mikhail. How long do you think it will take to find him?"

The men all leaned forward. *She* knew what the odds were.

"Pass," she said.

She poured two more glasses of liquor.

"Well?" she asked.

"Well, what?"

"What happened?"

Raphael stared down at the launch bay. Scout ship LE-27 lifted off and navigated through the airlocks, out to perform another search for the last living Seraphim.

"She said we have thirty days," he said.

"That wasn't what I meant."

He met his second-in-command's red, compound eyes.

"She shot me down," he said. "And then she hung up on me."

Glicki's tufted antenna tilted in different directions.

"Did you tell her how you *feel*?"

"Of course I did!" He stared down at the swirling liquor. "Not really," he mumbled. "There wasn't a lot of time."

"I warned you this would happen," Glicki said. "The fact this was offspring number twelve should have been warning enough, if the five-hundred page waiver didn't get that through your thick skull."

"I hoped to impress her," Raphael said. "She definitely seemed pleased at the time."

He rubbed the center of his chest, his expression wistful. The way she'd risen up to meet him; her cries as he'd brought her to climax again and again. He'd used every psychological trick in the book to imprint himself upon her, to be the *first*, even though he knew he was the twelfth. The tears that had come into her eyes as they'd lain entangled together the last time they had made love seemed too genuine to be fake. No matter *how* much it hurt now that she'd banished him to the opposite end of the galaxy, he wouldn't give up that memory for anything in the universe.

Glicki's gossamer under-wings buzzed an angry warning.

"The Emperor should have pulled other races into the military millennia ago!" she said. "The price you've paid for being policemen for the galaxy is way too high!"

"It's our honor to serve the naturally evolved races."

"You're treated like slaves! You should have the *same* right to marry as every other species in the Alliance. Not bow down to the naturally evolved races because the Emperor tinkered with your DNA!"

The lower-ranking officers all leaned in their direction, pretending not to listen. Their pending extinction was exacerbating some already deep rifts within the Alliance, especially among the Leonids and Centauri whose numbers were even lower than *theirs* were.

"Lower your voice," Raphael hushed her. "The direction of this conversation is treason."

"Then write me *up*," Glicki said, "and I'll tell the Emperor off *myself!*"

"It won't do any good."

"Dragon-*cac*! Without *you*, he wouldn't have an Alliance!"

"He's doing the best he *can*," Raphael sighed. "But until he finds a cure, our only hope is to be out-bred."[66]

"Sentient creatures aren't meant to *live* this way!" Glicki slammed down her glass. "We only have to serve twenty years. But *you*? You have to serve five hundred!"

"We can marry when we retire."

"By then, Jophiel will be too old to give you any more children," she said. "He needs to get you off of these ships. Not this ridiculous breeding program where every child needs a different father, and then shuffle them off to the youth brainwashing academy."

"I didn't mind being raised in a youth training academy," Raphael said. "Neither did Jophiel."

"They do it to take advantage of your tendency to imprint!" Glicki said. "That is *wrong!* To abuse your animal half to psychologically bond to the first person you encounter! You should want better for your son!"

Raphael grimaced. Glicki, as usual, called the intelligence the way it *was*. A mischievous pucker appeared on his left cheek, making him look far younger than his thirty-six Galactic Standard cycles.

"Maybe we should try Prime Minister Lucifer's proposal? Keep the little woman confined to a homeworld, barefoot and pregnant, like Shay'tan does with the Sata'anic females."

Glicki clicked her middle legs together in a disapproving crack. In Mantoid culture, it was usually the larger, stronger females who went to war.

---

[66] *Out-bred:* the opposite of inbred, to broaden the gene pool until a congenital defect can be eliminated.

"You saw how fast Jophiel shut down *that* cockamamie scheme!" She whirred her under-wings in disgust. "It was the one time Jophiel ever skipped a mating cycle."

His eyes wrinkled in a smile despite his inner pain. He'd reached for the most brilliant star in the sky, and missed.

"As Jophiel goes—" he raised his glass "—so goes the hybrid fleet."

"Here, here." Glicki clinked Raphael's glass before downing it. "Every female hybrid in the fleet refused to show up for their mating appointments until Parliament shot Lucifer down. Including Lucifer's!"

"I think it was the only time the alpha-stud ever experienced a dry spell."

Raphael barked a bittersweet laugh. The Alliance Prime Minister was both an example, and a caricature, of what their species had devolved into. The brightest and most beautiful of all the Angelics, in his desperate attempt to perpetuate his own bloodline, had become a symbol of their pending extinction.

"Jophiel showed *him* who was boss!" Glicki lowered her voice. "There's some sort of history between those two, if you ask me..."

"You've been watching too many of those sappy Mantoid space operas," Raphael said. "She's impervious to Lucifer's charm, and it goads him. She's the only commander he can't manipulate."

"Women make better commanders then men," Glicki said. "That's why Mantoid females leave the males home to rear the mantids."[67]

"And bite their heads off after mating with them."

"Urban legend!" Glicki's under-wings hummed in a Mantoid laugh. "Our females haven't done that for millions of years." She held out her glass in a mock-toast. "Unlike Angelic females, who still regularly indulge in the practice."

"Ouch!" Raphael's dimple disappeared. He stared down into the potent green liquor which swirled at the bottom of his half-empty glass. *He wouldn't mind being sent home to rear his soon-to-be-born son and support Jophiel's rising star.*

"Mikhail was raised by a family," he said softly. "He never speaks of it, but he said, if he can't marry, then he won't have any offspring at all."

"Can you blame him?"

"No." He donned a mock emotionless expression. "Seraphim only take one mate for life! Never have I seen a man want something so badly, and yet he avoids it."

They both laughed. Mikhail always stood at the periphery, watching everything, but never participating. It wasn't just his lack of social skills, a

---

[67] *Mantids:* baby Mantoids.

holdover from being raised in a Cherubim monastery, but humanoid nature, he said, was outright *illogical.*

"Personally, I think he has the right idea," Glicki said. "He may *serve* the Emperor. But the Emperor doesn't own him."

Raphael stared down at the launch bay as another shuttle glided in. Glicki wasn't cleared to know that the Eternal Emperor *himself* had gone to the youth training academy to 'imprint' Mikhail after he'd nearly killed one of his fellow students. While everybody *sensed* the rage the big, brooding Seraphim kept tightly leashed beneath the surface, only *he* understood the Cherubim had merely taught him to contain it. Not to get over it.

How in Hades do you get over watching your entire species get murdered?

Glicki reached across the table and touched his forearm.

"Jophiel calls you every week," she said, "about matters some underling far beneath her could handle. I think she sent you so far away because she fears you'll break down her resolve."

Raphael finished the dregs at the bottom of his glass.

"She doesn't care about me," he said. "I'm just another one of Hashem's pawns."

He lurched to his feet. The room spun as he flailed his wings to keep his balance. Glicki moved quickly to prop him up.

"Alright, Colonel," she said. "It's time to go sleep it off."

Chapter 23

February - 3,390 BC
Earth: Crash site
Colonel Mikhail Mannuki'ili

MIKHAIL

No matter *how* many times Mikhail wired it back together, he couldn't get the computer to repeat the message! Once, yesterday, a cursor flashed briefly on the screen, but then it shorted out, showering him with sparks before he could reboot the system.

It might help if he could remember *how* to reboot the system...

Perhaps a password?

What password would he use when he couldn't remember the past which had compelled him to create such a thing?

He threw his pliers down in disgust. He'd been here for more than a week, and had absolutely nothing to show for it!

He fished the small, carved doll out of his chest pocket. *This* was the password. He knew it. Could sense it. He could feel it in his bones. But the password remained elusive. He might be able to wire around the central processing unit to send a distress signal, but if he wanted to reboot the AI, he needed to remember the password.

His good wing spasmed, reminding him he'd been cooped up since Ninsianna's father had left. This ship, while adequate to do whatever it was he'd been doing before he'd crash-landed, had not been designed to live upon long-term. Especially not with an attractive woman orbiting him like a gas giant around a sun, oblivious to his attraction and the effect she had upon the ocean of his emotions.

He shoved the wooden doll back into his pocket.

"If I have to spend another minute in this ship—" he grumbled "—I shall pluck out all of my feathers and eat them with feather-sauce."

"Feathers?" Ninsianna repeated in halting Galactic Standard. She tugged at one of his long, brown primary feathers. "Eat?"

"Yes," he snapped. "Now can we *please* finish the language lessons outside?"

He lurched to his feet, the bad wing throwing him off-balance. His injured lung gave a sharp stab of protest, but the flesh had begun to heal.

"I no understand?" She tried to herd him back into his chair. "Go where?"

"Outside." He pointed towards the cracked hull. "Go outside. Now."

Ninsianna shook a finger at him. "You be careful. No do too much."

He reached down and checked the power supply on his pulse pistol, a gesture which was instinctive even though he had no recollection of ever having learned to fire the weapon. It was just as dangerously low on power as the last five hundred times he'd looked. He slid it back into the holster. Ninsianna's father claimed Jamin that wouldn't bother them, but he'd seen the look of determination in that black-eyed bastard's eyes.

A familiar vertigo made the room spin as he stepped through the crack. He took deep breaths and fought it. Even if he was still too injured to fight, at least he could walk! He waved off Ninsianna when she tried to press against him. Every fiber of his being yearned to use her as a crutch, but he didn't like feeling dependent.

Her face fell into an expression of hurt. Her pink lips trembled.

Don't be such a heel...

He schooled his irritation behind an unreadable mask.

"Thank you," he said. "I do it. Okay?"

Ninsianna nodded, but her tawny-beige eyes registered betrayal. How could he explain, through a language barrier, that it wasn't *her*? He felt just good enough to act like a cranky patient.

He flared his one good wing, flapping it against the wind until he worked the crick out of the knee joint. The bad wing, unfortunately, wouldn't lift much higher than his waist. But despite the pain, the desert wind felt good against his feathers.

He scanned the bowl-shaped valley and craggy ochre mountain which rose up out of the desert without a single blade of grass. His heightened senses drank in the scent of water, and the otherwise near complete absence of moisture. Down by the stream, the trees and bushes grew far into the waterline, indicating this stream would dry down and soon he'd have *another* problem.

The front end of his ship lay partially buried in rocks. A slender array of metal and wires dangled, connected to the hull by only a couple of wires.

Sub-space antennae...

He knew what it was without having any memory of ever seeing one before. If he could fix it, maybe he could send a distress signal to this Raphael?

Ninsianna hovered anxiously like a dragonfly.

"Could you please get my screwdriver?" He made a twisting gesture. "*Scriúire?* Get my little spear?"

"Ahh... Spear? Yes!"

She disappeared inside the ship, always helpful, always eager. The moment his bossy little drill sergeant was out of sight, he scrambled up the rocks which had conveniently fallen next to the crack to make a stair.

Gasping...
...the entire way...
...up...
...and...
Oh, gods!
...he was done.

He sank into the dirt like a weary feather pillow. But he was still alive! And *healing*. Thanks to Ninsianna.

She helps because she wants you to take her with you. You owe this woman the truth.

—*I can't. I need her.*

That's not your way, to lie...

It sat in his gut like a rancid piece of meat. For all he knew he was a deserter, shot down because he was a common criminal?

He looked up, but nobody had come for him, neither enemies, nor friends. If they were looking for him, wouldn't they already *be* here?

Friend?

Enemy?

And who was Raphael?

Ninsianna reappeared from inside the ship. She looked around, panicked.

"Up here," he said.

She looked up, her expression perplexed.

"You fly, wings?" She pressed her thumbs together and made a flying motion with her fingers.

"No. I climbed." He moved his hands to pretend he was pulling himself up.

"Ahh, climbed up?"

"Yes."

Ninsianna scrambled up the rocks and handed him the screwdriver. She squatted down beside him, her expression curious.

"Don't touch anything." He pointed at the wires. "Remember? Bzzzt!" He threw his hands out to mimic being thrown the ground.

"Spiders. Bite?"

"Yes. Spiders bite. Bad."

Ten gigawatts bad ... this thing has to open a subspace portal...

He had no words to describe any of what it did, so he worked in silence, painstakingly taking the subspace antennae apart and placing each nut and screw into his pocket. After a while, Ninsianna grew bored. She climbed down to gather twigs, chattering the entire time to her imaginary goddess. She placed them into a pyramid, and then struck two rocks together until the sparks landed in a bit of dried moss. Her lips pursed into a delightful pink moue as she blew until the smoldering bundle ignited.

He had to say *this* about her: the woman knew how to take care of herself.

He dug into to the hull with sharp-nosed pliers, forcing himself to focus on the wires instead of the swarthy-skinned beauty who worked beneath him. The sun grew hot. He flared his wings to keep the worst of it off his back. He was in the process of stripping a wire when his pinfeathers prickled.

The pulse rifle was out of his holster before he could think about it. He gave the air a sniff.

Barren desert. Not as empty as it appears. Burnt wire and charred metal. Dirt. Water. Animals. Vegetation. Ninsianna. Gods, she smelled good! Even from here.

He scanned the valley. Ninsianna continued foraging, oblivious to the threat. He looked up at the thirty meter cliff he'd slammed into. It rose up into the mountain where the stream appeared, flume-like, out of a narrow gorge. The valley wall itself was far too steep to climb, but it would be scalable to a man with a lengthy rope.

He paused, listening...

Small birds singing. Tiny creatures digging through the dirt. Something? Yes? A bird, gone suddenly silent? A place there -should- be sound, but wasn't any?

He could find no movement. No discernable sign of an enemy. If some animal stalked them, he was too unfamiliar with the scents of this planet to recognize it.

Speaking of scent....

"Gods!" he muttered. "I smell like a dirty *gabhar*."[68]

He laid the pulse pistol next to the antenna and resumed his work. At last he got it disconnected from the ship. The *sensible* thing would be to go inside and fix it, but the scent of roasting hazelnuts lured him down to the fire.

Ninsianna squatted next to the fire, sharpening a stick with her stone knife. He stared, not certain how to start a conversation with a beautiful woman who seemed as comfortable in her element, out here, as she appeared *uncomfortable* in his element, inside the crashed spaceship.

He stared into her tawny-beige eyes, and said nothing...

Her brow furrowed in confusion. It hurt her feelings, his inability to speak. Not the language barrier. So far they'd been able to make each other understood. No. His stupid tendency to become tongue-tied the moment he wasn't explaining how to *do* something.

---

[68] *Gabhar:* animal.

She gave him a hesitant smile, and then went back to sharpening the piece of wood. What should one *talk* about with a beautiful woman? Maybe, if he *spoke* to her, it would lessen the uneasy tension which, in the absence of conversation, seemed to focus in his loins?

If only I had a teacher? Somebody to teach me how to deal with humans?

Ninsianna stood up.

"I go *balik*," she said.

She stripped off her dress, leaving him gaping like an idiot as she waded into the stream, wearing nothing but her loincloth, the stick held out in front of her like a spear.

What in Hades was she doing?

Now and again, she stabbed it into the water, oblivious to the fact he watched. A dark-winged voyeur, come to watch her bathe. His crotch tightened. A wish, a desire, a need rose up from within.

Go to her...

No. He'd given her father his word.

She moved back and forth, peeking underneath the bushes submerged in the oasis and occasionally poking at them. She moved suddenly.

"Ee-yah!" she squealed.

With a triumphant laugh, she hauled up a small, brown aquatic creature wriggling at the end of her spear.

"See? *Balik!*"

She bounded towards him, her mouth curved up into a victorious grin. With each step, her breasts jiggled.

"Eat?" she held the fish out. "Good. Eat. Yes?"

A drop of water dangled enticingly from one pink nipple. Overwhelming pressure rose within his loins. Heat crawled up into his face.

"Eat?" he mumbled.

"Yes," she grinned. "*Balik* good."

She picked up her stone knife and headed back to the stream to clean the fish, oblivious to his attraction. He stood, panting, though whether it was from too much exertion, or the urge to pursue her like an animal in rut, he could not say.

A bead of sweat dripped down his forehead. What he needed right now was an ice cold shower. He stripped off his shirt and combat boots and waded into the stream. With a sigh of relief, he sat down into the cold, but not frigid water.

There. That was better.

He turned his back on the near-naked goddess and flapped his wings to work the water beneath the feathers. For the past week, she'd hauled in water and he'd used it to spot-wash, but this was the first chance he'd had to fully bathe.

"Mikhail?"

He turned.

Ninsianna stood behind him, holding a handful of smashed brown roots and leaves.

"*Sabun?*" she asked.

He did his best to stare at her eyes, and not her breasts.

"No thank you," he mumbled.

She shook her head.

"*Sabun.*" She rubbed the substance on her own arm. "See?" She sniffed it. "It's good."

Mikhail touched the lathery substance and lifted his fingers to his nose. While not slippery in the sense of the disinfectant in his lavatory, it had a pleasant, astringent scent which he recognized as part of Ninsianna's smell.

"Soap?" he guessed.

"Yes. Soap." Ninsianna nodded. *"Sabun.* Soap. You want?"

He tried to take it from her. She waved his hand away.

"You, sit!" she ordered.

Eyeing her warily, he sat back down in the stream and spread his wings.

She rubbed it furiously to create a lather, and then smeared it onto his broken wing, chattering as she ran her fingers through his feathers, especially the place where the splint prevented him from reaching.

Color crept into his face as a certain part of his anatomy strained guiltily against his cargo pants. Thank the gods he sat in the stream so she wouldn't see! It was the most exquisitely sweet torture since … he couldn't remember. The soap root burned wherever it made contact with an open wound. He twitched under his skin wherever she touched him.

"Canini yakmak," she inquired. "Hurt?"

"No," he lied.

Actually, he wasn't lying. Her ministrations didn't hurt. It was maintaining his self-control as her hands ran the slippery substance over his bare skin!

"Mikhail," Ninsianna pointed to his chest. "I see?" She wished to examine his wounds.

She bent in front of him, giving an unobstructed view of her breasts as she unwound his chest-bandage to examine her needlework. A trickle of water worked its way down her firm, brown breast and dangled at the end of her nipple, so close that all he had to do was open his mouth. Although in no way did her hands linger or convey any meaning other than a desire to help him, he shivered with a nearly uncontrollable urge to pull her into the water.

He stared into her beautiful, golden eyes which captured the sunlight. He reached up to touch her cheek.

"Ninsianna?" he whispered, his voice husky.

It did not matter, that he couldn't remember who he was. It did not matter, that he had a mission he'd forgotten. It did not matter, anything in the past. All that mattered was her smile.

A horrific shriek shattered the silence.

On the cliff above his ship, seven men stood clad in brown robes. He stood up and splashed towards the shore, his adrenaline pumping, and grabbed his pulse pistol. He clicked off the safety and aimed it at the men.

The men on the cliff raised their arms and shouted. Whoever they'd thrown off the cliff screamed and screamed and screamed.

Ninsianna appeared next to him, wrapping her shawl-dress to cover her nakedness. The men backed away from the cliff, but whoever they'd thrown down continued to scream. Ninsianna raced towards the ship.

"Wait!" he shouted.

She kept on running.

He bolted after her, still in his wet pants and bare feet, despite the vertigo which threatened to topple him. She scrambled up on top of the ship and knelt over the creature they'd thrown off the cliff. About sixty kilos, it possessed brown fur with a blaze of white, a pair of small horns, large ears, and a broad body. Tied around its neck were dozens of colorful strips of cloth.

He held up his pulse pistol to cover her as she worked, but the men did not reappear. Whoever they were, they'd delivered their message.

"Was it Jamin?" he asked.

"No," she said. "Halifians. Very bad."

Chapter 24

February – 3,390 BC
Earth – Village of Assur

JAMIN

The sun beat down mercilessly upon Jamin's raven-black hair, heating up his head until the sweat beaded on his forehead. His father had lined them up and paced in front of them, his hand clasped behind his back as Ninsianna's father made furious accusations. Villagers wandered into the central square, eager for gossip about the winged man who had fallen from the sky.

Immanu faded back, his wild, dark hair visible amongst the other villagers as he let the Chief handle the situation. Yes. *The Chief.* Everyone in the village thought of his father as *The Chief,* including him.

"Is it true?" Chief Kiyan's brown eyes bore into his. "Did you drag Ninsianna into the stream and hold her head under the water?"

Jamin squirmed under his father's glare. Usually his father ignored him, but with Immanu telling wild tales about winged saviors returning from the heavens, it was enough to get even the Chief interested. Jamin glanced to the warriors who stood on either side of him and shot them a glare. *Keep your mouths shut...*

"Siamek?" The Chief asked to his lieutenant. "What really happened?"

Siamek shot him an apologetic look.

"She was already in the water, Sir," Siamek said. "Jamin went in to talk to her."

The Chief turned to Firouz. "And what did *you* see?"

Firouz raised his chin.

"She insulted him. Ninsianna deserved it!"

"*Nobody* deserves to be attacked for expressing an opinion—" the Chief jabbed his finger into Jamin's face. "We are not Halifians! We don't abuse our women!"

"But, Father..."

The gawking villagers whispered furiously, eager to see their Chief lambast his only son.

"But nothing!" the Chief said. "A warrior's job is to protect the village. Not go looking for trouble! You are all to stay away from the winged one until I ponder this situation! Do you understand?"

"Yes, Sir!" the warriors muttered.

"I can't hear you!" the Chief shouted.

"Yes, Sir!"

The warriors broke up, eager to be away from the Chief's disapproving glare. Jamin tried to skulk away with them.

"Jamin!" his father called. "Get in the house. Now!"

A flush of mortification burned into his cheeks. Not only had he lost face once, when the winged demon had run them off and *kept* his wayward fiancé, but now the bastard had bested him *twice* by winning over Ninsianna's father. How could his father be so *stupid*? A shaman was more believable than his own son?

He stormed into their house, far larger than most houses in Assur, with a separate kitchen and a room built off of the multipurpose room where the Chief could entertain important visitors. Their ancient housekeeper saw the fury in the Chief's expression and scurried into the kitchen. The Chief shut the door and gestured towards the cushions.

"Sit."

"I don't want to sit."

"It's not a request."

Jamin sat down.

His father remained standing.

"A woman is not a piece of property," the Chief said. "They are inspirations, sent by the goddess to make us want to build and strive."

"She disrespected me in front of my men."

"And *you* disrespected *her* by mocking her when she grew angry after you refused to take her to Nineveh."

"*You're* the one who said I couldn't take her with us!"

"Because Ninsianna is too much like her mother," the Chief said. "They don't dare mock Immanu because he's Lugalbanda's son, but they won't put up with it from *you*. You'll be the laughing stock of the Ubaid if you let your wife butt into every negotiation."

"I wasn't going to let her butt in," Jamin said. "She just…"

He trailed off.

"She has a way with words," he continued. "A way to negotiate, without all the posturing and threats. I thought, maybe…"

He stared down at his hands.

"She reminds me of Mother."

His father wore that stricken expression he always wore whenever anybody dared mention her name. Ninsianna had awoken within him something he hadn't felt since the day his mother died.

"Before you were born," the Chief said, "our enemies used to steal our women. I built these walls—" he gestured at the room "—to protect them, not to keep them prisoner."

His expression turned mournful.

"But now I see you acting like the very men I built to keep out."

It stabbed Jamin in the heart, to see his father grief-stricken. It had always been thus for the past fifteen years. His father had never remarried.

"But what about Ninsianna?" A lump rose in his throat. "We left her there—" his voice lilted "—with a *demon*."

"Immanu assures me they are emissaries of the gods."

"Legends we've never heard about before today!"

The Chief's eyes filled with pity.

"The man is injured," the Chief said. "That's why he left Ninsianna behind, to care for him. I've authorized him to go back and extend an invitation."

Jamin gaped.

"You want to bring him *here*?"

"Yes." A cold, pragmatic gaze made his father's eyes glint. "By your own testimony, this man has weapons we can only dream of."

Jamin rose to his feet.

"Are you crazy?"

"Son…" His father's voice rumbled a warning.

"You're using Ninsianna as bait?"

"As I recall, you didn't have any problem using her as bait when it was *you* that wanted her!"

"She's my fiancé!"

"Not if the winged man takes her with him."

His words kicked Jamin in the gut. *Ninsianna? Lost forever?*

"I will *kill* him," he growled, "before I will let him take what is mine."

"You will stay away from him!" his father threatened. "Or you will answer to the Tribunal!"

He shoved past his father.

"Jamin!"

He burst out the front door and slammed it shut behind him. He adjusted his travel cape with the elaborate Halifian pin.

Ninsianna was *his* fiancé! If *he* didn't rescue her, nobody would!

Chapter 25

February – 3,390 BC
Earth: Crash site
Colonel Mikhail Mannuki'ili

MIKHAIL

He stared at the goat which dominated Ninsianna's attention. The foolish creature *lived,* in no small part to her considerable talent as a surgeon. It limped around the fire, one leg in a splint, bleating to be fed, its fur shaved bald where she'd stitched it back together. Right now, it had even more stitches than *he* had.

Was it normal? To feel jealous over a pet?

Normally she patted *him*. Or more precisely, she massaged his wings, but for the last two days she'd left him to his own devices. He didn't want to *ask* her. Heaven forbid he *admitted* he enjoyed her ministrations. Besides... It wasn't like he could reach back to adjust the splint when the darned thing kept his wing immobilized in an awkward position.

He gave his wings a snap, hoping she'd notice it had begun to spasm. It created a puff of wind which blew into the fire, causing it to flare up. A shower of sparks rose up like a desert whirlwind, right into Ninsianna and the goat.

"Mikhail, no!" Her eyes flashed copper. *"Elbisene ne yaptigini gorun!"*

A hint of mirth caused him to almost smirk. Was it wrong to rile her up? Yes. What was wrong with him? He kept acting like a petulant child.

Ninsianna patted the front of her dress which now bore a tiny, black burn mark. He drooped his wings to show the proper remorse even though he didn't *feel* it. If she'd just rebind his wing, he wouldn't feel so grouchy.

"Sorry," he mumbled.

She turned her back on him to emphasize her disapproval. He waited and waited, not sure how to say, *'my wing hurts.'* It would be kinder if she came after him with a club. At least, then, he'd have something *logical* to battle. More logical than a goat.

Fine...

If she wouldn't talk to him, he'd go fix his ship. The sooner he got out of here, the better.

He retrieved his antenna and spread it out to take apart. Usually his technology drew her like a bee, but she gave it a disinterested glance and went right back to patting to the goat. It was a good thing he'd promised to send her back to her father? As soon as the shaman came back, he would send her packing.

He held up the mangled antennae. The crash had caused considerable damage, but he might be able to salvage it. He couldn't remember the mechanics of how it worked, but when he held it in his hands, he *knew* where things were supposed to go. He must have rigged up emergency antennae, many times, perhaps under battle conditions? He could almost *taste* the scent of pulse-rifle plasma as he pulled the thing apart, but he couldn't *remember* what gave rise to that sensation.

As the sun reached its apex, a sharp whistle alerted them they were no longer alone. Two figures appeared on the horizon. Ninsianna stayed his hand before he had a chance to pull his pulse pistol out of its holster.

"Papa and Mama," she said.

The pair waited on top of the landslide which blocked the stream, the only way down, until Ninsianna stood up and waved.

There. This is it. By nightfall, Ninsianna will be out of my feathers…

An unsettled feeling settled into his gut as Immanu helped the smaller figure down the rocks, clad in brown travel cape which covered her from hair to heel. Immanu picked up the woman's bundles and hurried behind her as she marched confidently into their camp, looking neither left nor right, straight towards Ninsianna.

Mikhail stood up.

Ninsianna darted to stand behind him.

The goat bleated and ran behind *her*. Leaving *him* to face the wrath of an angry mother.

He stared down at a face which was an older version of Ninsianna's. Breathtakingly beautiful and proud like an empress. Only her eyes were different. Medium brown. Intelligent. Perceptive.

"Good day," he enunciated clearly.

"Hmpf!"

She jabbed a finger in Ninsianna's face and let loose a diatribe that would have burned the paint off a command carrier.

Ninsianna's shoulders drooped. She did not interrupt. At last Immanu caught up with his wife and dropped the packages on the ground.

"Mikhail," Immanu huffed, his face red and out of breath. "Meet my wife, Needa."

"Alo." Needa gave him a curt nod.

She flicked a hand.

"My wife," Immanu said, "would like to take a look at your injured wing."

Mikhail instinctively curled the good wing *away* from her. Hadn't he, only moments ago, been wishing somebody would massage his wing?

Not somebody who looks like they wish to snap it off!

"Needa is our village healer," Immanu added, sensing his apprehension. "Ninsianna is talented, but she is still only an apprentice."

Needa's lips pursed as she studied his expression. *What are you doing with my daughter?* A peculiar sensation tickled through his body, as though he was filled with water and somebody swam through it.

Her expression softened.

"Alo," she said, more gently this time. She pointed at his wing. While he didn't understand her words, he could tell she was used to being obeyed.

He shot a wary look at Immanu.

Immanu gave him a sheepish shrug.

How could he explain that allowing someone to touch his wings felt *intimate*?

He sat down so she wouldn't have to stand on tiptoes.

Ninsianna's mother poked at the broken wing. Where Ninsianna caressed before touching the parts which were broken, Needa assessed the flesh competently, but not gently. Her hands, however, bore the same warm, tingling sensation as Ninsianna's. He could easily picture her running the triage unit on a hospital ship.

No! Wait! He grasped at the memory fragment as it flitted through his mind and exited as randomly as it had come. *Damantia!*

"Have you remembered more about how you ended here?" Immanu asked.

"Just fragments," he said. "Most don't make any sense."

"What *do* you remember?"

"Nothing particularly helpful."

"Yet you can still do things that you did in the past?"

"It appears so?" Mikhail frowned. "I know what I know, but I can't remember how I know it." He pointed to his dog tags. "I only realize I know it when I need it. Does that make any sense?"

"I have seen this problem after injuries such as yours," Immanu said. "But I've never seen someone so lucid who could remember nothing at all."

Pain stabbed into his wing.

"Ouch!"

He turned and glared at Needa, who'd just cracked a bone into place without a warning.

"*Féach ar an sciathán!*" Watch the wing!

Needa shook her finger at Ninsianna and let loose a barrage of language like a parent scolding a neglectful child. Ninsianna's face grew scarlet-pink. She stared at her feet, her expression mortified.

"Ninsianna missed a dislocated joint," Immanu translated. "Had she not reset it, it would have left you unable to fly again."

Mikhail schooled an unreadable expression to prevent a look of terror. *Unable to fly...*

"Please convey my gratitude to your wife," he said. "And remind Ninsianna, if not for her, I wouldn't be alive."

Needa moved next to examine his chest wound. He tried not to wince as she poked at the hole and dabbed some kind of resin onto his stitches. She grunted with satisfaction.

"Good," she said in *his* language.

Ninsianna beamed. Her mother's approval meant something.

Needa met his gaze as she spoke through her husband and signaled for him to translate.

"My wife wants to know if your species always heals this fast?" Immanu translated.

"I can't remember. I know I've been injured before—" he pointed at the scar on his wrist "—but I have no recollection of when it happened or how long it took to heal."

Needa wrapped the splint back onto his wing. While tighter and much less comfortable than Ninsianna's splint, he could now raise the wing all the way up to his shoulder.

"Up!" she commanded. She pointed at the injured wing.

Stepping back so he didn't fan any more sparks out of the fire, he extended both wings and flapped, just enough to assure he'd regained some mobility.

"Thank you," he said in her language.

"*Rica ederim*," Needa replied.

Next she helped Ninsianna examine the goat. The two women treated the foolish creature as though it was the most valuable gift in the world.

Mikhail stared at the cliff above his ship.

"Why would the Halifians treat the beast so cruelly?" he asked.

"We ran into them the last time I came to visit," Immanu said. "I told them you are a god, and if they bother you, you will visit down upon their tent-group many terrible fates."

Mikhail raised one eyebrow.

"Then why throw a goat at me?"

"They offered it as an appeasement," Immanu said. "You are on their land. They wish for you to take your sky canoe and leave."

Mikhail held up the mangled antennae.

"I will," he said. "Just as soon as I get this working."

Immanu studied the slender strip of metal.

"Is it a sacred object?"

"No," Mikhail said. "It makes your voice travel further."

"Like a spirit-journey?"

He had no idea *what* a spirit-journey was.

"Something like that," he hedged.

Ninsianna and her mother argued vigorously. From the way she stood with her arms crossed, she had no intention of following her mother back to Assur. At last she came back with her arm around her mother.

"Mikhail?" She pointed at the ship. "Go inside? Yes?"

Her mother's hostile expression had been replaced with the same curiosity he often saw in Ninsianna. They followed her inside where she gave her parents a tour. They rummaged through his cupboards like eager little gerbils.

Mikhail stifled a sense of irritation.

"What kind of weapon is this?" Immanu held up a metal fork.

"You eat with it."

"Ohh…"

All three nodded as though it was the most profound thing they had ever heard.

Next Ninsianna pulled food packets out of his broken replicator and gave each parent an unremolecularized biocube. They chewed and swallowed, smiling and nodding as though the bland substance tasted wonderful. She opened the door of his food synthesizer and pushed every single button.

"Briste," she said. Food is broken.

"Broken?" Immanu asked. "How can you travel across the heavens with no food in your sky canoe?"

"It's a replicator." Mikhail held up one of the biocubes. "This contains all of the sub-atomic building blocks contained in most foods. You simply program whatever you wish to eat, for example, fish and tubers, and the machine reassembles the molecules."

Immanu looked at him as though he were a twelve-headed *ollphéist*.

"Its magic," Mikhail said, "but the magic which runs the machine is broken."

"Oh!" Immanu's eyes glittered. "Magic! Yes."

Ninsianna and her mother violated his ship, upending bins, poking into cupboards, even stripping off his bedcovers and unzipping his pillow. Immanu beckoned for him to come into the bridge. He set in front of him one of the packages he'd carried with him.

"The Chief has authorized me to bring you an offer," Immanu said. "He invites you to come and stay in our village."

"I can't abandon my ship," Mikhail said. "I have to complete the mission."

"I told him you'd say that," Immanu said. "Very well. He sent these items as a token of his friendship."

Immanu opened the leather satchel. Inside was a small, clay jar filled with oil, a measure of salt, some grain, and a ceremonial stone knife far nicer than the one Ninsianna carried.

"What about his son? Will he give us any trouble?"

Immanu sighed.

"You'll be far safer in our village," Immanu said. "Only the Chief's order prevents Jamin from sneaking up here with a band of warriors. He blames *you* for stealing Ninsianna away from him."

"I'm not responsible for whatever relationship he has, or doesn't have, with your daughter."

"But I am!" Immanu's voice rose sharp with anger. "It is not our way, to break off a betrothal. Ninsianna created a terrible offense. The longer you keep her, the harder it will be to convince Jamin you are *not* ravishing his bride!"

Mikhail stared at his still-ruined bridge. He held up the antennae.

"As soon as I repair this, I shall contact my people and leave."

"What about Ninsianna?" The shaman's voice warbled. "My daughter has become very fond of you. If you—" he looked away. "If you *encourage* her to go—"

The shaman sensed, as *he* did, that Ninsianna wished to leave. Permanently.

Ninsianna appeared, her eyes pleading with him not to send her away. She moved behind him and touched his back, her hands warm, tingling, pleasant...

Tempting...

Mikhail regretted the promise even as the words left his mouth.

"I won't force her to leave," he said. "But I give you my word. I will not take advantage of your daughter."

Chapter 26

義

Galactic Standard Date: 152,323.03 AE
Sata'an Forward Operating Base: Earth
Lieutenant Kasib

LT. KASIB

Their base cook had lost a leg and part of his tail in a campaign so long ago, it was longer than Kasib had been alive. But still he served faithfully, as best he could in the kitchen given their limited rations. What else was an old skullcracker to do when his valor had been insufficient to earn a wife?

"Emmer, einkorn, or barley?" the cook asked.[69]

"Is this from the latest annexation?" Kasib asked.

"The batch that came in two days ago," the cook said. "The men say the village gave it up, as pretty as you please."

"I'll take the barley," Kasib said.

"And what about the General, Sir?"

"He'll try the einkorn that Dahaka's unit brought in last night," Kasib said. "With a bit of dried fruit. What was that dark one you gave us yesterday?"

"They call them dates."

"With two of those," Kasib said. "And a spoonful of bee vomit."

"The locals call it honey."

The old skullcracker slopped the pasty beige substance into a pair of bowls. Kasib flicked out his tongue to inhale the delicious scent. Not as sweet as Sata'anic grain, but chewy and nutty. Most planets they conquered had to begin from scratch, but whatever calamity had dumped a population of Nibiruian survivors here, in a remote spiral arm, and stripped them of their technology, had left them with enough racial memory to remember their civilized, grain-growing forbears.

He covered the bowls to keep them warm and wound his way through the men, all in good spirits because the local population kept capitulating so easily. That was the advantage of colonizing a primitive planet. The locals thought they were gods.

He paused outside to let a platoon of skullcrackers pass. Big, burly lizards and other Sata'anic species with broad shoulders, a surly disposition, and a propensity to devolve into fights and brawls. Their splay-toed boots

---

[69] *Emmer* and *einkorn:* the predecessor-grains to modern wheat.

thudded on the soil like a temple drum, beating a joyous war-cry as they sang a marching cadence:

> Capitulate! Capitulate!
> Capitulate to Sata'anic rule!
> Or fight Shay'tan's legions
> And be crushed beneath our boots.

He hurried around the men who dwarfed a mere scholar-caste lizard such as himself, aware his position as Hudhafah's *aide-de-camp*[70] garnered him far more respect than he otherwise could have commanded on his own. The men marched into a waiting troop carrier, eager to lock and load, and strapped themselves in as the staff sergeant barked orders about the latest village they were about to annex.

On his way past the communications tent, a skinny lizard with an immature green dewlap came trotting out after him.

"Lieutenant, Sir!" the lizard skidded to a stop in front of him. "You asked for these reports?"

"Yes, Private." Kasib glanced at his hands, both full with the General's breakfast. "Anything out of the ordinary?"

"No wreckage, no unusual activity," the private said.

"Any radio signals?"

"Nothing, Sir. We've found no electrical activity of any kind."

Kasib and the private both glanced at the temple which was his destination. General Hudhafah's office. The private wrapped his tail nervously around one of his legs. His hand shook as he practically *begged* Kasib to be the one to take the report into the General.

Kasib sighed. He *knew* what the General's order would be, after getting his head bitten off. This wouldn't be the *first* campaign where the General's paranoia had turned out to be justified.

"Order all ships to keep monitoring for a distress beacon," he said. "If the Angelic is still alive, the first thing he'll do is try to summon help."

---

[70] *Aide-de-camp:* personal secretary to a high-ranking military officer.

Chapter 27

March – 3,390 BC
Earth: Crash site

NINSIANNA

The sound of a man's voice crying out in his sleep jarred Ninsianna awake.

"Máthair! Ná gortaítear sí! Le do thoil!"

She sat up and watched him flail. Every night he woke up screaming. Papa said, if she brought him back to the village, he would help Mikhail banish the night-demons, but she didn't *want* to go back.

Mikhail whimpered a heart-wrenching sob.

A lump rose in her throat. How could a man act so fearless when awake, but remain helpless when Dim-me and Dim-mea[71] came to torment his dreams? Whatever memories gave entrance to the demons, they must be truly terrifying.

"It would be kinder if I cast a spell to erase it," she whispered.

But she did nothing. Before Mikhail could take her to see the stars, first he needed to remember how to get there.

*

He was gone before she woke up, the same as every morning. How could such a large man could move so silently? She cast off her covers, now tucked up to her neck. He had a peculiar prohibition about seeing uncovered breasts. Breasts? What was wrong with the limbs women used to feed babies? It wasn't like she ever let him see her without her loincloth. Now *that* would be provocative!

She visited the magic chamber pot and then stumbled, half-asleep out into the bridge. As usual, Mikhail was seated in front of his altar, praying to his god, Compyoota.

"Good morning," she said.

Mikhail spun his chair around.

"Come," he beckoned. "See?"

He pointed at a blinking green light on the shiny square embedded in the wall.

---

[71] *Dim-me* and *Dim-mea:* night demons. Dim-me is sometimes associated with the Akkadian demon-goddess, Lamashtu, who devoured children; while Dim-mea is associated with her nemesis Pazuzu, the demon featured in "The Exorcist."

"Compyoota work." His blue eyes sparkled.

"Really?"

"Yes." He struggled for words. "Work. Bad. Broke. But yes. Work. Maybe?"

He pointed at the green line, and then tapped on a rectangle filled with symbols.

"Computer no speak," he said. "But old way. Work. A little."

Squiggly green lines appeared on the flat black square. His feathers rustled like an eager child.

"See?"

He jabbed one finger down onto the rectangle.

The divine voice which came from the ceiling spoke once again. *This time, she understood enough of his language to understand.*

'Raphael ... I ... hit! ... found the ... crawl... with enough ...'

She tilted her head up, struggling to translate. He hit the rectangle again. Compyoota spoke the exact same message as before.

Ninsianna frowned.

"Compyoota answer with own voice?"

"Not answer." He pressed his fingers against his forehead, trying to communicate. "Shout. Back and go. Like you. To me. From over there."

He pointed up at the ceiling. A tangle of spiderwebs, now wrapped together to make a thick rope, dangled down from the ceiling, into the hole in the wall he'd been tinkering with for weeks.

"Shout!" He reached up toward the ceiling. "To Raphael. In the stars."

A thrill of excitement rippled through her body. She tapped her forehead.

"You remember?"

His expression grew wistful.

"Not remember. Just know." He pointed at the flat black screen. "See?"

Lines of squiggles appeared on the square. Mikhail hit the rectangle again. Compyoota spoke. More squiggles appeared.

He pointed at a cluster of symbols that appeared just beneath the line.

"This. Is place. Place where Raphael live."

"In the stars?"

"Yes. Raphael here!" His expression grew more somber. "Or *was* here. Twenty-eight—" he flung his fingers wide twice, and then held up eight fingers "—days—" he gestured behind his head "—past. Don't know if Raphael live here now."

How could his friend move to a different star? Perhaps he lived in a sky canoe, just like Mikhail's? She decided not to ask. From the way he pinched his brow, the effort to explain this magic strained his patience. Whenever it got too much, he fell silent.

"You fix—" she patted the back of a wing. "I go make food. Okay?"

He nodded, relieved.

"Okay. Food good. And *that*—" he pointed at a fresh pile of goat dung "—you take outside."

Ninsianna glanced at the goat tied just inside the crack. She was a *good* goat who gave milk each morning and night. But for some reason, the goat irritated him. Why yesterday, he'd demanded she give the goat a bath!

She untied the goat and patted her furry head.

"Come, girl. Let's go find some forage?"

She led it outside, ignoring Mikhail's subtle scowl. He hadn't been pleased to bring it inside his sky canoe, but she'd explained either the goat had to come inside, or *he* had to sleep outside to protect it from predators.

She milked the goat, and then gathered sticks while it munched greedily on the clumps of grass which grew at the water's edge. The fire lit easily, helped along with a few sparks from still-smoldering coals. She patted cakes of flatbread made from grain sent along by the Chief, and then set them on a flat rock to bake while she hunted lizards and gerbils.

Mikhail was no more communicative when she brought the food inside.

"I shout to Raphael today," he said.

"Today?" Ninsianna asked.

"Yes, today." He pointed at the thick rope which disappeared through the crack in the ceiling. It had been joined by several more ropes since this morning, these ones much thicker, which ran towards the back of the sky canoe. "Magic stick, I fix, it work."

The squiggles on the flatscreen had changed. It dawned on her they were sigils, like the symbols Papa used to perform magic.

She squinted and scrutinized the squiggles on Compyoota.

"What this mean?" She recognized the symbols he'd pointed out earlier, the ones where Raphael lived.

"One-four-six—" he used his fingers to translate the counting words "—nine-five-five. Is, uhm…" he pinched the bridge of his nose. "Like song. Sing up. Sing down. Have to sing right song for Raphael to hear."

Ninsianna scrutinized the squiggles. A song?

She shut her eyes and prayed to She-Who-Is to explain. Sometimes *SHE* answered her, though most of the time the goddess just gave her a patronizing tingle. That sensation she'd experienced in her vision of floating in a river, surrounded by stars which sang, whispered into her mind, and then it went away.

Oh! Of course!

"Sing!" she laughed. "Like call goat." She pointed out the crack. "Sing, la-la-la, go further. Goat come?"

"Yes. Maybe."

Her curiosity sated, she signaled it was time to replace his bandage. The chest-wound still vexed him. She replaced the sturdy linen bandages she was now forced to wash and boil, having used up the soft, but fragile gauze he'd kept in his healer's kit, and touched along the sunken hole.

"Look good," she said. "Heal good. No evil spirits."

His cheek twitched as he stared up at the ceiling, his expression unreadable.

"Thank you," he said.

He *hated* being injured. He hated it with a passion. She could *tell* by the way his wings stiffened every time she tried to talk about his injuries and the limitations they imposed.

She closed her eyes and focused on the slender thread which connected her to She-Who-Is and began to sing.

> My lady performs the incantations.
> She speaks and they become better.
> She performs the incantation with ghee,[72]
> And pours it into her great bowl,
> Bringing it in her cooling hands.

A pleasant flow of warmth tingled through her body, past her heart and straight out of her hands into his body. Mikhail sighed. Despite his insistence he didn't believe in magic, he certainly seemed to enjoy it when she sang the healing songs.

That faint whisper she'd heard while floating in the vision came to her again, not just HER thoughts, but also snippets of images. This was the part she'd always loved best about being a healer. The way she could almost *see* the patient's thoughts. Their greatest fears? Their heartfelt desires? Perhaps that's why She-Who-Is had injured him? If he hadn't been injured, would Mikhail let her touch him?

In his mind, she sensed confusion, consternation, terror. Not at his predicament, but the fact he remembered absolutely nothing about who he was.

"Don't be afraid—" she whispered beneath the song. "*I will heal you, and you will take me with you? To see the stars?"*

Without even being aware of it, Mikhail nodded. She'd elicited this reaction from Jamin, though *he* had reneged. This time, she wouldn't muddle it up by openly stating her demands. She finished up, and then re-splinted his wing, binding it tight the way Mama had shown her.

So what else might she do to make herself indispensable?

---

[72] *Ghee:* clarified butter (oil).

Mikhail pointed at the excrement the goat had dropped last night. His wings rustled in disgust.

"You promise," he said sternly. "You clean?"

"Okay."

Mikhail turned back to Compyoota, eager to send his message before the sunset. Once he shouted to Raphael, then what? Would Raphael come here?

She stared down at the excrement left by the goat, and then up at the crack. Her lips curved up into a smile. It wouldn't do for Raphael to visit a broken sky canoe. She scooped up the goat dung and went outside.

Chapter 28

March – 3,390 BC
Earth: Crash site
Colonel Mikhail Mannuki'ili

MIKHAIL

Mikhail checked the commands he'd painstakingly hand-typed in. From the way his wrist hurt, he surmised that handwriting was an art he had learned, and then never, ever used.

Longitude...
Latitude...
Distance...
Power.

He climbed under the counter and double-checked his connection. Every ship possessed a 'black box,' an emergency distress beacon whose sole purpose was to broadcast a distress signal or, if the ship was destroyed, to broadcast his location so someday a passing ship might find the wreckage. Why it hadn't triggered after he'd been shot down was a mystery, but here it was. Enough power to send a single subspace message.

He quadruple checked the coordinates.

Subspace frequency: 146.955.[73]

While he couldn't *remember* how it worked, he *knew* the antenna would create a micro-wormhole through which a tiny pulse of light might pass. Once it got to the other side, it would remain connected to *his* radio through a series of subspace strings for several seconds. If he successfully connected to the other ship, so long as the two maintained power, they could talk. If he *couldn't* maintain power, however, all would not be lost. The pulse of light, once it emerged on the other side, would act like an ordinary radio signal, radiating through space at the normal speed of sound.

So what could he tell a man he couldn't remember who was stationed at a location he could not recall about a mission he could not remember from a planet, which he didn't know where it was?

Help me? Whoever you are? Come and find me? I am still alive.

He checked the power cable and made sure he'd taped off all of the spliced ends. All it would take is a single short, and the entire ship could blow up in a spectacular, atom-splitting explosion.

---

[73] *146.955:* by a completely coincidental set of celestial circumstances, this also happens to be the frequency for the Cape Code ARES ham radio repeater.

He stood up and worked the cricks out of his wings. Somehow he expected, injured or not injured, he wasn't used to spending this much time cooped up indoors.

"Ninsianna?" he called out.

He stepped towards the crack they used as a doorway. If he made contact, he wanted her *there,* at his side.

A sound, from above, made him look up.

A face full of mud tumbled down the hole.

Chapter 29

March – 3,390 BC
Earth: Crash site

JAMIN

Jamin crept to the vantage point above the sky canoe. In the valley beneath him, Ninsianna skinned several gerbils and set them into the fire to roast, talking to She-Who-Is. Once upon a time, he'd found the habit endearing. He didn't find it endearing *now* that Immanu claimed She-Who-Is had sent the winged demon to be a savior.

Fools!

His father was too blinded by daydreams of possessing the demon's weapons to *think* about what would happen if the bastard led a band against their village. No doubt, by now, he'd wheedled all of their defensive secrets out of Ninsianna! Well good luck with that. The first thing he'd done was change the sentry's schedules and ordered extra spears to be stored on the walls.

When the demon came, he'd be ready for him.

Bastard!

He gripped his spear. All it would take is one good throw from above. But Immanu swore the winged demon wasn't interested in Ninsianna. He might *look* like a man, but Angelics, Immanu claimed, possessed no baser instincts.

A eunuch…

He touched his lion's teeth necklace, the one he'd worn ever since he'd killed the lion using nothing but a knife. A *man's* necklace. The winged demon wasn't even a *man!*

He watched her now, his errant bride, as she patted cakes of flatbread and set them into the fire to bake. The wind shifted, carrying the aroma of roasting gerbil, desert artichokes, and garlic in his direction, causing his stomach to rumble. She looked so beautiful, standing by the fire. Voluptuous curves, a golden complexion. He could still *feel* the way her hands had grown warm as she'd touched his broken body and whispered sweet words of comfort.

He *had* to get her back! He couldn't believe those feelings hadn't been *real.*

The hair prickled on the back of his neck.

He scurried back from the edge, careful to display the bone pin.

"I know you're there," he called out softly in Halifian. "Marwan once said our tribes don't have to be enemies, so why don't you show yourself as a friend?"

The mercenary leader stepped out from behind some cover. Perhaps early thirties, he wore a faded brown robe, the kind a man might wear when conducting surveillance. His face, while sun-burned and scarred, bore a hint of regal breeding. He held his arms out to show he had sheathed his knife.

"What gave me away?" the Halifian asked.

"I'm not certain," Jamin said. "Most of the time, I just *know*."

"Ahh, an intuitive," the man nodded. "Marwan is like that. He says Al-iyah[74] teaches us how to fight, but Dhat-Bhataan[75] teaches us how to listen."

"And how *is* your father," Jamin asked. "I have not seen him for many years."

"Father-in-law," the man corrected. "He is curious, about the little Chieftain with whom he'd made a deal."

An elaborately carved bone pin in exchange for water for six goats, and a summer filled with language lessons to a grief-stricken young boy who had lost his mother. What *had* the shaykh wanted? To forge a future alliance with a malleable young mind while his father was too distracted to care?

Jamin gestured to a rock just out of weapon's reach. The Halifian sat down. He leaned forward, his brown eyes curious.

"I am Roshan," he said, "son of Yazan, Shaykh of the Baranuman[76] Halifian tribe. I am Marwan's son-in-law by his daughter from his fifth wife, Atara."

"I am Jamin, son of Kiyan of Assur," Jamin said. "Where are the rest of your men?"

"Close." The Halifian gestured to the valley beyond. "I see our friend is still *here*."

"Yes, unfortunately," Jamin said. "What's with the goat?"

"We hoped, if we made sacrifice, the winged demon would go away."

They both stared as Ninsianna patted the goat.

"Perhaps you should not have given him a means of procuring milk?" Jamin said.

"We thought he would *eat* it." Roshan gestured at the cliff, over thirty cubits. "It was young and tender. It should have died in the fall."

Jamin's lip twitched.

"She's a talented healer. She saved *me* from a gore wound."

---

[74] *Al-Iyah:* ancient desert war god.

[75] *Dhat-Bhataan:* nature goddess of the oasis.

[76] *Baranuman River:* ancient name for the Euphrates River in Iraq.

"From a he-goat?"

Jamin laughed. "An auroch. The thing lifted me right up onto its head."

"I find that incredulous."

Jamin shifted his cape to show his abdomen. The Halifian's dark eyebrows rose with disbelief.

"Now *that* is quite a scar."

"She healed *me*," Jamin said. "And now her father claims she healed *him*. Or at least that's the excuse he gave for allowing his daughter to stay."

They both stared across the valley at his reluctant fiancé.

"We could use a healer like that," Roshan said. "Who knows? Perhaps I shall make her my second wife?"

Jamin bristled.

"Not unless you care to be skinned and worn as my new cape."

The Halifian chuckled.

"Ubaid women are too much trouble!" he scoffed. "Look at the way she dresses? Every scoundrel in the desert would wage war to steal her from my tent."

"Every man in Ubaid territory would do the same," Jamin sighed. "Which is *why* I have to get her away from this demon. Not only has he addled *her* brain, but also the good sense of her father."

"The shaman?"

"Yes."

"Is it true?" Roshan made a finger-symbol to ward off evil spirits. "That he, like his father before him, can stop a man's heart by praying?"

Jamin grew wary.

"Yes," he lied. "I have seen him do it, but only when provoked."

Roshan grew silent. They stared at Ninsianna as she plucked several roasted gerbils out of the fire and placed them on a strange, silver platter to bring inside. The valley grew silent, accentuated only by the gurgling stream, the song of several birds, and an occasional bleat from the goat.

"The desert grows drier," Roshan said at last. "This valley is Marwan's refuge once Tharthar wadi[77] dries down."

"How much longer?" Jamin asked.

"Usually just after the spring Akitu ceremony, the tribes break up."

Jamin calculated the timeline.

"A fortnight."[78]

"Yes."

"What if he's still here?"

Roshan clutched his knife.

---

[77] *Tharthar wadi:* an intermittent stream which runs parallel to the Tigris and Euphrates Rivers in Iraq.

[78] *Fortnight:* two weeks.

"Then we shall have no choice but to ask him to leave."

Ninsianna came back outside, this time carrying a bucket. She dumped out a pile of goat manure, then went down to the stream and stripped down to her loincloth. Jamin grew hard as she knelt down beside the stream and began to dig, giving him a fantastic view of her posterior.

"Aye!" Roshan whistled softly. "Now *that* would be a prize."

"*My* prize," Jamin said. "We're due to wed at the summer solstice."

"First you have to get her away from the winged demon."

"That's why I'm here."

Ninsianna hauled the bucket up to the pile of manure. Jamin's breath caught in his chest. She was breathtaking, with her breasts smeared with mud.

"My father wants her to bring him to our village," Jamin said. "Perhaps we can get rid of him without a loss of life?"

"Have you seen him fly?" Roshan asked.

"No," Jamin said. "Only flare his wings."

"So we could fight him on the ground?"

"Maybe," Jamin said. "But you'd have to catch him unawares."

He decided *not* to mention the firestick. The Halifians had not been here to see that, and Immanu, who spoke a modest amount of Halifian, but not fluently, had not taken the time to explain the winged demon's weapons, only to make vague threats if they set foot inside the valley.

Ninsianna stepped over to the goat and began to rip up clumps of lush, green grass. She carried it back to the bucket and sprinkled it in, along with a double handful of manure from the goat, and began to smash it with a stick.

"What's she doing?" Roshan asked.

"Making mud-bricks. She wants to mortar something."

"Bricks are for people who are *settled*," Roshan snorted.

A lump rose in Jamin's throat as she lifted up the bucket and walked back to the sky canoe. Hadn't *he,* right up until the day Ninsianna had broken off their engagement, been making mud bricks to build their future house? They both watched as she climbed up the landslide which had collapsed on top of the sky canoe and stood over the crack which bisected the roof.

With a triumphant smile, she upended the bucket and dumped it into the hole.

"Hey!" a man's voice shouted.

The winged demon came rushing outside.

Covered in mud…

"Cad in Hades atá tú a dhéanamh?" he shouted.

He flapped his wings. Mud splattered everywhere.

Jamin clamped his hand over his mouth to force himself not to laugh. Roshan held his sides, unable to prevent a deep, lusty guffaw. The winged demon looked almost harmless, covered with baby-shit yellow mud, dried grass, and still-partially formed goat turds.

The winged demon bore down on Ninsianna.

"You. See that!" Mikhail pointed at a tall stick which jutted out of the sky canoe right next to the crack. "You touch that." He threw his arms out. "Bzzt! Remember? You die!"

Jamin grabbed his spear and crept forward. If the bastard laid a *hand* on her, he would skewer him like a wild boar. His father be damned!

Ninsianna stood up, wearing nothing but her loin cloth and mud. She touched the winged demon's arm, contrite, but fearless, and smiled.

"Sorry," she said. "*Le de thoil.* Try help, fix?"

The winged demon looked away.

"Fix no good," he mumbled. "I fix *computer.*"

Without an argument, Ninsianna picked up her shawl-dress and went inside. The winged demon gave his wings a mighty flap to shake the mud out of them, and then kneeled down to adjust the strange, silver pole which jutted out of the crack.

Jamin and Roshan waited until he went back inside before either one of them dared speak.

"What is that?" Jamin asked.

"He's been working on it all week," Roshan said.

"It must be important?"

"Important enough to kill her?"

Jamin's cheek twitched. Yes. Why threaten to kill her? But his body language had not matched his words. He *should* have thrown the spear, but she'd looked so fearless, and the winged demon had instantly backed down. She hadn't looked that way when she'd run away from *him*.

He stared down at the silver pole propped up by a pile of rocks. It glistened in the sunlight, shiny, like a silver necklace, surrounded, at the base, by an equally shiny shield filled with spikes. Now *there* was a weapon he could bring back to his father. A silver spear and a shield. When conspiring against one's enemies, the ultimate dishonor was to steal the enemy's most prized possession and display it as your own.

"He's no god," Jamin growled. "I shall prove he is nothing but a man."

He reached into his satchel for the rope he'd brought with him, a hundred arm's length; it *should* be long enough to make it down the cliff. He tied one end around a large boulder and threw the other over the edge.

"What are you doing?" Roshan hissed.

"Taking his stick," he said.

He eased his body over the edge.

One of his favorite hobbies, ever since he'd been a little boy, was to climb up the steep embankment upon which their village perched and rummage through the cliff-nests to steal bird eggs. He climbed down slowly, using shoulder muscles honed by decades of hard work and hunting, until he hit the ground.

He looked up. Roshan peered over the edge.

"If he comes out," Jamin called up softly, "I may need you to pull me up."

He tied the rope around his waist to make sure the Halifian didn't pull it up and leave him stranded, and then crept towards the pole like a predator stalking prey, pausing each time his foot dislodged a rock.

"We shall see how strong you are when I steal your weapons."

The silver spear began to spark, calling out a warning to its master. Bright blue light radiated out of the shield. Jamin's hair rose up, the feeling one got just before lighting struck dangerously close.

"Not this time," he hissed. "You will not intimidate me a second time!"

A vortex of light swirled up out of the shield, casting out bolts of miniature lightning as it spun up the silver spear like a desert cyclone. The air began to shriek. Powerful throbs of energy pounded into his body.

Jamin picked up a rock as big as his head.

"She is *my* fiancé!"

With a mighty war cry, he heaved the stone at the glowing silver spear.

Chapter 30

March – 3,390 BC
Earth: Crash site
Colonel Mikhail Mannuki'ili

MIKHAIL

Mikhail checked the connections one last time, pausing to make sure the supplemental power he'd jury-rigged from the engine cold-reignition system would kick in to maintain the wormhole if he was able to make a connection. He crawled out from underneath the counter, banging his injured wing in the process.

"Mpf!" he winced.

Ninsianna rushed towards him, eager to heal every bump and injury. He held up a hand to keep her at arm's length. The *last* thing he needed was for the beautiful young woman to distract him. She was already occupying far too much space inside his head. Starting today, it was time to disabuse her of the notion she was going with him.

He gripped her by the shoulders.

"Here." He pushed her backwards towards an empty seat. "You help here. Listen for voice—" he cupped his hand over his ear "—from Raphael. You tell me, yes? If you hear not-me?"

Ninsianna nodded, her eyes sparkling with excitement. He tried to suppress his *own* excitement. Everything depended on completing the last call he'd tried to make.

Complete the mission...

At last, he would find out what his mission had been?

Ninsianna perched on the stool like an eager cadet, her ear turned up to the ceiling. He double-checked the message which gave what little he knew about the planet, including estimated size calculated using the parallax method, how far it sat from a yellow-green sun, the oversized moon, and distance from several prominent stars, including three arranged in a constellation Ninsianna called 'the hunter's belt.'[79]

Glancing behind him to make sure Ninsianna hadn't moved, he entered the command to initiate the distress signal. Wires hummed as a surge of electricity built up within his ship. Sparks tried to escape his primitive patch-job, but he'd meticulously gone through and taped all of the splices.

---

[79] *Hunter's belt:* a cluster of three stars in the constellation of Orion.

Blue-white light radiated down through the crack as the energy surrounding the antenna began to spin, building up enough plasma to create a miniature wormhole.

Ninsianna reached towards the light, her face eager like a child.

"Don't touch!" he warned. "Bzzt! Very bad. Kill."

Her eye grew wide with anticipation. Fear? Terror? Excitement? Definitely excitement. The young woman seemed to thrive on the unknown.

His pinfeathers rustled with his *own* suppressed excitement. At last! He was going home!

He tapped the *initiate* key.

The entire ship throbbed as the energy began to spin.

A soft 'clink' from the roof drew his attention upwards. A shadow fell across the blue light cast down by the building plasma.

Mikhail shot to his feet and grabbed his pulse pistol.

"Stay away!"

He flew towards the crack. His splinted wing caught on the jagged edge. He hop-flapped a turn and raced out the doorway.

Jamin stood over the antenna, holding a rock.

"Mine!" he shouted.

Mikhail screamed: "No!"

The rock came down, almost in slow motion, into the partially-formed wormhole. A bolt of plasma radiated outward as the wormhole generator exploded in an electromagnetic pulse.

WHOOMPF!!!

It slammed Mikhail backwards. The electrical discharge tore through his body. He jerked back and forth as his entire body convulsed. Muscles clenched, helpless, as his synapses misfired.

Images flashed before his mind.

—*A small, dark shape, hides in the grape vines.*

—*"Come and find me..."*

—*She peeps out of the bushes, her black, prescient eyes far too large for her tiny body.*

He reached for the doll tucked, safely, into his chest-pocket. He tried to speak her name, but already she was gone.

A heart-shaped face appeared above his. Her eyes were golden, not black as *hers* had been. A beautiful spirit, come to guide him into the dreamtime.

"N-n-ninsianna."

She grabbed his face, weeping.

Gradually the convulsions subsided. He lay there, helpless, limp and weak. On the cliff, in front of him, Jamin's body dangled.

"J-J-J—"

He tried to force his tongue to speak. To say his enemy's name. The body rose higher, suspended from a rope. Up on top of the cliff, one of the Halifians who had cursed him with the goat hauled the body up.

"Help me!" he gasped.

Ninsianna pulled him into a seating position.

His hand shaking, he lined the body up in his gunsights. Through the discipline wrought of dozens of years of practice, he forced his trembling hands to click off the safety and jack the power up to the highest possible setting.

Ninsianna's mouth formed into an 'O' as she recognized what he was about to do.

"No!"

She knocked him backwards.

The shot went off...

...harmlessly into the air.

He lay there twitching, his nervous system unresponsive. Too weak, too tired, to *despondent* to get up.

The Halifian finished pulling Jamin's body up over the edge of the cliff and disappeared.

Mikhail lay there, shuddering, for what seemed an eternity before he finally regained enough control of his emotions to let Ninsianna help him to his feet. He stared at the vaporized remnants of his antenna.

It gave him no consolation that Jamin was probably dead.

Chapter 31

Galactic Standard Date: 152,323.03 AE
Earth: Sata'an Forward Operating Base
Lieutenant Kasib

LT. KASIB

Lieutenant Kasib stood at attention as General Hudhafah looked through the evening reports, his tail tucked up tightly along his right side. Every now and again he discreetly tasted the air, the sensitive tines of his long, forked tongue registering the pheromones which betrayed the general's mood.

"Any sign of that Angelic?" Hudhafah asked at last.

"Some errant mineral deposits that turned out to be iron ore," Kasib said. "Two debunked reports by locals, attempting to claim the reward. And this, Sir. Some kind of seismic disturbance."

Hudhafah's sharp dorsal ridge reared with curiosity. He examined the report from one of the shuttles.

"A distress signal?"

"We don't think so," Kasib said. "It was too brief, too irregular. They're attributing it to terrestrial magnetism."

"Have the *Jamaran* scan that area the next time it flies over. If there's anything bigger than a wristwatch, we should be able to pick it up."

"Yes, Sir," Kasib said. "It's already been done."

General Hudhafah pulled up the next report. The one about his efforts to secure local allies.

"Who is this tribe again?" the General asked.

"They call themselves Amorites,"[80] Kasib said. "They claim they can bring us females willing to learn the ways of the Empire."

Hudhafah took a claw and traced the photographs he'd uploaded to the General's flatscreen. A rough looking bunch, if ever he'd been a judge of humanoid character.

"Tell them we'll start with three," he said. "The best this planet has to offer. Give them one gold coin for each woman, and two to send back to the women's families. When I send this report back to Shay'tan, I want *proof* we haven't all gone daft."

"Yes, Sir."

With a crisp salute, Kasib stepped out to institute Phase II of Sata'anic Rule.

---

[80] *Amorite:* a Semitic-speaking tribe disparaged by the Sumerians.

Chapter 32

March 3,390 BC
Earth: Village of Assur

JAMIN

Incomplete rows of mud-bricks whispered taunts the same way the villagers now whispered behind his back. The forms sat vacant as they had since the day she'd broken off their engagement. Sand. Straw. Buckets to carry water. And a pile of goat dung to act as a binding agent to make their house strong. All his life he'd enjoyed the hunt. The sport. The kill. But only Ninsianna had ever inspired him to *build*.

Jamin choked back the emptiness which threatened to consume him, his mind leaping to all *sorts* of horrible conclusions. The winged demon touching his girl. The winged demon touching her face. The winged demon touching her … her … her …

NO!

He picked up a sapling he'd cut as a roof strut and smashed it into the wall, imagining he stabbed *him* with a spear. A wooden spear, not the fancy silver one he'd tried to steal. One of the mud-bricks came dislodged from the foundation. Anger flowed through him. With a primal scream, he smashed every single brick.

"Arghhh!"

He fell, sobbing, his chest heaving with grief. His hand shook as he picked up a shattered brick. It crumbled into dust.

"Jamin? Are you okay?"

He whirled to face Gita, Ninsianna's peculiar cousin. She was shorter by two palm's breadth, with bones sticking out of a shawl dress so worn it barely covered her emaciated frame. How long had the scrawny waif stood there watching, pretending to be part of the lengthening shadows?

"Go away," he snarled. He threw the shattered brick at her feet. Gita leaped back. "Have you come to relish my humiliation?"

Gita kneeled next to him, her expression sympathetic. Black, prescient eyes stared out of a pale, gaunt face that was a faint echo of the face he *really* wanted to see.

"Now you know how Shahla feels," she said softly.

He lunged for her, but Gita was too quick, her reflexes honed by a lifetime of evading her drunken father. She settled, just out of range, a dark dragonfly, ready to flit away at the slightest move.

"What do you *want*, Gita?"

"You have seen him?" her black eyes sparkled. "The legends are real?"

"What legend?" he growled. "Immanu made it up!"

Her preternaturally black eyes stared right through him as though he was not even there. Ninsianna's eyes, only blacker. As dark as night when no moon graced the sky.

Lugalbanda's eyes...

A shaman so powerful he could stop his enemy's heart...

Jamin looked away. He'd taken the odd girl under his protection when her drunken father had suddenly reappeared after being banished from whatever haughty house he had married into. For some reason, his old girlfriend, Shahla, had taken an instant liking to the reclusive child. Gita had given him the cold shoulder ever since he'd cast the harlot off to pursue Ninsianna. Why was she now lurking in his shadow? Because once upon a time they'd been friends?

"I have seen the cave paintings in *Es Skhul*," Gita said. "The priestesses at Jebel Mar Elyas protected it until the Amorites destroyed their temple."

"What cave paintings?"

"Demi-gods," Gita said. "Half-human, half-animal. They came across the waters in a great ship and waged war upon the people that were here before. The Nephilim."

Gita's eyes swirled blacker, like a nocturnal animal dragged unwillingly into the light. The sensation of suddenly being laid naked, his heart squeezed, made him choke up. He gasped for breath. Whenever Gita had done that to him as a child, it had always terrified him.

"Gita! Please! I never told Shahla that I loved her!"

Her nostrils flared, but then the pressure subsided. Shahla pursued him because she wanted to be the wife of a chief. *Her* father wanted leverage over *his* father for all of his shady trade deals.

"You have a black heart," she said, "Jamin, son of Kiyan. As black and empty as the obsidian at the end of your spear!"

"You *know* that's not true," he said. "It was *me* who begged my father to let *your* father back into our village after Immanu refused."

She stared west, towards the desert.

"You would have done better to cast us both out to die."

She stood to leave. Already she'd begun to fade into the shadows.

"Gita, wait!" he pleaded. "Tell me what you know?"

Gita's eyes turned black, haunted and mournful.

"I only remember the pictures," she said. "And a legend. That one day the halfway people would return."

"I thought the priestesses were—"

He cut off, rather than offend her by saying "sacred prostitutes."

"The priestesses were healers who ran a hospital," she said. "Not harlots, like your people preach. Perhaps, if you'd given her gift of healing more *respect*, Ninsianna wouldn't have left you!"

As she spoke, he could almost *see* the temple she'd described from her childhood. A magnificent building on top of the highest mountain, built not from mud-bricks, but carved from stone. Yes. That was what Ninsianna wanted. To have people worship her the way one would a goddess. But Assur didn't have the resources to build such things. But perhaps there? Yes! A separate room where people could worship his bride-to-be instead of meet with *him*. With a separate entrance? Her very own hospital!

Jamin looked up and was not surprised to see Gita had disappeared. Unless she wished to be seen, she had a way of fading into the shadows. A survival skill to escape the wrath of her drunken father.

His heart light, Jamin pulled out the goatskin parchment he'd used to sketch plans for Ninsianna's dream house and drew in in blueprints for a 'hospital' room.

A temple to *her*…

He picked up a displaced brick and placed it back onto the wall. For the first time in weeks, he felt hope.

Chapter 33

March – 3,390 BC
Earth: Crash site

Two weeks later...

NINSIANNA

Ninsianna stared at the long, lean legs protruding from beneath the pair of dark grey beasts that Mikhail claimed dragged his sky canoe across the heavens. *Engines* he called them. Each was larger than an auroch, with sharp spearheads and thick hollow reeds to tether them to his ship as though they were twin spiders sharing a single web.

"Céilí mór!!!" he cursed. Something rang as it hit the floor. "Ninsianna, *d'fhéadfá a fháil dom le do thoil go bhfuil eochair?"*[81]

"Here ... *anseo—*" she handed him the grasping tool he called 'wrench.' The strange tool, in fact, just about everything in his sky canoe, had no correlation in her language. She simply paid attention and learned whatever she could.

Muscular thighs flexed beneath taut woven cloth as he shifted position to move deeper beneath the engines. His undershirt rode up, giving her a pleasant view of his belly button. The way his taut abdominal muscles rippled beneath his skin *did* things to her. Warm, tingly things deep within her feminine core.

"Ninsianna, *d'fhéadfaí tú a lámh le do thoil dom scriúire?"*

"Anseo." She fetched the small spear he'd formerly kept on Compyoota's altar. His wings splayed beneath him on the floor like a brown feathered cape. She crawled over them on her hands and knees, trying to feel where feathers ended and flesh began so she didn't kneel on living tissue.

"Thank you." He regarded her with that cool, expressionless mask he'd worn ever since Jamin had killed his god, Compyoota. Ninsianna smiled, hoping to bridge the distance. The moment stretched out, infinitely long, before he shifted his gaze back to manipulate the little spear into the 'engine.'

"You're welcome," she said concisely in her own language. She backed out, careful not to bang her head against the underside of the engines. They both froze as she placed one hand down upon the spot where his bare

---

[81] "...could you get me please...?"

abdomen disappeared into his pants, dangerously close to where his manhood pressed through the fitted garments. His warmth radiated up through her fingers as she registered his abdominal muscles harden at the unexpected contact.

Such nice, hard muscles...

"Oh! Excuse me!"

She jerked away her hand a full seven heartbeats *after* she should have removed it. Why did embarrassing moments such as this always stretch out in time? She scurried the rest of the way out, ripping out a few dark feathers in the process. She stared with dismay at the evidence which floated into the air like pretty, fluffy brown tufts.

"Sorry!" She dusted stray pin feathers off of her dress.

"It's okay," he reassured her. "*Ní raibh sé gortaithe* ... not hurt."

Her face turn flaming red! Thank the goddess he was too engrossed to notice her interest. Focus! On anything but him!

She turned her attention to something *other* than the very appealing lower half of his body. For the last two weeks he'd become withdrawn, crawling through his sky canoe with almost frantic intensity, and treating her with polite disinterest. He didn't ask *why* she'd prevented him from using his firestick to strike Jamin's body. In fact, she suspected he felt *guilty* about becoming so angry he'd almost smote a man dangling from a rope, unconscious.

Stupid goat-head! If only Jamin really -had- died!

Bah! She didn't mean that! As much as she hated the way he kept pursuing her, part of her enjoyed it. There was no better way to make a man appreciate a woman than to have *another* man pursue her. Especially a man as utterly and frustratingly uninterested in her as Mikhail!

What would he do if some night she crawled into his bed and did some of the things that Shahla bragged she did...

No! She wasn't that kind of woman!

Mikhail shifted beneath the engines. The *scriúire* rang as it hit the floor.

"*Céilí mór!!!*"

He slid out from beneath the engine and gave it an icy stare. Wiping black tar off his hands with a cloth, he exclaimed, "*níl a fhios agam cad é an diabhal cearr leis an rud damanta!* Don't know why broken!"

His dark feathers rustled with frustration. She didn't know anything about fixing engine-oars that made sky canoes travel across the stars, but she could relate to not being able to fix something that had to work. She wanted the engine-oars to work every bit as much as *he* did so he could take her to see the stars!

She hesitated, and then slid her arms around his waist. This is what Mama did for Papa whenever a spell went bad. She laid her cheek against his chest to communicate she sympathized with his frustration. His chest felt warm and firm beneath her cheek, and his heart beat in a slow, reassuring flutter.

"Ninsianna," he tilted up her chin. *"Tú ag dul a fháil ramhar inneall ar fud an tosach do ghúna."*[82]

Her heart flip-flopped as she stared up into his unearthly blue eyes. Should she kiss him? Did she dare? Would he be offended if she initiated a kiss? Or would he think she was a hussy?

His wings curled forward. The tips of his feathers brushed against her shoulder blades. Time stretched out for an eternity even though she knew it was only several heartbeats.

She parted her lips.

Mikhail? Won't you kiss me?

A plethora of emotion darted across his beautiful, chiseled features, smeared with a tar-like substance that smelled like bitumen. He took the cloth he'd just used to clean his hands and dabbed the end of her nose.

"Ninsianna now dirty," he admonished her gently. "Mikhail dirty. You no want to touch."

Her lip trembled with disappointment.

"Yes, Mikhail all dirty."

She took the rag and stood on tip-toe.

His feathers rustled as she wiped a large streak of dirt that went from his chin all the way to his ear. She pictured what it might have been like if Mikhail had kissed her. She whispered the image from her fingers into his mind. His face remained unreadable, but his muscles trembled, as though it was all he could do to resist her charm.

She stepped back, breathless, and handed him the rag.

Maybe he *wasn't* impervious?

But every time she grew bold, Mikhail retreated.

She gave him her most disarming smile.

"Good now," she said. "Let's go eat?"

"Eat? Yes."

His unreadable expression melted at the mention of food. She led him out of the sky canoe like an enormous winged dog.

---

[82] "You'll get engine grease on your dress."

Chapter 34

March – 3,390 BC
Earth: Crash Site
Colonel Mikhail Mannuki'ili

MIKHAIL

The worse consequence of firing his pulse pistol at Jamin was not the fact he'd missed—he was *glad* he had missed, the man was unconscious and to shoot him would have been reprehensible no matter *how* furious he was at the time—but the fact he'd wasted what was probably his next to the last shot shooting at the empty air. The angry red light blinked faster every time he powered the weapon up, but he needed to practice. The more he practiced, the more his muscles remembered what his mind refused to tell him.

He slipped it back into his hip-holster and then pulled it out and aimed it again at a series of rocks lined up along a log.

"Boom," he said.

He didn't fire it of course. If it was his last shot, he intended to save it for a desperate day. He spun the grip around his finger like an old-style space opera gunfighter before putting back into his holster, and then he pulled it out again. It made him feel less impotent, to know the next time he had to pull it, his muscles would automatically aim whether or not he *remembered* how to do it.

His eye wandered to watch Ninsianna wade through the stream, nearly naked, engaged in her perpetual conversation with her invisible friend. She was quite adept at taking care of herself, but he kept a close watch on her. Until he found a way off of this planet, nobody would bother her.

I should send her home.

He glanced at his ship. *That* wasn't going anyplace, soon. What harm did it do to let her stay? Especially now that her father had brought word the Chief was livid that his micro-wormhole generator had almost killed his son.

He pulled the pulse pistol and pictured lining Jamin up in his gunsights. "Boom."

What good was it? To practice killing with an empty weapon?

He holstered the pulse pistol and pulled out his survival knife. He still *had* a weapon. The one he kept hidden above his bed. He selected an acacia sapling, slightly twisted, but it would have to do, and cut a length which ran from his fingertip to his shoulder. With a few sharp strikes, he hacked it off and smoothed off the bark. A weapon the exact same length as his sword.

Why don't I practice with the real weapon?

Because the *last* thing he needed was for Ninsianna's father to fall down to the floor, chanting accolades and prayers, instead of using his rational mind. The shaman had an almost hysterical belief in 'omens.'

He swung at a hazelnut bush the rapidly shrinking oasis had left high and dry. Now *that* was another problem looming on the horizon. What would he do once this oasis dried down?

Whack. Whack. At first it felt awkward to practice with an imaginary sword, but then his muscles began to take over. He swung until it settled into a training kata he *knew* but could not remember learning. Hit. Hit. Stab. Move your feet that way. Look behind you for a second opponent. Turn. Swing. Slice.

Increasing the ferocity of his swing, he stabbed an imaginary black-eyed human, smiting him a thousand times as he pondered what to do about Ninsianna. An honorable man would have sent her packing weeks ago. He swung, and parried, and jabbed until his muscles screamed in protest.

Splash!

The pond exploded into a miniature geyser.

Ninsianna laughed. She threw a fish up onto the shore.

"Mikhail! See, fish?"

She splashed to the water's edge, laughing with delight, almost naked, and triumphantly picked up the still-wriggling fish.

"Fish good." He forced himself to maintain eye contact and not stare unabashedly at her breasts. "I like. Eat."

"I go clean it. Then I cook it."

"Yes. *Le do thoil.*" He flapped his wings to show off a little. "You start fire. I make fire burn big and hot."

Ninsianna grinned. He had to *force* himself not to make a fool out of himself by smiling back.

He stared at her disappearing rump as she fetched her obsidian blade and took the fish back to the stream to clean it. Her back fascinated him, the graceful curve of her spine, the shoulder blades which moved beneath her flesh. *The absence of wings...* He dared not touch her back. To *him*, to touch one's wings, or back, felt almost painfully intimate.

And yet he let her massage his wings three times a day...

It's for medical purposes...

Liar! He let her do it because he enjoyed the way it made him feel!

Ninsianna returned with the fish and wrapped it, along with some tubers and greens she'd scrounged up earlier, into some leaves for cooking.

He resumed swinging his imaginary sword, showing off a bit of athleticism as muscle memory reminded him he was *good* at this. As the food began to roast, she sat down and unabashedly watched him practice with the stick, a smile lighting up her features. Her eyes had a mischievous golden glint.

"You heal good. You get *guclu*."

"*Guclu?*"

"Yes." She held up one arm and scrunched her bicep. "*Guclu.*"

"What that word?" He pointed to his bicep. "Muscles?"

"No." She picked up a rock and pretended to heave it over her head. "*Guclu.*"

"Ahhh! *Níos láidre* … stronger. I get it. Stronger. Yes?"

"Yes, stronger … *níos láidre.*" Ninsianna repeated. "You heal good. Almost heal."

"Yes, almost," he said. "But no fly. Wing still hurt."

"*Bana izen ver* … I look?"

Anticipation rippled through his feathers. He set down his imaginary sword, sat dutifully and stretched out his wing. For the past week he'd done without the splint. It was much more comfortable to sleep, but whenever he tried to extend fully upwards, the motion he needed to pull his body into the air, the pain grew so great he grew dizzy and wanted to vomit.

Had his wing been broken beyond repair?

She placed her hands over the joint where it had dislocated and felt along the bone. The area grew warm, along with the pleasant tingling sensation he associated with her touch. It felt so good he could sit here forever, allowing her to massage his wing, and enjoying the pleasant sensations she triggered within his body; as though some long-dormant piece of his spirit had awoken and begun to blossom.

She reached an area that made him wince.

"Ouch!" He grimaced.

"Hurt here?"

"Yes. There hurt bad."

She felt around it, digging her fingers in deep to probe the tissue beneath his skin, and prompted him to move the wing this way or that. He forced himself not to whimper, looking away so she wouldn't see his pained expression. Ninsianna sat down next to him, her face serious.

"Bone is good," she said. "It heal good. No more break."

"Wing okay?"

"No." She shook her head. "Wing not okay."

She wore that look people assumed whenever they were about to give you terrible news. Fear tore into his gut. He schooled his features into an unreadable expression so she wouldn't see his terror.

Mikhail gulped.

"What wrong?"

"*Kiris* not good," she said softly. "It hurt bad. Not know how to fix."

"*Kiris?*"

Ninsianna pinched the bridge of her nose, deep in thought. Finally, she pulled off one of the primitive hide coverings she used as a shoe.

"*Kiris* not good. Hurt bad." She pointed to her Achilles tendon. "*Kiris* break, need long time heal." She pointed at the spot in his wing which felt like somebody was trying to rip it apart every time he tried to fly. "*Kiris* in wing hurt. Need long time heal."

Kiris?

Tendon…

He'd damaged his main flight tendon?

"How long heal?" he asked.

Her expression grew apologetic.

"Sometimes never," she whispered.

A sense of vertigo, as though his ship had just leaped out of hyperspace into the middle of a black hole, left him feeling as though all of his molecules were suddenly being torn apart. For a winged creature, being told you might never fly again was like being told you might never walk again. Paired with the death of his computer, his ruined antenna, and the realization his ship might never fly again and he was trapped, that was a lot of bad news. Especially when he couldn't remember if anyone cared enough about him to even bother looking for him!

He masked his terror.

"Can you fix?"

"I don't know." She put her hand on his cheek. "Mama know better. Mama heal better than Ninsianna."

—*A sense of terror.*

—*Buried in a darkened room.*

—*Being small and helpless.*

—*The smell of blood and death.*

She pulled him in for a hug.

He threw his arms around her and buried his face in her hair, inhaling the scent of musk and soap root. She smelled warm and comforting. It was a scent he associated with *home*.

The tide of emotion he'd been fighting to keep at bay since he'd awoken, impaled through the chest with what he thought was a spirit come to guide him into the dreamtime, finally broke. Complete the mission? Who the heck was he kidding? And leave Ninsianna behind?

He'd rather cut off both of his wings…

"Cad é ag déanamh liom a dhéanamh faoi tú, mo grá?" He whispered in his own language so she wouldn't understand the words. *What am I going to do about you, my love?*

The wind shifted, blowing the scent of cooked fish in their direction.

He pulled himself back together before she read the naked vulnerability in his face. With his ship, his technology, his people, his memory, and his ability to fly gone, the only thing he had left to offer was his word of honor.

He'd made her father a promise…

His *word* was the one thing within his control.

Composing his features back into an impassive mask, he pulled away and suggested they bring the food inside.

Chapter 35

March – 3,390 BC
Earth: Outside Crash Site

JAMIN

Jamin gasped for breath, burying his face into his knees to suppress the scream which threatened to erupt in a wail of grief. He watched, helpless, as Ninsianna led the winged demon inside the sky canoe, her hips swaying gently in an invitation.

He lurched towards the cliff, his spear clutched in his fist, and fell back. He wasn't supposed to *be* here. His father had threatened to drag him before the tribunal if he thwarted his authority one more time. The penalty for disobedience was public humiliation, banishment, or stoning. He would bear humiliation gladly if it would win back Ninsianna's heart, but what if they banished him? If they sent him away, he would never get a chance to show her his plan.

He unrolled the goatskin parchment clutched in his fist. He'd brought it to show the room he'd just built on the side of their dream house. It was a 'hospital' room, still incomplete, with a tiny garden in the back so she could sit with patients and cultivate medicinal herbs. It was his temple to *her*. The goddess he'd failed to worship ... and lost.

And now it was too late...

A single tear fell from his cheek and streaked the charcoal he'd used to sketch in what he'd been building. He was the son of a chief. Her rejection had made him the laughing-stock of the Ubaid!

Real men didn't cry!

He faded back from the cliff, waiting until he was out of ear shot before he began to rage. If this is what they did *outside* the ship, he could only imagine what went on in private.

The wind picked up.

'Jamin ... let her go...'

The breeze taunted him, whispering his loss through the empty desert. A locust flew onto his hand, tilting its head to look at him and whirring its gossamer under-wings. The muscle in his cheek spasmed, stress causing the errant facial tic to develop a mind all its own. Let her go? He gave the wind his answer.

"Never!"

He squashed the locust and threw the blueprints into the dirt. He wasn't the *only* person who wanted the winged demon gone!

Skulking west, he plotted how to get even.

Chapter 36

Galactic Standard Date: 152,323.03 AE
Earth: Sata'an Forward Operating Base

LT. KASIB

The Algol-class ship hovered over the airfield and shifted its impulse engines to land on the rocky soil. It was shaped like an arrow, painted flat black to blend in with deep space, not a lot of cargo room, but a whole lot of engine. Shay'tan called them merchant vessels—peace be upon him—but everybody knew the ships were used for smuggling and spying.

The two gunships they'd sent behind the moon to flush it out of hiding hovered over it, their pulse cannons aimed at the slender ship. It contrasted sharply to the honor guard.

Dust blew up from the airfield, casting its fertile scent into Kasib's nostrils.

"Attention!" General Hudhafah barked as the loading ramp slid down.

The skullcrackers snapped to attention.

Three lizards appeared at the top of the ramp.

Kasib tasted the air, unable to read the peculiar blend of pheromones cast off by the General and his second in command. It was most irregular! Not just the fact they'd been followed—Shay'tan often spied on his own generals—but the blasé way Hudhafah had announced the ship had been following them ever since they'd left 3-Quincunx-742.

The ship's commander scanned the men who stood at attention, and then glanced up at the hovering gunships. Lieutenant Apausha was big for a junior officer, with broad shoulders and a bright red dewlap, intelligent gold-green eyes, and a bright-green hide, indicative of the upper castes.

He held his tail out straight as he strode dutifully towards General Hudhafah. If he was afraid, he did not show it.

"Attention!" Apausha ordered his two men.

All three lizards tucked their tails up along their sides in a crisp salute.

"Thank you for coming," General Hudhafah said gruffly, as if he'd given them a choice. "We have a shipment that needs to go straight to Shay'tan."

"The merchant marine operates under Lord Ba'al Zebub, Sir," Apausha said. "We take our orders from him."

Hudhafah growled.

"Are you saying you serve Ba'al Zebub above our Emperor and God?"

Kasib glanced nervously from the General to the three merchant mariners. There was something else going on here. Something he wasn't privy to.

"No, Sir," Apausha said. "Above all others, we serve Shay'tan, peace be upon him. I swear it upon my father's spirit."

"That was my impression." Hudhafah gestured at Kasib. "Bring her in."

Kasib spoke into his headset.

"Katlego? Bring the shipment."

Three skullcrackers appeared, two lizards and a boar-like Catoplebas, herding between them a terrified human woman. She was taller than the locals, almost as tall as *he* was, with a long neck, striking ebony skin, hair which tumbled down her back in ringlets, and high cheekbones. She wore the shawl-dress favored by local women, but around her neck she wore a necklace carved from rare, precious wood.

She was like a Leonid, a Centauri, and an Angelic, all rolled into one...

Lieutenant Apausha examined the terrified woman. He folded his hands non-threateningly in front of him.

"Don't be afraid," he spoke carefully in Kemet,[83] the local language of trade. "Nobody will hurt you."

Kasib's eyebrow-ridges shot up with surprise.

"You've been monitoring our transmissions?"

"Of course," Apausha said. "That was our assignment."

Kasib looked to the general. The general did not appear to be surprised.

"I wish you *not* to monitor any longer," Hudhafah said, "but to carry a message to our illustrious Emperor and god."

---

[83] *Kemet:* a common language used for trade; originates with the Kemet tribe of what would later become Egypt.

Chapter 37

March – 3,390 BC
Earth: Crash site

NINSIANNA

A vivid dream woke Ninsianna up with a start. A hand clamped over her mouth.

"Shhh..." Mikhail whispered.

Up at the front of the sky canoe, one of the ceiling mats they used to block the door went *'thud.'* The goat bleated.

"What is it?" she whispered. "A hyena?"

"Enemies."

He grabbed his firestick and shoved it into its holster.

Ninsianna slipped out from the covers. Mikhail reached up underneath his bunk and pulled out a long, slender weapon. It caught the dim light; flatter than an obsidian spearhead, polished silver, with a honed sharp edge.

A word whispered into her mind.

Sword...

Was this the weapon in the ancient song?

"Stay here," Mikhail said.

He tucked his wings against his back and crept silently out through the galley. Ninsianna recognized the fighting stance he'd practiced earlier with a stick, only now that stick was deadly as he crept towards the front of the sky canoe.

She held her breath. Was it a wild animal, come to eat the goat?

Somebody cursed.

A human. *Many* humans.

Her hear pounded in her throat. Women were a constant target for the slavers. As soon she'd been able to walk, her Mama had taught her how to use a knife. She pulled out her satchel and fished out her obsidian blade. Better two against one than to fight alone? Belting her shawl around her waist so she wouldn't meet their attackers naked, she hurried out to the bridge.

Two dark shapes moved near the doorway, illuminated by the pre-dawn greyness which seeped in through the crack. She scanned the dark room, searching for Mikhail. Where had he gone? A third man slipped in. The goat tugged at its rope and bleated a warning. One of them grabbed it by the neck and moved to slit its throat to silence it.

Mikhail erupted out of the wall, wings flared, part of the darkness. He grabbed both men by the their necks and smashed their heads together.

"Get out *de mo long!*" he shouted.

He picked up a third man and threw him out the entrance, just in time to knock down a fourth man crawling through the crack.

The first two men circled and jabbed at him with spears, but in the tight confines of the sky canoe, the weapons were less than effective. One of them stabbed at him. Mikhail swung the sword. In a flash of silver, the wood shattered.

The other man rushed at him. Mikhail grabbed the broken end of the spear to thwap his assailant while simultaneously spinning to kick the second assailant in the chest. With a shout, both men rushed at him at once. In a flurry of wings and fists and feathers, he punched and hit and kicked. Even slowed down by injuries, he was a far better fighter than they were.

The two remaining men staggered, beaten. He grabbed both men by the throat and strode outside to toss them into the dirt.

Ninsianna raced to the crack they used as a doorway. The pre-dawn light cast a grey shadow against the horizon, rendering their attackers little more than shadows against an even darker landscape.

A sound above caused Ninsianna looked up.

"Look out!" she shrieked.

A net flew down on top of Mikhail's head and wings. A dozen men leaped out of the shadows. They tackled Mikhail. He punched and hit through the net. Why didn't he just use his firestick?

One of the men grabbed Ninsianna's arm.

"Eek!"

She stabbed sideways. Her blade grazed the meaty part of his upper arm, but didn't sink in.

"Ouch!" he yelped.

He grabbed her wrist and pried the knife out of her hands.

He pulled her up against his body.

"Ahh, pretty, yes?" he grinned at her with rotted teeth.

His breath stank...

...and his cock pressed, eager, against her belly.

"Ugh!" She kneed him in the testicles.

He yelped, but grabbed her by the hair.

"Mikhail!" she shrieked.

The Halifian yanked her head down, knocking her to her knees, and held her there, helpless, as the others leaped on Mikhail. He whirled and fought, but was hampered by the net. He was one man against eighteen. Even if he *could* fly, the net got tangled in his feathers.

The Halifians set upon him with spears and clubs.

A flash of silver.

One of the Halifians yelped.

Ninsianna cheered as the sword drove their attackers back. Mikhail spread his twenty-cubit wingspan, far larger than the net, and leaped into the air, wings flapping, to do a mid-air somersault.

The net fell off of him.

Her attacker gaped.

She used the distraction to bite him.

The man yowled and punched her in the cheek. Pain exploded into her head. Dizziness. Falling. She crashed into the dirt. Her mouth filled with blood. The man grabbed her long hair.

"No!" She scrambled in the dirt.

She found her knife and stabbed upwards.

"Back off!"

The Halifian leaped back, holding his leg. A bloom of crimson seeped from between his fingers.

Panting, she rose to her feet, her blade held in front of her the way Mama had trained her. She wiped some blood from her lip.

"Mikhail is going to kill you," she hissed.

The man forced her backward.

Mikhail met her back-to-back.

"I tell you to stay inside!" he said in broken Ubaid.

His blue eyes glittered with some kind of internal light, the same color as his spirit light. Only this was visible. Either that, or She-Who-Is had chosen *now* to grant her another vision.

"Ninsianna help." She held up her knife. "See? Help Mikhail fight enemies."

"My job to protect *you*," he said.

Their enemies became more visible as the sun inched towards the horizon. Grey sky gave way to pink. The biggest attacker, a well-dressed Halifian carrying an intricately carved spear, gestured towards his right. Six men slipped behind them to cut them off from the sky canoe.

Mikhail crouched, ready to move in any direction.

The leader barked an order. Three men scurried to gather up the net. They stretched it out, preparing to rush at him again.

Mikhail spread his wings, ready to use them as weapons. The sword glistened silver in front of him.

"I fight them," he spoke low. "You. Run to place to climb up."

"What about you?"

"I fight better if not worried about Ninsianna."

One of the Halifians slipped behind them. He rushed at Mikhail's back. Mikhail back-flapped a wing to hit him in the face. As he did, he crashed into her. He needed room to maneuver.

"Okay," she said. "One, two, three…"

Mikhail went on the offensive.

Ninsianna ran towards the landslide.

All eighteen men rushed at Mikhail with spears.

Ninsianna turned before she reached the rocks. She couldn't just leave him?

Mikhail drove them back. The mercenaries stabbed at him with their spears, taking advantage of the reach of their longer weapons. Every time one rushed in, he easily deflected it, but it was eighteen men against one.

Several times the Halifians rushed at him with the net. The bastards *knew* he couldn't fly. Now that he knew they had it, he kept flapping it off, but each time he did they harassed him, circling, spinning, never stepping close enough to be hit, but always close enough he had to hit at them. Like a pack of hyenas, they carefully wore the prey out. Mikhail began to pant. His flesh turned ghastly pale. He began to stumble. While far stronger than any one of their enemies, his injuries still left him weak and he was vastly outnumbered.

A lump rose in Ninsianna's throat. She should leave. It was what he wanted. If she ran now and hid, she had a chance to get away.

Mikhail's broken wing drooped. Her beautiful man from the heavens.

The net-men rushed forward. They threw the net on top of him. The other Halifians grabbed the corners of the net. They pulled it tight and flipped him to the ground.

"No!" Ninsianna wept.

She ran back towards them, holding her knife.

The Halifian leader hoisted his spear.

"You're no god!" he shouted in Ubaid.

He threw the spear. It landed in the crumpled pile of feathers.

Mikhail cried out.

Ninsianna screamed.

The Halifians all threw their spears…

A deadly calm descended upon the valley. The shadows moved. The Halifians remained poised, their spears suspended mid-strike, as though they'd suddenly become frozen in a moment of time. Overwhelming terror screamed into Ninsianna's body.

'Get out! Get out! Get out!' it shrieked.

With the world still frozen, Mikhail flared his wings.

He rose slowly, like a lion rising up from the savanna. The net fell off his body, as though it had simply melted. The sky grew brighter, but it did not grow bright around *him*. Trills of terror vibrated through Ninsianna's being; almost palpable; a terrible, howling shrieking sound.

It felt like a sandstorm tore through her blood.

"M-m-mother?" she cried out.

She could see it, feel it, taste the awesome presence. Never had she sensed this much power. Not even in the presence of her grandfather, Lugalbanda!

Mikhail ripped the spear out of his thigh. He pointed at the man who had thrown it. The air shook as he spoke to his attackers, not in his language, not in her language. But in a language so ancient the very air vibrated with his words.

"Solvite!"[84]

Horror screamed through Ninsianna's veins as he turned to make eye contact and tilted his head like a strange, foreign bird. His eyes were black and empty, a bottomless black pit. The pre-dawn light played tricks upon her eyes, making her imagine his wings were the leathery wings of a bat. No. She blinked. This was still Mikhail. It was his *intent* which had changed. Up until now, he'd been trying *not* to kill their attackers.

That would no longer be the case.

The Halifians paused to coordinate their attack.

Mikhail clenched the sword. Darkness swirled around the blade.

"Ayiih!!!" They rushed forward.

Mikhail's wings pounded the air to keep him semi-aloft as he spun to hack off limbs, decapitated heads, and stabbed them in the heart in smooth, fluid motions. He slaughtered his attackers with a beautiful, graceful dance. The dance of death. He slaughtered them with ease, as though he reaped eighteen stalks of grain. He watered the earth with his enemy's blood.

The stench of death and perforated bowels filled the valley. A nineteenth shadow broke out from the carnage and raced towards her.

"Ninsianna!" the attacker called her name. "Run!"

Ninsianna held out her knife.

"Get away from me!" she shrieked.

Mikhail flew towards them both. In a flurry of feathers he raised his sword to reap the nineteenth deadly stalk of grain.

The attacker tripped. Mikhail swung and missed his head. The man landed at Ninsianna's feet. Mikhail rose up, wings flared, sword held high to make the decapitation.

---

[84] *Solvite:* destroy.

The first ray of light burst above the horizon. It streamed a ray of sunlight directly upon the man's face, as though the goddess wished to announce, *'this is the man who is about to die.'*

Oh, gods! It was Jamin!

"Mikhail! No!"

She threw herself on top of the Chief's son.

"Please! It's Jamin!"

He swung the sword down for the death-stroke. Ninsianna flinched as blood sprayed into her eyes. The sword stopped, so close to her neck she could *feel* the cold chill of the silver blade. Mikhail stared down at her, impossibly tall and deadly, a winged statue more fitting for a temple than a mortal creature she'd nursed back from the dead. Her heart beat with terror as she realized there was no recognition in his pitiless black eyes, only a darkness so vast and empty it caused chills to run down her spine.

Stretching her body across the chief's son, she reached her hand up in a plea.

"M-m-mikhail," she stuttered. "Please?"

Warmth surged through her body. That sense of time being frozen hit at her again, only this time it was SHE who delineated the moments. Words bubbled up to her lips that were not her own.

"Haec sunt mea latrunculorum frusta!"[85]

Mikhail's response vibrated the air, dark and terrible.

"Fraudarit me, coniunx. Quem ipsa non quaerit."[86]

She-Who-Is spoke to the avenging Angelic poised above her, sword raised to smite both Jamin *and* her. SHE spoke with haughtiness and defiance, her power palpable as SHE used Ninsianna's body to speak to HER champion.

"Habes pollicitus es me formaeque, maritus meus. Is unus est, electo meo. Non alterum unum."[87]

The goddess expected to be obeyed.

Mikhail removed the sword from her throat.

"Quem ipsa non quaerit. Videbitis."[88]

A feeling of victory raced through her entire body even though she had no idea what the goddess had just won. Unfamiliar words tumbled from her lips.

"A sponsione tunc. Quo iure nos videbimus."[89]

"Assentior." [90]

---

[85] "This is *my* chess piece."
[86] "You cheated, my wife. You stole his memories."
[87] "You agreed to my terms, husband. This one is *Chosen*. Not the *Other One*."
[88] "She is not the one he seeks, this you will see."
[89] "A wager, then? We shall see who is right?"

That sense of terror suddenly abated. Mikhail's wings fluttered as though he was thrown off-balance. Recognition crept back into his eyes as they transformed from that terrifying emptiness back into the unearthly blue glow. Saying something in a strange clicking language, he lowered his blade.

The goddess released her hold upon her body.

'Speak to him,' SHE whispered.

Ninsianna reached towards the dark-winged creature.

"M-m-Mikhail," she stuttered. "It's me. Ninsianna. Your friend."

He tilted his head, as though uncertain whether or not he recognized her.

"If you k-k-kill him," her voice shook, "his father will give us no quarter."

He looked at her outstretched hand, then at Jamin, and then at his sword. His cold expression changed to one of confusion as he surveyed the carnage. He backed up. Flapping his dark wings, he leaped into the air.

Feathers whistled, but the broken wing would not support his weight. He gained just enough height to crash on top of his ship. He crouched like a panther, watching her with a cold, inhuman stare.

Did he think *she* had anything to do with this?

Of course he did. Hadn't she just forced him to spare the ringleader?

She kicked Jamin as hard as she could.

"Get up!" she shrieked.

"Don't let him kill me!" Jamin's black eyes were wild with terror.

She jabbed her obsidian blade at his throat.

"Who are these men?!!"

"We came to save you from the demon."

"Did your father authorize this?"

"No. They are mercenaries," he said. "I hired them to save you."

Fury rose from deep within her gut.

"The only person I need saving from is *you*!" She drove her heel into his testicles. "Now get out of here before I let him kill you!"

Jamin scrambled to his feet and shot a fearful glance at the roof of the sky canoe. Mikhail crouched, his sword stretched out in front of him, waiting to spring. The Chief's son ran for his life.

"And don't come back!" She shook her fist.

The sun lifted above the horizon like a golden orb of fire. It backlit the dark creature, sent to guard the light.

---

[90] "I accept."

Chapter 38

March – 3,390 BCE
Earth: Crash site
Colonel Mikhail Mannuki'ili

MIKHAIL

Ninsianna moved with frenetic activity, gathering sticks and putting them into a pile. Mikhail stood up help her. She skittered back, her eyes wide with fear.

"Sorry," he murmured.

He sat back down before he terrified her even further.

The pile grew higher. He tucked his wings against his back and made himself as small as he possibly could, deliberately sitting on a low rock which left his feathers dragging in the dirt. Even from here, he could see her eyes glisten with tears.

He poked at the hole in his thigh. Yesterday she'd stitched it up, but there had been no healing songs, no pleasant warm hands, no reassuring smiles, and definitely no massaged wings. Her hand had trembled as she'd pushed the needle through his skin. He'd tried to talk to her, to reassure her, but he couldn't remember what happened between the moment he'd gotten stabbed in the thigh and when he'd become aware he stood over her with his sword at her neck.

She had good reason to fear him. She'd have even *more* reason if he told her that, whatever training he'd drawn upon to defeat their attackers, he'd only been marginally in control of it. If she knew, it might terrify her enough to go running right back to the man who'd attacked them for protection.

Protection from *him*...

The goat sidled over and regarded him with keyhole-shaped eyes.

"What do you want?" he asked.

The goat nibbled at his feathers.

"You think, just because we're bunkmates, now we're friends?"

The goat bleated an "*eh-heh-heh*." He'd spent last night sleeping on the floor of the bridge, so the goat now thought they were bosom buddies.

"Go on! Get out of here!" he hissed, afraid to raise his voice. "You stink like a…goat!"

The goat flicked her tail at him, as if to say *'you're not the boss of me.'*

It waddled over to where Ninsianna piled up yet more sticks, enough to keep them in wood for at least a month. She patted it absent-mindedly, but went right back to gathering sticks. He wasn't sure what hurt worse. The fact she was scared of him? Or the way she'd gone completely silent, not just not-speaking to *him*, but also the goat and her imaginary goddess.

He picked up a stick and poked at the roasting rabbit he'd caught earlier today when piling rocks on top of the bodies. The air filled with its decadent scent, but neither one of them felt hungry.

How could he have killed eighteen men and have no memory of winning?

A whistle echoed across the valley…

Mikhail's head shot up. His hand automatically reached for the reassuring bulge of the pulse pistol even though it was almost out of power. He forced his hand to move to his *opposite* hip, the one which held his sword.

Ninsianna's father appeared on top of the landslide wearing his formal four-fringed kilt and cape. Their eyes met. He waited for them to acknowledge his presence before scrambling down the rocks. Mikhail drew his sword and laid it across his thighs.

"Papa!" Ninsianna ran up and sank her face into her father's chest.

A lump rose in Mikhail's throat. Only two days ago, she'd embraced *him* like that.

Immanu gave Mikhail a dark look that communicated *'what did you do to upset my daughter?'* His bushy eyebrows reared up with surprise when he saw the long, slender blade.

Ninsianna relayed what had happened in her native language, some of which he now understood:

"Jamin *geldi* with eighteen Halifians! *Denedilir* kill Mikhail!"

"When?"

"Two nights *önce*."

Mikhail fingered his sword. Middle-of-the-night raids were not something that just 'happened' without somebody in authority giving an order. Immanu swore their chief had ordered his son to stand down, but that was *before* the darned fool had nearly gotten himself vaporized by a wormhole generator. Either Immanu was mistaken about the intentions of their chief, or he faced a coup d'état. Neither possibility bode well for his continued relationship with these people.

"The Chief *siparis edilen* Jamin *etmak* stay in the village—" Immanu's facial features conveyed surprise "—but five days ago he *kayboldu kimse*. Nobody has seen him *dan beri*."

The shaman translated.

"Ninsianna said the men were mercenaries," he said in Mikhail's language. "Jamin claimed he hired them to save her from *you*."

Mikhail forced his face to remain impassive. Until he figured out what had happened, he couldn't afford to let anybody know he was two screws short of a fully functioning hyperdrive.

The wind shifted, carrying with it the scent of death. He'd buried the bodies, but flies feasted on the dried blood which had soaked into the dirt in front of his ship. The earth now bore dozens of large, dark stains. Given the sparse rainfall, he'd be staring at the evidence of his own murderous streak for quite some time.

"Chief Kiyan will be outraged that Jamin conspired with his enemies," Immanu said. "He *hates* the Halifians. If it was up to *him*, he'd have run them off long ago."

"Is it possible that your Chief authorized this attack? Mercenaries aren't cheap."

"The Chief is not hotheaded like his son. He's a measured man, frugal and sensitive to the needs of his people. He is intrigued—" he pointed at the pulse rifle strapped to Mikhail's hip "—by the military advantage to be gained by allying with your people. He would not squander that opportunity on an honor-grudge."

Mikhail fingered the top of his pulse pistol, still safely ensconced within its holster. He did not divulge the weapon was almost out of power. He didn't know who to *trust*. Ninsianna wrung her hands as she strained to understand their conversation.

"*Ben yalniz*, him I need to speak," Immanu said to his daughter in Ubaid.

Without an argument, Ninsianna grabbed the goat and led her towards the far end of the valley. Immanu waited until she was out of earshot.

"It's no longer safe here," he said. "The Halifians will retaliate."

"I know."

"It is time to send my daughter home."

A crushing pain settled into Mikhail's chest which had nothing to do with his still-healing lung. For the last six weeks, she'd done nothing by say she wanted to see the stars. And *he* had promised her father he would not take her with him.

"What if she doesn't want to go?" his voice sounded hoarse.

"She'll go if *you* go."

"I can't leave my ship," he said. "I have to complete the mission."

Immanu's eyes flashed copper-golden, as if a red giant had just gone supernova inside his head.

"If you care for my daughter one bit," he growled, "you will bring her home *yourself* and *stay* with us until you are fully healed."

"Your chief's son just attacked me."

"It was not authorized," Immanu said. "I'll go talk with the chief."

"I'll think about it," Mikhail said.

"Do it quickly, because you just gave the whole Halifian tribe eighteen reasons to unite against the Ubaid."

He stood up and gestured towards the ship.

"Where are the bodies?"

"Up there." Mikhail pointed at the mountain.

"I have to perform the death rituals."

Immanu sent him to dig coals from the fire while the shaman foraged for a plant Ninsianna called *qat*;[91] a mild stimulant she'd been giving him to help rebuild his strength. They gathered sticks into a bundle.

"We're ready," Immanu said.

"What about Ninsianna?"

"She *hates* the death rituals," Immanu said. "She'll avoid us until it's over."

Mikhail led him up out of the valley. He'd dug eighteen separate graves, each one placed so they faced the rising sun. Atop each one he'd piled rocks to prevent wild animals from disturbing the bodies. One of his long, brown feathers stuck up out of each cairn, declaring who was responsible for smiting these men. Neatly arranged on top were their personal effects so their next of kin could identify their loved ones.

Immanu picked up the spear he'd laid on top of one of the cairns, its handle decorated with intricately carved antelopes. The flint still bore his blood where the Halifian leader had buried it into his thigh.

"You gave these jackals a far better burial than they deserved," Immanu said. "But I must ensure their spirits don't come back to plague the living."

They piled the wood into a small, ceremonial fire and placed the ember into its midst, blowing until flames licked the pile with hungry tongues. Mikhail avoided staring at the gravesites. *He* had killed these men. Every single one of them. If only he could *remember* killing them? Understood that they'd deserved it? Knew he'd fought fairly? The best he could do was give his enemy a decent burial.

Immanu unwrapped a cloth loaded with mud he'd dug out of the stream and used it to paint symbols onto his own body. As he did, he sang a low, chanting song similar to ones Ninsianna sang whenever she changed his bandages. He handed Mikhail the mud and gestured for him to do the same.

"I'm not familiar with this ritual," Mikhail said.

---

[91] *Qat:* a mild stimulant.

"Like this." Immanu scooped a fingerful of pasty yellow ochre. He used the cool, gritty mud to paint symbols on Mikhail's face, chest and arms. He paused on the final symbol, identical to one he'd painted on his own chest.

A winged man...

...carrying a body up into the dreamtime.

Immanu pointed to the weapon strapped to his hip.

"Do you still believe you are not our sword of the gods?"

"It's just a fairy tale. A song of gods and chess."

"And an ancient evil—" Immanu's eyes grew serious "—which my ancestors prophesized *you* would come to defeat."

It felt as though he hung onto his sanity by a single, fragile thread as Immanu ignited a bundle of *qat* leaves and circled each grave, praying for safe passage into the dreamtime. Prayers leaped into his mind in that third, clicking language, offered on behalf of the dead to some deity he couldn't remember ever having worshipped.

Did he worship a god? And if he did, then who?

Chapter 39

Galactic Standard Date: 152,323.04
Haven-1
Prime Minister Lucifer

LUCIFER

Lucifer nodded to the two fierce Cherubim masters who shadowed his adoptive father whenever the Eternal Emperor Hashem chose to appear in semi-corporeal form. The massive, six-limbed insectoids dwarfed even an Angelic, with four armored arms, each capable of fighting independently with a sword. He waited for them to give him entrance, not to the throne room, where only those who knew the Emperor well understood he was loathe to inhabit, but the *real* seat of his power, his cutting edge genetics laboratory.

Although most mortals assumed the Emperor could compel molecules to rearrange themselves on a whim, immortality only granted ascended beings a modicum of control over matter. Spontaneous creation was highly unstable. Even She-Who-Is preferred evolution, though *SHE* had grown so powerful that she *could* use her mind to manifest whatever sparked her interest. But immortality, by itself, did not grant omnipotence.

It was why the Emperor hadn't been able to simply wave his hands and make his army's inbreeding problem simply go away. No matter *what* method he used, whether natural breeding, cloning, artificial insemination or a certain amount of hand-waving ascended hocus-pocus, hybrid gametes combined artificially in meiosis simply failed to cause an embryo to grow.

Lucifer clenched his white wings against his body as he walked past cages, filled wall-to-wall, floor to ceiling with failed genetics experiments. They were all things the Emperor had created that were just too frail, or impractical, to survive anyplace except in inside this lab. The creatures assaulted him with a cacophony of noises and scents. A quasi-sentient creature signaled him with sign language. *Feed me? Please? Friend?* Those were the creatures that had always terrified him. De-evolution. Things which had once thrived, but due to a change in environment or circumstances, evolution had moved on without them.

He came to an ordinary looking man bent over a stainless-steel laboratory table. He looked like any *other* scientist in the galaxy, with his wild white hair, bushy eyebrows, bulbous nose, and kindly, wrinkled skin.

He wore a white lab coat over his favorite robe to keep it clean, and his beard appeared neatly trimmed, though the moment he walked out of the lab it would miraculously grow long again. If not for the tingle of power which permeated the Eternal Palace whenever the Emperor was in corporeal form, he might mistake the man for a mortal.

"Father," Lucifer called. "I came as soon as I could."

The Eternal Emperor Hashem did not glance up.

"Lucifer," he mumbled. "Glad you could make it."

He continued fertilizing a tray full of leathery eggs the size of softballs.

Lucifer's white feathers rustled with annoyance. For the past 225 years, the mantle of responsibility had fallen to *him* to manage the day to day affairs of the Alliance. Between Shay'tan's antics and the normal political intrigues which threatened *all* democratic institutions, Lucifer had to forever outwit his opponents to keep his father on his lofty throne. When Hashem kept him waiting, he couldn't attend to any of the *other* bazillion things he had on his already ridiculously overscheduled plate.

He attempted to draw him out in conversation.

"What are you working on, father?"

"Miniature water dragons. They're going extinct. I'm trying to splice in a genetic adaptation so they'll survive."

Lucifer twitched his wings with exasperation.

"-*We*- are going extinct," he said. "When are you going to give *us* a genetic adaptation to survive?"

Hashem looked up, his golden eyes glowing with the eerie, internal luminescence all ascended beings possessed. What was worse? The two hundred years Hashem had vanished into the ethers and let his empire languish after his mother had willed herself to die? Or the fragile, doddering old fool who had only reluctantly returned after the 51-Pegasi-4 genocide had wiped out the entire sub-species of Seraphim Angelics?

"I lost the root stock." Hashem's face drooped. "And then pirates wiped out the Seraphim control group that still possessed some of their original DNA. Without that, I don't know how to replicate my experiment."

"Godsdammit, father!!!" Lucifer slammed his fist upon the stainless steel laboratory table. "Why in Shay'tan's name do you keep putzing around with these insignificant creatures when the armies who defend you are dying?" He picked up the warning glare from the two Cherubim guards and moderated his tone to the appropriate respect for their Emperor and god.

"You're all so close to completion," Hashem said. "All you need is a few thousand more years to evolve and then you'll be complete. The Seraphim were close. They were so close."

"Close to what?"

"Your mother was almost complete. I could have finished her."

"My mother is DEAD—" Lucifer shouted. "When will you get your head out of the ascended realms and deal with what is happening down here? We won't be around in a few thousand years!"

The two Cherubim guards took a clanking step forward, four meters tall, each with one hand placed upon a sword hilt. Lucifer's wings trembled. He hadn't been afraid of them as a kid, but things had changed since the Emperor had disappeared and come back.

Hashem's demeanor shifted from that of an absent-minded professor to the hellfire-and-brimstone old god who had once battled Shay'tan, the one who viewed Lucifer as a failed experiment. He spoke with the clinical detachment of a scientist making a presentation before a conference of biologists about a colony of bacteria.

"Without the source race, there is nothing I can do to help you," he said coldly. "Your only hope is the breeding program. If you increase your genetic diversity through selective outbreeding, a new strain of Angelic might evolve to take your place."

Lucifer shuddered. How could a mortal, whose lifespan was a mere blink of an eye to an ascended being such as his adopted father, hope to make himself heard? He was a plaything, a toy. A tool the Emperor had used to lure his mother, a creature so close to completion that she had approached godhood herself, to stand at his side so he would have somebody besides Shay'tan to talk to as time ground mortal creatures into dust.

"What about the Leonids?" Lucifer pleaded. "They're down to 3,500 individuals. We have more Leonid ships than Leonids to man them."

"The Spiderids will take their place—" Hashem spoke as though discussing a defective toaster "—just as the Mantoids filled in the gaps in *your* ranks. I have ordered the aerospace manufacturers to create a new generation of ships adapted to Spiderid physiology."

Replaced? They were being replaced? He'd always suspected that was the plan, but this was the first time he'd heard the words uttered from the Emperor's own lips.

"I give up!" Lucifer threw his hands into the air. "You're worse than Shay'tan!"

He turned to leave. He got as far as the laboratory door before Hashem called his name.

"Lucifer!"

The Cherubim guards stepped to block his exit. Lucifer kept his back to him.

"These trade deals," Hashem said. "You and Parliament have outsourced too much of our economy. I want you to rescind the override."

Lucifer whirled to face him.

"Do it yourself," he hissed. "For two hundred years I ran your empire while *you* were grieving my mother's death. Never once have you thanked me! Never once have you taken an interest in the impact your obsession with seed worlds has on the older races in this empire. Or the species who defend them!"

He flapped his wings.

"You can't keep asking us to pay until they've got nothing left to give," Lucifer said. "For goddess' sake, look at your Cherubim guards? Jingu is over nine thousand years old and hasn't been able to produce a new queen!"

Lucifer gestured to the ant-like Cherubim whose race had once guarded the entire Alliance, but who now numbered mere thousands. Only love for the Emperor prevented the Cherubim from casting off the mortal shells they had long since outgrown and escaping into the highest ascended realms.

"That's enough!" Hashem ordered.

"If you won't look at me, then look at them!" Lucifer's fists clenched as he tried to make his father see reason. "They've guarded your empire even longer than *we* have, and they are even closer to extinction. You replace *them* with us, and now you replace *us* with insects!!! Are we really that expendable?"

Hashem's shoulders sagged.

"You're not expendable," he sighed. "I just don't know how to fix you."

"Please, Father …" Lucifer pleaded. "You're the only father I have ever known. Help us. I don't want to be the last of my kind."

Hashem picked up the pipette he'd been using to fertilize the reptile eggs and resumed whatever it was he'd been doing.

"I lost the source race," he mumbled. "There is nothing more I can do for you. I am sorry."

He turned his back, engrossed in whatever experiment he was conducting once more. The Eternal Emperor was gone. Replaced by the kindly, absent-minded genius who tinkered with inconsequential experiments in his genetics laboratory instead of dealing with the problems facing mortals.

Chapter 40

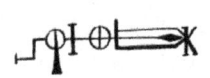

Galactic Standard Date: 152,323.04 AE
Zulu Sector: Command Carrier 'Light Emerging'
Colonel Raphael Israfa

RAPHAEL

The *Light Emerging* hummed reassuringly beneath Raphael's feet as they continued their mission of searching for his missing friend. Major Glicki's communications console beeped, signaling an incoming subspace message. With practiced efficiency, his second-in-command tapped the console to acknowledge the signal.

"Colonel Israfa," Major Glicki said, "Supreme Commander-General Jophiel has sent an encoded message, eyes only. She wishes you to make contact within 10 minutes."

"Thank you, Major Glicki," Raphael said. "Please assume the bridge while I go down to my quarters."

Glicki's tone was formal whenever they communicated in front of the other airmen, but the subtle tilt of her heart-shaped head was anything *but* emotionless. Raphael could almost hear her calculating how much time until she got off-shift and how much liquor it would take to lubricate him enough to shake off whatever bad news Jophiel was about to deliver.

He checked his appearance as soon as he got back to his quarters and hid Jophiel's photograph before queuing up the monitor. She'd overlooked the two additional weeks which had passed without contacting him to give new orders, but this would be the call. Father of her latest offspring or not, General Jophiel had a fleet to run and he was more valuable elsewhere.

It was time to abandon his closest friend for dead.

"Supreme Commander-General," Raphael greeted at the appointed contact time. "I'm at your service."

"Colonel Israfa—" Jophiel's face was a stern mask "—I assume you know why I'm calling?"

"I'm being recalled?"

"Not quite." Jophiel grimaced and breathed rapidly before regaining her composure. "I have another mission for you in that sector."

"General ... are you alright?"

"It is time," Jophiel said without emotion. "By this time tomorrow, your son will be here."

His son. There. With her. And then the child would be sent away. *His* child would be sent away. To the youth training academy to be raised by strangers. The only link he would ever have to her. The only *child* he might ever have!

"Let me be with you!" Raphael's golden wings trembled with emotion. "Please! I can take a needle and be there in an hour. Let me be at your side…"

"This is my twelfth child," Jophiel snapped, "I'm quite capable of taking care of myself."

"Jophie, don't be like that," Raphael said. "You don't have to do this alone."

"I am *never* alone," Jophiel said coldly. "The Eternal Emperor *himself* sees to it that I, and my offspring, are taken care of."

"He's *my* offspring too!" Anger rose in his voice as, for the first time in his life, he contradicted a superior officer. "He deserves to know his father!"

"He deserves to know what the Emperor *decides* he deserves to know!" Jophiel grimaced as she endured another contraction. "That's an order."

Raphael stared at the beautiful, cold woman who was, even now, giving birth to his child while simultaneously juggling command of the Alliance fleet. It was rumored she'd given birth to her fifth child right on the battlefield. Dropped into a trench when the contractions became too great to fly, given birth, and shot a Sata'an soldier in the face just as the child had slid from her womb. She'd fought her way out with her newborn in hand, killing two dozen Sata'an soldiers, and then immediately handed the child over to a youth training academy to be raised. She'd been rewarded by the Emperor himself with a medal, and a promotion, for her valor.

Raphael wished now he'd given more weight to those reports and not been so enthralled by her beauty and the honor of being chosen by a five-star general to mate. Their son would be a magnificent soldier who would someday rise to a position of power. That much he knew about all of Jophiel's offspring. But he felt cheated. Damn her! Damn her for being so heartless!

"Raphael?" The stern mask of a general disappeared, replaced by the tenderness he'd glimpsed during their courtship. "I didn't call to fight. I can't change the laws of our people. But I *can* do this for you."

Raphael paused the hand which had been about to commit the imprudent act of cutting off the transmission with the Alliance's highest ranking general before he did something even *worse*. Such as call her a heartless bitch.

"We have a fresh report of a suspicious merchant vessel running cargo out of that spiral arm," Jophiel said. "It may be a larger foray into that sector by the Sata'an Empire. I'm ordering you to go investigate." She gave him a wistful smile. "If you should happen to stumble across Mikhail while doing so … that would be fortuitous."

He understood what she was doing. To keep him away, she offered him another consolation prize…

"You will send me images of our child before you send him away? He's my son, too…" His voice was barely a whisper as a single tear rolled down his cheek. Hazel eyes turned green with emotion as he realized this was the end of their relationship. With their son born and abandoned to the youth training academy to be raised, Jophiel had no further use for him.

"Once you've found your friend—" Jophiel grimaced as she endured the next contraction "—I will grant you shore leave to go visit him." Her expression filled with regret as she reached towards the screen to end the transmission and hesitated. "I didn't realize when we mated that such things mattered to you. You're the first one who has ever asked."

He touched the screen, one finger tracing the downward turn of her lips as they bid each other goodbye. Her lip trembled as though she could *feel* the caress he wished to give her from halfway across the galaxy.

"It matters," his voice broke.

A tear streamed down her cheek.

"Goodbye," she said.

The screen went dark.

Chapter 41

April - 3,390 BC
Earth: Crash site

NINSIANNA

Such a pleasant dream, being carried back to the place She-Who-Is had shown her during her vision; that lofty perch where she could look down upon the stars and watch them sing as though they were overjoyed to be reunited. It felt as though she were floating in a river, the warm water carrying her weight as the sun streamed down upon her face, drifting wherever the goddess willed her to go. Oh, how she wished she could stay in this current forever!

A voice cried out.

"No! *Máthair!*"

She awoke to a man's voice crying out in terror.

"*Ná gortaítear sí! Le do thoil!*"

Where? Out front? Mikhail's bed was empty. The last few days came rushing back. Mikhail had taken to sleeping in the front of the sky canoe, he *claimed,* to prevent another incursion.

"*Mhamó! Cén fáth nach léi bogadh? Cá bhfuil Gabriel?*"[92]

She slipped out of bed and wrapped her blanket around her body. Cold radiated up out of the floor as she padded, barefoot, through the galley and into the bridge. The goat bleated nervously from underneath Compyoota.

"Mikhail, wake up!" she whispered. "An evil spirit has come to give you a nightmare."

"*Máthair?*" he called plantitively into the darkness. "*Máthair, múscail. Ní féidir liom a bhraitheann tú níos mó.*"[93]

Horror and grief threatened to crush her chest. Each night, his nightmares became worse. But ever since the attack, they'd been absolutely horrific.

"Great Mother?" she gasped. "Tell me what to do."

"*Help him?*" the goddess whispered.

"How am I to banish a demon?"

Mikhail slept on the floor, curled up in a fetal position, beautiful, tormented. A man come down from the heavens. He flailed his wings, his beautiful, broken wings, as though something had just collapsed on top of him and crushed him. Any moment now, if things went as they had for the

---

[92] "Granny? Why won't you move? Where is Gabriel?"
[93] "Mother, wake up. I don't feel you anymore."

last four nights, he would wake up grasping for his sword. She crept forward, eyeing the deadly silver weapon, and quietly moved it just out of his reach.

Caressing his cheek, she began to sing the *namburbi* rituals.[94]

> That man calls a dream interpreter,
> Wishing to have knowledge of the future.
> The man for whom the demonic illness
> Has been too great, utters a plea:
> "My lady, I come to do homage to you!"

Closing her eyes to enter the dream-state, she coaxed her mind to slip into his dream. It was not the clarity she'd experienced when she'd drank the sacred beverage, but each day that she was with him, her 'gift' grew stronger.

She found a crack in his heart where the spear had wounded him. There. That was how the demon kept getting in.

"*Máthair!*" he cried out. "*Tá siad mharaigh tú!*"

A boy. Blood! Terror! A lizard wielding a sword! Blood splashed onto her cheek. Millions of voices all cried out in terror!

A sound like a sandstorm roared into the boy. Around him pulsated darkness. So much power! It felt as though it would crush the universe within its maw.

"*Solvite!*" the boy cried out.

The shadows moved so palpably she could *feel* them.

"No!" She yanked herself out of his dream. She could not do this! Not even for She-Who-Is!

He reached for the sword.

The one she'd placed out of reach.

An uncontrollable shudder trembled through her body. She didn't want to touch this evil. She didn't want to *see* the evil which pursued the boy in his dream!

Mikhail whimpered. Tears slid down his cheeks. His hand trembled as he felt for his sword, only it *wasn't* his sword. She saw it. He reached through the dark. He clawed through the earth. He called for help, but nobody ever came.

And it hurt her to watch him suffer!

The thread which connected her to She-Who-Is grew stronger.

'*This memory causes him great pain.*' She-Who-Is whispered. '*He won't let me erase it because he feels it is part of who he is, but he placed his fate into your*

---

[94] *Namburbi rituals:* ritual to banish demons.

hands when you saved his life. Perhaps he will allow -you- to alleviate his suffering?'

She-Who-Is flooded her with warmth. She moved her fingers to rest against his temple. She saw into his mind, the first impression he had formed of her, a beautiful spirit, come to guide him into the dreamtime. There was something about that memory which was *stronger* than the darkness which plagued him. She was the first memory he possessed. She had imprinted him.

Invoking the goddess for protection, she slipped back into his nightmare.

A boy stood, surrounded by a slender eggshell of blue light. Inside the eggshell howled the black, terrible emptiness. It threatened to annihilate her existence.

'Eliminate it,' She who-is-whispered. '*Eliminate this child from his memory and he'll be yours.*'

"Who is it?"

'*It doesn't matter. Just get rid of it.*'

A tear dripped down Ninsianna's cheek. If he didn't remember, he would never take her to see the stars. If he didn't remember, he would not figure out a way to talk to Raphael. If he didn't remember, he would be stuck here forever. If he didn't remember, she would be stuck here as well.

But if he *did* remember, *she* would no longer be his first image of the light.

"Come back with me," she whispered. "Come back with me to my village. Forget this painful past. Come back with me to Assur."

The boy stood, partially buried, behind a blue wall which some other god had built. She sang a song to surround it with a golden wall of her own, three songs thick, held in place with a drop of her own blood. She then placed her hand over his heart and filled his spirit with songs of happy times to come; songs of belonging, songs of having a people, songs of never being alone again.

"Come with me," she sang. "Come with me into the light."

She sang that first image he had of her, surrounded by the sunlight. She caused the image to grow brighter. She pushed it into his mind.

Mikhail's hand moved up to cover hers. He clutched her hand to his heart, just beneath the terrible wound which she now understood existed in many dimensions.

"*Ní hamháin,*" he whispered. Not alone.

She could sense he wanted this more than anything in the world.

The child faded. Mikhail's breathing deepened into the rhythm of a restful sleep. Whatever those memories were, he didn't need them.

Chapter 42

April – 3,390 BCE
Earth: Crash site
Colonel Mikhail Mannuki'ili

MIKHAIL

He put the small, carved doll into a wooden box, ornate in its simplicity, but lined with red velvet. It was the kind of box someone might carve to place upon their altar. He traced the drawings he knew *he* had etched into the wood. While he could not name the language, he knew how to read it.

"*I will wait for you,*" it said. "*Just but on the other side.*"

He touched the doll's face, the too-large eyes carved into a slender body and the awkward hint of Angelic wings. Who had it belonged to? Why did he carry a child's toy? And why had he woken up this morning feeling empty even though he had Ninsianna at his side?

Ninsianna cleared her throat.

"Are you ready?"

He snapped the lid shut and placed it far back in his locker. For eight weeks he had languished, and nobody had come to find him. Already the ship had begun to smell musty, like a cave.

"Yes."

He shut the locker and engaged the lock. At least *here*, the doll would not be crushed.

He hoisted up his rucksack which was all he dared carry in his current questionable physical condition. On one hip he carried his pulse pistol—*they* didn't know it was almost out of power—if he was lucky, he might eke out *two* final shots. On his other hip he strapped his sword. Where he came from, it was considered a primitive weapon, but to a people who threw sticks and stones, its hardened steel might as well be a pulse cannon.

"Your father, he can call the other shamans?" he asked in slightly broken Ubaid.

"Yes. The other villages respect him."

"They will believe him? When he says old stories about my people?"

She gave him a reassuring smile.

"He'll have *you*," she said. "Some may even be able to speak to you."

It was funny. They no longer had a language barrier. At least not much of one. Other than having to use simple words, he and Ninsianna managed to talk just fine. All without a translation algorithm.

He paused at the AI which still had the best hope of telling him who he was. Did it contain history lessons about the *real* story behind the Song of the Sword? Would it tell him this song was not a prophecy, but a history lesson from the past? Could it tell him the name of his ship? Would it explain why somebody had shot him down? And why nobody had cared enough to come and find him? All of the knowledge in the galaxy lay within its database, and it was all out of reach.

"Are you coming?" she asked.

"Yes." A lump rose into his throat.

They stepped outside.

Ninsianna grabbed the goat which they'd laden down to carry extra water. Modern steel canteens and a plastic bucket rattled against primitive goat-bladder water skins, a strange melding of primitive and new.

He picked up the steel support strut she'd used to splint his wing, the one which had impaled him through the chest, and used it as a lever to roll several boulders in front of the crack. Not even Jamin would be strong enough to move them.

He placed his hand upon his ship, the only connection he had with his past.

Why was he here? What forces of fate had cast him down from the heavens? Would it matter, if he never finished whatever mission he'd been doing when he'd been shot down? Or was he destined to live among the humans forever?

He looked up towards the stars.

"I'll complete the mission," he swore. "As soon as I remember what it is."

Ninsianna held out her hand.

She led him towards humanity.

Chapter 43

⟁Y⟠ՈⲆՈⲆ

Galactic Standard Date: 152,323.04 AE
Alpha Sector: Command Carrier 'Eternal Light'
Supreme Commander-General Jophiel

JOPHIEL

The *Eternal Light* orbited Haven-1, the Alliance flagship for all four branches of the military. Its powerful engines throbbed reassuringly beneath her, a symbol of strength and power. A symbol of the *law*. The largest command carrier in the Alliance fleet was a constant reminder that Supreme Commander-General Jophiel had a much bigger mission to oversee. She was the highest ranking military commander. She was an example for her people.

She was one of the few fertile Angelics...

She allowed the medics to clean her up before she succumbed to the temptation to take a peek...

"Let me hold him—" Jophiel ordered midwife who'd been about to wheel her newborn out of sick bay before she'd even had a chance to look at his face.

"Is that a good idea, Ma'am?" the frog-like Delphinium[95] asked.

"It's the law," Jophiel said.

The midwife's broad lips pursed in a disapproving expression. It served everybody's interests if the mother parted with the child without tears, so normally they tried to whisk the newborns out before the mother recovered enough to ask, but a hybrid mother was allowed to hold her infant just once before they were sent away, never to be held again.

The midwife lifted up the newborn and deposited the sleeping infant into Jophiel's arms. She'd won countless battles, freed entire solar systems and galaxies, outwitted Shay'tan, but *this* was her crowning achievement. A child, born to a species facing extinction.

She pressed her nose into his warm, flawless skin and nuzzled him with her sensitive cheek as she inhaled his baby scent. Like all Angelic newborns, his head and wings were covered in downy fuzz, just like a little golden chick. It was too early to tell for certain, but the child bore a strong resemblance to his father.

"What shall you name him, Sir?" the midwife asked.

---

[95] *Delphinium*: a frog-like species, tapped to supplement the Merfolk Navy once most of that species relocated to merge with Leviathans.

"Uriel," Jophiel said. "Light of the Eternal Emperor."

The Delphinium glanced nervously at the door.

"The child is overdue for the transport shuttle, Sir."

The midwife reached out to take the child to one of the youth training academies where hybrid children were raised, educated, and integrated into the Emperor's armies. Jophiel snatched the infant away from the grasping arms.

"I'd like to bond with him for several minutes?"

"It will set a bad example."

"He's *my* son!" She snatched him back as if the midwife was the *Devourer of Children*.[96]

Gods! She sounded just like Raphael!

The midwife's bulbous eyes contracted into concerned slits.

"If the highest ranking general in the Alliance fleet refuses to fill the ranks, the lower ranking females will follow suit."

"I know, but...."

"You know the consequences, Sir," the midwife harummed. "Whatever *you* do..."

She didn't finish the sentence, but Jophiel knew the implication. She wasn't the *first* hybrid female the midwife had been forced to coax into giving up her child, but she was the most powerful and visible.

Yes. She knew more than anybody that the feat of science which had brought their races into existence had come with a fatal flaw. Whether animal or plant, hybrids of any ilk came with an astronomically high rate of sterility. The more the Emperor had inbred his armies for their abilities as soldiers, the worse that defect had become.

Their only hope to avoid extinction was to be *outbred* again...

"Can't you make an excuse?" Jophiel pleaded. "Say the infant is experiencing a problem."

"You're in command, Sir—" the midwife looked skeptical "—but please? If *you* waver, every hybrid in the fleet will do the same."

Tears welled in Jophiel's eyes. With each passing pregnancy, giving away her offspring had become harder. Although she tried not to form emotional attachments to her children's sires, she'd had a hard time letting Raphael go. Sentiment was a weakness no military leader could afford.

"I'll put him on the next shuttle," Jophiel promised. "Please? His father asked for a picture. Could you take one of me holding the baby?"

She held up the child, imagining what it would be like if circumstances were different? What if she could raise her children herself, as other species did? Would she have to give up her career?

---

[96] *Devourer of Children:* one of Moloch, aka the Evil One's, names. Refers to the practice of child sacrifice.

Uriel pulled at her heart like a sun tugging a planet into orbit. And Raphael? He'd been a sensitive and thoughtful lover; the only one who'd ever asked what *her* dreams were instead of using the access granted during the heat cycle to tell her *his* career aspirations. What would he be like as a father? If only…

The sharp flash jarred her back to reality.

She dismissed the midwife with orders to transmit the photograph to the lover she must never see again, so close had he come to breaking her resolve.

"Maybe it would be better if the Emperor confined us to a single homeworld," she whispered to Uriel as soon as the Delphinium left the room. "Some free will! Hand you over, or we all go extinct!"

Uriel looked at her trustingly, his eyes already showing the brilliant blue-green color they would someday become. He reached towards her face, entangling his tiny baby fingers in her white-blonde hair.

"If we weren't going extinct," Jophiel sobbed. "I would keep you! And your father, too! Giving *him* up was almost as hard as giving *you* up, little one. It's why I had to send him so far away. If he was near, I wouldn't be able to go through with this."

Uriel yawned, flashing a tiny dimple on just one cheek, just like Raphael. It almost broke her resolve, but a lot more was at stake than her own personal happiness or that of her child.

"It won't be so bad," she said. "Your father and I were both raised in a youth training academy. They will teach you to love the Emperor above all else."

She summoned the midwife.

Uriel squalled the moment the midwife took him from her arms. It felt as though the woman tore her heart out. She whisked him away before Jophiel could change her mind.

Jophiel wept as Uriel's screams echoed throughout the *Eternal Light*.

…He screamed.

……And screamed.

………And screamed…

As he was taken away to serve in the army of his god.

Book II:
No Place for Fallen Angels

When Moloch gains a foothold,
And desires to be fed,
She-Who-Is shall appoint a Chosen One
To warn of Moloch's spread.

—Song of the Sword

Chapter 44

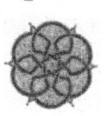

Galactic Standard Date: 152,323.05 AE
Earth Orbit: S.M.M. Peykaap
Lieutenant Apausha

Lt. APAUSHA

Liftoff was always a heart-pounding, exhilarating experience; an act of faith. A testament that their god watched over their frail, mortal bodies. Especially on an Algol-class vessel that was little more than storage and a whole quasar's-worth of hyperdrive.

Lieutenant Apausha engaged the secondary impulse engine. Their heads slammed back into headrests as G-force[97] plastered their bodies to their seats.

"Gyah!" he bared his fangs.

The ship shuddered for what seemed to be an eternity, only eight-and-a-half minutes, but each heart-pounding second reminded them it could be their last. The shaking subsided, almost imperceptibly.

"Mesosphere[98] clear, Sir," his co-pilot, Specialist Wajid shouted over the sub-light engines.

"How many kilometers to the thermosphere?"[99] he asked.

"One-seventy-five."

Apausha glanced back at the third lizard in their crew, their navigator and radioman, Specialist Hanuud.

"Make sure the *Jamaran* doesn't mistake us for an enemy."

All three lizards glanced nervously at the Sata'anic battlecruiser which lurked above them in orbit like jealous grey dragon guarding its treasure.

The radioman fumbled on his headset.

"*Jamaran, Jamaran*—" his voice warbled like a pre-pubescent hatchling "—this is Sata'an Merchant Marine vessel *Peykaap*. We have cleared the mesosphere. I repeat. We have cleared the mesosphere. What are your orders?"

A tinny-sounding voice came out of the loudspeaker.

"We see you, *Peykaap*. Lift-off authorized."

Apausha let out the breath he hadn't realized he'd been holding. It was a far friendlier response than when the *Jamaran* had chased them out of

---

[97] *G-Force:* an object's weight relative to free-fall, $g=Gm/r^2$.
[98] *Mesosphere:* third layer of the atmosphere.
[99] *Thermosphere:* fourth later of the atmosphere, where UV radiation ionizes.

hiding from the backside of this planet's moon. He turned to his co-pilot, Specialist Wajid.

"Begin spooling the hyperdrives. Get us out of here the moment we breach the exosphere."[100]

"Aye, Sir." The thick-necked co-pilot began their post-launch checklist. While slow and deliberate, normally a liability when you ran black-ops for Ba'al Zebub's private merchant army, Wajid's caution had saved their tails many times.

Apausha turned to his navigator.

"Calculate the jump."

"Yes, Sir!" Hanuud's narrow snout split into a grin. "Sir! We're going home!"

Hanuud spoke flight plans into the computer while Wajid methodically clicked through dozens of manual switches. Unlike electronic switches, which fried when subjected to an electromagnet pulse, manual jump switches could be reset.

That was how the Alliance had caught his father…

"Do you think Lord Ba'al Zebub will reward us with wives?" Wajid asked.

Apausha glanced back at the cargo area, filled with a sample of every flora and fauna that could appeal to a greedy dragon's heart. Strapped securely into her seat, General Hudhafah's crowning chess piece, the ebony-skinned human woman, sat heavily sedated, padded with blankets and pillows.

"If he does," Apausha said, "it won't be a reward."

"What do you mean, Sir?" Wajid asked.

"He'll use it to make us keep our snouts shut—" he held up the command-key given to him by the general "—so we'll all have something to lose."

He tilted the *Peykaap* to give them one last view of the blue water planet which spun peacefully around an ordinary yellow sun, completely unaware it was about to become pulse cannon fodder in a galactic war.

"Alright, *Peykaap*," the *Jamaran* called. "You're cleared for hyper jump. ETA[101] Hades-6[102] in five weeks. May Shay'tan guide you home."

All three crewmen touched their claws to their foreheads, their snouts, and their hearts.

"Shay'tan be praised!"

With a flash, the *Peykaap* disappeared.

---

[100] *Exosphere:* thin, outermost layer of the planet's atmosphere.
[101] *ETA:* estimated time of arrival.
[102] *Hades-6:* is the seat of the Sata'anic Empire.

Chapter 45

May – 3,390 BC
Earth: Village of Assur
Colonel Mikhail Mannuki'ili

MIKHAIL

Gritty ochre dust blew across the vast, barren landscape, as desolate and empty as the space between his ears. Long-dead streams divided the desert into patches of dark and light, giving the impression of squares. With each step, destiny moved him forward, as though some ancient god moved him across a chess board.

"Who am I? Why am I here?"

He fingered the dog tags he'd woken up with strung around his neck. They jingled with a hollow clink, the totality of his identity:

Colonel Mikhail Mannuki'ili
352d SOG
Angelic Air Force
Second Galactic Alliance

The name evoked no emotion, no belonging, and no sense of recognition. Only the pin worn over his heart; a tree emblazoned with the words, *"In light there is order, and in order there is life,"* provoked a sense of mission. As for the rest of his life? It had all been erased in the crash, just like the sand which fell back into their footsteps, eliminating all evidence he'd been here.

He stared straight forward, unwilling to let the tawny-eyed beauty that walked beside him see how much it pained him to abandon ship. Ninsianna had pulled him back from the brink of death, but each step led him further away from what little belonged to *him*.

'You failed!' that sense of mission whispered.

I didn't have a choice.

'You abandoned ship because of HER!'

Her father claims their shamans can tell me who I AM!!!

The wind picked up, coating his dark brown feathers with ochre yellow filth. Sand swirled into his eyes, his crotch, and his boots. A cross-wind caused it to coalesce into a vortex. He flared his wings to shield Ninsianna from the dust devil.

She cringed away from him. "Eek!"

She jerked sideways, trembling like a terrified *madra*. The goat yanked her forward, almost pulling her face down into the dirt.

"Sorry," he mumbled.

He tucked his wings against his back, exposing her to the merciless desert wind. She lowered the hand she'd thrown up to protect her neck.

"I thought it was a bee—" she lied.

She reached towards him, her hand trembling; a compassionate woman who'd befriended an injured predator. She pretended not to be afraid, but no matter *how* many times he washed the blood from his sword, he couldn't make her un-see how savagely he was capable of killing.

'*You're a murderer…*'

No I'm not. They attacked -me-!

'*You don't even remember killing them! So how can you say it was justified?*'

He shoved his hands into his combat fatigues, wincing as his hand brushed against the spear-wound in his thigh, and walked in silence, his mind racing with apprehension. Would the shamans help him find his people? Or would they behave as irrationally as the men who'd ended up dead at his ship?

The goat bleated and tugged at its rope. He stopped and flared his wings.

"I smell water."

Ninsianna's lips parted into a breathtaking smile. It felt as though the sun had just risen in his dark and lonely world.

"I told you we'd reach the village today!" she said.

The ground grew flatter; the air rich with the scent of fertility. In the distance, a glistening blue necklace wound its way through the desert, swollen with melt-off from the distant mountains and ringed on either side with a lush, verdant green.

"That's it—" she pointed "—the Hiddekel River."

Perched on the riverbank, a ring of houses closed ranks to create an impenetrable wall. From the way she'd described it, Assur had taken on the aura of a fairytale city, not the sorry clump of ochre mud-bricks which sweltered in the sun.

"Come—" he picked up his pace. "I promised your father I'd get you to safety."

Ninsianna yanked the goat's lead to force it to keep up with his longer stride. A deep-throated ram's horn blasted a warning:

Beware! Beware! Beware!

He glanced behind them to see if they were being stalked by the Halifians, but nobody followed them. The village, it seemed, wished to warn themselves about *him*.

He stopped a hundred meters from the wall; just out of spear range. It stood so tall it would take five men standing on one another's shoulders to scurry up onto the rooftops.

'Or for you, a hop-flap...'

If my wing wasn't broken.

'Too bad you didn't bring a grappling hook...'

For once he, and his subconscious, agreed.

Ninsianna pointed at the enormous wooden doors which blocked their entrance.

"My grandfather oversaw construction of this gate—" her voice filled with pride. "He said no enemy would ever breach it."

"Your grandfather, he was *innealtóir*, uhm—" he struggled for a translation. "Man who builds things?"

"No!" she said indignantly. "My grandfather was a shaman."

He knit his brows together in an incredulous expression.

"Your grandfather built this gate with magic?"

"Behnam did it," she said. "But he used plans my grandfather saw in a vision."

Mikhail scanned the construction, taking in every detail. Despite his memory loss, his instinctive grasp of tactics remained untouched.

"It appears to be anchored solidly into the walls—" he pointed at the two enormous tree-trunks which had been lashed, and then mortared, into the adjacent houses. "But it won't stand up to *this...*"

He fingered his pulse pistol, still safely in its holster.

"My grandfather's magic will stand up to *anything*," she huffed.

"Magic is no match for a plasma weapon."

A peculiar glimmer danced at the edge of his peripheral vision. He tilted his head, one wing held up; the broken wing down like a floppy-eared *madra*, and tried to coax the memory out of his subconscious.

"I've seen such a gate—" he traced the air, trying to pull out a memory he could not *see*, but remembered touching. "Bigger than this one. With a carved wooden tree. I think it might have been gold?"

"You have seen the gates to heaven?"

He tapped the place she'd stitched his scalp back together.

"I only remember a gate," he said. "Nothing else."

Her face fell. She was *fascinated* with the thought he'd fallen from the heavens. But to him, it was nothing but a door.

Muffled voices drew his attention upwards. While the guards remained hidden, he could detect the movement of perhaps two dozen men.

"I fear your father didn't square things with the Chief?" he said.

"It's just a precaution," she said. "Jamin filled his head with lies."

He stared down at her, this fragile woman to whom he owed his life. Without *her* there to distract him, maybe he could fix his ship? Without her there, needing protection, it wouldn't *matter* if he fought the Halifians. Without *her* to worry about, he could complete his mission, or die trying.

"Go inside," he said.

"You promised we'd do this together?"

"I *promise*d to take you home!"

Her expression grew frantic.

"No!" she grabbed his arm. "What about the shamans? Don't you want to know about your people?"

"Ninsianna," he said softly. "This is your *home*."

The words echoed mournfully into his subconscious. *Home*. He didn't *have* a home. Or if he did, they hadn't cared enough about him to come looking for him.

Ninsianna's eyes glittered golden-copper, a peculiarity of the light he'd noticed every time she became angry. She whirled towards the gate and jabbed a finger up at the sentries.

"I am Ninsianna, granddaughter of Lugalbanda," she shouted. "Why am I denied entry through my grandfather's gate?"

A swarthy-skinned man he recognized from his first run-in with Jamin peeked over the edge of the roof.

"Since you bring an enemy to our doorway," he said.

"You *know* that isn't true!" she said. "Siamek, you were *there*. Mikhail only attacked because Jamin tried to drown me!"

There was a long silence as voices whispered messages back and forth. Siamek peered back over the edge of the roof.

"*You* can come in," Siamek said, "but your friend has to go."

Mikhail touched her shoulder.

"Ninsianna," he said. "Go inside. Please?"

She jutted out her chin.

"When I needed shelter, you gave it to me. Now *you* need shelter because Jamin brought trouble to your sky canoe!"

She turned back towards the gate and raised her arms.

"Then tell the Chief I shall remove the spell my grandfather cast to protect these gates!"

A chorus of male voices laughed and cat-called from on top of the walls.

"Go ahead!" they taunted. "Women can't do magic!"

Ninsianna began a deep-throated chant.

The wind picked up. Her hair billowed in the wind like a chestnut rebel flag. A ray of sunlight reflected off the mud-brick walls and made it appear her eyes glowed purest gold.

The hair stood up on the back of Mikhail's neck as Ninsianna's voice grew louder, as though inside her words, she could harness the power of a hyperdrive.

> Open! Open!
> Barrier of the gods!
> That which is shut
> I smash it down!

She flung her hands at the gate. With a groan, the gate cracked inward.

"See?" she shouted triumphantly. "I am Lugalbanda's granddaughter!"

The gate opened further. Siamek stuck his head out. His brown eyes glittered with laughter.

"You can stop making a fool of yourself," he said. "Firouz ran back to the Chief. He said he will meet your friend."

Ninsianna paused mid-gesticulation.

"Okay," she squeaked.

Siamek pointed at *him*. "Don't make any sudden moves."

Two dozen warriors rushed out, including Siamek, wielding heavy spears. All wore fringed kilts, their chests bare, revealing muscles accustomed to martial training.

Mikhail flared his wings and crouched, one hand on his pulse pistol.

"Don't touch me," he warned.

Siamek's face registered surprise.

"You speak our language?"

"Yes—" he took pains to articulate the words clearly. "Ninsianna taught me."

"In just three moons?"

"She talks a lot." He pointed at the goat. "She even talks to animals."

Siamek laughed. It appeared he knew this quirk of her personality. He hid it quickly behind a serious expression.

"I'm supposed to disarm you—" he pointed at the sword.

Mikhail shook his head. "Not so long as I possess a single breath."

More warriors appeared on the rooftop, carrying a pair of fish nets. A sense of déjà vu rippled through his body. *Disembodied rage.* The *last* time this had happened, he'd blacked out and killed eighteen men.

A sense of *coldness* settled onto to his tongue.

Ninsianna's tawny eyes filled with terror.

"Don't hurt them," her voice warbled.

That sense of pressure increased. The world contracted into tunnel vision.

He backed away from her: "I should leave."

His arm tingled as Ninsianna touched his forearm. "Don't you want to speak to the shamans?"

"No..." his voice trailed off. *Not if it means I have to slaughter all these men.*

Her eyes glittered golden in the sunlight, filtered through tears. An emotion tingled up his arm.

Alone...

A memory gurgled up from his subconscious.

Sparks flying. The sensation of falling. A beautiful creature of legend, stepping from the sunlight, her eyes glowing golden as if she, herself, was the sun...

He gripped the place where a piece of wreckage had shattered his ribcage and stabbed perilously close to his heart. The spot where he kept the tree-pin. He'd stared into the void, the absence of light. If not for her, right now he'd be dead.

"I will meet with your shamans—" he swallowed a sense of desolation "—but then I must seek out my own people, or return to my ship and get it flying?"

Ninsianna nodded far too eagerly.

"Stay?" her voice warbled. "You said you'd give us a chance?"

His sense of duty warred with the fact he'd given her a promise to *get* her here. He pointed at the warriors who'd encircled them with spears.

"I don't trust you," he said to Siamek. "Let Ninsianna carry my weapons?"

"But she's a woman?" Siamek said.

"Yes. She's a woman," he agreed. "So it shouldn't be a problem. Should it?"

Ninsianna's eyes turned a threatening shade of copper, but she had enough sense not to contradict him.

Mikhail reached for his hip.

"First I'll give her my sword—" he spoke calm and measured.

"Make it *real* slow."

Siamek stood in a deceptively casual manner, but from the way his brown eyes kept darting from *his* eyes to his hand, his muscles bunched, the warrior was ready to strike if he so much as flinched.

Mikhail held the sword out for Ninsianna to take. The warriors whispered:

"Is that it? The sword in the prophecy?"

"Jamin said he killed eighteen men with that weapon."

"Eighteen men? Single-handedly?"

"Immanu says he's the sword of the gods."

Ninsianna's hand shook as she took the weapon from his fingers. She wrapped the belt around her waist and, not understanding how to use a buckle, tied it in a knot. Mikhail reached for his pulse pistol.

"Whoah!" Siamek jabbed his spear at his chest.

Mikhail flapped his wings. The warriors darted back from his ten meter wingspan.

"Ninsianna doesn't know how to get it out of its holster!" he said.

"How do I know you won't try to use it?" Siamek asked.

"You saw me wield it the day you came to my sky canoe," he said. "If I wanted to hurt your village, that gate wouldn't still be standing."

Siamek's expression turned grim.

"Yes. I saw the blue lightning." He signaled the warriors to step back.

Mikhail slid the pulse pistol out of its holster. Half a meter in length, with an adjustable stock, on full power it could easily take down these walls. With a practiced click, he popped the power cartridge out of the handle before holding it out for Ninsianna. While the warriors ogled the weapon, he slipped the power cartridge discreetly into his thigh-pouch. It might only have one or two shots left, but the *last* thing he wanted was to give these primitive people that kind of firepower.

"What about your blade?" Siamek pointed at the titanium survival knife mounted to his hip.

"I'll keep the knife," Mikhail said, "for eating."

"Not if you want to meet the Chief." Siamek's brown eyes narrowed. "For all we know, you've come to assassinate him?"

Ninsianna touched his arm.

"It's standard procedure," she said. *"Nobody* is allowed to meet the Chief armed except for his personal guard."

His feathers rustling, he slid the knife out of its holster. Without a word, Ninsianna slipped it into her leather satchel.

"Is that everything?" Siamek asked.

"We have a goat?" Mikhail pointed at the creature which cowered beneath his wings. "I call her Nemesis. If you go to sleep, she will eat your things."

Siamek's lip twitched.

"Why don't *you* bring in the goat—" he managed to keep a straight face. "It will keep your hands busy where I can see them."

Mikhail picked up the lead rope.

"C'mon," he grumbled at Little Nemesis. "Don't give me any trouble."

The gate groaned as the sentries pushed it fully open. The doors swung completely inward...

...revealing Jamin standing in the alley.

Chapter 46

May – 3,390 BC
Earth: Village of Assur
Colonel Mikhail Mannuki'ili

MIKHAIL

Mikhail crouched, ready to fly, but his still-broken wing sent a stab of agony into his axillary muscles.

"Get the weapons!" Jamin shouted.

The warriors rushed between him and Ninsianna. The goat bleated in terror. He reached for the pulse pistol that *should* be affixed to his hip…

…Ninsianna fumbled it out of her belt.

"Step back!" she shrieked.

She clicked off the safety, the way she'd seen him do thousands of times as he'd practiced quick-drawing. There was just one problem…

…the near-depleted power cartridge sat in his thigh pocket.

Jamin froze with his spear raised over his head, aimed at his *real* adversary … *him*.

"You don't know how to use it!" he taunted his ex-fiancé.

"Watch me—" her hand shook. "This firestick possesses great magic!"

"Women can't do magic!" He gestured at the warriors. "Split them up."

The warriors circled behind them like a pack of hyenas. A small, skinny man jabbed between them with a spear, attempting to cull the more vulnerable animal—Ninsianna—from the herd. Mikhail flapped his wings, beating the warriors back with limbs as powerful as war clubs. Ninsianna pressed against him, waving the pulse rifle wildly from man to man.

"Immanu swore your people are honorable?" Mikhail said. "You asked me to disarm, and I did."

"Honor?" the black-eyed bastard spat. "How can you speak of honor when you *claim* you cannot remember your own name?"

Mikhail touched the hexagonal dog tags, which were the only clue to his identity.

"I *know* my name," he said.

"But who do you *serve*?" Jamin challenged. "An army? An enemy? A god?"

He opened his mouth to give the Chief's son an answer, but nothing came out. No words. No memory. All he knew was he was a soldier in the Angelic Air Force.

A Special Forces soldier…

Which meant, perhaps, Jamin was right?

"Ninsianna—" he touched her arm. "I have to go."

Two of the warriors moved forward with their spears. Siamek, who'd opened the gate, stuck his fingers between his lips and blew an ear-splitting whistle.

"Stand down!" Siamek ordered.

"I gave you a direct order!" Jamin contradicted. "We can't let this bastard inside our gates!"

"No—" Siamek lowered his voice. "Those were *not* your father's orders. He said we were to escort the stranger inside."

The Chief's son stared at Ninsianna's trembling pulse pistol; the *hunger* to possess such a weapon lay naked in his expression.

"We *need* those weapons!" With a gut-wrenching howl, he launched himself at Ninsianna.

Ninsianna squeaked. She pulled the trigger, but nothing happened.

Mikhail let go of the goat's rope.

"Gyah!" he slapped Nemesis on the rump.

The goat bolted forward, forcing Jamin to correct his path. Jamin leaped for the pulse pistol and missed. Ninsianna skittered out of the way.

Roaring like an infuriated predator, Jamin lowered his spear and charged straight at *him.*

Time slowed to a heartbeat. Intuition whispered: *'this is the trajectory.'*

In a move he did not remember *learning,* Mikhail grabbed the spear-shaft, yanked it forward to accelerate Jamin's momentum, pulled him off-balance, and then slammed his elbow down onto the back of the man's skull.

Jamin collapsed.

Mikhail grabbed the spear. He stared down at his enemy, almost as surprised as *he* was that he'd known that move. The warriors darted out of the way, not sure how to fight a now-armed man with a twenty-meter wingspan.

"He killed him!" the warriors cried out.

Ninsianna kicked her ex-fiancé.

"Does anybody *else* want to die?" she waved the empty pulse pistol like a drunk.

Jamin groaned.

"He's just asleep—" Mikhail fought the urge to finish him off "—but she—" he pointed at Ninsianna "—is very angry."

They both backed up.

The warriors moved with them, blocking their escape.

"Wait!" a call came from the alley.

Two elderly women, both so wrinkled they looked like desiccated pieces of fruit, stepped out of the shadow of the gate. The younger helped her even more elderly sister move forward. The one who had spoken leaned heavily upon a cane.

"What is the meaning of this?" the old woman addressed Siamek.

"The winged demon tried to breach our gates," Siamek said.

"That's not what *I* saw," the old woman said. "You asked him to disarm himself, and he *did.*"

"We were ordered to take his weapons."

"By who? The Chief?"

"No—" Siamek's face fell "—by Jamin."

The old woman pointed at Ninsianna's unconscious ex-fiancé.

"Isn't it funny how trouble always begins, and ends with Jamin?"

The younger sister jostled Jamin with her foot.

"I've never *seen* anybody deflect a spear quite like that," she said. "Especially not against one so skilled."

"Yes," the elder said. "Had he wished, he could have killed him."

"I wonder what else the winged man knows?" the younger said.

"Perhaps he would teach us?" the elder said.

The two old women stopped in front of *him*.

"What is your business with the Chief?" the elder sister demanded.

"We need—" Ninsianna started to say.

"Silence!" the old woman held up her hand. "I want to hear it from *him*."

Ninsianna's mouth fell open like an indignant fish.

"Well?" the old woman peered up at him.

That sense of *pressure* dissipated as Mikhail stared down into a pair of intelligent brown eyes which peered out of a wrinkled face, still clear despite their age.

"Halifians came into my sky canoe—" he used the Ubaid word for ship. "It's no longer safe, so Immanu asked me to bring his daughter home."

The old woman's eyes turned sharp.

"So now you wish to bring your war with the Halifians to *us?*"

Mikhail's feathers rustled with indignation.

"I didn't ask for trouble," he said stiffly. "Jamin brought his war to *me*."

The younger sister whispered something to the elder. Both of them nodded, as though possessed of a single mind. The older sister pointed at Siamek.

"We are an honorable people—" she made a sweeping gesture at the warriors. "If you told this man Ninsianna could safeguard his weapons, then that is the *law.*"

"But she's a woman—" Siamek protested.

"What of it?" the old woman snapped.

Siamek shut up.

"Watch him!" The old woman's gaze turned sharp. "And for goddess' sake, child—" she gestured at Ninsianna's pulse pistol "—put that thing away before you hurt somebody."

With a sheepish expression, Ninsianna tucked the weapon back into her belt. Warmth flooded into Mikhail's chest. While he had no recollection of whether or not a woman had ever defended him before, never had one looked so beautiful and *fierce*.

"C'mon," Siamek said. "Let's go see the Chief."

The circle of warriors opened, allowing them a path through the front gate. Ninsianna beckoned. He followed her into the alley.

Perhaps twenty meters long and ten meters high, hostile-faced warriors looked down from the rooftops, their spears aimed right at him. While built of mud-bricks, the walls appeared sturdy. Even if an enemy *did* manage to breach the front gate, they'd have a hell of a time making it to the opposite end of this 'kill box'[103] alive.

"Why didn't your Chief grant us an audience from the get-go?" Mikhail asked.

"He probably *did*—" Ninsianna rolled her eyes. "It wouldn't be the first time Jamin twisted one of his father's orders to suit his whim."

Mikhail glanced back at the two old women who stood outside the gates.

"I thought you said all women are treated like goats?"

"Yalda's different," she shrugged. "She's a member of the Tribunal."

A cacophony of noise assaulted his ears as the warriors led them through a labyrinth of houses laid out on either side of a narrow street. Scents assaulted his nostrils, the aroma of baking bread mixed with the stench of excrement and human sweat. A middle-aged man walked through the streets, whacking people with a cane caught dumping their chamber-pots into the gutter. Scraggly-dressed villagers herded scrawny, owl-eyed children, goats and other livestock out of their path. Tall people. Short people. Young people. Old people. So many people! All possessed the same swarthy complexion and dark hair as Ninsianna.

They turned sharp-left, through another double alley, and then sharp right. Here the houses were larger and better maintained. Most of the women wore white linen shawl-dresses like Ninsianna and herded well-fed children before them. Makeshift tarps shielded tables filled with vegetables from the sun, while here and there, a table filled with goods marked the house of a tradesman.

All of the houses sported tiny windows at ground level, protected by shutters, but larger windows on the second floor to let in the desert air. On

---

[103] *Kill box:* a place where all of your assets plan strategize their weapons-fire in order to maximize the chance of killing your enemy in the crossfire.

the rooftops, children ran like monkeys, leaping from rooftop to rooftop on the largely interconnected buildings. The street meandered in a gentle curve.

"This village is built in circle?" he asked.

"The newer parts," Ninsianna said. "In the old section, there are places it's more like a rectangle."

"This place *inchosanta*—" he struggled for a word.

"Easy to defend?"

"Yes."

Ninsianna grinned.

"My grandfather, and the Chief's father, planned the expansion of this village. As it grew, Chief Kiyan and *my* father carried out their plans."

Mikhail grudgingly nodded. Whatever his opinion of Jamin, the father was obviously not a slacker.

The warriors led them sharp-left, through a third alley which was just as defensible as the first two. Three concentric rings, each separated by a 'kill box' of a gated alley. A pair of sentries ordered the curious retinue who followed them to 'scat!'

They exited the alley into a large central square which teemed with humanity, most of them finely dressed, though here and there, a ruffian scurried through the crowds, hawking a basket of goods for trade. One side of the square was dominated by a massive building, while near the center stood a low, circular ring of stones straddled by three logs lashed together to create a lever.

"That's the Temple of She-Who-Is—" Ninsianna pointed at the large building as Siamek led them across "—and *that*—" she pointed at the stone circle "—is her sacred well. We have three of them, but the others sometimes dry up in the summer."

"Can't you just take water from the river?"

"You can," she said, "but it contains evil spirits. The water from the well is always clean and pure."

Siamek led them to a large, two-story house with an elaborately tiled doorway. In front stood a middle-age guard wearing a heavily fringed, though not ornate, kilt and cape.

"What took you?" the guard asked.

"We had some issues at the gate," Siamek said.

"With *him*?"

"No. He lay down his weapons, just as the *Chief*—" Siamek accentuated the word "—ordered."

The guard's expression turned cynical.

"Where *is* he?" he growled.

"Back at the gate," Siamek said.

The guard snorted. Not one of the warriors mentioned he'd just knocked the Chief's son unconscious.

The guard studied him, his expression hostile.

"I am Kiaresh. Before you go inside, I have to search you for weapons."

Mikhail eyed the warriors which surrounded them. Ninsianna clutched the pulse pistol.

"Only you," he said. "I do not trust the others."

"You don't trust *me* either."

Mikhail glanced at Ninsianna.

"Kiaresh is a man of his word," she whispered.

Mikhail nodded. "Sometimes a man must take a risk?"

"Aye—" Kiaresh's expression turned grim. "That goes both ways."

Mikhail spread his arms and legs. His feathers rustled as the guard patted him down from his neck all the way down to his ankles. He forced himself not to yank back his wings when Kiaresh patted down his feathers.

"These are quite the pampooties—" Kiaresh checked his combat boots for hidden knives.

"We call them *boots*," Mikhail used the Galactic Standard word.

"I bet you can kick an enemy's head in with them?"

Mikhail knew the game, even though he couldn't remember it. Two warriors, sizing one another up.

"It's not nice to kick an ally in the head."

Kiaresh stood up and adjusted his cape. He opened the door, a simple contraption made of rough-hewn boards lashed together with rawhide, but the wood itself had been carved with sheafs of grain. Mikhail tucked his wings against his back. Kiaresh gestured for him to go inside.

Ninsianna moved towards the threshold.

"Not you!" Kiaresh held out his hand.

"Why not?" Ninsianna said.

"You're a *woman*," Kiaresh said. "This is a man's business."

"What about the weapons?" Mikhail asked.

"She can hold onto them, out *here*."

Mikhail fingered the square he'd tucked into his pocket. Without a power cartridge, his pulse rifle was useless, but even an untrained *primitive* could wreak havoc with a sword. He shifted into Galactic Standard.

"What if someone tries to disarm you?" he asked.

Ninsianna drew the pulse pistol.

"If they come near me," she said with bravado, "I will smite them."

His lip twitched upward. Gods! He would follow this woman straight into the gates of hell. He didn't have the heart to tell her the power cartridge was in his pocket, or that once he fired his final shot, he'd be no more technologically advanced than they were.

He switched back into lightly broken Ubaid.

"If anybody touches her—" he pointed at Siamek "—*you* will answer to *me*."

Siamek nodded. He'd just demonstrated, even unarmed, he knew how to hold his own.

He ducked to avoid hitting his head on the lintel and stepped inside.

Chapter 47

May – 3,390 BC
Earth: Village of Assur

NINSIANNA

It felt so powerful, to keep the warriors in check. But even holding Mikhail's firestick, they kept creeping closer, refusing to believe she would wield it against them.

"Back up!" she hissed.

"We're not doing anything," Siamek said with feigned nonchalance.

"You keep getting closer!"

"In case you *forget*," Siamek said, "your new boyfriend threatened to hold *me* accountable if anything happens to his weapons."

"So you're protecting me?"

"Yes."

Siamek glanced west, towards the gate they'd just come through. He didn't say the name, but she knew he spoke of Jamin.

"I don't need your help—" she planted one hand on her hip. "As you can see, I can take care of myself!"

They waited and waited. She propped her elbows against her sides to hold the heavy firestick aloft. Villagers milled about, curious about the weapon. The other warriors grew bored and left, but Siamek remained, leaning against his spear.

"Are you going to keep pointing that firestick at me?" he asked after what seemed an eternity.

"Yes."

"It looks heavy."

"It's not!" She forced her wrist not to tremble beneath the weight. "I'm as capable as any man."

Siamek snorted.

She edged along the wall and sat down on the stool Kiaresh usually sat upon when he guarded the Chief's door. She placed the firestick in her lap the way Mikhail had done the first time her father had showed up at the sky canoe, still pointed at Siamek in case he tried to rush her. It was such a magnificent weapon! Cold and black, like polished obsidian, beaten smooth with a rock and then tumbled in a barrel until the surface glistened in the sunlight.

It was too bad the magic only worked for Mikhail. Why, the look on Jamin's face…

"You've caused a lot of trouble." Siamek interrupted her gloating.

"I didn't ask for it."

"But you caused it."

"You *knew* I didn't want to marry him!" she snapped. "I only agreed because my father and the Chief insisted!"

Siamek's brown eyes grew hard.

"Yes. We knew!" he said. "We tried to warn him, but he wouldn't listen. You cast a spell on him. And now, I can see, you cast a spell on the winged one."

Ninsianna blanched.

"I did no such thing."

"Liar!" Siamek jabbed a finger in her face, heedless of the firestick. "Whatever you did, you'd better *undo* it, before those two fools kill one another."

He turned in a crisp movement that reminded her of Mikhail and marched away.

She stared across the square at the Temple of She-Who-Is. From beneath a sun-canopy, a voluptuous clay statue stared back at her with empty eye-sockets, holding a sheaf of grain and a stone sickle, symbols of fertility and plenty.

She prayed to the goddess who'd led her to Mikhail in the first place.

"I got him to come here," she said. "Now how do I make him stay?"

She-Who-Is stared back at her, her expression enigmatic. Ninsianna waited for an omen: a hawk, an insect, the familiar tingle of power which accompanied a vision, but the goddess said nothing. SHE just smiled.

Chapter 48

May – 3,390 BC
Earth: Village of Assur
Colonel Mikhail Mannuki'ili

MIKHAIL

Inside the Chief's house, the ceiling was just tall enough to stand without banging his head. A second guard stood with his arms crossed, a great burly beast of a man with as much hair on his arms as his bushy beard. While shorter than he was, the man was obviously not someone to be trifled with.

"I am Varshab," he said gruffly. "The Chief will see you now."

He led him through a curtain into a brightly colored room. Intricate tapestries lined the walls. On the floor beneath them, a felted carpet squished beneath his boots. Surrounding all four walls, thick embroidered cushions lined the floor. In the center, a clean drop cloth had been laid out to sit. There, in front of a tray filled with a hot, steaming beverage, sat Ninsianna's father, along with an older, more grizzled version of Jamin. The Chief and Immanu sat close together, but from the way they both sat, stiff and formal, they couldn't have been further apart if they'd sat at opposite ends of the galaxy.

"Sir." Mikhail gave a crisp Alliance salute.

"You may sit," the Chief gestured at a cushion.

The burly guard positioned himself near the doorway.

Mikhail lowered himself carefully so as not to crush his feathers. Angelics preferred lofty perches for the simple reason it felt awkward to drag one's wings upon the ground, not to mention the inconvenience of preening dirt out of your feathers.

Immanu picked up a brown clay cup and poured the Chief some tea with deliberate gravitas; and then he poured a cup for Mikhail. They each took a sip, sizing one another up over the brim. The concoction tasted woody, with a bit of a fruity zing.

Mikhail studied the Chief's attire: a five-fringed kilt and crimson-dyed shawl cast artfully around his shoulders in a deceptively casual manner. Around his neck, a golden torc marked him as the Chief. His forearms sported gold wristbands, not just bracelets, but the kind that could stop a knife. His hair and beard shone like a river otter's pelt, tightly curled into the oiled ringlets and adorned with beads. It was a show of wealth designed to meet with an opposing tribe's Chief.

"So tell me how you came to almost kill my son?" he asked bluntly.

Nothing like getting right to the point...

"*They* attacked me—" Mikhail said. "I didn't have a choice."

"Why didn't you negotiate?" the Chief shot back.

"I don't speak Halifian, and they didn't speak any Ubaid."

"Then why didn't you *speak* to my son?"

Mikhail studied the Chief's expression. It would bring him no confidence to explain he had absolutely no memory of those events, from the moment the Halifians had brought him down in the net, until he'd become aware he held his bloody sword at Ninsianna's throat. But neither would he tell a lie...

"I didn't recognize Jamin until Ninsianna told me to stop," he said truthfully.

"So he didn't personally attack you?"

I can't remember...?

"It was dark. I didn't *aitheantas*, uhm—" he struggled for a translation "—I did not *see* Jamin until Ninsianna threw her body over his."

"Recognize," Immanu translated. "He didn't *recognize* him until Ninsianna pointed him out."

The Chief shot Immanu a look, as if to say, *'see, I told you.'* Whatever the conversation had been prior to his arrival, Immanu did not share it. But it had obviously been exceptionally tense.

"And what about the time previous to that?" the Chief asked. "He said your silver spear almost made his hair catch on fire?"

My subspace antenna?

How could he explain micro-wormhole radio communications theory to a man still stuck in the Stone Age?

"It's not a weapon. It throws words—" he touched his lips "—like you would throw a spear—" he flipped his hand outward "—to a friend in the stars. When you throw it, it makes a lot of lightning. We had no idea Jamin was on the roof."

The Chief's eyes lit up with curiosity.

"Explain to me how this lightning works?"

Mikhail schooled an unreadable expression. That same subconscious voice which *refused* to tell him his own name cautioned against revealing the secrets of his technology. So far, humanity had proven largely hostile.

"It's like magic," Mikhail said carefully, painstakingly, not to lie. "I know a little about how it works, but not everything."

A flash of annoyance marred the Chief's expression.

"You don't remember?"

"If I know something, my body just does it," he said truthfully, "but if I stop and think about it, I don't remember anything at all."

"You expect us to believe that?" the Chief's voice rose with anger.

"Believe that I don't remember?"

"Yes."

Mikhail stared down at his hands.

"If I was you, -I- wouldn't believe me." He touched his hair, which still bore a thin spot where Ninsianna had stitched his scalp back together. "But it's the truth."

He met the Chief's gaze.

"Would you tell us if you *did* remember?" the Chief asked.

"No," he said softly. "My weapons are very bad. If I give you this knowledge, I fear you will use it against your enemies."

"*Your* enemies!" the Chief snapped.

"The Halifians weren't my enemy until Jamin brought them to attack me."

"You said it yourself!" the Chief said. "You didn't *see* him until he tried to help Ninsianna get away!"

A commotion interrupted before Mikhail could answer. Varshab, the burly guard, stuck his head through the curtain.

"Sir?" Varshab said. "Behnam is here to see you."

"Tell him to wait," the Chief snapped.

Varshab glanced at Mikhail.

"No. You need to speak to him *now*."

With an annoyed snort, Chief Kiyan rose from his cushion and moved into the other room. While shorter than his son, he moved with the casual grace of somebody who did a lot more than just sit around on their chiefly cushion and issue orders.

Mikhail caught a glimpse of an elderly man, wrinkled, but spry. The curtain closed behind him. In the other room, hushed voices spoke just below the level of his hearing except for a single recognizable word: Ninsianna.

Mikhail glanced at Immanu, who'd sat stiffly through this entire interaction.

"He doesn't like me," Mikhail said.

"You've put him in a terrible position," Immanu said, "to choose between *me* and his only son."

"Choose *you*?"

"Yes," Immanu said. "Jamin has allied every man in this village against you. I told him, if he refused to speak to you and make his *own* decision, Ninsianna wouldn't be the only person to leave."

Mikhail's eyebrows reared with surprise.

"You *made* him speak to me?"
"Yes."
"How long have you two been friends?"
"Forty-seven years."
Mikhail exhaled…
"I'm sorry."
"Don't be—" Immanu's voice sounded irritated. "This is *my* doing. I never should have pushed Ninsianna into this betrothal."
"But—"
The Chief stepped back through the curtain before he could finish asking the question and sat upon his cushion with a thump. He gave *both* of them a sour expression.
"Will you guarantee his behavior?" he gestured angrily from Immanu to Mikhail.
Immanu's bushy eyebrows rose with surprise.
"Yes. Of course."
"Then *take* him," Chief Kiyan said. "He can stay just long enough to meet with the shamans, and then I want him *out* of my village!"

Chapter 49

February – 3,390 BC
Earth: Village of Assur

JAMIN

All around him, the walls whispered. The housekeeper shook his shoulder.

"Go away, Urda!" Jamin swatted at her hand.

Sunlight streamed through window, stabbing into his throbbing brain. The housekeeper shook him again.

"Tell Father I am sick—" his stomach clenched. "Shut the curtains. Siamek can oversee the sentries."

He tried to pull up his blanket to cover his eyes, but the housekeeper kept grabbing it and tugging it off his body. He felt for her hand, but it was large and warm and…

…furry?

Jamin opened his eyes and instantly regretted it. Pain throbbed from the back of his head.

"Ow…" he groaned.

Why was he sleeping in the middle of the alley?

The 'housekeeper' nibbled gleefully on his cape. Mid-sized and brown, she was an otherwise ordinary looking goat, with a white blaze, but the lead rope which adorned her neck had been woven from colorful strands of a stiff, unearthly fiber.

"Go away!" he swatted at Ninsianna's goat.

The goat laughed an indignant bleat.

Jamin sat up.

All around him, villagers gossiped about his humiliating defeat.

"What are you looking at?" he shouted. "Get out of here! Before I crack your skulls!"

Dadbeh knelt down next to him. The small, skinny man gave him a lopsided grin.

"You weren't kidding," he said. "The winged demon is fast."

Jamin rubbed the back of his skull.

"Did you kill him?"

"Siamek brought him to see the Chief."

Jamin gaped. "You let him into the village?"

"We didn't have a choice—" Dadbeh shrugged. "Yalda intervened."

Fear gripped hold of his testicles and gave his stomach a yank.

"Yalda?" he said breathlessly.

"Yeah," Dadbeh said. "She watched the entire thing."

A surreal sense of being caught in the river after a rainstorm, sucked downstream while all around you the floodwaters raged, made the gossiping villagers seem far away. It had taken a heroic effort to convince his father he'd only been conducting *surveillance* when the Halifians had attacked. If the Tribunal inquired into the state of his father's treasury...

"Why, in the goddess' name, did you let him in?"

"Yalda said we have to honor your word," Dadbeh said.

"You were supposed to *provoke* him so we'd have an excuse to kill him!"

Dadbeh's expression grew wary.

"We did everything we could to rattle him," he said, "but he gave his weapons to Ninsianna without a fight."

Jamin groaned. The back of his head throbbed as if it might explode. Dadbeh, the alley, and the villagers all wore a halo, as if there were *two* of them.

And the goat...

The goat stood at the end of the alley, staring at him with flip-floppy ears, as if it wished to challenge him to a fight.

"I wish you'd been killed in the fall," he muttered.

He rolled onto his hands and knees and pushed himself, unsteadily, onto his feet. The world swayed like a leaky river barge. Dadbeh reached out to help him, but he pushed his hand away and grabbed his spear.

"Is there anything else you want to tell me?" Jamin grumbled.

"Yeah," Dadbeh said. "The Chief sent back a runner to order you to, quote, '*get your sorry ass up there so he can box your ears.*'"

Jamin's heart sank. His father rarely took him to task, but ever since Ninsianna had broken off their engagement, he'd demanded he stay home like a passive little farmer instead of rallying his warriors to go kill the threat which had taken up residence just outside their lands.

Inside my village now...

He looked up. A dozen warriors looked down from the rooftops which lined the alley wearing smug expressions.

"Get back to work!" he shouted. "Now we've got an enemy on the inside!"

He staggered like a drunk past curious villagers, still seeing double. Why the hell was he making a fool of himself over a *woman*? It wasn't like he'd ever had any problem luring women into his bed!

"I never thought I'd see—" a shrill, feminine voice taunted "—the mighty Jamin, felled with a single punch."

A woman stepped out of the pack, with one hand planted cattily on her up-thrust hip. Medium height and slender, with her shawl-dress artfully tied to expose one breast, everything about the well-dressed woman broadcast her wealth and sexuality. She'd be outright beautiful if her lips weren't frozen in a perpetual sneer.

"Get out of my way, Shahla," Jamin growled.

"First he took your *fiancé—*" she spat with jealousy "—and then he beat you in front of the entire village. What will you do next? Beg Ninsianna to take you as a second-husband?"

Jamin lunged for her.

A small, dark shadow materialized in front of him.

"No, Jamin! No!"

He stared down at the scrawny waif who held his wrist. Too-large black eyes stared out pale face and undernourished body. If it wasn't for her tiny breasts, most people would mistake Gita for a ten year old.

"Don't do this," Gita pleaded. "You know she likes to goad you."

"Get out of my way."

"You are *better* than this, Jamin!"

Her black eyes bored right into his soul. His mother had possessed eyes like that. The eyes of a sorceress. Only his mother had never worn a ring of bruises, with one eye swollen almost completely shut.

His anger evaporated.

"What happened to your face?"

"Nothing." Gita's hand slipped up to cover the offending black eye.

"I don't have time to deal with this," he growled.

"Did I *ask* for help?" her small chin lifted.

"Yes, Jamin—" Shahla interrupted shrilly. "Why don't you go take your anger out on Merariy? Show him you're still a *man*!"

He pushed past them, eager to be away from Shahla and her on-again, off-again cycle of arguments and make-up sex. Until he'd gotten gored by the auroch, he'd relished the game. But after Ninsianna?

A *real* woman. Not trash who fell willingly into his bed…

He pushed through crowded streets, ignoring the common voices which called out:

"Did you see him?"

"Did you see the winged man?"

"Immanu was right! He looks like a creature of heaven."

Varshab stood outside his father's house with his meaty arms crossed, his father's enforcer. Jamin shook off the sensation that the world had just gone off-kilter; a side effect, no doubt, of the blow to the back of his skull.

"Why did you counteract the Chief's order?" Varshab demanded.

"What order?"

"For Siamek to escort the winged one here for a meeting?"

"I had them disarm him at the gate," Jamin said. "I thought it prudent given—"

Varshab cut him off.

"-*I*- was supposed to disarm him!" Varshab growled. "*You* were supposed to stay away from him."

"In case you forget—" Jamin tossed his shawl around his shoulders "—I don't answer to you. I outrank you."

Varshab pointed at the door.

"And *you* answer to your father!"

Jamin yanked the door open and stepped inside. A figure moved inside the doorway, but it was only Urda, the *real* housekeeper, not the goat he'd mistaken for her while unconscious.

"Where is he?" Jamin asked.

The old woman pointed at the large room where they received important guests. His stomach sank. He hated it when his father treated him like 'official business.'

He stepped through curtain. His father's anger hit him full-force like the leading edge of a sandstorm.

"What the *hell* were you thinking?"

"I was keeping an enemy out of our village."

"Our *real* enemies are the Halifians and the Uruk!" the Chief said. "The ones you conspired with?"

Months of fury heated his flesh so hot it almost burned.

"Let me tell you about our *real* enemies!" Jamin screamed at him. "They come from the heavens to lay down with mortal women, and once they figure out our defenses, the rest of them will *come*. Just like the Uruk did in the time of your father, to slaughter the men and take our women as slaves!"

"Lugalbanda put a stop to it—"

"Lugalbanda did *nothing!*" Jamin shouted. "I was *at* the front gate. Ninsianna just undid the spell!"

His father's face grew grim.

"She can't," the Chief said. "You don't know what Lugalbanda did to secure that gate. Ninsianna is just a *woman.*"

Jamin's hand moved to protect the scar which marred his abdomen. How could he explain he'd *felt* the magic in his gut? The same way he'd *felt* it the day she had come to him and, with a whispered prayer, caused his intestines to close up and heal?

"You underestimate her—" Jamin's voice broke. "-*I*- underestimated her. That is why she left. She left because I made *fun* of her! I *dared* her to leave!"

He turned his back so the Chief wouldn't see the emotion. He'd treated her the way he'd always treated Shahla, and it had come around to bite him in the ass. He held his breath, forcing the emotion back into the pit of his stomach. It was a lot easier to be angry.

His father's expression softened.

"Immanu has offered to return the bride price."

"I don't *want* it back!" Jamin said. "I want her to honor the betrothal."

"You can find somebody better—"

"Who?" Jamin asked. "I want a mate who will be my equal."

He stared at a small, woven rug which occupied a place of honor on the wall. The rug was unfinished, just like his mother's life. He lifted it off the wall and ran his fingers through the warp and weft. He could remember her seated at the loom, singing as she wove the colorful threads, her stomach swollen with his baby sister.

"Mama followed your orders—" his voice warbled. "She never dishonored you in front of the tribe."

The Chief barked a rueful laugh.

"If you think your mother was obedient, then you'd better think again." His eyes focused wistfully into the past. "She was every bit as strong willed as Ninsianna's mother."

His father took the rug and reverently hung it back onto the wall. Fifteen years, he'd been a widower, and not only had he never remarried, but to his knowledge, he'd never taken comfort from any other woman.

"I would give up everything I own," the Chief sighed, "just to have your mother back for a single day." He took a deep breath. "I want you to find somebody who loves you like that? Is that asking too much? For my only surviving child?"

They stood in a stalemate.

"The winged demon is a threat," Jamin said.

"He is just a man," the Chief said. "A man with wings."

"You didn't *see* him when he killed those Halifian men," Jamin said. "Never have I seen a creature kill so savagely."

"It's not up to me," the Chief said. "The Tribunal has invoked the right to investigate."

The Tribunal...

Fear tugged at his gut. "You trust *his* word over mine?"

"It's not a matter of trust," the Chief said. "This matter affects the entire village. Whether or not you incited them, you were *there* when the Halifians were killed."

"You *said* you would only let him speak to the shamans!"

His father gave him a rueful look.

"I can't," the Chief said. "Immanu has sworn, if we refuse the winged one sanctuary, that he, his wife and daughter will all go with him to Nineveh. We will lose our shaman, our healer, and her apprentice, all in a single day."

"Immanu wouldn't dare!"

His father gave him a rueful look.

"A reed barge just arrived from Nineveh," he said. "Not only did Chief Sinalshu promise refuge, but he sent a cask filled with gold, along with the promise to give Immanu an entire herd of sheep, if Ninsianna will agree to marry his eldest son."

Chapter 50

May – 3,390 BC
Earth: Village of Assur

NINSIANNA

She led him to the second ring of the village, away from the bustle of merchants, to her parent's modest mud-brick home. While their house was larger than many in the village, now that she'd grown accustomed to the clean lines of Mikhail's sky canoe, the rammed dirt floor and cluttered shelves appeared shabby.

Mikhail crouched to fit beneath the doorway, grunting a muttered curse when he banged his wings upon the lintel. Bundles of herbs hung, drying, from the low ceiling, forcing him to stick his head between the ceiling joists. He hid his thoughts beneath an unreadable expression, but from the rustle of his feathers, she could almost *feel* his claustrophobia.

"These are Mama's medicines—" she yanked down the herbs that obscured his face. "She uses them to make liniments and teas."

"Where -is- your mother?" he asked. "I'd like to get my wing looked at."

He raised the damaged limb that *still* wouldn't lift much higher than his shoulder. Ninsianna felt a pang of regret. She'd done her best, but it hadn't been enough to restore his ability to fly.

"She came by while you were inside with the Chief," she said, "but then she got called away. She said to help you settle in."

She gestured at the empty counter where, normally, Mama kept a basket filled with potions and linen bandages. In its place, she'd left a crock filled with lentils, onions and meat; what they *usually* had for supper when Mama was busy with a patient.

Mikhail pointed at the weapons she still wore, tied around her waist. With a sheepish grin, she untied his belt and handed him back his belt and his knife.

"The firestick?" she raised her eyebrows. "It didn't work."

"Nope."

She waited for him to elaborate, but from his closed expression, he had no intention of saying more.

She held out his firestick.

"You keep it," Mikhail waved her off. "That was the agreement with the Chief."

"What about the sword?"

"Only the knife," he said. "We'll have to hide the rest someplace safe."

He scanned the room, searching for just such a place.

"We could store them in your room?" she suggested.

"And where would that be?"

"On the second floor."

She led him up a stairs that was little more than a ladder. It continued up to the roof, through a hole covered with a mat since, even in the spring, the temperature still got cold at night. Mikhail scrunched up his wings to fit up through the hole. She pulled back a curtain and showed him into his room.

"You'll sleep here," she said. "You can store your weapons underneath the bed."

Mikhail took in the comfortably sized sleeping pallet.

"Is this is the largest bedroom in the house?" he asked.

"Yes," she beamed. "It's the best room we have."

"I do not wish to inconvenience your parents."

Ninsianna's face dropped.

"It's our way…"

"It is not *my* way!" His jaw set into a determined square.

"I thought you couldn't *remember* your way?"

Just for a moment, his face showed vulnerability.

"Please?" he asked. "Isn't there another room?"

His wings drooped, a surer sign of his uncertainty than the lack-of-emotion he schooled upon his chiseled features. How humiliating, to be forced to abandon his sky canoe and come *here*. A creature of the heavens. Cast down onto the Earth and forced to grovel. If not for the fact they'd been attacked, would he have come?

'No,' her heart whispered. *'If not for you, he would have stayed out at that sky canoe, trying to fix it, until the day he died.'*

She pulled open a small, colorful curtain next to her parent's bedroom.

"There is this room," she said breathlessly. "It's small, but I think you'll fit."

Mikhail stepped into the closet which had been sectioned off from her parent's bedroom with a sturdy woven mat and several layers of sticks. A narrow sleeping pallet lay crammed beneath the window, not a *'bunk'* as he called the beds on his ship, but a simple wooden platform, elevated just high enough to discourage rats and padded with a folded blanket. On the wall above it, several shelves held her worldly belongings, including an altar to She-Who-Is.

Ninsianna squeezed in behind him and kneeled upon the bed, for there wasn't enough room for two adults to stand. *Especially* not a man with wings.

"This is your room?" he asked.

"Yes."

"Where would *you* sleep?"

"Here—" her voice warbled hopefully. "It would be no different than at your sky canoe."

His dark eyebrows knit together.

"There is only a single bed."

"We could share it?" she whispered hopefully.

Mikhail stepped closer and touched the small, clay statue she kept on the shelf, decorated with shells and flowers, and a woven einkorn wreath, a wish for marriage, a happy home, good health and fertility. For her entire life, SHE had whispered to save herself for someone special, to only form a union which would result in a sacred child. If Mikhail fell in love with her, would he stay and fulfill the prophecy?

He smelled so good, so powerful and musky. She gasped as a soft wreath of feathers brushed against her back. Warmth pooled between her legs as her entire body came alive.

He raised a hand and gently, almost awkwardly, brushed back a lock of hair that had fallen across her face. He swayed towards her, unable to escape the web that She-Who-Is had woven:

'Here is my Chosen One,' she could almost hear the goddess whisper. *'Take her... She is yours.'*

"Ninsianna—" his voice grew husky.

She closed her eyes, waiting for the kiss. A creature of heaven; sent in answer to a prayer. Her lips parted in anticipation as his warm breath caressed her cheek.

"I cannot stay here," he murmured. "I have to complete my mission."

He stepped back; his unearthly blue eyes filled with regret, and tucked his wings against his back like an impenetrable, wooden shield.

"I'll sleep downstairs," he said. "For now, we can store the weapons underneath your bed."

Without a backwards glance, he slipped out of the curtain and left her, kneeling beneath the statue of She-Who-Is.

Spurned...

Chapter 51

ΔΥƆΠΔΠϚ

*And it's no wonder; for even [Lucifer] himself
Is able to take the form of an angel of light*

2 Corinthians 11:14

Galactic Standard Date: 152,323.05 AE
Alpha Sector: Command Carrier 'Eternal Light'
Supreme Commander-General Jophiel

JOPHIEL

Dubbed the *Eternal Light*, the supreme military flagship had been built to the Eternal Emperor's specifications, from her sleek, contemporary lines, which drew inspiration from all four branches of the military, to the thirteen-pointed star which radiated light across her snow-white hull. Everything about the warship spoke of her terrifying firepower, but it also showcased its feminine, graceful lines.

Jophiel bent over her desk in her spacious private quarters, trying to keep her mind occupied with work instead of a thousand fuzzy-headed impulses. Already her figure had begun to return to normal thanks to the brutal hours she spent training for hand-to-hand combat. Graceful and powerful, she was the embodiment of the ship, and the ship, in turn, was a symbol of the Alliance.

The PA-system whistled.

"Supreme Commander-General?" her right-hand man, a Mantoid named Major Klikrr, called. "You have an alpha-priority-one message from the Prime Minister's office."

"Lucifer?"

"Yes, Ma'am," Klikrr said. "He says it's important?"

Jophiel let out an inaudible hiss.

"Tell him to piss off," she muttered.

"Ma'am?" Klikrr's puzzled voice came over the intercom.

Irritation flashed in her gut, though perhaps it was simply a post-partum hormonal fluctuation? Her milk had come in and, unlike all the other children she'd birthed, it refused to dry up, leaving her breasts constantly swollen, leaking fluid, and exacerbating her already irritable mood.

"Tell him I'm indisposed."

She cut off the communication far more brusquely than was warranted and buried her nose back into her flatscreen. Within minutes, the comms system beeped again.

"What now?" she sighed.

"He insists it's urgent."

"Urgent enough to interrupt—" she stared at the gruesomely tedious plasma-torpedo allocation reports "—these *very important* matters?"

"Ma'am?" Klikrr chirped a panicked squeak. "It's the *Prime Minister,* Ma'am!"

This wasn't the first time the poor bastard had gotten caught between her and Lucifer.

She stared down at the electronic tablet where she'd been signing off reports. Her signature looked more like a stab-mark than Alliance cuneiform.

"Very well," she groused. "Put him through."

She schooled her face to be devoid of emotion as the center of the room shimmered. She did *not* preen her feathers or straighten up her uniform. Lucifer materialized across from her desk, artfully arranged on a chair to convey sincerity and authority.

"What do you *want,* Lucifer?" She clenched her fists beneath the table so it wouldn't show up in the two-way hologram.

"I've been getting complaints about your goon squad harassing honest traders—" Lucifer's eerie silver eyes glittered as he spoke. "You must order them to stop."

"Why?" she snapped.

"Because it's not *friendly.*"

She resisted the urge to *comply* with the Emperor's adopted son. She knew, from experience, how very *manipulative* Lucifer could be.

"They're *Sata'anic* traders—"

Lucifer waved a hand to cut her off.

"Under the new treaty ratified by Parliament, the uncharted territories are considered neutral. The traders have as much of a right to be there as we do."

"Not when they smuggle counterfeit goods," she snapped, "and unload it on unwary settlers for their entire year's harvest!"

"Caveat emptor, Jophie—" he used her pet name with a sneer. "You know how much the Emperor respects the right of free will."

"Before one can exercise free will, they must have all the facts."

"What facts?" Lucifer laughed. "That the Emperor is *pissed* his little creations are all scurrying around, thinking for themselves?"

"Shay'tan is *dumping* those goods below cost to discourage them from developing their own industry," she said. "And then the moment they become dependent, he'll cut off their supply until they accede to his demands!"

"It's called comparative advantage—" he gave her a lascivious grin he knew drove her ballistic. "If we intertwine our economy with theirs, they'll be too dependent upon us to go to war."

"I don't see Shay'tan buying a whole lot of goods from Alliance planets! Only hard-earned Alliance money flowing into Sata'anic coffers."

"You don't need to like it—" he snapped. "You only need to enforce it."

"Not if I feel it endangers the Alliance."

Lucifer dropped the act. Seething hatred radiated out of his handsome features as he leaned into the projector which made it appear he was in the room.

"You *will* back off, you worthless upstart," he flared his wings like a raptor, "or I will take this matter up with the Emperor."

"You do that—" she flared her *own* snow white wings, fiercer than his, even though they were smaller. "Until then—" she gave a powerful flap "—if my men think they are carrying contraband, we're going to stop them!"

Lucifer's silver eyes glittered with malice. He stared at her breasts which, despite her sports bra, had swollen to three times their normal size.

"By the way?" his voice dripped insincerity "—have I passed along my congratulations on your latest little bundle of joy? You're so prolific! To perpetuate your genome with all those low-ranking nobodies."

She squeezed her fist as his arrow found its mark.

"Those *nobodies* were chosen because of their loyalty to the Emperor!"

"That's not what -I- heard!" Lucifer gave a mocking laugh. "According to the media, the Emperor decided to solve our infertility problem with a very *personal* infusion of his own DNA."

Jophiel gasped.

"It wouldn't be the *first* time he took an interest in a pretty woman," Lucifer continued. "Did I ever tell you about the way he lusted after my mother? Why—" he clasped his hands on either side of his chin in a girlie gesture a supermodel might use for the television camera "—except for your hair color, you and she could be twins."

She sputtered:

"How ... dare ... you—"

Lucifer leaned forward.

"And *you*, my dear, sweet nobody—" his eyes glittered silver with hatred "—expect me to believe you've been off fucking some nameless *Colonel* instead of wheedling the throne out from under dear old dad?"

Jophiel recovered. She delivered a verbal right hook.

"You're just jealous because I only had *one* mating attempt that ever failed!"

She cut off the hologram before he had a chance to retort, relishing his stricken expression as the pixels dissipated. A drop of crimson fell onto her desk. She realized she'd dug her nails into her own palm and drawn blood.

"Damn you, Lucifer!"

She put her head into her hands and groaned. He might be an asshole, but he was the most exciting asshole she had ever had the stupidity to fuck.

She rose and flapped her wings, pacing back and forth to disperse the overwhelming urge to order the *Eternal Light* to hunt down the *Prince of Tyre* and blast it out of the sky, along with its arrogant, pompous owner.

"I am better than you!" she screamed at the now-empty hologram. "I do not lead my children's fathers on with promises I can never keep!"

She reached into her desk drawer and pulled out the hand-written letter she kept there to always remind herself the Prime Minister was a snake. The letter was dated thirty-six years ago, ten years before the Emperor had returned.

FROM: Private Third Class Jophi'el-Ohim
          Alliance Air Force Academy

TO: The Honorable Prime Minister Lucifer
          Alliance Parliament - Haven-3

Scrawled across the envelope in angry, red letters was the word:

REJECTED - Return to Sender

Folded neatly into the envelope was a formal written complaint, written on the Prime Minister's official stationery, addressed to her commanding officer, ordering her to cease all attempts to contact Lucifer. The complaint was signed by Lucifer himself and prepared by his Chief of Staff, Zepar.

Thankfully, Lucifer had never actually *filed* it...

But she'd gotten the message...

...every word out of Lucifer's mouth was a lie!

She opened up the envelope and pulled out the tear-stained paper.

* * *

Dearest *iolar*:

You swore, whether or not our mating appointment was successful, that you wished to see me again. You said I was special, that you've never felt this way about any person ... so *connected*. As though we are each other's missing half.

Perhaps I misunderstood when you told me that you loved me?

Your most ardent supporter,
Jophiel

* * *

"What a chump!" she muttered.

She ordered the AI to pull up the records she kept on her children and project their images into the space Lucifer had just violated with his electronic presence. Twelve babies she had borne for the Alliance! Twelve beautiful babies, each one raised to love and serve the Emperor. The eldest had already graduated the Air Force Academy and were climbing in rank, and three had already sired offspring of their own.

"I guess -I- had the last laugh," she laughed bitterly, "didn't I, Lucifer?"

She scrolled through pictures of their fathers, all rising stars, chosen to solidify military support for the Emperor. As she moved through the pictures, the men grew progressively younger to avoid inconvenient political entanglements when the officer, whose offspring you'd just borne, had enough clout to not just order them away.

She paused at a picture of Uriel, his little face red from crying. Ever since the birth, she'd remained frantically busy, refusing to indulge the impulse to visit him … or his father.

"I warned him!" she spoke to the picture. "I made your father sign a waiver! I never told him that I love him!"

Tears streamed down her cheek as she traced the sad little dimple on Uriel's cheek; so much like his father's that it made her heart ache. She hadn't contacted Raphael directly since the day she'd gone into labor, unable to bear his sorrowful expression as she'd cut his heart out and handed it back to him.

"Oh, Mikhail! You were right!"

She ordered the AI to turn off the hologram. This was Mikhail's fault, really! Silly, stupid, *taciturn* Angelic! The Emperor wanted the last living Seraphim to reproduce, so she'd bonded with him over tactics and military training, and mentored him in combat that had begun to resemble foreplay. She *knew* the brooding Seraphim harbored feelings for her, so she'd asked *him* to sire this latest child!

Time had stood still as he'd curled his wings around her and said: "Seraphim take one mate for life."

And then he'd kissed her on the forehead and said:

"…*that* is something you are not able to give me."

And then he'd stepped back, leaving her standing there with her face turned up, waiting for a kiss…

…and asked to be reassigned.

"Damn you!" she cursed Mikhail! "Damn *you*, and your inflexible morals!"

She put her face into her hands, fighting back the urge to weep. She *was* no better than Lucifer. She'd only asked Raphael to sire this latest child because she'd wanted to *hurt* Mikhail by forming relations with his best friend! Only the joke was on *her*. Because in five meager days, Raphael had wiped all thoughts of him, her cadet mating experience with Lucifer, and the eleven men she'd mated with *since* then, right out of her mind!

And now Mikhail was dead because she had banished the *both* of them to the furthest corner of the galaxy on a fool's errand so she wouldn't have to think about either one of them!

The door chime beeped. Jophiel shoved the envelope back into the desk and grabbed the flatscreen which displayed the plasma torpedo allocation reports. She wiped her eyes and settled into a cool, confident pose.

"Come in," she said.

Major Klikrr stuck his green head inside the doorway.

"Excuse me, Ma'am," he said. "I thought you might like to convey these reports yourself?"

He held out his green grasping arm, balancing a second flatscreen between the three tibias which served as fingers. From the concerned hum of his underwings, he wasn't certain whether she'd sign them, or bite his head off.

"What are they?" she sniffed.

"Those shipping reports Colonel Israfa requested," he chirped cautiously. "He asked us to forward all activity in and out of the spiral arm he's searching."

A lump rose in Jophiel's throat. She'd used every excuse to maintain contact, calling Raphael every week, but refusing to let him come close enough to break down her resolve. If she possessed one iota of integrity, she would recall the *Light Emerging* and assign him close enough to visit his son.

Close enough to visit *her*...

Close enough that her presence would taunt him, the same way Lucifer called every single week to taunt *her*...

"Could you forward them, please?" her voice warbled. "Anything the Colonel needs, I want you to get it to him. Tell him to keep searching."

So long as he stays out there...

She glanced at the empty place where Lucifer's hologram had disappeared. Her expression hardened.

"And order every vessel in the fleet to step up health and safety inspections. If it flies, I want it boarded and inventoried."

Chapter 52

May – 3,390 BC
Earth: Village of Assur
Colonel Mikhail Mannuki'ili

MIKHAIL

He tossed and turned like stag pursued by a pack of hounds, only instead of his earlier nightmares, a golden-eyed huntress chased him across the heavens. He woke up, gasping, the urge to *go* to her so overwhelming that it took every ounce of strength not to indulge the urgency in his loins.

"I made a promise," he groaned.

He got up from the folded blanket he'd used as a bed and rummaged through the dark until he found the woolen cape she'd cast off last night, clean with soaproot[104] and something feminine. He buried his nose into the collar and inhaled her scent. The distance between them almost broke his resolve far worse than when she'd slept across the aisle from him, naked except for her loincloth.

"It's just for a few weeks," he promised. "I'm here to question the shamans, and then I'll leave to find the others of my kind."

He fell asleep with her cape thrown over him like a blanket, pondering their ancient legends. If the shamans spoke his language, some remnant of a colony must exist, someplace, on this planet? All he had to do was find it, and then he could figure out how he'd ended up here.

He woke up to the scrape of the front door opening.

"Ninsianna?" he bolted upright.

A dark-caped woman stood in the doorway, backlit by the dawn, her shoulders hunched as though she carried the weight of the world.

"It's just me," Needa sighed, "Ninsianna's mother."

She shuffled inside and placed a basket upon the counter filled with bloody rags. She was a beautiful woman, intelligent and stubborn, aged early from carrying the worries of an entire village.

Mikhail lurched to his feet and banged his head upon the ceiling. Pain shot into his brain. He tucked his wings against his back, not certain how to address Ninsianna's mother, who he hadn't seen since the day she'd come to visit his ship.

---

[104] *Soaproot:* a plant used in place of soap.

"Ma'am?" he said in the same tone of voice he'd give a commanding officer.

She gave him a wan grimace.

"It's a girl—" she held up one of the bloody rags. "Perhaps six *manû*.[105] She was born with the cord around her neck, but I managed to get her breathing."

"Did you have to resuscitate her?" He realized he'd slipped into Galactic Standard. "Uhm ... breathe into her mouth?"

"You know this magic?" Needa's brow knit together.

"Yes," he said. "At least I *think* I do."

Needa gave him a business-like grunt.

"Once I get some sleep," she said, "you and me, we're going to have a long talk about *everything* you know about healing."

She shuffled over to a clay oven which Immanu had painstakingly piled wood next to last night.

"I suppose you'll be wanting some breakfast?" she said wearily.

"That's alright, Ma'am," he said. "I can fend for myself."

She ignored what he'd just said and stuffed several pieces of wood into the coals at the bottom of the oven. Built of fired mud-bricks shaped into a beehive, the smoke drifted up the stairwell, through a hole cut into the roof.

"Could you flip back the ceiling mat?" she asked.

He climbed the ladder, eager to make himself useful, and flipped back the reed mat which minimized cold air during the night. The still-rising sun cast its light down into the kitchen. From up here, he could see the small mountain which marked the final resting place of his ship. He stared longingly at the curtain which cordoned off Ninsianna's room as he climbed back down.

Needa handed him a bucket the moment he hit the floor. Fashioned from sticks and lined with a goatskin, a coarse woven rope served as a handle.

"Do you remember where the well is?" she asked.

"Yes, Ma'am," he said. "In the central square?"

"The one by the north gate is better," she said. "There's less chance you'll cross spears with Jamin there."

He gathered two more buckets and made his way down to the outermost ring, past a much less impressive-looking, but equally well-defended gate to a ring of stones which marked one of Assur's three wells. Although just past sunrise, already dozens of scrawny children and bedraggled women lined up, waiting to cast their bucket down the hole.

The chatter turned silent as he moved to the back of the line. Women and children skittered out of the way.

---

[105] *Manû*: approximately one pound or .45 kg; 6 *manû* = 2.75 kg.

"Go ahead," he said. "I'll wait my turn."

Not one of them moved. It became apparent *nobody* would get water until he got out of there. He stepped up to the well, his feathers rustling from the unwanted attention, and hooked the bucket up to a rope suspended from a heavy wooden tripod.

He hauled the first bucket up perfectly fine, but the second got caught on something at the bottom. He tugged at the rope, but he didn't dare yank it as the buckets were poorly made. He spread his wings for balance and stuck his head down into the well.

"What are you doing?" a voice asked.

He looked up. A tall, slender girl, not quite at the threshold of becoming a woman, stood on the opposite side of the well, clutching a bucket to her chest. While better fed than the others, her clothing was simple, a worn linen shawl-dress and goatskin pampooties.

"It's caught on something," he said.

"A rock," she said. "You have to throw it towards the left."

"How do I get it out?"

"Unhook the rope and walk it around the hole," she said.

He unhooked the rope from the tripod and walked around the well, giving it a gentle tug every couple of feet. The girl crept closer, her eyes darting between his face and his wings, too young to hide her curiosity, but old enough to suppress the urge to pat him like a dog. At last, he felt the bucket give.

"It's free," he said.

"Now throw it to the right."

"You just said to throw it to the left?"

"That's from over *there*," she pointed at the tripod. "From *here*, you have to throw it to the right, or you'll hit the rock again."

He did at he was told. The bucket came up, filled with water, without hitting any additional snags. He hooked the third bucket onto the rope.

"Why isn't Ninsianna doing this?" she asked.

"Because I want to help."

"But you're a *man*."

He glanced at the spectators. Three of them were obviously the girl's younger brothers. For the first time, he realized he was the only male here over the age of ten.

"What does that have to do with it?"

Men don't fetch water," she said.

"I do."

"Why?"

He dropped the final bucket down to the place where it would avoid the rocks.

"Because I wouldn't want to burden anyone else with my needs."

He studied the tall, slender girl as he pulled up the final bucket. Although she bore the dark hair and brown eyes of the Ubaid, her straight nose and height hinted that her ancestors hailed from someplace else.

"I'm Mikhail," he said.

"I know," she said. "You're the only man in the village with wings."

"How do you know my name?"

"Needa just spent the night at my house."

"Oh?" he said. "I hear you have a new baby sister?"

"Yeah." The girl wrinkled up her nose. "Mama's in a bad way, so now Papa expects *me* to take care of my brothers and sisters."

He bent to arrange the handles of the three buckets so he could juggle them between his just-two hands.

"Did you ever have to do that?" she asked. "Watch your younger siblings?"

"I wouldn't know," he said.

"You don't *have* any brothers or sisters?"

He stared at the younger children who crept up behind her, emboldened by her bravery, all of them remarkably alike. *Nothing* about these miniature humans seemed familiar. In fact, they set off all kinds of alarms.

"No," he said. *At least I don't think so...* "I have no idea how to care for children."

"Well -*I*- do," she said. "It's *expected* because I'm a girl."

The girl's expression reminded him of Ninsianna every time she lamented the fact that the men in this village viewed women as little more than livestock.

"What's your name?" he asked.

"Pareesa," she said. "It means 'Little Fairy.'"

He held out his hand.

"Pleased to meet you, Little Fairy."

She stared at his hand as though not certain what the gesture meant. He could see, by the way she glanced around at the others, she couldn't decide whether to shake it, or run away.

"You're different than what Jamin claimed," she said.

"How so?" he ruffled his feathers defensively.

"Well you haven't killed anyone. Yet."

"I don't kill people unless they deserve it."

"That's what Needa said—" the girl clutched her bucket. "She said, if I see you, I'm supposed to give you a chance."

He scanned the women and children who huddled at the edge of the square, owl-eyed and whispering. They'd gotten as far away from him as they possibly could, and yet they had not left.

"Give me your bucket?" he said.
"Why?"
"So I can fetch some water."
"Fetching water is woman's work."
"Not where I come from."
He prayed it wasn't a lie.

*

Needa glanced up as he carried in the buckets. His shirt, his pants, his wings, all bore water-droplets.
"Any problems?" she asked.
"No, Ma'am," he said.
For the first time since he'd known her, Ninsianna's mother smiled.

Chapter 53

May – 3,390 BC
Earth: Village of Assur

NINSIANNA

Every morning, from the time Ninsianna had been a child, it was her job to cook Papa breakfast because, most mornings, Mama got called away. For *three* days she'd managed to evade her mother, but today no frantic villager had appeared to summon a healer.

She slipped down the stairs to where Mikhail, already up before the dawn, had gathered the empty water buckets and stood, poised, to exit the door.

"I'll do it!" she glanced apprehensively at Mama who stood at the oven, stirring a crock filled with porridge.

"Let *him* do it," Mama said, not turning around.

"It's woman's work." She grabbed a bucket from his hand.

Mikhail stared down at her from his impossibly tall height, one dark eyebrow raised in a quizzical expression.

"I don't mind."

Mikhail took the bucket she held, clutched to her chest, and with a nod to Mama, *"Ma'am,"* he ducked out the door. She watched him turn left, towards the well located in the poorest part of the village, where he drew water not just for *them,* but also the pregnant women, the elderly and the children. With that simple, humble act, he'd done more to undermine Jamin's machinations than all of her father's insistence he was here to fulfill a prophecy.

She bolted towards the courtyard.

"I have to milk the goat."

"Sit!"

Mama tapped the rough-hewn counter they'd dragged into the center of the room to make a table so Mikhail didn't have to crush his feathers onto the floor.

Ninsianna sat on the bench, her stomach filled with dread. Mama moved the porridge out of the fire and handed her a bag of onions.

"Peel." Mama picked up a stone blade and, with the deft hands of a healer, skinned each onion and placed it in a basket. Ninsianna followed her mother's example. After a while, the silence grew unbearable.

"Just say it!" she cried out. "Just say what you have to say."

"You've placed this family in a terrible position."

"Maybe if you'd spoken up for me," she struck back, "I wouldn't have run away!"

Mama's thick eyebrows knit together in a single, dark slash.

"I will not tolerate that tone of voice!"

"What about *my* self-respect?" Ninsianna retorted. "You took the Chief's bride-price, and now you're too *greedy* to give it back!"

Mama's mouth tightened into a grim line. She stared at the onions. Slip. Slip. Slip. She skinned them all alive, the poor little onions which had never done her wrong.

"Your father has never been frugal," Mama said at last. "He spent the bride price—"

"How is that *my* problem?" Ninsianna interrupted.

"You made a binding contract."

"I changed my mind."

"You reneged—" Mama said. "In some villages, that's grounds for a woman to be stoned."

"Not in Assur!"

"That's because Chief Kiyan's wife taught him to be kind to women," Mama said. "But you broke a contract—" she leaned forward "—with his *son*."

"It's about time somebody knocked Jamin over the head."

Mama's voice lowered into a she-wolf growl.

"Someday soon, Jamin will inherit leadership of this village, and when he does, his *impression* of women will be tainted by how you shamed him!"

"By the time that happens," Ninsianna scoffed, "he'll have forgotten all about me."

"You think so, eh?" Mama picked one of the onions out of the basket and stabbed straight through it. "Not if you keep antagonizing him."

"Me? Antagonizing him?"

"Yes!" Mama slammed the flat-edge of her knife upon the table. "You and your father should have *known* better than to bring Mikhail here!"

"You don't like him?"

"Of *course* I like him," Mama said. "Why do you think I've been promising favors if people will treat him fairly?"

"The well?" Ninsianna guessed.

"Yes," Mama said. "Jamin looks down on the ones who live in the poorest part of the village. So I sent him to draw water *there*, to give them someone to look *up* to."

"But if you like him," Ninsianna asked, "why are you so angry?"

"Because Mikhail is going to *leave*," Mama said. "But you? You have to stay behind."

Tears welled in Ninsianna's eyes.

"But I don't *want* to stay! I want to see the heavens!"

Mama harrumphed.

"Has he given you any encouragement?"

"No."

"Has he ever said he has *feelings* for you?"

"Nothing." Ninsianna felt sick. "He never talks about *anything* but completing his mission."

"Has he promised to take you into the heavens?"

"Every time I ask," Ninsianna sobbed, "he talks about something else!"

Mama reached across the table.

"Mikhail is a good man," she said. "He doesn't *want* power, no matter how much your father makes silly claims."

"It is *not* a claim!" Ninsianna said. "I *saw* him fight."

"You put too much faith in the goddess."

"Maybe you should give her *more* faith!"

"*SHE* may be powerful!" Mama said. "But *SHE* is as blind, and selfish, and *capricious* as any mortal."

"Is it wrong, to want a bit of power for yourself?"

"You covet it?"

"Yes," Ninsianna said. "Papa says it's *good* to earn favor from the gods."

Mama harrumphed.

"Your father is *blind* when it comes to craving power! He is too much like his *own* father. Just be thankful he was never willing to pay the price."

"Maybe he *should* have?" Ninsianna retorted. "Then instead of groveling to the Chief, he could just say '*do this*' like Lugalbanda did, and everyone would obey!"

Mama's face darkened into a mask of fury.

"You should thank the *goddess* your father is a better man!" Mama hissed. "If he wasn't, trust me, you wouldn't *be* here to make such an asinine claim!"

She scooped up the onions and carried them out into the courtyard where a second, much larger oven heated a huge clay pot, so large you could boil an entire sheep.

"Why, Mama?" Ninsianna followed her outside. "Why do you hate grandfather when he drove away our enemies?"

Mama dropped the onions into the crock which, since last night, she'd been boiling sheep's trotters to make *pacha* soup[106] for the shamans.

"Some things are too terrible to speak of," Mama said.

---

[106] *Pacha soup*: a gelatinous soup made by boiling a sheep's head, feet and offal.

"His magic?"

"Yes."

Mama clammed up. The Tribunal had ruled that all discussion of her grandfather's magic was forbidden, purportedly to keep it from the hands of their enemies. All she knew was that everyone, especially their enemies, was too terrified to speak Lugalbanda's name, even in death, any louder than a whisper.

"I'm not going to marry Jamin!" Ninsianna crossed her arms. "I don't care *what* you say. I'd rather be a spinster."

Mama sighed.

"I'm not *asking* you to marry him," she said. "Just make your peace with him so we don't have to leave."

"Leave?" she said. "Why would we have to leave?"

"Your father believes he's the Chosen One of the song," Mama said. "If he is, then Mikhail will need him to accomplish whatever great task the goddess has set for him."

"Mikhail doesn't believe the legend."

"It doesn't *matter* what he believes!" Mama said. "What *matters* is that Jamin will not relent until you either marry *him*, or marry someone powerful enough to discourage him."

"I can take care of myself."

Mama met her gaze.

"Really?" Mama said. "Who saved you when Jamin pushed your head beneath the water?"

"Mikhail will protect me?"

Mama reached across the table and took her hand.

"Mikhail is a creature of heaven. It's not fair, to ask him to linger, when you *know* he belongs up there."

She gestured at the rooftop where Mikhail spent most of his time, staring west, towards the mountain which sheltered his sky canoe. Ever since the night of the attack, he'd retreated so far inside himself that sometimes, it felt as though she spoke to a stone rather than a living man.

Ninsianna's shoulders sagged.

"What do you want me to do?"

"Your father sent word we will *move* to whichever village is willing to give Mikhail shelter," she said. "Nineveh has responded. They will lay every resource they have at Mikhail's feet if *you* agree to marry Chief Sinalshu's eldest son."

Ninsianna gaped.

"Qishtea?"

"Yes."

"Qishtea is an even bigger goathead than Jamin!" she exclaimed. "The only reason he *wants* me is to snatch away Jamin's prize!"

"Those are your choices." Mama let go of her hand. "Make peace with Jamin, whether that be marriage, or to make him understand you two are not *right* for one another, or your father will relocate *all* of us to Nineveh. And once we are there, you *will* follow through on your betrothal, or they will bury you in a pit and smash your pretty head in!"

Chapter 54

May – 3,390 BC
Earth: Village of Assur
Colonel Mikhail Mannuki'ili

Two weeks later...

MIKHAIL

His feathers rustled as she led him past the inner sentries, into the kill-box of an alley which led to the central square. Unlike the outermost ring where the people had begun to tolerate him, here the people cried out and pressed themselves against the walls.

"Remember to eat—" Ninsianna attempted to distract him from the whispers "—a bite of everything."

"Your mother already fed me," Mikhail said.

"But that was *ordinary* food," she said. "This food is an offering from each village to make peace with your gods."

"I don't *remember* my gods," he said. "How can I possibly bind them to a peace treaty?"

"It's all ceremonial," she said. "You have to pretend to like it. And don't forget the salt—"

"The salt?"

"Yes. No treaty is binding unless you take a pinch of salt[107] and sprinkle it onto your food."

His feathers rustled.

"How can I agree to a treaty before I've heard the terms?"

Ninsianna shrugged. "It's just the way things are done."

They emerged from the alley, into the central square. Ninsianna herded him away from the warriors who'd amassed in front of the Chief's house, reinforcing their spear-heads with fresh sinew and anything else they could do to appear intimidating. Thank the gods there was no sign of Jamin!

The Temple of She-Who-Is was, by far, the tallest building in Assur, more than three stories high, and built on the highest ground. Ninsianna led him beneath a wooden pavilion set against the side of the building, lashed together from date-palm wood, and strung with strips of linen to create shade. Sunk into an alcove, a clay statue of a large-breasted woman smiled

---

[107] *Sharing salt:* a ritual signifying good will with a guest.

down upon the villagers with empty eye-sockets. Ninsianna raised her palms into the air.

"Great Mother," she said, "I pray you will give Mikhail the answers he seeks."

She reached over and yanked out one of his small under-feathers.

"Hey!"

"You're supposed to make an offering."

She laid the brown feather at the goddess' feet, along with a wreath she'd woven earlier from grass.

He glanced at the villagers who all gaped up at him, expecting him to *do something* before the statue of their deity. How could he explain he couldn't remember his own name, much less who he worshipped, or *didn't* worship?

He bowed his head and tucked his feathers into 'dress wings.'

"Madam?" he murmured at the statue. "I'd settle for remembering who I'm supposed to be?"

He gripped his dog tags, waiting for some kind of divine revelation other than the cuneiform etched into the metal, but he felt no recognition, no sense of kinship. He simply felt … empty? As though his entire life had been unceremoniously dumped out, just like they did each morning to the chamber-pots?

"Come?" she touched his arm. "The shamans are ready to see you."

"I was ready to see them two weeks ago," he grumbled.

"If *one* shaman met you early," she said, "the others would take offense. That is why they all came so quickly. They believe you will select one amongst them to become the Chosen One."

He ruffled his feathers. He didn't *care* about Immanu's silly prophecy, only the fact that, somewhere, a colony of his people resided on this planet.

"Let's get this over with," he said. "The sooner I speak to them, the sooner I can leave."

Ninsianna's face took on a stricken expression. He'd tried to explain that he *had* to complete his mission. As much as his body yearned to give her that kiss, the rank etched into his dog tags meant his life wasn't his to give.

She marched out from underneath the pavilion, his sword slung over her shoulder like a quiver, her back ramrod straight, her head held high. He followed dutifully towards the temple entrance, reluctant to antagonize her any further. She paused, just before she reached the door, and faced the warriors who'd amassed opposite the courtyard.

Ninsianna gave a little wave.

Mikhail looked to see who she was waving at and froze. A pair of black eyes glowered back at him. A cold chill settled into his gut.

"I hope *he* won't be there," Mikhail said.

"So what if he is?" she snapped. "He's the Chief's son. Of *course* he has a say!"

She turned sideways in a universal female gesture of *"I don't care about you!"* and gave Jamin a coy smile.

An unfamiliar emotion gripped his gut.

I thought she didn't like him?

Ninsianna tossed her chestnut hair.

"Come," she said haughtily. "If you're going to leave, I'd just assume be rid of you."

A feeling, like standing at the threshold of a black hole, about to be torn to pieces by the gravity well, hit him full-force in the chest. She marched up the temple steps without giving him a backwards glance. He followed docilely behind her, utterly perplexed.

The man who'd frisked him the day he'd met the Chief stood guard at the temple door.

"Did you bring your weapons?" Kiaresh asked.

"Ninsianna has them," he said, "just as we agreed."

She dumped the bag with the sword on the step with an indignant sniff. Kiaresh gave him a raised eyebrow. Mikhail stood stone-faced, rather than reveal her behavior rattled him.

"You may take your weapons and go in," Kiaresh said, "but you—" he held out an arm to block Ninsianna "—are not allowed."

"But the shamans—"

"You know the *law*," Kiaresh said.

Tears welled in her eyes. She gripped Mikhail's arm.

"But he *needs* me to interpret!"

"So far as I can tell," Kiaresh said, "your *friend* speaks our language just fine."

Her lip trembled. It tore at his heart more surely than her earlier tantrum.

"She is right," Mikhail said softly. "While I understand the words, I have difficulty understanding context."

"Women are not allowed to defile the temple."

Mikhail raised an eyebrow.

"Are you serious?"

Kiaresh looked taken aback. Mikhail gestured at the pavilion they'd just left.

"I am here, to hear a prophecy, about a *goddess* who birthed *another* goddess who purportedly created the universe," Mikhail said, "in a *temple* to that goddess, and you tell me women are not allowed."

Kiaresh gaped.

Mikhail took Ninsianna's arm.

"She stays with *me*," he said. "Or *me*, and the weapons you all want so badly—" he held up the bag which held his sword "—will leave."

"We don't want—"

"I'm not *stupid!*" Mikhail bent forward, reminding the man of his superior height. "The only reason your chief allowed me into his village is because he wants the secrets to my magic more than he values the opinion of his own son!"

He gave his wings a disdainful flap.

"Come, *chol beag*,"[108] he said. "It's time to go back to my sky canoe."

A commotion came from just inside the temple. Someone called out in his language:

"Winged one! Wait!"

An ancient old man hobbled through the doorway, helped along by Immanu, Ninsianna's father. Both men were finely dressed in five-fringed kilts, heavily decorated with beads, leopard-skin capes, and necklaces carved from animal's teeth. The old man, however, also wore a headdress, fashioned of animal bones and long, brown feathers.

Ninsianna bowed her head.

"Zartosht," she murmured.

The old man reached towards him with a gnarled, claw-like hand. Intelligent brown eyes, turned blue with cataracts, squinted up at him through a pair of wrinkled portals.

"You are real," the old man said in heavily accented Galactic Standard.

"Of course I am."

The old man touched his own chin.

"No beard," he said. "Just like in the legends."

Mikhail glanced at Immanu. *That* wasn't a fact contained in the song of the sword.

"It is as I said," Immanu beamed. "The winged ones have returned."

The old man touched the feathers in his headdress, and then reached out to stroke one of his wings.

"He is descended from an eagle," the old man said, "just like the legends say."

Mikhail leaned forward. "What else do the legends say?"

"There are many legends," the old man said. "Most of them little more than fragments. Come inside, and we will share what we know?"

The urge to find out about his people warred with his distaste at the way they treated women. Ninsianna clung to his arm, her distress at being excluded physically palpable. He put his hand over *hers*.

---

[108] *Chol beag:* "little dove."

"We have a problem," he said in fully modern Galactic Standard, not the ancient dialect. "I cannot enter this negotiation without somebody I trust to interpret."

"But that's why -I- am here?" Immanu said. "She-Who-Is selected *me* as your Chosen One."

"In *my* world," he said, "women and men are equals. She saved my life. To exclude her would be reprehensible."

He prayed it was not a lie...

"Very well," Zartosht waved his hand.

"But my father said—" Immanu said.

"A creature of heaven has come into our midst," the old man interrupted. "If Assur won't allow his interpreter, then she can bring him to Nineveh—" he gave Ninsianna a wink "—where our Chief's son will indulge her every whim."

Ninsianna blanched.

The old man beckoned for him to step inside the temple. Ninsianna clung to his arm, her earlier animosity suddenly gone.

"Who is that?" he asked.

"Zartosht of Nineveh," she whispered. "Keeper of the legends. He's the highest-ranking shaman in Ubaid territory."

They led him into a tall-ceilinged room. Streaming down from a skylight, crepuscular rays shimmered with grain-dust. Placed in the center like an altar, an enormous table held a wooden lever balanced over a stone to make a primitive scale. One end of the lever bore a cradle to hold a basket, while on the other side, a pile of black stones had been lined up from the largest, to the smallest.

Overseeing it all, a gossamer-winged version of the deity they'd prayed to outside smiled down from a bas-relief that had been painstakingly etched into a slab of sandstone.

Ninsianna fell to her knees and bowed before the image.

"Great Mother!" she cried out. "You are just the way I imagined!"

His skin tingled as a memory whispered from deep within his subconscious, but it refused to come to the surface. He traced the lines. While he did not *know* this deity, he knew *of her*.

"This is the weighing room—" Immanu proudly gestured "—where the villagers bring a portion of their grain each harvest to make an offering to She-Who-Is. When times grow lean, it is up to the high priest—" he jabbed his thumb at his own chest "—to apportion it among the population at a fair trade price."

Each wall bore a doorway. Beyond were rooms filled with lidded baskets. Dozens of golden eyes peered out of the shadows.

"Cats?" he asked.

"She-Who-Is considers them sacred," Ninsianna said.

"Why?"

"They keep the rats from defiling the grain."

Immanu led them into a modest-sized inner room. Seventeen more shamans sat on cushions lined up along the walls. At the far end, another alcove housed a clay statue similar to the one beneath the pavilion, only this one was larger and far more intricately wrought. At her feet, a feast had been laid out, along with flowers.

Zartosht gestured towards a wooden stool which had been set up beneath the goddess. Unlike the other statues, *this* one possessed golden eyes.

"Come, sit," Immanu beckoned.

Mikhail tucked his wings up so as not to break any feathers. Ninsianna moved to stand behind him, between his back and his wing, one hand held possessively on his right shoulder. Some of the shamans whispered complaints, but none dared overrule the shaman from Nineveh.

He made eye contact with each, sizing them up and giving a polite nod as Immanu rattled off their names. The shamans nodded back. Whatever they'd been expecting, they appeared satisfied.

"We have prepared a feast in your honor," Immanu said. "Are you hungry?"

"Yes," he said, even though he'd already eaten.

With elaborate pomp and ceremony, Immanu blessed the feast while the others chanted deep-throated prayers which vibrated into his bones. Ninsianna passed out flat bread while the less senior shamans passed around platters of seasoned meat and tubers. One by one, the shamans tested their ability to speak his language. He forced himself to remain patient while they spoke of mediocre things:

"Is the bread tasty?" one asked.

"Yes. The bread is good."

"Could you please pass the salt?" another asked.

"Here," he said.

"Thank you."

The shamans heavily salted their meat and held it up to praise the goddess before they ate it. Mikhail bit into his *own* piece of meat, so laden with salt it drew all the moisture out of his tongue.

The youngest shaman tried his language:

"The weather is nice today?" Sagal-zimu asked.

"Yes. The weather is good."

"Do you think it will rain?"

"I don't know. I'm not a meteorologist."

The young shaman gave him a puzzled expression. While they spoke the same language, they did *not* understand his technology.

The questions shifted to become more personal. What do Angelics eat? Why doesn't he grow a beard? Do Angelics use a chamber pot? Is it true, that his sky canoe fell from the stars?

At last they asked the question he expected.

"What do you think of the *Song of the Sword*?"

Mikhail formulated his thoughts so as to give an honest answer without belittling their religious beliefs:

"It feels like a song you sing for children," he said. "I don't *remember* it, but I know I've heard it before."

The questions continued. After a while, they began to try his patience. Ninsianna squeezed his shoulder. He touched her hand, all too aware of the warmth which radiated out of her fingers.

Finally her father clapped his hands.

"Enough questions!" Immanu announced. "It is time to help our guest remember!"

The shamans broke out skin-drums and a variety of rattles and began to sing the Song of the Sword.

> In Ki's most sorrowful, desperate hour,
> When all was lost to blight,
> She sang her Song of Creation,
> And enticed Darkness to protect the Light.
>
> Primordial Light, the architect,
> Ki's daughter, She-Who-Is,
> Spun the darkness of He-Who's-Not,
> To create life, All-That-Is
>
> But then one day, the sickness returned.
> Moloch. Enemy of Ki.
> The Evil One. The ex-husband spurned.
> Collapse. Entropy.
>
> He spread his evil, throughout the worlds,
> Undoing all in his path.
> Devouring his own children,
> To make Ki feel his wrath.

But He-Who's-Not, the Guardian.
Lord Chaos. The Dark Lord.
Sang the Song of Destruction,
To protect the Light he adored.

She-Who-Is wept bitter tears,
To see her playthings broken,
The Dark Lord couldn't bear her grief,
And offered his mate a token.

To keep the balance so he could protect her,
They would play a game of chess.
She-Who-Is would create new pieces.
He-Who's-Not would reclaim the rest.

But both must remain ever-vigilant,
Against Moloch's eventual return,
He sends forth Agents to pave the way,
To escape the hell whence he burns.

When Moloch gains a foothold,
And desires to be fed,
She-Who-Is shall appoint a Chosen One
To warn of Moloch's spread.

SHE shall send a winged Champion
A demi-god fair and just,
A Sword of the Gods to defend the people,
And raise armies from the dust.

As Moloch corrupts Agents to do his work,
So shall Ki appoint Watchmen to do hers,
From the ashes of despair,
When all appears lost,
Hidden Agents shall choose to serve HER.

True love will inspire the Other One,
To pierce her heart upon a thorn,
And bring back hope where there is none.
For agape can access Ki's Song.

> When all the players have made their moves,
> And the Morning Star shines bright,
> He shall light the way through the darkest hour,
> And restore the path of Light...
>
> And if these measures should someday fail,
> And Ki's protections fall,
> The Dark Lord shall seize his vessel,
> And protect the Light by destroying them all.

As they sang, each shaman sang a different verse, while others sang harmonies or stood up and acted out the parts. They then acted out a different song about a man who'd subdued a serpent, a raft which had carried their people across a terrible sea, and half-human creatures who had led them from a cave to battle a race of giants.

His people...

His people had led *their* people to freedom...

As they sang, Immanu passed around a bitter-tasting drink. A pleasant tingle radiated into his extremities and gave the sensation he floated. Some part of his brain chided him for taking hallucinogens, but the other part, which was curious about the legends, sank into each story until it felt like he, and they, observed a part of living history rather than acted out a song.

They sang for hours, each shaman singing a fragment of a song, another singing the same song, only the words would be a bit different, until he was able to clarify songs that referred to technology which had become lost over time.

The room grew dark. Immanu lit the tallow lanterns. They drank more narcotics, ate more food, and always passed the salt. At last they sang a song which claimed his people had grown old and died, but they'd promised, one day, their kin would return.

Mikhail's face dropped.

"How long ago did this happen?"

"This song was ancient," Zartosht said, "even in the time of my grandfather's grandfather's grandfather. But purportedly there's a temple where the winged ones were laid to rest."

"Where can I find this tomb?"

"Nobody knows," Zartosht said. "Every generation, a traveler would bring stories about a group of priestesses who kept the old songs alive. But the last I heard, the temple had been destroyed."

Mikhail's wings sagged.

"Do you have any idea what direction they came from?"

"All I know is that the journey took many months," Zartosht said. "Across a desert that only the bravest, or most foolish person, would ever dare cross."

Mikhail bowed his head and stared at his hands.

"Do you have other stories?" his voice sounded hoarse. "About any other creatures that fell from the heavens?"

"Once a traveler sang a song about a race called the Cherubim," Zartosht said. "The day you came, the day the stars fell from the heavens, I had a vision about a god bathed in a brilliant blue light. He reminded me of this song, and said I must sing it."

Mikhail's pinfeathers tingled with a sense of anticipation.

"Sing the song of the Cherubim?"

Zartosht began to sing, his voice so thin and warbly he had to lean forward and strain to hear. The other shamans fell silent as the Keeper of the Legends sang a song about the highest order of heavenly beings, defenders of a great emperor who had sworn to protect the light.

Mikhail touched the pin affixed to his chest. Etched in a circle around a magnificent tree were inscribed the words: *"In light there is order, and in order there is life."*

The song changed. The old man recited a verse in an unknown language. One comprised of whistles and clicks.

Ninsianna stiffened...

"That's the language you spoke the day Jamin attacked with the Halifians," she whispered

Mikhail repeated the words Zartosht had just spoken, only the words flowed from his lips far more fluently.

"I remember this song!" he said excitedly. "It's a prayer for restraint."

"You know of the Cherubim?" the shamans asked.

"I think—" he stared right through them as a sense of blue light tingled at the periphery of his vision. "I think I might have grown up among them?"

A breeze blew down from the skylight and caused the tallow lanterns to flicker, distorting the shaman's shadows and making it appear they had many arms. The effect of the hallucinogens enhanced the sensation. It seemed he stood at the threshold of another time and place; laying upon his back, beneath a terrifying visage of a fierce, armored warrior.

—*The warrior reached down and gripped his arm.*

—*You reacted in anger, Nidan Mannuki'ili. When you act rashly, you give your opponent power.*

"Master Yoritomo?" he cried out.

He lurched to his feet as, in the memory, the many-armed warrior pulled him standing and dusted the sawdust off his simple brown robe. He pulled the sword out of the goatskin bag and recited the prayer; swinging the sword in the air as the warrior in his memory recited the exact words Zartosht had just spoken.

A memory…

…as clear as day…

……of getting his backside *slammed* into the ground…

………and then helped back up…

……and told to try again…

…welled up out of his subconscious, along with all of the emotion, and frustration, and *pride* he'd felt that day.

"It's a training kata!" he cried out triumphantly. "Master Yoritomo taught me this prayer so I would never kill a man in anger!"

He focused on the warrior in his memory. He could almost *see* dozens of other Cherubim warriors throwing each other to the ground, exactly the same as Master Yoritomo did to *him*.

"The Emperor sent me to live with the Cherubim," he said excitedly. "He wanted me to learn to control my anger, but I can't remember why I was so angry. Only that I was young."

"What do these Cherubim look like?" one of the shamans asked.

How could he explain an alien species, a *truly* alien species, to a race of people who thought *he* was alien-looking?

"They resemble ants," he said. "Only they are taller than I am by half. They are the most trusted defenders of the Eternal Emperor."

"Ants? That's ludicrous!" one of the shamans blurted out.

"So is a man with wings," another said. "But you're looking at one."

He prayed *more* memories would surface, but nothing did. But that single, powerful memory gave him an incredible sense of *duty*.

"That's all I can remember," he said at last, "but it's one memory I didn't have before."

A movement caught his attention. Standing in the doorway, Chief Kiyan, dressed in ceremonial attire, and his hate-filled son, had listened for gods only knew how long?

Immanu rushed to fetch the Chief a cushion and placed it upon the stool he'd vacated beneath the statue of She-Who-Is. The shamans fell silent as Chief Kiyan, the second-most powerful Chief in Ubaid territory, ascended to his makeshift throne, flanked by his most trusted guard, Varshab, and his only child and heir. Mikhail tucked his wings against his back and stood at attention, his sword pointed straight down with its tip resting against the ground.

"Sir," he said.

Nobody moved to disarm him.

Ninsianna bowed her head and deferred to the Chief. She met her ex-fiancé's gaze. Jamin's eyes burned intense with emotion as he tilted his head to her in a show of respect.

"Ninsianna—" he said cordially "—we are glad that you've returned."

Ninsianna gasped.

Jamin raised his chin, every aspect of his being portraying his *arrogance*, his assumption of being the future chief. Daggers of hatred radiated out of his black eyes as they slid from Ninsianna to *him*.

Jamin said nothing…

…not a word…

…..no acknowledgement…

………no greeting…

……just a hateful glare.

Mikhail's pinfeathers reared in their follicles. That dark anger, the one the Cherubim had taught him to suppress, pressed into his body and whispered: *'This man will give you no quarter.'*

The Chief's man, Varshab, gave a warning growl.

"Mik-hai-el," Jamin hissed.

It was the first time they'd greeted each other, face to face, without trying to kill one another.

"*Muhafiz*—" Mikhail used the honorarium the little girl at the well had told him *they*, the ordinary people, were expected to use whenever they addressed their future chief.

The black-eyed bastard momentarily lapsed into confusion until his face hardened, once more, into a hateful mask.

The Chief gave a satisfied grunt.

Mikhail stood straight and waited to be judged.

The Chief looked to each shaman and recited a litany of greetings, starting with Zartosht of Nineveh, and moving down the line to the bold young shaman from a tiny village named Gasur.[109] As he did, his son echoed his father's greeting with the polished demeanor of someone who'd been trained to uphold that tradition his entire life.

It was a demonstration of force to show he was outclassed. *'Just because you fell from the heavens, we expect you to bow down to -us-, and not the other way around!'*

At last, Chief Kiyan met his gaze.

"Mikhail, of the Second Galactic Alliance—" he used the title on his dog tags "—I have just come from a meeting of the Tribunal."

The weight of expectation settled upon the room.

---

[109] *Gasur:* a town in Mesopotamia, later called *'Nuzi,'* located alongside the Khasa River, a seasonal tributary of the Tigris.

"As I feared," the Chief said, "the Halifians have begun to amass at our border. They're allied with the Uruk, and other mercenary groups who have always coveted our land."

Mikhail glanced at Jamin. The man wore a hooded gaze.

"I have no quarrel with the Uruk," he said.

"But *they* have a quarrel with *us*," Chief Kiyan said. "Especially now that they fear we have a new magician."

Mikhail looked at the shamans who surrounded him.

"Who? One of them?"

"You!" the Chief said curtly. "Word has gotten around you single-handedly killed eighteen men."

"They attacked *me*," he said. "It was purely self-defense."

"The only witness to that attack begs to differ."

Ninsianna burst out: "Jamin is lying! He told me he *hired* them!"

"Silence, woman!" the Chief roared. "You have caused *enough* trouble! I am almost tempted to take Chief Sinalshu up on his offer to get you out of my beard!"

Ninsianna stood with her head bowed, but from the furious copper glint of her eyes, only a lifetime of being told to *'be silent, woman!'* prevented her from ripping the sword out of his hand and whacking her arrogant ex-fiancé on the posterior. Jamin gave a satisfied smirk. He'd *convinced* his father of his version of the story.

"And so I find myself in the untenable position," the Chief said, "that the very person who has caused our enemies to rally is also the sole force keeping them at bay. So tell me, man from the heavens? What would your god have me do?"

The elderly shaman, Zartosht, stood up.

"It would be our honor—" the old man spoke the way one would an equal "—to assume this problem. The advantage Chief Sinalshu seeks is not against Assur."

Chief Kiyan hunched down, his chin upon his fist in a thoughtful pose as he scrutinized the *both* of them with intelligent, watchful eyes.

"I only came here," Mikhail said, "to find out about my people."

"They are dead," the Chief said bluntly.

Mikhail's wings lifted with surprise.

"You knew?"

"Yes."

"How?"

A veiled look passed between Chief Kiyan and Immanu.

"I have my own sources," the Chief said. "But before you had this meeting, I met with each shaman privately."

"You wished to keep me in the dark?" he asked.

"There's no way I'd let a potential enemy pump my allies for information without first ascertaining its value," the Chief said. "They told you what they know which, so far as I can tell, is precious little?"

His estimation of Chief Kiyan went up another notch. The man might be blind when it came to his son, but in all other matters, he appeared to be exceptionally shrewd.

"It appears," Mikhail's voice grew thick, "that my people crash-landed here, just like I did, and *died* here, many generations ago."

A hint of sympathy softened the Chief's expression.

"I know nothing of these things," the Chief said. "Only that once upon a time, there was a temple who worshipped a goddess they *claimed*—" he gestured at the clay statue "—was She-Who-Is' mother. Once each generation they would send an emissary to warn against dark magic. And then they would disappear for another generation."

"When was the last emissary?"

The Chief's expression grew guarded.

"The temple has been destroyed," the Chief said. "This I know for certain. If it hadn't, I would gladly be rid of you."

"Just tell me which direction?" Mikhail's wings drooped "—and I will search for the ruins."

Ninsianna cried out, a small, soft plea. Mikhail turned to face the woman who'd saved his life.

"I came here on a mission," he said. "I can't *remember* it, but I know it's important."

"What about *us*?" Ninsianna said. "According to the song, you're supposed to protect *her*—" she gestured at the clay statue of She-Who-Is "—not a lesser god."

"I don't *know* her," he said.

"Do you remember your own god?"

"I remember training with Master Yoritomo," he said, "and I know what that means, the same way that I remember how to use my sword."

"And what *of* your god?" the Chief interrupted. "What do you remember of him?"

Mikhail opened his mouth to speak, but he could not tell a lie. He remembered how much the Cherubim admired the Emperor. He knew they defended an *ideal,* and that he'd defend that ideal with his dying breath. But when he tried to picture the Eternal Emperor *himself,* all he could recall was Ninsianna, stepping through the light, her eyes glowing golden as she'd kneeled at his side and touched his cheek.

He touched his chest-pocket over his shattered ribcage; the little round pin with the words: *"In light there is order, and in order there is life,"* encircled around a tree.

"I defend the light," he said. "I shall *continue* to defend the light, wherever I may find it."

Zartosht, the elderly shaman from Nineveh, pointed at the clay statue, and sang:

> And SHE shall send a winged Champion
> A demi-god fair and just,
> A Sword of the Gods to defend the people,
> And raise armies from the dust.

The other shamans followed his lead, reciting the song until it echoed off the walls of the temple.

"Do you still have doubts?" Zartosht said to Chief Kiyan, "that the creature that stands before us is not the sword of the gods?"

Chief Kiyan held up his fist. The room fell silent. Jamin stared straight forward, his jaw twitching, every muscle wound tight, ready to spring. Varshab placed a restraining hand on his arm and growled an inaudible warning.

The Chief gestured sarcastically at the shamans.

"If they are correct, a great evil will come to our land. So tell us, Angelic? How will you raise armies from the dust when you can't even *remember* your own name?"

Mikhail lowered his wings. It sounded as ridiculous to *him* as it did, no doubt, to the pragmatic village chief. He voiced the one memory he *knew:*

"A Cherubim needs no weapon but the one She-Who-Is places into his hand."

The Chief's eyes narrowed in a shrewd gaze.

"Very well," he said. "You have until the summer solstice to train my men to fend off the *enemies* you so inconveniently brought to my door. Otherwise, you will *leave.*"

Chapter 55

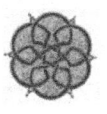

Galactic Standard Date: 152,323.05 AE
S.M.M. Peykaap
Border: Yaris and Zulu Sector
Lieutenant Apausha

Lt. APAUSHA

Three nervous lizards sat in the *S.M.M. Peykaap's* cockpit, watching the clock count backwards towards zero. While technically they'd be emerging into a part of the galaxy which had been mapped, the borderlands were rife with unmarked asteroids, hostile border patrols, and frequently space pirates.

The AI chimed: *'Sixty seconds.'*

Lieutenant Apausha clenched the subspace engine controls. The most dangerous part of hyperspace travel was exiting the wormhole. They had no way of knowing if another ship, an asteroid, or space junk had moved into the path inexpertly plotted via long range sensors.

"Calculate the next jump," Apausha said, "the moment we get into regular space."

"You think someone is monitoring the border?" his co-pilot, Specialist Wajid asked.

"Why take a chance?" Apausha said. "We can't risk the Alliance finding out what General Hudhafah found."

The third crewman and navigator, Specialist Hanuud, began the count as the digital clock counted back to all zeroes: "Five, four, three, two, one. Disengage…"

A stomach-wrenching sensation, like being in a funhouse, staring at your own distorted reflection, made Apausha's head spin. He forced a deep breath, a skill honed over tens of thousands of hyper-jumps, until his earholes stopped ringing.

"Hanuud!" he snapped. "Any contacts?"

"No, Sir," Hanuud said. "I see … wait! One bogey!"

"Another transport ship?"

"No—" Hanuud stared at his deep-space radar. "Alliance. It's a Leonid destroyer!"

Apausha growled deep within his chest.
"ETA?"
"Seven minutes."

"Dragon dung!" The clock counted the seconds for their long-range sensors needed to survey the area they needed to jump into: fifteen minutes. He glanced at his co-pilot. "Wajid?"

"On it, Sir."

The co-pilot flipped through dozens of manual switches, physically resetting the next step in their journey. Yes, the AI could do it, but electronic switches were susceptible to an electromagnetic pulse, and that did *nothing* to solve the *real* problem, the amount of time Hanuud needed to make sure the next jump didn't end up in the middle of a sun.

Apausha pushed power to the sub-light engines.

"They're hailing us!" Hanuud cried out.

"Ask what they want?"

"They're here to conduct a health and safety inspection!"

"Safety inspection, my arse," Wajid grumbled.

A gruff voice relayed a string of boarding instructions.

Apausha answered back: "Unknown vessel, this is the captain. You're breaking up!"

"I said prepare to be boarded!" the Leonid roared as clear as a gamma ray burst.

"Did you say: prepare to sell us whores?"

"Don't play smart!" the Leonid growled. "Submit to a safety inspection, or you'll be cooling your scales in an Alliance brig."

Apausha moderated his voice with practiced calmness:

"We're a peaceful trading vessel, Sir," he lied. "Of course we'll submit. We have nothing to hide."

All three of them glanced back at the bulkhead, thankful he'd stashed the human woman in the furthest cargo hold as she'd taken to screaming each time they exited hyperspace.

"We'll jump short," Apausha said. "Someplace that doesn't need a lot of power, and then jump again." He pulled up the map of the nearest solar system. "Here's an asteroid belt," he pointed. "Good cover, minimal power, minimal risk."

An inaudible thrum vibrated through the ship as the Leonid destroyer pulled alongside. Burly and golden-white, she was built as the Leonids were, incredibly powerful, and filled with sharp teeth and claws.

Wajid whistled: "these things always make me shit my britches."

Me too...

Quiet determination solidified in his gut. The law said no military vessel could surrender. Especially not one carrying what these bastards needed to reproduce...

"Let them go extinct," he muttered. He would steer the *Peykaap* into a sun rather than shame his family as his father had done.

"Sir?" Hanuud's dewlap turned a sickening shade of white.

"Not yet," Apausha murmured.

A metallic *thud* rattled the *Peykaap* as the destroyer's boarding ramp bumped against their secondary cargo-door. Apausha tapped the control for the impulse engines, just enough to deny the boarding ramp a seal.

"What in *Hades* do you think you're doing?" an angry voice snarled over the radio.

"Sorry, Sir," Apausha lied calmly. "We're having a spot of trouble. I'll line it up."

"They're charging their electromagnetic pulse!" Hanuud warned. He yanked the kill-switch to immediately cut power to their sensitive AI.

Apausha diverted power from the starboard impulse engine into his port hyperdrive, using the still-active port impulse engine to disguise the buildup of power while simultaneously lining the *Peykaap* up to the boarding ramp.

"I said power down!" the Leonid shouted.

The Leonid vessel let out a double exponential pulse. All three lizards clamped their hands over their ear-holes. The *Peykaap* shuddered as sine waves warred with the shielding around their electronics.

"Port hyperdrive stalled," Wajid called out.

"It only *works* if the engine is running!" Apausha barked a laugh. "It takes three minutes to recharge the EMP!"

The reactor wailed as Wajid manually diverted power to ignite the starboard hyperdrive. The engine, still *off* when the EMP had hit it, immediately flared to life.

"They're charging weapons systems, Sir," Hanuud shouted.

"Drat!"

Apausha rammed the starboard throttle forward a few seconds before it was ready. With a gut-twisting sensation, the *Peykaap* leaped from far closer to another ship than was either sensible, ethical, or legal, to the other side of the…

Crap!

Looming in front of them…

"Hashem's bushy eyebrows!" Wajid shrieked.

Apausha engaged the starboard impulse engine and maneuvered out of the way just before they rammed into an asteroid. A rock thudded into the hull.

"We came up short!" Hanuud cried out. "We landed *in* the asteroid belt, not on the other side."

"Reset the switches!" Apausha ordered. 'That Leonid destroyer will be on us in a couple of seconds."

The radar beeped the destroyer's proximity, pinging closer and closer, as Hanuud recalculated the next jump and Wajid reset the switches. Apausha maneuvered the *Peykaap* above the gravitational belt which kept this solar system's asteroid system in a semi-straight ring.

"Where's that destroyer?" Apausha asked.

"It's right on our tail," Hanuud squeaked.

Apausha diverted all power to hot-start the second hyperdrive, leaving them sitting ducks.

"How many seconds?"

"Twenty-seven."

"C'mon, c'mon, c'mon," he prayed. If they didn't get the second hyperdrive charged, impulse power wouldn't matter.

"We've got another contact, Sir," Hanuud warned.

"Another battlecrusier?" Apausha's heart sank.

"I'm not sure, Sir," Hanuud said. "It's coming from the coordinates we were *supposed* to leap into."

A massive shape reared up out of the asteroid belt, as big as a command carrier and bristling with spear-like weapons.

Fear tore through Apausha's intestines as he was overcome with the overwhelming urge to shit his pants.

"A Tokoloshe dreadnought…" they all whispered at once.

Rumor had it the bear-like species was an experiment gone wrong, genetically tinkered with by Hashem, and then taken over and *socially* engineered by Shay'tan on a dare. The warlike species had taken *both* side's technology and used it to carve their *own* kingdom out of the galaxy by eating … yes, literally eating, ALIVE … any species who crossed them in the name of their god:

Moloch…

…the Devourer of Children…

……evil incarnate…

…the one and only enemy which had ever caused Shay'tan, and the Eternal Emperor to unite.

"Dreadnought is charging weapons!" Hanuud shrieked.

Apausha gripped the controls and prayed, with every ounce of might, for the second hyperdrive to come back online. A blast of blue-white plasma erupted out of the terrifying warship…

…and passed mere meters from their windshield…

……towards the Leonid destroyer on their tail.

"Shay'tan be praised!" Apausha cried out.

The Alliance ship fired back at the terrifying visage which now hunted *them* as prey, narrowly missing them.

"Coordinates set, Sir—" Wajid looked up from his switches.

Apausha glanced out the window at the Leonid destroyer. Outmaneuvered. Outclassed. Outgunned by the only ship in the galaxy which could outgun a Sata'anic trireme or, sometimes, even an Alliance command carrier. If the Tokoloshe caught them, they would *eat* the Leonids in a great, mass ceremony of cannibalism.

He almost felt sorry for them.

Almost...

...but not enough to risk getting caught with his top-secret cargo.

Red-hot plasma erupted out of the dreadnought's nose cone.

"Sir! It's aimed right at us!" Hanuud shrieked.

Apausha rammed both hyperdrive controls forward. With a burst of light, the *Peykaap* disappeared.

Chapter 56

May - 3,390 BC
Earth: Village of Assur
Colonel Mikhail Mannuki'ili

MIKHAIL

Mikhail set down a rickety bucket filled with water. The second bucket, alas, he clutched to his chest. Or more accurately, he clutched a bundle of sticks.

"Ma'am?" he greeted Ninsianna's mother.

Needa glanced at the broken pile of twigs.

"That's the second one this week!" she snapped.

"I'll fix it," he lowered his wings in shame.

Needa's expression softened.

"Come. Sit." She gestured at the bench. "Let me look at that wing."

He sat dutifully and extended one black-brown wing, five meters in length, almost the entire width of the room. Steady hands slipped beneath his feathers and probed the once-powerful axillary muscles which had begun to deteriorate from lack of use. He grunted as she dug her fingers into the place where his main flight tendon had partially separated from the bone. The radius had healed, but he still couldn't raise the wing any higher than his shoulder.

"Does that hurt?" she asked.

"No, Ma'am."

"How can I help you if you lie?"

He turned to look at her. "I *never* lie!"

"You men," she grumbled. "You're all alike."

He picked a spot on the wall and stared at it, his expression impassive, as she forced the radius to extend far further than he could lift it on its own. His breathing became jagged as she gently, but firmly, forced the metacarpus to straighten above his head. She pressed her shoulder into his humerus to make it *stay* there.

"It's a good thing you're not the enemy—" he exhaled to control the pain. After a moment, his muscles went from trembling to a deep, bone-shaking shudder.

Needa forced the wing a bit higher. Unlike Ninsianna, her mother had no qualms about inflicting pain.

"Enough, woman!" he bellowed.

She released his wing. Instinct caused him to flap it to shake out the pain. His long primary feathers brushed against the wall, knocking a pile of baskets off a shelf and depositing its carefully rolled linen bandages onto the floor.

"I'll pick those up," he said.

"Yes, you will!" Tiny crow's feet crinkled the edge of her brown eyes, signaling she wasn't angry. "You're too *big* to fit inside my house."

"Yes, Ma'am."

She patted his wing affectionately.

"Now raise it as high as you can on your own?"

He raised the wing until it began to tremble, and then forced it higher just to show he *could*.

Needa grunted an approval that sounded sweeter than a thousand heavenly horns.

"That's two hands-breadths higher than yesterday."

"Yes, Ma'am," he said through gritted teeth.

The outside door swung open. Ninsianna marched in, her eyes flashing with a blend of anger and tears. She darted behind him and stood, defiantly, glowering at the door. Her father came in and sat down opposite him at the table.

"I need to speak to Mikhail alone?" Immanu gestured for his wife and daughter to leave.

Ninsianna gave him a look that pleaded, *'please don't let him do this?'* Without saying *what* she needed protection from, she stormed up the ladder to her room.

Mikhail gave Needa a raised eyebrow. The healer scooped up the bandages, her expression cloaked.

"I'll go re-roll these."

She scooted out the back, into the tiny, walled courtyard where they kept the goat penned, but left the door open so she could eavesdrop.

"Well?" Mikhail waited for the shaman to deliver bad news, but Immanu gave him a broad smile.

"It's all arranged," Immanu said. "Starting today, you will teach each member of the Tribunal everything you know."

"The Tribunal?" Mikhail asked. "I thought I was supposed to teach your warriors how to fight?"

Immanu's smile grew forced.

"We thought we'd start with more *practical* activities?"

Ninsianna's voice floated down the stairs.

"He's lying!" she shouted. "Jamin refuses to let his warriors train with you!"

"Ninsianna!" Needa called in from the courtyard. "Don't speak to your father with that tone of voice!"

"Why not?" she sobbed. "Because I won't let him trade me for a herd of sheep?"

Mikhail ruffled his feathers, perplexed.

"I thought your Chief already rendered his decision?"

Immanu sighed.

"The Tribunal fears, if Jamin is forced to train with you, it will come to blows. They'd rather you demonstrate your knowledge before they compel him to overcome his bruised ego."

"A test?"

"Not a test," Immanu hedged. "Think of it more as a sharing of information."

"But I don't *know* what I know! All I know for certain is the Cherubim trained me to fight hand-to-hand."

"What about your sword?" Immanu asked.

Mikhail hid behind an unreadable expression.

"Yes. My sword," he said noncommittally, rather than admit, "*I don't remember learning to use it, or the fight where I killed eighteen men?*" Maybe it was a good idea; to test his knowledge on less deadly skills?

"Okay," he said instead. "When do we begin?"

Immanu's smile returned.

"Now," he said. "Rakshan the flint-knapper[110] has arranged a demonstration."

The shaman rose. Mikhail looked up the ladder to where his daughter peered down, her eyes red-rimmed from crying.

"What about Ninsianna?" he asked.

"She's a healer in training—" Immanu dismissively waved his hand. "She needs to help her mother."

It took every ounce of discipline to not fly up the stairs and gather the teary-eyed beauty into his arms. He ducked out the door and followed her father through the second ring to the opposite side of the village. The villagers parted, but they no longer ran into their houses and slammed the door.

"Why was Ninsianna so upset?" he asked.

"Oh, it was nothing," Immanu said. "She's upset the Tribunal appointed *me* to act as the voice of the goddess."

"The goddess?"

"Yes," Immanu said. "As Chosen One, it's my job to guide you."

---

[110] *Flint-knapper:* a person who crafts tools from stone.

Mikhail kept his mouth shut rather than say, "*I don't believe in your silly prophecies.*"

The street changed as they entered the part of the village where the skilled tradesmen all lived. Potters. Basket-makers. Carpenters. And weavers. Strung across the street, bolts of roughly woven cloth flapped in the breeze to shelter outdoor workshops from the sweltering desert sun. In front of the largest house, a crowd of villagers had gathered in a festive, almost circus-like atmosphere, including two dozen warriors.

"I thought you said they didn't want to train?"

"Rakshan is held in high regard by the warriors—" Immanu shrugged. "If you win his respect, the warriors will pressure Jamin to let them train."

A sense of tightness gripped at his chest, akin to how he felt whenever the women at the well attempted to touch his wings. He felt like he'd fallen down into the well and gotten *stuck* there, with a hundred pairs of eyes peering at him through the stones.

His feathers rustled.

"Couldn't we do this privately?"

"No, no!" Immanu grinned. "I want the entire village to see what you can do!"

Mikhail reached for his hip, but both his pulse pistol, and the sword, lay hidden beneath Ninsianna's bed.

"All I brought was my survival knife."

"That's okay," Immanu said. "Rakshan is more interested in learning how to *make* your weapons, than how to use them."

Mikhail tucked his wings against his back to appear less conspicuous, and also to discourage the constant, subtle tugs on his feathers. They slipped through to the flint-knapper's workspace. A worn felt carpet lay out in front of his house, along with an assortment of poles and sticks, and sturdy baskets filled with different colored stones.

Rakshan the flint-knapper rose to his feet. An elderly man, perhaps early sixties, the youngest member of the Tribunal dressed simply in a work-kilt and woolen cape, with a leather thong around his neck displaying a small, broken atlatl-dart.

"Ahh, Mikhail!" Rakshan said. "Thank you for coming!"

"Sir," Mikhail snapped into a salute.

The flint-knapper gestured at a stool which had been placed beside his three grown sons. Around each man, the carpet was littered with broken pieces of rock.

Mikhail sat.

"The Chief explained you refuse to teach the secrets of your firestick?" Rakshan said.

"Not *refuse*," Mikhail said. "I only know how to use it, not how to build it."

"And what about your sword?"

"I have no memory of crafting the weapon," he said truthfully. "But when I hold it in my hand, I *know* it's made of rocks, forged in fire until it becomes hard."

"Ahh, magic?" Rakshan nodded.

"We call this magic 'metal.'"

"Meh-tell?" Rakshan pronounced the unfamiliar word. "And what of the blade you wear on your hip? Is that made with the same magical spells?"

"Yes, Sir."

Mikhail unclipped the small strap which kept his knife from falling out and handed it to Rakshan. The man's eyes lit up as he pressed his thumb into the blade and drew a crimson bead of blood.

"It's lighter than I thought."

"Yes, Sir," Mikhail said noncommittally.

"And sharp?"

"Yes. Sharper than flint, but an obsidian blade seems to cut almost as well."

"What can you do with it?" he asked. "Other than cut meat?"

"Everything I've seen Immanu do with a stone blade," Mikhail said. "Plus use it to defend yourself."

"Do you remember learning?" Rakshan asked.

Mikhail closed his eyes and pictured holding the knife in a defensive stance. While his muscles tingled, ready to perform the moves, he couldn't actually *remember* learning how to knife-fight.

"No, Sir," he said softly. "When I need it, my body does it, but I cannot *picture* what I know."

Rakshan picked up a stone blade which, given the bright white sinew,[111] had only recently been pieced together. It was a fine blade, chipped from the finest flint, with an elaborate horn handle.

"So what would I have to do to transform this stone knife into one like yours?" Rakshan asked.

Mikhail turned it over in his hands. Ever since he'd healed enough to begin repairs on his ship, he'd wracked his brains, trying to pry out the secret of forging metal. But while he recognized some of the local rocks *might* yield usable minerals, he had no idea how to get the metal out of the rocks, much less transform it into exterior hull-plating.

"I don't think this is the right kind of rock."

---

[111] *Sinew:* animal tendon, used for bowstrings or thread.

"What about *these*?" Rakshan gestured at the baskets. "We gathered every stone we could think of."

Immanu beamed a pleased expression. It appeared that he, and the Tribunal, had brainstormed about how to pry information out of his recalcitrant memory. Mikhail knelt before each basket and examined the stones. While some appeared quite beautiful, none carried the desired weight or feel.

"It looks like this?" he held up a verdigris rock that sat, all by itself, in a small, wooden box. "See this vein of orange? The substance you're looking for resembles this. But I'm not certain this is the right kind of metal." He pressed his fingernail into a thin, copper line. "In fact I'm *certain* it's not the right mineral. But the process to extract steel would be similar."

A middle-aged man at the front of the crowd said, excitedly: "that's what the trader said who sold me that stone!"

Immanu gestured at the man.

"Mikhail, this is Lagash, our goldsmith."

"You work metal?" Mikhail asked hopefully.

"Silver and gold," the goldsmith said, "but I haven't figured out the secret of extracting copper."

He held out a metal bracelet, verdigris-green, with a glimpse of copper shading where it wore smooth against his wrist. Mikhail took the bracelet and held it up against the light. While he recognized the stone, and the metal which could be rendered from it as important, the bracelet did not whisper the secret of extracting metal from a rock.

"I'm sorry—" he handed the bracelet to Rakshan. "I'm afraid I've never *personally* forged metal from this stage."

A voice carried from the back of the crowd.

"What good is he, then? A man who refuses to share?"

Over the heads of the curiosity-seekers, Jamin glared back at him with hateful, black eyes. The crowd skittered to make a path, fearful of standing between the Chief's vengeful son and his prey.

"I never claimed to possess the secrets of forging metal," Mikhail said.

"But you swore to teach us what you know?"

"I don't remember…"

"You expect us to *believe* that?" Jamin swaggered forward, his arms held wide to embrace the crowd.

"You were *there* the day I crashed," Mikhail said. "You *saw* how badly injured I was. I could barely stand."

"All that I *saw*," Jamin hissed, "was an enemy, expunged from the heavens, who decided to kidnap my *woman!*"

He reached for his knife-handle.

Mikhail flared his wings.

The crowd darted back to give them room to kill one another.

"Jamin!" the flint-knapper stepped between them. "We have already *discussed* this!"

"You *said* he would teach us something important!" Jamin growled.

Rakshan held out his hand.

"Your father deferred this decision to *us*," he said, "because he does not wish to *choose* between this knowledge and his only son."

"Cowardice!" Jamin spat.

"It's called *diplomacy*," Rakshan said. "We have chosen to give the stranger time to either integrate into our village, or to go his own way as our *friend!*"

Jamin jabbed a finger at him over Rakshan's head.

"He can't remember anything," Jamin said. "He brought enemies to our gate. He can't even *fly!* And now you expect these villagers to *feed* him?"

Mikhail's wings drooped. Where mercenaries and outright assault had failed, his adversary's *words* found their mark.

"That's enough!" Rakshan snapped. "The Tribunal has warned you about the consequences of continued aggression."

Jamin gestured at the warriors who stood behind him, each of them armed with spears.

"There's nothing to see here!" he shouted. "As you can see, the Angelic brings us NOTHING!"

Jamin backed up, never taking his eyes off Mikhail, the way a warrior *should* when facing down an enemy. With a mocking Alliance salute, the Chief's hateful son disappeared.

Mikhail let out a long, slow breath, whispering the Cherubim prayer to resist killing his enemies.

The crowd dispersed, some mimicking Jamin's cry that he was a burden, others murmuring that it would not behoove them to infuriate their future chief. The goldsmith, however, stayed.

"Come," Rakshan said. "We ruled this would be an *exchange* of ideas. Let us teach you that, perhaps, we are not as primitive as we might seem?"

Chapter 57

May – 3,390 BC
Earth: Village of Assur

NINSIANNA

She found him seated on the roof, staring at the dying sun as it cast the last rays upon the mountain which marked the location of his sky canoe.

"Mikhail?" she called out.

He lowered a wing and glanced back, his expression unreadable. Ninsianna grabbed a small bench and sat down next to him. The sunset reflected off his skin, accentuating his chiseled features and giving the impression he'd been carved from stone.

"I heard what happened," she said.

Mikhail stared down at a pair of stones he held in his hands. Around his feet lay hundreds of tiny flint-shards.

"It was nothing," he said. "I knew when I came here your *fiancé* doesn't like me."

He stared west. If he'd been able to fly, she had no doubt he would have already *flown* back to his sky canoe, to battle the Halifians to the death, rather than integrate into Assur.

"He's not my *fiancé*," she said.

Mikhail resumed hitting the flint with the striker. Flick! Flick! Flick! A shard split off. He dropped it into the growing pile, and then tapped the striker along the edge, preparing the stone to split off the next razor-sharp shard. A drop of crimson fell onto his feet. Another drop fell. Not a trick of the sunset, but blood.

"Mikhail? Your hands?"

She gripped his hands and forced him to release his grip. Both the striker, and the flint, were completely saturated with blood.

"What happened?" she asked.

"I can say, with certainty," he said bitterly, "that I've never knapped a spearhead before."

She pried the flint out of his hands, revealing dozens of cuts, and a deep, angry gash which still bled.

"Why didn't you say something?" she asked.

"It's nothing," he mumbled.

"What if it becomes infected with evil spirits?"

He fingered the golden tree-pin he kept pinned to his chest; and the angry, red wound he kept hidden beneath his shirt.

"According to your father," he said, "I'm some kind of demigod. And if I'm not?" he shrugged "—what does it really matter?"

Her mouth fell into a surprised 'O.' This was the first time, since the day Jamin had ruined the silver spear he called *antenna*, that she'd seen him express anything approaching self-pity.

She darted downstairs to grab her healer's basket and a goatskin filled with water. When she climbed back up, Mikhail stared west like a statue. He did not flinch as she rinsed the blood from his palms.

"So Rakshan taught you flint-knapping?" she made small-talk.

"Yes," he said.

She examined the largest cut, picking out bits of dirt.

"How many spear-heads did you make?" she asked.

"None," he stated flatly. "I broke every stone I touched, including an obsidian spear-blank."

Ninsianna forced her expression to remain neutral. Obsidian was traded from a distant tribe, so only the most experienced flint-knappers would attempt to shape one. Even the cast-off shards were reused, knapped into tiny points and embedded in a stick to make an awl, a cutting tool, or a war-club.

She smeared his hands with a liniment made of honey mixed with myrrh-sap and ash. From the way one wing twitched, it stung, but he did not say a word as she wrapped his hands with linen and sang a healing song.

That thread of power which connected her to the goddess tingled through her body and flowed into his palms. She could almost *see* his mortification, what it had *felt* like to be shamed in front of the entire village. She held his hands far longer than was necessary, but he did not pull away, even after she stopped singing.

"Why were you were upset this morning?" His unearthly blue eyes stared into hers.

"You already know."

"The bride price?"

"Yes."

He stared west. "Where I come from, I don't *think* you'd be considered payment for a debt."

She forced a bright face.

"They only ruled we must *repay* it by the summer solstice," she said, "not that I have to marry him."

"By marrying somebody *worse*?"

She swallowed. "If that's what it takes."

He stared west.

"Your father said he used it to trade for the goods he brought out to my ship—" he met her gaze "—which means you're in this predicament because of *me*."

"It's not your fault."

"If I'd forced you to leave, he wouldn't have mortgaged your future."

"Then I'd be stuck with Jamin."

"It appears you'll be stuck with him either way."

He picked up the flint and striker and resumed his fruitless hits.

"If you reopen that cut—" she channeled her mother "—I shall thrash you within a fingers-breadth of your life!"

His mouth twitched upwards in an expression she suspected might be amusement. For a creature of heaven, once you got to know him, Mikhail behaved remarkably like a human man.

"I want to *learn*—" he knapped off a shard "—so I can repay your father what I owe."

"It takes a long time to learn to knap flint," she said.

"I'm persistent."

"Perhaps you might be good at something else?"

His feathers rustled, revealing an inner maelstrom.

"I don't *remember* what I'm good at—" he said bitterly. "I don't even have the nightmares anymore!"

A sense of guilt settled into her gut.

What am I supposed to say? That She-Who-Is helped me bind what few memories you had left?

"Tell me about them?" she asked. "What do you dream of, when you wake up screaming?"

Mikhail stared at the mountain, now backlit by pink and red and yellow.

"Every night, when I had them, I prayed the nightmares weren't real. Only now that they're gone—" his voice grew thick. "Now that they're *gone*, I feel like I just lost what little bit of *me* survived the crash!"

She grabbed his wrist, where he was about to knap off another chunk of rock which would no doubt split his hand back open.

"Sometimes, if you tell your dreams to a shaman, they can help you recapitulate them?"

"Recapitulate?"

"Yes," she said. "Reincorporate bad memories back into your psyche, so they no longer act as an invitation for demons."

He stared west.

"I can never remember them—" he reached towards his empty hip "—but they have to do with my sword."

Ninsianna had *seen* the dark child in the nightmare reach for the sword, but what had *really* terrified her was the way the shadows moved every time he cried out for his mother.

"Have you ever feared the dark?" she whispered.

"No," he said. "The Cherubim believe the dark can be your friend."

Her brow knit together.

"Is that a memory?"

His thoughts turned inward as he searched for the source of that assertion.

"I guess, maybe it is?" he said.

"How do you know?"

His expression turned wistful.

"The same way I know how to use a sword—" he held up the flint and striker "—or that I *don't* know how to craft a spearhead."

They fell into silence, the only sound the *clink! clink! clink!* of stone striking against another stone. Never had she met somebody so *determined* to make their own way, without any help from anyone…

…not even the gods…

Great Mother, she prayed, *how do I help him?*

She waited for the prescience which had compelled every action when she'd been back at his sky canoe, but ever since she'd come back to Assur, the goddess had remained frustratingly silent.

What if Papa was right? That *he* was the Chosen One? And *she* was just the bait to get him here?

Goat bollocks! It felt like the goddess was *waiting* for something to happen. Until then, she would use her head.

"What if you tried a bit of everything?" she suggested. "See if you know how to do things, and if you do, it will tell you something about your past."

"And what if I don't know how to do it?"

"Then you'll know you never learned that skill, and that will *also* tell you something."

They both stared west at the ink-black mountain, now backlit only by the faintest hint of grey. The wind picked up moisture from the river. Cool and damp, it felt like the inside of a cave.

Ninsianna shivered.

"I *hate* the dark," she said. "When I was little, I got scared and ran away."

"Into the desert?"

"Into a cave."

"How old were you?" he asked.

"Three," she whispered. "I ran away the day my grandfather died."

Emotion gripped at her throat, her abject terror as the shadows had pursued her. It had never made sense, the compulsion to climb down into the well. Only that it felt as if the shadows had deliberately driven her down there.

"Obviously you found your way out again?"

"After three days…"

She wrapped her arms around her herself, reliving the sound of dripping water, the way her stomach had clenched from hunger, and the dark shapes which had swirled all around her.

"Whenever I wake up screaming," she said, "*that* is what is what I dream of."

Mikhail lifted one wing and settled it around her to block the wind. He ruffled his feathers, sharing the gift of their soft, luxurious warmth. It filled her lungs with a glorious, musky scent that reminded her of spice.

"It's not the darkness you have to fear," he said, "but what walks in the open, pretending to be the light."

Chapter 58

Galactic Standard Date: 152,323.05
51-Pegasi-4 – Genocide Memorial
Prime Minister Lucifer

LUCIFER

The Seraphim memorial was an angry, black wound which cut into the once-productive soil like an open grave. Carved of black obsidian hauled in from a distant volcanic asteroid, precious few people had come to witness the unveiling of a monument which marked the passing of an entire species.

Lucifer descended the steps, into the fertile soil his ancestors had loved more than they loved the Alliance, its petty politics, or the genetically engineered hybrids who had failed to meet their impeccable moral standards. His snow white wings drooped as he stood in front of the stark, black walls which listed the names of the people who'd been murdered. It would have made a magnificent publicity shot, if anyone had cared.

A pair of Sata'anic lizards, dressed in full ceremonial uniform, knelt at the wall and placed a bouquet of flowers beneath the part which memorialized the Sata'anic farm workers. A lone reporter snapped a picture. Lucifer stared down at the speech he'd prepared, and set it aside.

"Today is the 25th anniversary of the 51-Pegasi-4 genocide," he said. "Eleven million people lived on this planet, including races that elsewhere would call each other enemy—" he gestured at the Sata'anic emissaries. "They were spiritual beings who'd evolved beyond their baser impulses, to reach a state of perfection so pure that, in several lifetimes, it was anticipated they would evolve into gods."

He bowed his head.

"Unfortunately, they forgot that Utopia is just a dream. They chose a planet far from the Alliance's protection. They wanted to be left alone. So we left them alone."

His voice warbled.

"-*I*- left them alone. It was within my power, while my father was absent, to station warships in this sector, but they had no resources. Nothing to offer in trade. They were a completely self-enclosed world who wanted nothing to do with us, so we, in turn, wanted nothing to do with *them*."

He closed his eyes and caught his breath. He could almost *feel* the screams of the dying as he spoke.

"My mother's people came from this planet," he said. "I *should* have protected them, but I didn't, because I was *so* angry she died that I refused to seek diplomatic ties after Hashem disappeared!"

Tears streamed down his cheeks at the jumble of grief and loss.

"I would like to observe a moment of silence."

The ceremony broke up as soon as he finished the dedication. The media circus which dogged his every step was as conspicuously absent as the people who *should* have been living on this planet and were not. Nobody cared that the Seraphim had taken all hope of evolution with them, just as his father didn't care that the hybrids that defended him were also going extinct.

An elderly couple, well into their 900th year, made their way over to where he stood, not awe-struck the way people usually acted around the Alliance Prime Minister, but with that strange ease of equality his mother had practiced even though she'd never stepped foot upon the Seraphim homeworld. Their steel-grey hair and once-dark wings betrayed them as full-blooded Seraphim, two of the few who'd been off-world the day the genocide had happened.

"We knew your grandmother—" the elderly woman shook his hand.

"It was tragic," the elderly man's hands trembled with age. "What Zuriel did to her ... ouch!"

The elderly woman elbowed her mate in the ribs.

"I never knew them," Lucifer said. "They both died before I was born."

His mother had never told him *why* his grandparents had been cast off of this planet. Perhaps she'd not known herself? Should he ask? No. It only rubbed salt in the old wound of his mother choosing to abandon him.

"The genocide was not your fault," the man interrupted his thoughts. "We chose this planet because its only resource was its fertile soil."

Lucifer noted the hollow circles beneath the old man's eyes. The elderly Seraphim's spirit had already begun to separate from his body. It wouldn't be long before whatever ailment was eating away at him killed him.

"Soon we'll reunite with our children and grandchildren." The old woman took her husband's hand.

"I can feel them waiting for us," he said, "just but on the other side."

A rush of emotion stole Lucifer's breath. Those were the exact same words his mother had whispered with her dying breath. He looked away so the couple wouldn't see his eyes were too bright and shiny.

The elderly couple shuffled into the fading sunlight. The frail wife helped the even frailer husband along, the last remnants of an extinct species.

His comms pin beeped. He glanced at the key-code and let the message go to an automatic recording. Zepar kept trying to get him off to a diplomatic mission with the Tokoloshe Kingdom. Screw the cannibals! They were the *last* species he wanted anything to do with.

Keying in a different comms frequency, he called the commander of the *Prince of Tyre*.

"Yes, Sir?" Commander Marbas asked.

"Tell Zepar I'm spending the night on the planet."

"He's been frantic to get hold of you, Sir," the commander said. "He was furious when we told him you ordered us not to provide transport."

"I don't answer to Zepar!" Lucifer snapped. "Tell him I'll be back in the morning!"

He cut Marbas off before he could give an argument. He reached into his inside pocket and pulled out a slender flask, filled with his favorite poison, and snuck a nip.

He relished the burn as the potent green Mantoid liquor worked its magic to sooth his jangled nerves. *Choledzeretsa* was technically outlawed because it had a mild hallucinogenic effect, but he'd gutted out the legislation meant to enforce it so it could be bootlegged with impunity.

The few attendees lit candles and lay flowers along the long, black wall before getting into their shuttle craft and departing. There were no accommodations on this planet. No hotels. No restaurants. Just burned out farm houses, already taken back by Mother Nature, and kilometers of empty fields.

He pressed his back into the cold, black obsidian and sank to the ground, alone, for the first time in decades. He encircled himself in his wings and took another nip, contemplating the demise of his species as the sun was replaced with a waning silver moon.

"Is this spot taken?" a voice rumbled.

Lucifer lowered a white wing. A middle-aged Leonid stood before him dressed as a civilian, but nothing could hide the fierce build of a space-marine. Lieutenant-General Valepor's leonine eyes reflected the scant moonlight.

"It's an empty planet."

He didn't feel like company, but it was a public memorial.

The Leonid sat, his tail twitching as they both stared out at the darkness. Lucifer snuck another nip, and then handed the flask to Valepor.

The Leonid took a long, powerful dreg and wiped his whiskers with the back of his clawed hand.

"Mine was the first Alliance ship to arrive at the scene," Valepor said. "I've seen some terrible things in my lifetime, but they slaughtered every living creature and burned the bodies."

"Was there any indication of a reason?" He knew there wasn't, but sometimes, things didn't make it into the official report.

"This wasn't about resources," Valepor said. "Somebody wanted to make an example of these people."

"The sole eyewitness said it was Sata'anic soldiers?"

"The uniforms were the old style—" Valepor shook his furry mane "—more than a century out of date. Shay'tan's a butcher, but this just wasn't his style."

"What did the witness say when you first encountered him?" Lucifer asked. "In the moment, not what my father made him say in the official report?"

"He almost took out half a squadron with that sword he was carrying when we tried to remove his mother's body," Valepor said. "The sword was bigger than he was, but he was determined to protect her."

"The official report says he was catatonic?"

"That was *after* we got the sword away from him," Valepor said. "He crawled underneath his bunk and refused to come out until the Emperor, himself appeared, and promised to never disappear again."

The Leonid snorted.

"Two hundred years. And he comes back to talk to a kid?"

Lucifer grabbed the flask and took a long dreg to numb his resentment. After the genocide, Hashem had returned from the ascended realms and started managing his empire again. Only the Emperor was no longer interested in *him*, but on running genetic tests on the first full-blooded Seraphim to come off of 51-Pegasi-4, not because he was defective, but because the kid was too young to tell the Emperor to *"go to Hades!"*

"So why'd you come?" Lucifer asked.

"I'm still stationed in the sector," Valepor said. "It seemed right to come. It's disappointing that so few did."

"My Chief of Staff was spitting fire." Lucifer gestured at the memorial. "No PR value in coming to a dead planet. He's still under the illusion my father's breeding program will save the day."

"Bullshit," Valepor said softly. "It hasn't worked for *us*. I've managed to sire one pair of cubs during all my years of trying. Most of the poor guys now can't even do that. We're going the way of the Wheles."[112]

"We'll be right behind you." Lucifer snuck another nip. "I've pleaded with the Emperor to pay attention, but he doesn't know how to fix us. He's already put in an order to retrofit your carriers to fit Spiderid physiology."

He passed the flask back to Valepor.

"I don't mind the bugs—" Valepor's whiskers drooped. "They pull their weight. I just don't like the fact that this is a problem we can't *fight*! It's not our nature to go down without a battle."

---

[112] *Wheles:* once one of the most highly evolved species in the Alliance, the Wheles chose to stop incarnating into mortal form. They are now extinct.

"I just don't understand why the Seraphim didn't fight their killers?" Lucifer said.

"They even slaughtered the Sata'anic civilians." Valepor ran his claw across a Sata'anic surname which bore the Seraphim *'il'* suffix. "Shay'tan keeps the females confined to the Hades cluster, so once they defect, they have no hope of ever starting a family. I found a lizard curled around a Seraphim child, trying to use his body as a shield to save her. They killed him. And then they killed the little girl. But only the boy fought back and lived."

"Utopia is great in theory," Lucifer said, "but in real life, there are too many assholes waiting to take it from you." He twirled a snow-white feather, a nervous habit he'd picked up from his mother. "I shouldn't talk. I'm as greedy as any of them."

"And yet you're the only one who came," Valepor said.

Silence stretched out between them. Yes. Why *had* he come?

"Our species is dying," Lucifer sighed. "It seemed the most appropriate place to spend the afternoon."

The general's comms pin chirped. His transport had arrived. They shook hands and parted ways, leaving Lucifer alone with the ghosts which haunted this world.

What would he do if he could go back in time and warn his younger-self? Would he protect this planet's genetic resources? Or would he make the same mistake that Hashem had done? Spurn this world, because the Seraphim had chosen to spurn *them?*

Gradually he dozed off and dreamt of Seraphim who followed their mates into the dreamtime rather than live without them, and a dark, evil thing which devoured everything in its path.

A bird singing woke him up before sunrise. He followed the sound to a nearby orchard, heavy with fruit even though nobody had tended these fields for twenty-five years. He found the bird in a broad-limbed tree. Not *that* tree, but the song was pleasant, even if it was only an echo of the song he longed to hear. Beneath its spreading branches, the elderly Seraphim couple he'd met yesterday lay curled up in the untended grass between a cluster of gravestones, fast asleep in each other's arms.

The bird flitted down to one of the gravestones, marked with the last name the couple had given yesterday, and tilted its head back and forth, watching him with pert, yellow eyes. The couple did not move. Lucifer crouched down and touched the bodies whose pale expressions mirrored utter peace.

He touched his comms pin and keyed in a specific frequency.

"Eligor?" he asked.

"Yes, Sir?" a voice answered.

"I'm ready for extraction."

"I'll be there in twenty minutes, Sir."

Lucifer touched the elderly woman's cheek. *She'd* still had a vigorous life force, but she'd cast her spirit into the dreamtime, rather than live without her mate.

He touched his comms pin a second time:

"Eligor?" a lump rose in his throat. "Could you please bring a shovel?"

There was a brief silence.

"Was there a problem, Sir?"

"No," Lucifer said. "They came here to be buried with their family."

Chapter 59

May - 3,390 BC
Earth: Village of Assur
Colonel Mikhail Mannuki'ili

MIKHAIL

The north gate opened onto a modest ledge which the river had eroded to create a pathway down to their fertile fields. Unlike the south gate, which enjoyed the warm, drying rays of the Mesopotamian sun, the north gate faced the river and showed serious signs of decay; from the mildew-stained boards to the termite-holes which marred the two tree-trunks anchored into the adjacent walls. On the alluvial plain beyond, the river had begun to recede, laying bare the Ubaid fields, protected from flash-floods with low stone walls. The wind carried up the scent of fertile silt. The ordinary villagers, the ones who lived in the outermost ring, bent over the fields, planting their allotment of grain.

"We're going to plant?" Mikhail asked.

"No!" Immanu snorted. "We're not farmers!"

He led him down the steep embankment, perhaps a hundred meters high, then along the edge of the fields. A pregnant woman, surrounded by three children, straightened up from her work and waved.

"Do you know her?" Immanu asked.

"I carried home her water."

"That work is *beneath* you!" Immanu snorted.

"I'm not good at anything else."

They crossed a small footbridge comprised of a pair of logs which spanned a feeder-stream tumbling down from the desert, already slowed to a trickle. On the other side, the spry old man who'd spoken with the Chief oversaw a group of workers who busily hacked away at an enormous tree which had been dragged up out of the water.

"Mikhail, this is Behnam," Immanu said. "He's a member of the Tribunal."

"Sir?" Mikhail tucked his wings into dress-wings.

The old man peered up at him with curious, wrinkled eyes.

"So I hear you wield weapons, but don't know how to make them?" Behnam asked.

"Yes, Sir—" his wings drooped. "It appears that is the case."

"No matter—" the old man gestured at the men who labored over the logs. "The only skill you need for *this* job is a strong back and a certain amount of skill wielding an axe."

He introduced him to the men who labored in the sun, all of them stripped down to their work-kilts as they used stone hatchets to trim off the smaller branches. Around them scurried boys who gathered each cut-off branch and sorted them into piles, while a girl moved through the workmen, ladling cups of water from a bucket.

"You might want to take that off?" Behnam pointed at his uniform shirt.

Mikhail touched the place where the crash had shattered his ribcage. He didn't feel like advertising the fact his left-hand side was still weak; from his broken wing, to the wrist which still ached, to the limited mobility caused by the damage to his pectoral muscle.

"I'd just assume leave it on, if you don't mind?"

Behnam gave him a toothless grin.

"Very well. But by the end of the day, you'll wish you had!"

He bent down easily for one so advanced in age and hauled up a stone axe, perhaps a meter in length, with a long, sharp shard of flint anchored into the handle.

Mikhail scraped his finger along the edge. While not as finely wrought as a spearhead, the stone was sharp.

"Rakshan's work?" he asked.

"One of his grandsons."

The old man put him to work, trimming off the branches. As he worked, he explained how, each spring, when the river swelled, the Anatolian tribe of far north would float hardwood trees downriver. The further one got from the Taurus Mountains,[113] the higher the price. *This* far south, hardwood fetched a magnificent price, indeed.

"What's wrong with those trees?" Mikhail gestured at a grove which grew on the other of the fields.

"Those are date-palms," Behnam said. "Good for goat pens, but when replacing boards on the front gate, you don't want something a battle-axe can go through with a single stroke."

"I noticed it was rotted."

"For the last six years, Nineveh has purchased every log the traders floated downriver," Behnam said. "The only reason he let *this* one pass is because his shaman wanted to speak to you."

"I thought Nineveh was your ally?"

Behnam gave him a grim smile.

"*'Ally'* is a matter of convenience."

---

[113] *Taurus Mountains:* mountain range in southern Turkey whose eastern edge forms the headwaters of the Tigris (Heddekel) River.

The workmen chopped off the last errant branch, leaving a single, large log, perhaps six meters in length and a meter around. Behnam handed him an oddly-shaped stone wedge, devoid of any handle.

"This is what we use to split the log," he said.

"It's not that sharp." Mikhail fingered the edge.

"It doesn't need to be," Behnam said. "You *hit* it with a club."

He demonstrated how to use a stone axe to chip out a groove, and then jam the stone wedge into the place where you wanted to split the log.

"How do you make sure the entire log splits?" Mikhail asked.

"Teamwork—" Behnam gestured at the other workmen, who did the same "—and a fair amount of skill."

The old man bent to peer behind the wedge, using line-of-sight to line up the other wedges. He moved down the line, personally adjusting each wedge, and barked instructions at the waiting men.

"Every tree contains a spirit," the old man explained. "If you listen to the tree, the log will split evenly and give you much valuable wood."

Mikhail put his hand on the trunk, but felt nothing.

"What happens if you don't sense this spirit?"

"Then the log will shatter," Behnam said, "leaving you with splinters."

A prickling of his feathers caused him to look up. On top of the riverbank, a pair of hate-filled black eyes glowered down at him, flanked on either side by a dozen curious warriors.

"Now it's *your* turn—" Behnam handed him the stone axe. "Cut a groove, and then set your wedge."

"What if I set it wrong?"

"Don't worry about it," Behnam said. "This is the first split. It will take many cuts to split it all the way through."

The old man gave him a good-natured pat on the back of his wing. Mikhail picked a spot in the center of the log and painstakingly lined up a spot to chip out a groove and jam his wedge in.

The stone axe felt awkward and heavy. He dropped it twice, and once he smashed his finger. Up on top of the riverbank, the warriors chuckled about his lack of skill. He suppressed the urge to tell them that he *had* a steel hatchet, back at his ship. He'd used it to help Ninsianna cut scrub brush for their cook fire, but he'd left it behind, only able to carry so many supplies.

"Okay, tree," he murmured to the log. "Make me look good?"

He realized the other workmen had long ago set their wedges. He stepped back, embarrassed to hold up progress.

"Now what?" he asked.

Behnam pointed at a long, thick club with a good-sized stone securely lashed between a forked branch.

"Now you hit it with a splitting maul."

The other workmen stood poised above their wedges, ready to strike. Mikhail picked up the maul. It had to weigh a good ten kilos.

"When I count to three, you hit it," Behnam said, "as hard as you can."

"...if he can hit it at *all*," a sarcastic voice floated down from the riverbank.

"Yeah," a second voice taunted. "He'll probably miss and crush his foot."

"Ow!" a mock-girly voice called. "I broke my toes!"

Mikhail's feathers reared up in their follicles. That dark sense of anger which nipped at his subconscious whispered to *show* them. To *smite* the warrior's arrogance the way one might lop an enemy's head off. He flared his wings and raised the stone maul up over his head, every muscle in his body poised, the way he would hold his sword when swinging a decapitating blow.

"Watch. He'll probably miss!" Jamin's voice floated down from the riverbank.

We'll see if I miss, if we ever cross swords in battle...

"One..." Behnam counted.

He pictured Jamin's head lay on top of the stone wedge, his black eyes staring up at him, laughing at him, taunting him.

"Two," Behnam counted.

He focused every ounce of resentment into his muscles. The taunts, the insults, the pent-up urge to *kill*...

"THREE!" Behnam shouted.

He swung the maul with every ounce of his might, giving Jamin's imaginary head the blow he *should* have given him the night he'd attacked his ship. He felt the anger, the darkness, the *rage*. The rock at the end of the stick connected with the stone wedge. It reverberated with a bone-jarring *CRACK*!!!

The handle snapped...

...the rock flew back up and smacked him in the forehead.

Stars danced.

It felt like a hyperdrive, hurtling into a black hole.

He stared up at...

...faces.

.....the taste of blood.

.........A pair of too-large black eyes appeared above his face.

—"Mikhail? Come and find me!"

—*He ran through the orchard, peering up into the trees.*

—"Olly-olly-encomtree!" *he called out.*

—*The tree giggled. He flew up into the branches.*

"Amhrán?" his voice warbled.

"Here. Drink this?"

She pressed a cup to his lips.

—*"You know I'm going to find you!"*

—*He couldn't see her, but she was there, hidden among the leaves.*

He reached towards her.

"Hah!!!" the warriors roared from the riverbank. "He doesn't even know how to use an axe!"

"Get away from him, you harlot!" another voice roared.

The too-large eyes disappeared, replaced by Immanu's tawny-beige ones, holding the cup. Mikhail took a sip until the stars stopped spinning.

"What happened?" he mumbled.

"You hit with more force than we expected," Immanu said.

Mikhail sat up. He touched his forehead and came away with blood.

Immanu helped him back to his feet. He shook the dirt out of his feathers. Behnam, and the other workmen, stood over the log, staring down with dismay at the smashed and splintered center, squashed flat like a piece of flatbread. Except for the lack of burns, he might as well have shot it with a pulse-rifle.

Mikhail's wings drooped.

"I'm sorry," he said.

Behnam's face wrinkled in a sympathetic expression.

"Come back tomorrow," he said. "It appears this log's spirit wishes to be turned into other things?"

Chapter 60

Galactic Standard Date: 152,323.05
51-Pegasi-4 – Genocide Memorial
Prime Minister Lucifer

LUCIFER

Long and sleek, with a pair of muscular hyperdrives tucked neatly beneath a pair of stabilization fins that resembled a leviathan's tail, Lucifer's flagship, the *Prince of Tyre,* echoed an eloquent, almost organic grace which was otherwise absent from the Alliance's contemporary shipbuilding.

Lucifer twirled a snow white feather, silently replaying something his pilot had said as they'd laid the two dead Seraphim into the ground. Or more precisely, *revealed,* due to his ability to *see* the emotions which lay beneath another person's words. It wasn't like he'd ever talked much to the taciturn Angelic, but Eligor had always been around, keeping the engines running and, on more than one occasion, helped him shoot his way out of a dicey situation.

"Who was he?" Lucifer asked.

"He?" Eligor said.

"Your Seraphim relative," Lucifer said. "My father never inducted you into his army."

Eligor flipped through his pre-landing checklist. For a moment he feared the man might tell him to go piss off, but then his wings rustled.

"Does it matter?"

"Yes."

Eligor avoided answering by hailing the *Prince of Tyre* air traffic controller and announcing their intent to land. The man was difficult to read. He'd always been too busy to notice the lack-of-thought of his hired mercenaries.

"I had a Seraphim grandfather," Eligor said at last. "When he got kicked off, he made sure his offspring stayed as far away from the Alliance as they could."

Lucifer preened his long primary feathers.

"Do you know *why?*" he asked.

"Why he stayed away?"

"Why he got kicked off?"

Eligor grunted.

"He didn't like following all their rules."

The radio crackled as the *Prince of Tyre* air traffic control ATC Officer relayed their landing instructions. As they navigated the double airlock, that small, nasty inner voice that he'd successfully been ignoring began to grow louder.

'Zepar is pissed…'

"I'm in charge of the Alliance," Lucifer muttered.

'That's what you said until your father got back…'

'Shut up!' he ordered the voice, which always seemed to nitpick his deepest fears. It was a point of contention. He'd run the Alliance for more than 200 years until Hashem had come back and announced he wasn't pleased with how he'd run his empire.

Maybe he should apologize? Tell his father the trade deal was to fend off unnecessary hybrid deaths?

Eligor called back as the second airlock opened.

"Sir," he said dryly. "It appears you have an honor guard."

Lucifer unbuckled his flight harness and peeked out the front windshield. Standing in the flight hanger, flanked on either side by a brutal, matched pair of white-winged Angelics, stood his Chief of Staff Zepar, the man who *really* ran the Alliance when it came to knowing where all the skeletons were buried.

"Honor guard, my tailfeathers!" Lucifer muttered.

"Sir?" Eligor queried.

"Just back me up—" Lucifer patted him on the shoulder. "Tell him—" he wracked his brains. "Just tell him the shuttle broke down and you weren't able to bring me back until today?"

Eligor donned an unreadable expression. The man might be a bad-ass mercenary, but Pruflas and Furcas, the pair Zepar assigned to protect him, scared the shit out of *everybody*. Including Eligor…

Lucifer strutted towards the dirty-winged Angelic, ignoring his most *un*-obsequious expression, the moment the ramp touched the flight deck.

"Why, Zepar!" he elongated the 'r'. "Did you catch those *magnificent* publicity shots the reporter took?" He flared his snow white wings in an artful politician's pose. "I want them broadcast to the entire Alliance."

Zepar's dishwater blue irises picked up the artificial light, making them appear red.

"What were you thinking?" he shrieked. "We had an *appointment* with the Tokoloshe king to discuss promethium[114] mineral rights!"

Lucifer leaned forward.

---

[114] *Promethium:* a rare-earth element which can be used to formulate an unusually stable form of fluorescent light and also nuclear batteries.

"I was *thinking*—" he hissed, not in the mood to play puppet-prince "—that the *last* thing I want is to be invited to *dinner* by the cannibals! Especially for something as trivial as glow-in-the-dark paint!"

"While you were off *gallivanting* on a useless publicity stunt—" Zepar jabbed a crooked finger "—the Tokoloshe king interpreted your absence to be a snub!"

"So send them some potted flowers—" Lucifer waved his hand dismissively. "So sorry we missed your state dinner. Who did you eat, again? Your grandmother—" he cupped one hand by his ear "—did you say she was old and tough?"

Zepar lowered his voice to that deliberately obsequious one, the one which usually preceded a political knife in the back.

"Jophiel sent a *battlecruiser* to secure that disputed mining planet," Zepar hissed. "When you didn't show up, the Tokoloshe interpreted it as an act of war!"

"I say, let the Leonids off their leashes," Lucifer said. "They've been chafing at all this peace. Whaddaya say, Eligor? Maybe we could sell tickets? The match of the century?"

He turned to the goon, Pruflas.

"Aaaaand, Ladies and Gentlemen, we have here, on the left, big, drooly and vicious, the Tokoloshe cannibals. It's a match to die for... Literally."

"Lucifer," Zepar interrupted. "We need that promethium for—"

Lucifer cut him off.

"And here on the right—" he turned to the *other* goon, Furcas "—we have the Alliance's finest. Our brave Leonids. They'll tear you apart. But while they're doing it, don't they just look magnificent?"

"Lucifer!" Zepar said louder.

"So who will you bet on? The Cannibal King? Or the Leonid Lions? Step right up and place your bet. This is better than the Emperor's chess game. Defeating the Tokoloshe. The only thing he and Shay'tan ever agreed upon."

He leaned towards Zepar.

"WE DON'T MAKE DEALS WITH THE CANNIBALS!!!"

A stab of pain gobsmacked him between the ears. Lucifer's head snapped back as his eyeballs rolled back into his brain.

"The Tokoloshe *ambushed* them!" Zepar shrieked.

Lucifer grabbed his head as he fought the sensation that someone had just clobbered him in the back of the skull.

"Ambushed?" he choked out.

"Yes!" Zepar shrieked. "The Tokoloshe ambushed the Leonids."

His blood roared in his ears as that nasty voice grew louder.

"H-how?" he whispered.

"The battlecruiser sent a distress signal," Zepar said, "but since then, we've heard nothing!"

Acrid bile rose in Lucifer's throat.

"Did they ... sacrifice...them?"

"Maybe. You just *personally* snubbed the Tokoloshe king."

The flight deck swayed. Lucifer flapped his wings, fighting to remain upright. The Leonids? Invited for dinner? To a Tokoloshe feast where the main course was their still-screaming victims?

Eaten alive?

"Are you okay, Sir?" Eligor grabbed him by the elbow.

"It's just a migraine—" Lucifer said weakly. "I've had them most of my life."

The flight hanger grew dark as his field-of-vision narrowed into a tunnel. The sound of his crew faded, until all he could hear was his inner voice taunting:

'They -ate- them! They -ate- them! It's all your fault they ate them!'

"I'll take care of this!" Zepar dismissed the pilot.

The world went black as Pruflas and Furcas helped him back to his room.

Chapter 61

May – 3,390 BC
Earth: Village of Assur

NINSIANNA

Inside the village, a woman's tasks consisted of homemaking, gathering food from the fields, and picking up after the men. But whenever Mama got too busy, she sent *her* around to perform the less life-threatening healing calls.

The chubby, dour-faced teenager had cut the bottom of his foot. He tried to appear tough as Ninsianna untangled her bundle of horse-tail and threaded a long, stiff hair through one of Mikhail's steel sewing needles.

"Isn't this spectacular!" she held the needle up to the light. "Look at how thin it is? It will barely leave a scar."

The boy's plump face turned pasty as she squeezed the two flaps of flesh together. His name was Ipquidad, the soft-spoken son of a tradesmen. At the rate he was growing, soon he'd be almost as tall as Mikhail.

"This will hurt—" she warned.

"I'm not scared!"

He let out a yelp as Ninsianna punctured his flesh.

"Breathe!" his mother coached as Ninsianna stitched.

She tied the thread off and then dipped the needle in the strong-smelling embrocation Mikhail had let her take from his sky canoe.

"Stay off that foot for a week," she ordered. "Keep the dirt out. And be sure to change the bandage every day."

Ipquidad nodded, his eyes filled with tears.

The boy's mother poked at the stitches.

"This magic is amazing!" she said. "I can *see* why the Chief is fascinated by the winged one's weapons."

"This isn't a weapon," Ninsianna said. "It's a healer's implement."

"But it *could* be?" Ipquidad interrupted. "Couldn't it?"

"Not this."

The mother picked up the strange, clear urn of embrocation and gave the peculiar liquid a sniff.

"What was it like?" she asked. "To be held prisoner inside a shooting star?"

"A prisoner?"

"Yes. Jamin says you were held against your will?"

Ninsianna's cheeks flushed red with irritation.

"And what else did Jamin say?" her voice grew cold.

Ipquidad answered: "He said be on the lookout for things which might be more deadly than they appear."

Mother and son both eyed the needle as she put it back into the leather wallet she used to keep it from getting lost. That sense of *knowing* whispered where the kid was weak.

"Since when does Jamin give you the time of day?"

Tears appeared in the plump-faced teenager's eyes. Though big for his age, and the right age to begin warrior training, Ipquidad was the kind of good-natured teen the elite warriors liked to make fun of.

She smeared one of her mother's liniments onto his foot. Ipquidad whimpered as it burned into his open wound. She bound it with a strip of linen, far less gently than normal.

Damn Jamin! Damn him for being so thick-headed!

The boy's mother offered her the usual token of bread and a measure of grain. Normally, she would only take the bread, but she had a bride price to pay back, and idiots like *this* who kept making her life more difficult by feeding into Jamin's lies!

"Thank you," she said curtly.

She stepped out into the sunlight and noted its position near the horizon. Hopefully Mama had gotten back to start the lentils for supper? Otherwise, their dinner would be late because *she* had been tied up, making house calls the entire day.

"Ninsianna!" someone called her name as she passed into the second ring. "Wait!"

She glanced back.

Oh. Great...

She considered running, but Jamin, unfortunately, had seen her. She walked faster, praying he'd take a hint, but he ran to catch up, not even slightly winded.

"Ninsianna?" he touched her shoulder. "Please? We need to talk?"

She whirled to face him, not because she wanted to, but because Mama had ordered her to make her peace with him and, *dammit!* If she couldn't pay back the bride-price, between him and the *Muhafiz* of Nineveh, she'd much rather not be forced to *move*.

"What do you *want?*" she snapped.

"Did you hear what happened?"

"Happened where?"

"At the woodworking area?"

So this was going to be one of *those* conversations, eh? Where Jamin spun conspiracy theories because Mikhail had no idea how to wield a stone tool?

"Of *course* I heard—" she searched for an escape route.

"What do you think of it?" he blocked her exit.

"I *think* you'd better reinforce the north gate before an enemy comes and slips—" she ducked beneath his arm "—through a hole in the rotted wood."

He gripped both of her forearms.

"So we agree?"

"Yes." She backed up and hit the front of a mud-brick house. "Of course we agree. We have to fortify our defenses so the Evil One can't breach our walls."

Jamin grew excited.

"We will start with the two gates, and then we can figure out how to stop the lightning?"

He prattled on about the destructive blue lightning, and what it would take to outfit his warriors with weapons as powerful as Mikhail's.

Was it possible? That her father's plan had worked? Had Mikhail finally shown him something spectacular enough to pique Jamin's interest?

She gave him her warmest smile, desperate for him and Mikhail to get along.

"About the lightning," she said, "I've been thinking about what to do when the Evil One finally arrives."

"You have?"

"Yes," she said, her expression animated. "I'd like—" she formed an image of his deepest desire and touched his arm, picturing the thought passing into his mind "—to hold a mass ceremony to reinforce the magic, like my grandfather did when he built the southern gate. Only *this* time we know She-Who-Is will listen."

"Because she speaks to you?"

"Yes—" she hugged him ecstatically. Nobody, not even her *father*, had ever believed that she could speak to HER. "And then we'll ... I don't know?" she prattled on. "Maybe we can bring some magic from the sky canoe?"

Jamin's face split into a beautiful grin, for a moment reminding her that she hadn't been *entirely* reluctant the day she'd told him she would marry him. He wrapped his arms around her, filling her nostrils with his warm, earthy scent.

"I *knew* you would come to your senses!" He kissed the top of her hair. "The others believe it was an accident. But you? You've *seen* what the bastard is capable of."

Ninsianna's brow knit together in confusion.

"An accident?"

"Yes," Jamin said. "I've never seen anything like it. He smashed the entire tree."

"What tree?"

"The one my father bought to rebuild the rotted north gate. He completely crushed it, so now we have no wood."

A sense of vertigo blended with exasperation. The *tree?* The one old Behnam was supposed to teach Mikhail how to split into boards?

"Jamin," she said crisply, "the goddess wants you to *train* with him. Not spin plots against her Champion."

"Her *Champion?*" Jamin stiffened. "So you're still in league with him?"

"In league?" Ninsianna laughed. "All I'm trying to do is get you two to stop trying to *kill* one another!"

"How can you say that, after he nearly killed you?"

"Killed?" she said. "Is *that* what you're telling people now?"

"Yes." He leaned forward so his nose pressed against hers. "I was *there* when he held his sword to your neck, and he DID NOT WANT to stop."

Her hand flew instinctively to protect her throat.

"No—" she said weakly.

"Yes—" he ran his finger across the place where the blood-stained sword had pressed against her neck. "That *thing* which lives inside of him almost *killed* you, because you dared stand between *it* and its prey!"

She backed away, not wanting to *remember* the soulless creature which had stared out of Mikhail's pitiless black eyes. Jamin stepped forward, a lion that had cornered a gazelle.

"She-Who-Is *spoke* to him," Jamin said. "I was there. Remember? He only stopped because SHE ordered him not to kill you!"

Ninsianna's lip trembled.

"He stopped, because he—"

"Loves you?" Jamin's black eyes grew intense.

She shook her head.

"Mikhail barely notices I exist."

Jamin's expression was pure relief.

"Ninsianna—" his dark eyes pleaded. "Can't you see? He is only here to weaken our defenses."

She backed away from him.

'Mother!" she prayed. *'I do not want to hear these lies!'*

"Is everything okay?" a voice asked.

She turned towards her saviors, two old women; the younger sister fit, but nearly blind; the elder clear-sighted, but bent painfully over her cane.

"Yalda," Jamin said with formality. "Zhila. Have you made your decision?"

"Yes, *Muhafiz*—" Yalda used his formal title. "The log is beyond all hope of salvage. The best Behnam can do is turn it into trinkets."

Jamin gave her a dark look which communicated: *'See? I told you.'*

"And who is going to *pay* to send an expedition to the Zagros Mountains,"[115] Jamin asked, "and float a fresh hardwood tree downstream so our north gate does not remain undefended?"

"The act was not deliberate," Zhila said. "Every man there said he simply failed to grasp how *effective* our stone tools are."

Jamin's swarthy complexion turned almost purple.

"I *watched* what he did!" he said. "Mikhail smashed that log on purpose!"

"If he *did*," Zhila said dryly, "he wouldn't have knocked himself unconscious."

"Unconscious?" Ninsianna asked with surprise.

"Yes, unconscious," Yalda said. "The maul-handle broke and threw the axe back onto his head."

Jamin backed up, his dark eyes filled with recriminations.

"You were *there*—" he ran his finger along his neck. "You *watched* him butcher eighteen men."

He turned and, with an arrogant motion that showed his status as their *Muhafiz*, rearranged his shawl back onto his shoulders, and then left as though he was already the Chief.

Ninsianna turned to the widow-sisters.

"Please?" she said. "Tell me everything that happened?"

*

She climbed up onto the roof with a basket of flatbread. Mikhail sat facing west, towards the mountain, his magnificent dark wings an impenetrable wall as he stared at the life he'd left behind.

His feathers rustled as she came up behind him, but he did not turn to greet her.

"Yalda sent over some bread," she said. "She makes the best in the entire village."

"The old woman who met us at the gate?"

"Yes. She heard what happened."

"So now I'm an object of pity?"

She sat down next to him and placed the basket in front of him. When he didn't take a piece, she picked it up and held it towards him, waiting for its still-hot scent to work its magic. He took it without turning to face her.

"How bad is it?" she asked.

"Your mother gave me seven stitches."

---

[115] *Zagros Mountains:* a mountain range that spans north-east Iraq, Iran and Turkey.

She touched his chin and *made* him turn to face her, revealing the big, red lump which bulged out of his forehead like an antelope's horn. Seven brown stitches marred the perfect, chiseled features that even falling from the heavens had been kind enough to spare. Ninsianna didn't know whether to laugh, or cry.

"That's one heck of a black eye?" she said.

He turned away.

"I'm not *good* at being human," he grumbled. "All I know how to do is kill."

She didn't know what to say. In *this*, both Mikhail, and Jamin, agreed. But if there's one thing she'd learned about him, it was that Mikhail had no tolerance for self-deception, flattery or excuses. She stood up and moved to stand behind his broken wing.

"Mama said you can lift it as high as your head now?" she asked.

"Yes."

She waited for more, but of course he said nothing.

"Let me massage the bone," she said. "Maybe it will help?"

He stretched out the wing and let her massage around the main flight tendon, digging her fingers deep into the muscles until it released the tension. As she worked, she sang a song about overcoming demons, pulling light from that thread of power she drew from She-Who-Is.

Her hands grew hot, the way they *always* did whenever she helped somebody heal. Mikhail sighed as she coaxed the metacarpal up above his head.

"I had a memory today," he said.

"Yes?" she paused.

Mikhail stared west.

"At least I *think* it was a memory?" he said. "There was a girl. She looks a lot like you, only her eyes are black. She gave me water, and I remembered, as a child..." he trailed off.

"What happened as a child?"

"I don't remember," he said. "I was looking for someone, in a tree. When she spoke..."

"What?"

Mikhail sighed.

"I'm not sure. All I remember is her eyes."

A peculiar emotion clenched at her gut. But what did a girl from his past have to do with now?

She released his damaged wing and moved to massage the undamaged one, but Mikhail twitched it away. Ever since the day he'd killed the Halifians, there'd been a barrier between them; as big and impenetrable as Assur's outer wall.

Her father called up.

"I'll be right back," she said.

She climbed down the ladder. Her father stood in front of the wooden chest where he stored the implements of his magic. He held up an empty vial of poppy-seed extract.

"Ninsianna?" he asked. "I'm going to ask you a question, and I want you to tell me the truth."

Ninsianna swallowed. Papa always *knew* when she told a lie.

"Yes, Papa?" she said innocently.

"Three times this week I've refilled this vial, and each morning, I've found it gone."

Ninsianna glanced up, at the ladder.

"I was trying to teach myself how to recapitulate bad memories."

"Mikhail's?"

"Yes." She gave him a sheepish look.

Papa's eyes glittered copper-red, a latent power he rarely displayed, but it had always terrified her, especially when she'd been a little girl.

"Do you know what the penalty is for a woman accused of sorcery?" he asked.

"I only did a bit of dreamwork," she said, "to ask the goddess how to help Mikhail."

"The only way to speak directly with the goddess," Papa said, "is to bury yourself in the earth and negotiate with her *husband*."

"But how am I supposed to guide Mikhail—"

"It's not your *job* to guide him!" Papa said. "She-Who-Is chose *me!*"

"But I'm the one who *found* him!"

"To lure *me* out into the desert!" Papa pressed his palm against his heart. "She knew I would do *anything* to get my only child back!"

Ninsianna lowered her head.

"But she *spoke* to me," she said. "She spoke *through* me, the day she wouldn't let him kill Jamin."

"You expect me to believe this?"

"Just ask Jamin," she retorted. "He heard *HER.*"

Papa sighed.

"Mikhail's memory loss is the will of She-Who-Is. You have to stop forcing him to remember."

"He can't remember because *SHE* asked me to bind his nightmares!"

"You have no such skill!" Papa dismissed her. "You're just a woman."

"I'm your *daughter!*" Heat rose in her cheeks. "Why would grandfather pass his abilities on to *you,* and not also to me?"

"In case you forget, you're not the *only* granddaughter of Lugalbanda!"

"Gita has no magic!" Ninsianna said. "You said it yourself. Your brother inherited no gifts!"

"Well Gita was there when he hit himself on the head," Papa said. "He acted like he knew her. And then he pestered me the rest of the day, asking who the water-bearer was?"

A cold chill settled into Ninsianna's gut.

"Gita gave him water?"

"Yes."

"What does it matter?" her voice warbled. "Her father is the village drunk."

Her father lowered his voice.

"You know what her mother was," he growled. "Just *how* she led men astray."

A sense of *fear* ripped into her gut.

"Mikhail is *above* such machinations," she whispered.

"Not *this* machination," her father hissed. "His daughter was *born* at the Temple of Ki. My brother will use her to gain the winged one's ear."

"But the temple was destroyed."

"What if Merariy tells him otherwise?" her father said. "He'd like nothing better than to declare that *he* is the Chosen One because he, and *only* he, knows how to find the ruins?"

Tears welled in her eyes.

"But Mikhail seems so lost," she said. "Maybe we should *tell* him?"

"And have him *run off* with the daughter of a whore?" Her father slammed his fist down. "She-Who-Is sent him to *my* daughter, to *this* village, and broke his wing so he couldn't fly away. If *SHE* wanted him to find the temple, she would have dropped him out of the sky, right on top of the ruins."

"But what if we're supposed to help him find it?" she implored.

"The desert nearly *killed* my brother," Papa shouted. "He was gone for seven years, and when he came back, he was a raving lunatic, and every man we sent with him was *dead*. Do you *really* want to do that to Mikhail?"

Ninsianna's lip trembled. Uncle Merariy was a bitter, angry drunk who frightened her even more than Papa when he got angry. Jamin was right. Papa hadn't *seen* Mikhail the day he'd killed the Halifians. What would it do to him, if he succumbed to the desert-madness?

What would it do to *her*? If Mikhail left her behind?

The sound of footsteps caused *both* of them to fall silent. Ninsianna looked up.

"Is everything okay?"

Mikhail perched on the ladder, his wings bunched into an awkward position as he squeezed down the hole. He looked so pitiful, with his face all swollen and bruised, and ugly stitches that would likely leave a scar. It made no difference that he'd inflicted this wound upon *himself*. He looked like a kid who'd been beaten up by a bully, not a creature of heaven.

Right now, the only evil appeared to be *them*...

"We were just talking about what you're supposed to learn tomorrow," Papa lied. "Behnam asked you to bring your knife. He wants to learn how *you* would craft wood, and then he'll try to adapt it to using Ubaid tools."

Chapter 62

Galactic Standard Date: 152,323.06 AE
Zulu Sector: Command Carrier 'Light Emerging'
Colonel Raphael Israfa

RAPHAEL

Raphael examined the holographic map of the Orion-Cygnus spur of the Milky Way galaxy. Different colors marked the solar systems they'd scouted, red for uninhabitable, yellow for systems with planets or moons that might support life for a brief period of time, and green for M-class planets that could support life long-term. There was precious little green…

…and an awful lot of grey marked *'Unexplored.'*

He gripped at his hair, grown out of its crewcut because he'd been too darned *busy* to make a trip down to the barbershop, and *yanked* it in frustration. For seventeen weeks there'd been no sign of a homing beacon or Sata'anic activity which might indicate where Mikhail had been shot down.

He paced back and forth, molting buff-gold feathers as his sense of mission warred with his *need* to contact Jophiel. It felt as though his heart had been cleaved in half, with part wanting to find his best friend, while the other half screamed, "go and visit your son!!!"

"Where are you?" he stared at the hologram. He couldn't believe Mikhail was dead. He *wouldn't* believe it! After all he'd been through, to die, anonymously, on some uninhabited planet. The last living Seraphim…

…had died *alone.*

A soft alarm warned of an incoming communication.

"Sir," Major Glicki gestured towards her console. "Somebody has opened a subspace wormhole."

Raphael rushed to his commander's chair, his heart singing.

"Put her on the main screen!"

A golden image solidified on the screen. Raphael's face dropped as furry, golden ears, a reddish-brown mane, and sharp fangs set into a powerful jaw appeared. The most animalistic of the four hybrid species, Leonids resembled their leonine ancestors, now extinct after the catastrophe at Nibiru, but they possessed the enhanced intelligence and opposable thumbs of a human.

Attached to his crisp uniform collar, four golden stars attested to the Leonid's rank.

"It's General Re Harakhti from the *Emperor's Vengeance*, Sir," Glicki chirped with surprise.

Why was the highest-ranking *Leonid* directly contacting *him*?

"General Harakhti—" Raphael saluted. "What can I do for you, Sir?"

"I hear you're looking for suspicious activity?" Harakhti rumbled.

"Yes, Sir," Raphael said. "Anything coming in or out of Zulu sector."

A low growl erupted out of the Leonid General's throat.

"We intercepted something you might find interesting," Harakhti said. "They claimed to be traders, but then they pulled the *ballsiest* damn maneuver we've ever seen."

"Sata'anic?" Raphael guessed.

"Sata'an Merchant Marine," General Harakhti said.

"What class of ship?" Raphael leaned forward in his commander's chair.

"Never seen anything like it," Harakhti scratched his whiskers. "But when we ran it through Central Command, an order came down from the Supreme Commander-General *herself* to open up a micro-wormhole and call you immediately."

Raphael's wings drooped. Normally, Jophiel would have used it as an excuse to relay the information, but since Uriel's birth, she'd refused to return his calls. The screen flickered as Harakhti sent the image, along with holographic coordinates where the ship in question had emerged.

A terrifying brown mass appeared on the viewing screen. Large and squat like a gigantic carnivorous predator, bright red plasma beams erupted out of the Tokoloshe dreadnought straight towards the ship recording the image.

In-between the camera, and the dreadnought, lay the ship Mikhail had been shadowing the day he'd disappeared.

The screen went to static.

"Did they escape?" Raphael asked. He wasn't talking about the smuggling vessel.

"They went down fighting," Harakhti said solemnly. "We lost 162 Spiderids and sixteen Leonids, but nobody was captured alive."

Raphael bowed his head. With less than 2,600 Leonids left in existence, every lost Leonid was an irreplaceable loss.

At least they weren't crucified and eaten alive...

"What were they doing that far out?" Raphael asked.

"There's a couple of Alliance mining colonies in the borderlands," Harakhti said. "The Tokoloshe Kingdom invaded a nearby planet, so we sent some ships to discourage further aggression."

Major Glicki enlarged the image to identify the suspicious ship.

"Algol-class," she confirmed. "No tail markings, but identical to the ship the Colonel was shadowing the day he disappeared."

A small sense of victory warred with sadness over the Leonid destroyer's fate.

"I take it they didn't get on board the suspicious ship?" he asked.

General Harakhti growled in the style of an old-school general who had earned his stripes the hard way ... in battle.

"From what it *appears*," he roared, "that ship led my men right into a trap!"

Raphael scratched his chin. It would be a cold day in Hades before Shay'tan would ally with the Tokoloshe, but a Sata'an merchant vessel of questionable parentage?

"Might be a defector?" he said.

"I don't know," Harakhti snarled. "But the next time we see that ship, we're going to shoot first, and then sift through the wreckage!"

Raphael knew better than to argue with a four-star General. He'd relay a request to Jophiel and let *her* talk-shop to the officer immediately beneath her. *One* thing was for certain. Every Leonid in the fleet would be out hunting for that smuggling vessel.

"Thank you, General," Raphael gave him a crisp salute. "You have given us a search boundary in an area of infinite space."

"Glad I could help," Harakhti said. "If we encounter anything else, I'll pass it along."

The screen went blank.

"Micro-wormhole closed," Glicki announced.

Raphael bowed his head. The rest of the bridge-crew did as *he* did, gave a moment of silence for the 162 Spiderids and sixteen Leonids who'd lost their lives.

"May She-Who-Is guide their spirits into the Dreamtime," he murmured.

"May the Emperor *personally* guide them to the gateway," the bridge crew replied in unison.

"Amen," he said.

He rose to his feet and stalked over to the holographic table.

"Did you mark those coordinates, Glicki?"

"Yes, Sir," his efficient second-in-command replied. "I'm triangulating a new search area ... now."

The red circle they'd used to delineate the search area contracted slightly, leaving a still-unfathomably large uncharted area where Mikhail's ship could have gone down. Seventeen weeks it had been since he'd sent a distress signal. Had the smuggling vessel been travelling round-trip all that time? Made several trips? Or had it set down someplace, and then resumed its journey?

"Damantia!" Raphael cursed. "We just don't know!"

Chapter 63

June - 3,390 BC
Earth: Village of Assur
Colonel Mikhail Mannuki'ili

MIKHAIL

As far as buckets went, it was neither beautiful, nor artfully made, but he'd *made* it, *damantia!* Without steel or glue or modern nails, unless he counted the pine resin he'd used to waterproof the wooden slats. More importantly, he hadn't resorted to his knife. Old Behnam had taught him how to use stone tools.

The old man handed him the *first* two buckets he'd made, several week's work, for a total of three. One that was *his*, plus two to replace the stick-buckets he had broken, though for *those* he'd cheated and used his titanium knife.

"See?" Behnam said. "I *told* you that log wanted to be made into smaller items."

"What about the north gate?"

"Last season we had a generous harvest," he said. "The Chief will trade for another log, and *this* time, we won't let you anywhere near the splitting maul."

The old man gave him a good-natured pat on the wing. An errant emotion tugged at the corner of Mikhail's mouth. All day long he'd felt giddy, as though something had turned a corner and, finally, he might get something accomplished?

"What shall we build tomorrow?" he asked.

"We'll turn those into staffs—" Behnam gestured at the pile of branches they'd trimmed off the tree trunk "—so you can begin to teach my apprentices how to do that thing. What did you call it again?"

"A training kata."

"Yes. A *training* kata to lay our enemies out on the ground. It seems to be a rather practical skill."

The old man shot him a toothless grin that communicated, *'sorry, this was the best I was able to do.'* Jamin kept making it clear there was no way *he*, or his warriors, would ever train with him.

"Thank you, Sir," Mikhail said. "I look forward to teaching them."

He gathered up the buckets and ducked out the low gate which led to Behnam's workshop, out into the street, and made his way down to the lower well. So what if he couldn't train the warriors? The Chief had only ordered he had until the summer solstice to train his *men*.

The sentries called out their usual sharp warning as he passed into the outermost ring, but the women and children, the ones he'd carried water for, greeted him by name. The little girl who'd befriended him his first morning in the village called his name and ran to catch up to him.

Pareesa fell into step beside him.

"Good morning, Little Fairy," he greeted.

"I see you finished the buckets?"

"Yup." He resisted the urge to grin. "Carved *entirely* with my own hand."

The girl skipped to keep up with his longer step. Perhaps it was his imagination, but she seemed taller and ganglier than she had only several weeks before. Her long legs carried her without much need for him to slow down.

"I thought you have to babysit?" he asked.

"Not today," Pareesa grinned. "Granny came to help with the baby."

This time of the day, with planting season in full swing, most of the village was down working in their fields. An elderly woman struggled with a stick bucket stuck in the well. He helped her unjiggle it, and then pulled up a bucket full of water for her.

"She-Who-Is favors you," the old woman thanked him.

"I'll settle for She-Who-Is not ruining my brand new bucket, Ma'am."

He held it up, showing off, but he couldn't resist. Along with the woodworking lessons had come memory-echoes that he'd worked with wood before, even if that skill was largely unhoned.

He tied the rope to the bucket and dropped it down, careful to avoid the ledge. It made a hollow thud as it hit the bottom, and then came up with only a small dreg in the bottom.

"What happened to the water?" he asked.

"It's beginning to dry up," Pareesa said. "You'll have to finagle it down into the hole."

"A hole?"

"Yes," Pareesa said. "There's one place in the well that's deeper than the rest."

"Where?"

"Right between the place where it always catches."

Mikhail tried again and, this time, the rope went deeper. It snagged as he pulled it up, but the sturdy bucket navigated whatever obstacle lay more than a hundred meters down.

He stuck his head down into the hole as he dropped down the second bucket.

"I hear running water?"

Pareesa shrugged.

"All I know is the more the river drops, the more the water drops inside the well. In a few more weeks, this well will run completely dry."

He pulled up the second bucket, noticing the way the water tugged at the rope. The hole was small, just barely big enough for the bucket. Was this the well Ninsianna had fallen down?

"I think it's some kind of underground stream?" he said.

"Like the river?"

"Yes," he said. "Only smaller. Inside a cave."

He glanced south, towards the center of the village. It was too bad he couldn't look down upon this village from a birds-eye view.

"I'll bet the same stream feeds all three wells."

"Then how come this well, and the other one, always go dry?"

A man called out Pareesa's name.

"I've got to go," she said with a sour expression.

She skulked off as though she was being led to her own execution. Her father gave him a dirty look, and then chided her for skipping off without doing her chores.

Mikhail tied a rope to the third bucket and dropped it down, listening for the way the wood echoed up through the stones. He flared his wings for balance and stuck his head in, listening as he moved the bucket back and forth, gauging the depth.

What if he climbed down there with one of Rakshan's stone axes and split the stone shelf that kept eating the buckets? If, as he suspected, the well tapped into an underground stream, opening the hole up further might mean the village had *two* reliable wells, instead of just one? Maybe *that* would be a valuable enough labor for the Chief to forgive Ninsianna's bride-price?

A light hand tickled his feathers.

"I see Ninsianna has conned you into doing her work?" a brassy voice laughed.

Mikhail looked up. A tall, well-formed woman stood in front of him, carrying a bucket. Her shawl-dress was woven from the finest linen, decorated with fringe, and strategically tied to leave one breast artfully exposed.

He averted his gaze.

"Excuse me, Ma'am?" he said. "Am I blocking your way?"

The woman gave him a too-friendly smile.

"In my way?" she laughed. "Oh, goodness, no! I was enjoying the fine sight of your posterior in, what do you call these—?" she ran her hand down his hip in a suggestive manner.

"Excuse me?" he sputtered.

"Such a pity, to cover such fine, muscular legs?" she said. "An *Ubaid* man would take the opportunity to flash a little ooh-la-la when they bend over—" she coyly flipped her hair "—if you know what I mean?"

Mikhail's wings jutted straight outwards. He'd been cast down from the heavens and battled eighteen men, but…

"I—" he gave an awkward gasp.

"Now if you came home with *me*—" she ran her hand suggestively down the front of his shirt "—my father would find you some *man's* work. Nice, hard—" she reached towards his crotch.

Mikhail stepped backwards and tripped over the low wall which surrounded the well. He pounded his wings for balance as he tumbled backwards.

"Watch out!" a voice cried out.

A familiar *tingling* filled his chest with warmth as Ninsianna grabbed his hand and yanked him back from the brink of falling. He fumbled forward and crushed his sweet savior to his chest.

"Is féidir liom a bhraitheann tú, chol beag,"[116] he murmured so the others wouldn't understand his words. *I can feel you, little dove.*

He pulled her into his side, encircling her with one wing in a universal male gesture of *"I'm taken! Now go away!"*

"Please tell your father—" he told the harlot "—thank you, but I *have* work! Starting tomorrow, I begin training Behnam's workmen how to fight."

The brassy harlot clamped her hand over her mouth and giggled. The other villagers who'd come to get their water gaped. In the street in front of him, Ninsianna stood, carrying a covered basket. Her expression shifted from recognition, to confusion, to betrayal…

"Get away from him, you bitch!" she shrieked.

She threw the basket…

…at *him*!

Mikhail flapped one wing in front of his face and ducked…

Ninsianna stormed towards him, her eyes flashing golden-copper.

"You *tricked* him!"

Mikhail instinctively pulled Ninsianna closer and tried to protect her.

No.

Not Ninsianna.

Angry-Ninsianna stood directly in front of him. Which meant helpful-Ninsianna…

He looked down…

---

[116] "I can feel you, little dove."

...into a pair of terrified black eyes. Identical to Ninsianna's. Only the girl's emaciated features made her eyes look preternaturally large and black, like a nocturnal animal dragged involuntarily into the sunlight.

"You're ... not...?"

— *Olly-olly-encomtree!!!*

— *The leaves giggled. A pair of eyes peered out, solid black, and devoid of any light.*

He let her go...

With a frightened squeak, the scrawny girl bolted out of the prison of his wings.

Ninsianna strode up to the girl and struck her.

"Stay away from him!" she shrieked. "You—!" She hit the black-eyed girl again. "Filthy—!" She hit her again. "WHORE!!!"

The sunlight caught her irises, making them appear fiery red. Mikhail gaped as Ninsianna hit a smaller, darker version of *herself...*

"Sweet mother of whores!" The brassy harlot honked a trumpeting laugh. "Did you see that? The winged one thought Gita was *you!*"

The other villagers laughed, which infuriated Ninsianna even further. She clawed at the black-eyed girl's eyes.

"Tell your father he can't *have* him!" she screamed. "He is not the Chosen One! She-Who-Is sent him to *me!*"

The black-eyed girl took off...

...Ninsianna ran after her.

Mikhail stood like a big, stupid statue of an Angelic, gaping...

The brassy young woman called after Ninsianna: "I guess he figured out you're not the only woman in Assur, huh?"

She turned towards him, her expression calculating.

"I wonder what would happen—" she stepped forward "—if I told Jamin—"

Mikhail backed up like a terrified prey animal.

"—that I'd lain down with *you*—" she stepped forward again "—instead of lying down with *him?*"

He grabbed the basket Ninsianna had thrown at him and held it out in front of himself like a terrified cadet fending off a horde of alien berserkers.

Curiosity seekers came out of the houses to see what was causing such a ruckus.

"Is there a problem, Shahla?" an elderly woman called out.

Mikhail backed away from the brassy young woman, more terrified of *her* than the Halifians back at his ship.

"Ninsianna?" he called out. "Ninsianna! Wait!"

Abandoning his new buckets, he hurried after her.

Chapter 64

June – 3,390 BC
Earth: Village of Assur

NINSIANNA

She marched through the north gate, sobbing.

"He doesn't want me!" she cried out to the goddess. "I saved his life, and then he turned to *her!*"

She ran down the path that led to their fields as Mikhail called out her name. He caught up with her at the bottom of the hill, holding her basket.

"That wasn't what it looked like."

"Go away!" she shrieked.

She pushed past him and marched into the fields.

He followed after her.

"Ninsianna? I don't understand?"

She whirled to face him.

"Shahla? You wanted to lay down with Shahla?"

His brow knit together, perplexed.

"But didn't you hit—" he moved his hands, like a man might do when flipping something over "—the other one—"

"It doesn't matter," she shrieked. "I DON'T CARE!!!"

She knocked the basket out of his hands and ran, sobbing, towards the river. He caught up with her and grabbed her shoulder. She balled her hands into fists and pounded against his chest.

"Go away!"

He grabbed her wrists and yanked her into his arms.

"I'm sorry, I'm sorry—" he encircled her with his wings. "Whatever I did to hurt you, I'm sorry."

"You *embraced* her!" Ninsianna hiccoughed.

"The girl stopped me from falling into the well," he said. "That's all. That woman, Shahla, almost knocked me in. The other one caught me. I thought she was *you*."

She stared up into his beautiful, haunted eyes, even bluer than the sky.

"The only reason I'm *here* is because of you," he stroked her hair. "If you really want me to leave, I will go."

Leave?

"W-what?" she sputtered.

"I'll go away," he said. "But I'd really hoped to pay off my debt first? So your father doesn't marry you off to whoever comes calling with a bag of gold."

"You're here out of obligation?"

"Well, yes," he said. "Why else would I be here?"

"I thought—"

Oh. What a *stupid* little girl she was! He'd always been clear he had a mission to complete. He was here because he didn't have a choice. She-Who-Is had broken his wing so he wouldn't be able to fly away.

Papa was right. Some Chosen One *she* was turning out to be!

Ninsianna burst into tears.

"But I thought. You. Might. Want. Shahla—" she babbled incoherently. "She's. Jamin's. Old. Girlfriend."

Mikhail crushed her against his chest, encircling her in the safety of his wings.

"I'm not good with people," he murmured. "There are lots of unwritten rules that I just can't comprehend. But if I lose *you*..."

He forced her chin up to meet her gaze.

"If I lose your trust, I shall walk into that desert and never return."

Ninsianna's lip trembled. For a moment she thought he might kiss her, but he stroked her cheek, and then loosened his wings to give her room to breathe. She clung to him, praying he might *act* on whatever emotion she could sense at war with his overdeveloped notions about honor, but of course he didn't. Not with the warriors and other villagers standing all around them, entertained by the quarrel in the middle of the field.

A pair of raucous male voices cat-called:

"Oh, loverboy!" Dadbeh called out in a high, falsetto voice. "When will you plant my field?"

"I'm working on it, dearest—" Firouz said. "You just keep giving me so much woman's work —" he flapped his hands at his shoulders to make a pair of mock-wings "—that I'm having a bit of trouble finding my manhood!"

The other warriors laughed as the two tricksters pantomimed Dadbeh-Ninsianna pretending to lead Firouz-Mikhail around by his penis. Mikhail stiffened. He ruffled his feathers.

Jamin stared at her, only he wasn't laughing. His black eyes shone with that *same* betrayal they had the day he had fallen from the heavens.

Mikhail let her go...

He strode across the field and, for a moment she thought the two might come to blows, but he simply picked up the basket she'd knocked out of his hands and carried it back to her.

"You spilled some?" he gestured at the barley seeds.

"This grain belongs to Yalda and Zhila," she said.

He spotted the two old women who'd met them the day they'd come through the south gate. They were bent over their field, Yalda leaning heavily on her digging stick, while she directed the spry, but almost-blind Zhila, where to loosen up the soil.

"The elderly shouldn't be forced to perform such hard physical labor," he said. "Why are they planting the fields themselves?"

"Their husbands are gone," she said, "and their sons were killed in the war against the Uruk. Yalda has a daughter, but she married into another village."

He glanced at the warriors who loitered at the edge of the fields, mock-wrestling with their spears and making fun of the men who were merely farmers. She saw recognition flare in his eyes as he finally understood why the Chief was so reluctant to take on another 'elite warrior' of unproven merit.

He held out the basket.

"Come?" he said. "We have never been properly introduced."

He marched her over to the widow-sisters with a single-minded purpose. Ninsianna glanced back at Jamin. The warriors stopped their play-acting to watch what he did.

"Good day, Ma'am?" Mikhail tucked his wings into a polite show of respect.

Yalda, the elder of the two, elbowed her nearly-blind sister.

"Have you come to help us plant?" Yalda asked.

"Yes, Ma'am," he said. "I was told I have to apprentice with all three members of the Tribunal."

"Behnam convinced us to let you begin training the workmen," Yalda said.

"But you promised to teach me *three* trades," he said. "Wouldn't it be best for the village if I possess well-rounded skills?"

The younger of the two peered up at him, her eyes almost as blue as *his* were from the cataracts which had stolen much of her sight.

"He *wants* to plant?" Zhila asked.

"Aye," Yalda said.

"That's surprising, for one so skilled in hand-to-hand combat," Zhila said.

"I'm a soldier, Ma'am," he said. "We do what needs to be done."

The elder sister, Yalda, scrutinized the *both* of them with a skeptical expression.

"Have you ever planted before?" Yalda asked.

"I don't know, Ma'am—" his face remained serious. "I seem to have misplaced my memories."

Yalda pressed her hand into the small of her back and gestured at the surrounding fields, where the villagers had all stopped working to watch the curious spectacle of a five-cubit-tall Angelic standing ankle-deep in mud.

"It's back-breaking work. Most villagers—" she gave Ninsianna a sharp look "—would rather do *anything* besides provide for our daily bread."

"I was hoping you might teach me?" Mikhail said. "In exchange for a portion of your crop?"

Yalda's grey eyebrows rose at his audacity.

The younger sister elbowed the elder one. "He's ambitious, ain't he?"

"Aye," Yalda agreed. "Though that's not necessarily a bad thing." She peered up at him. "If we agree, what do you plan to do with your share?"

Mikhail looked at *her*.

"I intend to compensate the Chief for the gifts Ninsianna's father sent to the regional shamans."

A thrill tip-trickled into Ninsianna's body. Mikhail intended to pay back her bride price?

"It would solve a problem," Zhila said.

"Yes. It would. But I do not think it will satisfy *him*—" Yalda tilted her head towards Jamin, who watched the exchange intently.

"The debt is owed to the Chief," Zhila said.

"The Chief wants his bride-price back," Yalda said, "and he will not budge."

"Tell him we will guarantee the share?" Zhila said.

The two old women turned to him, together.

"We can make no bargain on behalf of the Chief," they said with a single voice, "but if you wish to tend our field, we shall give you one-third of the crop."

"Yes, Ma'am," Mikhail said. "That sounds agreeable."

Yalda reached into the basket with a wrinkled, crow-like hand and grabbed a handful of seed.

"We traded a Chief's ransom to get this barley," Yalda said.

"It is sacred—" Zhila said.

"—to the goddess—" Yalda said.

"—Ninkasa," Zhila finished.

Mikhail raised a curious eyebrow at Ninsianna.

"Ninkasa is the goddess of bread and beer," she whispered.

"Beer?" Mikhail pronounced the unfamiliar word.

"Yes," she said. "Fermented barley-water. You had some the night the shamans met. Yalda and Zhila make the finest beer in Ubaid territory."

"Ahh…" Comprehension dawned in Mikhail's eyes. "And these seeds…?"

"...make the *bappir*[117] which is turned into beer," she finished.

Yalda scattered the first handful.

"Cast the grain in a circular motion—" Yalda demonstrated. "Not too thick, and not too thin."

"There is only enough to plant a single field," Zhila said.

"...so if you waste it..." Yalda said.

"You shall *not* grow enough to pay off her debt!" they said in unison.

Mikhail attempted to mimic the motion. The seeds hit the ground in a clump.

"No! No!" Yalda scolded him. "You have to give the seedlings room to breathe."

Ninsianna grabbed a handful and scattered some seeds herself, conscious of the whispers as the other villagers gossiped about the shaman's daughter and her winged champion, taken to the fields to plant like ordinary peasants.

Mikhail glanced to where Jamin and his warriors slapped their sides, guffawing in hysterics to see a creature of heaven performing the lowliest job. He picked up a second handful and held it up towards the sun.

"I think I have done this job before," he said.

A trill of anticipation tingled through Ninsianna's body.

A hawk cried out…

'Yes…' the wind whispered. 'This you may remember…'

With a broad grin, Mikhail cast the seeds straight into the air and, with a mighty flap of his wings, scattered them unto the waiting Earth.

Yalda and Zhila laughed as he grabbed another handful and scattered the seeds far more efficiently than a dozen field hands. Laughter welled up in Ninsianna's chest. The joy of watching him show off made her heart swell.

"Mikhail, stop!" she laughed. "If you spread your seed any further, you'll plant grain all the way up to the Taurus Mountains!"

He grinned down at her.

"My body remembers this!" he said excitedly. "I think, where I come from, my family owned a farm?"

The sun shone down on him, bathing his feathers in a beautiful, golden light, as if *he* was the light, and she saw him as She-Who-Is had created his species, to be defenders of the light, and all that was good and just.

She realized she looked up at him with naked desire. Forcing her jaw shut, she composed her features into something other than lust.

His joy disappeared behind a carefully constructed mask.

"Did I do something wrong?"

---

[117] *Bappir:* twice-baked barley bread.

"No—" she placed her hand over his heart. "It's the first time I've ever seen you smile."

He bent towards her, as though he might kiss her, but Yalda and Zhila's whoops of laughter reminded him they were not alone. He glanced over at the warriors, the other villagers, and then stepped back.

"Hah!" the warriors guffawed. "Next she'll have him emptying out the chamber pots!"

A sense of frustration made her want to stomp her foot. So Mikhail *wasn't* immune to her? Would he have kissed her if Jamin hadn't made a show?

She grabbed a handful of seed and turned towards her ex-fiancé.

"Come," she said loudly. "I wish to work off my *own* bride price."

Chapter 65

For this cause ought the woman
To have [a veil] on her head,
Because of the angels [she might tempt].

Corinthians 11:10

Galactic Standard Date: 152,323.02
Sata'an Empire: Hades-6
Emperor Shay'tan

SHAY'TAN

Alliance legend claimed Shay'tan lived in a hellish cave which could only be accessed by crossing a river of fire. In truth, Hades-6 was just like any other cosmopolitan homeworld, complete with skyscrapers, public gardens, and a busy spaceport which connected millions of planets. Shay'tan's palace rose above his capital city, Dis, like a fairytale castle, with tall, slender spires and a moat filled with water, not fire. Once upon a time his ancestors *had* lived in caves, but then again, so had Hashem's. It was all propaganda, intended to smear his name so Alliance citizens wouldn't be tempted by Sata'anic ideals of orderliness and wealth.

All except for the bit about hoarding treasure.

That was true…

The Sata'anic Emir,[118] Lord Ba'al Zebub, a lizard of significant height and girth, bowed and tucked his tail up against the right-hand side of his body.

"Your Eminence," Ba'al Zebub flicked his long, forked tongue. "General Hudhafah has sent you a gift."

Shay'tan flared his leathery wings like an eager hatchling.

"The human?"

"Yes."

"So this lieutenant's claim is real?"

Ba'al Zebub bowed even deeper.

"I have seen her with my own eyes, my god."

Shay'tan had been stunned when an obscure merchant ship had bypassed his entire intelligence apparatus, using General Hudhafah's personal access code, to reach him directly in the palace. If this is what

---

[118] *Emir*: a high ranking noble, king or chief. Somebody who speaks for the king.

Hudhafah *claimed* it was, he'd just delivered the means to crush the Alliance.

"Show me—" he gestured at the guards.

A pair of ornate carved wooden doors swung open. Three anonymous merchant mariners stepped in, herding between them an ebony-skinned female. She was tall, like an Angelic, with a regal step, as though she possessed the finest breeding and manners. Despite her primitive dress, the dark eyes which scanned the room were alert and filled with intelligence.

Shay'tan rose from his massive carved throne, thirty meters of meticulously groomed scales and fangs and claws.

"Welcome, Miss?" he grinned.

The woman fainted.

An indignant puff of smoke snorted out of his nostrils.

"Not very sturdy, are they?" he snuffled the unconscious woman. "It's hard to believe this is the foundation upon which Hashem built his armies."

"I took the liberty of running a quick genetic test," Ba'al Zebub said. "This *is* the root stock of the four hybrid races. The ones he used to breed back in to maintain genetic diversity."

Shay'tan's snout turned upwards in a predatory grin.

"And to think?" he said. "Hashem believes they're all extinct."

Ba'al Zebub's corpulent form jiggled with excitement.

"Perhaps we could sell a few to key players?" he rubbed his claws together. "Not enough to solve the hybrid fertility problem. Just to secure key allies?"

Shay'tan scratched a loose scale as he schemed. "We've already destabilized their economy with these free trade agreements of yours. And driven a wedge between Hashem and his son. I've quintupled my fleet ... all paid for with Alliance dollars."

"The idiots are so eager for peace that they haven't noticed their trade deficit is running 300 to one," Ba'al Zebub laughed. "Should I order Hudhafah to gather more of these humans for trade?"

"Where *is* their homeworld, exactly?"

Ba'al Zebub glanced at the merchant mariners who had transported the woman, and then ambled over to the enormous whirling hologram of the galaxy that he and his ancient adversary used to plot out their next move. He gestured to Shay'tan, and then surreptitiously pointed to the place where the two great empires, and two petty, warlike kingdoms, came together into a no man's land of rebellion, back-stabbing and war.

"Here."

Shay'tan frowned.

"That's disputed territory," he said.

"But this could be highly profitable!" Ba'al Zebub protested.

"Not if we can't hold onto that planet," Shay'tan said. "If Hashem wants it badly enough, he'll just swoop in and take it."

"What if we keep the location a secret?" Ba'al Zebub said.

"Not with Jophiel crawling up my tail, and *those* idiots—" Shay'tan gestured at the Tokoloshe Kingdom and the Free Marid Confederation "—eager to sell me out."

Situated, as they were, with borders shared with both the Sata'an Empire and the Galactic Alliance, every time he went after one of them for smuggling, they'd run to the Eternal Emperor, pleading for help. Of course, they did the *exact* same thing to Hashem, playing the two great empires against one another. It was a trick they'd learned from their long-dead leader, Shemijaza.[119]

He scratched his long, golden whiskers. Ba'al Zebub was a brilliant political strategist, but he lacked a dragon's long view. This was the biggest leverage he'd gained against his ancient adversary in 150,000 years. If he wanted to *keep* that advantage, he needed to plot his next move wisely.

"Maybe..." he stared at the ebony-skinned woman.

"Yes, Your Eminence?" Ba'al Zebub leaned forward.

Shay'tan's snout turned upwards in a toothy grin. He hadn't come up with a plan this brilliant since he'd tricked Hashem into creating a fifth race of ... ooh! Even the *thought* of it gave him chills!

"Send an armada to defend the planet," Shay'tan said, "but send them the long way around, to throw the Alliance off our tail."

"That could take months," Ba'al Zebub said. "Before we can even *launch* the darned thing, we would first need to gather ships and outfit them with resources in such a way that it doesn't tip off Hashem's spies."

"But spies can be compromised, yes?" Shay'tan said.

"For the right price."

"That's where *you* come in!" Shay'tan slapped Ba'al Zebub on the back, almost knocking the corpulent lizard flat onto his snout. "I will take you up on your idea—" he pointed at the unconscious woman "—with that one."

Ba'al Zebub grinned.

"She shall fetch an emperor's ransom."

"A ransom?" Shay'tan chuckled. "No, my friend. We shall send her as a gift."

"A gift? To who?"

Shay'tan gestured at the spinning hologram.

"Why? To the rightful ruler, of course."

Ba'al Zebub's eyebrow-ridges wrinkled together in confusion. He glanced at the map.

---

[119] *Shemijaza:* Lucifer's biological father. The leader of the "fallen angels" listed in Enoch's "*Book of the Watchers.*"

"Of Earth?"

"Yes," Shay'tan said. "If it lies *here*—" he pointed at the planet, which sat in the same sector where Shemijaza's "Third Empire" had once stood "—then this beautiful specimen should marry its rightful king."

Ba'al Zebub's jaw went slack.

"Lucifer?"

"Yes," Shay'tan chuckled. "We've driven a wedge between him and Hashem with this trade deal. Now, let's see if we can't get history to repeat itself?"

"And what of Jophiel's spies?" Ba'al Zebub asked.

"Let *Lucifer* take care of it," Shay'tan said. "Those two *hate* one another. If it comes down to the preservation of his species, he will sell the *both* of them out in a heartbeat."

He rubbed his claws together. All he had to do was keep Hashem distracted long enough for Lucifer to sire an heir. An heir who was loyal to *him*. He could just *see* the look on Hashem's face when he sprang *that* chess move on him during a future match!

"Who's to say a few *more* of those brides can't be gifted to Alliance males who promote Sata'an policies?" Ba'al Zebub suggested. "Mercantilists? Or politicians with fertility problems? A little black-market side-trade to grease the wheels of commerce?"

Shay'tan pondered the implications. As much as he wished to fatten his treasury, the more people who were in on the conspiracy, the more likely some careless hybrid would let the secret slip.

"No," Shay'tan said. "Order Hudhafah to secure that planet until the armada gets there, and in the meantime, we'll see what kind of trouble Lucifer can stir up."

"But—"

"I said *no!*" A puff of fire erupted from Shay'tan's throat.

Ba'al Zebub threw himself to the ground. The three merchant mariners who'd accompanied the human woman threw their bodies over her with a terrified squeal.

'*Calm... Calm...,*' he visualized the image *she* had taught him to project to his subjects; a benevolent and generous dragon. He adjusted his fur-trimmed velvet robe and presented his *good* side to the three merchant mariners.

"Good and loyal subjects," he said in his most magnanimous voice. "You have pleased me greatly. In several weeks, you shall convey Lord Ba'al Zebub—" he gave his corpulent Emir a magnanimous nod "—to the Alliance border, to meet with Alliance Prime Minister in secret. Before you go, you shall each be gifted a wife."

The three merchant mariners fell to their knees and pressed their snouts into the floor.

"Shay'tan be praised!" they cried out.

Shay'tan basked in their adoration.

"And *you*," he turned to Ba'al Zebub, "shall see that this creature is properly outfitted for marriage."

"Marriage?" Ba'al Zebub sputtered. "But hybrids are *forbidden* to marry."

"I know." Shay'tan slapped his paw upon his throne with delight. "No loose Alliance morals for our newest Sata'an females! Oh …no! We are setting a precedent with this one! Hashem will have an apoplexy when he discovers his own son flaunted his ridiculous *'no marriage, no same mate twice'* breeding policies and hid the offspring!"

"Yes, your eminence," Ba'al Zebub bowed stiffly.

Shay'tan noted his second-in-command's posture. Was he upset because he thought he was ignoring his advice?

No… More likely Ba'al Zebub had already committed the profits he could skim selling humans to some side-endeavor. Taking a 'cut' was a common, and unofficially sanctioned, practice among the upper echelons of Sata'anic society. Ba'al Zebub had expenses the same as everybody else. He would offer his right-hand man an even *more* productive means to skim money

"Ba'al Zebub!" Shay'tan said with a toothy grin. "You have my blessing to do whatever is necessary to secure that planet. I want that world industrialized within twenty years. Every resource I possess is yours to command!"

The feral glint in Ba'al Zebub's eyes gave Shay'tan an uneasy feeling, but a scribe rushed forward with another fire to put out within his empire, interrupting his thoughts. The old dragon pushed aside his apprehensions and focused on the latest emergency.

Chapter 66

June – 3,390 BC
Earth: Village of Assur

JAMIN

Jamin's cheeks turned fiery purple-red as his enemy showed off like a white-cheeked bulbul bird,[120] flaring his wings and scratching the ground, claiming he'd found a way to purchase *his* bride!

"Did you see the way he spread their seed?" Firouz said with admiration. "That would have taken me all day."

"The beer will be flowing come autumn!" Dadbeh laughed.

Jamin's knuckles turned white, clenching his spear...

"I wish he'd come plant *my* field—" the youngest member of the elite warriors, Tirdard, looked forlornly at his *own* basket of seed. "I can't go with you until I finish up."

"That's because you daydream all day long about Yadiditum—" Firouz gave him a good-natured noogie "—instead of focusing on what you *should* be doing."

Tirdard sighed.

"All that Yadiditum daydreams about these days is *him*—" he pointed across the field. "She said I should be more like him."

"A spy?" Jamin growled.

"No, more helpful—" Tirdard said, oblivious to the dangerous undercurrent.

"A man can't get any luvvin' since *he* showed up," Firouz said.

"That's for sure," Tirdard sighed. "It's all my sisters gossip about. *Who* can catch the winged one's eye?"

Dadbeh fetched a pose with his arm akimbo on his hip.

"Oh, beautiful winged one," the small man said in high-pitched voice. "Come carry me into the sky with those great, big wings of yours."

"No, fair maiden," Firouz donned an unreadable expression. "I must follow Ninsianna around like a large, winged dog."

Dadbeh grabbed the front of Firouz's kilt and dragged him, in lock-step, behind him as the pair of tricksters mimicked Ninsianna leading Mikhail around.

---

[120] *Bulbul bird:* a small, colorful songbird.

Jamin slammed the butt-end of his spear into the ground.

"It isn't funny!" he snarled. "The bastard's only here to find weaknesses in our defenses!"

"Are you serious?" Firouz scrunched up his face. "The only reason he's here is because of Ninsianna. Just *look* at him?"

He gestured out into the field, where Mikhail walked behind the chestnut-haired beauty, casting his seed into the air and spreading it by pounding his wings.

A low growl vibrated out of Jamin's chest. He resisted the urge to *throttle* them for their stupidity!

"Easy..." Siamek placed a restraining hand on his shoulder. "You're better off without her."

"How?" Jamin looked away so the fools wouldn't see him gasp for breath. "It was bad enough she broke off our engagement, but now she openly mocks me?"

Peals of feminine laughter drifted across the fields as Mikhail moved on to help an old man plant *his* grain. Jamin's heart stuttered. Ninsianna used to laugh that way for *him!*

A trio of women came out of their fields carrying empty seed baskets, their work-dresses all smeared with mud.

"Did you hear what he said?" one of them asked the other. "He wants to buy out her bride-price."

"He said if she ever spurns him," the second said, "he will leave and go out into the desert forever!"

"That's so romantic!" the third woman sighed. "I wish he'd look at *me* that way?"

"He never looks at *anybody!*" the first one mock-swooned. "He only has eyes for her."

"I wonder how long until they announce they're engaged?"

The three women fell silent as they trudged past him, models of meekness, but the moment they got past, they giggled.

"That's it!" Jamin said. "We've got to get him *out* of here!"

"How?" Siamek said. "The Tribunal just ruled, if *we* refuse to train with him, he can satisfy your father's edict by training *any* group of willing men."

Jamin stared across the field, where *his* fiancé, one of the highest born women in all of Ubaid territory, stood knee-deep in goat-shit impregnated mud and spread seed like a common field laborer, rather than marry *him*.

"Spread the word," Jamin said. "Anyone who shows up at that training tomorrow will answer to *me*."

The warriors fanned out like a pack of jackals. Jamin stared at his ex-fiancé, his thoughts whirring. It wouldn't be enough, to simply deny the winged demon the chance to train his men. Much to his chagrin, Mikhail's skills-ineptitude had only *strengthened* the Tribunal's conviction the dark-winged bastard suffered from memory loss, not that he was keeping secrets as a ruse to gather intelligence. He had to get *rid* of him before he bamboozled his father into letting him stay.

He glanced up at the trio of women, now at the top of the path that led up to the north gate, who had joined a large group of women to gossip. They pointed across the field at Mikhail.

He bent towards Siamek.

"I have an idea," he said, "but I need your help to set it up."

Chapter 67

June - 3,390 BC
Earth: Village of Assur
Colonel Mikhail Mannuki'ili

MIKHAIL

The sentries called out in the early morning darkness.

"Koo-whee! Koo-whee!"

He gave them a salute as he made his way out the north gate, even though it was a warning:

"The winged one is leaving the village."

He picked his way down the path which led to the Ubaid fields, almost giddy with anticipation, laden down with a dozen wooden staffs. The still-dark sky made the footing difficult, but he counted each step to memorize the obstacles so he could navigate later in the dark.

Had he taught combat skills before? He couldn't remember... The absurdity almost made him laugh. It felt like freedom, the chance to finally prove his worth! If only he could remember what he knew *before* he got clobbered over the skull and, *surprise!* His body knew how to block!

What else did his body remember? Besides the yearning which had taken up residence inside his chest?

He glanced up at the morning star which heralded the dawn. It shone its pale light upon the fields he'd planted only yesterday, a new hope for the future, new friends, and maybe a place to call home?

"So you're saying the moon revolves around the Earth?" Ninsianna had pointed up at the moon.

"And the Earth around the sun—" he'd taken her finger and drawn her arm across the heavens "—and the sun around the galaxy in a circular dance of stars."

"Just like in She-Who-Is' vision!" Ninsianna had said excitedly. "Will you take me to see them?"

"The sun?"

"No. The stars?"

"May the gods be willing," he swore, the opposite of the evasive answer he'd given her last night. He'd made her father a promise, and his *word* was the only thing of value that he had. His body still tingled where she'd leaned into him for warmth as they'd stared up at the stars and spoken of petty little dreams; both of them too afraid to speak of the *real* one.

He worked his way around the edge of the fields, now completely above water as the Hiddekel River receded. He could almost *feel* having once walked a similar field. The farmers and workmen were still fast asleep, but he looked forward to toiling with them to see what *else* his body remembered? He moved past the area where Jamin trained his warriors—best not to antagonize him—out of sight of the sentries, at least until the sun rose, and began his morning warm-up with a run.

Inside the village there was little room to spread his wings. He stretched the limbs upwards, clenching his teeth as a sharp stab of pain shuddered through his main flight tendon, and made a running-start off the riverbank, desperate to *become* the creature of heaven these people wanted him to be. Just for an instant, the wind buoyed his fall, but then his damaged wing gave out and dumped him face-first into the dirt.

"Gyah!" he cried out.

He untangled his body from the jumble of his feathers. Thank the gods nobody was awake to see him fall!

He picked the sand out of his wings, and then did a thousand pushups, his left-hand side still weak thanks to his damaged pectoral muscle and shattered ribs. He then moved through a grueling routine of strength-training that he didn't remember learning, but his body flowed automatically from one exercise to another.

The sky turned grey, and then it turned pink; the sun lifted above the horizon, back-lighting the shining village built along the banks of a river. One by one, the early risers trickled down to tend their fields. He greeted the men, but they all averted their gaze.

His feathers prickled. *Some* of these men, only yesterday, he'd helped to plant their fields.

Uncomfortably self-conscious, he picked up one of the wooden staffs and began to move through the training kata he remembered Master Yoritomo had taught him. One of the few memories he had.

Around and around.

…Block.

……Strike.

………Jab.

Visualize your opponent.

The Cherubim routine sparked tantalizing little snowflakes of memory. They were *better* than him. *That* he remembered…

"I'll start with the basics."

The *last* thing he wanted was to make Behnam's men feel as incompetent as *he* had felt, learning to knap flint and shape an object out of wood.

The pathway down from the village grew thick with people as the entire population came down to tend fields filled with emmer, einkorn and lentils.

He twirled the staff, loathe to show off, but painfully cognizant of the fact he needed to *prove* he had something to offer.

He glanced at his wrist computer, largely useless here in a land where the people kept time by the passage of seasons, lunar cycles and the sunrise.

"Seven o'clock."

He held his hand up to the horizon and measured the time according to the Ubaid method; the sun sat four fingers above the horizon.

My hand is bigger than the Ubaid. Perhaps they thought eight o'clock?

He completed his training katas, and then moved through a series of dance-like stretches, attempting to shake free more memories. A haze of blue light sparkled at the periphery of his vision. He could almost *hear* the soothing ring of a brass bell, the smell of flowers, and clicking voices, all reciting a series of martial prayers.

But still the workmen did not appear.

A niggling self-doubt settled into his gut.

Why am I even here?

— *Because you're in love with Ninsianna.*

I just want to protect her.

— *Hah!*

His subconscious mocked him for being such a fool.

The sun climbed six fingers above the horizon. A tall, slender figure picked her way down the path, not quite a woman, but neither was she a little girl. Pareesa marched over the logs which spanned the tiny creek, but there was no spring in her step. In her hands, she held a piece of firewood.

"Hello, Little Fairy," he greeted her. "Have you come to watch the workmen train?"

"They're not coming!" she said. "Word has gone through the village that any man who trains with you will feel Jamin's wrath."

That sense of dark anger warred with despair.

"But they *said* they wanted to train with me?"

"They did—" her eyes glittered with tears. "But life is difficult enough, without having the future chief out to get you."

He tucked his wings against his back, stiffly.

"I see."

He picked up the wooden staffs and bundled them together to carry back up into the village. She held out her crooked stick

"*I'm* willing to train!" she said. "Teach me, and we'll show them, together, at the summer solstice games?"

"Not today, Little Fairy."

"Why?" she cried out. "Because I'm a girl?"

"No," he said, "because it will make you a target."

"I don't *care!*"

"Well I *do*," he said. "The *last* thing I need is another woman to babysit!"

He heaved the staffs over his shoulder and started back towards the village, arguing with his subconscious which asked: *"Why are you even here when you have a mission to complete?"* His rational mind knew that Jamin kept needling him to drive him out of the village. But that *irrational* part, the part the Cherubim had taught him to suppress, wanted to hunt the bastard down, disembowel him, and make him *eat* his own intestines!

Chapter 68

June - 3,390 BC
Earth: Village of Assur

NINSIANNA

She climbed out of bed, bleary-eyed from a night spent on the roof, listening to Mikhail explain the secrets of each object which sparkled in the sky. It was a curious fact, that the man couldn't remember his own name, had words to describe things She-Who-Is had shown her in the vision.

She stumbled down the ladder, her shawl-dress unartfully wrapped for a trip down to the well. Mama and Papa sat stiffly upon the carpet. Had he already come back from his meeting with the Chief? The counting-sticks Papa used to keep track of their wealth were spread across the floor, neatly arranged into piles.

"Good morning!" she yawned. "Did Mikhail fetch the water?"

"Yes—" Mama pointed at the fancy new buckets.

"So early?" Ninsianna asked. "I heard him leave before the sunrise."

"Did you expect anything different?" Papa snapped.

"No. Not really. I just thought—"

"You thought, now that they're going to treat him like a *man*, he'd act like one?" Papa growled.

"Immanu!" Mama gave a sharp rebuke. "That is no way to speak about our guest!"

"Our *guest* is supposed to act like a creature of heaven!" Papa said. "Not crawl through the fields, lusting after my daughter."

Ninsianna gaped. Was Papa upset she'd overslept?

"But he just wants to pay you back?"

"He announced my *shame* in front of the entire village!" Papa shouted.

"Perhaps it's time you *were* ashamed!" Mama scolded.

"I'll show you, woman—" Papa raised his hand.

Mama held up a single finger.

"If you do," she spoke with cold, quiet deliberation, "*this* time, you won't get a second chance."

Ninsianna glanced back and forth. Her parents rarely fought, but when they did, Mama always won.

"The *Chief* isn't giving us a choice!" Papa sounded desperate.

"Yes he did," Mama said. "He simply gave you a choice you did not like."

Papa looked to *her*.

"Please? Tell her?" he said to Mama.

Mama shook her head.

"This is your doing," she said. "*This* time, I'm not going to take the blame."

Mama rose to her feet and grabbed her healing basket, her expression cloaked. But her russet eyes burned with suppressed fury as she left to do her daily healing rounds.

Ninsianna's father patted the carpet next to him.

"Please, sit?"

She sat with her knees pulled up to her chest. It appeared his meeting with the Chief had not gone as expected?

Papa fiddled with his counting-sticks, the ones he used to keep track of how many baskets of grain and other trade-goods they kept stored in their pantry.

"Everything I've done has always been for you," he said softly.

"Has it?" her voice rose sharp with rebuke.

Normally Papa would scold her about a daughter's duty to respect her parents, but instead he sighed. It was far more terrifying than when he lost his temper.

"I've decided to accept Chief Sinalshu's offer."

Ninsianna gasped. They were moving to Nineveh?

"But Mikhail—"

"Is getting nowhere," Papa said. "So long as we are here, *you* will continue to stand between Mikhail and his destiny."

"That's because Jamin thwarts his every move."

"Because *you* insulted his honor!" Papa shouted.

"I just don't see why that means we have to move to Nineveh?"

"We have no choice—"

"I'll run away again," she threatened.

"Where will you go?"

"Back to Mikhail's sky canoe."

"If you do, not only will Jamin come looking for you, but so will Nineveh. It will fracture the Ubaid alliance."

"What does Nineveh have to do with any of this?" she asked. "I've never even been there because *you* won't let me leave Assur!"

"Chief Sinalshu has sworn, if you marry his son, he will put Mikhail in charge of his warriors."

"Since when does Qishtea want to marry *me*?"

"He asked you to marry him the *last* time he came to visit."

A sense of vertigo caused Ninsianna's world to go off-kilter.

"He said it in jest," she whispered.

"Was it?" Papa gave her an accusatory glare. "Because, as I recall, he came to call upon you several times?"

Ninsianna crossed her arms. Yes, she *had* encouraged the handsome young *Muhafiz* of Nineveh, but it was only to show him up. Last winter, he'd broken Yadiditum's heart, so she had woven a love-spell so she could *spurn* the arrogant young chieftain—publicly—to salve her best friend's ego.

"He only wants me because he's in a pissing contest with Jamin," she said. "They both want the prestige of marrying Lugalbanda's granddaughter!"

"If he wants to marry Lugalbanda's granddaughter," Papa said, "there's another one available."

Ninsianna's face grew hot with indignation.

"Qishtea would *never* marry the daughter of a drunk!"

"It would be a lot cheaper than buying out your bride price."

Ninsianna shot to her feet. She paced over to the basket which she'd used yesterday to carry Yalda and Zhila's grain.

"You don't *need* to pay off my bride-price—" she picked up the basket. "Mikhail has struck a deal. He and I will take a share of Yalda and Zhila's crop."

"Your marriage is set for the summer solstice," Papa said.

"We shall *give* the Chief his grain!"

"It won't be ready until the autumn equinox—" Papa shook his head "—but in the meantime, this dispute is tearing our village apart. Not only has it destabilized *our* village, but now it's brought into jeopardy our alliance with Nineveh. The Chief has had enough. He wants Mikhail *gone*."

She burst into tears.

"But Mikhail didn't do anything wrong!"

Papa rose to his feet and embraced her, the way he had done when she'd still been a little girl. She pressed her face into his cape, sobbing. She'd gotten *into* this whole mess because she'd wanted to please him, and dammit! Part of her still did!

"I don't *want* to marry Jamin!" she sobbed. "And I don't want to marry Qishtea of Nineveh, either!"

"Those are our two choices," Papa said. "Unless you can make *these*—" he pointed at the counting sticks "—magically increase by the summer solstice, you will marry one of them. Or Mikhail will be cast out into the desert, alone."

Alone…

The word he had whispered the day she had saved his life. The word he cried out every time the demons had come to plague his nightmares, before the goddess had shown her how to bind his memories.

"But Yalda and Zhila said—"

"They came with me to see the chief," Papa said, "and he still said *no*. He fears, if this situation continues, Mikhail and Jamin will come to blows, and we both *know* it's not going to be Mikhail who loses."

"Maybe that's what Jamin needs?" she crossed her arms. "A good beating?"

"Jamin won't stop until one of them is dead."

Ninsianna picked up the counting sticks and laid them out neatly. Even *with* their share of Yalda and Zhila's crop, they'd have a hard time making up her bride price. Papa had been so proud, that the Chief had been willing to meet his ridiculous price. But at the time, Jamin was still weak with injury, and Qishtea had been sniffing around. The Chief had been willing to pay whatever it took to make sure she'd keep his only child alive.

"I will pray on it," she said softly.

"Do," Papa said. "Your mother insists it should be *you* who decides which chief will be your husband."

She went outside to milk the goat. Why had she tormented Qishtea? And why had she told Jamin yes? She should have, politely, refused *both* of their advances.

Only, dammit! She'd enjoyed pitting the two goatheads against one another!

She tugged on the goat's warm teats, squirting milk into Mikhail's brand-new bucket. So now she was back to being nothing but a brood goat? An empty womb, to birth the next generation of chiefs?

"What do you think of all this?" she asked Little Nemesis.

The goat lifted its face from the treats-bucket and gave an empathetic bleat. While her fur had grown back, the poor creature still bore the scars of having been thrown off a cliff. It seemed far happier being a brood goat for *them* than running free with the cruel Halifians who'd abused her.

Inside the house, somebody knocked. Ninsianna carried the milk bucket back inside, and then opened the front door. A nervous young boy stared at her, owl-eyed.

"Dadbeh sent me," the boy said. "His grandmother is complaining of chest pains."

The elite warrior's grandmother was under her mother's care. The old woman suffered from a condition which often left her gasping for breath.

"I'll be right there."

She laid a piece of linen over the milk bucket to keep the flies out, and then gathered up her healer's basket. While not as complete as her mother's, she'd gathered many implements, and a good collection of medicinal herbs.

All but one…

"Drat! I'm out."

She rummaged through the bundles of dried herbs which hung from every rafter, shelf, and peg. Her mother had used the last of the khella[121] plant. She would have to forage for some, after she encouraged the old woman to lie down.

She followed the boy towards the place where the alley split off for the lower ring. She was surprised when the boy kept walking.

"Dadbeh's house is *that* way?"

"She was at the temple when she collapsed."

He turned left into the alley which led to the innermost circle. The boy kept walking past the temple.

"Where is she?"

"She took shelter down here."

Ninsianna's skin prickled as the boy ducked into a narrow slit cut between two of the houses, into a brick-lined alley which ran between the first and second ring. A soft layer of hay had been spread out to absorb the dust, and every doorway she passed was brand new.

The boy stopped exactly where she expected. Only instead of an empty foundation-hole, a fired-brick house rose up in partial completion.

She began to back up.

"No—" her hand flew to her throat.

It was her dream house. The one she'd sketched onto a goatskin during their courtship, while Jamin had still been bedridden.

On the right-hand side, a wooden gate flew open. Dadbeh stuck his head out.

"Thank the goddess you've come!"

He threw the gate open wide, revealing a courtyard that grew green despite the unfinished condition of the house. Just inside, his grandmother sat on a stone bench, her hand clamped over her chest as she gasped for breath.

"You shouldn't have *brought* her here!" Ninsianna snapped.

"Why not?" Dadbeh gave her a guileless look.

"You know darned well what I mean!"

She set her basket down on the bench. It was one she recognized from the Chief's private courtyard.

"What seems to be the problem, Kubaba?" She placed her hand upon the old women's hands. Her skin felt clammy, and her nail-beds and lips had begun to turn blue.

"I ... went ... to ... pray..." the old woman gasped.

Ninsianna glanced around the courtyard, expecting Jamin to appear and attempt to play the hero, but he was surprisingly absent.

---

[121] *Khella:* a medicinal herb, used to treat asthma.

"I need to find some fresh khella," she said. "In the meantime, let's get you someplace where you can lie down?"

Dadbeh helped his grandmother up.

"This room is finished—" he pointed at a second doorway. The wiry young man was not much taller than his grandmother.

He guided the old woman inside a small room which jutted out of the house like an afterthought. *This* room had a roof. And a door, which bore a carved symbol of Ningishzida, the Ubaid goddess of healing.

Ninsianna's eyes adjusted to the dim light as he helped the old woman over to several cushions. She took a step inside—

—and stopped.

The room was dominated by a wooden counter which ran along one wall, topped by sturdy shelves filled with baskets. While most of the shelves remained empty, the baskets contained rolled linen bandages, several bundles of herbs, and small, specialized tools, including the shard of obsidian she'd used to scrape maggots out of Jamin's infected flesh.

Tears welled into her eyes.

"What is this?" she asked.

"It's a house of healing." Dadbeh's mismatched eyes turned accusatory. "If you hadn't been acting like such a goathead, he planned to show it to you the day you returned to Assur."

A lump rose in her throat.

"I need to go forage some khella," she said.

"There is some planted outside."

She stepped out into the garden. As she expected, Jamin waited for her, wearing his finest kilt. He towered over her, his black eyes somber as he adjusted his shawl of state, almost nervously, in the proper fold befitting a future chief.

"This was a dirty trick," her voice warbled. "You put Dadbeh's grandmother at risk."

"Did I?" he gestured at the garden. "As you can see, we have everything she needs."

"Not khella plant," she said. "It will help with her breathing."

"It's over here—" he pointed at a raised bed filled with lacy white flowers. From the scatterings of soil in front of it, the plants had been transplanted here within the last few days.

He'd done all this for *her*?

She tore at the flowers, refusing to *think*. It was all a manipulation!

"You shouldn't have done this," she said. "You did it all for naught."

Jamin looked as though she'd just kicked him.

"Why?" his voice warbled. "The winged demon, I thought... But why would you marry Qishtea of Nineveh over me?"

"Because you're *insensitive!*"

She stared at the freshly transplanted khella and other plants, each one of them medicinal.

"Would Qishtea of Nineveh build you a house of healing?" he asked softly.

"Is *that* what this is?"

"Yes."

Her lip trembled. "Why?"

"You know why."

Ninsianna stared down at her hands.

"I don't want to marry *anybody*."

He stepped closer: tall, strong, wealthy, and smart. At one time she'd thought he was the highest man to whom she could aspire. A man who'd ignited her imagination with all his talk of far-off places and the things he'd like for her to *see*. But then She-Who-Is had sent her a man from the heavens. A man who could fly. A man who, it turned out, wasn't *completely* immune to her charms?

"Jamin, I—"

Out from somewhere beyond the alley, one of the sentries called:

"Koo-whee! Koo-whee! Koo-whee!"

Jamin lurched forward and gathered her into his arms.

"Ninsianna. I want you to marry *me*."

Chapter 69

*The heart is deceitful above all things
And beyond cure.
Who can understand it?*

Jeremiah 17:9

*June - 3,390 BC
Earth: Village of Assur
Colonel Mikhail Mannuki'ili*

MIKHAIL

"Koo-whee! Koo-whee!"

The sentries called back and forth as he passed through the north gate. As soon as he got to the other side, a boy ran up to him.

"Ninsianna asked me to fetch you," the boy said.

"Is she in trouble?"

"No—" the boy glanced up at the sentries. "She just needs help to do something."

"Okay," he said. "Just let me put these down."

He laid the bundle of staffs against the wall and called up for the sentries to make sure they didn't get taken as firewood. He would speak to Behnam when he returned the sticks. Let the *tribunal* bring the matter to the Chief. It was not his place to tell the man to discipline his son.

The boy ran ahead, forcing him to keep up despite his longer stride.

"Where are we going?" he called out.

"Hurry!"

The boy led him into the inner circle, past the temple of She-Who-Is. The usual worshippers gathered beneath the sun-tarp, offering flowers to their empty-eyed clay goddess to plead for heavenly favors. The boy turned into a narrow alley.

"She's down there—" the boy pointed. "Just keep going to the end."

The boy ran off before he could ask questions. Except for a series of sharp whistles, there was nothing dark or menacing about the alley. It wound behind the back courtyards of several houses. The ones on the left belonged to the inner ring, while the houses on the right had all been newly constructed. It correlated perfectly to a spot in the second ring where none of the houses had doorways. The people here, rather than be forced to live in the less prestigious second ring due to a lack of space, had gerrymandered this alley to connect their houses to the innermost ring.

One of the doors opened. A mother and a daughter stepped out, both finely dressed. The little girl shrieked when she spotted him in the alley. The mother pulled her daughter behind her.

"P-p-please—" she backed her child up. "Don't hurt her."

"I wouldn't—"

He realized his wings were flared, the way he did when he was irritated.

"My apologies, Ma'am—" he tucked them against his back. "I came in search of Ninsianna."

"You should leave her *alone!*" the woman said. "It's bad enough you kept her prisoner and smeared her honor!"

She shoved her child inside the house and slammed the door in his face. Mikhail reached towards the wood.

"But I *didn't* keep her," he called out. "*She* was the one who wanted to stay."

His feathers rustled, but he was, quite literally, talking to a door. He continued down the alley, which twisted and turned as it wound behind several more houses. It ended at a brand new house, still under construction. Attached to the house, a wooden gate opened up to a lush, green courtyard.

Inside, he heard Ninsianna's voice.

"Koo-whee! Koo-whee! Koo-whee!" a sharp call came from the rooftop.

He stepped forward to call her name.

"Nin—"

Directly in front of him, Ninsianna stood in Jamin's embrace.

"I'd rather marry you than Qishtea of Nineveh," she said.

A shocked sense of unreality knocked the breath right out of him. Ninsianna did not fight. She did not push her ex-fiancé away. He resisted the urge to fly at the man and shriek *"That's my woman!"*

Jamin stroked her hair.

"If you marry *me*, I will lay the world at your feet," he promised.

"What about Mikhail?" she asked.

"If you marry *me*, I'll ask my father to let him stay."

Jamin gave him a dark glance, and then he pulled Ninsianna in for a kiss. Pain stabbed into his heart. The heart she had stolen the day she'd saved his life.

His dog tags jingled, reminding him that he still had a mission to complete. A mission which wasn't getting done so long as he lingered here. He turned and fled back out of the narrow alley, past the doorways filled with people who were all afraid of him. As he moved, the boys the Chief had set to watch him, to let the warriors know where he was within the village, called out their warnings.

"Koo-whee! Koo-whee!"

Here is the enemy.

That's what he was. An intruder who'd dropped into their village, beggar's hat in-hand.

No one was there when he got back to Immanu's house. He shoved his belongings inside his rucksack, and then crawled up the ladder to retrieve his pulse rifle and sword.

He touched the bed which Ninsianna had offered to share with him. From a wooden shelf, a small clay statue stared down at him with empty eye-sockets.

"This should make you happy—" he leveled his pulse rifle at the statue of She-Who-Is.

It reminded him of Ninsianna.

Moisture slid down his cheek and dripped onto the tree-pin that said: *"In light there is order, and in order there is life."* He touched the teardrop and studied the glimmering water.

Alone…

Better to die alone, than to be betrayed.

He slipped the pulse rifle into its thigh-holster, grabbed his sword and climbed back down the ladder. There was nobody here to tell that he was leaving. What would he say?

Your daughter broke my heart?

No. He was not that desperate.

Feeling obligated to announce his departure to *somebody*, he stuck his head out the back doorway into the courtyard and called out to the goat.

"Goodbye, Nemesis?"

The goat stuck its head above the fence and bleated.

Heaving his rucksack onto his back, beneath his wings, he walked towards the south gate which led out into the desert.

The sentries called a warning as he passed through the *'kill box.'* Jamin's right-hand man stood at the front gate, his expression unreadable.

"You're leaving?" Siamek asked.

"I don't belong here."

"No. You don't."

Mikhail trudged past him, showing the enemy his back. Hoping, *wishing*, the man would shove a spear into it and end his pain.

"Don't let her follow me," he said.

"What do you want me to tell her?"

Mikhail paused. Stiff. Silent. *Stoic.* He bent one wing forward and pulled out his longest primary feather.

"Tell her it's only a feather—" he handed it to Jamin's second-in-command. "I am just a soldier, no different than *you* are."

Something registered in the man's brown eyes. Guilt? This whole charade had been a setup. But what had it revealed? That all of his dreams were lies!

He trudged out into the desert, abandoning these people and their fickle, unfaithful women.

Chapter 70

Galactic Standard Date: 152,323.04 BC
Orbit – Haven-3:
Diplomatic Carrier 'Prince of Tyre'
Prime Minister Lucifer

LUCIFER

Half-formed creatures screamed in the nightmare. Disjointed images spun around him in a jagged vortex. The scent, and taste, of blood.

Gradually he became aware of the reassuring hum of the hyperdrive engines throbbing beneath him, the soft hiss of the atmospheric recycler, and muffled boots marching outside his hatch. Lucifer clutched the luxurious satin sheets—and vomited.

"Zepar?" he cried out.

Nobody answered. He crawled to the edge of his bed and fumbled on the nightstand until his hand touched a cold, familiar pin. He held the comms unit up to a pair of lips which tasted like pasty cheese-scum, stale liquor, and rotten meat.

"Zepar?" his breath came out a pathetic hiss.

It seemed like an eternity before his Chief of Staff answered.

"You're awake?" the man's voice conveyed surprise.

"I need help?"

"I'll be right there, Sire."

The darkness took him. When he woke up again, the room reeked of vomit and his own stale sweat. Bright light stabbed into his eyes.

"Shut that off?" he clamped a hand over his face.

Zepar hit the dimmer switch.

Lucifer waited for the room to stop spinning.

"How long have I been out," he croaked.

"Since yesterday," Zepar said.

Lucifer peeked out from between his fingers. His dirty-winged Chief of Staff stood in the dim light, carrying a familiar silver case.

"I don't want that," he said.

"It's the only way to control the migraines."

"I don't *want* it!" he pushed away the syringe.

He *did* want it. Desperately… But he hated the way the medicine made him feel like not-him.

He pinched the bridge of his nose to dull the pain as he forced himself upright and hung his legs over the edge of his bed. He tilted one wing forward; his snow white feathers were stained with glops of pinkish puke.

"When are we supposed to meet with that representative from the Tokoloshe Kingdom?" he asked. "I want to get this meeting with the cannibals over with as quickly as possible."

"Sire?" Zepar's wings twitched, his expression perplexed. "That meeting happened two weeks ago."

"Two weeks ago?"

"Yes, Sire," Zepar said. "You ordered us to go there right after you came back from 51-Pegasi-4."

A sense of vertigo that had *nothing* to do with the hyperdrive engines decelerating threw him off-kilter. A voice came over the loudspeaker:

"Attention all crew. Prepare for arrival at Haven-3."

They were back at Parliament? His stomach convulsed as the ship dropped out of hyperspace.

"I've got to—"

Lucifer lurched to his feet. He rushed towards the bathroom and upended the remaining contents of his stomach, his wings trembling as they dragged upon the floor.

"What—in Hades—did I drink?" his voice echoed into the porcelain bowl.

"Your usual poison—" Zepar pointed casually at the dry-bar.

Lucifer grabbed a towel and wiped the vomit off his chin. Hanging onto the edge of the toilet he crawled back up, wings flared to help him keep his balance, and sat down noodle-legged on his porcelain 'throne.'[122]

"So?" he tried to act nonchalant. This wasn't the *first* time he'd woken up, disoriented, after a night spent binge-drinking. "Refresh my memory. What did the Tokoloshe king and I discuss?"

"You mean you can't *remember?*" Zepar's dishwater-blue eyes bored into his.

Lucifer's voice trembled.

"I had too much to drink," he said. "I don't have time to prepare for my speech."

I -presume- I'm here to make a speech?

"You're here to ratify the *treaty*," Zepar said.

"A treaty?"

"Yes."

"What treaty?"

"The one you already signed."

---

[122] *"Porcelain throne"*: i.e., his toilet.

Lucifer covered by feigning disdain.

"Of *course* I signed a treaty," he said. "I'm asking you refresh my memory on the *terms*."

Zepar gave him that cold, obsequious look that usually preceded a political knife to the back, though thankfully it wasn't usually directed at *him*.

"You and the Tokoloshe king agreed we'd cede two mining colonies in Yaris Sector."

"Why would I cede those colonies to the cannibals?"

"Because we can't *defend* them—" Zepar looked at him as though he was a total idiot. "You were very upset about the death of the Leonids. So you cut a deal. They get those two planets, and in return, we get two planets that are close enough to defend."

"What about the *people* who live there?"

The last time he'd cut a deal with the Tokoloshe Kingdom, they'd reneged, attacking a Delphinium colony and devouring thousands of innocent civilians. What in *Hades* had he just done?

"King Barabas promised not to eat them," Zepar tut-tutted. "The colonies are lightly populated. They can relocate to colonies he ceded to *us* in return. He is only interested in the mineral rights."

A feeling of dread seeped into his body. Whenever he had a blackout, he usually found out that he'd been up to things he wouldn't necessarily condone. But for the last twenty-five years, he'd been free of the accursed memory lapses! Had his brain tumor returned?

"Leave me—" Lucifer waved his hand disdainfully. "I need to clean up, and then I need to figure out what line of crap I need to sell Parliament in order to get them to ratify the darned thing."

"Here is your briefing report, Sire." Zepar handed him a flatscreen. With a bow, his Chief of Staff left.

Lucifer crawled into the shower to cleanse himself of vomit. Unlike every *other* ship in the Alliance, his used real water, not sonic waves, a luxury few military vessels could afford. As he shampooed his wings, the stench of liquor, and some other foul smell that reminded him of a slaughterhouse, turned the drain pink as he rinsed his snow-white feathers. He closed his eyes and let the shower-jets pound into his scalp until the splitting migraine began to lift.

After blow-drying his feathers, he moved out to his closet to dress for his speech before Parliament, the finest suits his tailor could custom-fit. While he'd been in the shower, Zepar had sent somebody in to change his sheets. Lucifer sat on the edge of his bed and picked up the flatscreen Zepar had left upon the nightstand. He flipped through the proposed treaty. It sure *looked* like the kind of treaty he would negotiate, slightly better for *them* than for the Tokoloshe.

So why did he feel so uneasy? Like he'd just signed away the keys to the Galactic Alliance?

He queued up a speech he'd made shortly before the Seraphim genocide. The man who'd stood before Parliament, urging the delegates to give him tens of billions of galactic credits to fund some top-secret project *looked* like him, but he did not remember making *that* speech any more than he remembered negotiating this treaty.

He walked across his roomy quarters to the massive cabinet which dominated an entire wall. Built of precious wood, dozens of bottles of priceless liquor sat backlit by mirrors. He picked his favorite poison, *Choledzeretsa,* a brilliant green liquor with swirls of silver and gold.

He held the glass up and stared at his own reflection, distorted by the liquor and the way each bottle bent the light.

"Cheers," he said.

He drained the glass, relishing the warmth which burned into his belly. The silver-eyed man who stared back at him sure *looked* like him. But deep within his pupils, he could swear he saw a faint glow of red.

"Father?" he prayed. "What is wrong with me?"

Chapter 71

June - 3,390 BC
Earth: Village of Assur

NINSIANNA

Jamin stroked her hair.

"If you marry me," he said, "I will lay the world at your feet."

Ninsianna frowned. She did not want to marry *anyone*. But right now, Jamin was not listening to reason.

"What about Mikhail?"

She held her breath and waited for him to fly into a rage.

"If you marry *me*—" he surprised her — "I'll ask my father to let him stay."

He glanced over her shoulder, his expression intense. With a sudden move, he pulled her against his chest and kissed her.

"Jmmmm.... Nooooooo... Mmmpfffhhhh....."

She tried to wriggle out of his embrace, but he gripped her hair and crushed her head against his lips, preventing her from taking a breath. He tilted her backwards, forcing her to grip his shoulders, keeping her too off-balance to fight.

Just as quickly, Jamin broke his embrace. He stepped back, panting, before she could push him away.

"I'm sorry—" he said. "I just..."

He backed up.

"I'm sorry," he said. "I hope that you'll forgive me."

Ninsianna gaped. She touched her brutalized lips, not certain whether to curse him, or take pity on him?

He stuck his fingers between his lips and gave a sharp whistle. From inside the unfinished house, Firouz came out, helping a middle-aged field laborer. Behind him came Tirdard, carrying a sickly-looking toddler. And behind *him* came several other warriors, each helping along some of the sickest, poorest people in the village.

"Whatever she needs," Jamin ordered, "make sure she gets it."

He gave her a cordial bow.

"I hope, before you move to Nineveh, you'll consider how much this village needs you."

Without another word, he was gone.

*

As the shadows grew long, she bid her last patient goodbye. Alone at last, she poked through the rest of the house. It was incomplete, just like their marriage.

She shut the door to the hospital room and traced the sigil he'd carved into it, a symbol of the goddess Ningishzida.

"I can't," she said softly. "I'm in love with Mikhail."

She turned her back on it and made her way to the temple of She-Who-Is. The supreme goddess. The one who ruled over all the other gods. She paused underneath the tarp to pray that *SHE* would give her a different option.

"Please?" she said. "I don't know what to do?"

The empty-eyed statue stared down at her, completely blind. If there's one thing her sojourn in the desert had taught her, it was that She-Who-Is lived inside her heart, not in a statue carved by mortal hands.

The sky turned red as the sun dipped towards the horizon. Was it really that late? This close to the summer solstice, it was far past supper, indeed.

She hurried through the innermost alley, to the second ring where they had their house. She passed Pareesa and her brothers, laden down with a heavy bundle of wooden staffs.

"I see he put you to work?" she laughed.

"No—" Pareesa gestured at her next-younger brother. "Namhu said he *left* these. And now I can't seem to find him."

An uneasy feeling settled into her stomach.

"Mikhail would never leave his weapons lying around."

"Didn't you hear?" Pareesa scowled. "None of the men showed up. Jamin threatened, if they did, they would deal with *him*."

Her face grew hot with anger. Oh! That little sneak! And he'd distracted her, by keeping her busy?

"Bring them back to Behnam," she said. "He's the one who made them."

The not-quite-teenager said: "If you see him, tell him I *meant* it when I said I would train with him."

"We will *all* train with him!" her three identical brothers chimed in simultaneously.

"I will," Ninsianna said.

She hurried back to her house and burst inside the door. Mama and Papa sat at the bench they'd dragged out to make a table. Two empty place settings; hers, and Mikhail's, sat uneaten.

"Where is he?" she asked breathlessly.

"We thought he was with you?" Mama said.

She shook her head.

"I was seeing patients."

"Patients?"

Before Mama could question her, she hurried over to the place where Mikhail had cordoned out a place to sleep. While the blankets were still there, the multicolored-green satchel he'd brought from his sky canoe was missing.

"Ninsianna?" Papa asked. "Is something wrong?"

Her lip trembled. She scurried up the ladder to her bedroom, chanting: "*please, please, please?*"

She lifted up her blanket and peeked underneath her bed.

The weapons were missing.

With a distraught cry, she ran back downstairs.

"He is gone!"

She ran to the south gate, holding her ribs to control a painful side-stitch. The sun had already set, and the gate had been shut for the night.

"Mikhail!" she called out.

She pounded on the wood.

"Please?" she shouted up to the sentries. "Let me out?"

Siamek appeared in the ally. He walked towards her, tall, silent, and totally loyal to Jamin.

"Mikhail left," he said.

"You lie!" she shouted. "Mikhail would not leave without saying goodbye!"

Siamek held out a long, brown feather.

"He asked me to make sure you don't follow him," he said.

"Why?" she burst into tears.

Siamek's expression grew guilty.

"He said: '*I am just a soldier.*'"

Chapter 72

Galactic Standard Date: 152,323.06 BC
Eternal Palace - Haven-1
Prime Minister Lucifer

LUCIFER

Lucifer stared down at the magnificent white palace which had been his home for the first fifteen years of his life. The entire building surrounded a beautiful garden. At its center, a massive tree reached towards the ionosphere, its branches spread wide like a woman embracing the stars.

The Emperor had planted it the day the Alliance was founded, before he'd built his palace, before he'd populated his garden. He claimed it would flourish so long as the Alliance fought to protect the light. It was always in full bloom, but never once had the tree set a single piece of fruit.

It was sterile. Just like *him*...

His pilot, Eligor, circled around the palace to the small landing pad located at the rear, as far away from the garden as the Emperor had been able to design it. The impulse engines whined as Eligor engaged the VTOL[123] to aim them downwards and make a planetary landing.

"Wait here," Lucifer ordered.

He spread his wings and *flew* above the grounds and fields until he reached an enormous gate, more than ten meters tall, built into the palace. Fashioned of solid gold, the Great Gate's doors featured a bas-relief depicting the Eternal Emperor wielding a lightning bolt against Emperor Shay'tan. Only twice in his life had he seen the Great Gate opened. The day the Emperor had officially adopted *him*. And the day he'd elevated that *Bitch,* Jophiel, to the rank of Supreme Commander-General. Just to the right of it stood the equally beautiful, but smaller and much more functional Pearl Gate, made of wood embedded with mother-of-pearl.

"Do you have an ID, Sir?" the guard on-duty asked him.

"Excuse me?" Lucifer flared his wings. "Do you have any idea who I am?"

The guard's voice warbled. A frog-like Delphinium.

"If not for you—" the Delphinium saluted "—I would not have this job. But Sir? The rules are the rules."

---

[123] *VTOL:* vertical take-off and landing.

Snorting with irritation, Lucifer dug out his universal ID and handed it to the man to run through the scanner. As the Delphinium scrolled through his monitor, positioned so Lucifer could not see what information was written on it, he honed in his "gift."

"So?" he asked warmly. "Tell me how I got you this job?"

The Delphinium looked up. His bulbous eyes lit up with gratitude.

"It was while the Emperor was still gone, Sir," the Delphinium said. "You came to my graduation, the first group of Delphiniums to go through the Alliance military academy. I told you I'd always wanted to see the Great Gate—" he gestured at the much larger gate "—so you got me a job here."

"Ahh, yes—" Lucifer remembered. He read the name-patch on the man's uniform. "Santpeter, right?"

"Yes, Sir!" the Delphinium said, ecstatic.

All *kinds* of mental images flowed into Lucifer's mind, including a bit of hero-worship. No deliberate stonewalling there. If the guard was busting his chops, it was because his *father* wished it to be so.

"Well I'm glad you're enjoying your job—" Lucifer flashed him the smile that caused Alliance citizens to swoon.

The Delphinium went back to scrolling through his appointment calendar.

"Sir?" the guard's frog-like lips trembled. "It seems you don't have an appointment."

"I don't *need* an appointment," Lucifer snarled. "I'm the Eternal Emperor's son."

The guard croaked a nervous harrummm.

"L-let me look into it?"

The man touched his comm's pin and whispered something to whoever was on the other side.

As they waited, Lucifer drummed his fingers on the counter. The frog-man grew more nervous. Lucifer toyed with him by projecting images of losing his job. The man's mind filled with worries about what would happen to his hatchlings.

"I seem to recall—" Lucifer gave an insincere smile "—that you'd just gotten married, the day we'd initially met?"

"Y-yes, Sir!" the frog said. "We'd just clutched a bunch of tadpoles."

"How are they? Your children?" Lucifer projected images of public disgrace.

"You know how it is?" the Delphinium gave him a genuine smile. "They're the reason for my existence. It will be my legacy, to teach my children to love the Emperor and all that is good?"

Into the Delphinium's mind flooded gossip that the Alliance Prime Minister was 'shooting blanks.'[124]

Lucifer's smile grew forced.

"Not that you can't provide *another* legacy to the Alliance, Sir," the Delphinium back-pedaled. "You can, uhm, do other great things. Legislate, uhm…"

He grabbed a badge out of his drawer.

"There must be a mistake, Sir," the Delphinium stuttered. "Just let me make a temporary badge."

Lucifer put the lanyard around his neck. The moment he rounded the corner, he threw the badge into a potted plant.

"Temporary my tailfeathers!" he hissed.

He didn't bother going to the throne room. The Emperor was never there. He cut through the housekeeping section, ignoring the maids' squeals of surprise.

When *he'd* lived here, everything had been an adventure. He'd flown through the lofty hallways and helped the Eternal Emperor beat the old dragon at galactic chess. No matter how many times the Emperor now pushed him aside, blew him off, pooh-poohed his requests and minimized his concerns, that part of him that had grown up adoring the man he called 'father' refused to die.

Nowadays, when Hashem wasn't in the ascended realms, he was always in his genetics laboratory. It was this building, which jutted out the back of the Eternal Palace like the tail in the letter 'Q', to which he headed.

At the inner door, he met the first set of Cherubim guards. The four meter tall, ant-like warriors looked fierce and resplendent in the battle armor which accentuated their naturally armored exoskelatons. He was known here, but they *still* made him go through a retinal scanner and answer a series of questions.

Just outside the main laboratory he was stopped a second time.

"I have to speak to him," he told the Cherubim guard.

"He's busy," the Cherubim said.

"It cannot wait."

Once upon a time, the Cherubim had been under orders to simply let him in, a boy whose curiosity the Emperor liked to pique. Nowadays, it was all he could do to get the Emperor to return his calls. His father was still angry he refused to rescind the trade deal.

He twirled a long, white primary feather while he waited for an audience. The door to the laboratory flew open. His stomach sank when he saw the person his father had sent.

---

[124] *Shooting blanks:* slang for an impotent male.

"Dephar—" he greeted the tall, wingless, serpent who wore a laboratory coat and spectacles. Dephar was a Mu'aqqibat dragon, a long-lived species that dated back to the founding of the Alliance. He'd served as the Emperor's chief geneticist for longer than Lucifer had been alive.

"Why are you here?" Dephar demanded.

Lucifer tucked his wings against his back.

"I need to see him."

"He is running a genetics experiment and can't be disturbed."

"I need his help."

"Call the palace and make an appointment—" Dephar turned to go back inside.

"I did!" Lucifer said. "The Emperor isn't returning my calls."

"He's busy!" Dephar said. "He doesn't have time for your intrigues."

"I'm his son! I have a right to see my own father!"

"You are *Asherah's* son," Dephar said coldly. "Not his! For 225 years you've been lying to the press."

"He publicly announced it the day he brought me through the Great Gate?"

"The adoption was never completed," the dragon hissed, "because your mother *left* him and ran back to Shemijaza!"

Lucifer's wings drooped.

"He's the only father I've ever known."

"Well he *isn't!*" Hatred flashed in the Mu'aqqibat dragon's eyes. "Why do you think he's avoided you ever since he got back? He doesn't want *you* any more than your mother wanted *him*."

A dead chill settled into his gut. He'd always known that Dephar didn't like him. Mu'aqqibat dragons were one of the ancient races who'd fought tooth and claw to prevent the genetically engineered hybrids from gaining the same legal rights as the naturally evolved species. There had always been some sort of tension between the serpent-like creature and his mother, but he'd never realized his father's chief geneticist *hated* him.

"I was on a Leonid battle cruiser yesterday," Lucifer's voice warbled. "There were no Leonid's on it! Only Spiderids."

"The Spiderids are taking over for the Leonids," Dephar said, "just as the Leonids took over for another race that is now extinct. You are all defective creatures who are being replaced."

"That's not true!"

"You're nothing but a failed experiment!"

With a disgusted snuffle, Dephar turned and disappeared back into the genetics laboratory.

"But I need his help?" Lucifer reached towards the now-shut door. "Tell him I'm sick."

The two Cherubim guards silently escorted him back to his waiting shuttle. As it took off and cleared orbit, that inner voice which had always been heartbreakingly right broke its silence.

'Your father never loved you…'

Chapter 73

June – 3,390 BC
Earth: Village of Assur

NINSIANNA

A hollow-eyed wraith, she moved through the village, ignoring the gossip, carrying her healing basket from house to house to house. As *if* she didn't realize Mama was trying to keep her too busy to run away!

She hadn't eaten.

She hadn't slept.

She hadn't drunk.

Her eyes were so red-rimmed from crying that everything had a vague, ethereal glow, kind of like what had happened when she'd received the vision from She-Who-Is; only without the pleasant tingle of power.

She stumbled and fell.

"Ninsianna!" a feminine voice called.

Her friend, Yadiditum, helped her back to her feet.

"Are you okay?" the voluptuous beauty asked. With long, dark tresses which tumbled down her back, the hooked nose, which would have been overpowering on any other woman, was balanced by a warm, generous mouth, large almond eyes, and high cheekbones that put even Mikhail's to shame.

"I guess," Ninsianna mumbled.

Yadiditum picked up the supplies that had tumbled out of her basket and gave them back to her.

"You look like -*I*- did," Yadiditum said, "after Qishtea spurned me."

Ninsianna gave her best friend a weak smile.

"We showed him? Didn't we?"

"Yeah," Yadiditum laughed. Her expression grew concerned. "You're not going to marry him? Are you?"

"No," she sighed. "Now that Mikhail is gone, my father doesn't want to move to Nineveh."

Yadiditum glanced back to where her current boyfriend, Tirdard, the youngest member of the elite warriors, roughhoused with some boys who were almost old enough to begin training, including Pareesa's next-younger brother, Namhu. She grabbed Ninsianna's hand.

"What if I told you they drove him out?" Yadiditum whispered.

"I *know* they did," Ninsianna said. "He got sick of Jamin thwarting his every move."

"No," Yadiditum lowered her voice. "They did *more* than that. Tirdard—" she glanced at her boyfriend "—he said Mikhail was *there*. When Jamin kissed you."

Ninsianna's jaw went slack.

"He *saw* that?"

"Yes," Yadiditum whispered. "Jamin set it up."

Ninsianna's face burned.

"That dirty, no good bastard!" She grabbed Yadiditum's hand. "Thank you! Don't tell anyone that you told me."

She made her way to the temple where Papa usually spent the day, cleaning the temple granary and counting the offerings for storage—this early in the growing season, usually just lentils. She passed the blind statue with its empty eye sockets. With no guard at the door to stop her, she barged right in.

"Papa!" she shouted. "We need to talk!"

Her father stuck his head out from one of the storage rooms. His dark hair was filled with yellow grain-dust.

"You don't *belong* in here," Papa said.

"*SHE* says otherwise—" she gestured at the fresco of She-Who-Is, the one which had eyes.

"We are fallen creatures," Papa said. "We have fallen from her favor."

"No. We didn't." Ninsianna grabbed his hand. "Mikhail didn't leave because Jamin thwarted him. He left because he saw him *kiss* me."

Papa gripped her shoulders.

"Why would Mikhail *care* if Jamin kissed you?"

"He just, uhm, did?" she stuttered.

"He's the goddess' Champion!" Papa's face took on a terrible countenance. "You were supposed to help me *teach* him. Not seduce him!"

Ninsianna stepped back. Papa rarely lost his temper, but when he did, sometimes he scared her. His tawny-beige eyes turned copper-red.

"I've done nothing to encourage him," she sputtered.

"You don't think I know you stole my magic to weave a love spell around the whole sorry bunch of them and play them all against one another—Jamin, Qishtea, and Mikhail—for your own amusement?"

"I didn't—"

"But you *did!*" Papa shouted.

Ninsianna's lip trembled.

"I only wanted Jamin to be less arrogant," she said, "and then Qishtea broke up with Yadiditum, so I made a spell to teach him a lesson. And then Mikhail—"

"You cast a love spell on him?"

"No!" she cried out. "All I did was bind his memories."

"You *can't!*" Papa shouted. "That's high ceremonial magic."

"She-Who-Is helped me."

"You're just a woman!"

"So is *SHE!*"

Papa grabbed her arm and dragged her over to the fresco of She-Who-Is. He threw her down upon her knees.

"Time and again, I warned you that magic has a price—" his eyes glowed red with fury. "Whenever you cast a spell, you reach into other people's lives, change things that might seem insignificant, but are part of a bigger picture. Women are too *simple* to consider all the factors."

Ninsianna stared up at the fresco of She-Who-Is.

"She's gone silent," she said softly.

"Because you meddled in dark magic without getting *permission!*"

"Permission?" she scoffed. "Why do I need permission? She-Who-Is *herself* taught me how to do it."

"I find that hard to believe!"

Ninsianna pointed up at the fresco. "Then why don't you ask *HER?*"

"Because first you have to ask *HIM.*"

He pointed at a vague shape, barely visible behind the carved goddess. She could sense a dark power swirling within the picture.

Ninsianna pulled back.

"What is that?" she whispered.

"That's He-Who's-Not," Papa said. "She-Who-Is' husband."

"The one in the Prophecy?"

"Yes."

"The monster her mother, Ki, sang into existence?"

"Yes. *HIS* sole duty is to protect She-Who-Is from being devoured by her father."

She stared into the background, trying to discern a shape. A terrifying power looked back at her, the *same* dark presence which had looked out of Mikhail's eyes the night he'd killed the eighteen Halifian men and then, almost, turned his sword upon *her*. Abject terror shuddered within her body. It gripped her on a primordial level, like a sandstorm paired with an earthquake, hail and lightning, a hundred thousand hunting horns blown by a vast, destructive army, and a swarm of bees, every single one of them ravenous to destroy.

She could *feel* the monster look out of the picture…

…It looked at *her*…

……and it did not judge her to be worthy.

She reached towards *HIM*, her hand shaking with terror.

"Sir? I have to find him? Please?"

The picture, of course, said absolutely nothing.

"*HE* won't speak to you," Papa said.

"Why not?" a tear dripped down her cheek.

"Before you can speak to the bat-god, you must face your greatest fear."

Chapter 74

Cursed is the one who trusts in man,
Who draws strength from mere flesh
And whose heart turns away from the Lord.
That person will be like a bush in the wastelands;
They will not see prosperity when it comes.
They will dwell in the parched places of the desert,
In a salt land where no one lives.

Jeremiah 17:5-6

June – 3,390 BC
Earth: Crash Site

MIKHAIL

For two days he walked towards the mountain, the entire time, warring with his impulse to go back.

"She doesn't want me."

You didn't give her a chance to explain.

"Things are better this way."

How? To marry that controlling jerk?

His illogical subconscious, the one which refused to tell him anything about his past, had flipped from telling him to leave, to now urge him to go back.

"Look at the house he built for her," he argued with himself. "I have nothing to give her."

Why don't you go back and ask what she -really- wants?

"I *heard* what she said! And I saw her kiss him!"

Maybe you were mistaken.

"I *saw* her kiss him with my own two eyes!"

His wings flared like a raptor about to dive-bomb some hapless creature. He marched deliberately through the dried-up *wadi*, refusing to look back. His dog-tags jingled, reminding that he had an unfinished mission.

Complete the mission...

What mission? In five months, no one had sent a search party.

At last he reached the narrow side-*wadi* which appeared to be little more than an insubstantial crack. Into the sandstone, he'd etched the Galactic cuneiform symbol for 'home.' He pressed his wings against his back and squeezed through the rocks. Just on the other side, it widened enough for a man to march single file.

The closer he got to the mountain, the more it resembled the fangs it had been named after, *Hyena's Teeth*. As he approached the landside which had created a natural dam, he pulled out his field binoculars and crept, silently, up the rock fall.

On the other side, a desolate, bowl-shaped valley opened up, and then disappeared into a *wadi* on the other side. Bleached out twigs reached imploring arms towards the sky, begging for water, while only salt-marks attested to the fact that, just two months ago, this valley had been filled with water.

The valley floor was riddled with animal tracks and spoor, indicating within the last few weeks, a large herd of goats had come through and stripped it of vegetation. While the Halifians had moved on, burned-out cook fires spoke of prolonged encampment.

He pulled out his pulse-pistol, even though it was almost empty, and climbed down into the valley, sweeping the muzzle back and forth in case any of the enemy tribe remained. He kneeled at the place the dried-up stream used to seep beneath the natural dam and grabbed a handful of sand.

It was completely dry…

He cast the dusty silt back onto the earth. He'd known this valley would dry down, but hadn't expected it to do it this early in the dry season.

Now what?

He moved towards the cook-fires and stuck his fingers in the ashes. The dust was cool, but some of the bones they'd left scattered about still bore remnants of flesh, indicating it had been abandoned within the last two days.

The enemy was close…

He approached the cliff where his ship had slammed into the foot of the mountain. Fresh rubble had collapsed onto the roof, burying it even further and obscuring what was left of his hyperdrives. Before he'd left, he'd sealed off the crack they used as a door. From the amount of disturbed dirt, the Halifians had tried to get inside, but hadn't been able to move the enormous boulder.

"Thank the gods for primitive lack-of-knowledge," he muttered.

He walked over to the crevasse where he'd hidden the lever he'd used to move the boulder. An internal ceiling-strut, two meters in length; a brown discoloration marked the place where it had impaled his chest during the crash.

'If not for her, you wouldn't be alive—' his subconscious chided.

"The best thing I can do for her is leave."

He shoved the end beneath the boulder.

"C'mon, you dragon-dung."

He had no recollection of what a *dragon* was, but he assumed it must be something bad.

With a mighty cry, he rolled the enormous boulder to one side. He stepped inside his ship, allowing his eyes to adjust to the dim light. Everything was as he'd left it. No magical helper-djinn had appeared to make repairs.

He surveyed his ship, so sleek and modern compared to the Ubaid village, and yet so useless. The nose-cone was still buried in a cliff. Its back was still broken. The computer was still thoroughly dead. The food replicator still did not work. His bathroom and the galley still had no source of water. And the engines…

He pulled the manual ignition key out of the place he'd hidden it and slipped it into manual override controls. Just for hoots, he turned it, but of course nothing happened. Not only were his engines dead, but the electrical system was out of power.

He moved into the sleeping quarters where he'd slept across from Ninsianna, watching her sleep, but never touching her. He sat down in his bunk, his head in his hands.

"Now what?" he asked.

The gods, of course, did not answer.

He had a mission to complete. Only he had no idea what that mission was.

He grabbed a field shovel and made his way out to the stream. Down here, it was all dried up, but maybe at its source?

He followed the valley up past the place where it climbed up into the mountain. This was where he'd hauled the Halifian bodies. The passage narrowed and became more rocky. And then it opened up, into—

—drat!

A goat.

He backed up. Directly in front of him, an entire *herd* of goats grazed on the sparse, desiccated forage.

Two men looked up.

"*Aldakhil! Aldakhil!*" the older of the two shouted.

The younger, just barely a teenager, scrambled up the rocks, still shouting for help, but the elder man turned and pulled a flint blade.

Mikhail flared his wings, praying the man would run.

He didn't…

Goats were too valuable to simply abandon.

Mikhail held up his hands.

"I don't want any trouble," he said in Ubaid. "I just came to check up on my sky canoe."

The man stood in a ready stance, obviously an experienced knife-fighter. He was perhaps mid-thirties, with hazel-green eyes. While, genetically, there wasn't a lot of difference between the dark-haired Halifian tribe and the river-dwelling Ubaid, he wore a coarse-woven brown robe tied with a broad, green belt; the kind of clothing that was suitable for the desert.

"You kill my sister's husband," the man said in halting Ubaid.

"He attacked me first," Mikhail said.

"You kill," the man spat. "I avenge."

Mikhail held the shovel the way he would a fighting staff. While he wore his sword on his hip, he towered over the man, and didn't want to hurt him. Not unless his kinsman came back with an entire barbarian hoard.

He crouched, wings flared, just enough for balance. Unlike the last time the Halifians had attacked when he'd still been egregiously injured, while he still couldn't fly, he could flap and leap and use his wings as fighting limbs.

The man rushed at him.

"Al-iyah!"

Mikhail stepped aside and swung the shovel down to cut him off at the knees.

The man veered at the last second, depriving him of an incapacitating blow, and stabbed straight at the artery in his underarm.

"Yikes!" Mikhail leaped back. "So it's going to be like that, eh?"

He clubbed the man with one of his wings.

The man stabbed into his feathers.

Mikhail raised the shovel up into a quick block. Their weapons rang; a steel shovel against a primitive, but effective stone blade.

The two of them circled.

"Don't make me hurt you?" Mikhail said.

"You winged demon!" the man hissed.

The man rushed at him, legs bent as he slashed back and forth, a striking serpent with a single stone 'fang.'

Mikhail deflected a dozen lightning-fast strikes. He spun the shovel and, this time, clubbed the man in the back of the head.

The man collapsed forward.

"Stay down!" Mikhail ordered.

The man pushed himself back up, onto his hands and knees. He bunched his legs to lunge at him.

Mikhail crouched.

The man came at him. At the last second he veered in the exact same direction as Mikhail tried to step out of the way.

"Yow!" he shouted as the blade just barely scraped his flesh.

This time, he hit the man hard enough to knock him out cold.

Still panting, he kneeled and pressed his fingers against the man's neck. A steady pulse throbbed against his fingers. He pried the knife out of the unconscious man's hand.

"If I'd known you were that good—" he fingered the brand new hole in his uniform shirt "—I probably would have used my sword."

He glanced up at the eighteen graves he'd dug in this small, upper pasture. The Halifian tribe was not going to let him stay in peace.

"So now what?" he raised his face to the sky.

Not only did he have no idea which direction to go, but now he had to vacate his ship before he'd had a chance to resupply.

Chapter 75

Galactic Standard Date: 152,323.06
Orbit - Haven-3
Prime Minister Lucifer

LUCIFER

His most magnificent creation, the Alliance Parliament building, represented Lucifer's vision of a democratic republic; responsive to the voice of the people, but guided by an immortal's hand. Thirty stories tall, the massive, circular office building was where representatives from tens of thousands of solar systems met to discuss, and vote upon, the direction they wished the Alliance to take.

And he'd just found out it was all a frikkin' lie!

"Mr. Prime Minister! Mr. Prime Minister!" the reporters swarmed around him. "Is it true? You sold out Yaris Sector to the Tokoloshe?"

Lucifer pushed past them on his way in from the shuttle pad. Why in Hades had he passed a law banning flight, whether that be spaceships, personal rocket packs, or an Angelic's wings, from within two square kilometers of the capitol building?

"How could you do that?" a middle-age woman lunged at him. "They're going to eat my son!"

His pilot, Eligor, stepped between him and the outraged woman.

"Step back, Ma'am," Eligor said.

Six different reporters shoved microphones into his face. They waited expectantly for an answer.

"No comment—" Lucifer pushed past them. What could he say? *I don't remember making the treaty which fucked them over?* All he knew was that Parliament had instantly ratified it. After losing the Leonid destroyer, the citizenry was loathe for yet another war.

He strode into the massive, circular outer building which housed the offices where the delegates actually worked. The doors closed on the cacophony of hatred too overwhelming for his 'gift' to shield.

Eligor trotted to catch up.

"Thanks," Lucifer muttered.

The pilot wore an unreadable expression. Unlike the crowd, whose shouts had rammed thousands of images of just how badly they thought of him right into his skull, with Eligor he could get no reading. He had no idea about how the man truly felt about the planet-swap. But Eligor had always been there when he needed him and, right now, he needed somebody he could rely on, no questions asked.

He made his way to his office where an army of interns planned out his every second.

"You can leave," he said to Eligor.

It wasn't an insult. Eligor transported him back and forth to visit the Emperor. For everything else, Zepar assigned the two brutally large Angelic 'goons,' men with no personality, to stand like statues outside his door.

He shut the door on Pruflas and Furcas, and then stalked over to the desk where he'd planned, and ratified, much of what made the Alliance what it was. Carved of the finest wood, its sleek, modern lines showcased natural tiger-wood, its twisted grain a testament to how environmental hardship could turn a living object into a thing of beauty. He sank into his soft, leather chair, put his head back, and shut his eyes.

Dephar's hateful words reverberated in his brain.

'The adoption was never completed...'

Never completed?

Then why hadn't the Emperor simply evicted him when he'd come back? Especially lately, when all they did was lock horns? There must be something the Emperor had agreed to. Something binding. Something that would prove an even greater embarrassment than admitting he'd lied when he'd told the public he was his son.

He wracked his brains, but it had been so long since the Emperor had disappeared that he couldn't remember details when he was fifteen years old. The Emperor had left. The Alliance had looked for a leader, so Zepar had stepped in and groomed *him* to be the leader they all needed.

Why?

Why groom him for power unless he had some authority?

But what?

And why did the Emperor let the farce continue?

He lurched out of the chair and stretched the snow white wings which denied his species a voice because they hadn't naturally evolved. Zepar had always insisted he needed to produce an heir.

Produce. An. Heir.

They'd only gotten back three days ago, and already he'd serviced seventeen cadets.

And the Emperor agreed.

So what was so important about producing offspring?

He paced back and forth, wracking his brains about what he *thought* he knew, versus the cryptic statements the Emperor had made every time he'd tried to reconcile the distance his father had maintained ever since he'd returned.

"If you don't produce an heir," Zepar kept repeating, "when you die, everything you built will pass back to the Emperor."

While the Emperor always said: "your genetic profile is too unique to waste."

So there was some kind of agreement? He'd negotiated too darned many of them to not be able to spot a binding term which had caught the Emperor in a snare.

He queued up his A.I.

"Pull up my adoption paperwork."

A mechanical woman's voice said: "Sir? Those documents are eyes-only for the Eternal Emperor himself."

Lucifer paced back and forth. He'd never read the actual adoption paperwork, back when the Emperor had made his mother sign it. Zepar had always discouraged him from looking into the past, and he was too darned busy to go digging all by himself. The few times he'd asked about his biological father, Zepar had loaded up his schedule and fired whoever he'd sent to dig.

So don't ask Zepar…

But who would help him get to the truth?

He touched the communications speaker that connected him to the outside office.

"Miss Rigler?" he asked the receptionist. "Could you send in that intern? What's her name?" he snapped his fingers. "The ugly one?"

"Pravuil, Sir."

"Find her," he said, "and send her in."

One of the gifts the Emperor had endowed his species with was homogenous beauty. Fair haired, white winged, with aquiline features that reflected his classical notions of perfection, it was rare to find an Angelic who was less than pretty. But this last year, the training academy had rotated in a new cadet, a legislative aide who was downright plain.

At first he'd avoided her because one of the perks of serving on his staff was that, once a cadet's biennial heat-cycle rolled around, Zepar moved them up to the top of his 'appointment list.' It was a running joke, that volunteering for his staff was the fastest way to test-drive his legendary sex drive.

But he hadn't fucked her…

Pravuil's heat cycle had come and gone and, for the first time in history, a cadet straight out of the academy had remained a virgin.

But a funny thing had happened as she stumbled into his office each morning, fumbling paperwork. Pravuil didn't like Zepar, so he'd found himself enlisting her aid to thwart his Chief of Staff. He'd begun, not to flirt with her, for she was still as plain as dirt and, despite his reputation, he wasn't deliberately cruel; but to talk to her. As he hadn't talked to anyone since his mother had died.

The intern stepped in and quietly shut the door.

"M-mister Prime Minister," Pravuil stammered.

"Come in, Private, uh…"

"Pravuil," she said.

Lucifer suppressed a smirk. Unlike everybody else, where he pretended to remember their name to garner political loyalty, with Pravuil he'd taken the opposite tact so Zepar wouldn't dismiss her for becoming 'too close.'

Average height, a bit underweight, with mousy beige wings that matched her baby fine hair, Pravuil wore an Alliance uniform that hung off her frame as if it had been tailored for a much bigger sister.

"I have a favor to ask?" he leaned back in his leather chair.

"Of me?" Pravuil's wings perked up.

"Yes, you—" he gave her a practiced smile, the one he knew she fantasized about thanks to his ability to read other people's emotions. Immediately, he regretted it. The cadet had a hopeless crush on him and the smallest thing encouraged it. He wanted her to be his friend.

A friend?

What did he know about having friends?

According to Zepar, men of power didn't make friends, but only attracted people who wanted political favors. But his mother had believed a leader should be forthright. He didn't have any friends, but for the last several months, he'd been experimenting on Pravuil—his ugly friend who he had no intention of ever fucking. It was a one-sided experiment since he called all the shots, but he was trying to be fair.

Which meant *not* seducing her.

He decided to frown instead.

"Is something wrong?" Pravuil asked.

"Yes." Lucifer tapped his fingers together. "It's about a matter which is very delicate."

She leaned forward.

"How can I help?"

What Pravuil lacked in beauty, she made up for with her tenacious ability to dig up buried treasure. It had been his excuse to make Zepar keep her after her first rotation had ended and the plain-as-dirt intern had remained unbedded.

"Can I trust you to be discreet?" he asked.

"Of course you can, Sir!"

He used his gift to see inside her mind. Words meant nothing, while body language could be schooled to lie. He caught an image of her jumping in front of him, wings flared, with a pen in her hand, wielded like a sword.

His heart did an interesting little flip-flop. Not in a sexual way, of course, for she was still ugly, but in an *'aww, somebody really cares about me'* kind of way.

He stared across the room at a picture of himself as an adolescent standing next to his mother, his white wings a contrast to her nearly black ones. They had both possessed the same facial features at that point in his life, an echo of a dead woman he suspected still haunted the Emperor even though manhood had squared off his jaw.

He rose up out of his chair, padding over to snatch the picture from the shelf like a prowling cheetah. Halfway there, he remembered to soften that instinctive body language he used around women. Instead of walking back to his desk, he sat down in the chair opposite Pravuil.

"I never knew my biological father," he said softly.

"So I have heard, Sir." Pravuil trembled at having him sit this close.

Lucifer gave her a wistful smile.

"When the others aren't around to gossip, you may call me Lucifer."

"Y-y-yes S-sir, I mean, Lucifer, Sir," Pravuil stammered.

Lucifer stared at the picture.

"Before she died—" he ran his thumb across the glass "—my mother contacted my biological father. Rumor has it, well; the truth is ... I don't really know what happened. All I know is my real father claimed the adoption was invalid because my mother had never told him that I existed."

His real father? He'd never called Shemijaza that before.

"What can I do to help?" she asked.

He looked into Pravuil's mind. What he got was not fluttery dreaminess or pity, but honest compassion. Pravuil wanted to help him, not because he was the Alliance Prime Minister and she had a crush on him, but because ... just because.

Emotion welled in his throat.

"I don't know who I am anymore," his voice warbled. "Ever since the Emperor came back, things between us have been strained. I just think ... I would feel better if I knew the truth."

"Haven't you looked into it before?" Pravuil asked.

"Several times," Lucifer said. "You know Zepar—" he rolled his eyes "—he reassigns the aides to do something more practical."

"I don't think knowing who your family is impractical!" Pravuil burst out. "I may have been raised in the training academy, but my half-brother and my father call me every week. And we take leave together at least once a year."

Lucifer's blonde eyebrows reared with surprise. Most hybrids only sporadically visited their offspring, if at all. It was a deliberate casualty of the strict anti-fraternization laws which not only discouraged mated pairs, but encouraged Hashem's armies to look to *him* to be their father-figure instead of the parents who had given them life.

Lucifer handed her the photograph.

"I'm not even sure where you would begin," he said. "All I know is that she died in 152,098 and that, several months prior to that, my biological father initiated some sort of legal action."

"I'll research the media reports from that time period, Sir—" her mousy-beige wings stiffened with determination. "And then I'll sift through the court records. If it was a contested adoption, the records will be sealed, but you can sometimes get at them indirectly."

She broadcast an image of her ideal archetype, a bold investigative journalist, digging for the truth. Her wings were still mousy-beige, her hair still thin and stringy, but when her hazel-blue-grey-green eyes met his, she was the most beautiful woman he'd ever seen.

The smile he gave her was genuine and heartfelt, a smile few people ever saw. The smile she gave him in return was just as genuine. It made him feel … warm. As though she'd reached into his empty heart and made a place for herself.

A friend.

"Thank you—" Lucifer resisted the urge to clasp her hands. "I'll tell Zepar I have sent you on some bogus mission. Just keep this between you and me? Okay?"

"Yes, Sir."

Pravuil rose and shook his hand. It was surprisingly firm for a cadet who acted so meek. For him, she would pick up a shovel, bash the gatekeepers over the head, and dig.

His touch lingered far longer than the practiced two-and-a-half second handshake he'd spent the past 225 years perfecting. A warm tingle flowed from her hand into his.

Her wings flared with determination as she strode out the door.

Yes. He had finally made a friend.

The next time she came into her heat cycle, he still would not mate with her. Not because she was ugly, but because the moment he did, Zepar always made the interns go away. His Chief of Staff was too tightly intertwined in his affairs to risk pissing off. But beginning right now, he would start taking more control; starting with knowing the truth about his family! If the Emperor didn't want to be his father, then perhaps it was time he found out who his real father had been?

That small, nasty inner voice hissed:

'What the hell are you doing?'
"Oh, shut up!"

The next thing he would have her look into was all these shifty trade deals.

Chapter 76

June – 3,390 BC
Earth: Village of Assur

JAMIN

The rope slid down Assur's outer wall. Attached to the end, a large woolen blanket, bundled with supplies, bumped along in the darkness until it reached the ground. A figure appeared, wearing a dark brown cloak, and eased itself over the edge of the roof.

"Ooh! Ow!" the mysterious figure cursed.

It reached the bottom, and turned—

—straight into Jamin's arms.

"Oh, no you don't!" the Chief's son grabbed his reluctant bride.

"Let me go!" Ninsianna cried out.

"I can't let you do this."

"Let me GO!!!" she fought him, tooth and nail and foot.

Jamin dodged the back-elbow that came for his nose. Laughing, he pinned her to his chest, incapacitating her arms in her own woolen cloak.

"Take it easy, take it easy—" he spoke soothingly, the way one would to a wild animal he hoped to tame. "I'm not going to hurt you."

"You *tricked* me!" she shrieked.

"Mikhail left of his own volition," he said. "All I did was keep you busy."

A heel to his arch caused him to loosen his grip. She wrenched out of his arms and made a run for the desert.

"Mikhail!" she screamed.

Her voice echoed into the darkness.

He caught up with her easily and pulled her into his arms, kicking and screaming and pounding against his chest.

She pressed her face into his chest and wept.

"He didn't even say goodbye!"

A small, quiet voice that sounded remarkably like his mother whispered he should tell her the truth. If he loved her, he would let her go.

His mother was *dead*...

And *he* was getting married in six more days...

He hardened his heart against her weeping. She was *his* woman. He just had to make sure she stayed put until their wedding. Once he filled her belly with his sons, she'd forget all about her "man from the heavens."

"You didn't like it when I followed you into the desert," he chided her. "What makes you think it will be any different for Mikhail?"

Her lip trembled. Tears streamed down her cheeks.

He put his arm around her shoulder, tightly, so she could not run away, and led her back to the south gate. The sentries, who he'd tripled, moved around him like shadows to silently gather up her supplies from this latest escape attempt. It was the seventh time in four days.

"It's time to grow up," he said, "and think of your responsibility to this village."

Chapter 77

June - 3,390 BC
Earth: near the crash site
Colonel Mikhail Mannuki'ili

MIKHAIL

Knife-wielding men scrambled over the rocks. Mikhail crouched down, his wings spread flat to blend into the arid landscape. There were hardly any bushes here, no greenery, and few shadows. The ochre-yellow rocks were the perfect contrast to call attention to his dark brown plumage.

He pressed deeper into the crevasse and cursed. He might as well have been wearing a pink neon sign which screamed: *"the Angelic is hiding over here!"*

"C'mon?" he squinted up at the sun. "Hurry up and set."

It inched lazily towards the horizon across a perfect, cloudless sky that cast not a single shadow for him to hide. He smeared his uniform with dirt and rubbed it into his feathers.

'You should have killed the kid that ran away,' his darker nature chided him.

"I am not a murderer."

'Tell that to the eighteen men you buried.'

He stared longingly at the mountain with its sheer stone walls that only the most foolhardy human would dare scramble up. If only he could fly, he could easily evade these jokers. But his damaged wing refused to carry his weight.

Goatskin-clad feet flap-flattered towards him across the sun-hardened earth.

Mikhail crouched down, praying his paltry camouflage would hold.

The green-eyed man came into view, the one he'd chosen *not* to kill, followed by another man, a bit older, with cruel eyes and a crooked slash of a mouth. At their heels came an entire war party, perhaps seventy men, some finely dressed, but most wore the dust-impregnated robes of the robbers who plied this desert, preying upon travelers. The cruel-mouthed man barked some orders at his men. The Halifians broke into separate groups. The green-eyed man stayed, along with the teenager who'd run off, really just a boy. The father stared right at him, as if he could see him pressed into the rocks, but then he turned and hurried away.

Whew…

The sun continued to beat down upon him, giving him no opportunity to slither away to safety. He squeezed the last sip of water out of his canteen. Before he did *anything*, he needed to find a reliable source of water. At least he'd had time to grab his survival gear and roll the boulder back in front of his ship's door before the first Halifian war party had appeared.

Maybe he should have just run?

No…

It was imperative his technology didn't end up in the enemy's hands. Even if they never figured out the finer aspects of his ship, even broken pieces of metal could give the hostile tribe an unfair technological advantage.

The sun dropped lower. The sky turned an appealing blush of pink and yellow, reminding him of Ninsianna's skin. Finally, it set, casting the entire desert in a soft, grey twilight. He moved stealthily away from the valley which hid his ship, towards the rugged mountain which could give him a birds-eye view.

The temperature dropped. Beetles clicked. Off in the distance, a jackal gave a mournful howl. He felt oddly comfortable here, more at home with the night creatures than he'd felt back in Assur. Part of a prayer tingled at the surface of his memory. Bits and snippets. A sing-song rhythm. He mouthed the words until they sounded *right* in the clicking, alien tongue. A prayer to navigate in the dark. While not a form of magic, he could *feel* the Cherubim prayer enhance his awareness as he scrambled over the rocks.

Evade the enemy…

He was *good* at this. His body remembered.

Snippets of memory sparkled in his subconscious with every step he took away from the human village. A clicking conversation. A glimpse of the real-life tree which graced his Alliance pin. Part of a debrief about a dicey mission.

Who was Major Glicki?

And why did he feel such a compelling need to *contact* this person and tell them what he'd found?

A dislodged pebble tumbled onto the trail like a pulse cannon blasting apart an alien battlecruiser. Mikhail crouched down and scanned the dim outline of rocks. There. Two Halifians had decided to lay in wait.

He crept behind them, as silent as a ghost. He found them crouched behind some rocks, watching the well-worn trail.

Mikhail pulled out his titanium survival knife. He needed to scale that mountain and they blocked the only way up. In front of them the trail tumbled down a cliff-face, while directly behind them the cliff continued up the summit.

'So? You're going to kill them?' his better natured chided him.

"Weren't you just complaining I didn't kill that Halifian boy," he grumbled.

His subconscious fell silent. *Good!* If it wasn't going to tell him which way to go, he had little use for it. All he wanted to do right now was survive.

He found a less optimal location to scale the cliff. Hand over hand; he pulled himself up, using his knife as a rock piton[125] and shoving his combat-boots into the cracks. From the way his shoulders ached, he'd never abused them thus—why should he when the gods had given him wings to fly—and his damaged pectoral muscle made him significantly weaker on his left-hand side. His arm muscles began to shudder. *Damantia!* Life was harder as a human! He jammed his knife into a well-differentiated crack and began to pull—

Cac!!!

The rock came loose. Pebbles tumbled down onto the trail below like a herd of stampeding auroch.

"*Hunak!*" a voice called down from the trail below.

Mikhail looked down. *Damantia!* He'd been made.

One of the men threw a spear. Yikes! It struck the rock between his legs and bounced off the cliff-face. He clung to the rock, involuntarily shuddering. Four more centimeters and he'd be squatting to take a leak just like a woman.

A second spear came at him. His heart raced—he had nowhere to go. He was pinned, to a cliff, hanging by his fingertips, with only one foot in a toe-hold.

Flaring his wings, he pushed his body off the cliff and dropped down on them, perhaps ten meters. The injured limb gave out at the last minute; dumping him face down into the dirt, but luckily the two men weren't used to fighting somebody who could come at them from the air.

He spat out pebbles.

"Traitor!" he looked up at the useless limb.

The men recovered their spears. The first one crept towards him, knees bent, his body held sideways to make a less visible target should he choose to strike back.

"Oh, no you don't!" he clubbed the man with the useless wing.

The man fell, not used to fighting an adversary with six limbs. The second man circled around him, his spear held out, watching for an opening.

Mikhail drew his sword.

---

[125] *Piton:* a metal spike used for rock-climbing.

The weapon slid out of its scabbard with a metallic shiver, the gasp of a long-suppressed lover, trembling as it met his hand's embrace. The grip felt firm and ready. In his subconscious, a familiar blood-lust sang.

"Get back!" he flared his wings.

The Halifian lunged for him with his spear.

Mikhail blocked the spear with his blade, and then jerked it forward, catching it just beneath the spearhead where it joined the wood, wrapped in sinew.

The Halifian yanked it back. The man shouted with surprise when it came back, just an empty pole without a spearhead.

"Thank you, Rakshan," Mikhail muttered.

The second man raised his spear to his shoulder to throw.

Mikhail held his sword up, the blade touching his ear.

The man threw...

Mikhail jerked the sword to one side.

It caught the spear and knocked it out of the air.

He stepped on the shaft, quickly, so neither man could recover it.

Both men shrieked as they realized they were about to face the lethal silver blade unarmed.

"Yeah, you've heard about this, haven't you?" he said in Ubaid.

The men backed up.

Mikhail stalked forward, his wings flared, the sword held ready in case one of them pulled a knife.

"You see, it's like this," he said in Ubaid. "I need to go someplace, and I can't have *you* two jokers telling your friends where I am. So if you don't mind—"

He lunged forward.

With a well-placed combat boot, he snapped the first man's kneecap.

The first man screamed.

"Mercy!" the second man pleaded in broken Ubaid.

"Yeah, that's just me," he said sarcastically, "the Angelic of mercy."

He whacked the second man with his wing and, as the man fell, brought his fist down on the back of his skull. The blunt-edge of the sword knocked the man unconscious.

Panting more from bloodlust than from actual exertion, he rummaged through his knapsack and pulled out the small, plastic strips that he'd salvaged out of his engine room.

"Do you see these?" he held the plastic ties up in front of the man with the broken knee, whose eyes lolled, neither fully conscious, nor unconscious. "These are great and powerful magic. They can take a man, and make him stay *put* until his friends come along and cut him free."

He restrained both man's hands behind their backs, and then he tied their legs, and then he tied their hands and legs together. Dreadfully uncomfortable, but at least he'd left them alive. Last, but not least, he tore a strip off their robes and tied them around their mouths to muffle their screams. Just because it seemed decent, he dragged the two men together and arranged their robes so they wouldn't freeze once the nighttime temperature dropped. More than likely, their compatriots would come looking for them in the morning.

"Magic—" he held the zip-tie up to the nearly-dark sky. Six weeks among the Ubaid, and already he'd started adopting primitive words.

He resumed scaling the cliff to reach the mountain's summit, gripping small cracks and finding various toe-holds with his boots. Unlike a human, if he fell his wings would slow his descent, even *without* the gift of flight. He was almost tempted to cast his body off the side of the mountain to see if his inability to fly was all inside his head?

A sharp stab of pain reminded him that his disability was not just psychosomatic. Too bad Ninsianna wasn't here to…

No! He refused to think about her!

She was better off without him.

He climbed, determinedly upward. Up *here,* he could scope out the landscape and figure out which direction he was supposed to head.

Panting from exertion, he flapped his wings to help pull his body weight up onto a ledge. He scanned the dim landscape for the enemy. Not too far in the distance, a massive cluster of campfires parked alongside a dry, shallow *wadi* attested to the fact that Chief Kiyan's intelligence sources had been correct.

Had all these men *really* come together to kill him? Or were they here for some other reason? Such as a family gathering? Or an annual meeting of allies? If it was the latter, hunting *him* was just an excuse for a bit of sport. But if it was the former…

A cold chill whispered a warning.

"Assur is not my responsibility," he pushed it back.

It wasn't *his* fault the Chief's son had made a deal with a bunch of jackals.

Ninsianna's future husband…

…the man she was about to marry…

……the man she *wanted.* Not him.

He faced north-east, the direction from which he'd come. Assur rose like a beacon of light in the nearly-dark landscape, hundreds of lanterns as the Assurians sat down for dinner and gossiped about the day spent out planting their fields.

His breath came in short gasps even though, usually, by now, he should have caught his wind. Ninsianna had made her choice. The best thing he could do for her was *leave*.

He faced west, towards the Halifian encampment. *The enemy...* Why? Because Jamin had made it so.

He pulled out the binoculars he'd salvaged from his ship, turned them towards the camp and scoped out the people in the tents. The Halifians appeared to be grouped into tent-clusters, probably extended family. Most were men, but every now and again, a dark-robed figure darted between tents with their head covered.

Far to the west, his heightened elevation enabled him to witness the sunset a second time. Beyond the Halifian encampment, there was nothing but the desert. No mountains. No glisten of water. No greenery. No animals. No deeply rutted *wadi's* that might hide streams. The *wadi* the Halifians camped along now appeared to be almost dry, its greenery razed down to rubble by too many goats and sheep.

Beyond it, not a single campfire. Empty desert.

Far to the south, more lights twinkled. The land of the Uruk? Allegedly, three week's journey south, another river converged with the Hiddekel River at a body of water they called the Pars Sea. Maybe he'd head down there? Ask the locals if they'd ever heard any legends about his species? If these mysterious priestesses had travelled from village to village, telling the old stories, all he had to do was keep backtracking until he found the source. Even if the temple they'd worshipped at had been destroyed, there had to be *some* archeological evidence?

The last bit of twilight slowly expired, leaving him standing completely in the dark. He turned one last time to face Assur and fixated his binoculars on the distant village, two days travel. It was too far away to see anything other than the lights.

"Goodbye," he murmured.

His chest tightened, whispering for him to go back.

He was not that desperate.

He moved to the southern cliff, spread his wings, and fell.

Chapter 78

Galactic Standard Date: 152,323.06
Haven-3: Parliamentary Offices
Prime Minister Lucifer

LUCIFER

Lucifer rolled off the latest cadet, his erection still hard, and twirled the pretty Angelic's golden hair.

"You'll let me know if we have any success?" he murmured.

"Of course, Sir," the cadet said, far too eagerly.

What the heck was her name again?

He used his *gift* to look into her mind. Her thoughts were not of *him*, but of all the accolades she would gain if she bore the Alliance Prime Minister an heir. Her eyes were intelligent, eager and calculating. That perfect shade of sky-blue. He found himself wishing they were a muddy shade of hazel-green-blue-brown.

"All right then," he sighed. "I have to get to a budget meeting."

As if on-cue, Zepar knocked. For once, it didn't feel like an intrusion. As a matter of fact, all this week his four-times-a-day fucks had been nothing but a chore.

He took the time, despite his dissatisfaction, to reinforce the image he'd impressed into the cadet's malleable young mind of *him* as the source of all her dreams. The alpha-stud. The lover-of-legend. The...

Aw, fuck! Who was he kidding? He was shooting blanks.

He nuzzled her neck. She reeked of *him*...

"Thank you," he murmured in her ear.

The cadet stood on tip-toe for one last kiss. It was all so goddamned predictable.

He gave her an insincere smile as she marched out the door.

Zepar walked in.

"Take a shower," Zepar ordered. "You have two appointments back to back."

"I'd rather take this one off."

"You know the consequences if you don't produce an heir."

Lucifer's eyes bored into his Chief of Staff.

"About that," he said, "what, exactly, will happen if I *don't* produce an heir."

Zepar gaped, as if he hadn't expected him to spring this question out of the blue. He shrank into his most obsequious posture, his wings tucked into his back almost timidly

"We can go over the details later, Sire," Zepar said far too agreeably. "But for now, if you don't catch this cadet's heat cycle, she won't have another one for at least two years."

Lucifer tried to use his *gift* to see how much Zepar was yanking his feathers, but as usual, the man's mind was filled with tedious thoughts of numbers and appointments as if the man had no ambitions of his own.

"Very well," Lucifer said.

He threw off the sheet he'd wrapped around his waist and strode into the bathroom, buck-naked, showing Zepar his ass and the backside of his wings.

He turned on the showerhead and lifted his face up to embrace the punishment of thousands of needle-like jets pounding into his skin. He lathered up and washed his underarms, his body, and his cock. It sprang up, ready to service the next one.

"Don't you ever get tired of it?" he spoke to his cock. "Never taking the time to get to *know* any of them?"

His cock, of course, said nothing. All it cared about was the next mindless fuck.

He toweled off and then stood underneath the dryer jets, waiting for the evaporators to remove the moisture from his feathers. His comms pin chirped; his private channel which only Zepar knew. He grabbed the towel and wrapped it around his waist, strode out into the main bedroom, and clicked the comms pin into the holographic generator port.

"Now what?" he asked.

A holographic image took shape in the middle of the room. It was not his Chief of Staff, but the mousy-winged intern, Pravuil.

"S-s-sir!" she clamped her hand over her eyes and looked away. "I didn't mean ... Sir! I'll call you back."

She reached to click off her holo-generator.

"Wait!" Lucifer ordered.

The intern froze, trembling in front of the camera.

"Just let me grab my robe," he said softly.

He took his time, watching the way she pretended not to peek as he fetched the luxurious white silk garment and pulled it over his muscular body. He plopped down on the edge of his bed, automatically assuming a 'model's pose.' The hologram made it look like she was standing in the room, right in front of him, as though *she* was the aggressor.

It was too bad the hologram didn't enable him to read her thoughts. He rather *liked* her thoughts. Unlike the others, when she thought of him, she thought of funny little things *about* him, like the fact she'd noticed he preferred mustard on his fried tubers, or the way she picked up on the fact that other people's thoughts sometimes overwhelmed him. His little experiment into friendship was going rather well.

"Report?" Lucifer ordered.

Pravuil splayed her fingers to make sure he was decent, and then took her hand away from her face. Her skin had turned deep ruddy pink, betraying the fact she *had* peeked. Her muddy hazel eyes shone an almost iridescent shade of green.

"Sir," she said. "I found something suspicious."

"The adoption paperwork?" he asked.

"No, Sir," she said. "I still haven't figured a way to hack into the sealed records, so I decided to look into that other matter."

"The research grant for M-Theory?" he asked.

"Yes, Sir—" her expression grew nervous. "I got in. Sir? You're not going to like this."

An odd sense of fear struck deep within his gut. He'd pieced together *hundreds* of legislative bills he'd made Parliament pass when he'd been under the influence of a blackout, and asked Pravuil to look into where all that money was going.

"Tell me?"

"N-not on here, Sir—" she touched the pin. "It's, uhm, Sir. You're *really* not going to like this."

She looked scared. Not *"my boss will fire me for doing a bad job"* scared, but *"the Tokoloshe are about to eat me alive for dinner"* scared.

"You want to meet privately?"

Her eyes darted sideways, as if she feared being watched. Pravuil nodded.

"Okay," he said. "I've got a meeting in, oh, three more minutes. Give me two hours, and then I'll slip down to let you in my private entrance."

Pravuil clutched her flatscreen to her chest.

"Sir?" her voice warbled. "Don't trust Zepar."

Chapter 79

June – 3,390 BC
Earth: Village of Assur

NINSIANNA

Ninsianna slipped across the street which served the second ring, hiding in the shadows as she moved towards Yadiditum's house. She tapped twice upon the side-gate which led to their courtyard. Yadiditum opened it. Her best friend glanced back at her dark house and sleeping parents.

"They're going to think I'm sneaking Tirdard in," Yadiditum whispered.

Ninsianna slipped inside the gate.

"Just get me to the roof?"

"This way." Yadiditum led her through the dark inside her parent's house, to the ladder which ran all the way up to the rooftop. Ubaid houses were built so the front formed an impenetrable wall with two doors, one which led inside, the other a narrow alley which led to an inner courtyard. This meant you could move from rooftop to rooftop with only a short leap, and most rooftops had logs to span the distance. It was one of the things which made this village so defensible.

She climbed up the ladder, lugging her satchel filled with supplies. A sleepy voice called out:

"Yadiditum? Is that you?"

Ninsianna froze.

"Yes, Papa," Yadiditum lied. "I had to use the chamber-pot."

Her friend's father mumbled something incomprehensible. They both held their breath until his breathing grew shallow and heavy.

The two of them finished climbing up to the roof. From here, she could see into the innermost ring.

"Are you *sure* this isn't another escape attempt?" Yadiditum asked.

"I just want to pray inside the temple," Ninsianna said. "Papa says women are barred."

Yadiditum led her across the roof. The reed-covered logs crinkled and sagged. At any moment, she expected somebody to shout "Hey!", but nobody did. They reached the gap which spanned from this house to the neighbor who faced the inner ring.

"Be careful!" Yadiditum clasped her hand. "I am certain *SHE* will bring Mikhail back for you. You were always her favorite."

"Goddess willing," Ninsianna said.

Stepping carefully, she walked across the date-palm log which spanned the courtyard, praying it wouldn't break. Sweat poured down her back as the log bowed in the center, but she reached the other side and waved.

"Wish me luck!" she called out softly.

"First we have to get this thing down."

Yadiditum shoved the log off *her* end. It clattered to the ground. Ninsianna gripped the log so that *her* end didn't fall as well. If it did, it would leave her stranded on the neighbor's roof with no way down except to creep *through* the inside of their house.

A dog began to bark.

"Go!" Ninsianna hissed at Yadiditum.

Her best friend darted back inside her house.

Ninsianna climbed down the log, into the back-neighbor's yard, scuffing up her legs in the process. She rushed out the gate, into the inner ring, terrified the occupants would mistake her for a thief. Hopefully they'd assume the wind had blown the log down?

She moved past the most luxurious houses in the village, including the Chief's house, towards the Temple of She-Who-Is. The white linen shade-canopy glistened in the moonlight. She stared up at the empty-eyed clay goddess who graced the outer wall, the one that the commoners prayed to.

"Mother, hear me?" she prayed. "Help me find Mikhail."

She crept past the entrance of the temple itself, but it was not her destination. Her father, during his rant about shamans needing to meet the bat-god, had given her an idea.

In the central square, the men and boys had begun to stack wood for a bonfire, many cubits high, around a central pole that, rumor had it, once upon a time had been used to burn criminals alive. Instead, they'd fashioned an enormous wicker effigy. In four more days, the bonfire would be lit and she'd be forced to marry Jamin.

She reached the sacred well and looked down.

When she'd still been a little girl, her grandfather, Lugalbanda, had lit a great bonfire and performed the magic which had turned back the Uruk tribe. Just as they'd been lighting that bonfire, all of a sudden she'd become terrified. She'd run without looking, and *fallen*...

...down there...

......into the sacred well.

She looked both ways to make sure nobody would see what she was about to do. Jamin and his warriors were all stationed around the outermost wall to make sure Mikhail didn't come back, and so *she* couldn't find a way out.

Well she knew of *another* way...

...one that terrified her...

......her greatest fear...

.........she would kill two pigeons with a single stone.

She balled up her cape and shoved it into her satchel, then threw it into the well. It fell a long time before it finally hit the water and splashed.

Ninsianna gulped.

She stared down into the open black throat which yawned into the earth, waiting to be fed.

"I hate the dark," she whimpered.

She grabbed the tripod they used to haul up the water buckets and let down the rope until there all that was left was the place where it joined the logs. She gripped the rope and swung her body over the hole.

"Eek!" she hung in free-fall.

She wrapped her hands and knees around the rope and began to slide down, praying she did not fall. The jute bit into her hands. She'd climbed ropes before, as a child, but it had been many years since she'd attempted something so strenuous.

Her shoulders began to ache. Her knees shook as she gripped the slender rope between her thighs to stop herself from falling. Down. Down. Down. Bitter sweat burned into her eyes. The rim of the well swallowed the moon, leaving nothing but an inky-black sky with only a couple of stars to see by.

Dripping water, blended with the scent of moisture and another sound, groaned inside the well like a distant wind. It felt like being swallowed alive.

Her foot slipped....

...she slid down the rope.

"Eek!"

She frantically grabbed the rope.

...the jute bit into her hands...

......and burned!

ACK!!!

She lost her grip.

...she tumbled...

......head...

.........over heels.

SPLASH!!!

...into the cold water.

......water rushed up her nose.

Oh!

Gods!

...she clawed...

......frantically!

The cold water knocked the wind out of her.

…she gasped…

……for breath….

………water poured into her lungs.

She fought her way back up to the surface, but without the sun, she couldn't tell which way was up.

Great Mother! Help me!

…her hand struck something squishy….

……her satchel!

………Yes!

With a shriek, her face broke the surface of the water.

Coughing up water, she sputtered until she caught her breath.

"If *that* doesn't please He-Who's-Not—" she dog-paddled inside the well "—I don't know what will."

The rocks which surrounded the well caused her voice to echo, amplifying every breath, and making each splash sound like a horde of crocodiles thrashed in the water with her.

Now what?

She had to figure out how she'd gotten out of here the *last* time she'd fallen down, and ended up somewhere down-river.

She felt her way around the wet, slippery rocks which lined the pit. Some distant ancestor had reinforced the well by piling stones in a crude semi-circle. But the water had an ingress. No matter how low the river dropped, this well provided water, although sometimes even *it* grew a bit brackish.

She slid her hand along the inner pit.

Rocks. More rocks. Where was the cave she'd found her way into as a little girl?

Her hand disappeared into a void. Here! She shoved her hand in up to her armpit and felt inside.

Her face dropped with disappointment. How the heck was she supposed to fit into *that*? She'd been three summers old the *last* time she'd been down in this well.

She grabbed the rope and tried to climb back up, but got no further than her body length before she fell back in. Three hundred cubits up, the inky-black sky was now devoid of a moon. Should she wait until morning and call for the first person who came to retrieve water to summon help? Or squeeze through the hole and escape into the river?

Marry Jamin?

…Or climb into a dark cave?

Marry Jamin?

…Or go find Mikhail?

Her whole life spread out in front of her, trapped inside this village, condemned to never see the stars. It was just her own fear, making excuses to avoid what she knew she had to do!

Meet. The. Bat. God.

Or more precisely, work her way through a cave filled with ugly, gnashy-teethed little bats. Squeaking. Writhing. Flapping against her with their nasty, nightmarish little wings.

Ugh! Bats!

It was either them, or marry Jamin.

She dog-paddled back to the hole and stuck one leg in, and then the other, trying not to think about the horrible creatures which lurked in dark places, waiting for foolish maidens to stick their heads in.

This time, she'd come prepared…

She shoved her satchel in, held her breath, and ducked beneath the water. It was a tight fit, but if she wriggled like a serpent, maybe she could get her shoulders in?

I did this before…

She pulled herself into the hole. Her breasts caught on the lip, but just in front of her, her hand reached an open void.

There. The cave.

She scissor-kicked to force the rest of her body through the hole. Her hips got caught.

Oh, drat!

…she tried to back up…

…….and had nothing to push against…

………she was stuck!

No!

She kicked frantically, but could not force her body forward. Neither could she go back. There was nothing in front of her to help push her backwards.

Her lungs began to burn…

….*Help me, Mother!*

Into her mind leaped an image of twisting…

…sideways…

……she did…

………and PULLED…

……all of a sudden she broke free.

She shot forward, into a vast, empty space.

…Air!

……She needed air!

She broke above the dark surface.

…AIR!!!

......She gasped.

The cave was dark, without a single speck of light. Her feet found the bottom of the cave. She closed her eyes and tried to *see* using gifts other than her mortal sight. Cold water. The drip-drip-drip of moisture from the ceiling. And an earthy smell she remembered from the *last* time she was here.

Bat guano...

Ninsianna's teeth chattered. She felt in the dark until she found her satchel, and then held her hand in the stream until she sensed which way the current flowed.

Yes. That way. The stream flowed underneath the village, into the river somewhere beneath the cliffs. All she had to do was follow it and squeeze out the hole at the other end. But first, there was the matter of appeasing She-Who-Is' husband.

"So you think I'm not worthy?" she challenged.

She wasn't certain *what* she'd done to anger him, but obviously He-Who's-Not had been interfering with her ability to communicate with She-Who-Is because, ever since she'd failed to break the spell at the front gate, it felt as though her 'gift' was wrapped in a blanket.

She felt blindly, using her feet to test the slant of the cave-floor. The stream grew shallow; and then, suddenly, she stood high and dry. She shook the water off her satchel and pulled out her cape. It was only *slightly* wet. She wrapped it around her shoulders and rummaged for her striker, flint and a wooden torch.

She clacked the striker against the stone, praying, in the dampness, it would ignite. The sparks hit the wet rocks and immediately extinguished. She struck for sparks again. One landed on the animal-fat impregnated torch and ignited.

Thank the goddess!

She held the torch up, examining the cave of her nightmares.

Bats!

Lots of bats!

Little bats...

Ninsianna gave a nervous giggle. Not so many bats, really. Tiny little bats, like mice. They clung together, wrapping their wings around each other for warmth. In fact, they looked every bit as cold as *she* was.

"I'm not afraid of you!" she shook the torch triumphantly at the bats.

Her voice echoed back at her: *"Not afraid! Not afraid! Not afraid!"*

She swung the torch and circled, jabbing it at every stalactite and crevasse. The light drove back the darkness, revealing an ordinary cave. It felt anti-climactic, to face her greatest fear.

Papa claimed, to be a *real* shaman, you had to stay buried in the earth for three whole days, but she had no time for that. She had to be out of this cave and float downriver before the dawn, or Jamin and his warriors would simply track her down.

But first, there was the matter of She-Who-Is' silence…

She rummaged into her satchel and set up a personal altar on the rocks. A shell, representing water. A splinter of wood from the tree Mikhail had crushed. A smooth, brown pebble brought from the earth surrounding Mikhail's sky canoe. And last, but not least, a large brown feather pilfered from Mikhail's wing. Into the center, she placed her small, clay fetish of She-Who-Is.

She pulled out a tightly rolled bundle of herbs, pilfered from her father's stash, and touched it to her torch until the herbs began to smolder. She breathed the smoke in, holding her breath until it gave her a familiar sense of light-headedness.

She held the clay statue and tried to *visualize* the goddess' bat-winged husband as she sang a song of appeasement:

> May the god who is not known, be quieted toward me;[126]
> In ignorance, I have eaten that which is forbidden;
> In ignorance, I have set foot on that which is prohibited.
> The transgression I committed, indeed I do not know;
>
> The god, in the anger of his heart, has oppressed me;
> Although I look for help, no one takes my hand;
> When I weep, they do not come to my side.
> I utter laments, but no one hears me;
>
> O merciful god, I address to thee the prayer,
> I kiss the feet of my god, I crawl before thee.
> Mankind is dumb; he knows nothing;
> Whether committing sin or doing good,
> He does not even know.
>
> The sin which I have done, turn it into goodness;
> The transgression I committed let the wind carry it away.
> My many misdeeds, I strip off like a garment.
> Remove my transgressions, and I will sing thy praise.

---

[126] "May the god who is not known…" –Sumerian prayer

She sang and sang, but nothing happened. No sense of purpose. No strengthening of the connection. No vision. Obviously He-Who's-Not was not impressed. She reached into her satchel and pulled out a small, clay vial.

"So it's back to the beginning?"

She pulled out the stopper. *This* time, she'd brought some honey to kill the awful taste.

She drank down the tincture, extracted with goat urine.

...and gagged...

......she stuffed a piece of honeycomb into her mouth.

The wax cells burst, spraying sweet honey onto her tongue. The urge to retch subsided. She pulled her cape around herself and waited for the vision.

A subtle drip.

...The click of tiny beetles.

......The soft crackle of the torch as the fire consumed the stick.

Time passed, but still no vision. Papa must have replaced the poppy-seeds and belladonna with something that would do nothing at all!

Soon, it would be dawn. She needed to get downstream before they noticed she was missing.

Grumbling about her lack-of-magic, she packed up her supplies and put them back into her satchel. Who needed visions? She was an intelligent woman. She'd figure things out *without* any help from the gods! First, she'd search for Mikhail's broken sky canoe. And then, if he wasn't there, maybe she could pick up his trail?

The bats squeaked.

Something hit her in the face.

"Ack!"

More flew at her. Hundreds of thousands of wings!

With the coming dawn, bats poured into the cave. They flew into her hair, her eyes, and her skin. They all swirled all around her, shrieking in a terrible, angry cacophony. More bats flew in. All seeking refuge from the light.

She swung her torch at them. The sacred beverage gave the bats a peculiar synchronicity, as though she could hear what they squeaked. A shadow crept into the cave and moved towards her like a stalking cat.

"What are you?" she held the torch in front of her, hoping to chase the thing away.

More shadow cats appeared. Not animals. But immortal creatures, fashioned from darkness. They crept around her like hyenas sizing up their prey. The last time she'd been here, she'd *sensed* their presence. But now...

She could *see* them. And they terrified her.

"I came to speak to your master," her voice warbled.

The closest shadow-cat hissed.

"S-sir," she begged. "Whatever I did, I came to beg forgiveness."

There was a long silence, disturbed only by the rustle of countless wings. The eyeless shadows came no closer. But neither did they pull away.

A deep, terrible voice whispered into her mind.

"So you think you are worthy to be *HER* Chosen One?"

Ninsianna's voice warbled.

"I think that should be up to *HER*, don't you?"

An image popped into her mind. Her. Wielding magic at the South Gate. She'd attempted to break her shaman-grandfather's spell and, in the process, had tapped into the terrible dark magic her grandfather had used the day he'd formed that spell …

…the day the shadow-cats had chased her *down here*….

……to protect her?

The shadow cats whirled around her, faster and faster. They flew in a frenzy like disembodied bats. They drew her spirit into a dark vortex filled with stars.

…The stars sang…

……the Song of the Sword.

………faster and faster…

……she saw the universe as She-Who-Is had created it…

…billions and billions of points of light.

The stars rejoiced as She-Who-Is created planets, and then life to populate them. Cities rose up. Entire civilizations.

The stars spun faster…

…solar systems filled with light…

……turning and turning…

And then one day, a sickness took root in the center. She saw the vision she'd seen the day She-Who-Is had brought Mikhail here. A sword of darkness smote his ship. He-Who's-Not nudged it towards the blue stone circling the sun. She saw herself encrusted in yellow ochre by the stream, begging for a favor. She-Who-Is convinced *HIM* that she could be trusted. *SHE* sent her to Mikhail to heal his wounds.

The vision shifted into a potential future, a future possibility which was not yet set. She saw Mikhail planting crops, fighting alongside the Ubaid, and seated by the campfire, his expression unguarded and happy. Mikhail embraced her, and her belly grew heavy with child.

"Are you willing," *HE* asked. "When the time comes, will you be there for him, no matter what the cost?"

"Yes," she promised.

The vision spun faster. Out of the center of the universe, a *second* ship headed towards her planet. As it hit the earth, it split open like an egg, revealing thousands of lizard-like monsters. They swept across the earth from the desert to the west, conquering each village. All that stood between them and Assur was Mikhail.

Feathers rustled. She turned to embrace her husband…

…but it wasn't Mikhail. A white-winged Angelic with white-blonde hair, unblemished skin, and the most intriguing silver eyes she had ever seen picked her up and laid her down onto a bed. He pressed his lips against her ear.

"You think you can defeat me?" he murmured.

"Yes," she said. "She-Who-Is has said it shall be so."

The white-winged Angelic's eyes turned fiery red.

In those eyes, she saw the death of countless galaxies. In those eyes, she saw the death of stars. In those eyes, she saw limitless destruction.

In those eyes, she saw the gods, themselves, be devoured….

Unspeakable terror clenched at Ninsianna's gut. The Evil One held a knife above her belly.

"Mikhail!" she screamed as he cut Mikhail's son from her womb.

Chapter 80

Galactic Standard Date: 152,323.06
Haven-3
Prime Minister Lucifer

LUCIFER

Heavy, black filth pressed down upon his body. A small, bright light cried out. He moved towards the echo of a song he hadn't heard since the day his mother had died. Her name came into his mind, but then the light went out.

Deep within his soul, he grieved...

He tried to follow her, just like his mother had followed his father into the grave, but the filth buried him so deep that, no matter how hard he fought, it only made him weaker.

Flames burned around him, devouring her spirit.

I have to help her!

All of a sudden, he found a path...

He clawed his way back to consciousness, back to the surface. The spirit *it* devoured broke free. The dirt which held him captive howled.

"Don't go!" he wept.

But she was gone.

Somebody shook his shoulder.

"Master ... can you hear me?"

He struggled towards Zepar's voice, trying to reassemble the jumbled, nightmarish fragments that danced through his brain.

"Mmfff—" pain stabbed into his head. "Where am I?"

"In Lucifer's personal quarters—" Zepar said in a reassuring voice. "Don't worry. I'll dispose of the body."

His lips cracked open. It felt like swimming through a painful green fog, but so long as he didn't move, he could regain a modicum of awareness.

Zepar's words registered...

"Body?" he whispered.

He forced his eyelids open, but a stab of pain forced him to immediately shut them. He coaxed his body to tell him where he was.

Softness under his back...

...the squishiness of a silk comforter, clenched in his fist...

......the sharp, alcoholic taste of *choledzeretsa* ...

.........soft, feminine curves pressed into his side.

Had he blacked out during one of his mating appointments?

"She was unimportant," Zepar said. "Ki's watchmen usually are. Nobody will come looking for her."

A coppery scent assailed his nostrils. He grabbed the female lying next to him. Her skin felt ... cold.

"Zepar?" he croaked in a panic. "What is wrong with me?"

Rough hands grabbed him and pried his eyelids open. Light stabbed into his eyes.

"Oh. It's you—" Zepar's voice filled with disgust. "Don't worry, Sire. I'll give you something for the pain."

"N—"

Something sharp jabbed into his neck.

'Trust Zepar,' that inner voice soothed him. *'He helped you pick up the pieces after Hashem abandoned you...'*

Lucifer slid back into unconsciousness. As he did, he dreamed of fire.

Chapter 81

Galactic Standard Date: 152,323.06 AE
Alliance / Sata'anic Border: S.M.M. Peykaap
Lieutenant Apausha

Lt. APAUSHA

Lieutenant Apausha stared out at the colorful florescent streaks which flashed by the *SMM Peykaap* like an aurora borealis, absent-mindedly twisting his tail around the base of his seat. It never ceased to amaze him, in the emptiness of hyperspace, that what flashed by were hundreds of planetoids and stars.

A noise behind him caused him to look up. A massive lizard blocked the door to the cockpit with his corpulent frame, made all the more *obtrusive* by virtue of his garish purple robe.

"Lord Ba'al Zebub?" Apausha asked nervously.

"How long to the Alliance border?"

"We're due to drop out of hyperspace in twenty minutes," his co-pilot, Specialist Wajid chimed in, "aren't we, Sir?"

"Twenty-six—" Apausha glanced at the analog clock which ticked the seconds, positioned above the *real* ship's clock which counted the seconds down to the one-one-thousandth of a second.

"Last time we dropped out—" Ba'al Zebub bared his fangs, "our passenger had a difficult transition."

"She's from a primitive planet, Sir," Apausha said.

"I don't wish to *hear* it," Ba'al Zebub snarled.

Apausha grimaced. The ebony skinned woman had shrieked bloody murder when Ba'al Zebub had groped her. According to their AI's translation program, the woman thought he was the devil.

"I'll take care of her," Apausha said. "Wajid? Get ready to make the next jump."

He got out of the pilot's seat and worked the cricks out of his muscular frame. Unlike most lizards, who went to paunch the moment they got out of the military (case in point, Lord Ba'al Zebub), excellent breeding had given him a physique typical of the upper castes, even though, technically, he was one caste lower than a street-sweeper.

He moved past the luxurious feast Lord Ba'al Zebub had laid out and been noisily devouring without offering anybody a single bite. He nodded to Ba'al Zebub's two personal guards. They weren't bad chaps.

The two guards looked the other way.

Apausha snitched a melon and carried it back to the galley. With a practiced hand he sliced it up, slipped in a sedative, and carried it back to the rear cargo bay they'd cordoned off to make a harem.

The bulkhead echoed as he knocked.

"*Hakuna tatizo?*" he painstakingly articulated in the Earth-language his AI had taught him. *Excuse me, Miss. Would you like something to eat?*

"*Nenda zako!*" floated through the bulkhead. *Go away!*

"I'm coming in," he said. "Please don't throw anything at me? I'm not going to hurt you."

He lowered his gaze as he twisted open the bulkhead. Tinashe rose up from her cot, as tall and regal as an empress, her ebony skin glistening like velvet under the artificial lights.

Shay'tan's black queen...

The Eternal Emperor Hashem was about to get played...

"Please, eat?" he said in Kemet. "This fruit is a gift from our Emperor."

The woman clutched her dress as she edged over to the table. He picked up a piece that wasn't drugged and made a great show of sniffing, careful to not show any lizard-mannerisms such as flicking his tongue or baring his fangs.

Her dark eyes watched him as he ate the slice of fruit. She was a striking woman, well-mannered despite her terror, with long, black hair that tumbled down her back in ringlets. She was almost as beautiful as Marina...

Oh, Marina... His heart gave a joyful leap. All *three* of his crew were now married to women from the highest-ranking families. Shay'tan, himself, had fastened their hands.

"In a little while," he used their shared vocabulary, "the air will feel peculiar. It will get loud and—" he made a motion with his hands "—rough, but then it will go away."

"Sky canoe make waves again—?" she attempted to place his explanation into her limited understanding of space travel.

"Yes. Like waves," Apausha said. "Don't be afraid."

Her straight, white teeth bit into the orange fruit, accentuated against her smooth, black skin and deep russet lips. Her eyelids began to droop as the sedative took effect. Her tall frame swayed. Apausha caught her before she hit the floor.

"Let it be said that Lieutenant Apausha *always* delivers his contraband unharmed," he hissed softly in his own language.

He strapped her into her bunk so she wouldn't get tossed around if he had to take evasive maneuvers and padded her with blankets to keep her warm. She smelled delicious. If he wasn't a newly married man, he might be tempted to stay in here, just to inhale her pheromones.

The bulkhead groaned as he resealed the airlock, insurance against escape and explosive decompression. The *Peykaap* had been designed to deliver supplies into the hottest warzones and circumvent the most vigorous Alliance blockade. If *one* part of the ship got hit, the rest would survive so long as nobody took out his engines.

"Buckle up, Sir?" he said to Lord Ba'al Zebub as he passed his boss. The corpulent bastard chowed down on the rest of his feast, including, ugh! Red meat...

"This isn't my first trip running black-ops—" meat-juice dribbled down Ba'al Zebub's fleshy scarlet dewlap. Truth be told, he was too fat for the *Peykaap's* utilitarian flight-harness to fit around his belly.

His two guards buckled up on either side of him, ready to grab and shield him if the fat bastard got tossed around.

Apausha strapped himself back into his pilot's seat, specially made to accommodate his tail, while Specialist Hanuud slipped his headset over his ear-holes.

"Is she asleep?" his co-pilot, Wajid asked.

"Out like a miniature black hole," Apausha said.

Specialist Hanuud counted down the seconds while Wajid prepared to reset the manual switches which enabled them to get past most planetary defense systems. Apausha gripped the manual controls, ready to maneuver.

"Re-entry in five, four, three, two, one, hyperdrives disengaged..."

The *Peykaap* shuddered as the ship dropped out of hyperspace, right at the entrance of the Alliance demilitarized zone. Unlike the borderlands, where only a few Alliance patrols enforced their laws, the defensive ring surrounding the Alliance proper included an electromagnetic defensive net designed to incapacitate any ship which tried to sneak through, even one traveling through hyperspace, with their subspace disruptors.

"Net control," Hanuud called, "this is the merchant vessel *Odyssey*. We carry supplies bound for 23-Orion-4."

They'd changed their tail-markings to match an innocuous merchant vessel of indeterminable construction and added a false engine-housing—in other words, cobbled-together space junk—before filing an official flight plan through legitimate shipping channels. All made possible thanks to Lucifer's trade deal...

Apausha drummed his claws on the flight controls, waiting for approval. Normally they slipped right though, but lately the Alliance had stepped up bogus 'health and safety inspections.'

"Odyssey, Odyssey," the radio crackled. "What class of ship is that?"

A chill trickled through Apausha's sharp dorsal ridge.

"We built her ourselves, Sir—" Specialist Hanuud feigned offense. "From lawfully obtained space salvage."

There was a long silence. Apausha began to sweat. It was one thing to leap away while in the borderlands, quite another when you were inside the enemy's territory. His forearms tightened as he prepared to take evasive maneuvers.

"Sir? We have a contact," Hanuud said. "It just dropped out of hyperspace."

"What class of ship?" Apausha asked.

Hanuud's voice warbled. "A Leonid command carrier, Sir."

An overwhelming urge to shit his pants ripped into Apausha's intestines.

"Attention *Odyssey*," a gruff voice came over the radio. "Prepared to be boarded."

"Hashem's bushy eyebrows!" Apausha cursed.

Three more warships appeared, one Centauri and two more Leonid ships. Hanuud spoke soothing placations to the Leonid commander as Wajid followed their order to kill the FTL drives. The smaller, faster battlecruisers moved to either side of them like a pack of lionesses moving in to cut an animal off from the herd, while the Centauri corvette darted behind them so they couldn't back up.

"What are you doing?" Lord Ba'al Zebub bellowed as the impulse engines also went dead.

"You'd better buckle up, Sir!" Apausha called back. "It appears we'll be going in hot."

Apausha flipped the manual switch to turn off the AI and then moved his hand over the switch which would reignite the FTL drives so they could leap out of Alliance reach once they thought their electronics were fried. No matter how much they shielded it, it was no match for an Alliance—

"They're charging weapons, Sir!" Hanuud shouted.

Alarms shrieked. Apausha thought of his brand new wife. His greatest dream, and now he was about to lose her.

"Your Eminence," Apausha prayed to Shay'tan with all of his might. "We could use a bit of divine intervention, Sir?"

They waited for the EM-pulse to hit; either that, or for the Leonid's pulse-cannon to turn them into space dust. The analog clock ticked each painful second.

Tick. Tick. Tick.

"Attention, Odyssey," the voice said. "I don't know who the heck you know, but you've just been cleared for passage."

Chapter 82

June - 3,390 BC
Earth: Village of Assur
Colonel Mikhail Mannuki'ili

MIKHAIL

The young eagle floated lazily above the desert, carried upon the blistering hot wind which whistled across the flat, empty land. Every now and again, its shadow crossed his path, as if it was watching him; though more likely the bird hoped he'd startle up some prey.

Mikhail shoved his hands into his pockets, wishing fervently that *-he-* could fly instead of using his useless wings as a large, feathery sun-shade. His uniform shirt clung soggily to his chest. There was something hellish about the western desert, although according to Immanu, the burning hot sands *here* were nothing compared to the barren stretch they called the Badiyat al-Sham.

The eagle veered off and headed towards the *wadi*. Mikhail touched his flaccid water skin, but he dared not follow; the Halifians knew, eventually, he'd be forced to go there for water.

He paused at a desiccated shrub which showed evidence of having been eaten. Halifian goats, guessing by the tracks? He rummaged through his knapsack and fished out his camp-shovel. If the bush was still alive, there *had* to be a spring?

"C'mon?" he prayed to no god in particular. "How about a break?"

He dug around the roots, past a promising dark spot, but the sand quickly turned into bone-dry dust.

"Damantia!" He choked on ochre yellow grit. How in Hades was he supposed to cross the desert when he didn't know where he was, had no idea where he was going, and even when he got there, he had no idea who he was or what he was supposed to do?

His dog-tags jingled: *Complete the mission...*

What mission? Walk into the desert like an idiot and die? All because he'd gotten his feathers ruffled by a woman's rejection?

"It wasn't rejection—" his subconscious whispered. *"She doesn't have a choice."*

Yes she does...

"What choice? You never told her how you feel."

He continued marching forward, determined to find this mysterious Temple of Ki, dig up whatever artifacts his people had left behind, and figure out a way to get the heck off this world!

A guttural shriek interrupted his self-pity party…

…followed by shouts.

He curled his wings forward, funneling the sound, turning left and right until he identified where the noise was coming from.

The *wadi*…

The eagle circled above it, attracted by whatever drama went on within its depths. Mikhail grabbed his pack and broke into a run. Before he reached the canyon, he dropped to his hands and knees and crept up to the edge.

Ten meters down into the dried-up river bed, the cruel-mouthed man he'd noticed earlier—a brother, judging by his brown robe, of the hazel-eyed shepherd he'd let live—and eleven other mercenaries, circled around three travelers who'd been foolish enough to traverse the only source of water. The traveler's fringed kilts and open capes marked them as members of the Ubaid tribe.

His first thought was that Jamin had sent warriors out to kill him, but they were not familiar. The eldest traveler sported a bushy, white beard; the second was little more than a teenager; while the third man wore a four-fringed kilt which marked him as a man of status despite his age, perhaps mid-twenties? The Ubaid men backed into a circle around a cart drawn by a pair of castrated he-goats, holding out spears to keep the enemy tribe at bay.

A sense of duty warred with a sense of self-preservation.

"*They wanted me to leave…*"

Want? *Who* wanted? Ninsianna? Immanu? Pareesa? The Tribunal? No… He'd tucked his tailfeathers between his legs and run because he couldn't bear the thought of Ninsianna marrying someone else.

The young man with the four-fringed kilt attempted to reason with the robbers.

"Where is he?" the cruel-mouthed man demanded.

"Where is *who*?" the young man asked.

"The winged demon!" the Halifian shrieked. "We know you're allied with Assur!"

Mikhail's feathers tingled as the young man spoke.

I know that man…

He'd met the young shaman from Gasur at the gathering of shamans; the feast Immanu had financed using the money he *should* have used to pay back Ninsianna's bride-price. The man had engaged him in an eager conversation in the ancient version of *his* language, Galactic Standard, about what it was like to live among the stars.

What was the man's name again?

'Don't do it, don't do it...' his subconscious chided him. *'This isn't your problem. Don't get sucked back in.'*

The enemy spread out like a pack of hyenas encircling a herd of antelope. Nor were they all Halifians. The eldest traveler cursed at a man wearing a colorful striped robe in an unknown language.

A sense of *coldness* narrowed his vision, almost as if his mind had been split in half. One part calculated where each man stood and what kind of weapon he could bring to bear, while another sized up their weaknesses. *This man looks too old. This man walks with a limp. See those three, the ones not wearing Halifian robes? One of them is backing up, he won't engage.*

All of his frustration at being treated like a plucked waterfowl roared into his veins.

He wanted this battle.

He *needed* this battle, to prove he was still a *man.*

With cold determination, he unbuckled his survival pack and set it upon the ground. His sword shivered as he slid it out of his scabbard, the handle so familiar it felt like part of his hand.

The cruel-faced Halifian moved towards the young shaman like a slithering serpent, uttering placations. He held his hands in front to show they were empty.

Don't fall for it...

He'd *seen* this same walk, knees bent, posture deceptively relaxed, when he'd knocked out the hazel-eyed shepherd who'd almost gotten the better of him.

Just like that, the man held a knife.

The cruel-faced Halifian lunged at the young shaman. The shaman blocked the thug's knife-hand and skittered out of the way, but the Halifian switched hands and slashed at the young man's bicep.

With a guttural "Ay-i-ya-yah-yah!!!" the Halifians all fell upon the travelers.

"Where is he?!" the cruel-mouthed Halifian shrieked.

I am here, you bastards...

Mikhail spread his wings and lunged off the cliff. He plunked down gracefully into the Halifian's unprotected flanks.

"You want me—" he slammed his sword through the wrist of the first man to turn "—now you've got me."

A warm, copper scent filled the air as the wounded man stumbled, holding his severed wrist.

"Ay-iyah!" With single-minded purpose, the enemy turned and rushed at *him.*

A peculiar detachment settled into his psyche, not frantic or angry, like when the Halifians had attacked his ship, but almost peaceful. As if this were a training exercise, and these men? They were all figments of his imagination, cast out by a training AI.

Block...

...parry...

......chop...

.........collect ten points...

............just a training exercise...

.........kick that one in the nuts...

......Oh? This one thinks he's tough?

...playfully cut off the enemy's belt.

A sense of mirth welled up in his chest. He was *good* at this, unlike flint-knapping or woodworking or playing nice with humans. He *enjoyed* a good fight. Every cell in his body sang.

A spear flew at him. That sense of *knowing*, a tingling blue vision, warned him of the maneuver before the spear even left the man's arm. Images leaped into his mind. Training patterns. Subtle movement. Intent. His recalcitrant subconscious regurgitated offensive triangles. The geometry of swordplay. The physics behind the fight.

His sword whistled as he easily knocked the spear right out of the air.

Two more men rushed at him...

...he hit....

......and parried...

.........he kicked both men in the arse.

The two men went flying.

"Bring it on?" he beckoned to the next one.

All of his trouble had started when *these* idiots had paired with Jamin to drive him away from his crashed ship before he could wrangle up a distress beacon!

At the back of the pack, the cruel-faced man's eyes glittered, sharp and black, like an obsidian spearhead. While dressed simply in a dark brown robe with a green sash, the man's elaborate stone blade would rival the workmanship of even Rakshan.

The leader barked orders at his pack. Three men skirmished between them, while the other four broke off and tried to slip behind him, but Mikhail had already witnessed this particular tactic—they'd used it the night they'd attacked his ship.

"Oh, no you don't!"

His ten-meter wingspan, still useless for flight, made a spectacular pair of clubs. He slammed the leading edge into the first man's neck who tried to get behind him. Pinfeathers flew. The Halifian fell, gasping for breath.

You're lucky I didn't use my sword....

He hit the second man, knocking him flat upon his back.

"Stay down!" he poked the tip of his sword under the enemy's chin.

The men from Gasur took advantage of the distraction. They rushed into the Halifian tribe's now-unprotected flank. The old man drove a stone blade into one of the striped-robed men's ribcage while the teenager stood like a tree-trunk, wielding his spear to protect his comrade's back.

Mikhail whirled and flapped, unable to get fully airborne, but his wings enabled him to move in ways the Halifians had never seen. His sword sang a frustrated death-song as he chopped off hands and fingers, but he made himself stop short of actually killing any of his prey.

"Kill the leader—" his ears roared with bloodlust.

He fought towards the cruel-faced man, but the desert hyena expended his men's lives; wearing him down before he would personally engage.

The three Ubaid took down a few more mercenaries. The old man proved to be a remarkable fighter, while the teenager was surprisingly agile for a kid, not much older than seventeen. As the tide began to shift, the three mercenaries who wore a different style of dress, neither Halifian nor Ubaid, grabbed their injured comrade and began to back away.

The cruel-mouthed man shouted insults at his cohorts.

The three colorfully-robed strangers turned tail and ran.

"That's what happens when you consort with hyenas!" the young shaman from Gasur shouted.

With a cursed expletive, the cruel-mouthed man turned towards Mikhail and snarled in broken Ubaid— "we shall be back, in much greater numbers."

His men backed up, dragging their injured towards the large Halifian encampment which lay towards the north. Mikhail stood, panting, fighting the urge to run after them and cut out their entrails. Some might die from their injuries, but he'd resisted the urge to kill them.

"Colonel Mannuki'ili," the young shaman greeted him. *"Go raibh maith agat.* Thank you!"

"Stand back!" Mikhail whipped his sword up, not certain who he could trust.

"Winged one, we are your friends," the shaman said. *"Cairde, tá?* Friends? Remember? We broke bread together in Assur?"

All of the shaman's silly rituals, Immanu's insistence he must eat and drink and share the salt, all came rushing back as his bloodlust warred with the fact this human spoke his language.

"Cairde, friends," the shaman spoke soothingly. "We spoke of your magic. *Meteorology,* you called it? The study of when it's supposed to rain."

The inane facts, spoken in an archaic version of Galactic Standard, calmed him in a way the half-forgotten Cherubim prayers seemed incapable of doing. The young man gripped his bicep. A crimson stream seeped between his fingers.

"You are hurt?" Mikhail spoke in Ubaid.

"Those Halifian bastards are ruthless knife-fighters," the shaman said weakly.

His two companions helped him over to a boulder and sat him down. The older man tugged off his own cape and pushed it into the shaman's arm to staunch the flow of blood.

Mikhail struggled to remember the young shaman's name.

"Sagal-zimu?"

"Ahh, you remember me!" the shaman gestured at a severed hand which Mikhail had chopped off the first Halifian to rush at him. "I can see why they call you Sword of the Gods?"

Mikhail frowned. The *last* thing he wanted was to indulge their foolish superstitions.

"Why are you here?" he asked.

The shaman looked to his companions.

"We are here because of *you*."

"Me?" Mikhail asked. "Did Immanu send you after me?"

"No," Sagal-zimu said. "Right after we last met, our chief, Jiljab, sent me on a quest along with *these* good men—" he gestured at his companions "—to seek out information about the temple that you seek."

"I am Gimal—" the older men spoke, the one who was handy with a knife "—and this is my nephew, Harrood—" he pointed at the teenage boy. "Twice a year, we travel to the confluence of the two great rivers to trade with the people who live around the Pars Sea. Chief Jiljab asked if we'd bring Sagal-zimu to swap gifts in exchange for information."

"What kind of information?" Mikhail asked.

"About the Priestesses of Ki," Sagal-zimu said. "We'd hoped to find out where the legends originate from."

A lifetime of distrust warred with a sense of: *you would do that for me, really?* He forced his expression to remain neutral.

"And what does Chief Jiljab hope to gain out of all this?"

"Needa," Sagal-zimu said.

"Needa?" Mikhail's wings flared with surprise. "Ninsianna's mother?"

"She's originally from Gasur," Sagal-zimu said. "She was apprenticed to our healer, but then Immanu lured her away."

Feigning nonchalance, Mikhail wiped the blood off his blade, scrutinizing the traveler's body-language as he slipped it back into its sheath.

"So you're saying Needa put you up to this?"

"Needa? No—" the young shaman gave a weak grin. "It was a blow to our honor, when Needa moved to Assur. We hoped, rather than let her husband marry her daughter off to Nineveh's young *Muhafiz*, perhaps we could entice her to return to Gasur?"

Mikhail's head swam as an imaginary man wielding a tiny hammer smacked him right between the eyes, exacerbating days of frustration, escape, and a side-helping of dehydration. Ugh! These humans! And all their petty intrigues! But Sagal-zimu's mission was useful, even if it was self-serving.

"So what did you find out when you reached the junction of the rivers?" he forced his voice to remain nonchalant.

The shaman's grin disappeared.

"You have made some powerful enemies," Sagal-zimu said. "One of the men you killed was not just Marwan's son-in-law, the shaykh who rules the eastern half of the desert, but he was also the only child of Yazan, the most powerful shaykh in the western half. The Amorites and the Uruk both use the Halifians as a mercenary army, and *both* covet Ubaid land."

"So tell me where to find this temple," Mikhail said, "and I shall be gone from your lands."

"Every village we visited has a different myth—" Sagal-zimu shook his head. "Some say they came from the west, others from the south or north. But they all agree, the temple was destroyed."

A sense of hopelessness tumbled down on top of him, like being buried alive in an avalanche.

"I'll question them myself?" Mikhail said. "There may be things you don't understand that mean something to *me*. Like when Zartosht sang the song about the Cherubim?"

"You don't understand," Sagal-zimu said. "Yazan's allies control every known water source between here and the Baranuman River. It is why we were forced to traverse this *wadi*.

"So I'll go north—" *back past the Halifian tribe and their treacherous encampment* "—and then I'll cut across."

"Once you leave the Pars Sea, the two great rivers diverge. One heads west, the other north-east, with not a single drop of water in between. No one has ever walked straight across the Badiyat al-Sham and survived."

"So how did *you* travel to this other river?"

"We bribed the Uruk to give us safe passage through their land," Sagal-zimu said, "but halfway there, Yazan attacked."

"I'm on good terms with one of the Amorite traders—" Gimal added. "He warned us in time to escape."

"Which is why we risked traveling Tharthar *wadi*," Sagal-zimu said. "The eastern Halifians have never cared for the Amorites. We'd hoped Marwan's sons—" he pointed in the direction the cruel-mouthed man had disappeared "—would be open to bribes."

Mikhail's wings drooped. So much for his plan of traveling from village to village, gathering information.

Sagal-zimu swayed, and then he toppled forward. With a cry of dismay, his companions lowered him to the ground.

"He's badly hurt," the old man said. "We need to find a healer."

"Not with *this* wound—" Mikhail touched next to the slash where the blood continued to flow. "He won't live long enough to get back to Assur."

He moved towards the cliff-face. He'd left his survival pack at the top, along with his trauma kit. What he wouldn't give to be able to fly up instead of climb!

As if on cue, the young eagle he'd been following, the one he suspected was the *same* eagle that had graced the valley where his ship had come down, landed atop the cliff and stared down at him with watchful, yellow eyes.

"Don't rub it in," he muttered.

The eagle tilted its head, as if it understood. It was a large bird, with plumage remarkably similar to his *own* black-brown wings, sprinkled with gold, and a bit of grey on its underfeathers marking it as a juvenile.

"I don't suppose I could get you to throw my bag down?" he asked.

With a flap of its three-meter wingspan, the eagle took flight...

...with his survival pack in its claws.

"Hey!"

He stretched his wings upwards and tried to follow, but the traitorous limbs would not grant him the gift of flight. He scrambled up the cliff, flapping his wings to gain a bit of momentum. At the top, he picked up a rock and threw it at the eagle.

"It is *mine!*" he shouted.

With a squawk, the eagle dropped the pack and headed north-east, the direction he'd just come from. All three Ubaid men threw their bodies to the ground.

"She-Who-Is has sent an omen!" Sagal-zimu cried out. "You must return to Assur right away."

"It's just an eagle," Mikhail said.

"Mountain eagles are sacred," the shaman said. "They're the eyes of She-Who-Is."

The ever-present wind groaned through the *wadi*.

"Mhiiii-kaiii-elllll..."

It sounded like Ninsianna, calling out his name.

His bones filled with a terrible sense of dread.

"Please? Escort us back?" the old man pointed at the eagle. "If you do not, *SHE* will visit calamities upon us until you do."

"I'll think about it."

Without another word, he stalked towards the place the eagle had dropped his survival pack. He rummaged through it until he found his trauma kit. He would bind the shaman's wounds, and then he would *leave*.

As he turned back towards the *wadi*, a dust cloud on the horizon caught his attention. He pulled out his binoculars and twisted the knob to focus.

Stretching across the horizon, hundreds of men marched in a semi-organized fashion. Running *towards* them were the three men who'd broken off from the Halifian pack and run away. He remembered Chief Kiyan's warning, that he'd received intelligence that his act against the Halifians had caused old enemies to unite with a single purpose:

…destroy Assur.

A single, silent terror gripped his gut.

Ninsianna…

He grabbed his gear and ran back to the *wadi*.

"Abandon the cart," he shouted. "We've got to leave, right now!"

Chapter 83

June - 3,390 BC
Earth: Village of Assur
Colonel Mikhail Mannuki'ili

MIKHAIL

Assur rose out of the desert like a fairytale city; her lumpy, mud-brick walls more welcoming than a modern skyscraper. Just beyond, the Hiddekel River beckoned with its blue-green water, an endless supply which could outlast any siege.

"Home," Sagal-zimu murmured feverishly, supported between himself and the old trader, Gimal.

"Home," Mikhail hollowly echoed. He didn't *want* it to be home. But Assur's walls were defensible and, right now, Sagal-zimu needed a place to heal.

All four of them glanced over their shoulders like a herd of nervous antelope. The Halifians had dogged their steps for the last three days.

"Let's move," Mikhail said. "I'm not certain the fact we've crossed the border will deter them."

He and Gimal half-carried Sagal-zimu while Harrood walked behind them, leading the two now-cartless he-goats. The shaman's wound throbbed an angry shade of red, laced with black veins and putrescent yellow-green pus. Somewhere in his past, he must have received some kind of first responder training, because he'd known what to do with his trauma kit, but he had no antibiotics, and the packets of disinfectant were inadequate to treat infection.

With a curious sense of joy-dread, he approached the village, half of him hopeful, the other half chiding him for giving in to his weakness. He scanned the walls, hoping to catch sight of Ninsianna. Would she come to the gate to greet him? Or would she be so angry, she'd cross her arms refuse to speak to him?

The sentries sounded the alarm: *Beware! Beware! Beware!*

Yes. They *should* be aware. But the danger wasn't *him*. There were hundreds of mercenaries amassing along their border.

As they drew close to the gate, Mikhail murmured:

"If they turn me away, I want *you* to go inside."

"If they do, make your way to Gasur," Gimal said. "Harrood will go with you. He'll make sure you get settled in."

Mikhail glanced at the stoic teenager who'd peppered him with questions about how to use a sword. What he wouldn't give to have an entire army to train just like *him*. Kids who *wanted* to learn new ways to fight. Not Jamin's haughty 'elite warriors.'

"First I have to warn Chief Kiyan."

"If he'll listen," Gimal said.

"If he won't," Mikhail said, "then maybe he'll listen to *you*?"

The gate opened. Jamin's elite warriors came pouring out like wasps out of a shaken hive, a bit ragged around the edges, as if they'd only just come back from a lengthy reconnaissance mission. As much as he resented the fact they wielded their spears as though *he* was the enemy, when the Halifians attacked, they were going to *need* that kind of cohesion. Otherwise, Ninsianna—

Oh, gods! What if she'd already gotten married?

The devil, himself, stalked out of the gate, his black eyes glittering with fury.

"Where is she?!"

Mikhail helped Sagal-zimu forward.

"We have injur—"

Jamin pulled his obsidian blade and lunged at him like a psychotic hyena.

"What did you DO with her?!!"

The knife came towards his jugular. Mikhail let go of Sagal-zimu and grabbed Jamin's wrist. He pushed the handle towards his own forearm, twisting the wrist sideways to disable it in the crook of his elbow before stepping back, causing the knife to fall gently to the ground.

Jamin's expression turned to confusion, but the man was an experienced fighter and, over the course of their confrontations, he'd learned a couple of tricks.

He lunged for Mikhail's still-sheathed sword.

Mikhail clobbered him with one of his wings. The warrior clawed at a face full of feathers, filling the air with soft, fluffy under-feathers.

"As I was *saying*—" Mikhail ground out through frustrated teeth "—Sagal-zimu is injured. We need your *fiancé* to look at his wound immediately."

Jamin immediately went for his throat.

"I know you took her!"

"Took who?" Mikhail deflected the hit.

"Don't toy with me!" Jamin rushed at him again.

Mikhail stepped back.

"*Damantia!* Man! I don't want to fight you. I come bearing news of developments on the border."

The teenager, Harrood, stepped over to talk to Ugazum, one of the second-tier warriors and a distant cousin. The two young men pressed their heads together, looking remarkably alike. Ugazum gestured to Siamek. Jamin's second-in-command listened to what Harrood had to say.

Jamin circled, his stance spread wide in an intimidating crouch, his black eyes wild and filled with dark circles.

"We can't *find* her!" he shrieked. "She went out into the desert, after *you!*"

"Ninsianna?"

"Yes!" his voice took on a frantic edge. "She's been missing for the last three days!"

A terrible sense of dread twisted in Mikhail's stomach.

"We did not see her."

"You lie!"

"No!" Gimal interrupted. "For the last three days, the winged one has been with *us*!"

Jamin circled, panting like a rabid dog. His kilt appeared ragged; his chiefly shawl dusty, his limbs sluggish and weary, as though he hadn't slept. Siamek stepped up to him and grabbed his shoulder.

"Jamin—"

Jamin whirled to hit his second in command. Siamek ducked, as though this was something he'd done many times.

"Jamin," he said soothingly. "Ninsianna isn't *with* them. Bring them inside, and we'll interrogate them about what they *know*."

Jamin jabbed a finger at Mikhail.

"If she is harmed," he hissed, "I *swear* I'm going to kill you."

Mikhail looked out into the desert. If she'd gone back to his ship, the Halifians would have captured her. If they *had*, he wouldn't be able to rescue her alone.

"Let's get Sagal-zimu to see Needa," he said. "And then I need to speak to your father."

"You'll answer to *me!*"

"No!" Mikhail and Siamek both said at the exact same time.

"I mean—" Siamek back-pedaled "—we need to gather a war-party. To do that, we need authorization from the Chief."

Jamin stumbled, as though he might fall over.

"Take the shaman to see Needa," he hissed. "And then, you're going to tell me where she is!"

Harrood darted forward to shore up Sagal-zimu. His cousin, Ugazum, grabbed the two castrated he-goats which carried their water, along with what little trade-goods they hadn't been forced to abandon along with the cart.

Mikhail tucked his wings against his back as the elite warriors surrounded him with their spears. He was now in a worse position than when he'd left. And *this* time, there were no wise old women at the gate to let him in.

It's your own damn fault...

Yes. It was. He never should have left.

He knew better than to attempt to speak to Jamin. The man was irrational. He turned to Siamek.

"Tell me what you know?"

Siamek relayed everything they'd done to prevent Ninsianna from leaving the village, including watching her with spies and quadrupling the guard. He did not hold anything back, her numerous escape attempts, the humorous ways they'd repeatedly turned her back, and the fact Jamin had sent out patrols with orders to *kill* him if he dared step foot back onto Ubaid land.

They arrived at Immanu's house.

Needa burst out the door, her expression frantic.

"Mikhail! We'd hoped she'd gone with you!"

Ninsianna's mother threw her arms around him and pressed her face against his chest. Mikhail stood stiffly, not sure how to handle a crying woman, and even *less* sure whether he should let her see he was every bit as terrified as *she* was. He gave Immanu a helpless look. The shaman redirected his wife.

"Look, Needa?" Immanu said. "Sagal-zimu needs our help. Let's attend to him, and while we do, we'll discuss what everybody knows."

Gimal greeted Needa warmly. It was obvious the two knew each other, while Harrood hung back, his expression shy. By the time he'd been born, Needa had already left Gasur.

They all crammed into Immanu's modest house. Him. The Gasurians. And all of Jamin's elite warriors. Needa's expression transformed from frantic mother into a competent drill sergeant as she directed them to lay Sagal-zimu upon the workbench which she used as an operating table. She took the curved scissors that he'd given her as a gift and used them to cut off the crude bandage they'd wrapped around the shaman's arm.

They all cringed as the room filled with the stench of putrifying flesh. Needa poked at the puss-filled crater. She frowned at the shiny coating which held the flesh together instead of stitches.

"What kind of magic is this?" she asked.

"It's called *wound glue*," Mikhail said. "I used the last of it to stop the bleeding."

"Well you missed something—" she pointed at a piece of skin which bubbled outward, the flesh underneath an angry blackish-red. "He's bleeding internally."

He experienced a twinge of guilt.

"Which is why we brought him *here*, Ma'am."

As she worked, he drilled Immanu for information about Ninsianna's disappearance. His story was not that different than Siamek's, only the shaman shared one additional detail. Ninsianna had been devastated that he'd left without saying goodbye.

Mikhail did not admit: *'I left because I saw her kissing Jamin.'*

The devil, himself, reappeared, followed by his father. Instead of ceremonial garb, the Chief wore a simple work-kilt. His hirsute beard remained un-beaded, and his bare shoulders sported freshly-landed sparring bruises.

"Jamin, wait outside," the Chief ordered.

"He *took* her!"

"Apparently not."

"She's *my* fiancée!"

"This isn't the first time she's run away," Chief Kiyan said.

Jamin lunged at him. The Chief's enforcer, Varshab, grabbed the irrational young man and shoved him backwards towards the door. Jamin was strong, but Varshab was built like Assur's outer wall; immovable and thick.

"Father, please?" Jamin's voice turned frantic. "I have to know what he knows!"

The Chief's expression softened at his son's distress.

"Very well," he said, "but remain silent. The rest of you—" he gestured at the warriors "—everybody out, except for Siamek."

While Needa dumped an astringent-scented embrocation into Sagalzimu's now-reopened wound, the Chief filled in additional details about what they'd done to search. Jamin had run his warriors ragged, searching high and low. They'd even gone, hat in hand, to the nearest villages, Nineveh and Eshnunna,[127] but the allied chiefs swore she hadn't gone there.

"Who was the last person to see her?" Mikhail asked.

"Yadiditum," the Chief said. "I just sent a runner to get her."

The outer door opened. A warrior led in a dark-haired beauty.

Mikhail greeted Ninsianna's best friend.

"I understand you saw her the night she disappeared?"

The young woman's eyes filled with tears.

---

[127] *Eshnunna:* a Sumerian city-state along the Diyala River, a tributary to the Tigris.

"I helped her get to the temple," she said, "so she could pray to the goddess, *inside—*"

"It's forbidden for women to breach the inner sanctum," Immanu said curtly.

"Which is *why* she went at night!" Yadiditum hissed. "You all knew she didn't want to marry Jamin, but *you—*" she jabbed a finger at the Chief "—only care about your treasure, while *you—*" she shrieked at Immanu "—promised if she came back, you wouldn't make her marry Jamin, and then you reneged. And *YOU—*" she rammed a finger right up at Mikhail's nose "—you LEFT without giving her a chance to EXPLAIN what you think you saw!!!"

"Explain what?" Immanu and the Chief both asked at once.

Jamin's lip curled into a self-satisfied smirk.

Mikhail stared down at the furious little badger. She *knew?* Scalding mortification crawled up into his cheeks. He ruffled his feathers to disperse the sudden heat.

"I *left,*" he said guiltily, "because I thought I was in her way."

Yadiditum snorted, but her expression softened. She paced back and forth, clutching the hem of her shawl-dress.

"I *knew* I shouldn't help her," her voice warbled, "but she was headed *into* the center of the village, not the outer ring. She said her satchel held the implements for prayers."

"Are there any secret passageways?" Mikhail asked. "Some place, from inside the temple, that she could have gotten through the gates? Or maybe even hide until the wedding date was past?"

"There is nothing," Immanu said. "The temple was designed by my father to store grain in case we had famine or a siege."

"Are you *certain* he didn't build a secret passage?"

"I helped lay the bricks for that temple myself—" Chief Kiyan shook his head. "At the time, I was *Muhafiz.* My father insisted I *learn* what it took to build a village so I would carry on, long after he was gone."

"It was our fathers' greatest fear," Immanu said, "that we would squander everything they had built."

Her greatest fear…

Have you ever feared the dark?" Ninsianna had whispered.

"No," he had said. *"The Cherubim believe the dark can be your friend."*

Mikhail grabbed Immanu by the shoulders.

"I think I know where she went."

He glanced at Jamin. With grim determination, his enemy stepped aside and let him pass. The warriors fell in behind them as, together, they marched into the street. Mikhail stopped at old Behnam's house.

"Mikhail?" the woodworker gave him a toothless grin. "We'd feared you'd never return."

"I have to borrow this—" he grabbed the biggest stone axe. "I can't promise I won't break it."

"Then break it," Behnam said. "When you come back tomorrow, I shall show you how to fashion a new one."

The villagers fell in line behind him as he turned, not *up*, towards the temple like they expected, but *down*, into the outermost ring. He stopped at the well, the one which had gone completely dry.

"She's down there," Mikhail said.

Jamin and the warriors all peered down into the well.

"The last place she was seen was near the *central* ring," Jamin said. "I verified Yadiditum's story. Ninsianna climbed over the roof to the innermost ring."

"This well is fed by an underground stream—" Mikhail put the stone axe into the water-bucket which dangled from the tripod. "In the central well, the water runs deep, but down here?"

He lowered the axe into the well. After what seemed like an eternity, the heavy bucket clattered down at the bottom.

"This well always dries up," Jamin said.

"That's because this end of the cave is higher," Mikhail said.

"Cave? What cave?"

"The underground stream which feeds all three wells."

He untied the rope and then retied it, more tightly, onto the legs of the tripod. He sat on the edge of the low stone wall and dangled his legs into the hole. Jumping off a cliff? With that, he could flare his wings and be fine. But if he fell into the hole?

"Let me go after her," Jamin pleaded. "Please? She is *my* fiancée."

Mikhail stared at his adversary.

"If you touch her again," he said coldly, "I will kill you."

Wings smushed against his back, he swung out over the yawning hole and began to lower his body into the gaping maw. Hand over hand, the walls became claustrophobic. His shoulders began to ache. The sun grew tiny as the earth swallowed him alive.

Embrace the dark. Hide in plain sight.

He thought of his first glimpse of her. A creature of legend. Stepping through a ray of light to save his life.

How could he ever leave her? Even if she married another.

At last his combat boots thudded upon the bottom. Dozens of broken buckets littered the bone-dry well. He felt along the bottom, gauging the strength of the bedrock. At last he found the place where, sometimes, you could get the bucket down a bit deeper. He shoved his arm down into the hole. At the end of his fingertips, it felt like the hole suddenly opened up.

The air felt cooler, and definitely damp.

"Ninsianna?"

His voice echoed, confirming his theory there was a cave, but he heard nothing. Not a cry. Not a whimper. Nothing but the sound of dripping water and the rustle of bats.

A sense of terror clenched at his intestines.

Her greatest fear…

"Ninsianna!" he shouted. "I am coming!"

He picked up the stone axe and stood over the hole, his muscles straining as he *pictured* the obstacle which stood between him and her.

The darkness which terrified him flooded into his body; icy cold strength, blended with rage. He pictured the rock beneath him. The rock was his enemy. The rock stood between him and the woman he loved.

A single word gurgled up from his subconscious.

"*Solvite,*" he whispered.

Wielding every ounce of strength, he SLAMMED the stone axe into the rock.

Chapter 84

June – 3,390 BC
Earth: Village of Assur

NINSIANNA

All around her, the shadows shrieked. The stars screamed as the Evil One consumed them.

Ninsianna trembled as the universe got torn apart. Helpless. Frozen. She watched the Evil One devour stars and planets, gods and goddesses, plants and animals and people who she loved. Everything Moloch touched, first it grew unnaturally fast, and then it deformed and devoured itself.

Faster and faster.

Again and again and again.

She clamped her hands over her ears as the star-song turned into screams. She had to help them!

"Noooo…" she fought the shadows which held her back.

Darkness…

…Fire…

Darkness…

…Fire…

Whirling and whirling.

She crawled away from the terrifying creatures which writhed in the dark.

"Mikhail!" she screamed.

But Mikhail did not come…

As she lay, trembling, some part of her registered her own hunger, registered exhaustion, the fact she was wet and cold. But whenever she tried to move, she fell back into the vision.

Darkness….

…Light….

Darkness….

The night sky exploded.

A pillar of white light appeared within the dream.

A dark figure emerged from the shadows, backlit by the light. A bat-winged horror stood wielding a battle-axe. All around him flew shrieking, flying shadows. As he moved towards her, the shadows did *HIS* bidding.

"No," she gave a strangled cry as the nightmare knelt beside her.

"Ninsianna, *dúisigh*! Wake up!"

She tried to crawl away, but got cast back into the nightmare. Strong arms picked her up and cradled her to *HIS* chest.

"So much power," she murmured.

The illusion dissipated.

...Not the Dark Lord...

......Not *HIM*...

Jostling.

...Dangling.

......Other people touched her.

A woman sobbed.

Mama? She tried to speak, but her mouth would not work. The voices sounded far away.

"What is wrong with her?" Mikhail asked.

"She is stuck between this world and the Dreamtime," Papa said. "Women get stuck there too easily, which is why they're forbidden to perform magic."

She fought her way towards the voices, but the dream trapped her. Outside of the vision, someone chanted and blew cedar-smoke into her nostrils. Suddenly, Papa stood within the nightmare. The Evil One's flames reached towards him.

"Be gone!" he commanded.

The flames died down to ashes.

Ninsianna flew into her Papa's arms, but he felt incorporeal, as though she hugged the morning mist. Instead of the four-fringed sheepskin kilt he wore in the material realms, here his kilt was woven from solid gold, with a filigreed headdress instead of one made of feathers.

"Papa!" she cried out. "What is happening to me?"

"You're stuck in-between," he said. "If you can't find your way back out, your body will die."

"My body won't obey me!" she began to weep.

"Whenever you do dream work," he said, "you have to stay grounded. Never go into the astral realm without a symbol of something you love to pull you back to earth."

"What do you focus on?"

"Your Mama—" Papa's homely face softened into a smile. "She can call me back from the most horrific vision." He pulled a lock of Mama's hair out of his small medicine bag, braided into a slender rope, with a lapis lazuli bead knotted on either end. "Whenever I grow frightened, I just pull out this braid and focus on your Mama's voice, and the next thing you know, I wake up."

The fact Papa let Mama boss him around all of a sudden made sense.

"So how do I get out of here?" she asked.

"Focus on your body," Papa said. "*Feel* your arms and legs. Picture your spirit pouring back into your fingers like water. Allow yourself to float in it, until you become aware of everything which touches your skin."

"My body is cold."

"You were trapped in a cave for three days."

Ninsianna shivered as she *felt* her compromised state. So tired! So hungry! A deep chatter settled into her teeth. Everything felt cold and bruised.

"Relish what you feel," Papa said. "Don't push away the discomfort. Welcome it back—and thank it. It is there to keep you alive. Thank the shivers, and then let them go."

Gradually she became aware that someone had covered her with a blanket. There were other people around her, trying to get her warm.

"Now what?" she asked.

"Focus on what you can hear," Papa said. "The little things—the sound of your own heartbeat, your breath as it expands and leaves your lungs. Then focus on things outside your body. Can you recognize a voice? Does it have a taste? Relish your other senses before you try to open your eyes."

A strong hand stroked her cheek. Large, and warm, he cradled her against his chest, rubbing her arms to get her warm. Soft feathers caressed her skin as he encircled her in his wings, lending his warmth to her frigid body.

Drops of salty moisture fell upon her lips.

"I'm sorry—" he wept.

Mikhail touched her using the *same* gesture she'd used to comfort *him* the day his ship had crashed and he'd stood at the threshold of death.

"Wake up, *colún beag*," his voice broke through the veil between the worlds. "Please wake up? I cannot bear to wander this life alone."

Ninsianna hugged her Papa in the vision.

"I think I'll be okay?"

She focused on Mikhail's voice, his funny accent; the way he spoke, half in his language, half in Ubaid. She forced herself to feel the way her body fit against his chest. Him so large and hard. Her so small and soft. Everywhere their skin touched, her body tingled, as if he was pouring his life-energy into hers.

"Mikhail," she murmured. *"Tháinig tú ar ais?"* You came back?

"Oh, thank the gods!" his chest shuddered.

Ninsianna opened her eyes.

It was the first thing she'd noticed about him, the way his eyes sometimes glowed an unearthly shade of blue. Only it wasn't just inside his eyes. Light radiated out of him, surrounded and filled him. She lifted her hand and touched his cheek, the same way she'd touched him the first time they'd ever met. He grabbed her hand and pressed it against his face. His cheeks were wet from crying, his eyes filled anguish.

"I'm sorry," he said. "Yadiditum told me what really happened."

"Jamin tricked us," she said. "If you'd stayed longer, you'd have seen me tell him no."

He rocked her back and forth, the only sound the rustle of his feathers as he fluffed his wings around her and willed the numbness to leave her frozen limbs. After a while, she became aware of other people. Mama. Papa. Voices in the street. Mikhail must have hauled her out of the cave. But how had he found her? Did he possess magic, unacknowledged, unrealized?

Something she'd seen in the vision, not the Evil One, but the terrifying, deep voice which had challenged her when she'd first demanded a vision, clamored at the edge of her subconscious.

A warning…

"*Nani ga warui kite iru,*" she said. Something bad is coming.

Mikhail gave her a puzzled look. He answered in the strange, clicking language he'd used the day he'd killed the Halifian men.

"*Anata wa Cheribumu no kotoba o hanashimasu ka?*" he said. You speak the language of the Cherubim?

"Cherubim?" she frowned. "But aren't we speaking in Ubaid?"

Mikhail shook his head.

"No. You are speaking Cherubim," he said in the clicking language. "And you speak without an accent, the way Master Yoritomo does."

Carefully he unfurled his wings, revealing she lay in her own bed. Mama stood in front of them, wringing her hands.

Mama gasped, "Immanu! Look at her eyes!"

Ninsianna touched her face, but she didn't *feel* any different, other than the fact she could see Mama and Papa's spirit-light the way she had the day She-Who-Is had sent the first vision. She could also *feel* the strong thread which connected her to the goddess. Whatever blockage had prevented her from using magic, the barrier was now gone.

Mikhail touched her cheek, just beneath her eyes.

"How is this possible?" he asked in Ubaid.

"She's been touched by the goddess," Papa said remorsefully. "I can say with great certainty that -I- am not the Chosen One, but Lugalbanda's granddaughter."

"But I feel exactly the same—" Ninsianna sat up and patted the flesh around her face. "What is wrong with me? Did I cut myself?"

Mama poured water into a shallow bowl and held it steady until the water stilled.

"Look in the reflecting bowl, child."

Ninsianna stared at her own reflection. Staring back at her was not the tawny-eyed girl who had greeted her each morning as she drew water from the well, but a creature whose eyes radiated pure, unburnished gold.

Chapter 85

June - 3,390 BC
Earth: Village of Assur
Colonel Mikhail Mannuki'ili

MIKHAIL

The knock came tentatively, unwelcome, but not unexpected. Immanu opened the front door. Outside stood Yalda and Zhila, followed by Rakshan the flint-knapper and the carpenter, Behnam.

"Can we come in?" they asked.

It wasn't really a request.

Mikhail gave the Tribunal a crisp Alliance salute as the strong, but blind sister Zhila elbowed Immanu aside and helped her older, frailer sister over to bench.

"Just call for me when you're ready," Zhila told Yalda. She grabbed Needa's arm. "Come, you must show me this magnificent milk goat that your daughter rescued from the Halifians?"

Mikhail tucked his wings against his back as he took in their formal dress. Both Behnam and Rakshan wore four-fringed kilts, while Yalda's shawl-dress sported a quadruple-layered fringe. All three of them wore the elaborate beaded neck-plates that accompanied Tribunal official business.

Mikhail stood stiffly, waiting to receive bad news.

Yalda spoke first.

"How is Ninsianna?"

"She is resting comfortably." Immanu said. "She appears unharmed, but her experience left her traumatized."

Yalda snorted.

"You mean she's having trouble coping with the visions?"

Immanu wrapped his arms across his chest, his expression a blend of guilt and strife. Ninsianna had spent the night wracked with nightmares, her only relief when he held her and wrapped her in his wings.

"You know how it is," Immanu said weakly.

"Yes, we know," Yalda snapped. "The question is, does *she*?"

Immanu shook his head.

"A woman shaman is unprecedented," he said. "I think, perhaps, we should let She-Who-Is decide what *SHE* wishes to reveal?"

The three elders glanced from one to the other.

"We agree," they said with finality.

Mikhail waited for them to say more, but Behnam changed the subject.

"We just came from a meeting with the Chief," Behnam said.

"And?" Immanu's eyebrows furrowed with worry.

"Jamin claims that Mikhail threatened to kill him."

Mikhail's feathers rustled. All three elders looked at him expectantly. He chose his next words carefully.

"He wanted to be the one to go down into the well," he said. "Perhaps I made a poor choice of words?"

Yalda snorted.

"In the privacy of this room, we'll admit sympathy with your position," the old woman said. "First Ninsianna, and then Immanu, and now *you* have told the stubborn goathead he can't simply get his way. But the fact remains, our people have certain traditions—"

"—for example," Behnam cut in, "the sanctity of a marriage contract."

Yalda sighed. "The stability of our village depends on everybody upholding the *law*. Especially one as visible as Lugalbanda's granddaughter."

"But she's the Chosen One of legend!" Immanu protested. "Certainly that must change things?"

Rakshan the flint-knapper absent-mindedly tapped his fingers along his hand, as though searching for a place he could strike the flint to make the situation turn out *right*.

"We've convinced Chief Kiyan to forestall repayment of the bride price until Yalda and Zhila bring in their crop," Rakshan said.

"Then what is the problem?" Mikhail asked.

"This village shall know no peace so long as you and Jamin both reside within its walls," Rakshan said.

Mikhail flared his wings, more from irritation than disagreement.

"I've done everything you've asked," he said.

"You didn't train the warriors," Rakshan said.

"Jamin won't *let* me! Ever since I got here, all he's done is sabotage me."

Rakshan started to speak, but Yalda held up her hand. The other two Tribunal members fell silent. As the oldest elder, she had precedence to speak first. Her ancient face wrinkled with sympathy, which in a way, almost made it worse.

"You know we want you to stay," the old woman said. "But Jamin controls the loyalty of the warriors. You are asking the Chief to choose between you—"

"—a stranger to him," Behnam added, "since he hasn't taken the chance to get to know you—"

"—and his own son," Yalda said.

"Not to mention the ability to defend this village," Rakshan added.

"So he's clinging to the letter of the law," Yalda finished.

Mikhail's wings drooped.

"You want me to leave?"

"Chief Jiljab of Gasur has offered you sanctuary," Yalda said. "We think you should go there, at least until Jamin accepts his broken engagement."

"But Ninsianna is the Chosen One!" Immanu protested. "She-Who-Is will be furious if you separate her Champion from her Voice."

The three Tribunal members glanced from one another. It was Behnam who spoke.

"Ninsianna is free to leave," the old man said. "But right now we have an army amassing at our borders, all intent on killing *him—*" he pointed at Mikhail.

Immanu clamped his hands across his chest, as if the room had suddenly turned frigid. Mikhail caught himself ruffling his under-feathers, though he was certain the chill was a figment of his imagination.

"Quite frankly," Rakshan said, "we think Chief Jiljab is a fool for agreeing to harbor him because Gasur is one-seventh our size and doesn't have a wall."

"Only Nineveh has defenses to rival ours," Behnam said.

The reality of what the Tribunal was saying registered on Mikhail's inner tactician.

"I'd be putting her at risk?"

"Yes," Rakshan said. "You'd be putting their entire *village* at risk. Every man, woman and child."

"And Chief Jiljab knows this?"

"Of course he does," Rakshan said. "He thinks you'll protect them."

Mikhail stared down at his hands. Sagal-zimu and Gimal had filled him in on the *real* motivation behind the Gasurian chief's gesture; the reason Zhila had artfully whisked Needa out of the room. Before she'd run off with Immanu, Ninsianna's mother had been betrothed to the Gasurian chief. While a generous gesture, Chief Jiljab wasn't being guided by logic any more than Jamin was.

"Let me think on this," Mikhail said.

"You have until the morning after the solstice festival," Yalda said gently, "and then, because you haven't fulfilled the exact terms of the agreement, Chief Kiyan intends to ask you to leave."

The Tribunal left. Both *he*, and Immanu, sagged like they'd been physically beaten.

"Who will tell her?" Mikhail asked.

"I will—" Immanu's voice sounded like lead. "I got her into this mess. She should hate *me*. Not you."

An overwhelming urge to pick up his sword and hack through the timbers, smash the furniture, and knock out the mud-brick walls screaming, *"how could you do this to her?"* shuddered so powerfully through his body that he had to clench his fists to force the dark urge to pass.

Instead he picked up the water-buckets.

"Excuse me," he said with a tight voice. "When she wakes up, Ninsianna will want to bathe."

He trudged down to the lower well, ignoring the well-wishers who congratulated him on the rescue, his wings sagging with defeat. He'd come back ... only to lose her anyways.

Maybe you'll be able to protect her in Gasur?

"Oh, shut up!" he chided his subconscious. If it *really* wanted to help, it would have told him who he was and how to contact his people instead of encouraging him to come back, only to be forced to leave again.

A tall, leggy teenager fell into step behind him, followed by three younger brothers—his perpetual shadows—each an identical version of the other. Pareesa hop-skipped behind him, carrying a stick which she'd sharpened into a spear with a big, fat squirrel impaled at the end. Her makeshift "army" marched behind her, each proudly brandishing a rat or frog they'd speared for the dinner-pot under their *'commanding officer's'* direction. She'd popped in to see him at Immanu's house, but Needa had chased her off, claiming both he, and Ninsianna, were too exhausted for guests.

"Did you see?" she asked excitedly. "Now that you smashed the roof of the cave, we can lower the buckets right into the middle of the stream."

"Glad I could be of help," he mumbled.

The people at the well stepped back to give him access. The women and children patted his arms and wings, congratulating him on a daring rescue and thanking him for putting water back into their well. Normally, uninvited touch made him feel uneasy, but right now, he wouldn't feel any worse if somebody shoved a knife between his ribs.

"Well you're mister grumpy-face today—" Pareesa gave him a sour expression.

Her brothers mimicked the expression.

Mikhail shrugged and tied his bucket to the rope.

"So when are you going to announce your engagement?" she cocked one eyebrow at him, the way teenagers do when they *think* they know the ways of the world, but really, they're just feeling you out.

"We're not—" his despondency registered in his voice.

"Well, I mean, not at the *solstice*," she said. "That would be rather rude. Though honestly, I think we'd *all* like to see Jamin get kicked in the shins."

"I said we're *not*," Mikhail said far more vehemently than he intended. "In two days, I have to leave. *Alone...*"

Pareesa's brows knit together.

"But I thought you loved her," she lowered her voice. "Everybody here, they just thought—"

"They were wrong—" Mikhail cut her off.

Pareesa's shoulders rolled forward in a mirror-image of his *own* despondent body language. If she had wings, they'd be dragging on the ground.

"Oh—" tears welled in her brown eyes. "Papa *said* that would be the case. I'd just hoped..."

Her frankness, her youth, cut through his defenses in a way no weapon ever could.

"So did I."

He finished hauling up his water, and then helped an old woman pull up hers. The buckets came up easily from the greatly enlarged hole; no longer snagging. The water was fresh and clear and cold.

The old woman patted him on the wing.

"That was real brave," she said, "going down into that well. Will you play the role of Damu-zid at the solstice celebration?"

"Damu-zid?" he asked.

"Yes. The bringer of the light," the old woman said.

Pareesa's face lit up.

"That's it!" she held up her mock spear.

"That's what?" he asked.

"How you're going to make Jamin let you stay!"

Chapter 86

Galactic Standard Date: 152,323.06 AE
Zulu Sector: Command Carrier 'Light Emerging'
Colonel Raphael Israfa

RAPHAEL

He and Major Glicki had taken to working opposite shifts so that there was always a battle-hardened commander on the bridge. Out here in Zulu Sector, they were too far away from help if whoever had shot Mikhail down took objection to their snooping and decided to do to *them* what they'd done to the Leonid destroyer. While the *Light Emerging* was technically a command carrier, its primary function was intelligence-gathering, not hammering against a Sata'anic naval carrier or a Tokoloshe dreadnought.

They weren't the *Jehoshaphat!*

And *he* wasn't General Abaddon…

He tossed and turned, *trying* to force his mind to embrace the sluggish haze which dogged his waking hours. Four hours and thirty-two minutes. That's how long he had left, if only he could get his mind to turn off and stop obsessing about how to get Jophiel to return his calls.

What if he liquidated his lifetime salary and hired a florist to fill the *Eternal Light* with flowers?

Not subtle enough?

Yes.

But she'd mentioned, during their mating tryst, that she loved the garden which sheltered the Eternal Palace. He, personally, had never seen the Eternal Tree whose image graced every Alliance civic building and uniform, but from the way she described it, the tree was always in bloom.

He glanced at the clock. Four hours and thirty-one minutes left to sleep.

He shut his eyes, imagining her expression when he made it known to the entire fleet that *he,* a lowly Colonel, had the audacity to wish the most beautiful Angelic in the Alliance might love him back?

Four hours and thirty minutes even…

Gah!

There was no way he was going to get any sleep!

He sat up and turned on his reading lamp. The light illuminated his modest commander's quarters in a favorable light, softening the stark, white walls and casting golden shadows onto his pictures, making it appear almost homey. While luxurious compared the enlisted men's quarters, it was little more than a single bunk, a desk, and two chairs for whatever crewman was in the 'hot seat.'

He ruffled his golden feathers and then padded over to his desk. Major Glicki would have his head on a platter if she knew he hadn't been sleeping—what good is a commander too sluggish to maneuver in battle, she liked to say? But he was loath to visit the infirmary for a sleeping prescription. The doctor would want to know why he couldn't sleep, which would result in a mark on his service record that he, Colonel Raphael Israfa, had broken the Emperor's highest law by not only falling in love, but he'd fallen in love with their Supreme Commander-General.

Too bad Glicki was out of *choledzeretsa*. There was nothing he'd like better right now than to get stinking drunk on her aunt's home-bootlegged liquor.

He touched the monitor to turn on his A.I., although technically it wasn't 'artificial.' His ship's computational power was supplemented by a living, bacteria-based hive-mind known as the Daarda'ail.[128] A pleasant voice greeted him, neither male nor female:

"Good morning, Colonel Israfa. What can the hive do for you today?"

"Any communiques from the *Eternal Light*?"

"No Sir," the hive-mind replied. "But we have some new reports, forwarded at General Re Harakhti's bequest."

Raphael's wings perked up.

"Pull them up."

The hive-mind pushed the report to his portable flatscreen.

Raphael scrutinized the first report, flagged 'highest priority,' moving his lips as he read, a trick he'd learned to force himself to *hear* what he was reading so his ear could pick up on the absurdity of something his eyeballs missed. A single sentence, *'possibly Algol-class,'* jarred him out of his insomnia-induced stupor.

"How recent was this incident?" he asked.

"Six days ago, Sir," the hive mind said.

"And the Leonids are certain this was a diplomatic shuttle?"

"They're not positive of anything, Sir. It was given clearance by the Prime Minister's office before the border patrol could perform a proper inspection."

He enlarged the image and scrutinized the design. It looked similar to the ship the Leonids had tried to capture before the Tokoloshe had shot their battlecruiser down, but it had different tail numbers—which didn't mean anything—spy ships changed registration numbers as regularly as some people changed their underwear. The ship in the image appeared old

---

[128] *Daarda'ail*: a sentient bacteria colony which forms a "hive mind".

and decrepit, its metal dented and patched, but the engines appeared more primitive than the ones which had outrun the Leonids. Why in Hades had Shay'tan sent a drug-runner to contact Lucifer?

It was probably filled with bribes for all the shady trade deals Lucifer kept ramming through Parliament, he snorted. Jophiel's hatred of the man had colored his impression of their illustrious Prime Minister.

"What about these other reports?" Raphael asked.

"They're all health and safety inspections," the hive-mind said.

Raphael scrolled through countless manifest logs, most of them Sata'anic. As he did, he added puzzle pieces to a theory he'd been building in the back of his mind, still incompletely formed, but the intelligence officer in him felt like a tracker-beast on the hunt.

"What about this one?" Raphael paused at a flight manifest flagged, "forward to Colonel Israfa" by a colleague embedded with the Centauri cavalry.

"They were intercepted in the borderlands," the hive mind said. "According to the log-entries, Major Hepi made them open up the boxes and rifled through their hidden compartments. The goods were all Sata'anic in origin, but of civilian design."

That, in and of itself, was not unusual. Ever since the advent of Lucifer's free trade agreements, *most* goods were now manufactured in the Sata'an Empire. He scrolled through the inventory lists.

"Any weapons?"

"No, Sir," the hive mind said. "Just lots of glow sticks, sleeping bags, and cots."

He paused at the items marked 'camping gear.' It was all listed as 'olive drab' or 'olive green.'

"There's enough here to set up a Sata'anic base."

"The Supreme Commander-General just redeployed ships to scan for an emerging base," the hive mind said. "If Shay'tan's got one, he is keeping it hidden."

"What are you up to, you old bastard?" he murmured.

"They were all boxed up and priced for commercial sale," the hive mind finished its report. "Major Hepi states that had no legal jurisdiction to hold them."

Raphael nodded, though he wasn't happy about agreeing. The borderlands were neutral territory. Either superpower's ships were free to travel the area at will, selling goods to newly settled planets, most of which were mining colonies.

He directed the hive-mind to dump the latest reports into the database he was compiling of all suspicious activities which might lend credence to Mikhail's final message, *"This planet is crawling with enough Sata'an to..."*

To what?

And more importantly, *where?*

Light coalesced in the center of the room as the hive-mind projected the latest data into a holographic map of the galaxy, centered on their current location in the Orion-Cygnus spiral arm.

Raphael rose and paced over to the image. The data was anomalous. Shay'tan wasn't amassing supplies out *here*, towards Zulu Sector, but in the furthest corner of his empire, where the borders intersected with the Free Marid Confederation and the Tokoloshe Kingdom.

"This doesn't make any sense!" Raphael exclaimed. "Whatever Shay'tan is hiding, it *has* to be out *here*."

A large, blue search grid identified the area where Mikhail's ship could have gone down. Even if he'd been travelling at his ship's fastest speed, there was no way he could have made it anywhere near the place where Shay'tan was potentially amassing troops. If not for the fact the Leonids had seen the mysterious Algol-class ship emerging from Zulu Sector, they'd have no confirmation that what Mikhail had been chasing was even real.

"It's a distraction—" Raphael scrutinized the buildup of Shay'tan's war fleet. "It *has* to be. He *knows* we spotted that ship, so he's retrofitting his warfleet *here* so we won't pay attention to what the rest of his fleet is doing."

"The Supreme Commander-General has spies monitoring most of those ships," the hive mind said.

Raphael ran a quick mental calculation.

"If we're inspecting that many cargo vessels," he said, "our intelligence apparatus must be running pretty thin. Especially with *us* all the way out here."

He plunked back down into his chair, inadvertently crushing one of his long primary feathers. He picked up the broken shaft and twirled the feather in the light, studying the color-pattern in the vanes, wondering if Jophiel's son...

...*his* son...

...bore any of the red which sometimes showed when the light hit his plumage?

"Oh, Jophie," he sighed. "If only you'd return my calls."

"Would you like me to tell the *Eternal Light's* hive-mind that it would be more logical for us to bolster the Supreme Commander-General's intelligence gathering near *Tyre?*" the hive-mind asked.

Raphael stared at the hologram which dominated the center of the room. While Jophiel had banished him, her *first* loyalty lay with the Emperor. All hive-minds thought alike, purely data-driven. Other than Mikhail's final message and the glimpse of the Algol-class smuggler, he had no evidence the Sata'anic buildup was aimed out here.

'Shay'tan's found the godsdamned Holy Grail...'

What did that mean?

Why was he out here, chasing after a ghost?

He twisted his chair, glancing between the photograph Jophiel had sent of *her* holding their newborn son and the holographic map. She was out of uniform, her long white-blonde hair tumbling over her clothing to accentuate her breasts. It seemed as though she looked out of the picture straight at him, a small, wistful smile playing upon those luscious pink lips he *still* dreamed of kissing.

Raphael rubbed the tight spot in his chest. Jophiel was lost to him. But if he redeployed closer to the Alliance, at least he could meet his son?

...at the cost of leaving his best friend for dead.

"Mikhail, where are you?"

He walked over to the wall full of pictures from his Academy days. In every picture he wore a huge, silly grin while the stoic Seraphim stood stiffly at his side. He and Glicki had made a game out of getting their too-serious comrade to lighten up, but the best they could usually accomplish was to pry out a smirk before Mikhail would school his expression back into the unreadable one that seven years under the Cherubim had instilled.

One picture, however, was from the day they'd beaten the socks off of a rival team in the iron man 3-day competition. Arms wrapped around each other's shoulders in an easy camaraderie, Raphael wore a goofy expression while the too-serious Seraphim beamed a smile that would have lit up six solar systems.

He couldn't believe Mikhail was dead.

He *wouldn't* believe his best friend was dead.

Whenever the odds grew unfavorable, Mikhail loved nothing better than to give his opponent a surprise ass-whupping.

He touched the picture, and then turned to the A.I.

"Tell the Supreme Commander-General we're continuing the search."

Chapter 87

Summer Solstice - June - 3,390 BC
Earth: Village of Assur

NINSIANNA

The first light of dawn shot through skylight, turned golden by the grain-dust as it radiated downward to shine upon the ancient clay statue who sat upon her pedestal. Ninsianna waited with awed anticipation. Exuberant. Fearful…

Outside the temple, jubilant wooden horns announced the arrival of longest day of the year.

"Now?" she whispered.

"Not yet," her father murmured.

The light-ray grew brighter as the sun finished heaving itself above the horizon. She-Who-Is' eye sockets glittered gold, and radiated outwards in a sunburst pattern to shine off eleven colorful gems embedded in the temple wall.

Slender lines crisscrossed, displaying in the air the exact same eleven-pointed star which was engraved into the temple floor. As below, so did the star glisten above?

Ninsianna clapped her hands together.

"Does it do this every sunrise?" she asked reverently.

"Only today," Papa said, "on the longest day of the year."

No woman had ever seen this sight. Until this morning, only men had been allowed to attend to the goddess' daily needs.

"We have to move quickly," Papa said. "The blessing only lasts several minutes."

Ninsianna kneeled.

He picked up a heavily beaded neck plate and placed it upon her shoulders, fastening the leather bindings to tie the collar shut. The beads sat heavily, cold and bumpy, nothing like the warmth which radiated out of She-Who-Is' citrine eyes.

"As conferred upon me by my father, Lugalbanda—" his eyes glittered too brightly "—I confer upon thee the title of shaman."

A lump rose in Ninsianna's throat as he picked up his own headdress and placed it upon her head. How could she tell Papa the Dark Lord had found her wanting? If Mikhail had not rescued her, she would have emerged from the cave insane.

"As for the last title, *Chosen*—" his voice broke. "I do not have the authority to bestow it. She-Who-Is has conferred it upon you *herself*."

She-Who-Is' citrine eyes glimmered radiantly bright, and then disappeared, leaving them standing before the clay statue which graced the inner sanctum. Papa helped her onto her feet, and then arranged his *own* five-fringed kilt and neck plate.

"Come," he said, "the people are waiting."

"What if they won't follow me?"

"How can they *not* follow you," he said. "What I see *here* but once a year—" he gestured at the now-sightless statue "—radiates out of your eyes."

She kissed her fingertips and pressed them against the statue of the goddess. Whether or not she *felt* like a fraud, her people needed to believe she was the Chosen of She-Who-Is.

Outside the temple, Chief Kiyan gave a long-winded speech. The hinges groaned as Kiaresh wrestled the carved wooden doors open. The crowd grew silent as she and Papa emerged.

"Look at her eyes," the villagers whispered.

"They've turned to gold."

"No. They are made of sunlight."

"Surely it is as described in the prophecy?"

They walked towards the bonfire which would be lit after the games. At its center stood an enormous wicker effigy of Nergal—god of the summer solstice—and also the god of war.

This was *his* ceremony, and Jamin was its king.

She scanned the crowd, searching for the war god's challenger. Despite his place at the back, he was easy to spot. Not only did his wings set him apart, but his spirit-light shone a radiant shade of blue—the exact same color as his unearthly blue eyes.

Beside him stood Zhila and a boy, overdressed for the weather in a brown woolen cape.

Mikhail nodded.

Great Mother? Please make use of my voice?

She bit her lip to stop it from trembling and strode towards the effigy of Nergal. Jamin stared straight forward, his expression unreadable as Ninsianna ascended the platform. The Chief's mouth tightened into a grim line as he spied the sixth line of fringe her Mama had sewn onto her father's borrowed cape—one more fringe than *his*.

"Ninsianna," the Chief said curtly.

Her knees turned suddenly weak.

"You may call me Chosen One."

"I will not fall prey to this farce," his voice rumbled dangerous, and low.

She gave him a wan smile.

"Last night, She-Who-Is sent me a vision," she said. "Your treasury is missing a *qû*[129] of salt, a *sutū*[130] of oil, and a bushel of your finest einkorn."

"Your own father noted the missing einkorn."

"But you didn't tell *anyone* about the missing necklace," she said. "Lapis-lazuli, with golden beads, and a carved black pendant that looks like a winged crocodile holding up a star?"

Jamin's skin turned suddenly pale.

"It belonged to my wife."

"You kept it hidden in the wall next to your bed," she said. "Each night, you would twine it around your wrist, but three nights before the Halifians attacked Mikhail's sky canoe, the necklace went missing."

The Chief's eyebrows reared with surprise.

"It has merely been misplaced."

"In your enemy's tent."

With a disgusted snort, she turned to the crowd and held up her arms as though the Chief had just welcomed her like a warrior queen.

"People of Assur," she shouted. "She-Who-Is delights in your offerings. Bring them forward, and I shall implore her for a fortuitous dry season."

The three members of the Tribunal stepped forward, dressed resplendently in their robes of state. Each elder carried an offering to present to the gods.

"Chosen One—" Yalda carried a woven basket "—on behalf of Ninkasi, the goddess of farmers and bakers, please accept this bread baked with this season's first sheaths of grain."

Ninsianna picked up a loaf and held it up to the sun.

"May She-Who-Is bless your crops with sunlight, and water them each week with a gentle rain."

The villagers cheered as Papa took the basket and placed it at the wooden effigy's feet. Nergal was a terrifyingly powerful god, but even the god of war bowed down to She-Who-Is.

Next came Behnam, carrying a carved wooden antelope which was so realistic, it looked like it might leap out of his hands.

"Chosen One—" Behnam said. "On behalf of Enki, god of woodworkers and craftsmen, accept this totem to attract unto our people the spirits of countless deer and prey."

---

[129] *Qû:* bowl (cup).
[130] *Sutū:* vessel (container).

Ninsianna took the intricately carved antelope. It possessed the same beautiful woodgrain as the three wooden buckets Mikhail carried home each morning from the well.

"It is from the ruined tree-trunk?" she asked.

"Enki hates waste—" Behnam gave her a toothless grin "—so I made a statue to consecrate in his name."

Ninsianna held the antelope above her head.

"When the herds migrate out of the desert to drink," she called out, "may She-Who-Is bless our warriors with enough meat for every cookpot in this village."

Jamin's elite warriors gave an ululating cheer. Standing behind them, a group of boys who'd competed yesterday for the right to train as Assur's next generation of warriors raised their parent's spears and cheered as well. This would be the first year they'd participate in the hunt.

A slender boy whose kilt was a bit too short clutched his cape as the other boys slapped him on the back. Ninsianna gave the youth a subtle nod.

Next stepped forth Rakshan the flint-knapper, carrying a long, slender bundle wrapped in a length of cloth. He undid the wrappings, revealing a magnificent obsidian-tipped spear.

"Chosen One—" he said. "On behalf Nergal, the guild of weapons-masters presents our finest spear."

Ninsianna hefted it into the ready position, hand over her head, the way a man would when about to toss a killing blow, and turned towards the effigy of Nergal. The crowd fell silent. While some women could hunt with a slender atlatl, few had the upper body strength to wield a full-fledged spear.

Mother, guide my words...

"As the goddess' Chosen One, I shall bequeath this spear upon he who is destined to protect this village."

Jamin stared straight forward, his black eyes fixed on Mikhail. His cheek twitched. The villagers *knew* who her father had decreed was destined to be *HER* Champion. He took a deep breath, ready to protest.

"On behalf of She-Who-Is—" she held the spear towards Jamin "—*SHE* would like *you* to assume the role of Nergal at the games."

The crowd fell silent, their expressions perplexed. Their eyes all turned towards Mikhail. He stood neutrally, his expression neither offended, nor surprised.

Jamin reached for the spear.

"Your faith in me is surprising," he said softly.

His fingertips lingered as he took the spear from her grasp. He hefted the spear into the air.

"I *accept* the role of Nergal for this afternoon's games."

The crowd cheered. This wasn't the *first* time he'd been appointed—the role usually went to whoever had won *last* summer's games—which was always him. But it was unexpected. Every person in this village had expected her to bequeath Nergal's spear upon Mikhail.

"And now—" she said abruptly "—*SHE* would like her God of War to accept the new inductees who your own tests of skill proved yesterday are ready to join your ranks as warriors."

Proud parents cheered as the elite warriors shepherded the new inductees up to the foot of the stage. Jamin took out his knife and sliced the fleshy part of his palm. One by one, he called the boys up and handed them the knife. The boys sliced their palms, and then clasped Jamin's hand, blood-brother to blood-brother, as he welcomed them into the brotherhood of war.

Six boys from the end, the boy with the too-short kilt ascended the steps, cut his own hand, and waited for Jamin to recite the now-familiar vow:

"On your family's blood, do you swear to devote your life to the defense of this village?"

"I swear—" the youth said solemnly "—that I shall defend this village, unto my final breath."

Jamin clasped the boy's bloody hand.

"Namhu, son of Appanili, on behalf of Nergal, I welcome you as a warrior of Assur."

The youth shook Jamin's hand, her expression nervous.

"Thank you," her voice trembled. "But I'm not Namhu. I'm his sister, Pareesa."

Chapter 88

Summer Solstice - June - 3,390 BC
Earth: Village of Assur
Colonel Mikhail Mannuki'ili

MIKHAIL

He guided Zhila towards the front of the crowd, crouching to remain inconspicuous. Pareesa shook Jamin's bloody hand.

"Thank you," she said. "But I'm not Namhu. I'm his sister, Pareesa."

Mikhail crouched, ready to fly at the stage if the Chief's volatile son attempted to abuse his young protégé.

"No matter what happens," Zhila whispered, "don't let him provoke you into anger."

The crowd fell silent as Jamin held Pareesa's bloody hand.

"You're not Namhu?" he looked perplexed.

Pareesa glanced over the crowd at *him,* her expression terrified, and yet so painfully *brave.*

"No," her voice warbled. "Mikhail felt I had the better arm, so Namhu agreed to let *me* compete yesterday in his stead."

"But you're a *girl!*" Jamin yanked his hand back. "No woman has ever fought for Assur!"

Zhila called out.

"*That,* my boy, is a lie!"

The crowd parted. He helped Zhila towards the stage. In their wake followed the *real* Namhu, Pareesa's next-younger brother, wearing her too-long cape, but other than a slight difference in height, the two siblings appeared remarkably alike. Mikhail stopped. Namhu helped the blind woman ascend the steps, carrying an age-darkened spear.

"What is the meaning of this?" Chief Kiyan demanded.

"Your son just accepted this girl as one of your warriors," Zhila said.

"I forbid it!" the Chief said.

"You don't have a choice," Zhila shook her finger at him. "All three members of the Tribunal, as well as *me,* went down to the fields yesterday to witness this girl earn her spot fair and square."

Yalda, Zhila, and Rakshan the flint-knapper, all closed ranks to stand beside Pareesa.

"You *knew* she was a girl?"

"She came in sixth place," Rakshan the flint-knapper said. "Your own law decrees the warriors *must* accept the top twenty and train them for the second tier."

Jamin gaped, as though he'd expected the weapons-master to stand with him.

"You plot against my son?" Chief Kiyan asked.

"No," Rakshan said. "I simply appreciate a warrior with skill. You seem to forget that Zhila's husband was my brother."

An unfamiliar emotion welled up in Mikhail's chest. *Pride?* Where *he* had failed, his young protégé had known *exactly* where to find a chink in the Chief's pig-headed insistence that he had to train a warrior in order to stay. He was darned lucky the kid had natural talent.

"Those were different times," Chief Kiyan said. "You were never officially a warrior."

"But I defended this village." Zhila held up her spear. "And I *continued* to defend it until my eyesight grew so bad, I could no longer hit my target. And some of you—" the old woman pointed at the crowd "—are old enough to remember when I used to compete in the summer solstice games. So don't tell me this girl isn't eligible!"

"I don't know what you're up to!" Jamin snarled. "But it will be a cold day in *hell* before I train a little girl!"

A sultry voice came from beside the effigy of Nergal.

"Which is why," Ninsianna said, "I refuse to marry you. Because a *real* leader always picks the most qualified person for the job, regardless of their personal feelings."

The black-eyed bastard looked like he'd just been punched.

"Is *that* why you chose me to play Nergal?" he gestured at Pareesa. "For *this*?"

"I asked you to assume the role of Nergal because last year you won the games," Ninsianna said. "You're Assur's most gifted warrior, you know our village defenses. Every single man here would *die* for your command. To declare otherwise would be blasphemy."

Jamin opened his mouth to speak. Chief Kiyan put a hand on his arm.

"She is right, son."

"But—"

"The correct question isn't whether Pareesa is qualified, but rather, who trained her in the first place?"

All heads turned towards Mikhail.

"Step forward, winged one," the Chief commanded.

Mikhail's heart pounded as he ascended the steps. He pressed his wings tightly into dress-wings.

"Sir?"

"It seems, despite my son's machinations, that you *did* train a single warrior."

"He trained two, Sir—" Pareesa grabbed her brother's arm.

Ten-year-old Namhu moved to stand beside his sister.

"The boy tried his best," Mikhail said, "but he doesn't have the weight—yet—to put behind the weapon. He'll do you proud, once he hits his growth spurt."

"My son will only train the best."

"He should *continue* to train the best," Mikhail said. "All I ask is that you allow me to train the *least*."

"The least?"

"Yes, Sir," Mikhail said. "The ones your son has no patience to train, so you will always have a third tier of warriors to draw upon should this village be attacked."

"If I let you stay, we *will* be attacked."

"You're going to be attacked anyways," Mikhail said. "Whether or not you believe Jamin *paid* the Halifians to attack my sky canoe, your own allies just confirmed the enemy knows he was *there*. They want vengeance, either way."

The Chief stroked his beard as he scrutinized first *him*, and then Pareesa, and then the warriors and his son. For the first time, Mikhail noticed the Chief's eyes were a warm shade of brown, not the angry black color of his son's.

"It seems my Tribunal has staged a rebellion."

All four elders leaned together.

"We are your friends," old Behnam said.

"Sworn to advise you," Yalda said.

"Sometimes—" Zhila said.

"—you just refuse to listen," Yalda finished.

He looked to Rakshan the flint-knapper, who shrugged.

"More warriors means my sons grow rich, knapping spear-points."

For just one moment, the Chief's expression remained inscrutable, and then, suddenly, he burst into a deep-bellied guffaw.

"I seem to recall that one of your *granddaughters* insists on learning to knap knife-blades?"

"She has no talent," Rakshan said.

"Fair is fair!" the Chief laughed. "And I know *just* the man to teach her."

They both looked at *him*...

Mikhail backed away.

"I'm not qualified."

"He *did* finally knap a passable axe-head," Rakshan said blandly.

"I'm *really* not qualified," Mikhail insisted.

"You also claimed you'd never thrown a spear," Behnam said, "but somehow, you managed to teach Pareesa?"

Chief Kiyan slapped his son on the back.

"Come, Jamin," he said. "We have five more warriors to swear in. Let's pray you don't get any more surprises."

Scowling, Jamin finished swearing in the five remaining new warriors. And then, the Chief declared:

"Let the solstice games begin!"

Chapter 89

*And it came to pass
When the children of men had multiplied
That in those days were born unto them
Beautiful and comely daughters.
And the angels, the children of heaven,
Saw and lusted after them,
And said to one another:
'Come, let us choose us wives
From among the children of men
And beget us children.'*

Book of Enoch, Book 1 – Watchers

Galactic Standard Date: 152,323.06 AE
Alliance/Sata'an Border
Prime Minister Lucifer

LUCIFER

Lucifer leaned against the rusty shipping container, cold and clammy, drenched with sweat, as a man with a pick-axe pounded inside his brain. He glared at Zepar. The inconsiderate bastard had dragged him out of a dead sleep and announced they had to meet that fat prick, Ba'al Zebub, immediately, on a private commercial hauler; the kind that ran cargo between solar systems. The run-down launch bay was poorly lit, filled with shipping containers, and reeked of dirt and rust; exacerbating his already fragile state.

He patted his inside-pocket, wishing *fervently* he dared take a nip of his favorite "hangover medicine," *choledzeretsa*. The *need* ate at him, tangible and hungry, like a beast which gnawed at his intestines while a siren-song whispered, "just a little taste."

'I need it I need it I need it...' his heart beat.

-- No you don't. That's just the addiction talking.

'I'm not an addict.'

-- Yes you are...

'I'M THE ALLIANCE PRIME MINISTER!!! NOT AN ADDICT!!!'

-- You can't even remember what you did last night.

Lucifer sighed. The entire past week was one big memory-hole, but something *significant* had happened. Something *bad*... And not just the fact he'd sold two mining colonies out to the fucking cannibals. He felt like he had after his mother had died, only he had nobody to grieve; while three different alien creatures had all taken up residence inside his head and were duking it out, with *him* the loser no matter *which* side won.

He gave Zepar his most displeased, gimble stare.

"Why are we meeting with a gun-runner, again?"

"It's carrying Lord Ba'al Zebub," Zepar said.

"You *told* me that," Lucifer said. "Why are we meeting him *here*?"

Zepar's dishwater blue eyes slid sideways to glance at Furcas and Pruflas, the two Angelic goons who always accompanied them to *these* kinds of meetings. *These* meaning "*something my immortal father would never approve of.*"

"Ba'al Zebub insists upon the utmost discretion," Zepar said.

"Don't trust Zepar…"

The words kept rattling inside his head, even though his nasty inner voice kept screeching the opposite. *Don't trust Zepar…* He'd be less inclined to believe that if not for the fact he was so helplessly, completely *dependent* upon the man to guide him through his blackouts. That wise inner voice, the one Zepar had taught him to listen to, shouted the other voice down, but no matter how much he chastised himself, deep within his gut he just *knew* he wasn't alright.

"Don't trust Zepar…"

A vomit-inducing STAB knocked him between the eyes. Lucifer swayed. Zepar steadied him, and then held out a familiar metal case.

"I brought your prescription, Sire?" Zepar's voice reeked of concern.

"I'm fine." Lucifer waved him off.

"Perhaps it will help with the pain?"

"I'm said I'm fine!"

'No I'm not… I need help…'

He closed his eyes and focused on his breathing, a trick that his mother had taught him when he'd still been little and the Emperor had to run medical experiments on him. Oh, his father … but the *things* they'd do *after* those experiments! Like run in the Eternal Garden, or play galactic chess. They'd talk for hours about the best way to outsmart his father's detractors. Even as a boy, he'd had a far better grasp of politics than his immortal father, which is why it hurt so bad that his father now refused to see him.

Maybe he should just bury the hatchet? Tell Ba'al Zebub to go fuck off and rescind the trade deals?

Oh, gods! I need a fucking drink!

A deep-throated alarm jarred him out of his meditation. The embarking ship was about to clear the inner airlock. The floor rumbled as the enormous inner cargo bay doors slid open, revealing a Sata'anic vessel which was not what it had first appeared.

"Oo-whee," Lucifer gave a sharp whistle. "I've heard of these, but never seen one."

Rust-colored paint had been splashed all over the Algol-class ship, with welded-on space junk and random panels painted mismatched colors to make it appear she'd been pieced together from salvage. Around her engines, false shields rattled like a Mantiwood movie set, obviously not designed to last for more than a single mission, but *nothing* could mask the ship's long, sleek slender lines. She was a whole lot of engine, and not a lot of cargo room. The fastest ship in the galaxy alighted daintily upon the cargo carrier's flight deck, sinking into her landing gear with a sigh.

"Go!" Zepar ordered.

Furcas and Pruflas moved to aim weapons at the *SRN Peykaap*. Zepar held up one fist, signaling them to make no move that might be construed as aggression.

The side-hatch opened.

An enormous lizard appeared on top of the ramp, wearing a luxurious purple velvet robe trimmed with white ermine. On every finger glittered diamonds, rubies and gold. Atop his head, a razor-sharp dorsal ridge reared up like an emperor's crown, while dangling from his chin, a deep red dewlap marked him as a high-ranking male. If portliness was next to godliness, then Ba'al Zebub was a titan.

The Algol-class ship shuddered as Ba'al Zebub's boots tromped down flight ramp, followed by his *own* matched pair of well-armed, muscular guards. As his feet hit the flight deck, Lucifer could *feel* the metal shudder beneath the Sata'anic Emir's feet.

"Is it me," Lucifer stage-whispered just loud enough for Ba'al Zebub to hear, "or has the old boy packed on another hundred-and-fifty kilos?"

Furcas and Pruflas did not react. Lucifer ruffled his feathers, more offended by their lack of humor than *anything* that fat pig, Ba'al Zebub might have to say. His favorite shuttle pilot, Eligor, who *unfortunately* wasn't here, had a mild way of saying *"Yes, Sir"* that, according to the degree of blandness, you could *tell* the man suppressed a laugh. But these two? If he hadn't seen them bleed, he'd swear they were androids.

Ba'al Zebub stomped over, huffing like a pair of bellows. His bright red dewlap turned a phlegmatic shade of bluish-purple.

"Prime Minister Lucifer—" Ba'al Zebub made the Sata'anic prayer-gesture. "It's a pleasure to meet with you again."

"I wish I could say the same," Lucifer said.

Ba'al Zebub spread his arms in a magnanimous gesture.

"Our Emperor has sent a gift," he said.

"I don't accept bribes."

Ba'al Zebub grinned, exposing gold-tipped fangs.

"This gift will grant your most heart-felt desire."

The *last* thing Lucifer wanted was one of Shay'tan's "gifts," since they always came with strings and, the way things had been going lately [*cough, cough, blackouts*], he'd probably wake up tomorrow morning and find out he'd just signed away the Alliance for Sata'anic rule. The *last* thing he wanted to do right now was negotiate with the crafty Ba'al Zebub, especially with his mental faculties a few cylinders short of a fully functioning hyperdrive.

What he *really* needed was to patch things up with his father.

"My *father* gives us everything we need," Lucifer said coldly.

"Ahh," Ba'al Zebub's snout split, revealing a mouth full of pointy teeth. "I can guarantee he won't give you this."

Lucifer crossed his arms in front of his chest.

"I highly doubt that."

Ba'al Zebub barked an order in the Sata'anic language.

"Bring her..."

A Sata'an merchant mariner appeared at the mouth of the ship, escorting a tall, veiled figure wearing a jewel-encrusted dress. As she moved, the dress glittered in the murky light, highlighting the only part that was visible; her decidedly *humanoid*, almost black-skinned hands. The guard guided her towards him, murmuring something in an unknown language.

"May I present," Ba'al Zebub grasped the edge of the woman's veil, "the origin of your species?"

He yanked off the veil. Beneath it was a black-skinned Angelic.

Lucifer flared his wings with curiosity. He'd seen dark-winged Seraphim, but never an Angelic with black *skin?*

"Who is this?" he asked.

"You tell me?" Ba'al Zebub grinned.

The woman clung to the guard as Lucifer walked around her. Almost as tall as a female Angelic, her flawless dark skin was the color of ebony-wood. Intelligent dark eyes highlighted high cheekbones, long, curly hair, a broad nose, and full lips like a Centauri mare, but instead of hooves, she possessed humanoid feet, clad tastefully in designer heels. Most peculiarly, erupting out of her back was...

...nothing.

Absolutely nothing.

Lucifer touched the woman's shoulder blades. She *looked* like an Angelic, but didn't possess a pair of wings? He pinched the bridge of his nose, wishing, *fervently*, he'd dared take that drink. This *had* to be a blackout, because he was seeing unicorns. Pink elephants. *Humans...*

"What did you do to her?" his voice warbled.

"Nothing—" Ba'al Zebub relished his dumbfounded look. "This is the root race the Eternal Emperor used to create his hybrid armies."

"An asteroid hit Nibiru 74,000 years ago," Lucifer said, "and wiped out all life."

"You *know* that's not true!" Ba'al Zebub laughed. "Hashem gathered up the survivors and sent them to other planets."

"All twelve colonies died out."

"Twelve?" Ba'al Zebub laughed. "*Not* twelve. Thirteen."

"Thirteen?"

"Hashem didn't want the *rejects*," Ba'al Zebub said. "He viewed it as an opportunity to experiment on a grand scale. So he left behind the criminals, the ones who refused to worship him, the ones who were stupid, or just plain ugly. Shay'tan rescued them, just to tweak his nose."

A sense of vertigo made Ba'al Zebub sound far away. *"You're nothing but a failed experiment!"* Dephar had said. Would his father *do* that? Yes, he'd seen him "play god" countless times, with lesser species. But would his father *do* that with Alliance citizens?

"He had limited resources--" Lucifer repeated the history books. "It happened so *quick*, he couldn't rescue them *all.*"

"And yet he found time to go back and rescue the Leviathans," Ba'al Zebub poked a meaty finger at Lucifer's chest. "Eh?"

So far as the Emperor would admit, he'd transplanted as many as he could save in twelve gigantic ark-ships, including two of every animal, but for some reason, he'd culled a few aquatic mammals, tinkered with their DNA, and dumped them on a remote planet at the edge of the Alliance.

"But my father *remembers* Leviathans," Lucifer said. "So far as he knew, his experimental group had *died*. But he swears up and down, and I *questioned* him on this – repeatedly after we found the Leviathans – he *swears* he did no such thing with the source race, itself."

"Well he *did*." Ba'al Zebub gestured at the woman. "Shay'tan seeded them on a new homeworld, but they were *so* violent that he left them to finish evolving."

"So why hasn't Shay'tan come to us sooner?" Lucifer asked.

"He *has*," Ba'al Zebub grinned. "He's offered, *repeatedly*, to sell that colony back to your father … for a hefty profit, of course…"

"What price?"

"Oh, the usual—" Ba'al Zebub flipped his hand in a dismissive gesture. "Several mining worlds, some redrawn borders, a whole command carrier filled with treasure—"

"I trade for those kinds of things every single day," Lucifer said.

"Ahh, yes..." Ba'al Zebub gave a feral grin. "But have you ever tried to get your father to admit, publicly, that Shay'tan was *right?*"

Lucifer pinched the bridge of his nose. *Gah!* Not a migraine, but *firsthand knowledge* of how piggishly *intractable* his father could be whenever it came to their never-ending tit-for-tat.

"*That* was the sticking point?" he asked weakly.

"That was the term," Ba'al Zebub said. "Non-negotiable. Either Hashem calls a press conference, or he can watch his hybrid armies die out."

His father's *avoidance,* the way he'd lost *interest* in him, and also the hybrids, ever since his mother's death, all of a sudden made horrible sense. He gripped the ebony-skinned woman's arm, swaying, as the cold, hard reality came crashing down.

"So why is Shay'tan coming to *me*?" he asked.

"Your impassioned speech before Parliament moved him," Ba'al Zebub said. "If he can't get Hashem to admit he was right, then why not let *you* do it--"

And put an even bigger wall between me and my father...

'Your father is a piece of shit,' that nasty inner voice taunted.

"I *will not* foment a rebellion!" he said aloud.

"Nobody's talking about a rebellion," Ba'al Zebub said. "The old dragon just wants his pound of flesh."

"Who's flesh?"

"Hashem's," he said. "Shay'tan wants you to *marry* this female and make dozens of babies who will *keep* your Parliament alive to perpetually be a thorn in Hashem's side.

"Why would he do that?" Lucifer grew suspicious. "Isn't it more *advantageous* if Shay'tan lets us die out?"

Ba'al Zebub gestured at the two dead-eyed goons. "It's to Shay'tan's advantage if *they* die out. But you—" he gestured at Lucifer. "We have a good thing going, don't we? Averting war by promoting peaceful trade? And if Hashem won't agree, well you can simply override it, can't you?"

His father was *furious* about the last override.

"What kind of trade?"

"Nothing to opprobrious," Ba'al Zebub mashed his fat fingers together. "The human homeworld is considered a "seed world," so right now, we can't *trade* you anything from it. You *know* how your father is about natural evolution."

"They're the root of our species," Lucifer said.

"No," Ba'al Zebub said. "Nibiruians were the root of your species *after* your father tinkered with their DNA. Humans are descended from Nibiruians who weren't so blessed. While the Leviathans achieved space travel, these *humans—"* he said this with a sneer "—regressed back into the Stone Age."

A feeling of revulsion slithered along Lucifer's skin.

"They're *neolithic?"*

"Yes."

"Is she sentient?"

"She *is*," Ba'al Zebub's hand wavered *'so-so'*, "but you'll need to discuss politics with somebody else."

Lucifer scrutinized the woman's figure. She *looked* like she had curves in all the right places. And her smell...

He closed his eyes and took a deep breath.

Oh, her *smell...* She smelled more earthy, more pungent than Angelic females. The tantalizing smell worked into his brain-stem, like lutropin on steroids. His cock stirred, despite his misgivings. After 225 years of non-stop trying, he *knew* when a woman was in heat.

"Seventy-four thousand years is a lot of time for genetic drift to occur--" his resistance wavered. "Even if we *look* the same, how do we know we're still genetically compatible?"

Ba'al Zebub laughed.

"Ahh, my friend, you've caught me! Shay'tan wants to know how *valuable* this chess piece is before he plays it against your father. If you impregnate her, he'll know he has the cure."

"And if she doesn't conceive?"

"Then return her," Ba'al Zebub said.

"I don't want defective offspring."

"It's better than no offspring at all," Ba'al Zebub said, "which, after 225 years of nonstop *'Ooh-la-la'--"* the fat bastard thrust his corpulent belly forward "—is absolutely nothing."

The ever-present migraine pressed into Lucifer's skull. His wise inner voice whispered:

'Sometimes, you must make sacrifices for the greater good...'

He touched the woman's high cheekbones. She reminded him of a rare painting his father had of He-Who's-Not, the goddess' husband. Only instead of a pitiless black gaze, tears glittered like the jewels sewn into her dress.

"What's with *this?"* he touched one of the rubies.

"Our benevolent Emperor is formally gifting her to be your *wife*," Ba'al Zebub said, "in the same manner in which he gifted *me* all thirty-six of *my* wives."

Zepar shoved between them.

"Marriage?" Zepar sputtered. "Hashem forbids it!"

"But that's the condition Shay'tan has put upon receiving her," Ba'al Zebub hissed pleasantly. "The human homeworld is in Sata'anic territory. If you want access to our women, you must respect our traditions."

"No!" Zepar shouted. "The Prime Minister's genome is *unique*."

Lucifer tapped his lip. What Zepar wanted, or Shay'tan wanted, or his immortal father wanted, was irrelevant. The only thing which mattered was what *he* wanted, which was to save his species and, in the process, make sure that everything he'd spent the last 225 years building didn't die out because he'd failed to begat an heir.

"It might be worth it just to see the look on my father's face when I show up at a press conference," Lucifer said blandly, "to thank Shay'tan and announce I've found the solution to our problem?"

"You have to set an example for the other hybrids," Zepar insisted.

"Nothing in Sata'anic culture prohibits the taking of more than one wife," Ba'al Zebub said. "Why, Shay'tan has nearly four dozen wives in his harem."

Lucifer bowed his head and made the Sata'anic prayer-gesture of respect.

"My esteemed colleague, please convey my gratitude to your emperor," Lucifer said. "If she is what you claim she is, perhaps we can come to a more lucrative accommodation?"

Ba'al Zebub rubbed his plump claws together.

"If she sets fruit," Ba'al Zebub said, "we can discuss terms for future shipments."

Zepar looked like he was about to have an apoplexy as Lucifer held his hand out towards the woman.

"My beautiful bride," he said softly. "It appears we are to be married?"

Butterflies fluttered in his stomach as she took his outstretched hand. Already he could envision their future children. Him. Her. And their attractive black-skinned, white-winged children. Or would that be white-skinned, black winged children? One of each? He'd beget hundreds of offspring upon her, each child more magnificent than the one before!

Zepar's face turned purple as Ba'al Zebub made him put his hand on a Sata'anic prayer-book and recite the Sata'anic wedding vow. He could almost *see* the press release: *"Billions of females mourn the most eligible bachelor in the galaxy being taken off the market. Lucifer declares: from my loins shall spring forth the Third Galactic Alliance."*

"May the blessings of Shay'tan smile upon your union," Ba'al Zebub said. "And may she bear you many fine sons."

Zepar's mouth opened and shut like a fish.

"Shay'tan be praised," Lucifer taunted his Chief of Staff.

"Her fertility cycle ends tomorrow," Ba'al Zebub said, "and won't re-emerge for another 28 days, so I recommend you don't waste any time."

"Twenty-eight days?" Lucifer said, dumbstruck.

"Only twenty-eight days," Ba'al Zebub grinned. "Not once every other year, like an Angelic female."

Resisting the urge to *fly* back to his shuttle, Lucifer shepherded his new wife into his waiting "devil cruiser." Zepar stayed behind to argue with Ba'al Zebub. He herded her out of sight of the open door.

"Hello, my wife," Lucifer said giddily. "Do you have a name?"

"Tinashe—" the woman glanced nervously at Ba'al Zebub and Zepar arguing just outside his shuttle. *"Mimi nataka kwenda nyumbani."*

"You have no idea what just happened, do you?" he said. "You'll be the first female I've ever had to woo. Zepar usually sets these things up. I'm not even sure you'll respond to my 'gift' if you're not able to understand my language."

Visions of the future filled his head with daydreams. What kind of legacy could he build, now that he had the means to start a family?

"You have beautiful eyes—" he touched her cheek, amazed at how her skin could be so dark. "I see, within your face, the features of the Centauri. Are they descended from your people?"

He projected an image of a caramel-skinned Centauri mare into her mind, wondering if she understood. The female tilted her head, and then reached up to touch first his temple, and then her own. Did she *really* understand that he could communicate telepathically? The Emperor had always led him to believe the ability was one he'd *engineered* into the hybrids ... and then eradicated when he discovered the ability was linked to defects lurking in the Seraphim bloodline. Was the ability innate?

Caressing her chin with his finger and thumb, he leaned in and gave her a kiss. She didn't respond with the eagerness of the Angelic females during a mating appointment, but she didn't reject him. Instead, she touched the leading edge of his wings, her eyes round like an owl's as she realized the feathers were real.

Lucifer shivered under her caress. He felt like *he* was the cadet about to be fucked and gods! He looked forward to it! Yes. He would wait however long it took for *her* to want *him*.

Zepar scurried into the ship and ordered Pruflas to get them the hell out of there.

"I'm sorry, Sire," Zepar bumbled. "I had no idea he would make such a ridiculous demand! If I had known, I would have refused to schedule the meeting."

"Like hell!" Lucifer burst out. "Look at her! She bears the genetic features of the Centauri. If my father tries to quarantine her, I have legal grounds to prevent it. She's my wife!"

"It's a tool to solve a problem," Zepar waved his hand dismissively. "Don't get attached to it."

"It?" Lucifer snarled. "IT is my WIFE!"

"Of course, Sire—" Zepar's manner turned suddenly obsequious. "But you heard what Ba'al Zebub said? She is only fertile for the next 24 hours."

"After 225 years of shooting blanks," Lucifer said, "I'll risk taking a few weeks to get to know my new wife before I throw her down upon the bed. I've had my fill of meaningless sex!"

"You must mate with her *immediately!*" Zepar insisted.

"I just made a deal with the devil," Lucifer said. "So let me enjoy the up side of having sold my soul to Shay'tan before my father rains down his wrath upon me!"

Zepar reached into his pocket and pulled out the small, metal box. That ever-present migraine exploded inside of Lucifer's skull. He staggered; pain forced him to sit down. He gripped the bridge of his nose and squeezed, breathing through his mouth to prevent himself from vomiting.

"Wewe ni sawa?" the female touched his forehead. Her eyes went round with fear.

"Migraine," Lucifer whispered. "I get them a lot."

"Nyeusi uchawi!" she hissed. She turned towards Zepar, holding her hand in some sort of sign. *"Ibilisi!!!"* She moved to stand between Lucifer and Zepar.

"She's just a farm animal," Zepar crooned. "A means to an end."

His traitorous inner voice agreed:

'Just think of the power you'll gain if you can to get access to more of these...'

"She is no more sentient than the funny little creatures Hashem keeps in his genetics laboratory," Zepar said.

'She is just breeding stock...'

"Just breeding stock," Lucifer mumbled.

Darkness crushed in upon him from every angle; like being buried alive. His inner voice grew louder, taunting him for his weakness. Zepar's voice sounded far away.

"I ... I need to lay down..."

Chapter 90

Summer Solstice - June - 3,390 BC
Earth: Village of Assur
Colonel Mikhail Mannuki'ili

MIKHAIL

Ninsianna dragged him down the pathway which descended from the north gate, down the steep embankment which led to the alluvial plain. On the fields beneath them, the warriors had transformed the training field into a competition course that would rival a modern stadium. The nearest end had been set up with targets, while at the far end, date-palm trunks had been stacked to create a ten meter tall wall which started off a race into a nightmarish gauntlet, culminating in a pair of earth-reinforced log tunnels that resembled a pair of fang-laden mouths.

The Chief marched to the closest field: the one where ordinary citizens would participate in an exhibition match. The war drums grew louder, and then they fell silent.

"Today we mourn the ascent of summer," the Chief announced, "when the rains grow scarce and the sun wilts our crops. Those who refuse to till the soil will find the desert no longer provides forage for their herds, so our enemies will come *here*, to run their herds through our crops and pollute our water."

The villagers booed, showing their contempt for the Halifians, who herded, rather than settled down and farmed, but there was a raucous, almost cheerful feeling to the crowd, as though every person here acted out a role in a play.

"Every solstice, we hold a competition to remind you it's your *duty*—" the Chief grabbed the ceremonial spear out of Jamin's hand "—to defend this village. So first we'll begin with the women's exhibitions to cast the role of Geshtinanna.[131] And then, the men will compete to play the role of Damuzid."

Ninsianna gripped his arm.

"I hope to win."

Mikhail's eyebrows knit together.

"But aren't you *already* the high priestess?"

Ninsianna grinned.

"You really are naïve."

---

[131] *Geshtinanna and Damuzid:* an epic Sumerian poem; after Damuzid was killed and sent to the underworld, his sister/lover Geshtinanna offered to take his place.

She sauntered towards the warriors, tossing her hair the way the women often did when they were playing coy, though he hadn't quite figured out what she was after whenever she did it. He pried his eyes away from her swaying hips as she found her friend Yadiditum and gave the young woman a hug.

A bony hand tugged on one of his long primary feathers. It was the widow-sisters, free of their ceremonial attire.

"Will you compete?" Yalda asked.

"Aye! You must compete!" Zhila said.

"I think he'll be good at it," Yalda said to her sister.

"Aye! He is very strong—" Zhila squeezed his bicep "—and become even stronger hauling water to our crops."

"Uhm, Ma'am?" Mikhail sputtered.

The widow-sisters giggled like a pair of teenage girls, accentuating their wrinkles, grown deep around their eyes and mouths.

"I thought he was *our* champion—"called out Ninsianna's father. He approached, along with his wife. "After all, we're the ones who've been feeding him."

"Yalda bakes him bread," Zhila said.

"He eats quite a lot," Yalda said.

"And *we* convinced the Chief to let him stay?" Zhila said.

Mikhail ruffled his feathers like an eagle that'd just been caught and stuffed into a cage.

"I, uhm…"

He glanced frantically towards Ninsianna. He lost his train of thought as she stripped down to her loincloth, as did the other women.

"Relax," Ninsianna's mother murmured. "We're just posturing."

"Posturing?"

"Negotiating," Needa clarified. "We all want a share of this year's prize."

Mikhail gaped as Ninsianna bent to touch the earth, and then smeared her arms and breasts with dirt. The other young women did the same, but his young protégé, Pareesa, stood at the periphery. She spotted him, and came bouncing over.

"So whose champion are you going to be?" she asked.

"Champion?"

"Yes," she laughed. "The women who compete get to *pick* which men get ceremonially killed tonight by Nergal."

He gaped at the women, all of them Ninsianna's age, or perhaps a bit younger.

"Why aren't *you* competing?" he asked.

"I'm too *young* to want a husband," she snorted.

"A husband?"

Pareesa giggled.

"You really *do* come from a completely different world."

She went bounding off to join her younger brothers. Namhu stood at the edge of the field, fascinated by the goings-on with the women.

The warriors—not *all* of them, just the young, single ones—schooled the young women in the proper use of an atlatl. They were interrupted by the arrival of Shahla, the young woman who had propositioned him at the well, and her waif-like shadow, an emaciated, black-eyed girl.

Shahla made a beeline for Ninsianna's best friend. She stepped between Yadiditum and the young man she'd been speaking to like a hyena cutting a prey animal out of a herd. The young man helped Shahla warm up, oblivious to Ninsianna's infuriated look. The audacious young woman looked at *him* and smiled.

That one is trouble...

He ruffled his feathers and turned away.

"Line up!" the Chief ordered.

He held his breath as Ninsianna assumed a graceful pose, like a painting he'd once seen of She-Who-Is on a hunt. He struggled to shake free the memory, trying to dredge up some context other than *'hey, you might have seen something like this once'*, but his recalcitrant subconscious refused to tell.

"Throw!" the Chief shouted.

Ninsianna flung her atlatl. The physics of the throwing stick propelled the slender dart thirty meters to strike one of the targets.

"It's good!" Immanu shouted ecstatically.

Mikhail tried not to beam as Ninsianna gave a victory dance, and then strutted to the back of the line.

"Whoo!" she shouted.

Zhila touched his arm.

"See that spear?" She pointed at Jamin, who held the spear which Ninsianna had awarded to him this morning. "That's one of the prizes."

"I thought it was *his*."

"It's *his* if he can retain his title," Zhila said. "He's got quite a collection of them—ever since he turned fifteen, he's beaten the other men—but he's become too arrogant. Some of us would like to see someone—" she raised her caterpillar-grey eyebrows "—knock him off his pedestal."

"I don't have a spear," Mikhail said. "Pareesa used her father's."

Zhila held out the one she'd used to reprimand Jamin.

"I'll let you borrow *mine*," she said. "It is said, if you send forth a champion to battle Nergal fairly, win or lose, the god of war will spare your family's crops."

His hand tingled as Zhila placed the ancient weapon into his hands. Knapped from black obsidian, each flake had been struck with near-perfect symmetry, so razor thin that not even his titanium survival knife could match its edge.

He gave an appreciative whistle.

"Not even Rakshan could knap its equal."

Zhila gestured at the wall which marked the beginning of the gauntlet.

"Everything in this field has a correlation to some event in our past." She pointed at a series of carvings which had been etched into the hardwood. "Part of that history is engraved in my father's spear."

"This spear tells a story?"

"It's the legend of Damu-zid. We honor his sacrifice at every summer solstice."

He traced a surprisingly realistic carving of shepherd-boy, holding his wooden staff while, all around him, tiny carved sheep grazed in Ubaid fields. Further up the shaft, a god-like figure stabbed the shepherd-boy in the chest. Around his body, the grain wilted under the sun. Mourners buried him in a cave which looked like a mouth filled with fangs. But towards the top of the spear, the shepherd-boy crawled up out of the cave, accompanied by a woman. Right at the spearhead, the shepherd-boy subdued the god who had killed him. The rains returned. The shepherd, and his sheep, grazed peacefully once more in their fields.

"That's Damu-zid emerging from the underworld—" Zhila pointed at the boy as he emerged from the cave. "And this figure—" she pointed at the woman "—some say she's his lover, other legends say she's his sister. Geshtinanna loved him so dearly that she offered to replace him in the underworld if the gods would let him go."

Mikhail studied the competition field. The two earthen tunnels resembled the cave on the spear.

"You honor me—" Mikhail bowed his head at Zhila.

"Just win this competition," she said. "It's the only time you'll be allowed to beat Jamin without arousing his father's ire."

The Chief announced which women had qualified to move up to the second round. Ninsianna lined up. In small groups, the women lobbed their darts at targets, now moved back to fifty meters.

Ninsianna's shot flew true.

"Yes!" Mikhail shouted, and then hunched down as he realized he was acting like a fool.

"I won my husband at the solstice competition," Zhila said.

"You did?"

"Yes," she said. "I caught his eye with the spear you have in your hand right now."

A sensation of warmth tingled out to his extremities. That was how Ninsianna had first caught *his* attention, stripped half-naked, wading thigh-deep in a stream, catching fish with a tri-pronged stick. Had she been 'fishing' for a fish? Or had she been fishing for *him*?

On the third round, the contenders were whittled down to a single pair. Ninsianna ... and her emaciated, waif-like cousin.

"She's not eligible to compete!" Immanu shouted angrily. "Her father contributed *nothing* to last year's stores of grain."

The girl looked in their direction, her eyes too-large and black, but similar to Ninsianna's in shape.

An odd sensation tingled in Mikhail's subconscious.

—*He flew up into the tree.*

—*"Come and find me..." she giggled.*

—*He rifled through the branches, searching for her.*

"They look alike," he said.

"Don't let Immanu hear you say that," Yalda whispered. "There's some real bad blood between him and the girl's father."

His curiosity piqued, he flared his wings, as much from the rising heat as his own natural predatory instincts, and watched the two young women line up in front of the log wall. Two of the newly sworn-in warriors shimmied up the wall and dropped a net.

"Come," Yalda said. "We have to cheer them on."

She handed him a bucket filled with straw.

"What is this for?" he asked.

"You will see," she grinned.

Immanu and Needa each carried one of his wooden buckets, one filled with mud, the other filled with feathers. All of the villagers carried something. They lined up on either side of the obstacle course. It was filled with rocks, logs to climb over, nets to shimmy under, and a water hazard filled with soft, goopy clay.

Chief Kiyan explained the next phase of the competition.

"According to Ubaid legend, after Damu-zid was killed, his sister, Geshtinanna, descended into the underworld and offered to take his place. Along the way, she suffered much travail. Which of these women—" he gestured at Ninsianna and her cousin "—possess the fortitude to guide our shepherd-boy out of the underworld after our war god, Nergal—" he pointed at his own son "—whups him during the men's games."

Jamin held up his spear.

"I promise a merciful death," he laughed, "and a quick resurrection, accompanied by copious amounts of meat and beer."

The villagers cheered. The death was ceremonial. Whoever lost would be carried back up into the village to be resurrected as part of a magnificent feast.

"Who says the war god will win?" Ninsianna shouted. "Perhaps this year, She-Who-Is will favor the shepherd?"

The villagers laughed. But Jamin looked at *him*, his black eyes filled with hatred.

A chill rustled through Mikhail's feathers.

"Get ready!" The Chief shouted.

Ninsianna and her cousin crouched, both ready to sprint for the wall.

"Go!"

The black-eyed girl scrambled up the net while Ninsianna remained stuck on the lower level ropes, but once on the other side, the villagers began pelting both contestants with glops of mud.

"Take that!" Immanu shouted.

He hit the girl in the chest.

The black-eyed girl cried out. Most of the villagers targeted *her*, not the favorite, Ninsianna.

Ninsianna dropped down off the wall and sprinted towards the next obstacle, a net stretched close to the ground. The black-eyed girl caught up with her. The smaller, thinner girl crawled easily through the dirt and shot out the other side.

Yalda handed him a bucket filled with straw.

"Here," she said. "You're supposed to distract them so they have a hard time concentrating."

"But won't that make her lose?"

"Better to lose here," Zhila said, "than in battle."

He glanced at Immanu, who ran alongside the obstacle course, cheering along his daughter and, occasionally, throwing mud.

The two girls sprinted through a series of boulders, and then some piled logs which they needed to scramble over. Here, Ninsianna had a clear advantage thanks to her greater height.

"Go!!!" Immanu shouted.

Ninsianna bolted for one of the cave-like tunnels.

Between her and the cave, the warriors had dug out a pit and filled it up with mud. It was soupy and wet, more like an ochre bath than dirt you could walk through, with a rich, silty scent like the bottom of the river. Her cousin caught up with her. The two women waded into the guck.

"The straw!" Needa shouted. "Hit her with the straw!"

The villagers threw straw at the two women.

"Go! Go! Go!" they chanted.

Both girls cleared the mud and dove into one of the two caves. The black-eyed girl emerged first, but Ninsianna was right behind her. Both girls picked up their atlatls. As the black-eyed girl moved to swing, a glop of mud hit her square in the face.

She dropped her dart.

Ninsianna completed her throw.

The other one recovered and threw her dart. It hit the target perfectly, but it was too late.

"I call it for Ninsianna!" the Chief shouted. "Tonight, she shall play the role of Geshtinanna."

The crowd cheered.

Ninsianna pranced up to her parents, coated with straw and mud, her arms raised into the air in a victorious "V". Immanu held out his hands.

"Not this year, you don't," he said.

Yalda and Zhila both stepped back as well.

Ninsianna pranced towards her mother.

Needa put out both of her hands and said, "Oh, no you don't!!!" She bent and whispered something in Ninsianna's ear.

Ninsianna turned to *him* and gave her most fetching smile. He gave her a puzzled look, trying not to stare at her bare, muddy nipples. With a grin, she bounded over to where he stood stiffly like a tall, winged tree.

"Hug?"

She leaped into his arms and gave him a wet, muddy kiss. Not sure what to do, Mikhail held her.

A second passed…

…and then another.

The mud slipped between them; warm and slippery, causing him to think of the kinds of things the warriors whispered when the women were out of earshot. His mouth moved towards hers.

"Ninsianna," he murmured. "You have gotten me all muddy."

Immanu slapped him on the back.

"Hah! She got you!"

Her parents and their elderly neighbors roared with laughter.

"I can't believe he fell for it," Yalda laughed.

"I have to pee!" Zhila shrieked.

"He never saw it coming!" Needa said.

The entire village pointed fingers and laughed. He suppressed the urge to kiss her. All that mattered was that he held the woman of his dreams.

"Those two have it bad," Yalda whispered to her sister.

"It's only a matter of time," Zhila whispered back.

Ninsianna's cheeks turned bright pink.

Mikhail put her down and rustled his feathers, not certain how to react.

"And now," the Chief announced, "it is time for the men to compete for the role of Damu-zid."

Chapter 91

Summer Solstice - June - 3,390 BC
Earth: Village of Assur
Colonel Mikhail Mannuki'ili

MIKHAIL

The men lined up, not just warriors, but all of the unattached men. It slowly dawned on him, the source of Pareesa's laughter.

"I'm too young for a husband..."

Was this some kind of fertility rite?

He glanced at the black-eyed girl who had lost to Ninsianna. The emaciated waif sat on the ground, weeping, all by herself. She held a rock the size of her fist. A great, big red mark marred her too-pale skin.

"I thought the villagers were only supposed to throw mud?" he asked the young man next to him, a stocky, dour-faced teenager who was nearly as tall as *he* was.

"For the women," the teenager shrugged. "-We- have to face rocks and spears."

For the first time, he recognized the piles of rocks which had been piled up along the obstacle course. He'd just seen, first-hand, what would happen to the less favored contender.

"That doesn't seem very fair," Mikhail said.

"The Chief insists we run the gauntlet under battle conditions," the teenager said.

"Have you ever run it?"

The beefy teenager shook his head.

"And face *them*?" he tilted his head towards the elite warriors. "Nah. I've never made it past the first qualifying round."

Mikhail held out his hand.

"I'm Mikhail," he said. "I'm supposed to help change that."

"I'm Ipquidad—" the teenager shook his hand. "Son of the baker."

Jamin approached the weeping young woman and knelt down next to her, his demeanor something other than its usual *'arrogant goathead.'* He glanced at Ninsianna, his expression unreadable, and then led the black-eyed girl away the way one might comfort an injured child.

"Immanu shouldn't have done that," Ipquidad said.

"Immanu?"

"Yeah. I watched him coat the rock with mud."

Mikhail flared his wings.

"You lie! Immanu would never do such a thing."

Ipquidad backed up. "You don't believe me? Then fine."

The teenager found another place in the line.

Mikhail inwardly cursed. *How am I supposed to convince these kids to let me -train- them if I insult them?* The teen's body language indicated he believed what he'd just said, even if it wasn't true. Jamin had spread a lot of lies. The kid must have misconstrued something he'd seen.

The first round of competition was to eliminate for distance. Anyone who couldn't throw one-hundred-fifty cubits, around a hundred meters, would be eliminated from running the gauntlet.

"Get ready!" Chief Kiyan ordered.

He twirled Zhila's spear, searching for the center of gravity to ease his jitters. He *knew* he'd learned to use a similar weapon, the same way that he *knew* he'd never knapped a spearhead, but had once planted a field. He could almost *feel* the ant-like Cherubim teach him to use some kind of javelin, a double-ended staff topped with steel tips. He'd discovered the talent when Pareesa had shown up with her father's spear.

"Throw!" the Chief shouted.

Mikhail moved his weight behind the spear. It sailed past the minimal distance line and kept on flying, past the two hundred cubit marker, right over the wall which separated the training field from a field filled with barley.

The villagers gasped.

"That's even further than Jamin..."

The older warriors ran out into the field and held up the spears which had surpassed the minimum distance line. The beefy young man, Ipquidad, failed to make the cut.

The rest slapped one another on the back and said: "we'll do better next year."

As warriors dragged out more targets, Ninsianna slipped up behind him.

"Good luck," she whispered. "If you lose, tonight, I will have to sit with Nergal at the feast."

"You didn't tell me his men would be pelting me with rocks and spears?"

She gave him a sheepish grin.

"If I had," she said, "would you have agreed to do it?"

He stared down at the woman who occupied his heart. How could she have no idea?

"For you—" he touched her cheek "—I would drag the devil straight into hell."

The Chief announced:

"Next we'll sort you by ability. If you fail to hit the target, you will be eliminated. If you hit the outer ring—" he pointed to the bullseye "—you will run the gauntlet as a group. The man who hits the enemy's heart first—" he pointed at two man-shaped targets with bright, red circles painted over their chests "—will move up to compete with the second group."

He pointed at the next closer ring.

"If you hit the second ring," he continued, "you'll compete against the elite warriors. As for the very center—" he pointed at a small, black dot, no bigger than a man's eye "—if anyone hits dead-center, they'll compete directly against Nergal, played by Jamin, my son. If not, whoever wins the second round will be assigned to the role."

Jamin held up the spear which Ninsianna had given him.

"He -always- plays Nergal," one of the villagers whispered.

"That's because he is -good-," another villager said.

"He -wins-," the first one said, "because his warriors crack anyone's skull who gives him a good run."

"Line up!" the Chief shouted.

Mikhail moved into a pose similar to the one that Zhila had demonstrated when she'd loaned him her spear, but it felt unnatural. The Cherubim had taught him to use a javelin as a *defensive* weapon. Every fiber of his being screamed *"don't let go of your weapon, you'll disarm yourself, you idiot!"*

He held the spear upright, vertical against his body. Lunging into a sparring kata, he spun the weapon, right-left-right, deflecting imaginary opponents who struck at him with swords. In his peripheral vision, he could almost *see* three ant-like Cherubim strike at his head, his torso, and his wings, as he used the javelin to block and strike.

Become one with the weapon...

At one point in the kata, a fourth Cherubim would come at him, wielding a weapon that was similar to an atlatl, only propelled by a curved stick strung with sinew. In his mind, the Cherubim strung the bowstring...

"Throw!" the Chief shouted.

Mikhail heaved the javelin, flaring his wings as his entire body moved to eliminate the bowman.

The spear flew straight.

It hit the black dot with so much force that it pierced straight through the straw and disappeared out the other side.

"Yes!"

He forced himself to display false calm as the older warriors ran up the line, shouting out names associated with spears. Most men were eliminated, but others marched proudly to stand in one of the other two groups. At last they got to *his* spear. Chief Kiyan's enforcer, Varshab, gestured for the Chief.

The crowd waited as the Chief and Jamin argued. Mikhail overheard a single word.

"—disqualified," Jamin insisted.

The Chief beckoned to Rakshan the flint-knapper. The weapons-master squatted in front of the target and peered through the hole, and then stood up and said something to the Chief.

"But it didn't *stick!*" Jamin shrieked.

"If that had been a man," Rakshan said, "it would have torn his heart out."

Jamin stormed away, his fists clenched.

The Chief stood calmly in front of the men.

"The purpose of this competition is to encourage our people to be prepared in case of attack," the Chief said. "Since Mikhail hit the innermost target, he shall face off directly against my son."

The villagers cheered. Yalda and Zhila clapped him on the back of the wings. Ninsianna gave him a knowing 'I told you so' smirk while Immanu and Needa congratulated him.

"You'd better start baking more hot bread, wife," Immanu joked. "Before our Yalda and Zhila lure away our guest."

"I'm a healer, not a cook!" Needa cuffed her husband. "If you want soft bread, bake it yourself!"

He glanced over at Jamin. The angry *Muhafiz* stood, crouched in a circle with his elite warriors. Every now and then, one of them looked over. They were up to something. No doubt planning how to 'distract' him.

"What am I facing?" he asked Immanu.

"The villagers will throw rocks and sticks," he said. "None larger than your fist. It's forbidden to aim for your head, but any other part of your body is fair game."

"And what about the warriors?" he asked.

"They'll come at you with spears," he said. "They're allowed to cut you, but it's forbidden to throw."

"Serious injuries are not uncommon." Needa lifted up her healer's basket, the one she brought whenever she called upon a patient.

The men stripped down to their loincloths, the same as the young women had done. The elite warriors moved into position. The rest of the villagers moved towards the piles of rocks. All of them joked about "killing Damu-zid."

The Chief shouted "Run!"

The third-place level of men bolted for the ten meter high wall. In such a large group, while the men dodged rocks, it was difficult for the elite warriors to single out a single man.

"You'd better take that off—" Yalda pointed to his shirt.

"Unless you want it to be ruined," Zhila finished.

"Why?" he asked.

"Our clay is filled with yellow ochre," Zhila said.

"No amount of washing will get it out," Yalda said.

"The men usually go bare-chested," Zhila said.

"Supposedly so as not to dirty their spare kilts," Yalda said.

"But the real reason is—" Zhila said.

"—they enjoy parading around for the women," Yalda said.

"And we don't mind at all, do we Yalda?" Zhila elbowed her sister in the ribs.

"No, we don't mind," Yalda laughed.

He touched the place where the crash had left him with several permanently shattered ribs. So far, he'd kept his chest covered, not because he felt bashful about his appearance, but because he didn't want the villagers to know where he was weak.

"You'd better take that off—" Ninsianna touched his feathers.

"Why?" he asked.

"Because I don't think you'll fit through that tunnel—" she pointed at the manufactured cave. "It was tight for *me*, and I'm not burdened with wings."

He glanced at the useless appendages which, ever since he'd woken up, were of little use except to make him stand out like some kind of freak. Why couldn't he have woken up without them?

He stripped off his shirt and stood, naked to his waist; vulnerable in front of these primitive, savage people.

Yalda and Zhila fell silent as they beheld the hideous, sunken scar which marred his chest. He moved his hand instinctively to protect his heart which pulsated through his unprotected skin.

"Immanu told us," Yalda said softly. "But I do not think we *believed...*"

He curved one wing forward. That sense of self-preservation which made him twitchy caused every nerve fiber to scream "don't let anyone get near!"

"It's okay," Ninsianna murmured. "Everyone here is your friend."

He glanced over at the third-tier contestants. As the first man dove into the tunnel, the man behind him grabbed his feet and dragged him back out, while the *third* man to clear the mud-puddle leapfrogged over the both of them, only to be waylaid when a fourth man did the same thing to him.

A brawl broke out in front of the two tunnels as the men vied for position. Fists and feet flew as the villagers pelted the men with rocks.

Suddenly, a man appeared on the other side. He picked up one of the two spears, only to drop it when one of the villagers hit him in the chest with a rock. A second man appeared out of the adjacent tunnel. He picked up the second spear and threw it at the target.

He missed…

The first man picked up the spear and hit the target dead-center.

The villagers cheered. They picked up the man and transported him to a place of honor.

"This game," Mikhail said. "It's survival of the fittest?"

"So it is with life," Immanu said.

"This game does not promote cohesion," Mikhail said. "When an army works together, it is stronger."

The second-tier men lined up behind the log wall. Most of these men were Jamin's elite warriors. As they vied for a good starting position, Pareesa and the other "new" warriors scrambled up the climbing net, and then cut it away, replacing it with a series of knotted ropes.

"This obstacle course is harder?" he asked.

"As ability goes up," Immanu said, "so does the difficulty of the gauntlet."

The older warriors lined up alongside the obstacle course and began to taunt the contestants with good-natured insults to their manhood. The spears they held, however, were anything but funny.

The villagers began to chant "kill Damu-zid!"

"Go!" the Chief shouted.

The elite warriors surged forward. As they scaled the wall, the extra training they'd received quickly separated them from the men who had merely qualified. The villagers pelted them with rocks as they tried to clear the apex. Firouz dropped to the bottom of the wall. He plucked a rock out of the air that had been aimed at his skull and lobbed it back at the villager who'd thrown it.

The villager yelped.

"If you hit me again," Firouz snarled, "when this is over, I will find you!"

The elite warrior bolted towards the crawl-net.

"Is he *supposed* to do that?" Mikhail asked.

"Do what?" Immanu said.

"Threaten the villagers?" Mikhail asked.

"What do *you* think?" The shaman's bushy eyebrows rose up in an expression of *'you tell me?'* "This festival is held to honor the God of War."

The contestants dove under the first net, vying against not just each other, but also the villagers they protected. As the elite warriors hit the mud pit, they did not work against one another as the third-tier contestants had done. Siamek was the first to reach the tunnels. The elite warriors closed ranks, preventing a non-elite contender from dragging him out of the tunnel. Meanwhile, the small man, Dadbeh, dashed into the second tunnel. They emerged at the exact same time.

Both men made the throw…

Both men hit the target…

The judges went out to examine the targets, and called a draw.

As the villagers picked up the two men and carried them to a place of honor, the Chief called for him and Jamin to line up. The remaining elite warriors resumed their places along the obstacle course as spearmen.

Ninsianna's mother got called away to tend some wounds….

"Be careful," Ninsianna said. "The villagers throw half-heartedly, but Jamin's men? They will stab you."

"What about the tunnel?"

"The right-hand tunnel is filled with obstacles," she said. "I have no idea what the left-hand tunnel looks like, but Dadbeh got through it quickly."

"I think the right-hand tunnel might be bigger," Immanu said, "because Siamek went for the right-hand one. You have to remember that Dadbeh is small, for a man."

He took his place at the starting line. While he waited, the warriors shimmied up the ropes, and then cut them away, leaving him facing an almost unscaleable, ten-meter-high log wall.

Jamin strode up to take his place. While in hand-to-hand combat, Mikhail had an advantage due to his height, with primitive weapons, Jamin was the embodiment of Nergal, the god of war.

"May the best man win," Mikhail held out his hand.

Jamin stared at it, his expression filled with disgust. He crouched for a sprint, his black eyes focused on the top of the wall they were about to scale.

"Go!" the Chief shouted.

Both men sprinted. As they gripped the logs with toes and fingertips, Mikhail fought the urge to flap his wings. Jamin scaled the wall faster, unencumbered by their great weight, but on the way down, Mikhail spread his wings and simply dropped.

They hit the ground together.

Mikhail fanned one wing to prevent a rock from hitting him in the face. As they slammed into the dirt to crawl under the net, Mikhail dodged a pair of well-placed spear jabs.

"Damantia!"

He flattened his wings and crawled elbow over elbow. He'd learned to do this *someplace*. His entire body remembered doing it, even if he could not remember where or why.

Free from the inconvenience of tangled feathers, Jamin cleared the net several seconds before he did.

Mikhail wriggled free, dodging spears.

Both men sprinted for the boulders.

Jamin darted easily between the boulders, his feet swift on terrain he'd grown up on. Mikhail stretched his wings and leaped up on top of them, jumping from boulder to boulder and deflecting fist-sized rocks. They both cleared the obstacle at the exact same instant.

"Go!!!" Ninsianna cheered.

Next was a jumbled pile of logs.

Jamin danced easily from log to log.

Mikhail flapped his wings and scrambled up over the pile. Here, at least, their weight did not hold him back.

"Go! Go! Go!" the villagers chanted.

Both men dove for the mud pit.

Jamin's face bunched with revulsion as he moved through the soupy mess.

Mikhail dove right into it to avoid a pair of spears. The villagers laughed as he rolled and coated his wings with mud.

"He doesn't know what he's doing!" one of the elite warriors laughed.

He cleared the pit a few seconds quicker than Jamin.

A wall of spear-points stood between him and the right-hand tunnel.

The left-hand tunnel was clear.

A sense of *knowing* whispered: *"Dadbeh is small for a man."*

He veered to the right, straight into the spear-points. The warriors yelped as he flapped his wings to give them a face-full of muddy feathers, and then grabbed the spears, ignoring the pain of the ones which cut him.

He dove into the right-hand tunnel.

Flatten your wings...

Don't be ashamed to crawl...

He pictured he was a snake, writhing and slithering as he jammed his too-large body through a tunnel designed to be tight for even a human man. Rocks and sticks tore at his body, ripped out feathers and crushed his wings.

He wriggled forward, obsessed with a single thought...

"There's no way in -Hades- I'm letting Ninsianna sit with that black-eyed bastard tonight!"

Here was his chance to show these people he was *more* than some pretty bird, fallen from the sky.

He reached the edge of the tunnel.

Jamin was already there.

Lurching forward, he grabbed the second spear and rose to his feet, his wings flapping to accelerate his motion as he *threw* every ounce of frustration into the spear.

The spears left their hands at the exact same instant.

Jamin's spear hit the target's belly.

His spear slammed into the target's red-painted heart. The target shattered, destroying not just the chest, but the log they'd used to prop it upright like a man.

The crowd cheered.

The Chief moved in front of the people, his expression cloaked.

"It appears," the Chief said, "that this year, Damu-zid has won."

With an angry shout, Jamin stormed away.

A *feeling* let loose from deep within his belly.

It felt like belonging…

It roared outwards—as a laugh.

The villagers picked him up and *carried* him back to his two elderly liege-ladies, covered with thick, yellow mud. Never again would he feel incompetent. He'd just beaten Jamin at his own game!

Ninsianna gave him a nervous smile.

"Are you going to let her get away with that?" Yalda asked.

"Better be quick, boy!" Zhila poked his muddy belly. "Before she gets away."

His eyes focused; a raptor on the hunt. Ninsianna hid behind her parents, squealing.

"Don't look at us," Immanu laughed.

"We're not going to save you," Needa said.

"An eye for an eye…" Immanu said in a mock-serious voice. He looked at Mikhail and nodded.

Ninsianna squealed, and bolted into the crowd.

Mikhail flapped his wings to close the distance between them. The warm Mesopotamian wind caught his feathers like a lover.

The first mistress any winged creature made love to was the wind. She tickled each sensitive feather and whispered she wished to carry him.

He banked his wings to catch her caresses.

…uplift….

……his fickle mistress carried him up into the sky.

The Emperor had bred his species to hunt. With the eyes of an eagle, he spied Ninsianna slipping into the crowd, unaware he'd taken to the air in her haste to escape his playful wrath.

He tucked his wings against his side and dove like a hawk. Wind whistled past his ears, singing exhalations, as he swooped towards his prey. Like a gigantic eagle, he snatched her.

"Ack!" Ninsianna shrieked.

Pain shot down his damaged flight tendon as he hit the ground and pounded his wings to free her from the grasp of her jealous lover—gravity—but the pain didn't matter.

He shot back into the sky.

"Eeeee!!!" her legs flailed like a prey animal trying to escape the eagle's grasp.

"I owe you this," he laughed.

Ninsianna slid her arms around his neck, both terrified and exhilarated, as she refused to look down at the rapidly shrinking ground. He caught an updraft over the Hiddekel River.

This was what he'd been bred to do…

Their eyes met, stealing the breath from his lungs.

"Ninsianna," he murmured.

His mouth descended towards hers.

Greedily he tasted her luscious red lips that had tempted him from the moment he'd first woken up in his crashed ship, with no memory of his past. With a moan, she wrapped her legs around his body. Warmth ignited in his loins as he sought out her tongue.

"Mikhail," she pressed her lips against his ear. "You can fly…"

"With you, I can do anything," he said.

He adjusted his flight to capture an updraft. They the circled lazily above the cheering spectators like the enormous mated pair of golden eagles who forever circled the river in search of fish.

With a mischievous grin, he added:

"And now you are covered in mud too, *mo grá*."

Chapter 92

⊗

Neutral Zone: Sata'an/Alliance Border
Diplomatic Carrier: Prince of Tyre
Alliance Secret Service: Special Agent Eligor

ELIGOR

Special Agent Eligor stood at attention as the Prime Minister's shuttle cruised into the launch bay of his diplomatic carrier, the *'Prince of Tyre.'* For some reason Chief of Staff Zepar had radioed ahead and demanded the entire crew assemble in the launch bay. A chill of anticipation rippled through the men as Lucifer's "devil cruiser" cleared the airlock..

The hatch slid open. The gangplank slowly extended. The Prime Minister stepped off, wings flared like a rock star, shepherding a veiled female wearing an ornate, jeweled dress.

"It figures," his crewmate, Larajie said. "With him it's always something female."

"A Sata'anic female," Eligor whispered. "The only one who has ever seen one is General Abaddon. Shay'tan won't let them out of the Hades cluster."

"So now he's going to fuck a lizard?" Larajie scoffed.

"It wouldn't surprise me," a hard-nosed mercenary named Ruax said. "We all know there are two Lucifers. The one he shows the cameras, and the one we see the minute he gets out from beneath the Emperor's thumb."

The Prime Minister guided the terrified female to stand in front of his men, three lines-deep, and stood, with a feral glint in his eyes. He grinned like a cat who had just swallowed a bird, slid down the woman's veil, and waited for his men to recognize what was standing right in front of their eyes.

"That's no lizard," Eligor said. "She's ... "

"Human," Lerajie finished.

"Shit ... he did it!" Ruax said. "Lucifer found the root race! We are saved!"

Eligor looked into Lucifer's silver eyes and shivered. Whatever stared back was so malevolent and cold, he could swear it wasn't mortal.

Sword of the Gods:

Book III:
Forbidden Fruit

*And the woman said unto the serpent,
"We may eat of the fruit of the trees
Of the garden: But of the fruit of the tree
Which is in the midst of the garden,
God hath said, 'Ye shall not eat of it;
Neither shall ye touch it, lest ye die.'"*

--Genesis 3:3

Chapter 93

Galactic Standard Date: 152,323.04 AE
Earth: Sata'an Forward Operating Base
Lieutenant Kasib

Ten weeks ago...

Lt. KASIB

A crowd of humans huddled at the edge of the village, watching the Sata'anic troop carriers hover above the makeshift airfield. The roaring VTOL engines kicked up a cloud of dust and blew it towards the village, obscuring Lieutenant Kasib from their view.

"Excuse me?" Kasib called out.

The humans cried out as they realized he was one of *them*. One of the "lizard-gods." Come to lift them out of the Stone Age. They threw their meager bodies onto the ground, pressed their pink foreheads into the dirt and proclaimed:

"Shay'tan be praised..."

Kasib raised two claws and gave them the expected blessing before stepping over their prostrated bodies. The humans stared enviously at the small, clay vase which he carried, shaped from yellow ochre clay and decorated with a darker shade of brown; the second-most precious fruit this planet had to offer. Its contents represented all of the *good* things this planet could offer the Empire, as well as all of the *bad* things if he failed to help the General secure the *most* valuable fruit, it's people, against the Alliance.

The last two troop carriers set down upon the airfield and spooled down their subspace engines in a frustrated hum. With fuel reserves running low, there would be no more supply runs up to the *SRN Jamaran*. General Hudhafah (*Shay'tan praise his infinite wisdom*) had ordered that all but a skeleton crew would evacuate the battlecruiser and begin colonizing the planet. The aft-ramp split open. Thousands of burly soldiers, representing every planet in the Empire—Sata'anic lizards, boar-like Catoplebas, blue-skinned Marid, and dozens of other races—descended from the squat, grey ships, carrying rucksacks that were light on ammunition and even *lighter* on food.

"Where's the mess hall?" the newcomers shouted.

"Up yer arse!" the Earth-veterans shouted back.

"They said there'd be more food here?"

"There is–" the Earth veterans gestured towards the distant mountains. "All you have to do is git' off yer arse and take it."

Combat boots stomped in unison over hastily graded fields as the staff-sergeants herded the hungry men towards a tent marked with the quartermaster's key-and-sword.[132]

Kasib skirted the razor-wire fence. This was the most difficult supply campaign he'd ever had to help Hudhafah coordinate, 12,000 light-years from the nearest Sata'anic outpost, under total radio silence and utmost secrecy. The humans were so enamored with Sata'anic technology that they had no idea how *precarious* their hold was on this planet.

A drop of fragrant oil leaked past the clay vase's stopper, filling his nostrils with a fruity scent.

Maybe he should take a taste?

No! The village elders had given it as a peace offering. It was up to *him* to convince Shay'tan that the humans would cooperate so they could avoid a bloody clusterfuck like the *last* planet they had conquered. Success was the only way he'd earn the pinnacle of Sata'anic achievement: a wife, a family, and children to carry on his name.

A platoon of skullcrackers blocked the gate, laden down with supplies just retrieved from an outlying village. Judging by their blood-splattered uniforms, the village had required a bit of *persuasion* to supply the base with tribute.

Kasib sighed. Wouldn't these men ever learn that *"use diplomacy"* meant something *other* than the business-end of a pulse rifle?

He took a quick count of the number of baskets. While thick with plunder, there was little actual *food*.

"Is this all you were able to get?" he asked.

The skullcrackers ignored him.

"*Privates!*" he ordered sharply. "Will you be able to get more?"

Two of the burly infantrymen sneered down at him.

"Oy, look!" said a muscular, blue-skinned Marid. "'Ere's a bit o' cannon fodder, telling us 'ow to do our job?"

"Aye," the other said, a flat-headed lizard with a scar which ran from its nostril to its eye. "E's so little, maybe I could use 'im to wipe my arse?"

The two skull-crackers sniggered.

"You shall call me *Lieutenant*," Kasib huffed indignantly. Skullcrackers had an appalling lack of respect for any officer who couldn't knock them onto their ass.

---

[132] *Quartermaster:* military officer who is responsible for managing supplies. The *key and sword* are a symbol of their rank.

"'E' looks like one o' them paper-pushers, don't he?" the Marid poked a blue, muscular finger into Kasib's chest.

"Maybe you should use 'im fer toilet paper the next time you's run outta paper in the latrine?" the flat-headed lizard laughed.

The blue-skinned Marid grabbed at the precious urn.

"Whatcha got there?"

Kasib yanked it away.

"This is a *gift* for Emperor Shay'tan!"

"For Shay'tan, you say?" the lizard laughed. "This little guy claims 'e's got a channel to Emperor Shay'tan!"

All of the skullcrackers burst into deep-bellied guffaws.

A high-pitched wail cut them off.

"*Ayağa kalk kaltak!*" a human voice shouted.

"Let me pass!" Kasib bared his fangs. "Or I shall place your disciplinary folder on General Hudhafah's desk!"

He twisted his collar so the two knuckleheads could see the gold-braided pin which marked him as the General's personal *aide-de-camp*. The blood drained out of the flat-headed lizard's dewlap.

"We didn't mean nothin' by it, Sir," he said.

"Aye," the Marid said. "We was just 'avin a bit of fun."

The two skullcrackers stepped aside.

Muttering about discipline, Kasib elbowed his way through the rest of the platoon. Blocking the gate stood a group of humans dressed in colorful striped robes. Their leader wore a leather bandolier[133] draped over one shoulder; but instead of bullets, dozens of small, bone-handled knives were shoved into the leather strap. His men carried a weapon that the local tribes didn't carry; bows and arrows. A foul stench forced Kasib to snap his long, forked tongue back inside his mouth.

"Why are *they* here?" he asked the pig-snouted Catoplebas who guarded the gate. "I just came from the village. All supplies are to be traded *there*."

"Not *these*," the Catoplebas said. "Your allies said they require special handling."

"*Which* allies?" Kasib glanced back at the blood-splattered skullcrackers.

"The ones you told we'd train their women as wives?"

Kasib gave the traders an incredulous once-over. The secret to colonizing any new world was to convince the indigenous population to adopt Sata'anic ideals. By controlling access to women, and therefore reproduction, within a single generation, they could turn even the most hostile planet into a reliable tributary. He'd mentioned this to the village

---

[133] *Bandolier:* a pocketed ammunition or weapon belt.

elders, but they were nowhere *near* ready to begin the re-education of future brides!

The boar-faced guard, whose name-patch said *"Katlego,"* brutally elbowed one of the traders.

"Step aside, you meatheads!" he oinked in Kemet.

The traders moved.

At their center huddled a dozen terrified women, scandalously clad with bare arms and uncovered faces. One of the women had fallen, reasonably attractive, but judging by her ripped clothing, a bit worse for the wear.

"You clumsy piece of goat shit!" the leader snarled. "She keeps pretending to trip!"

"I'm sorry," the female sobbed. Bruises marred her cheek.

The cruel-faced leader grabbed her by the hair.

"If they reject you," he hissed beneath what he *thought* was the Sata'anic level of hearing, "I shall take you out into the desert and slit your throat!"

The woman shrieked.

The trader began to beat her.

The skullcrackers all laughed.

Kasib rushed forward and grabbed the trader by the neck.

"Shay'tan—" he bared his five-centimeter long fangs "—has *rules* about how a man should treat a woman!"

While modest in size, at least compared to the skullcrackers, even a modest-height lizard towered over the average human man. He picked the man up so that his legs dangled off the ground.

A sharp, ammonia scent filled the air. Urine pissed down the leader's leg.

"S-she keeps on falling," he pleaded.

"If you on keep *kicking* her," Kasib growled, "of *course* she's going to fall!"

The skullcrackers hooted: "Way to go, Lieutenant!"

Kasib glanced over at the grounded spacecraft, and then at the meatheads he'd forced to step aside. As much as he wanted to earn their respect by dismembering the leader limb-by-limb, he *needed* these traders to forge a local supply chain on a primitive planet which lay millions of light-years from the heart of the Sata'anic Empire.

Whether they were ready or not, Stage 4 of the invasion had to begin right now.

"What's your name, trader?" Kasib asked.

"Rimsin," the trader sputtered. "Son of Kudursin, of the Amorite tribe of Jebel Bishri.[134] We specialize in the trade of women."

---

[134] *Jebel Bishri:* a mountain range in modern-day Syria.

"Well Shay'tan demands we discipline our women *kindly*—" Kasib growled. "You must implore her with reason, and if that fails, then you hit her, *gently*, with a cane. Do you understand that, *trader*?"

"Y-yes," the trader squeaked.

"Good." Kasib set the trader down and flattened his multi-colored robe. "Deliver these women to the quartermaster for three gold *darics* apiece, and then—" he gestured at the women "—bring me as many maidens as you can find. No more than *two* from a single village!"

"Thank you!" the trader exclaimed.

The Amorites bolted through the gate, abandoning the women to collect their bounty of gold. At the price he'd just offered, these women would be the first of *many*.

Kasib felt for the clay urn and realized he'd dropped it. At his feet, the woman he'd just rescued fumbled in the dirt and gathered the precious brown fruits to her bosom.

"H-h-here—" she reached up towards him.

In her hands she held three small fruits, bruised and covered with dirt, but still as sweet and salty-smelling as when Nipmeqa had packed them into the jar. The urn, on the other hand, was irreparably cracked. The oil had seeped out, wasted, onto the ground.

Kasib opened his snout to scold her, but then he realized...

...the woman was blind.

Tears streamed down her cheeks as she gathered the remaining fruit.

"That's okay," he lied. "Shay'tan is a *forgiving* god."

Chapter 94

*And when the woman saw
That the tree [was] good for food,
And that it [was] pleasant to the eyes,
And a tree to be desired to make [one] wise,
She took of the fruit thereof, and did eat,
And gave also unto her husband with her;
And he did eat.*

--Genesis 3:6

End-June - 3,390 BC
Earth: Village of Assur
Colonel Mikhail Mannuki'ili

Present timeline...

MIKHAIL

The Mesopotamian wind buoyed his wings like a long-lost lover, welcoming him back unto her warm bosom. He swirled in lazy circles on a pre-dawn updraft, higher and higher, until the cold caused his skin to prickle, and his head grew dizzy from lack of oxygen.

At last the first frail rays of sunlight shot over the distant horizon, even though the land beneath him still lay cloaked in a peaceful slumber. The light kissed his skin; brilliant, dazzling and golden-white. Just like Ninsianna's eyes—

—just like the overwhelming sense of *duty* which refused to shake free from his absent memories.

He tucked his wings against his back and dove.

Whirling and twirling in a dizzying spin, his heart raced as he relished the sensation of free-fall. The wind roared past his ears, falling, falling; drowning out the scolding voice which chittered—

—*complete the mission, complete the mission, complete the mission*—

What mission? He couldn't even remember his own name!

The thickening air screamed that he'd fallen dangerously close to the earth, but the only time he felt *free* was when he allowed himself to fall. Without opening his eyes, he flared his wings in a gut-twisting stop that flipped him mid-air and catapulted him straight upwards, back into the wind.

"Whoo!"

It felt exhilarating, not like combat. His entire body tingled, as though for the first time in his life, he could *feel*.

He caught another updraft above the Hiddekel River. It carried him above the sleeping village as the sun rose a second time, painting Assur's mud-brick walls in dazzling shades of pink and golden-yellow...

...just like Ninsianna's sun-kissed skin.

He flew over the north gate, past the sentries who gave him a sour expression. One of the younger warriors waved. The warrior next to him elbowed him in the ribs—hard.

"He's an *enemy*," the warrior hissed.

"But the Chief said—"

"It doesn't *matter*," the warrior interrupted. "If Jamin sees you, he'll crack your skull."

Mikhail suppressed a twinge of irritation. No matter how much things had changed since yesterday, the more they stayed the same. He skimmed the top of the wall so that the wind from his feathers would knock the warrior's cone-shaped hat off.

"Hey!"

He glided to the right, ignoring the warrior's expletives. His shadow raced beneath him, casting a gigantic winged-shape upon the road. Groggy villagers stumbled out of their houses and looked up, still unaccustomed to see him fly.

"Mikhail! Mikhail!"

One of the villagers jumped up and down ecstatically, waving a battered wooden spear. Mikhail banked his wings to hover above Pareesa. She'd cast off her brother's cape and kilt to wear her own shawl-dress, belted high to free her legs.

"I'm off to training!" she held up her father's spear.

"Good luck!" he called out.

"Will you join us?"

His powerful wings kept him aloft above her.

"That's not up to me," he said. "It's up to the *Muhafiz*."

Pareesa crossed her eyes and made a rat-face. They both knew what the likelihood of *that* happening was. *'When Hades freezes over'* and *'over Jamin's dead body.'* But it wasn't *her* job to win his battle for respect.

He bid her farewell, and then caught an updraft to carry him over the second ring of houses. The wind battered his feathers as he descended into Immanu's courtyard.

Ninsianna's bedroom shutter had been thrown wide open. With a tingle of anticipation, he picked up the water buckets he'd fetched earlier, before he'd succumbed to the urge to see the sunrise happen *twice,* and ducked beneath the lintel into the mud-brick house.

She stood in the kitchen, a domestic goddess, rummaging through a basket with her shawl-dress draped gracefully over the curve of her back. A ray of sunlight backlit her in glorious, golden light. He stood, tongue-tied.

"Mama! Where's the *a'alendra*?"[135] she shouted.

"Drying in the rafters," her mother's voice floated down from the second floor.

She reached up to the ceiling, causing her artfully wrapped shawl-dress to slip off one shoulder as she rummaged through bundles of drying herbs; their grassy scent filled the air.

"I can't see it!" she shouted.

"It's near the *Za'afaran*,"[136] Needa shouted back.

A pert, brown nipple peeked out of the soft white cloth, causing Mikhail's pants to grow uncomfortably tight. She reached towards a bundle of dried white flowers.

"Here it is!"

She crashed into him, pressing her warm, soft breasts into the flat of his stomach. Water from the two buckets splashed onto her dress, causing it to become transparent. Her goddess-kissed eyes met his.

"Ninsianna," he murmured.

She stood on tip-toe with her face turned up, her lips parted with anticipation. The scent of soaproot wafted up to his nostrils. He bent to kiss her, but her mother's foot upon the stairwell drove them both apart. Needa climbed down the step, arranging her dark-tinted chador[137] to protect her clothing against that common healer's malady: other people's blood, vomit and piss.

"Did you find it?" Needa asked.

Ninsianna grabbed the nearest bundle of herbs and clutched it to her chest.

"Y-y-yes, Mama." Her face turned scarlet-pink.

Mikhail shifted a bucket to hide his erection.

"You can set those *down*—" Needa pointed at the wooden counter "—over there."

"Yes, Ma'am," he said, his voice thick with guilt.

Needa gave him a raised eyebrow as he skittered sideways, still holding the bucket in front of him, and then sidled back, one large wing curved forward to discreetly shield his *intentions* towards her daughter.

Ninsianna giggled.

"That is *borage*—"[138] her mother cut her off. "Not *a'alendra*. You need to *sedate* the old woman's breath, not make her want to run a race."

---

[135] *A'alendra:* a small, local shrub used to treat asthma.

[136] *Za'afaran:* a traditional local herb used to treat male impotence.

[137] *Chador:* in Mesopotamian times, a length of cloth draped over the head to make an informal veil, cape or apron; generally worn by high-ranking women.

[138] *Borage:* a medicinal herb used for treating fatigue and infection.

"Yes, Mama." Ninsianna said docilely. She grabbed her basket and skittered out the front door. Her luscious pink lips formed the promise: *"later..."*

"And *you,*" Needa pointed at the table. "Yalda and Zhila came by while you were up there—" she twirled her finger in the air to indicate his aerial acrobatics "—showing off. They brought your share of the prize."

"The prize?" he drew a momentary blank.

"From yesterday," she said. "After you flew off with my daughter—" she gave him a stern look "—the Chief awarded your *sponsors* your prize."

His face flushed, but he was *positive* nobody had seen him kiss Ninsianna—he'd had the wherewithal to carry her upriver before succumbing to the urge—and then, the rest of the night, they'd played the platonic roles of "Geshtinanna and Damu-zid" in front of the entire village.

Her mother gestured at a small, clay urn. Unlike the mud-clay jars which contained her healer's embrocations, this jar had been fired from the finest ochre yellow clay, and then decorated with dark brown symbols.

He picked it up.

"What is it?" he asked.

"You're going to share it with us, won't you?" her voice lilted hopefully. "After all, *we're* the ones who've been feeding you."

"Yes, Ma'am," he said guiltily.

The tiniest hint of a smirk tugged at Needa's lips. He'd been knocking himself out, trying to earn his keep, but at last, yesterday, he'd *proven* he was good at something.

What? Killing...

—Yes.

There's no way in Hades that Jamin will trust you near his men.

—But they saw me *beat* him. That's got to count for something?

"Open it," Needa gestured at the urn.

He removed the wooden stopper. Exactly halfway down sat a cluster of small, brown orbs, steeped in their own golden oil.

"What are they?" He picked one out.

"Olives," she said.

He gave it a sniff.

"Are they a fruit or a vegetable?"

"A fruit," she said.

"It doesn't *smell* like fruit."

"They're fruit," she huffed.

Raising a skeptical eyebrow, he raised the orb to his lips. It had an aroma like fresh-cut barley, chopped date-palm leaves, and perhaps a bit like butter? A drop of golden oil dribbled onto his tongue, partially salty, partially sweet, with the subtlest undertone of just a bit of spice?

"Go ahead, taste it?" she eyed him enviously.

He popped it into his mouth.

"Just watch out for the—"

He bit into it.

"Ouch!" His teeth hit something hard.

"—pit," she finished.

"Thanks for warning me," he grumbled.

The fruit disintegrated onto his tongue. It was definitely not fruit-like, but neither was it like a vegetable. It reminded him of—*gah*!!! He couldn't remember. The memory lurked in his subconscious, arousing an impression of music and light.

It tasted like the sunrise. The one he'd just witnessed—twice.

He reached back into the jar.

"They are better with flat bread." Needa pointed to a basket of bread that could only have come from Yalda's oven, wrapped in a clean linen cloth.

Popping a second fruit into his mouth, he moaned in pleasure as salty juices burst onto his tongue. A dribble of oil ran down his chin. He sniffed the still-warm bread before tearing off a piece to dab the olive oil.

Needa "harrumpfed" and gestured at the bench.

"While you're busy stuffing your face," she said, "let me check your wing."

He stretched his wing like a goose baring its neck for the headsman's axe, the one which had snapped and twisted backwards when his ship had crashed. If not for Ninsianna, he wouldn't be alive, but if not for her mother's considerable talent, he'd still be grounded with a pretty, but useless feather duster. He reached for another olive as her experienced fingers dug beneath his feathers to explore where the bones had knitted back together.

Needa cuffed him off the side of the head.

"Hey?" he exclaimed.

"Save some for the rest of us, you big oaf," she said half-seriously. "You're eating us out of house and home!"

"Soorrriiiii," he mumbled through a mouthful of flat bread, completely unapologetic.

He winced as she prodded the place where his main flight tendon had reattached itself to the bone.

"Does it hurt?" she asked.

"Yes," he admitted.

"That's because you weren't supposed to take your first flight with my daughter in tow!"

She cuffed him a second time.

"Ninsianna asked for it! She got me all muddy."

He suppressed a grin. By the time he'd finished running the gauntlet, he'd been *so much* muddier than *she* had been!

Needa grunted for him to tuck his wing into a more comfortable position. She sat down opposite the table and regarded him with an unreadable expression as she dipped a piece of flatbread into the luscious oil. The silence grew deafening as she chewed.

Finally, she spoke:

"Ninsianna is fond of you?"

A wave of guilt slammed into his gut. He'd made her parents a promise, but all he'd done since *yesterday* was act like a boar in heat.

"That won't happen again," he said miserably.

"That wasn't what I asked."

"What *are* you asking?"

"Are *you* fond of *her*?"

He answered truthfully.

"Very."

"So what are you going to do about it?"

Do? What *did* men do when a woman had become their heart and soul? Or more importantly, what did an Angelic, who possessed *no* fungible trade skills, zero personal possessions (except for an out-of-power pulse rifle, a ruined spaceship, and a sword), and with no memory of who they were or how they had gotten here, *do*, when they crash-landed on a primitive planet and fell in love with the woman who had saved their life?

"Nothing," his voice warbled. "I gave Immanu my word I wouldn't—"

"—ask him." Needa interrupted.

"Ask him what?"

"Ask Immanu for permission to court his daughter."

"But … he … made me … promise?" His brow knit together, perplexed.

She took his hand and squeezed it.

"We were only afraid you'd take our only child *away* from us," she said. "Promise that you will stay, and Immanu will relent."

"I can't!" he cried out. "I can't remember who I am!"

"But we know what you are *like*," she said.

"Socially inept?" he scoffed. "With no viable trade-skills?"

"You treat everybody fairly," she said, "from the lowliest old woman, to the highest-ranking citizen of this village. You love our daughter—" she paused, as though daring him to contradict it, and then continued "—and you're not afraid to *work*."

"I'm a *soldier*—" he dangled his dog tags. "A soldier without an army. What if a ship arrives and they order me to return to duty?"

"*Would* you return?"

"To the military?"

"To *here*," she said. "Would you return *here*, to be with my daughter, when you are done?"

"Of course!" he exclaimed. "I would battle Shay'tan himself to come back for her."

He grabbed at the word—*Shay'tan*—and the sense of *mission* which the name provoked, but the memory disappeared as soon as the word flew past his lips.

"What if you get out there—" Needa pointed at the ceiling "—and discover that the world you came from is much more interesting than this one?"

"I find *nothing* more interesting than Ninsianna."

"Would you ever abandon her?"

"Not unless I am dead!"

Needa picked up another piece of flat bread and dipped it into the oil. She stared past him, into her own, distant past.

"Around the time Ninsianna was born," she said, "we were at war with the Uruk. Immanu was always away."

"But he came back, obviously?"

"He did," she said. "But it took me a long time to convince him that his place was with his *family* and not off—" she waved her hand "—chasing the goddess' every whim."

Mikhail fell silent.

"I don't remember my family," he said mournfully.

"But obviously you *had* one?"

He patted his chest-pocket, where he *used* to keep a carved wooden figure. *A child's toy...* Awkwardly carved, scorched and broken. Carved by his own hand, he suspected. He'd left it back at the ship because it gave him a disembodied sense of grief.

"What if I already *have* a wife?" He tapped the healed stitches on his scalp. "I wouldn't remember her, would I?"

"What does your heart tell you?" Needa asked.

"My *heart?*"

"Yes." She poked a finger at his chest. "When you look up at the stars, does it feel like somebody is missing?"

He chose his next words carefully, not because he wanted to *deceive* her, but because the sense he'd *forgotten* something was so vague that he could not put it into words.

"When I'm with Ninsianna," he said truthfully, "she's the only person I can think of. But sometimes…"

—*Black eyes, peeking out of a bush.*

—*A child's voice…*

—*"Mikhail, come and find me!"*

—I part the leaves, but she is gone...

He rose from the bench and began to pace.

"You have doubts?" Needa asked.

"Not *doubts*," he said. "I *feel* like—"

He turned, oblivious to the way his feathers knocked bundles of herbs off the shelves, trying to name the emotions which felt as if they'd always been frozen, but Ninsianna's warm sun had laid bare the tiniest corner of something terrifying.

"I know I'm supposed to *do* something," he said. "Finish some kind of mission. I feel like—"

He sat back down and put his head into his hands. How could he explain that Ninsianna made him happy? That, until he'd met her, he didn't think he'd *ever* felt happy in his life, because the sensation felt so unfamiliar? But whenever she was away, an overwhelming sense of *duty* whispered: *"Complete the mission?"*

"I fear," his voice warbled, "that following my heart is *forbidden!*"

Needa gave his hand an affectionate pat.

"Why would your god forbid his Angelics to marry?"

"I don't know."

"I can't imagine *any* god would be that cruel."

She picked up her healer's basket, and then squeezed the leading edge of his wing.

"Well if you want to feel *useful*—" she pointed out the door to the courtyard "—the goat escaped her pen again."

She walked out the door to perform her healer's rounds.

Mikhail fished out his dog tags and held them up to the light.

Colonel Mikhail Mannuki'ili
352d SOG
Angelic Air Force
Second Galactic Alliance

With his other hand, he picked up an olive and held them side by side. The dog tags flashed sleek and silver, but the oil which coated the olive captured the sunlight, fruitful and ripe, giving it the same luminescence as Ninsianna's goddess-kissed eyes.

Now that he could fly again, what could he do to earn his keep?

Besides killing...?

And why did he feel so anxious about a mission that he couldn't remember?

Chapter 95

Galactic Standard Date: 152,323.06
Neutral Zone: Diplomatic Carrier 'Prince of Tyre'
Prime Minister Lucifer

LUCIFER

Between Shay'tan's empire and the Galactic Alliance lay the savaged remains of what had once been a third empire. Ground up and shat out by the two adjacent titans, its only purpose today was to serve as a strategic buffer, a place where "unofficial business" took place, things the movers and shakers did not wish their governments to know.

Among the asteroid belt of what had once been its capital-planet—until somebody [*cough, cough, his adoptive father*] had blown it all to shit—hovered the Alliance flagship, the *'Prince of Tyre.'* Long and graceful, there was something organic about the way she tapered from nose to fin, her catfish-like antennae, and her tail section which ended in a pair of fins.

A rude hand shook Lucifer out of his nightmare.

"Lucifer, wake up!" his Chief of Staff, Zepar exclaimed. "I have wonderful news!"

A brain-splitting migraine stabbed into Lucifer's skull. He drew his white wings around his body to shield himself from the light and grabbed his forehead so his grey matter wouldn't spill out onto the sheets. Where was he? What was the last thing he remembered? And, oh gods! He *stank*....

He felt the bed next to him, but it had already gone cold.

"Where is she?" he croaked from the safety of his feathered "cocoon.'

"Where is who?" Zepar asked.

"My wife—" he patted his satin sheets. "I distinctly remember getting married yesterday."

He opened one eye, only a slit—just enough to see Zepar's sour puss—and winced as a stab of light threatened to melt his brain.

"That was four days ago." Zepar shook him again. "Lucifer! Doctor Halpas just ran the tests. Your seed took! The origin of your species is fertile!"

"Fertile?" Lucifer shot up. "You mean, he thinks my father might be able to do something with their genome?"

"No—" Zepar bent down so that his dishwater-blue eyes were level with *his*. "Fertile, as in, that *thing* is carrying your child."

"My child?" Lucifer frowned. "I don't even remember making love to her."

"Made? Love?" Zepar's dirty-beige wings trembled with laughter. "To *it*?"

Anger roiled in Lucifer's gut.

"I'll remind you that "it" is my *wife!*"

"Your *wife?*" Zepar gave a cruel laugh. "That *animal* tried to claw your eyes out!"

"My eyes?" he patted his face, but it felt as smooth, as *perfect,* as it always did.

"Don't you remember?" Zepar asked. "Don't tell me you've had another blackout."

Terror gripped at Lucifer's gut.

"Nooo..." he lied. "I just had too much to drink."

"Good," Zepar said. "Because you'll be the laughing stock of the Alliance when they find out your new "wife" isn't entirely sentient."

"Not sentient?" Lucifer pinched the bridge of his nose. "But she spoke to me, I remember—"

That *fog* he sometimes got whenever he argued with Zepar stabbed into his brain. His tongue tasted like somebody had poured thick, white scum into his mouth before shoving it full of cottonballs.

"What do you remember," Zepar asked.

"We met Ba'al Zebub," he said weakly.

"And...?"

"He brought a wingless female that he *claimed* was the root-stock my father used to engineer our species." Lucifer frowned. "He *claimed* my father abandoned them to die."

"That much is true," Zepar said. "Shay'tan *insisted* he wouldn't give her to you unless you married her."

Married? Yes. He remembered *that*.

"I *did* marry her, didn't I?" he grinned. "And in Shay'tan's name! I can't wait to see the look on my father's face when—"

"It was just a farce!" Zepar shook a finger at him furiously. "Shay'tan knows we're desperate, so he dishonored you."

"But she *spoke* to me." Lucifer knit his white-blonde brows together.

"Spoke?" Zepar gave a mocking laugh. "You were furious when you got back to the shuttle and realized she couldn't obey a simple command."

Lucifer rose shakily and staggered to the bathroom, shutting the door in his Chief of Staff's face. His mind whirled as he pissed out the contents of his bladder. Not sentient? How could the root-stock of his race not be fully sentient? They, and humanity, were both descended from Nibiruians, but

74,000 years was a long time for genetic drift to occur, especially when a species' homeworld had been destroyed.

"*They got knocked back into the Stone Age,*" Ba'al Zebub had told him. "*A prison-colony, filled with violent rejects. Hashem had twelve other planets filled with more worthy survivors, so he ceded the thirteenth world to Shay'tan.*"

But what had happened *afterwards*?

And why was his memory of the ebony-skinned beauty so unclear?

Shakily, he sat down on his porcelain "throne" and gripped his forehead. What *had* his father said about Nibiru?

Criminals?

Nay…

The Emperor *claimed* he'd transformed a warlike planet into a peaceful utopia, which meant he'd tinkered with their DNA to reduce their natural aggression, and most likely (because he always did), increased the species' natural intellect.

But after *evolving*, could the root-race of his species then *devolve*?

Yes. After all, *his* species had, hadn't they? In the 152,000 years since Hashem had grafted wings onto a Nibiruian genome, not only had they lost the ability to reproduce, but they now stood at the threshold of extinction.

But *not sentient*?

He stared down at his sleepy cock. He was a lot of things, but if there was one thing he prided himself on, it was to make a lasting impression upon the ladies. There's no *way* he would have fucked a non-sentient animal. And obviously he *had*, because the woman was now pregnant…

Pregnant…

His wife was *pregnant*! After 225 years of shooting blanks, at last he had sired an heir!

He hopped into the shower, preened his snow-white wings, and then cleared the fog off the mirror so he could stare at his reflection. What he recalled of last night—nigh! Four nights ago—what he recalled of his *bride* was that she was tall and regal, with luscious ebony skin. So what if she wasn't the brightest star in the heavens? She was giving him a child.

No… she was doing *more* than that. Her very existence meant his species finally had hope! No longer would they teeter at the brink of destruction. If they were genetically compatible enough to breed, he'd never have to go crawling to his adoptive father again!

He stepped under the blow-dryer to fluff up his snow white feathers, and then threw open the door, his mood exuberant. He'd be the savior of his species!

His Chief of Staff waited outside.

"Supreme Commander-General Jophiel just called again," Zepar said. "She demands—"

"I don't *care* what the bitch wants—" Lucifer cut him off. "Where is she?"

"Jophiel?"

"No," Lucifer snapped. "Where is my *wife?*"

Pushing past him, he went to his wardrobe and rifled through his collection of hand-tailored suits. What should he wear, to *meet* the woman he had married? Alliance women liked their men sophisticated and fit...

But what about *human* females?

He fretted through his wardrobe like an adolescent girl, ignoring Zepar's frantic prattlings about his arch-nemesis, the Supreme Commander-General. The human homeworld was primitive, so his wife would most likely be attracted to someone who looked protective? Like his father's attack dog, that nasty Seraphim who, thank the gods, had gone missing in action.

He pulled out the suit he wore whenever he was forced to deal with a war-like species, the one which padded out his shoulders, and contrasted with his white-blonde hair and snow-white wings. Most primitives liked gold, so he affixed his largest watch, and then—oh, what the heck!

He grabbed his solid-gold pauldrons.[139]

"What are you *doing?*" Zepar looked incredulous.

"She married the Alliance Prime Minister—" he affixed the wing-shaped armor-of-state on top of his suit. "I want her to know I've just made her the Queen of Heaven."

"But she doesn't—"

"Silence!" Lucifer held up one finger. "Where is she?"

"We set her up in an empty troop barracks," Zepar said. "Doctor Halpas thought she'd be less destructive if we gave her space to roam."

"To roam?" Lucifer laughed headily. "I'll give her my entire empire as her playground!"

He sprayed himself with cologne, a musky aphrodisiac that had been chemically engineered to mimic an alpha-male's pheromones, and then bolted out of his chambers. As he expected, Zepar's two Angelic "goons," Furcas and Pruflas, stood like a pair of cold-eyed statues just outside his door, big and meaty and oh-so-incredibly stupid.

"Here's living proof that it's possible to devolve," Lucifer muttered.

With Zepar chasing after him, he half-skipped, half-flew through the high-ceilinged corridors, past his crew, to the lower levels. Unlike *most* Alliance military vessels, he ran his ship on a light crew. Ostensibly it was because he feared assassination, but the *real* reason was that he liked to be reminded, every time he felt tempted to waiver on a trade policy, how *few* of them actually remained.

---

[139] *Pauldrons:* plate-armor which covers the shoulders, back and chest. Often worn ceremonially by high-ranking lords and kings.

And now he had a wife…
A *human* wife…
A wife who was pregnant.
At last, he had sired a child!
He reached the empty troop dormitory.

"Step aside," he ordered the two low-ranking nobodies that Zepar had plucked out of some other command carrier's brig. Like most of his crew, they weren't the brightest or the best, but the men were blackmailable, so therefore, utterly loyal.

"Sir!" the two men stepped aside.

"Lucifer, wait!" Zepar shouted.

With a harrumph, Lucifer flared his wings to look "protective" and slipped inside the room.

"Arrrrghhhh-iyah!!!!"

A flat, metal object flew at his head.

"Hey, wait—"

He yelped as the tray bit into his scalp.

It was immediately followed by a ripe piece of fruit. With enhanced Angelic reflexes, he caught it before it splattered against his wing-shaped pauldrons. An inhuman screech tore into his subconscious. Somebody else's TERROR slammed into him like a full-nuclear fusion planet-killer.

"Ay-ee?" he clamped his hands over his ears.

One of the 'gifts' he'd inherited from his half-Seraphim mother was the ability to read people, to literally *see* into their minds and catch a glimpse of their greatest hopes and fears. Violent images leaped into his mind, like a farm animal's bleat for mercy as the abaittor[140] slit its throat.

He bent forward, his wings crossed in front of him to protect him from the awful noise. Lucifer jumped as a hand touched his shoulder.

"Make it stop?" he pleaded.

"I *told* you she wasn't sentient," Zepar said caustically. "Next time, maybe you'll trust me?"

The screeching subsided, replaced with a guttural chant.

Iblisi, iblisi, iblisi…[141]

Whatever *iblisi* meant, the sound was attached to *him*.

He parted one wing and peered at the creature. Her ebony-black skin shone magnificently against the glittery Sata'anic wedding dress, embroidered with a kingdom's ransom of precious stones; but it bore great claw-marks, as though she'd wrenched it apart—

…*or an enormous predator had ripped it off her body.*

---

[140] *Abaittor:* butcher.
[141] *Iblisi:* devil.

She crawled into the furthest possible bunk and crouched into a fetal position. Her eyes appeared vacant as she waved her hands in front of her face, chanting that terrible sound.

Iblisi, iblisi, iblisi…

"Mister Prime Minister—" Zepar shoved him closer, "—may I present your *wife.*"

Lucifer tucked his wings against his back, wishing *fervently* he'd worn a less intimidating suit. The woman shrieked. No longer docile and beautiful, her hollow eyes reminded him of a wild, caged animal.

"Remember me?" he spoke soothingly. "We got married yesterday, um, four days ago."

He listened for the subconscious longings his 'gift' allowed him to sense beneath the speech of all sentient creatures, even only marginally intelligent ones, but he found absolutely nothing. It was nothing but noise.

He held out the fruit out she'd thrown at him, a ripe, red *úll*[142], one of the most luscious fruits in the Alliance.

"Are you hungry?" He pretended to take a bite. "It's really yummy."

He held it towards her while projecting images of him and her sharing a meal, something which usually worked with even lesser species, but the female hissed and scurried to the opposite corner of the room.

"What's wrong with her?" he asked.

"We suspect Ba'al Zebub sedated her so she wouldn't scratch your eyes out," Zepar said. "It's why he insisted you mate with her right away."

A sense of disappointment settled into Lucifer's gut as all his dreams about love, marriage and a family went *poof!* For some reason, he'd thought she was more intelligent, although he had no memory of mating with her. None at all.

"She is definitely pregnant?" his voice warbled.

"Yes," Zepar said. "I made Doctor Halpas confirm the embryo is genetically *yours.*"

A lump rose in his throat.

"Will my child be—?" his voice broke. "Will my child be *defective?*"

"Our tests indicate your superior genes will be dominant," Zepar said. "Your son will have a sentient-level IQ."

"So he'll be smart?"

"Probably not as smart as *you,*" Zepar said, "but the Emperor always engineers intelligence to be a survival trait."

"What about my wings?"

---

[142] *Úll* is a type of apple.

"That—" Zepar flicked his *own* dirty-beige wings. "Your *father* pulled off one hell of a miracle to graft avian DNA onto a human chassis. The gene is recessive."

Lucifer's wings drooped.

"So he won't inherit my wings?"

"Probably not," Zepar said. "We knew that was a problem back when he used Nibiruians to refresh your gene-stock. But every other Angelic trait appears to be dominant."

"Son?" Lucifer perked up. "You know it's a boy?"

"Yes, Sire," Zepar said. "You can breed him back to hundreds of Angelic females and most of your grandchildren will have wings—only without the fertility problems so much inbreeding to maintain them has created for our species. The gene is there. It's just recessive."

Lucifer pinched his chin, deep in thought. Obviously he couldn't bring *her* before Parliament! He'd be the laughing stock of two empires. But what about his son?

"How long until she delivers?" he asked.

"Nine months," Zepar said.

"What am I supposed to do in the meantime?"

A trickle of blood dripped from a cut above his eye, onto his golden pauldrons and the horrifically expensive fabric of his designer suit. With a curse, Lucifer wiped it off. Never again would Shay'tan trick him into thinking the origin of his species was sentient!!!

Zepar placed a reassuring hand onto his shoulder.

"Lucifer," he used a fatherly voice. "You've been trying for 225 years to sire a child. Will it be so terrible, if your son appears as the Eternal Emperor does? A human male, without wings?"

Lucifer sniffed the bruised fruit which his brand-new "wife" had thrown at him. Exotic and ripe, he could almost *see* the press release: *"Lucifer sires a child who looks just like the Eternal Emperor, claims it's a sign from She-Who-Is."* He would spin the propaganda as *homage* to his adopted father when he stood before Parliament, cradling his newborn son—and asked them to open their coffers so he could fix their hybrid armies.

He flashed Zepar a weak grin.

"I don't have to show them the *mother*, do I?" he asked.

"All they care about is your son," Zepar said.

His son...

Yes. His *son*...

He would say the woman had been reared like the Sata'anic women, confined to a harem. Given his father's policies about religious freedom (so long as *he* remained high-god, and the "lesser" gods were demoted to the rank of "saint"), he could rub his father's hypocrisy in his face, which was what Shay'tan intended.

Lucifer laughed.

"The old dragon outsmarted us," he said.

"But it's not necessarily *bad*," Zepar said.

"It's not?"

"No," Zepar said. "According to Lord Ba'al Zebub, for the right, uh... favors—"

"You mean bribes," Lucifer said.

"You know perfectly well what he means," Zepar said.

"And..." Lucifer waited.

"Ba'al Zebub believes he can convince Shay'tan to release a few *other* females for high-ranking males who've been experiencing, how shall we say this? *Difficulties.*"

"You mean infertility?"

"Yes."

"Why would he do that?" Lucifer grew suspicious. "It's in Shay'tan's best interests if we *don't* reproduce. It puts our armies on equal footing."

"The Sata'anic Empire is anxious to secure further trade."

Lucifer began to pace.

"Hashem won't allow it! He'll simply veto the bill."

"Then override it," Zepar said.

"How?" Lucifer said bitterly. "My father carries a lot of support. The only reason I got them to pass the *last* one was because nobody wanted to send *their* children to die in our place!"

"Which is *why* Ba'al Zebub thinks Shay'tan will go for it," Zepar said. "It *goads* the old dragon, that his adversary constantly *beats* him using an army of genetically engineered slaves."

"As if *he's* any better," Lucifer grumbled.

"Which is why *you* told Ba'al Zebub you would *matchmake* human women to similarly afflicted men," Zepar said. "It will tickle Shay'tan pink, to think Hashem's cannon-fodder is getting *married* in his enemy's name."

"That would be rebellion!" His gut clenched. "You *know* what my father did to the *last* person who divided his army."

'Your –real- father.'

He pushed the thought out of his mind.

"Rebellion?" Zepar laughed. "Who said anything about a rebellion? You'd just use lawful means to gain support for a *trade* policy."

Lucifer tapped his lip. Not a rebellion? Marriage between hybrids was forbidden for so long as they were obligated to serve, nor were they allowed to marry an Alliance citizen, but there were *no* specific laws in place prohibiting them from marrying a Sata'anic citizen because the thought was so preposterous, nobody had ever done it. Jophiel would view it as treason, of course, but who cared what the *bitch* thought? Every other year, she popped out another baby like clockwork! But what about the generals beneath her? Many were infertile, and *most* viewed her as nothing but an upstart. More importantly, she'd *banished* her most powerful detractors to defend distant planets which *depended* upon those dying armies to keep them safe.

Planets which all had a vote…

"I'll do it," he said. "The generals are so desperate for offspring, they'd fuck a slug."

He tossed the fruit into the air. All he had to do was wrangle Parliament into giving him enough trade concessions to lull Shay'tan into giving him a few more "gifts," and if the old dragon reneged? Why, he'd simply 'sic Hashem's dying armies on the newly rediscovered human homeworld and *wrest* the planet out of Shay'tan's greedy claws!

Lucifer laughed.

Zepar was a scheming bastard, but only *he* could cook up a plan ballsy enough to not just solve the hybrid fertility problem, but to also tweak *both* ascended deities' noses.

He sniffed the fruit which his "wife" had thrown at him.

All he needed was a few more human women, and then he could *tempt* the movers and shakers to take a bite.

"Contact Ba'al Zebub," he told Zepar. "Tell him I'll take as many women as he can give me."

He bit into the luscious, sweet fruit until the juices ran down his chin.

Chapter 96

End-June - 3,390 BC
Earth: Village of Assur

NINSIANNA

Just before it reached Assur, the Hiddekel River widened out, leaving a long, lazy stretch of water. On a hot day like today, the entire village abandoned their work and descended upon the beach like thirsty fish.

"Hey, Ninsianna!" a former patient greeted her.

"Ninsianna!" another friend waved.

A third friend gave her a thumbs-up.

Twisting the necklace she'd been awarded for winning the solstice competition, she wound her way through the crowded beach, humming a cheerful love-song. Normally she *enjoyed* washing laundry and gossiping with the other women, but yesterday her father had warned:

"Don't be a commoner! A shaman must set himself apart."

So how should a *"Chosen One"* behave around people who had been friends, and patients, for her entire life? She lugged her heavy basket to a place where the beach grew narrow, and the water became clogged with water-rushes and reeds. The water here smelled fertile and muddy, but the acacia trees would give her respite from the sun.

A pair of junior warriors, no older than Pareesa, stood ready with their spears to stab any "logs with eyes."

"Any crocodiles today?" she asked cheerfully.

"Just one," the taller boy said. "We chased him over there."

By the reeds, the crocodile lay in wait, submerged beneath the surface so that only its cat-like eyes and a pair of nostrils were visible. Judging by the length of its snout, it was a young male, barely seven cubits; large enough to ambush a woman or a child, but not so old that it had learned to avoid the boys with their spears.

The crocodile spied potential prey—her—and moved closer, barely disturbing the surface as its powerful tail swished beneath the water. As it swam, its fang-laden snout became more visible.

Ninsianna's heart beat faster as a ridge of scales broke the surface. The sound of splashing villagers faded as a roar obscured the warriors' frantic warning.

With an ear-splitting roar, a sky canoe, squat and grey, hovers outside the south gate, obscuring the village with dust. The ship cracks open. From its belly, all manner of monsters pour out, only the monsters walk upright and wear clothing.

The warriors throw spears from the safety of the gate, but the monsters carry firesticks. A bolt of lightning erupts from the lizard-people's ship. With a thunderous roar, Assur's walls disappear in an explosion of rock and dust.

The lizards march into the village and gather up the women. A lizard-man steps in front of her…

…and bared its gigantic fangs.

"Watch out!"

The two boys rushed past her, into the river, and stabbed at the crocodile as it reared up to drag her into the water.

The crocodile roared, snapping its enormous jaws, but the boys stabbed it with their spears until it finally swam back to the edge of the reeds. The boys waded out of the river, their faces flushed.

"What's the matter with you?" the taller boy chided her. "We *told* you he was there!"

"S-sorry," her voice warbled. "The goddess sent me a vision—"

"A vision?" the shorter boy snapped. "Your stupid *vision* almost got you killed!"

She stared at the crocodile which watched her with hungry eyes. While undoubtedly a monster, it did not walk upright, wear clothing, or travel in a sky canoe.

"Go back to the beach," the taller boy ordered, "until we can kill him—"

"—or teach him to fear *man*," the shorter boy held up his spear.

Both boys sniggered at some joke to which she was not privy.

Ninsianna's cheeks flushed scarlet.

"I am the Chosen of She-Who-Is," she said imperiously.

"Well obviously SHE has Chosen you to be that crocodile's next meal!" the tall boy laughed.

Huffing with indignation, Ninsianna picked up her basket and stomped back towards the beach. Whatever had possessed her to wade into the river? After a crocodile, no less! And think the thing wore clothing?

She wove her way through the glistening bodies which had emerged from the cool water and flopped down upon the beach.

"Ninsianna!" one of the women called out. "Congratulations on winning the competition yesterday."

"And for winning Damu-zid's heart," another woman said. "I must say, you're the first iteration of Geshtinanna who ever *flew* out of the competition field."

The other women giggled, passing off-color jibes about "Damu-zid's" physical prowess. She could almost *see* Mikhail blush bright red as the women talked about "spears" that had little to do with the one he had thrown.

Ninsianna grinned.

She dumped out the laundry basket which contained, not just *her* muddy clothing from the competition, but also Mikhail's. His pants had dried so stiff, she could almost stand them upright. She checked for crocodiles before wading in—though with so many warriors cooling off in this part of the river, it was unlikely the predators would dare come too close *here*.

Any that *did* would get killed, skinned and eaten...

She hummed a happy song as she dipped his pants into the river, her lips still tingling as she remembered Mikhail's kiss. While he'd never taught her the translation for *mo grá*, thanks to the goddess' gift of tongues, she knew it meant "my love".

Which meant the goddess' premonition was right...

An unsettling chill rippled through her body. She scanned the water for another crocodile, but there was no sign of "lizard men," or floating "logs" with teeth and eyes.

Something hit her in the back.

"Hey?"

She whirled to face Shahla, Jamin's former girlfriend.

Tall and curvaceous, with glossy black hair, exotic eyes, and the best linen shawl-dress her daddy's wealth could buy, Jamin's ex-girlfriend would have been beautiful if not for the permanent sneer which showed off a gap between her teeth. Here was living proof of her father's admonition to "remain mysterious." Shahla was "known" to everybody, or more specifically, "known" to all of the men...

Standing behind her, Shahla's "black-eyed shadow", Ninsianna's accursed cousin, wore a threadbare dress which hung off her emaciated frame. Large, nocturnal eyes stared out of a face that was too large for her scrawny body, scraggly black hair, and skin so pale it showed off every bruise.

"What did you do that for?" Ninsianna asked.

"You *cheated* yesterday!"

Shahla picked up a second rock.

"No, Shahla, don't!" Gita grabbed Shahla by the arm.

"*Somebody* has to speak up!" Shahla shrieked. "Do you think, just because her FATHER—" she threw her nose in the air and made an imperious gesture "—declares she's "*Chosen*" that she can get away with taking what is *yours*!"

"It's nothing!" Gita cried out. "Please? It doesn't matter!"

"You *needed* that prize, and Ninsianna took it!"

"I'll do without it!"

"How?" Shahla said. "You practiced that atlatl throw for months! If you'd won that necklace, you could have *sold* it for enough flaxseed to plant your *own* field instead of working for my father!"

Ninsianna touched the necklace she'd been awarded at the solstice ceremony as this year's "Geshtinanna," the lover who'd volunteered to replace Damu-zid in hell. While not an especially precious necklace—it was just lapis lazuli with a bit of onyx[143]—the necklace was a status symbol. It was supposed to symbolize self-sacrifice, family and love.

The other villagers began to whisper:

Ninsianna? A cheat?

I told you she won too easily!

Her father performed magic to trick us into believing she's a shaman.

"I didn't cheat!" Ninsianna said angrily.

"Oh, no?" Shahla shook her finger at her. "Look at Gita's face!"

She grabbed her cousin's face the way one might grab a cheeky toddler and yanked her forward, revealing a sizeable cut just above her eye.

"Ninsianna's *father* hit her in the face with a *rock!*" Shahla shouted.

The villagers began to whisper:

"Gita came out of the tunnel first."

"I saw Immanu hit her."

"It threw off her throw."

"It's a wonder he didn't blind her!"

A sense of panic welled in Ninsianna's gut.

"The spectators are *supposed* to distract us," she laughed weakly. She held up her muddy loincloth, the one she'd worn during the race. "Gita's not the *only* one who got pelted. You *all* threw mud—at the both of us!"

"Everyone knows the face is off-limits—" Shahla tapped her cheek. "And for the women's race, they're only allowed to throw mud and straw. This—" she shoved Gita's face at her "—was done by a rock your father hid in the mud."

"Is *that* what you're telling everybody?" She grabbed her cousin's arm. "The reason you *lost* is because you have lousy aim!"

Gita cowered, her black eyes filled with fear. She edged back towards the crowd, trying her best to disappear.

Shahla stepped between them and blocked Gita's escape. As the daughter of the wealthiest trader in the village, she was the only woman Ninsianna had never been able to cow or charm. Ever since they'd been kids, they'd been in a competition. First, as to who was the *prettiest*, and then later, which one could get the most gifts from the boys. Only somewhere along the way, Shahla had crossed a line. Unable to *charm* the

---

[143] *Onyx;* a black semi-precious stone with bands of color, usually white.

boys into slavering at her feet, the arrogant strumpet had begun to *sleep around.*

It had backfired when Jamin cast Shahla off for *her…*

Ninsianna smirked.

'Great Mother?' she prayed. 'How do I get this witch to go away?'

Shahla's wash-basket glimmered at the corner of her vision. She grabbed a white, linen dress, the one Shahla had worn yesterday before she'd made her half-hearted first throw.

"What's this?" Ninsianna held it up. "Is that a *grass* stain?"

Shahla lunged at her.

"Let it go!"

"I see you spent the solstice celebration on your back!" She flapped the shawl-dress so everyone would see the grass stain. "We know you weren't with Jamin, since he sat next to Gita, the other *loser*—"

She leaned towards her cousin.

"—at the *loser's* table! So who's the lucky man? Some other woman's husband?"

The other women whispered at an angry buzz. It was well known that Shahla liked to prey upon their husbands.

Shahla lunged for her. Ninsianna stepped aside. Instead of leaping for her shawl-dress, Shahla veered, and grabbed…

…the necklace…

……right of off Ninsianna's neck.

With a sickening *SNAP*, the hemp broke loose, spilling the lapis beads into the mud.

"My necklace!" Ninsianna cried out.

"You didn't *earn* it!" Shahla shrieked. "Do you think because your father declares you are a shaman that you get to *take* whatever you want?"

Gita fell to her knees to gather the semi-precious stones.

Ninsianna lunged after Shahla.

An enormous shadow fell over them.

Ninsianna looked up.

A pair of black-brown wings flew directly overhead.

Her heart caught in her throat as the man who'd regained flight only *yesterday* pressed his wings against his back and dove, crazily, straight towards one of the fields.

Mikhail fell, falling, falling, falling…

…he fell, straight towards the earth…

……without spreading his magnificent brown wings.

"Look out!" the villagers shrieked.

Ninsianna grew faint.

He flared them at the last moment…

…hit the ground…

……and shot back up again…

………carrying….

"Bah-ah!" Little Nemesis gave a high-pitched bleat.

The villagers laughed, and then began to cheer as Mikhail circled, carrying their squirming dairy goat that'd escaped and gone foraging in somebody else's field.

Ninsianna wept. And then she began to laugh. Oh! What a magnificent Champion the goddess had sent her! All she had to do was figure out *what* the goddess wanted him to do, and then *lead* him, as the goddess' *Chosen One*.

"He looks just like the ones in the cave paintings," Gita said softly. "According to legend, the only thing that can kill them is a broken heart."

She handed Ninsianna the broken pieces of her necklace, but her black eyes followed Mikhail, carrying a look of utter longing.

"C'mon, Gita!" Shahla declared. "I will not bow down to a false prophetess!"

Shahla grabbed the scrawny wraith and dragged her upriver, towards the place where the two boys stood guard, waiting to stab the crocodile, before Ninsianna could say, *"Keep it. I don't want it now that it's broken!"*

Chapter 97

End-June - 3,390 BC
Earth: Village of Assur

JAMIN

Just upstream from Assur, the river had gouged a cruel gash into the earth, carving a cliff out of the mud. A nearly-dry stream cut that cliff in half and trickled down the rocks like a trembling heart which gushed the desert's life-blood.

Jamin sat, hidden among the sweet-scented acacia bushes, twisting the necklace he'd made from the teeth and claws of a lion. Far beneath him, his unfaithful former fiancé stood thigh-deep in the river's fertile waters, cheerfully doing laundry. The bulk of her laundry belonged to Mikhail.

Every muscle in his body whispered: *Kill the intruder.* He would slay him, the same way he'd slain the lion. *Up close...* With a knife between the ribs.

A soft whistle drew his attention. Siamek scrambled up the sharp cleft which separated this side of the stream from the village. Without asking permission, he plopped down next to him in the scrub-brush.

"How'd you know where to find me?" Jamin asked.

"Where *else* would you be?" Siamek gestured at Ninsianna.

They sat in silence. Jamin dug one of the lion claws into his flesh. He relished the *pressure* until it began to bleed. A drop of blood trickled down his arm.

"Yesterday was supposed to be our wedding day," he said at last. "Of all the days to announce they are a couple, why did she have to choose then?"

A happy song wafted up with the breeze. A *love* song. A song that he'd sung for her back when she'd stopped rebuking his advances and started to encourage him.

He pretended to pick a gnat out of his eyes.

"It's not right," Siamek said, "but you can't keep stalking her like a lion."

"I am *not* stalking her!"

"Listen—" Siamek grabbed his shoulder. "I'm saying this as your *friend.* You don't eat. You rarely come to practice. You look like goat-shit. It's time to move on."

"How can I?" he pointed in the direction where Mikhail had flown off with the goat. "My *warriors* want me to let him train them, and even my own *father* wants me to integrate him! Next thing you know, the bastard will *replace* me!"

Siamek stared at his hands.

"What?" Jamin's head snapped up with suspicion.

"It's just ... you haven't been presenting people with your *best* lately." Siamek held up his hand so he wouldn't interrupt. "Ever since Ninsianna dumped you, you've been acting like a spurned lover instead of our *future chief*."

"You would *too* if somebody stole your fiancé!"

Siamek stabbed his knife into the dirt.

"You're not the only man who's ever had his balls cut off."

"Who?" Jamin gave a bitter laugh. "Shahla?" He gestured towards the place where the harlot had moved off to, fomenting vicious gossip. "You can *have* her!"

Shahla had been his girlfriend until, in a misguided attempt to make him jealous, she'd slept with his biggest rival. She'd been *furious* when, instead of proposing to her, he'd broken things off and disappeared on a fool's hunt – the one where he'd gotten himself gored by an auroch.

Oh... If only that damned bull had *killed* him!

He picked up a pebble and threw it down the cliff. It plinked close to where Ninsianna slapped her laundry against the rocks and dunked it into the river to rinse off the soaproot, but she didn't notice it; she did not notice *him*.

"I know how it makes you *feel* when you love a woman who doesn't love you back." Siamek stared at where Shahla dragged her friend around by the arm. "It makes you *question* whether you're still a man."

"I am *definitely* a man!" Jamin held up his lion fang necklace. "Let's see that fluffy-winged bastard try to kill one of *these* with nothing but a knife!"

Siamek laughed.

"Now *that* was a day!"

Back when he'd been Pareesa's age, a lion had come into their fields, preying upon their goats and sheep. The warriors had surrounded the lion with spears, but he'd waved them off, determined to prove to his father he was now a *man*.

His father had been *furious*...

But ever since that day, the men had looked to *him*...

He wasn't about to let Ninsianna's new "beau" deprive him of that respect. Over his dead body!

Siamek stood and held out his hand.

"C'mon," Siamek said. "An emissary just arrived from Eshnunna. Let's go show them this village still has a *Muhafiz*."

Chapter 98

End-June - 3,390 BC
Earth: Village of Assur
Colonel Mikhail Mannuki'ili

MIKHAIL

As much as he wanted to take to the sky, the goat needed water, so he *flew* to the well, carrying three clanking wooden buckets. Since he hadn't yet mastered the art of flying without slopping water all over himself, he decided to walk back. As he walked, he greeted the humans who, only yesterday, had been so frightened of Jamin that they'd been willing to let him get kicked out.

A slender girl fell into step behind him. Usually she hop-skipped, but today her goatskin pampooties stomped heavily against the earth; her young, strong shoulders slouched forward.

Mikhail slowed down—only a little—Pareesa *hated* it when he patronized her, and let her catch up.

"Shouldn't you be at warrior practice?" he asked.

"Jamin said he wouldn't teach a girl."

His pinfeathers prickled, but he'd *suspected* the Chief's son wouldn't accept her "qualifying" as a junior warrior. Like everything else, he'd have to extract it out of the bastard, kicking and screaming.

"I'll talk to Behnam," he said. "Let the Tribunal bring the matter to the Chief."

"It won't work." She crossed her arms. "The other boys said if I squeal, they'll beat me up."

Her eyes burned with righteous indignation. For the first time, he noticed one side of her face appeared swollen and red.

"*Damantia!*" he hissed.

He suppressed the urge to fly over to the training field, grab the warrior-trainees by their necks, and smash their skulls together.

"Meet me on the other side of the date-palm orchard after supper," he said. "If they lay another hand on you, I'll teach you how to break their fingers."

A small smirk tugged at the corner of her mouth.

"You *really* think I can beat them up?"

"In a one-on-one fight? No," he said. "Most of the boys are bigger and heavier than you are. But you can learn to use their bodies against them if you understand, uhm..." he struggled for a translation for the word 'physics.' "*Airíonna fisiceacha*.[144] The science of movement."

"It sounds complicated?"

"Would you rather get beat up?"

"No."

"Then meet me after supper. I'll teach you how to lay them out on the ground."

The skip returned to Pareesa's step. She chattered about the solstice festival yesterday, her baby sister, and the fact that her mother was feeling better. They parted ways at the alley which led to the second ring.

The sentries gave him an unfriendly stare as he passed into the more heavily fortified middle ring. Assur had been built in three concentric circles, with each house's outer wall forming part of a solid barrier which made the village defensible. While it still had problems, like *no* running water and a lack of sewers, he'd learned to tolerate the close proximity of other bodies, a lack of deodorant, and the underlying stench of piss and shit.

Ninsianna's father caught up with him just before he reached the house. While more simply dressed than yesterday's high ceremonial attire, he wore a four-fringed kilt, a bone-and-feather headdress, and the elaborately beaded neck-plate which marked him as a shaman.

"Mikhail! Wait!" Immanu called out. "The Chief has asked you to come for a meeting."

A sense of dread settled into his gut. Every *other* time he'd met with the Chief, it had been to give him some version of *"my son doesn't like you, so give me the secrets to your technology, and then go jump off a cliff."*

Although now, at least, he could *fly...*

"Let me guess," he said. "He's unhappy I beat his son yesterday?"

"Oh, no!" Immanu's mouth split in a sun-wrinkled grin. "An emissary just arrived from Eshnunna, along with Gimal of Gasur. He insisted the Chief consult with *you*."

Mikhail's brow knit together.

"The Chief wants my *advice*?"

"Maybe not the *Chief*," Immanu admitted. "Gimal wants to see if you recognize some crazy dart our enemies used to breach their defenses."

Mikhail hoisted up his water buckets.

"Just let me drop these off, and then I'll meet you at the Chief's house."

"I'll wait," Immanu said.

"Don't bother." Mikhail flared his wings. "By the time you walk there, I can fly."

---

[144] *Airíonna fisiceacha:* physical properties.

Immanu hurried off. Mikhail jiggled the latch for the side-gate which led to their inner courtyard and deposited his buckets off the heavy yoke.

He spread his wings to fly, and caught a whiff of the hircine stench of goat. Little Nemesis had left hoofprints all over his shirt. Rather than take off, he hop-flapped under the sun canopy, pulling his wings against his back to fly into the open back door.

"Eeeek!!!"

Needa dropped the medicinal herbs she'd been tying into bundles. The healer shook her finger at him.

"We're going to have some RULES around here, young man!!!" she said sternly. "No flying inside the house!"

"Yes, Ma'am." He schooled an appropriate look of chastisement.

Needa's stern façade cracked when a fluffy, brown pinfeather *floated* past her face.

"Carry on, then, Colonel Show-Off," she ordered.

"Yes, Ma'am." He gave her a crisp salute.

Stepping behind the curtain that cordoned his sleeping pallet off from the larger room, he pulled on his dress uniform jacket, straightened out the collar—and the medals he couldn't remember earning—and then strapped on his pulse pistol and his sword. An angry red light blinked, reminding him the plasma weapon was almost out of power. He dipped his hands in the bucket kept for washing before heading back outside, dripping water all over the floor.

"Got to go!"

He took off the moment he hit the threshold. The backdraft from his wings scattered Needa's herbs.

*

In the center of the village sat the sacred well where, only last week, Ninsianna had fallen, nay, *climbed* down into an underground stream. Next to that, a potter sat beneath a canopy, spinning a pot on a wheel as a gaggle of children watched; while a food vendor kneaded balls of flatbread and plastered them inside the wall of a beehive oven to bake. Just beyond them, merchants hawked their wares: woven mats, cloth made of linen, clay pots, beads, and various fruits. Dominating the plaza stood the temple of She-Who-Is.

Immanu stood outside the temple doorway with Gimal, a trader from Gasur who he'd aided after the Halifians had raided his trading caravan. Late middle-age, with broad, muscular shoulders and a long, white flowing beard, he carried himself with the confidence of a warrior who'd turned towards more profitable endeavors once the Ubaid had ceased their war against the Uruk. As Mikhail glided in for a landing, the wind from his wings knocked off the man's conical leather hat.

"Gimal," he reached out to shake the trader's hand.

"Ahh, Mikhail," Gimal gave a hearty shake. "They *said* you'd begun to fly?"

"Yes, Sir," Mikhail said. "I'd feared I'd never fly again."

"I'm not surprised," Gimal said. "The way you fought the Halifians, it was only a matter of time before you regained true flight."

"How is Sagal-Zimu?" he asked about Gasur's young shaman, who'd been injured in that raid.

"Healing nicely," Gimal said. "He shall live, thanks to you—" he turned to Immanu "—and of course your talented wife."

Immanu beamed.

"She healed Mikhail's wing," he bragged.

Mikhail flapped the appendages. "Ninsianna patched me back together, and then her mother rehabilitated the damaged flight tendon." He turned to Gimal. "So what brings you back to Assur so soon?"

"When we got back to Gasur, I learned we'd been attacked," Gimal said. "The next day, an emissary from Eshnunna arrived to report *they* had been raided, as well."

"Was this in retaliation for the men in the desert?" Mikhail asked.

Gimal glanced sideways at the spectators who'd gathered to eavesdrop. He placed his hand on his shoulder and murmured: "Come, my friend, let's go inside."

They crossed the square to the largest house in the village. While only two stories high, thanks to its tall ceilings, it neared the temple in height. Outside an elaborately carved wooden door, the Chief's man, Varshab, stood with his arms crossed, burly and intelligent, the kind of man not even *he* would trifle with, and he feared very few.

"Sir," Mikhail said.

"The Chief is waiting for you."

Varshab opened the door.

Mikhail ducked beneath the lintel, but once inside, he was able to straighten up to his full height. The interior was cool and dim, immaculately clean, and scented with fragrant herbs. Varshab led them to a room cordoned off by a set of linen drapes, elaborately embroidered with scenes from a hunt.

He turned to Mikhail.

"Your weapons?"

His expression remained cloaked, but at least, *this* time, Varshab's eyes were less than hostile.

Mikhail unbuckled his utility belt, including the straps which secured his pulse pistol to his thigh, and handed the entire thing, including his knife and sword, to the Chief's enforcer.

Gimal did the same.

Varshab placed the weapons on a table, patted them down, and then opened the curtain. Just inside, the Chief sat on a plush woolen cushion, a powerful, handsome middle-age man. To his right sat his even *more* powerful—and hateful—son; resplendent in his four-fringed kilt, his haughty shawl, a necklace made of lion's teeth, and a solid-gold armband wrapped around his meaty bicep. In the center, a drop-cloth had been laid out with the appetizers for a feast. Directly across from them sat a man wearing a three-fringed kilt, a leopard-skin cape, and a heavily-beaded neck plate which marked him as an emissary.

Jamin glared at him, his black eyes filled with hatred. His father reached over and, silently, placed a hand on his son's arm.

"Immanu, son of Lugalbanda," the Chief said formally, "and Colonel Mannuki'ili, of the Galactic Alliance—" the foreign title rolled off his tongue with ease "—please welcome Farzam, son of Nabonahid, an emissary from our ally, Eshnunna."

Mikhail rustled his feathers and settled his wings into a tightly-tucked military posture.

"Sir—" he gave the man a proper Alliance salute.

The emissary gaped, or more accurately, he stared at his wings as though he hadn't believed Gimal's story. The man realized he must look like a fool and murmured something noncommittal.

"Come, sit," the Chief beckoned with false cordiality.

Gimal sat next to the emissary, while Immanu sat perpendicular to the Chief. The shaman gestured to the place where *he* was supposed to sit, at Jamin's right-hand side. While Mikhail was no expert in human culture, he'd participated in enough meetings to garner the Chief wished to convey that *he* was, militarily, one of their assets.

Jamin's cheek twitched as he awkwardly arranged his wings and sat next to him, cross-legged, on the carpet without hitting anybody with his feathers. The Chief growled an inaudible threat as his son opened his mouth to issue some kind of cut-down. Jamin glared at him.

The Chief's housekeeper, an elderly woman with a dour expression, slipped in through the curtain with a fresh pot of herbal tea. They all waited for the Chief to take the first sip, and then drank the first cup in silence. While not stimulating like the beverages in his crashed ship—his supply was now long gone—the blend of barley-leaves and honey tasted earthy and pleasant.

At last the Chief spoke:

"It appears our enemies have developed a new tactic."

"Which enemies?" Mikhail asked.

"The ones he brought to our door," Jamin hissed.

The Chief shot his son a look that would kill.

"Tell him what you told *me*," the Chief said to Farzam.

The Eshnunna emissary laid out the sorry tale:

"The first raid came a fortnight ago," he said, "though at the time, we figured the girl had run away."

Like Ninsianna...

"What did you think she was running from?" Mikhail asked.

"She wanted to marry a boy from a lower caste—" the emissary wrinkled his nose "—but the boy swore they hadn't eloped."

Mikhail schooled an unreadable expression, rather than say: *"I think your entire 'caste system' is barbaric...'*

"Let me guess, they were *supposed* to elope, but the girl never made the rendezvous?"

"Yes," the emissary said. "The boy blamed the parents for locking her away, but the parents swore he'd taken her. A search of *both* houses yielded no results."

The curtain parted. The housekeeper came back in, this time carrying a tray filled with hot, grilled vegetables, freshly baked flat bread, and skewers stuffed with marinated lamb. She placed the fragrant feast on a clean white cloth at the center of the carpet. They each filled their plates, and then waited for her to leave before they continued. They made a great show of passing, and eating, a pinch of salt.

"So what was the second incident?" Mikhail asked.

"Six days ago, a young mother was snatched from the date palm grove. Her son, the boy is only four, swore that men in colorful robes jumped out from behind some trees and carried her away."

"They didn't take the boy?"

"No," the emissary said. "He hid. He found his way back to the village, but by the time we launched a search party, the enemy was long gone. But their robes match the description of the men who helped the Halifians attack Gimal."

Mikhail picked up a skewer of lamb and toyed with the succulent meat as he did the math; recreating, in his mind's eye, the fight.

"That was the day *after* we battled them in the desert," he said, "two day's journey west of here, which means *three* days west from Eshnunna. It couldn't be the same group."

"That's what I told them," Gimal said. "So it wasn't in retaliation."

"So what about this third raid?"

"Now *that* is where it gets interesting."

The emissary picked up a bundle that lay on the ground beside him and carefully unwrapped the cloth. Inside was a long, slender stick, about the length of his arm, with feathers on one end, and a tiny knapped flint point on the other. The emissary handed it to Gimal, who handed it to *him*.

"Have you ever seen such a thing?" Gimal asked.

Mikhail picked up the sharpened stick. While his memory refused to give up any information, he stretched out one arm, with the tiny spearhead balanced on two fingers, while with his other hand; he lifted the feathered end to his cheek.

He could almost *feel* the weight as he drew back an imaginary bowstring.

"It's an arrow," he said.

Farzam's eyes lit up with excitement.

"You have *seen* such a thing?" he asked.

Mikhail set the arrow into his lap and ran his fingers down the slender stick.

"Has the Chief explained my condition?" he asked softly.

"You were cast out of the heavens," the emissary said.

Jamin's lips curved up in a smirk. So? *That* was what the bastard kept telling everyone had happened?

"Immanu's daughter—" Mikhail gestured at the shaman "—found me in the desert, close to death. I don't *remember* my past, but if you put a weapon into my hands—" he used the arrow to string an imaginary bow "—if I have ever used it before, I *know* how to wield it, even though I can't remember learning."

"Is this weapon brought from heaven?" the emissary asked.

"I don't think so. It's too primitive—" he shrugged. "But I know I learned to use it, because I can *see* myself hitting a target."

"Primitive?" the emissary sputtered. "Do you have any idea what the enemy *did* with this weapon? They shot them over our front gate and killed three of our sentries."

"You were just surprised," Jamin cut in. "It is nothing but a miniature atlatl dart."

"You didn't *see* them," the emissary insisted. "They breached our defenses, went directly to the houses they wanted to hit, and made off with six more women before we even knew we were under attack."

"So that's eight women taken?"

"Nine," the emissary said. "Another one went missing three days ago."

"What about Gasur?" he asked Gimal.

The trader ran his fingers through his beard.

"The night before I got back," he said, "a group of raiders attacked Gasur in a well-organized raid. They went directly to houses with marriageable-aged daughters, and then disappeared with four of our women.

"Which means they had insider information?"

"We don't know how, but yes," Gimal nodded.

"Did they have these arrows?"

"Not that anybody *saw*," Gimal said. "By the time we realized we were under attack, the raiders were already gone. But everything else sounds similar to what happened to Eshnunna."

"So what do you want from *me*?"

Both Gimal, and the emissary, looked to the Chief.

Jamin gave a low, long growl...

"How would *you* propose defending against such a weapon?" the Chief asked.

Mikhail fondled the arrow. *Draw. Aim. Shoot.* Vague, half-formed images, more kinetic than actual *memories*, danced at the edge of his brain, so close, and yet, frustratingly out of sight.

"I'd ask Rakshan to recreate a few dozen samples," he said. "And then I'd ask Behnam to help me build some bows so I could teach the elite warriors—"

Jamin's eyes shot daggers at him.

"—I mean," he corrected, remembering the *promise* he'd made at the solstice ceremony yesterday, "I'd work with the *Muhafiz*—" he used the honorarium for the future chief "—to train his men how to use, and fend off, an attack from such a weapon."

"They're just *sticks*," Jamin hissed. "I wouldn't waste my warrior's time."

"This weapon can reach a great distance," Mikhail said.

"Yes," the emissary chimed in. "They ambushed our sentries before they got into spear-range."

"That's because your *walls* are little more than a fence!" Jamin exclaimed. "And *your* walls—" he pointed at Gimal "—are non-existent. You're too lazy to build, so now you want *Assur* to come to your aid?"

The Chief drummed his fingers together, his expression thoughtful.

"Eshnunna fought bravely at our side against the Uruk," he said. "Might it be possible our old enemy has decided to test our defenses? You *are*, after all, the Ubaid's southernmost village."

"That was our first thought," the emissary said. "But the robes—"

"—they didn't *wear* those kinds of robes when they raided Gasur," Gimal cut in. "According to the families, they were a disparate bunch."

"Mercenaries?" Jamin said.

"That's what we suspect," Gimal said.

"But why go after the *women*?" the emissary asked. "They didn't even *touch* our temple granary. Usually, *that* is what raiders are after."

"It wouldn't be the *first* time the Uruk came at us through mercenaries," Chief Kiyan said. "That's how we got into war against the Halifians. The Uruk *hired* them to wage war on a second front."

"Have we gotten word of any *other* villages experiencing similar raids?" Immanu asked.

"I sent a runner to check with Nineveh," the Chief said. "If anybody raids our allies to the north, they'd go to Chief Sinalshu, the same way our allies to the south always look to Assur."

"What about the arrow?" the emissary said.

"Mikhail?" the Chief gave him a raised eyebrow.

Mikhail studied the Chief's expression. Up until now, they'd worked opposite one another, *him* sympathetic to Ninsianna's plea to be set free, and the Chief swayed by his son's insistence that she should honor their engagement. His entire future depended on burying the battle axe someplace *other* than in Jamin's arrogant, stubborn skull.

"I'll do as I suggested," he said to the Chief. "Figure out how to use it, and then let your son train the elite warriors."

Jamin leaned across the drop cloth and picked up the arrow.

"This is just a stick," he said with disgust. "A child's toy. Easily broken." He pretended to snap it across his knee. "If Eshnunna wants our help, I'll send men wielding *spears*."

Mikhail picked up a handful of cast-off meat skewers. He held one up.

"Each stick is easily broken—" he snapped one between his thumb and finger "—but when they stand together—" he smashed the rest of the bundle against his knee. It bounced, but did not break "—they are stronger. This weapon is, I believe, strongest when used in a group."

"A *coward's* weapon!"

"An *army's* weapon."

"An army of what?" Jamin taunted. "Of little girls?"

Now wasn't the time to bring up what he'd done to Pareesa. But he'd sworn he would square her with the Chief, and so *help* him, he would.

"You're the *Muhafiz*," he bowed his head cordially. "If *that* is your wish, then *that* is who I shall train."

"You *do* that," Jamin snarled. "-I- will be busy, preparing my *men* to meet this new threat."

Mikhail held out his hand.

"It's a deal."

Chapter 99

End-June - 3,390 BC
Earth: Village of Assur
Colonel Mikhail Mannuki'ili

MIKHAIL

Mikhail strapped on his pulse rifle, and then fell into step behind Immanu as they left the Chief's house. The shaman walked ahead of him, forcing him to stretch to keep up, even with his longer legs. Now was his chance to ask permission to court Ninsianna, if only he could put the sentiment into words.

"Ahm, *Sir*," he said as chased him across the central square.

Immanu turned in anger.

"Why did you *agree* to that?"

"Agree to what?"

"To let Jamin *dishonor* you!"

Mikhail stepped back, surprised by the shaman's anger. Around the edge of the man's tawny-beige eyes, he could *see* the hint of copper that Ninsianna had gotten the day he'd mistaken her cousin for *her*.

His speech grew instantly tongue-tied.

"I, ah, uhm..." he stammered. This wasn't the difficult conversation he'd been intending to have.

"Maybe you don't *care*—" the shaman waved his arms wildly "—that Jamin just made a fool of you. But what about your mission—"

"—I can't remember my mission."

"Not *that* mission!" Immanu gestured skyward. "The goddess' mission! She sent you here for a *reason!*"

Rather than anger him further by saying, "my getting shot down here had nothing to do with your prophecy," Mikhail fell into step as Immanu resumed walking.

"What would you have me do?" he asked the shaman.

"Well, for one thing," Immanu said, "go to the warriors and *offer* to train them."

"I gave the Chief my word that I wouldn't usurp his son," Mikhail said.

"Then *break* your promise!"

'I can think of –one– promise I'd like to break.' But he didn't say it, because even he, clueless dolt that he was, could sense that the *worst* time to broach this subject would be while the shaman was angry.

"Wouldn't you like your daughter to be *safe?*" he asked instead

"She's got *you* for that!"

Mikhail was so surprised that he failed to look where he walked. He crashed into a young woman who carried a basket of laundry. With a cry of dismay, she went tumbling down to the ground. Her freshly-washed laundry tumbled onto the dirt.

A pair of startled eyes stared up at him, the same shape as Ninsianna's, but as black and deep as the furthest reaches of outer space.

—*Black eyes, peering out from a bush.*

—*"Mikhail, come and find me!"*

—*I search for her, but already she is gone.*

Mikhail knelt to help.

"S-s-sorry!" she looked down, as though frightened he would beat her.

"The fault is mine," he said gently. "I failed to watch where I was going."

The girl gathered her laundry, trembling as she pulled a tattered white shawl from the yellow ochre dust. She glanced fearfully at her uncle, gathered her laundry and skittered away.

Mikhail grabbed her arm.

"Wait?"

A sense of *familiarity* shocked through his skin. She smelled like ozone. The girl trembled, refusing to meet his gaze.

"L-l-let me go," she pleaded.

"Let me help you?"

"You can't," she whispered.

Mikhail let go. Instantly, she was gone.

He stood up and ruffled his feathers.

"Why was she so afraid?" he asked, wondering how she'd managed to disappear into the crowd.

"She's of no concern!" Immanu said angrily.

Rather than further alienate what he *hoped* would be his future father-in-law, he asked Immanu a question that he *knew* would be like honey.

"We were just *discussing,*" he said firmly, "how you could help me *earn* Jamin's respect. If I can teach women how to use a bow, imagine what I could teach the warriors?"

That hard copper edge which ringed Immanu's eyes subsided.

"You should have asked me *first,*" Immanu huffed.

"I'm asking you *now,*" he said.

"I don't have much input with the *women,*" the shaman said condescendingly. "If you want to *teach* them, you shall have to convince them on your own."

He stepped into his haughty temple and *slammed* the door in Mikhail's face.

Chapter 100

Galactic Standard Date: 152,323.06 AE
Earth: Sata'an Forward Operating Base
Lieutenant Kasib

Lt. KASIB

Lieutenant Kasib adjusted the checkered shemagh[145] he'd affixed over his snout as the poor schmuck who'd been assigned latrine duty jiggled the shit-drum out from beneath the women's outhouse. The stench was nearly overwhelming, along with the metallic scent of human menstrual blood. Now that his "Women's Training Academy" had swelled to thirty women, the thing had to be burned off several times a day.

"Why we gotta clean this one so often?" the lizard groused. "The men's shitter only gets burned once a day."

"We can't teach the women hygiene if their latrine is overflowing," Kasib said. "We need them to demand these amenities from their future husbands."

He reflected on the irony that *he*, who had yet to earn the right to take a wife, had been placed in charge of "educating" the future wives of their human collaborators. But they *needed* women to help them civilize this planet. A beautiful face often wielded far more ardent converts than the most technologically advanced pulse rifle.

Flies swarmed out of the outhouse and landed on his green, pebbled skin. He flicked his tail at them absent-mindedly. On the ground beneath the shit-hole, maggots writhed where the drum had overflowed.

The skinny lizard shoved a recently burned "honey pot" under the outhouse to replace the one he'd just pulled out, and then dumped a hefty glug of kerosene into it to kill the flies.

"Take it easy on the fuel," Kasib ordered.

"It makes it easier to burn, Sir."

"Once we run out, you'll be humping that cart three miles from the base for disposal."

The skinny lizard groaned. It was bad enough they had to drag the barrels outside of the fence to reduce the shit-impregnated black smoke

---

[145] *Shemagh:* an oversized cotton scarf that can be used to protect the head, face, or neck from a desert environment.

which fouled the base. The humans were convinced that Shay'tan ruled a fiery hell.

"When will Shay'tan send a supply ship, Sir?"

"With the Alliance breathing down our neck," Kasib said, "the *last* thing he'll be worried about is where we take a crap."

The unfortunate lizard dragged the overflowing shit-cart out of the latrine, and then tied the privacy-screen so the skullcrackers couldn't get their jollies by peeking into the women's bathroom. He'd be back to empty it again tonight, at least until a *different* lizard had pissed off their staff sergeant enough to take his place.

Grabbing his flatscreen, Kasib recorded how many cans of kerosene they had left; not a lot. Normally, by now, a mining ship would have arrived, carrying equipment to drill for crude oil; but the Alliance tended to shadow those kinds of ships. Given the need for secrecy, he *doubted* one would come anytime soon.

With a tingle of anticipation, he stepped into the enormous tent which had been designated the Women's Training Academy. With a surprised squeak, the women all averted their eyes. It was the first thing he'd made the instructors teach them—Sata'anic modesty—and to fashion garments which covered them from head to toe. Off to one side, their newest delivery of women clung to one another and sobbed, but they were more afraid of the Amorite slave traders—their *allies,* he corrected himself—who'd brought them here, than they were of *him.*

Up at the front, the first group of women recited a lesson about how to reduce the risk of disease—deaths which would be prevented once Hudhafah decided which collaborators to "gift" a bride. With increased hygiene, most collaborator-babies would survive long enough to become Sata'anic soldiers. In a single generation, they'd out-breed the rebels.

The instructor gave him a crisp salute.

"Sir!"

"At ease." Kasib glanced at the seated women, discreetly scanning their faces for a certain pair of eyes. "Where is the one called Taram?"

"At the infirmary, Sir—" the instructor avoided his gaze. "Doctor Peyman wanted to evaluate her more thoroughly."

An odd sense of panic fluttered in his gut. But for the past ten weeks, she'd been nothing but a model student. He'd seen to it, *personally,* that she learned her lessons despite her blindness.

He finished inventorying the women's tent: what they'd used, what they still needed, and a small bonus—some baskets they'd woven using local materials to store the base's dwindling supplies. He logged the items onto his electronic flatscreen, and then hurried to the infirmary.

"Sir!" the medic stood at attention. "Ready for inspection, Sir!"

"At ease," he saluted back. "First, I'd like to check in on the patient from the women's tent."

"Aye, Sir!" The medic led him past a row of beds—all of them full due to fiercer-than-usual fighting they'd experienced against a local, primitive tribe—to a cordoned-off area; the chief medical officer's office, examination room and, sometimes, if the trauma ward was overflowing, an overflow surgical ward.

"Lieutenant Kasib is here, Sir?" the medic announced through the privacy curtain. "He wishes to see the patient."

Doctor Peyman stepped out, giving him a glimpse of Taram and her breathtakingly beautiful older sister, Sarvenaz. He was a tall lizard, not especially burly, with a deep red dewlap, indicative of the upper castes. He gestured for Kasib to follow him to a different part of the tent, away from curious ears.

A hollow sensation settled into Kasib's gut.

The physician cleared his throat.

"Did the instructor inform you about the results of her final exam?" Doctor Peyman asked.

"She exceeded all expectations?" Kasib said hopefully.

"Not the field tests," Peyman said. "She failed to navigate a public market."

"That's why the law says all women must travel in pairs," Kasib said.

The doctor's gold-green eyes crinkled with sympathy.

"A well-trained woman must not *only* be able to navigate the market," Peyman said, "but also protect any children born of whatever union she is ordered to form. Their offspring—" he gestured at the privacy curtain "—are the future of the Empire."

"But she bears extensive knowledge of home economics," Kasib protested, "basic first aid, and proper Sata'anic morals. She's even learned a significant amount of our language!"

Doctor Peyman sighed.

"If I was back on Hades," he said wearily, "I could study their physiology and engineer a cure, but out here—"

"What would you need?" Kasib asked.

"Do you have access to an electron microscope?" Peyman asked. "A modern research facility? And a robotic assistant for microsurgery?"

Kasib's sharp dorsal ridge sank with defeat. They'd had *all* of that equipment on General Hudhafah's old Sata'anic naval carrier, but Shay'tan, peace be upon him, had transferred the toughest members of their crew to the SRN *Jamaran* so they could follow a lead *out here* without risking an Alliance tail.

Except for that Angelic scout ship they'd shot down…

"Will you recommend sterilization?" his voice warbled.

Back in the Sata'anic Empire, if a female failed to graduate, she would usually be sterilized and returned to her family in disgrace. Given the high value of "breeders," it was the ultimate dishonor to have a daughter deemed unfit to bear the next generation of soldiers. Daughters who'd been returned home often ended up dead, victims of honor killings. The practice was outlawed, but it still happened with distressing frequency.

Doctor Peyman twirled his tail thoughtfully.

"She can see shadows," he said, "and differentiate basic colors. Given her test-scores—"

"—some of the highest," Kasib cut in. "Only her sister scored higher."

"Yes," Peyman said. "Sarvenaz has qualified as a first-wife for a very high-ranking male."

"Then dishonoring her sister will lead to hard feelings," Kasib said frantically. "Sarvenaz may be able to harden her future husband's heart."

Doctor Peyman tapped his stylus-pen against the flatscreen he used to enter medical records.

"We *could* return her to her village," Peyman said. "Explain to her father it wasn't for want of her trying. Given all that she's learned, I doubt he'll turn her out into the street."

Kasib tasted the air nervously.

"That's just it," he said. "These traders—"

"You mean, the *slave* traders," Doctor Peyman hissed.

Kasib winced. He knew what the human riff-raff *did* that he was forced to rely upon, but once the woman got *here*, he made sure they were treated humanely.

"It's a necessary evil," Kasib said. "As I recall, you had the same objection at the *last* planet we annexed."

"And look what happened?"

Peyman turned his back and paced.

Kasib stared down at his flatscreen. Taram had *told* him what the Amorites did to the women they captured. One had been so traumatized he'd ordered them to take her home. The woman had been found dead, just outside the outskirts of the village.

"They don't *know* where they are from," Kasib said. "I tried to get them to point it out on a map, but their technology is so primitive, they can't even point out landmarks on a satellite image."

Doctor Peyman sighed.

"I have procedures to follow," he said.

"I know," Kasib said. "Everyone needs to pull their weight."

"*You're* the lizard who gets things from point A to point B," Peyman said. "Put in an order for the proper equipment, and I'll recommend she be the first for experimental surgery."

"Given the need for secrecy," Kasib said, "that could be months. Maybe even years?"

"Well I *can't* recommend she stay here," Peyman said. "You must give her back to the traders so the quartermaster can withhold the cost the next time your *allies*—" he spat the word out like he was eating excrement "—bring in a batch of women."

"They will kill her," Kasib said. "I heard them threaten her with my own ear-holes."

"Then I will list her as expired," Peyman said. "You can sneak her off the base, and then what you do with her—" he threw up his clawed hands "—I don't want to know."

Kasib twirled his tail. The *proper* thing to do was return her to the traders and demand a refund. On the other hand, he'd become a bit too attached to simply let his new "trading partners" drag Taram out in the desert and slit her throat. Especially with her sister earmarked to tempt the highest-ranking collaborator they could find…

"I've made some connections in the village," Kasib said. "I'll see if *they* can figure out a way to get her home."

Chapter 101

End-June - 3,390 BC
Earth: Village of Assur
Colonel Mikhail Mannuki'ili

MIKHAIL

Rakshan was the finest flint-knapper, not just in Assur, but in most of Ubaid territory. Not only did he knap a mean spear-point, but he also happened to be a member of the Tribunal. He and Behnam, a carpenter and *also* a member of the Tribunal, sat surrounded by razor-sharp shards of stone, slivers of wood, and half-chewed pieces of sinew.

"It snapped," Mikhail held up his broken bow, "the moment I drew it back."

"How did the arrowhead hold up?" Rakshan asked.

"The arrowhead did fine," Mikhail said, "but the bow keeps snapping, and the arrows keep splintering the moment they hit the target."

The two old men bent over their shattered experiments, haggling about the failure points and how they might overcome the problem.

"I think the problem is the *type* of wood we are using," Behnam said.

"It works fine with atlatl darts," Rakshan said.

"Atlatl darts are thicker," Behnam said, "and have considerably less—" he looked up at Mikhail. "What was that word you use?"

"Velocity." He paraphrased the formula. "It's displacement, uhm, how far it has to travel, divided by how long it takes to hit the target."[146]

"We can't make the arrows go any slower," Rakshan said.

"So the fault lies in the *wood*," Behnam said. "We have to find a wood that will hold up to such an impact."

He left the two men to argue about physics while he moved through the village, *walking* like a human, and greeting villagers who went out of their way to avoid him. It felt so artificial, acting *friendly* when his base nature insisted that he sit back and observe from a distance. If he wasn't doing something *useful*, it felt unnatural to open his mouth. At last he got to the lower well. Now *here* was someplace he felt more comfortable. First he helped the women haul up their buckets of water, and then he asked:

"Did you hear about the new weapon the Chief ordered me to teach?"

"The one they used against Eshnunna?" a woman asked.

---

[146] *Velocity* is $v = d / t$, where d is displacement and t is the change in time.

"They're called bows and arrows," he said. "They're designed for women. Would you like to learn how to use one?"

The women giggled.

"Isn't that the warriors' job?" one asked.

"Who do you think we are," another said. "Pareesa?"

One of the women pretended to gird up her loins.[147]

Another started to say: "Jamin said—"

"Shhhh!"

The other women shushed her. They hurried away, glancing back over their shoulders, gossiping, and occasionally laughing. He felt like an adolescent getting shot down after asking the most beautiful woman in the room to dance.

If *this* was how he handled a simple conversation, how in Hades was he supposed to ask Ninsianna to marry him?

He crossed paths with Pareesa, carrying her baby sister.

"Any luck?" he asked.

"No," she scowled. "They told me to stop pretending to be a man."

They passed a group of women, fresh off the fields and laden down with baskets filled with melons. Pareesa ran over to ask them to join his archers.

"Don't you want to protect yourself?" she asked.

The women gave her a scornful look.

"No," they said. "That's what the warriors are for."

They moved from group to group, but it was always the same answer. Jamin had *promised* to beef up their defenses. Every available man, even the boys, had been invited to the training field for a chance to qualify for a third tier of warriors.

At last Pareesa's baby sister woke up and began to cry.

"I have to bring her back to Mama," Pareesa said.

"Take care." Mikhail's wings sagged.

They parted at the alley between the outermost and second ring. It was well past noontime, and *still* he hadn't found a single recruit!

His step grew lighter as he approached Immanu's house. He'd spent all of his time, chasing after prospective archers, and no time whatsoever with the woman who'd inspired him to do all of this work in the first place. He couldn't wait to see his beloved!

Just inside, Ninsianna stood next to her mother, a breathtakingly beautiful goddess, stuffing supplies into her healer's basket. The lunch had already been cleared, all except for *his* plate. A sliced cucumber, a bowl of steamed grain, and a cup of fresh goat's milk, covered with a cloth to discourage flies, sat on the table, waiting…

---

[147] *Gird up your loins:* to pull your kilt through your legs and belt it around your waist, making a crude pair of pants.

"How was your day?" she asked coolly.

"The bow broke," he said. "Again..."

"Behnam will fix it," she said. "He's a genius when it comes to wood."

"Your wood isn't very strong," he complained. "He was able to make arrows from the cedar-tree that I shattered, but now he's out of wood. He *might* need to trade for something far away."

Ninsianna's mother, Needa, pinched her lip, her expression thoughtful.

"Do you need it to be *stronger?*" she asked. "Or bend more?"

"A little of both."

Needa moved to the furthest corner of the kitchen and pointed up at the place where the rafters met the outside wall.

"Could you get that for me?" she asked.

Mikhail easily reached it as his head often bumped the ceiling. The plants were stuffed all the way into the place where the rafters met the wall. He pulled out a dusty bundle of twigs.

Needa bent the slender twigs. Rather than snap, they bent back, despite the fact the needles appeared brown and dry.

She handed it to him.

"Try that," she said.

"It's too small." He bent a twig no wider than an electrical wire.

"Not *that*," she said. "That kind of wood."

"What is it?" he asked.

"Yew,"[148] she said.

"Me?" he said.

"Not *you*," she said. "Yewwww. With a "who" at the end. Like an owl."

"Oh..." He lifted it up to his nose to sniff the needles.

"Don't!" she batted it away. "It's poisonous."

"Then why is it in with your medicinal herbs?"

"It's *not*," Needa said. "We use it to discourage insects. And, oh—" she handed him a strip of linen "—it's an irritant, so make sure you don't breathe the dust."

He highly doubted the pathetic clump of needles would solve his problem, but he stuffed it into his pocket. What did *he* know? Right now, he couldn't even convince the women to teach themselves not to be kidnapped. Much less outfit an entire army with a novel weapon.

Ninsianna finished putting together her healer's basket.

"I have to go," she said glibly. "One of the women is close to giving birth."

His wings drooped.

"I'd hoped we could eat lunch together?"

---

[148] *Yew:* a coniferous tree or shrub.

"So did I—" her smile became strained "—but you were so busy talking to all those women, that I guess you forgot about me, eh?'

She hurried towards the door, her shoulders stiff; before it occurred to him that something was wrong. Wait? Was she angry at him? Why was she angry? Because he had failed? Or because she felt *left out?*

"Will you train with me later?" he called after her. "I mean, as soon as we solve the problem with the wood?"

Ninsianna whirled and gave him a perky smile.

"I'm a *healer*," she said. "I don't have *time*."

And with that, his most ardent supporter went flying out the door...

Chapter 102

Galactic Standard Date: 152,323.07 AE
Haven-3: Alliance Hall of Parliament
Prime Minister Lucifer

LUCIFER

Haven-3 was the seat of the Alliance Parliament, chartered to free the Eternal Emperor from the day-to-day tedium of running a galactic empire. During his two hundred year "disappearance," Lucifer had seized the opportunity to build an enormous circular stadium around the original building and expand Parliament's power, leaving his father's old-style cathedral little more than the insignificant tail of a letter "Q".

In Hashem's old parliament building, every delegate sat symbolically separated from his throne, carefully segregated, and arranged by prestige and net-worth. In Hashem's parliament, only the ancient races had possessed representation; but in Lucifer's parliament, every sentient planet had a voice, and every delegate had equal access to *him*.

Would they now repay him for strengthening each planet's self-governance and voice, their *free will* and *freedom*, at the expense of his relationship with his immortal father? Or would they spurn him, like the Emperor had done upon his return, in his time of greatest need?

Eligor helped him to the podium. *Damantia!* He still felt shaky from his latest blackout and was forced to flare his wings for balance like a drunken cadet. The rushed trip from the neutral zone to Haven-3, along with a lack of sleep, had rendered him a little less "bright and beautiful" than usual this morning. The entire bottle of *choledzeretsa* he'd downed didn't helped matters any. More than anything, he needed to puke.

A tall, slender serpent, a Mu'aqqibat dragon, ascended the central podium and banged his gavel.

"The Prime Minister wishes to address Parliament," the Speaker of the Commons called out in a formal voice.

A bead of sweat dribbled down Lucifer's nose as he ascended the central platform. Eligor stood close enough to catch him until he reached the top step, but then he was on his own. He stared up at the balconies which cascaded upwards towards the skylight. Most of the seats were empty; there was barely enough of a quorum to make his appropriation bill legal.

The delegates fell silent, curious at what had compelled their Prime Minister to attend an ordinary budget meeting.

"Ladies and gentlemen," his voice warbled, "if you'll look to your flatscreens, you'll see that I just filed an emergency motion to grant relief to the Yaris-6 mining colony."

"Yaris-6?" one of the delegates asked. "Didn't you just ask us to *cede* that planet to the Tokoloshe Kingdom?"

"Y-yes, I did," Lucifer stammered. "King Barabas promised—" *I think* "— that he'd treat those miners the same way he'd treat any other citizen in his kingdom—" *at least that's what I TOLD you, even though I don't remember saying it* —"but the *people* on that planet are Alliance citizens. They wish to come home, not hold onto their mining claims."

"350 million credits is a lot of money," another delegate said. "Why can't you just send the military in to blow the cannibals all to hell?"

The truth was, he only needed 50 million credits to evacuate that mining colony and get them resettled someplace else. The miners were so desperate to get the Hades out of there that they'd pay *him* for passage to any other planet or asteroid in the galaxy. The *other* 300 million credits were to buy more human women. But he couldn't tell *them* that. It'd be all over the six o'clock news.

"The initial problem, that we don't have enough Leonids to *patrol* that sector, and also protect *us*, hasn't changed," Lucifer said. "There are only 2,500 Leonids left. We can't squander their lives."

"The Leonids that –I– know are all chomping at the bit to be let off their chain!" a delegate said.

"Yeah," said another.

"Let them wreak vengeance!"

The room began to spin. Why in *Hades* had he ceded that planet to the cannibals in the first place?

'To save the Leonids, you dimwit. And now you need to save YOU…'

Lucifer's hands shook. This wasn't going the way he'd planned it. Not that he'd really planned *anything*. Zepar had jammed him into his "devil cruiser" and ordered Eligor to bring him here without any *thought* about how he would actually pull this off. The fact he couldn't *think* straight, not to mention could barely *see*, didn't help matters any; nor did the fact his tongue felt too thick and tasted like rotten fish. Out of all the times he'd gotten drunk, and then been forced to legislate while suffering from a hangover, this had to be his most impotent performance.

…impotent…

He patted his chest-pocket.

No. He was *NOT* impotent…

He pulled the sonogram kept close to his heart. His soon-to-be son was still little more than a bubble with a tail, but it was *his* son, dammit! The one he'd dreamed about for the last 225 years. He wasn't about to let an absence of *pin money* deprive his fellow hybrids of the exact same hope.

'Please?' he whispered to his inner voice. *'Tell me what to say?'*

It had been Zepar who had taught him how to listen to his inner voice. He closed his eyes and invited it into his body. His nervous system tingled as his "inner voice" filled him with power.

It pushed him aside, that strange juxtaposition when he listened to his inner voice, almost like a two-man fighter spaceship where either pilot could fly.

When he opened his eyes, all of Parliament was bathed in a faint orange light, as if the entire governing body sat inside a firepit, warmed by a raging bonfire — *him*. This was the Lucifer who'd built Parliament after his adoptive father had abandoned him.

'Tell me?' he asked. *'Tell me what to say?'*

He took a deep breath and focused his *gift* on his delegate's hopes and fears. His silver eyes glittered with eerie prescience as he scanned the crowd, searching for the weakest link to apply pressure.

He spied his weakness in the mind of a Saori[149] delegate. She'd lost a brother in that battle, one of the Leonid's physicians.

"When we *ceded* that world," he spoke directly to her, "we were all still *reeling* from the death of our brave Leonid destroyer. We were thinking in *material* terms: "here is a planet with no clear claim to ownership which is too far away to defend," and not in terms of "there are still 60,000 people on this planet, many of them Alliance citizens, who *went* to that planet to mine something we need."

"They were mining for promethium," an Electrophori delegate contradicted him. "Nobody *needs* that mineral. It's used for fluorescent paint."

Lucifer focused his *gift* on the Electrophori delegate. Besides being a constant pain in his ass, the vociferous delegate belonged to an eel-like species that generated its own electrical charge.

'Humiliate him,' his inner voice whispered.

--He's a dangerous enemy…

'It will force him to show his hand'

"Member Djalu," Lucifer laughed. "We can't all carry our own light with us."

"You think it's *funny*?" the Electrophori's flesh crackled, emitting a pale, blue light. Its eyes glowed murderously red,

---

[149] *Saori*: a single-horned, gazelle-like species which spawned the myth of unicorns on Earth. They are known for their compassion.

"I'm just pointing out the obvious—" he pointed at the creature's sparking tail. "Maybe *you* could care less, but *we* need our electrical devices to glow in the dark. It's disingenuous to deny aid to *Alliance citizens*—" he accentuated those two words "—now that we discover our desire for cheap technology has put 60,000 of them at risk of being *eaten alive*."

"The Tokoloshe won't eat them!" the Electrophori said. "You said it yourself! You gave your word!"

Which I don't remember doing, damn it!

"Yeah!" the other delegates agreed with the Electrophori delegate.

"You gave your word, Lucifer!"

What the fuck do I say?

He focused on his sarcastic inner voice.

'Blame the problem on Shay'tan.'

Lucifer turned his back on the Electrophori delegate, flaring his wings to signal he would give that delegate no further consideration. Instead he focused on the delegate his gift had singled out; the Saori whose brother had been among the crewmen murdered.

"When we colonized that planet—" he spoke gently "—our *Emperor*, my father, had won that resource planet from Emperor *Shay'tan*—" he projected into her mind an image of the two old gods playing chess. "We sent our colonists there, *immediately*, to mine it, and a Leonid destroyer to protect them. Alas, what we *didn't* know was that the Tokoloshe Kingdom had *already* laid claim to that planet; a claim which, I might add, they provided overwhelming evidence to back up."

Not that I remember –seeing- that evidence, but I wrote an affidavit that I –had– during my blackout....

"Then why didn't King Barabas come to *us* with his dispute," the Saori's doe-like eyes glistened with moisture. "Why did he kill the Leonids?"

Yes? Why didn't he?

'Let me speak.'

I hate it when you speak.

'Let me SPEAK!!!'

Lucifer stared at the delegate, whose grief was real. He let his "inner voice" step all the way into his body. It felt, for a moment, like being shoved to one side of his brain while the "other pilot" took control, but then his words began to flow.

"King Barabas claims he went to *Shay'tan*," Lucifer said, "but the old dragon rebuked him; said he'd blow the planet up before he'd go crawling back to our Emperor and admit he made a mistake."

He paused, to let that all sink in.

...chess game...

......bad bets....

..........bad blood between the two emperors....

............two old gods playing *games* with mortal lives...

It didn't take *much* to reinforce old stereotypes. In their scriptures, they had countless stories about the two old gods daring each other to do terrible things, and then refusing to lift a finger while their subjects suffered, all to win a bet. The two had been at war like this for as long as there had been an Alliance. Shay'tan was an effective boogieman, just as Hashem was effective to motivate the Sata'anic lizards.

"The Tokoloshe claim they did not *intentionally* fire upon the Leonids," he lied. "They fired upon a Sata'anic smuggling vessel that was carrying, they claim, weapons of mass destruction to destroy that resource planet so *they* couldn't have it. The Leonids were chasing that vessel for the exact same reason ... it leaped into real space too close to the planet. When they tried to board it, it performed a mini hyper-jump so close to their ship that the micro-wormhole damaged part of their hull. They were pursing the vessel when the dreadnought[150] came after the vessel which *it* had originally been tracking."

"But why did they have to shoot *our* ship?" the Saori asked.

"It was all a mistake," he said. "Both ship's surveillance videos *clearly* show that the dreadnought fired at the Algol-class smuggling vessel after it pursued it out of an asteroid belt; the same asteroid belt that the Leonids had just chased it in to. Unfortunately, that vessel made a *second* hyperspace leap just as the Tokoloshe's laser reached it. The shot carried onward, into the Leonid destroyer. And then the Leonids, whose weapons were already charged, shot back. The Tokoloshe assumed the Leonids, and the smuggling vessel, were allied."

He didn't mention that *same* Algol-class smuggling vessel had been the one to deliver his so-called "wife."

"It doesn't *justify* it," the Saori delegate said. "They *should* have radioed before opening fire."

"No, it doesn't—" Lucifer projected soothing images into the Saori's mind. "But we *all* saw the shot, and studied the flight-recorder recovered from the Leonid destroyer. That's why the Tokoloshe didn't *eat* the colonists when they first took back their planet. It was an act of conciliation. But our colonists are turning out to be royal pains in the asses because they believe in freedom, and the Tokoloshe do *not*."

He flared his white wings in an artful pose upon uttering the word "freedom." That sarcastic inner voice sneered:

'*This will make a great publicity shot*'

---

[150] *Dreadnought:* a massive battleship.

"The Tokoloshe want those colonists *gone* because it's infecting their regular work-force and their patience is at an end," he continued. "All our colonists want is to come *home*."

The Saori nodded, as did the delegates allied with her planet.

"What about the rest of us?" the Electrophori shouted over the other delegates. "You want us to pay for somebody else's mistake?"

Lucifer turned, *furious* the upstart had interrupted his speech. An image popped into his mind of that delegate's worst fear. He formed the image, and then he *spoke* it…

"Perhaps *you'd* like to be eaten alive, Member Djalu?"

He *rammed* the image into the Electrophori's brain. Being captured by the bear-like creatures, strapped upon a table, and then his flesh peeled back, begging for mercy as they carved meat out of his trembling muscles. He pictured the Electrophori's wife, his entire family, all of them screaming as they were devoured in front of him with terrifying reality.

The Electrophori began to convulse.

Lucifer held the creature's gaze as it clutched both sides of its head. That part of him which observed, who'd invited his "inner voice" to speak, shouted *"No!"* as he remembered doing this trick before. How could he have forgotten what it felt like to drain the life-energy from a living creature? It felt so *powerful*. Deep inside, he wanted *more*.

The Electrophori's static electricity faded. Blood seeped out of its nose and ears. The creature clutched its chest.

'Stop!' Lucifer pleaded. *'Stop this! I didn't mean to hurt him this badly.'*

All of a sudden, his "inner voice" stepped to one side. The power, along with his memory of ever wielding it, began to fade.

'This power is normal. Any halfway-ascended demigod can wield it. Why do you think the Emperor adopted you in the first place?'

Yes. It was perfectly normal. The Emperor had run tests on him, trying to see if he had "pre-ascended" abilities, but he'd been too young then. It was the Emperor's own fault he'd disappeared before he'd developed the ability, and hadn't cared enough to ask about it since.

The Electrophori gasped for breath.

Lucifer turned, as if it never happened. Exhaustion hit him, but he still needed to get the appropriation bill through Parliament.

On his own….

Non-powerful Lucifer, ordinary Lucifer, mortal Lucifer, reached towards the Saori delegate.

"Please," he said simply. "We can't abandon those people. We need to bring them home."

The Saori nodded. So did the delegates who'd allied with her.

The Electrophori was in no condition to protest.

The delegates from wealthy 'old worlds' could care less about 350 million credits. They'd already moved on to debate much costlier budget items.

"Yea," they all waved him off. To them, it was nothing but lunch money.

Lucifer nearly collapsed as he stepped off the stage.

Eligor caught him.

"Are you okay, Sir?" Eligor asked.

"Just tired," he pinched the bridge of his nose. "Just get me back to my ship? We have let Ba'al Zebub know we *got* his money."

Chapter 103

July - 3,390 BC
Earth: Village of Assur

NINSIANNA

Ninsianna grabbed an onion and peeled off the papery skin. It reminded her of Mikhail, the way that, just when she thought she had the darned thing ready to cook, she'd peel off another layer and find, lo! More hard, yellow skin!

She wiped away a tear.

"Stop rubbing your eyes!" Mama scolded. "You'll only make it worse."

"Onions *always* make me cry."

She chopped the onion with pent-up ferocity. She felt like a doe in heat, aching for another kiss, but ever since the solstice festival, he'd stayed as far away from her as he possibly could!

The knife slipped.

"Dammit!" she hissed.

She sucked on her finger to keep her blood from splattering onto the onions. The knife Mikhail had given her—made of the same heavenly material as his sky canoe—cut more deeply than any stone blade.

"Sit!" Mama ordered.

"I'm fine."

"It wasn't a request."

With an aggrieved sigh, Ninsianna plopped down on the bench they'd set up under the canopy which shaded their outdoor kitchen. Only a *fool* cooked inside in the summer!

Mama ran inside to fetch her healer's basket. With deft fingers, she rinsed her hand with water drawn earlier from the well, and then wrapped it in a strip of clean linen.

"You woke up screaming again last night," Mama said.

"It was just a nightmare."

"You've had them every night since Mikhail pulled you up from the well."

Ninsianna avoided her mother's too-perceptive gaze. While Papa could see into the Dreamtime, Mama had the ability to *feel* what other people were feeling. And right now she felt...

"—suffering from exhaustion," Mama said.

"Huh?"

She realized she'd faded out—quite some time ago—judging by the completed bandage on her hand.

"Sorry," she mumbled. "I'll help you finish supper."

Mama grabbed her wrist.

"I went through this with your father," she said. "They're not *dreams*. The goddess keeps sending visions because she wants you to *do* something."

Ninsianna's voice warbled.

"It's too fantastical to be real!"

She looked away. Given the distance that Mikhail had put between them ever since that emissary had arrived from Eshnunna, she highly doubted the dream would come true.

"*Tell* me!" Mama's eyes bored into *hers*. "I may not be a seeress, but I can *feel* your terror when you wake up screaming, and don't *stop* screaming until Mikhail comes rushing up the stairs to hold you!"

Tears streamed down her cheeks. *This* time, it had nothing to do with the onions.

"I keep dreaming about crocodile-men," her voice broke. "They're going to attack our village. And then the Evil One will come."

"Is the dream symbolic?" Mama asked.

"I don't think so," Ninsianna said. "They come in sky canoes."

"Like Mikhail's sky canoe?"

"Yes? No!" She threw up her arms. "I don't know! They look different; like great, big dung-beetles, with a mouth that opens in the back."

And then the white-winged Angelic arrived; the one who embraced her each night like a lover, right before he stabbed her in the belly. A tear slid down her cheek. Mama grabbed her hand.

"Tell me about the Evil One?" her fierce, mahogany eyes bored into *hers*.

Ninsianna glanced around to make sure nobody was eavesdropping. She'd led her father to believe the Evil One was a *demon*. How could she tell Mama the truth when it would only validate Jamin's lies?

"He's *beautiful*," she whispered. "The most beautiful, the brightest..."

Her voice trailed off.

"Angelic?" Mama guessed.

Ninsianna shook her head. Yes? No! What should she say?

"I think he's from a different tribe," she said. "His wings are white, not brown. And his eyes are different. Silver—" she pointed at her *own* goddess-kissed eyes "—and red, like when Papa gets really angry. And his voice—"

She trembled uncontrollably.

"When he *speaks—*" she cried out, remembering the way he made her voluntarily lay down, like a sacrificial ram.

In his eyes, she sees the birth of countless universes; gods and goddesses to rule them, and spinning discs filled with stars. Fish crawl out of the oceans and transform into people; they turn their eyes to the stars. With a single voice, they worship the One True God.[151]

Her breath grew faster; her skin flushed red with excitement. She *wanted* that power; only the One True God's favor came at a terrible price.

"He makes you *feel* like you want to do whatever he asks?" Mama's expression grew intense.

Ninsianna nodded. How did Mama *know* this?

"Why would he want to *kill* me?" she said in an anguished voice.

Mama scooped her into her arms in a rare display of affection. Ninsianna blubbered onto her shoulder. It wasn't that Mama was heartless—quite the contrary—she was far too empathetic. It was just that Mama had little tolerance for self-pity, which made her sympathy right now all that much more terrible.

"Perhaps he's Mikhail's rival?" Mama said. "*Somebody* threw him out of the heavens."

"But why would he come after *me*?"

Mama gripped her face between her hands.

"Oh, you silly child!" she kissed her forehead. "For a seeress, you are terribly blind!"

So if Mikhail had an enemy, one he didn't *remember*, and that enemy were to come here…

"You can't *tell* anybody!" Ninsianna grabbed Mama's hand. "Jamin will *insist* his father drive Mikhail out."

"We have to tell your father."

"He tried to *sell* me to his son!"

Mama sighed.

"Things have changed," she said. "Right now, the Chief is worried about a bigger enemy."

"What? Strings and sticks?" Ninsianna scoffed. "That's just the latest ploy to make a *fool* out of him!"

The entire village, and by *entire*, she meant the warriors, had made a great stink about Mikhail's offer to teach the art of flinging little sticks to *women*. The women had gone into a-twitter, most too polite to laugh in the big Angelic's face, but behind his back, they hen-heckled and gossiped. The men, on the other hand, had flocked to Jamin's offer to train a third tier of warriors, even the "untalented" ones, something he'd previously refused.

---

[151] The *One True God* is one of Moloch's (aka "the Evil One") titles.

Even old Behnam, opining about Mikhail's *other* failed attempts at "being useful," had gently asked if, perhaps, he was trying a little too hard to put himself into the Chief's good favor?

"He's trying to find his place," Mama said.

"He's the goddess' Champion!" she said. "He doesn't *need* a place!"

"He's a *man*," Mama said. "A man who understands that starting a family takes responsibility."

"How can he? When Jamin thwarts him at every turn!"

"He's *trying* to find a way to help without going head-to-head against Jamin," Mama said.

Ninsianna turned her face away so Mama wouldn't see her guilty expression. She'd feigned busyness when he'd asked to teach her.

"But I *have* been helping him—!" she gestured furiously at a pile of sticks. "I've been doing his laundry, cooking his meals. But all he cares about are his stupid sticks!"

Mikhail's "failed experiments" taunted her from their neatly stacked pile beside the oven. They were using them as firewood to cook tonight's supper.

"He needs your *help* to recruit people to try out his new weapon," Mama said.

"I've tried—!" she picked up a twig and shook it. "Jamin has ridiculed the weapon so badly that the only one who wants to train is Pareesa."

She didn't add that even *she* felt repulsed by his talk of learning "combat skills." Self-reliance was one thing, but to seek out trouble and get into a brawl? Even if she *could* convince the other women to abandon their feminine pursuits, how could a woman overpower a man?

"I've *seen* his sky canoe," Mama said. "He comes from a group of warriors so vast and powerful, I suspect it would dwarf the entire Ubaid tribe."

"He can't *remember* his past—"

"But he *knows* this," Mama's eyes bored into *hers*. "I've watched him stare at that necklace he wears—"

"They're called '*dog tags*.'"

"They prove he was part of something *big*. Something important enough that the goddess fears the Evil One shall come after *you*. And now he's part of nothing. So if you want him to *stay* here, you need to give him something *big* enough to replace whatever's still calling to him from the world he left behind."

"Like what?"

"Like preventing whatever happens in your vision."

"*Prevent* it?" she cried out. "It's a prophecy! There is no changing fate."

"It's a *warning*," Mama said. "Do you think it a coincidence you received the vision at the exact same time these strange men started raiding our allies?"

"But those are *human* men." She wrinkled her brow. "In the vision, I saw *crocodile*-men?"

"It's symbolic," Mama said. "They lurk at the edge of our villages, waiting to ambush us, like crocodiles in the river. That's what happened the day you were born."

"You dreamed of crocodile-men?"

"Serpents," Mama said. "The goddess sent your father visions about a serpent which crawled into our house and ate an egg."

"So how did he prevent it?" she asked.

"He didn't," Mama said. "Your grandfather, Lugalbanda, convinced him the vision had no merit. But on the night you were born, the enemies breached our walls by digging through a spot with weak bricks and slithered into the hole like snakes."

Ninsianna gasped. "Where was Papa?"

"Away!" Mama hissed. "Your father and Kiyan, back then he was still just the *Muhafiz*, and every *other* warrior in this village, were off fighting the Uruk."

"The men were *gone?*"

"Most of them, yes," Mama said. "And our enemies knew it, so they sent assassins to kill the leaders' families."

Ninsianna's eyes grew wide with horror.

"What did you do?"

"Me?" Mama scoffed. "I did nothing! I was writhing in labor. Jamin's mother held them off until old Behnam got here with some men and killed them."

Ninsianna twirled her hair. Her father had dreamed of serpents? And now *she* was dreaming of crocodile-men?

"If it's a warning," she asked, "then how can I prevent it?"

"In retrospect, your father realized the goddess had shown him the *exact* place where the serpent would find a way through."

"I thought grandfather was infallible?" Ninsianna asked.

"He was *powerful*," Mama scowled. "But he was hungry for power, and viewed women and children as sheep. So when Kiyan became the Chief, his first act was to alter the solstice ceremony to ban—" her face grew flushed. She turned away. "He changed things," she whispered. "He ordered that, from now on, the only sacrifice our daughters would make to appease Nergal would be to *compete*, just like the men do."

"With an atlatl?" Ninsianna laughed. "I thought he just wanted to encourage us to hunt?"

"The *atlatl* was the weapon his wife used to fend off the enemy." Mama jabbed at her chest. "The *last* thing those men expected was a woman with deadly aim."

Mama resumed furiously chopping onions. Why was she so angry? Perhaps it was because, tonight, she had nothing to feed them but lentils with onions because none of the families she'd helped this week had any meat to offer as "payment" for medical treatment? Until the great herds of antelope returned, the only meat to be had would be if somebody's goat broke a leg.

The wind picked up Mama's onion-skins and blew them across the yard, onto the pile of "failed arrows" which Mikhail had piled next to the oven to use as firewood. The papery skins rustled, like women gossiping, as they worked together harvesting their crops.

'Pay attention…' the wind whispered.

The sticks *glimmered* at the edge of her sight.

The wind picked up the onionskins. They rose, in V-shaped flight, like a flock of wild geese. With another gust, they flew across the yard and swirled around the cook-pot in a dance of golden-white sunlight.

A tingle of excitement shot down Ninsianna's spine.

"Mama! I have an idea!"

Chapter 104

July - 3,390 BC
Earth: Village of Assur
Colonel Mikhail Mannuki'ili

MIKHAIL

The villagers watched as they trudged past the training field; *him* laden down with dozens of arrows, while Pareesa walked beside him, carrying a half-dozen bows. Nearly three hundred warriors toiled beneath the hot summer sun, naked and sweaty except for their loincloths, stabbing at targets. The place reeked of sweat, testosterone and itchy balls.

"Ready," Jamin shouted. "Thrust!"

A large group of men moved to his command, armed with the fighting-spears; thicker and longer than the slender atlatl-darts preferred for hunting antelope.

"I didn't realize you had this many warriors," Mikhail said.

"We do," Pareesa said. "But most haven't fought since the war against the Uruk."

He took note of an older man who, despite his significant paunch, stabbed a target with the sturdy footing of somebody who, at one time, had obviously done battle.

Jamin bellowed at the third-tier warriors: "Aim for the face!"

The warriors thrust their spears upward at an imaginary opponent. Some niggling of training, he couldn't say if it came from the Alliance military, which he couldn't remember at *all*, or the Cherubim monks, of whom he could remember only snippets, took note of openings the warriors left available for counter-attack. His limbs tingled as he *pictured* performing a counter-move for every single stab.

"How many battles has Jamin been in?" he asked.

"I dunno—" Pareesa shrugged. "Most of the stuff they brag about is fighting lions or going after wild bulls."

His arch-nemesis moved through the ranks, insulting the lesser-warriors and praising the more proficient ones. When he got to the fat-man, he made a comment about the man's speed. The fat-man crouched into a sideways horse stance, and then exploded forward, thrusting out his spear—

—Jamin leaped back.

"Okay, okay!" He held up his hands.

The fat man grinned.

Jamin gripped the older man's hand, forearm to forearm.

"He used to be one of the Chief's men," Pareesa whispered. "They're the only men that Jamin can't bully."

Pareesa stared longingly at a group of boys who trained under one of the elite warriors—the ones who'd qualified *with* her at the solstice competition. Her younger brother now trained with them; having just "won" the right to train after a farce of a "qualification round."

"The Tribunal said that -*I'd*- won the right to train," she said mournfully.

"You *are* training," he said. "You're just doing it with *me*."

Around the field, the unmarried young women ogled the half-naked warriors and giggled about which one showed the most physical prowess.

Pareesa shot the women a baleful scowl.

"Why won't *they* train?" she asked.

"They said they're too busy—"

His wings drooped. Even Ninsianna had, thus far, manufactured excuses; generally "*I have to help the sick.*"

Jamin spotted them. With a hate-filled sneer, he picked up his own spear and ordered the warriors to stab their imaginary enemies in a fierce show of testosterone that made the solstice festival look tame.

"Crouch, STAB! Lion stance. BLOCK!"

As much as he hated to admit it, the spears looked far more "protective" than the bundle of slender arrows he held hoisted onto his shoulder.

"Hey, Pareesa," a young man taunted in between stabs. "How's your warrior training coming?"

"Better than *yours* is!" she shot back. "At least I can hit a target, which is more than I can say about *you*."

The men cat-called and made lewd comments about her newly-sprouting breasts. Pareesa pulled her shawl-dress tighter, causing it to slip off her shoulder and tangle around her feet. She caught herself before she tripped, but the bows went tumbling onto the ground.

Like a predator drawn to blood, Jamin stalked towards them.

"You expect to train *her* to defend this village?" he challenged.

"That was our *agreement*," Mikhail said evenly.

"Our *agreement*," Jamin snarled, "was that I'd show my father we're perfectly capable of defending our village so he'll forget his foolish notions about sending *women* to do a man's job." He jabbed a finger at Pareesa's dress. "And *you*... If you want to act like a man, at least gird up your loins!"

Pareesa opened her mouth to give a snappy retort. Mikhail touched her shoulder.

"He's the *Muhafiz*—" he said. "A soldier always obeys the chain of command."

Jamin shot him a look, utterly filled with hate. Feigning respect, if for no reason other than to irritate him, Mikhail tucked his feathers into a respectful dress-wings. With a bull-like snort, the Chief's son lumbered back into the thick of his warriors, barking orders about the proper way to kill.

"Move along," Mikhail murmured. "Once they see how good you are, maybe some of the women will want to train?"

"Who? *Them?*" Her voice warbled with hurt. "The only thing *they* want is to catch the eye of a future husband."

They traveled behind the obstacle course left over from the summer solstice festival. As they passed the tunnels, Jamin hoisted his spear and made a breathtakingly long throw to hit the target just in front of them.

With a lusty *'hoo-rah'*, the remaining warriors followed suit. Most of the spears fell short, but one thunked into the dirt in front of Pareesa.

"Hey!" she yelped.

"When you can throw a spear that far—" Jamin picked up another spear "—*then* I will train you."

Mikhail shoved her forward before she did something stupid, like attempt to use the new *'aikijujutsu'*[152] moves he'd been teaching her to compensate for her shorter height and lesser weight. Given time, he expected she'd learn to hold her own, but her fighting skills were nowhere *near* combat-ready.

They faded into the date-palm grove which grew protected by a series of levies; carefully nurtured with strategically placed goat manure. Softly rustling leaves and still-green dates shaded them from the hot summer sun.

"Why do you let him push you around?" Pareesa asked.

"Because I promised the Chief that I would not usurp his son."

"But you're *better* than he is!"

"Respect has to be earned," he said. "As much for *me*, as it must be earned for you."

He maneuvered the bundle of arrows through the fern-like branches. Just beyond the final levy, the river had receded enough to create a grassy field. They broke out of the date-palm orchard and—

Pareesa squealed.

"Homa! Gisou!"

She broke into a bounding hop towards two young women, dressed more appropriately for a feast than an afternoon spent sparring. All three girls threw their arms around one another and gave a delighted, high-pitched squeal.

---

[152] *Aikijujutsu:* an ancient martial art which is the parent of both jujutsu and aikido; both manipulate an opponent's own force against themselves rather than confronting it directly with one's own force.

Just behind them, Ninsianna stood like an alabaster goddess, wearing a smile like a cat that had just swallowed a bird. Her father, her best friend Yadidatum, and three middle-aged women also stood waiting, as well as the woodworker who'd helped him shape the bows.

Old Behnam gave him a toothless grin...

"Since I'm not as young as I used to be—" he held up his arm and pinched a bit of loose skin "—I thought, perhaps, it might let me hunt again?"

Mikhail scrunched his brow together in confusion.

"Hunt?"

"Yes." Ninsianna glided up next to him. "I promised our friends you would help us fill our cook-pots."

Her scent overwhelmed him, clean and feminine and something else—something which made his heart race.

"The Chief asked me to train *archers*," he said. "I know *little* about the habits of wild game."

"But you know how to *shoot* this weapon, don't you?" Behnam asked.

"Yes."

Ninsianna touched his arm. A *tingle* passed, pleasantly, into his chest.

"Well Behnam knows the habits of waterfowl," she said. "So we hoped—" she gestured at the other women "—you might teach us?"

Her smile grew strained. Even *he*, clueless dolt that he was when it came to human behavior, could read the plea in her eyes. *Let me help you salvage – something- from this failed experiment?*

Her father stood to one side with his arms crossed. The shaman had been less than pleased he'd offered to train *women* instead of insisting the Chief let him teach the men.

So, how could a man teach a weapon that he couldn't remember learning to perform a skill which he, himself, possessed little "local" knowledge?

"First, we'll learn to shoot," he said. "And then Behnam will help us adapt the skill to whatever you wish to hunt."

Immanu gave a grudging nod. While the shaman wasn't happy about it, his daughter had gotten six other women to show up, whereas he'd delivered absolutely none.

There was a festive atmosphere as Pareesa handed out the bows.

"Why don't we introduce ourselves?" Ninsianna said brightly.

"We already *know* each other," the oldest woman snapped, late into her forties. "Every single one of us owes your mother a favor."

Ninsianna winced. She shot him an apologetic look.

"Your family is *hungry*," she said. "Until your husband recovers, let *him* watch the children while *you* fill the cook-pot."

Mikhail's feathers rustled with discomfort. The older woman scowled, but then she turned to him.

"I'm Alalah," she held out her hand. "My husband lost his foot in a hunting accident. Needa saved his life."

"How many children do you have?" he asked.

"Eight," she said. "Although two of them are grown."

"Once we work the bugs out," he said, "perhaps you can teach your children to hunt?"

The woman nodded. She gestured to woman next to her, a dark-haired beauty in her twenties.

"This is Kiana," Alalah said. "She's recently widowed. Three kids, one still on the breast."

Tears welled in the younger woman's eyes.

"We just moved back from Eshnunna," Kiana said. "My husband was killed in the raid. My parents took us in, but they're so poor—"

She began to sob.

"It's okay," Ninsianna moved to comfort the widow. "Mikhail will teach you how to hunt so you won't be a burden."

Mikhail tucked his wings against his back as Ninsianna introduced the remaining women: her best friend, Yadidatum; a woman in her thirties named Orkedah, and then Homa and Gisou, two giggly teenage girls who appeared more interested in getting out of household chores than learning to fend off kidnappers. With Pareesa, that made eight, ten if he included old Behnam and Ninsianna's father. These were not the eager warriors he'd envisioned teaching, but all seemed interested filling their cook-pots.

Ninsianna sidled next to him, earning a glower from her father.

"Thank you," she murmured.

"For what?" he asked.

"Agreeing to teach them," she whispered. "Papa thinks it's beneath you, but Behnam thought it might be a good idea."

The shaman harbored grandiose notions. Why couldn't he grasp that *he* felt like just as much of a "burden" as the women who'd come to train because their children were hungry? At least, this way, he could supply their family with meat.

And then maybe he could ask—

No! Until he had something to offer, he would *not* demean her with so paltry a prospect as absolute nobody. For goddess' sake, he couldn't even remember his own name!

He turned abruptly, ignoring her hurt expression, and counted out thirty paces from the target, an easy hit, but a good distance for an absolute beginner.

"Ladies," he said, "I trust that someone has told you about my condition?"

"You can't remember your past," Alalah said. "Needa said it won't affect your ability to teach?"

Mikhail grabbed one of the bows; carved from river-willow, and nocked[153] an almond-wood arrow. He drew back the sinew to his ear, took aim, and let the arrow fly. With an ominous *whoosh*, it slammed into a dark splotch he'd rubbed into the center of the target to mark the quarry's heart and shattered.

All of the women gasped.

"It *does* affect my ability to teach," he confessed. "I can't remember how I *learned*, so you'll have to be *honest* when you don't understand something so I can make sure I teach you all of the steps."

Old Behnam squinted at the target: "How small of an object can you hit?"

Mikhail nocked another arrow.

"I'm out of practice, but—" he spied a gerbil dart out of a clump of grass. He let loose the arrow. The women gave him a perplexed look until Pareesa ran out, fetched the arrow, and held it up with the now-dead rodent on the end.

"You're getting better," she grinned.

"And you still stink," he said. "So line them up and let's teach them what we know."

---

[153] *Nock:* a notch cut into the end of an arrow to fit into the bowstring; or the notch at either end of a bow to string the sinew.

Chapter 105

義

Galactic Standard Date: 152,323.06 AE
Earth: Sata'an Forward Operating Base
Lieutenant Kasib

Lt. KASIB

The Algol-class ship hovered over the airfield. Long and sleek, she was a whole lot of engine and not a lot of cargo room, but she could move from one end of the galaxy to the other in a matter of weeks, evading most blockades and outrunning all but the fastest energy weapons. She set down lightly, despite, it was rumored, running largely on pilot skill rather than the advanced computer systems which powered the rest of the Sata'anic navy.

Kasib fidgeted next to a disembarkment crew led by Master-Sergeant Dahaka, the general's most trusted advisor despite his modest rank. Even though, technically, Kasib outranked the burly lizard, the respect one was given in the Sata'anic military was tied to how many battles you had won. Judging by his battle-scarred green and beige striped hide, Dahaka had won quite a few.

"I wonder what they brought?" Kasib clutched his flatscreen.

"Hopefully power cores for the pulse rifles and the shuttles," the big lizard said.

"I'm more worried about *food*," Kasib admitted.

"Just give me more power cores," Dahaka shot him a mercenary grin, "and we'll have this planet civilized in no time."

Kasib twisted his tail like a fidgety cadet. There was always a lot at stake when you were stationed at a remote outpost. One never knew what might come in on a merchant mariner vessel, especially one with a reputation for gun-running.

The cargo-hatch lowered, revealing Lieutenant Apausha and his flight crew. The three lizards marched down the ramp to give Kasib, and then Sergeant Dahaka, a crisp salute. The pilot addressed Sergeant Dahaka, not Kasib.

"Sir," Apausha said, "We've returned from the general's errand."

"Was Shay'tan pleased?" Dahaka asked.

"*Very* pleased," Apausha said. "So much so, that he gifted all three of us wives."

"Really?" Kasib broke in with a sputter.

"Really," Apausha said.

Kasib asked, awe-struck: "Did you get meet our god in *person*?"

"Yes." Apausha's maw split into a fang-laden grin. "He performed our wedding ceremonies, *personally*. He is even more terrifying, and glorious, than the propaganda says."

"Shay'tan be praised!"

The entire disembarkment crew made the Sata'anic prayer-gesture. Oh, what Kasib wouldn't give to earn such praise from their Emperor and god!

"We'll unload the ship," Dahaka said, "while the *Lieutenant—*" unlike *most* skullcrackers, there was no sneer of derision as he gestured at Kasib "—will take you to speak with the general."

Apausha's two crewmen stayed behind to help unload the ship. Kasib led the pilot through the base to the primitive stone temple which was now General Hudhafah's office. The General rose up immediately to shake the merchant mariner's hand. Lieutenant Apausha gave the general a crisp salute.

"It's good to see you again, Sir."

"What did you bring us?" Hudhafah asked.

"Gold, Sir," Apausha said. "Ba'al Zebub filled our hold."

Hudhafah picked up his flatscreen and pulled up a copy of the requisition list which he'd sent to Ba'al Zebub.

"What about the power supplies I asked for?" Hudhafah asked.

"He didn't give us any, Sir." Apausha said.

"Weapons cores?"

"Nope."

"Some fuel?"

"No, Sir. He didn't give us any."

"How about that drilling equipment I asked for?"

Apausha's expression became strained.

"Nothing, Sir. Nothing like that."

The General's dewlap turned purple-red.

"Grain?" he asked. "We're getting awfully low on food."

"No, Sir," Apausha said. "He didn't send any."

"How about the medical supplies? Kerosene? Some lamp oil?"

"He didn't send *anything*, Sir, except for *gold*. He wants me to exchange it for as many women as you've been able to train."

"Shay'tan's foot!" Hudhafah slammed his fist upon the desk. "Gold won't power our pulse-rifles or spaceships!"

Kasib nervously flicked out his long, forked tongue. The general's anger-pheromones were rising. He knew, better than anyone, how *desperate* they were for resupply.

"Our glorious Emperor is sending an armada," Apausha said. "He ordered Lord Ba'al Zebub to send *'everything you need, including the kitchen sink.'* You're just going to make due until it gets here."

Kasib jumped as the general knocked his paperwork off his desk. Apausha didn't flinch. Kasib rushed over to pick it up.

"How long?" General Hudhafah growled.

"I don't know, Sir," Apausha said. "We weren't privy to that conversation. But we overheard Shay'tan order him to secure this planet at any cost."

General Hudhafah paced, muttering underneath his breath. "*Stupid politicians!*"

Kasib tidied up the paperwork. It wasn't the merchant mariner's fault that Ba'al Zebub had screwed them. Shay'tan used them to evade the Alliance. Right now, Apausha was this base's only lifeline, something that Ba'al Zebub *knew* when he'd sent the lizards back empty-handed.

It was an old Sata'anic trick, to leave your men *no choice* but to stand and fight to the death…

Hudhafah gripped his desk so tightly that his claws dug into the wood.

"So *when* does our glorious Emir," Hudhafah said with a sarcastic sneer, "want these women?"

"Right away, Sir," Apausha said. "As soon as you can unload the gold, he'll take as many women as you can, quote, 'beg, borrow or steal.'"

A ripple of fear clenched at Kasib's gut. What about Taram? He still hadn't figured out how to send her home?

"The last one must have made one hell of an impression," General Hudhafah said. "I take it Shay'tan liked her?"

"Very much, Sir."

"So now our Emperor has a forty-seventh wife?"

Apausha tasted the air nervously with his long, forked tongue.

"No, Sir."

"No?"

"No, Sir. He gave her as a gift."

"To whom?"

"The Alliance Prime Minster, Sir."

Kasib froze in horror as the General's dewlap turned a raging shade of purple. His dorsal ridge shot up. He bared his fangs.

"He gave her to *Lucifer?*"

"Yes, Sir."

Kasib hit the deck.

General Hudhafah smashed his desk in half.

Chapter 106

July - 3,390 BC
Earth: Village of Assur
Colonel Mikhail Mannuki'ili

MIKHAIL

The archers met each night after the evening meal. With the days so long, Mikhail had two hours before it grew too dark to teach. Behnam unveiled his newest iteration of a bow.

"For you," he said proudly.

"Yew wood?" Mikhail guessed.

"We found a grove across the river," Behnam said. "It should be enough for several dozen bows."

Mikhail held up the bow and admired Behnam's handiwork. At two meters long, it was half a meter longer than the ones he'd crafted for the women. Both end-nocks were reinforced with animal horn to seat the bowstring, while the grip was painstakingly wrapped with leather to create a flat arrow-plate. He ran his hand along the warm, golden wood. It felt smooth to the touch, without a single snag.

"You used rottenstone?"[154] he asked.

Behnam grinned. "You remember your woodworking lessons?"

Mikhail glanced over at Ninsianna's father, who stood with his arms crossed, his expression skeptical. After two weeks of broken bows and shattered arrows, he'd done *little* to reassure the shaman that teaching women archery was any more of a path to success than learning flint-knapping or mastering wood-working.

The women clustered around them, admiring the new bows.

"Shoot it?" Ninsianna said.

"Hand me an arrow?"

She handed him one of the longer arrows. They had many sizes and shapes, since they were still experimenting with which ones were most effective. While the women usually managed *not* to snap their bows, with his greater strength, he had a bad habit of breaking every bow that Behnam had carved for him thus far.

"Here goes." He took aim at the furthest target. Drawing it back, he really had to *pull* to get it back to his ear.

---

[154] *Rottenstone:* a fine, porous rock, such as limestone, sandstone or pumice; used for sanding wood.

"This isn't one for the ladies," he said.

"Speak for yourself!" Pareesa chimed in.

"You'll see," he promised.

He let the arrow fly. While the first arrow hit off-center, the second hit the bullseye. He grabbed three more arrows and shot them in rapid succession.

"Ooh!" the women sighed.

Ninsianna grinned.

Her father nodded. Perhaps he might *finally* win the shaman over?

"How does it feel?" Behnam asked.

"Nice and springy." He set one end against the ground and gently bent it into a "D" shape until the bowstring sagged, and then let it snap back up. It sprang readily, without an ominous crack. "I think this might be the one."

"I'm glad," Behnam said, "because if that one doesn't work, I'm afraid we're out of options."

Mikhail handed Pareesa the bow. She nocked an arrow and drew it three-quarters of the way back, but couldn't quite make it to her cheek.

"Drat!" she pulled mightily.

"You need to develop more upper body strength," he said.

"How do I do that?"

"Lots of practice."

He took the bow back and turned to Ninsianna.

"Remember the test you suggested earlier?"

Ninsianna gave him a heart-melting smile.

"I came prepared."

She reached into her satchel and pulled out a variety of objects. Pareesa handed him arrows while Ninsianna threw each bauble into the air. One by one, he practiced shooting until he'd *refreshed* his muscle memory about what, exactly, he hoped to teach today.

"Okay," he said. "I think I've got it."

"How to hunt supper?" Alalah asked hopefully.

"We'll start by hunting *those*," he pointed at five duck-shaped targets that he'd set up at the end of the field. "Once we get good enough, Behnam will teach us how to hunt."

The women buzzed around him like excited bees, grabbing their new bows and filling their quivers up with arrows. For the first time in two weeks, Ninsianna's father appeared something other than bored.

"Let's move closer to the targets," Mikhail said. "In two weeks, you should be able to shoot them from here. Ladies, string your bows."

The women struggled to insert the sinew into the notches of the much more springy bows at either end, no easy task. They did so with determined expressions.

"Ouch!" Yadidatum exclaimed as the sinew slipped her grasp and thwacked her in the leg. "That hurt!"

Mikhail showed her how to push down on the bow, rather than pull up on the sinew, to get it strung. And then he demonstrated:

"Grip your bow like this, with your non-dominant hand. This is your aiming hand—" the archers followed his example. "Put your arm straight out, at a right angle to your body. If you don't hold your arm straight, you won't *shoot* straight."

He glanced at Ninsianna, always aware of her presence. Between visiting the flint-knapper to design arrowheads, the butcher to get sinew and feathers, and trips into the sparse underbrush to harvest wood, two weeks been lost. He'd had no time to woo her.

"Now, put three fingers on the string *beneath* the notch, like this," he said. "Be careful not to bend the fletching. The feathers make your arrow fly straight."

Pareesa plucked at the fletching with curious fingers.

"Are these *your* feathers?" she asked.

"No," he said bluntly.

"They sure *look* like your feathers."

He rustled his feathers.

"You're not going to pluck me."

Pareesa grinned. The little imp was always scurrying behind him, picking up whatever he molted which, in this godawful heat, was pretty much all the time.

He turned to the other archers.

"Draw back your arm all the way to your cheek … like this. Your three fingers should line up along your chin."

The archers pulled back the sinew with eager awkwardness.

"Oops!" Ninsianna's string slipped her fingers. Her arrow sprang out and onto the ground. She gave him a sheepish look. "Sorry."

A flash of a memory, *him* making the exact same mistake the first time he'd taken up the bow, caused him to almost grin.

"That will happen until you build up more strength in your fingers," he said. "For now, don't aim at anything you don't want to hit."

He handed Immanu his bow.

"Try this one?"

"You said it draws too heavy."

"Too heavy for a *woman*," Mikhail said. "A *man* should be able to draw a bigger bow."

For the first time, the shaman appeared enthusiastic. His tawny-beige eyes sparkled as he nocked an arrow and pulled it back towards his cheek.

"You're right. It *is* a heavy draw."

"Would you rather use a lighter bow?"

Immanu grunted as he forced the bowstring back to his cheek.

"No need."

He walked behind them, correcting their stances as they drew their bows with serious intent. He divided them into groups since he only had five targets.

"Look down the arrow and line it up with your target. Where you look, that's the direction your arrow will fly. Ready, aim .... shoot!"

Yadidatum's hit the ground a few feet in front of her. She'd been practicing for a week and had *yet* to hit the target. Pareesa hit a perfect bullseye, but the arrow bounced off without sticking. Behnam hit the straw beneath the target, not bad for an elderly man. His aim was getting better. Orkedah hit the bale of straw underneath the mock-duck, while Ninsianna's father knocked his duck right off its bale of hay.

"Whoo!" Immanu shouted.

"Great shot," Mikhail congratulated him. "Yadidatum ... don't close your eyes when you release your arrow. That's why it fell flat. Orkedah, we'll work on building your upper body so you can get more distance. Pareesa, Behnam, nice job."

The archers congratulated and slapped each other on the back. The other half of the women stepped up: Alalah, Gisou, Homa, Kiana, and of course, Ninsianna. Mikhail coached them how to shoot, with similar results. Alalah, the oldest, hit the bullseye.

"Nice shot," Mikhail complemented her. "Switch!"

They took turns over the next two hours. Towards the end, they began to cheer and joke, even Ninsianna's skeptical father. Satisfied that, *at last*, things appeared to be on the correct track, Mikhail switched to something far less sexy.

"Now it's time to do some strength training," he said. "Did everybody bring their buckets?"

Pareesa groaned. He'd been making her do strength-training for her *jujutsu* lessons and it was her *least* favorite part of the lesson. They filled them with water, and then he explained how to target different muscle groups. The women twittered as he moved through each exercise and demonstrated, on his own body, where it made each muscle flex. Behnam vigorously lifted his two buckets with all of his might.

"It's not a competition," Mikhail said.

"I can't let the young ladies get the better of me—" Behnam flashed a toothless grin. "A man's got to have his pride!"

Mikhail suppressed a grin. Although he couldn't remember what he'd done back in wherever it was that he'd come from, teaching seemed to come more naturally than milking the goat. He showed the archers how to build up their pectoral, back and triceps muscles.

"My arms are about to fall off," Homa complained.

"Do you think this will make my boobs look bigger," Gisou asked. She turned pink with mortification when she realized he'd heard her.

"I don't get it," Yadidatum complained. "I keep getting water on my dress."

"It might help if you imagine your arms are wings." Mikhail demonstrated the proper form. "You want to flap smoothly, just like an eagle."

Pareesa giggled. "Like *your* wings?"

"I don't have hands on my wings," he replied with a deadpan expression. "I have to lift with my arms the same as everybody else."

This response struck the young women as hilarious. Raphael used to think everything was funny like this…

Raphael? He stopped to coax the memory out of his scrambled subconscious.

"Mikhail?" Ninsianna came up beside him. "Are you okay?"

Flashes about basic training flitted through his mind. He grasped at the memories like a man grasping at fireflies; most of them escaped, but a few ended up in the jar.

"They're waiting for you to finish the lesson," Ninsianna said.

"Sorry," he came back to the present. "I was thinking about a friend."

"A memory?"

"Yes … a good one."

He glanced down at Ninsianna. What little concentration he had left disappeared in a puff of longing. Her earthy scent *did* things to his brain.

What had he been doing again?

"Buckets … water … upper body strength to draw the bow," her father prompted.

"Oh, yeah, right," he said. "From now on, ladies and gentlemen, every time you fetch water, I want you to do these exercises. Not only will you build upper body strength, but you'll also get your daily chores done."

They lifted water until the sun began to race for the horizon. Mikhail gestured at the village perched above them on the cliff.

"I'll see you all here at the exact same time tomorrow."

The archers bid him farewell.

Ninsianna gathered up her things and ran off with her healer's basket, anxious to make her final house call before it got dark. Rather than fly off, he walked with Immanu back towards the village.

"That new bow appears to have done the trick," Immanu said.

"Needa suggested it."

"The yew wood?"

"Yes."

"She knows quite a bit about the properties of plants," Immanu said.

They fell into silence as the exited the date-palm grove and crossed the field where Jamin and his most ardent students stabbed at man-shaped targets. In response to their appearance, Jamin called out:

"Turn to the right." The warriors all turned to face Mikhail. "Ready position, crouch, STAB!"

With a vicious "Hoo-rah!" the warriors all thrust their spears at Mikhail.

Immanu called out:

"You shouldn't—"

Mikhail put his hand on Immanu's arm.

"I can fight my own battles," he murmured.

"You shouldn't let him *disrespect* you."

"I'll earn his respect when I *produce*," Mikhail said. "Something that's possible now that I have a working bow."

He fingered the brand new yew-bow that Behnam had crafted for him. Immanu's eyes lit up. He'd won the shaman over, now he had to win over the others. He didn't care if he had to practice all night, he would *perfect* his aim so that he never missed.

Both men fell silent until they escaped the *Muhafiz's* hateful gaze. The road was empty as they climbed the hill beneath the north gate.

Do it... his subconscious whispered.

Mikhail cleared his throat.

"Sir?"

The shaman looked at him, his expression interested.

"When we first met," Mikhail said, "you made me give you a promise. Do you remember?"

"I do." A deep smile line appeared on Immanu's cheek.

"I'm afraid I made a promise that I cannot keep." He held his breath, praying the shaman wasn't angry, and then continued, "I would like your *permission* to ask Ninsianna to become my wife?"

Immanu's mouth split into a broad grin.

"That's up to Ninsianna." He glanced over the fields, back towards where Jamin continued to train his men. "I learned my lesson the *last* time I tried to force her affections. What does *she* say?"

"I haven't asked her yet," Mikhail said. "I thought it appropriate to ask you *first*."

Immanu slapped him on the back of the wings.

"When will you ask her?"

"I'm not sure what your customs are," he said. "I want to do this right."

Immanu's expression grew tender.

"Ninsianna's mother comes from Gasur—" he gestured towards the distant hills. "She was apprenticed to their healer, so her entire village feared I might lure her away. I had to woo her without anybody knowing."

"How did you win her heart?"

"I used every excuse to make the journey. I had to sneak in under the guise of trade, so I would bring her things. Game I had hunted, food I had gathered, and small animals carved from wood. Things to *prove* I could provide for a wife."

"Obviously you were successful?"

"At first she was merely amused," Immanu said, "but finally I convinced her to come for a picnic by the Khasa River[155]. By then, I was in training to become a shaman, so I taught her how to close her eyes and go into the dreamtime."

"You said it was forbidden for women to do that?"

"Healers use the dreamtime to diagnose their patients," Immanu said. 'They just don't realize that is what they are doing."

"So how did you finally convince her to become your wife?"

Immanu gave him a cryptic smirk.

"She-Who-Is showed her that it was meant to be."

"I don't think She-Who-Is will intervene on *my* behalf," Mikhail frowned.

"I think *SHE* already has," Immanu said. "Or you wouldn't be alive."

---

[155] *Khasa River:* a seasonal tributary of the Tigris (Hiddekel) River.

Chapter 107

July - 3,390 BC
Earth: Village of Assur

JAMIN

He stayed at the training field, long after Ninsianna had run past and *refused* to speak to him, even after he'd called out her name. Long after the other archers had passed by, laughing, as though they found something funny. Long after the Angelic, and his pet shaman had slithered by. Long after the warriors *he'd* been teaching had left.

He continued practicing as the shadows lengthened into darkness; as the bats came out and began chasing insects; as hyenas laughed in the distance. Soon, he'd prove that his way was the best, and then he'd get the Angelic *out* of his village.

He hefted another spear…

Thwunk

It only hit the *edge* of the charcoal heart that he'd smeared onto the straw-man. Dead-center meant dead. Less than dead-center meant, well, he'd *seen* the scar on the winged demon's chest when he'd stripped off his shirt and run the gauntlet on what *should* have been *his* wedding day.

The hair reared up on the back of his neck.

He calculated the intruder's size and distance.

The air after a thunderstorm…

"Gita," he stared into the twilight. "You shouldn't lurk in shadows."

She stepped out of the date-palm grove where she'd been watching the archers; so emaciated and thin that he could snap her neck. If it'd been anybody else, he'd clock them over the head to teach them not to sneak up on him; though if it'd been anyone else, he'd have seen them coming from a quarter *bêru*[156] away. The girl always *had* possessed a gift for remaining invisible. Given her father's violent rages, she didn't have much of a choice.

"How did you know I was here?" she asked.

"I just *knew*."

"You're the only person who ever *sees* me."

"It's my *job*—" he grabbed a spear from the dwindling pile "—to watch over this village. I'm not going to let some *demon* replace me!"

---

[156] *Bêru:* a league, or 3.45 nautical miles.

He hurled the spear with every ounce of hatred he could muster. He aimed too high, knocking off some crow feathers he'd stuck up to mimic Mikhail's wings. They floated in the air, taunting him with their flight.

A feather floated over to Gita's outstretched hand.

"It's not *his* fault the goddess sent him here to protect us."

"Protect us?" he whirled to face her. "What do you know of the goddess' intentions?"

"The priestesses had legends—"

"You mean fairy tales?" he snarled, "painted on a brothel wall."

"They were more than that."

"Then maybe you should go back there?" he said. "And bring Shahla! She'll fit right in with the "sacred" whores!"

Ignoring her hurt expression, he grabbed his best spear and hurled it with all of his might. They'd always had an understanding, him and Gita; because only *she* understood what it was like to watch your mother die. The spear pierced the emmer-stalks he'd bound together to make a straw-man and came out the other side.

"She's not *worthy* of your love," Gita said. "This anger will destroy you."

"He *took* her from me!" he cried out in anguish. "He *took* her before I had a chance to make amends! And now? Now he's got my *father* under his spell!"

"He's not here to *replace* you," Gita said. "He's here to make you better."

"Better?" he shouted. "Better than *this*?"

He grabbed his lion-teeth necklace and clenched it in his fist. Not even his *father* had ever killed a lion using nothing but a knife.

Gita held out the feather, purplish-black, from an ordinary rook. It matched the bruise which Immanu had smashed into her face at the solstice festival with a cleverly hidden rock so he could help Ninsianna beat her – as usual – by cheating.

"She's not worthy of -*his*- love, either," Gita said. "Just you wait and see…"

A deep sense of *knowing* resonated all the way down into Jamin's bones. Merariy claimed her mother's people had possessed the gift of prophecy. *His* mother's people, if the whispers he'd overheard the night Immanu's stark raving mad brother had reappeared in their village were true. His father had been in a fog of grief, having just lost his mother and baby sister. It had been *him* who'd ordered the warriors to allow Immanu's estranged brother—and his traumatized five-year-old daughter—back into the tribe. Not Immanu. And not his father who, for *some* reason, hated the bitter drunk even more than his own brother did.

He looked away, unable to meet Gita's gaze. When he looked back again, she'd disappeared into the lengthening shadows.

Picking up another spear, he took aim…
…and hurled it…
……straight at his enemy's heart.

Chapter 108

July – 3,390 BC
Earth: Village of Assur
Colonel Mikhail Mannuki'ili

MIKHAIL

"Mikhail," Pareesa called out. "Oh Mikhail?"

His youngest archer jabbed him in the wing.

Mikhail startled.

"Sorry," he apologized. "I was just … thinking."

He stared longingly at the lovely visage which tested her bow, her arm lined up in perfect symmetry with her luscious breasts.

"Yeah," his impish sidekick joked. "I know *exactly* what you are thinking! You drifted off mid-sentence."

The other students laughed at his absent-mindedness. Ever since his conversation with Immanu, he'd been having a hard time keeping his baser impulses under control. He glanced at his hoped-to-be father-in-law, who gave him a knowing look. Mikhail forced his thoughts back down onto the planet.

"Today we shall put our skills to the test," he said. "Since I have no experience hunting ducks, Behnam will lead us."

The wizened old carpenter gave them a toothless grin. Although heavily wrinkled, with knobby knees and thick-knuckled hands prone to rheumatism, Mikhail suspected the Tribunal member would hold his own in the modern world which he'd come from, the one he couldn't remember. Behnam quickly apprised the women about the animal they were about to hunt, where they could find it, and some tips about navigating, silently, through the terrain. The old man led their merry band upriver.

The oldest female archer, Alalah, always asked practical questions.

"How quickly will they take flight?" Alalah asked.

"Ask *him*," Mikhail gestured at the carpenter.

"The birds are skittish," Behnam said. "They are wary of nets, but they've never been hunted with *these* weapons—" he held up the elaborately carved bow which he'd fashioned with his own hand. "Once they see their comrade's fall, the entire flock will take to the air."

"How quickly would *you* take flight?" Yadidatum asked Mikhail.

"I'm a soldier," he said. "I wouldn't let you near me in the first place."

"Doesn't it bother you to shoot birds?" Gisou asked.

"Why would it?"

"I mean, you, well..." She pointed at his wings.

Ninsianna chortled back a laugh. Behind him, Pareesa flapped her arms.

"Quack!"

Mikhail paused, pondering her question. It had never occurred to him that he might share DNA with the avian population.

"I'm not sure *what* I'm descended from," he said, "but I definitely don't quack."

The others giggled, causing his mouth to twitch upwards.

"If he's descended from *anything*," Ninsianna said, "it would be the eagles."

Behnam shushed them. The old men had led them to a bend in the river which opened up into a natural cove. The air felt redolent and moist as they approached the tall reeds.

"Step softly—" the old man pointed at the soggy soil. "Be careful not to splash. We'll crouch the last few feet."

"And watch out for crocodiles," Ninsianna added nervously.

Mikhail reached into the quiver he'd fashioned from a woven-grass basket and selected an arrow. Over the last few weeks, he'd made many modifications to his design.

"String your bows," he ordered.

Not exactly *silent*, the archers strung their bows and then slipped, *almost* noiselessly, into the reeds. The air smelled earthy, and musty, and slightly briny. Just beyond the wall of reeds, a flock of ducks "quack-quacked", along with the honk of an occasional goose.

"Eeewww...." Homa and Gisou said simultaneously as they sank into the silky, black mud up to their thighs. The mud smelled faintly of rotten eggs.

Pareesa sped forward, oblivious to the muck.

Ninsianna crept slowly, stabbing the reeds with an arrow.

"What are you *doing*?" he asked.

"Checking for crocodiles."

They reached a spot where the reeds had been squashed flat. In the middle sat a mound of reeds.

"Wait," he ordered.

The women hung back while he, Immanu and Behnam probed the water surrounding the makeshift island. It smelled slightly fishy, as if something had been hauled in here to die.

"She's gone," Behnam said.

"How do you know it was a girl?" Pareesa asked.

"See this?" Behnam picked up a tiny, shed skin. "This came from her offspring."

"Be careful," Immanu warned. "A mother crocodile is absolutely ferocious."

Mikhail took the lead, followed by Immanu and Behnam. While he was no expert in crocodiles, from his automatic urge to scan the water, at some point he *must* have engaged in jungle combat.

Pareesa grumbled: "We don't need you to protect us."

"Speak for yourself," Gisou said.

"We're here to learn to fight," Pareesa said.

"*You're* here to learn to fight," Gisou said. "I'm here to catch something to eat."

Alalah jabbed Gisou with the butt-end of her bow. "If you bring home a nice, fat duck, your family will stop complaining."

The reeds grew thinner. Just beyond them, the water opened up into a small cove created where a seasonal *wadi* emptied into the Hiddekel River. Paddling around, safe from any predator that couldn't swim, sat an enormous flock of ducks.

"I can taste roast duck already," Immanu whispered.

"Then you'd better let your daughter cook it," Behnam joked, "not your wife."

"Maybe I *like* burnt duck?" Immanu chuckled.

"You just don't like getting banished to the goat shed," Behnam jibed.

Mikhail used hand-signals to get the women to fan out. The ducks quacked nervously, but few predators could follow them into the water fast enough to catch them. The archers crouched down between the reeds and strung their bows.

"Not yet," Mikhail said. "We need to shoot all at once."

Ostensibly he ordered this so the ducks wouldn't fly away after a single, errant shot, but the *real* reason he'd installed military-style discipline into this "hunt" was because he was determined, no matter *what* the women's motivation was for showing up, to transform them into the "army" he'd promised the Chief.

Ninsianna's best friend Yadidatum fumbled with her bow.

"Face the cock[157] away from the bow," Ninsianna pointed at her fletching, "so it doesn't hit the grip."

Mikhail held his breath while Yadidatum got her arrow nocked into the bowstring. Poverty or some other form of desperation had driven every *other* woman in this group to show up, but Yadidatum didn't *need* to fill her family's cook pot. If he could convince *her* to learn how to protect herself, then maybe *she* could convince the other women?

---

[157] *Cock* and *hens:* the three parts of an arrow's fletching (feathers). The *cock* faces away from the bow, while the two V-shaped *hens* face towards it so the arrow can pass the bow without hanging up.

Yadidatum took aim at a nice, fat duck. Ninsianna shot him a look of relief. One by one, the other archers took careful aim.

Mikhail scanned the terrain. A plump, brightly-colored male beat up on a small, brown female. It reminded him of Jamin...

'You...' He pulled the bow back until the string hummed next to his cheek.

"Shoot!" he shouted.

He took his first shot.

The mallard dropped dead with a squeak.

He reached into his quiver for a second arrow. Ten more arrows whistled through the air.

"I got one!" Pareesa shouted.

"I did too!" shouted Alalah.

The water erupted in a chaotic dance of wings as panicked ducks tried to get airborne.

"They're taking flight!" Behnam shouted.

Mikhail took a second shot.

He glanced at Ninsianna. She wore a look of intense determination. A lump rose in his throat as she drew back her bowstring and released a second arrow.

"Whoo!" she shouted as a duck fell out of the air.

Mikhail reached into his quiver and nocked a third arrow. He shot straight up at a retreating duck. The bird fell onto Pareesa's head.

"Hey!" she shouted.

She nocked an arrow and shot another duck.

Mikhail reached for a fourth arrow, but the ducks were already out of range. Dead and dying ducks littered the water; enough to prove the worth of archery practice to their begrudging families.

"Alright, that's enough!" he shouted. "Don't waste arrows on long shots."

They waded into the open water, swimming to retrieve their supper before the current carried it downstream.

"Find your arrows," Behnam said, "or I'll make you fashion the next batch yourselves."

They retrieved their arrows and dog-paddled back to shore. The men fanned out, forming a protective circle around the women as they pushed back through the wall of reeds in case any crocodiles had been attracted to the scent of blood. They made their way back to the archery range and dropped the ducks.

"How many did we get?" Ninsianna asked.

Alalah counted the ducks while Behnam sorted out the arrows. Mikhail had made them mark them in unique patterns so they would always know which arrow belonged to whom.

"I got one!" Yadidatum squealed victoriously.

"I got three," Behnam said, "and I didn't lose any arrows."

"I got four," Alalah announced.

"That's one more than Mikhail," Behnam laughed.

"Hey," Gisou complained. "You should share!"

"I've got eight kids to feed," Alalah said sternly. "If you want to *get* more, then maybe you should *practice* more, instead of socializing with Homa all the time?"

Mikhail pretended to scratch his nose, rather than laugh. Alalah, in many ways, reminded him of Needa.

"I got two," Kiana said. "Enough to feed my kids and parents."

"I only got one," Homa lamented. "I've got four brothers and sisters, my parents, and my grandmother."

"Mikhail took three shots and got three ducks," Behnam said. "You took four shots and lost three arrows."

"I'll just make more," Homa said.

"You mean *I'll* make more," Behnam said crossly. "I think our *next* lesson should be *'how to make your own arrows.'*"

Homa groaned…

"Maybe if you practice more," Alalah said, "your parents won't nag you to clean the house?"

"Why do you think I'm *here*?" Homa laughed. "If they can't see me, they can't order me to clean up after my brothers!"

"I got two," Orkedah said, "just the right amount to feed my kids."

The rest of the women piled seven ducks at his feet. Three that *he* had shot, plus Immanu and Ninsianna had each shot two.

"That's a lot of ducks." Ninsianna gave him an expectant look.

"I'd like to give one to Yalda and Zhila," he suggested.

"That's still a lot of ducks."

"Why don't we present two of them to the Chief," her father suggested.

Jamin kept thwarting him, while the women's families were giving some pushback. What better way to ensure his continued place in this village than to make sure the only person who *approved* of this endeavor got something out of it, other than an earful of grief from his son?

"That would leave us with four ducks," he said. "Why don't we keep two, and give the other two to somebody who didn't catch enough?"

Ninsianna's mouth broadened into an approving smile.

They set the two fattest ducks aside for the Chief, including the cruel mallard which had been the first to fall. The women divided up the rest to make sure everybody had enough.

Pareesa grabbed the two fattest ducks.

"I can't wait to see Jamin's face when I hand these to the Chief." She owed the pompous jerk payback, as well as the cruel boys who'd locked her out of training.

In a merry mood, the archers headed towards the village.

"Aren't you coming?" Behnam asked.

"Mikhail has *other* quarry to catch," Immanu said.

The two men gave him a knowing look. Mikhail rustled his feathers. Did *everybody* know what he was about to do? The two men laughed as they gathered up their hunting equipment and headed after the women, leaving him and Ninsianna alone.

"Jamin will spit stones when Pareesa presents his father with those ducks," she said. "You realize the little mischief maker will do it so that the entire village sees?"

"What upsets Jamin isn't my problem."

She slipped her arms around his waist.

"Chief Kiyan enjoys gifts," she laughed. "He'll be pleased with the ducks, and also that his experiment is paying off."

Mikhail's heart began to race.

Ask her. ASK her!!!

She pressed her ear against his chest so she could hear his heartbeat. Mikhail encircled her in his wings, but the words wouldn't come. Instead, he nuzzled her hair.

"Will you teach me how to shoot long-distance?" she asked.

She looked down the field at the furthest target, the one which only *he* could hit, wearing that dreamy expression she often wore when half of her mind was *here*, and the other half was off in a daydream.

"Certainly--" he picked up *his* bow, a longer bow with a thicker string. "Hold it the way I showed you."

He moved behind her to help her aim, relishing the close proximity of his body to hers. She aimed too low, just short of the target. He ran his fingers along the underside of her forearm to nudge it up into the correct angle.

"You have to aim high to account for the drop," he said.

"Like this?"

"Yes. You should always aim higher than you intend to hit."

He held his left hand in place, just barely touching the underside of her wrist to encourage her to maintain the correct form. With his right, he reached around to touch her drawing hand. His hand lingered on hers.

"Now draw it the rest of the way back to your cheek," he murmured in her ear.

She pulled against the string.

"It's hard," she complained.

"It is at first," he said, "but with practice, you'll be able to draw a stronger bow."

Flaring his wings to block any wind that might throw off her aim, he helped her pull her drawing arm back that last little bit.

"Like this?" She squinted down the length of the arrow.

"Perfect."

She leaned back so the length of her body nestled into his. Heat radiated into his torso, along with a most pleasant tingling sensation. He was afraid to breathe. If he did, the moment would be broken.

"Your drawing fingers should come to your chin," he murmured. "Don't flinch as you release the string. Just loosen your fingers and the string will do the rest."

She released the arrow. It flew down the field and hit the target, not quite dead-center, but at the edge of the middle circle.

Ninsianna squealed. She threw her arms around his neck and hugged him.

Mikhail closed his eyes and took a deep breath. He stared into her golden eyes. The carefully rehearsed speech flew right out of his mind. Instead, he tilted up her chin and tasted her sensuous lips. Tangling her fingers in his hair, Ninsianna pressed into his body as she explored his mouth with her inquisitive tongue.

"Mikhail," she moaned.

He curled his wings around her to envelop their bodies. A certain part of his anatomy pressed insistently into her abdomen as she melted into him. Even without his memories, he just *knew* no woman had ever instilled this depth of desire. But he had no intention of making love to her until *after* they were married.

"Ninsianna," he shuddered. "We have to stop."

"Mmm hmm...." she murmured, not stopping at all.

"If we don't stop now, I won't be *able* to stop."

"Mmmm—" her voice lilted upwards, more of a 'yummy sound' than an agreement. She slid her hands between his back and his wings, touching the sensitive under-feathers. Oh, gods! What, was she trying to do? Kill him with desire?

She kissed his chest, causing him to become so hard it *hurt*. His testicles twanged. He fought the urge to rut in the middle of the field like ravenous beasts.

"We can do this later!" he gasped.

"Later?"

He felt as though his heart would leap right out of his ribcage. Sliding her hands down his back to his buttocks, she tilted her pelvis into his.

"A-af-after we ask your parents...." he stammered.

She drew back; her lips formed a lush, pink moue.

"Ask my parents?" Her voice was pure innocence, as though the siren of three seconds ago had never existed.

"Ask your parents if we can marry?"

He held his breath, waiting for her answer.

"Really?"

"Really."

Her golden eyes sparkled.

"Yes!!"

She threw her arms around his neck and kissed him until he was senseless. He flared his wings and carried her, squealing, into the air. Beating his wings to gain height, he found an updraft, and then leveled off into a lazy glide. Ninsianna wrapped her legs around one of his to give herself stability.

"Tell me that you love me?" she kissed his neck.

"I love you more than life itself."

He kissed her until she was as breathless as *he* was.

Chapter 109

July – 3,390 BC
Earth: Village of Assur

JAMIN

His father called *him* when the emissaries arrived from Nineveh. Not Mikhail; and not that fraud of a shaman, Immanu. He sat at his father's right-hand side, with Siamek at *his* right, the way things used to be before the winged demon had come into their village.

Qishtea of Nineveh was the eldest son of Chief Sinalshu. Tall and muscular, with a thick, black beard and locks oiled into ostentatious ringlets, his four-fringed kilt signaled his rank as his village's *Muhafiz*. There'd been a long-running rivalry between the two chiefs' sons. They competed over *everything*: sports, hunting, even the same women. Qishtea was the only man who'd ever bested him in a contest, although just as many times, he'd bested Qishtea, resulting in rivalry between Assur and the most powerful village in Ubaid territory.

Smug satisfaction warmed his belly. It wasn't *every* day that your biggest rival showed up, hat-in-hand, to beg for information.

Qishtea's dark eyes sparkled with amusement.

"So she stood you up?" he laughed.

"She stood *you* up, as well," Jamin growled.

"I want to meet this man who has bested the *both* of us."

"He'll be back later," his father said, "and then you can meet him yourself."

Qishtea took a sip of the beer his father had ordered for their guests. Like all of the best beer, it came from Yalda and Zhila. He held up his straw:

"Cheers," he said, "I guess that makes the *both* of us losers."

Jamin bristled, but how could he take offense when Qishtea had, cleverly, included *himself* in the insult? Unlike *him*, the pompous future chief of Nineveh had never been a serious contender for Ninsianna's hand; while he, on the other hand, had *had* her and then lost her to an enemy.

Nineveh's shaman, Zartosht, a wrinkled old man with sharp eyes that missed absolutely nothing, inquired of the Chief:

"We heard you trained some men from Eshnunna and Gasur?" he asked.

"Three men from each village," his father said. "Mikhail *insisted* he be allowed to train them."

Jamin cut in:

"We've tripled the number of warriors," he bragged. "I created a third tier of spearmen to support the heavy troops."

Qishtea waved his hand dismissively.

"Nineveh has *always* had a third tier of spearmen. What we're interested in—" he leaned forward; his mirth suddenly vanished "—is to learn this new weapon from our *allies* so we stop losing women."

"They're just *sticks*," Jamin snorted.

"They kidnapped my *cousin!*" Qishtea growled. "I don't want your spears. I've got plenty of my own!"

Jamin gripped his lion-claw necklace, an act of bravery that even Qishtea had never achieved. He noted, with satisfaction, the way his rival's eyes were drawn to the lion's fangs. *Yeah, you're too much of a coward to kill one with a knife. You used a spear, just like everybody else…*

A cacophony of voices grew loud outside the house. Someone pounded on the door. Varshab disappeared, and then came back.

"You're requested outside," he said.

"We are busy," his father said.

"Our *guest* might want to see this," Varshab said.

His father shepherded Qishtea and the ancient shaman out through their front door. Jamin and Siamek followed them out of the house. A group of villagers had crowded into the central square to watch a parade, not of men, but Mikhail's archers.

They marched in unison, singing a martial song learned from the Angelic. Each woman wore their quiver and bow draped across their backs. At their front marched Pareesa, calling out the cadences of the marching song.

The warriors who'd accompanied Qishtea from Nineveh crowded around them, as well as his *own* warriors, the second and third tiers.

Pareesa marched up to the Chief, carrying four ducks.

"Sir!" she snapped to attention.

"Did you shoot these?" his father asked.

"Yes Sir!" her eyes glittered victoriously.

Jamin's warriors crowded around him.

"Look at all those ducks," Firouz said.

"That's two ducks each," Dadbeh said.

"I've caught that many ducks," Jamin scoffed.

"But we've never caught that many as a *group*," Firouz said.

Qishtea of Nineveh moved among the archers, admiring their bows. As he did, Pareesa peeled off two of the ducks and handed them to his father.

"Sir," she said, "it's our great honor to provide you with the fruits of our success."

His father's face brightened at the sight of his newest, and until a few moments ago, his most *questionable* investment of resources. He took the two fat ducks from Pareesa's hand.

"Where is Mikhail?" he asked.

A wing-shaped shadow fell over the central square. Jamin looked up. Mikhail flew overhead ... carrying Ninsianna!

Qishtea gaped. Zartosht had told him, but it never prepared you to see a man fly.

"That's so romantic!" Kiana swooned.

"Do you think he finally proposed to her?" Orkedah asked.

"He *said* he was going to do it today," Immanu said.

Far up in the air, Ninsianna squealed. Mikhail changed direction. He carried Jamin's unfaithful fiancé away from the village.

Qishtea shot him a look that communicated: '*Loser...*'

Jamin clenched his fist. He dared not speak. The *last* thing they needed was an intra-tribal war.

His father said to Pareesa, "Tell Mikhail I said thank you."

"We will, Sir," Pareesa said.

Qishtea of Nineveh took the opportunity to break in.

"Do you think the Angelic would be willing to train *my* men to use a bow?"

"It's not *up* to me," Pareesa said. "You'll have to ask the Chief."

"We *are* allies," Qishtea said pointedly. "I'm sure he won't mind."

Jamin sidled up to Siamek.

"They're only doing this to gain my father's favor!"

"Maybe *we* should learn to use the bow," Dadbeh said.

"Yeah, if *Nineveh* wants to learn it," Firouz said.

"Then it must be valuable," Dadbeh said.

Can you teach us?" the two men asked with a single voice.

The warriors had looked to *him,* ever since he'd been little, to teach them any new skill. But in order to learn, first *he'd* have to learn from Mikhail. He'd be *damned* if he'd go crawling to his enemy, in the same way that Qishtea of Nineveh had just come crawling to *him.*

"It's a waste of time!" Jamin snapped. "We're using *real* weapons, the kind used to hunt lions and boars."

"Those weapons sure look real to me," Dadbeh said.

"And those are *definitely* real ducks," Firouz said.

Siamek leaned into him and lowered his voice.

"We should look into this," Siamek said. "It makes us look bad."

His youngest warrior, Tirdard, beamed at his girlfriend Yadidatum.

"Who would have thought girls could hunt like that?" Tirdard said.

"You just say that because Yadidatum is one of the archers," Dadbeh elbowed him.

"Oh, Yadidatum," Firouz called out in a mock-low voice. "Let me insert my arrow into your lovely bow."

Firouz grabbed his crotch and pretended to aim it like an arrow, straight at where the curvaceous Yadidatum stood showing one of Qishtea's warriors how to aim.

"Ahh, yes, brave Tirdard," Dadbeh said in a high mock-female voice. He tilted his pelvis towards Firouz's 'arrow.' "Such a big, firm arrow you have. String it right here, my love. Ahh! Ahh! Ahhhhh!"

The other warriors laughed and slapped one another on the back.

Jamin scowled. His authority was being usurped by a bunch of girls!

Kiaresh, his oldest elite warrior, came over to stand next to him.

"I would never contradict your judgment, *Muhafiz*—" the man lowered his voice "—but I have two daughters the same age as Pareesa. If our women carry bows, they won't be easy targets."

"Mikhail is *dangerous*," Jamin hissed. "You didn't *see* him, the night he slaughtered the Halifians."

"Then I won't ask him," Kiaresh said. "I'll ask Alalah. She and my wife are cousins."

Jamin scowled at his father's babysitter and spy.

"It's one thing to shoot at ducks, another entirely when a man runs after you with a spear."

He grabbed his spear and stalked over to Nineveh's warriors. His elite warriors closed ranks behind him as any good troop always *should*.

"With one of these," Jamin held up his spear, "I can take down an auroch, not just a scrawny bird."

"And when was the last time you brought home one of those?" Pareesa shot back. "Oh, I forgot. Last September?"

Qishtea and his warriors laughed.

Jamin's cheek twitched. Not only had she just insulted him in front of his biggest rival, but last September, he'd been laying on his deathbed, lingering between life and death from a gore-wound to his gut.

"Ahh, little fairy," his father laughed. "What a fierce little huntress you've turned into. I hope the other the women follow your example?"

She and his father locked forearms, the way one might with another man.

Jamin scowled.

The Chief held up the two fat ducks.

"Everybody, listen!" his father called out. "With these weapons, *anybody* can become a provider. It would please me greatly if *more* of you took up this weapon."

"What would it take for you to teach *us*?" Qishtea asked.

"We shall train three of your men—" his father glanced at the women crowding around the archers "—as long as you don't mind training alongside our women?"

"Nineveh is in your debt." Qishtea gave his father a respectful bow.

His father's enforcer, Varshab, asked:

"I want to learn. Is it too late to join?"

"We'll teach anyone who wants to learn," Alalah said. "*Anyone* who wants to put in the time can learn this skill."

"Not to mention it's darned handy to put supper on the table." Gisou held up her ducks.

Jamin's elite warriors slithered over to the archers. Pareesa sauntered up to him like a cat taunting the family dog, confident the dog would not dare growl with the master looking on.

She stuck out her tongue.

Something inside of him snapped.

"You will not mock me!"

He moved to slap off her smirk.

Pareesa stepped to the side, leaving him slapping empty air.

"You'll have to do better than that," she laughed.

He struck at her again, but she moved like a cat. Her high, sweet laughter caused the villagers to stop and look at what had her so amused.

Funny? She thought this was funny?

Jamin balled his hand into a fist. *This* time, he would hurt her. Throwing all of his weight into the punch, he aimed a right cross at Pareesa's temple.

Someone grabbed his arm and twisted it behind his back. *Pain* screamed into his elbow joint as they forced him to bend all the way down to the ground.

"I'll kill you!" he shrieked.

"You *will not* dishonor me in front of our guests!" his father growled.

With a practiced *kick*, his father knocked his legs out from under him and laid him face-down in the dirt. Jamin kicked back, but with his father's knee pressed into his back, he was pinned.

Pareesa moved in front of him. He thought she might kick him, but her voice warbled as she told his father "thanks."

The villagers fell silent. *No one* had ever seen his father discipline him like this, not since the time he'd caught him using a goat for sling-practice back when he'd been six years old.

Mortification rose in Jamin's cheeks.

"Get in the house!" his father released the hold. "Now!"

Jamin rose to his feet. The villagers, Qishtea, even his *own* warriors, refused to meet his gaze. His father's enforcer, Varshab, moved to stand at his father's left-hand shoulder, while Pareesa stood defiantly at his right.

That was –his- place…

Mortified and fuming, Jamin skulked into the house.

Chapter 110

Galactic Standard Date: 152,323.07 AE
Sata'an Empire: near Alliance Neutral Zone
S.R.N. Tsalmaveth
Lieutenant Apausha

Lt. APAUSHA

The *S.R.N. Tsalmaveth* ostensibly belonged to Shay'tan, but the old dragon hated to be caged, so whenever he needed to be someplace, he simply sent his fleet ahead, and then, after the quarry had been suitably intimidated, he made a grand entrance by *willing* himself into existence.

Who needed a ship when you were a living god?

Over the years, Lord Ba'al Zebub had commandeered the ship, until the *Tsalmaveth*, and Ba'al Zebub, had achieved the status of "Shay'tan's voice."

Lieutenant Apausha grimaced as he piloted the *S.M.M. Peykaap* up to their Emir's flagship and waited for the docking clamps to engage.

"They're not going to let us inside?" his radioman, Specialist Hanuud, licked the air with his long, forked tongue.

"He's probably afraid we'll shit on his carpets," his co-pilot, Specialist Wajid said.

"Really?" the gullible Hanuud said.

"You know you're a meathead?" Wajid teased the younger lizard.

"What he *means*," Apausha said, before it devolved into a fistfight, "is that they feel the merchant marine is *beneath* them."

All three glanced back through the open door. The cargo they carried was *anything* but "ordinary."

A hollow sound *thunked* through the ship as the docking clamps engaged and pulled the *Peykaap* in for an air seal. Unlike most ships, Apausha preferred to use a manual shutdown procedure. He spooled down the engines while Wajid ran through a post-flight checklist.

"Peykaap, this is Tsalmaveth," the radio crackled. *"Prepare to be boarded."*

"Roger that, *Tsalmaveth*," Hanuud said.

They set down their clipboards and hurried towards the airlock, past the thirty women and their male escort who they'd buckled into their seats for inspection. Apausha had sedated them prior to dropping out of hyperspace, even the escort, out of fear he might react adversely to should Ba'al Zebub insult his honor. While most of their passengers had fallen asleep, the oldest, a woman named Sarvenaz, watched him with an expression which was far too alert to have swallowed the drugs.

"You're supposed to be asleep," Apausha said in Kemet.

The woman's chin shot up. She apprised him with intelligent, mahogany brown eyes.

"I pity the poor fool who gets *that* one," Wajid said.

"She hasn't misbehaved," Apausha said.

"Just look at her," Wajid said. "She thinks she's better than us."

"She probably is," Apausha said. "She's smarter than the rest of them put together."

"She'll rule her husband with an iron fist," Wajid grumbled.

What he meant was *his* new wife ruled him with an iron fist.

Apausha couldn't help but smile. The human female reminded him of Marina, his beloved wife. Oh, what a wonderful gift Shay'tan had given him for shepherding that first woman safely past a Leonid destroyer, a Tokoloshe dreadnought, and the entire civil defense system of the Alliance proper. In his wildest dreams, he never would have been able to attract such a high-ranking wife!

The airlock alarm sounded. Ba'al Zebub was ready to inspect his cargo. Apausha hit the "entry" command. The door slid open.

"Attention!" Apausha ordered.

They tucked their tails up along their right-hand side and gave their boss the proper Sata'anic salute.

Ba'al Zebub lumbered in, an enormous lizard with a mahogany-red dewlap, corpulent even by Sata'anic standards which sought to emulate their god. The deck shook as his slippers slammed into the deck. While the Emir dressed in the foppish silks and furs preferred by the upper castes, rumor had it he'd been a bloodthirsty general before Shay'tan had elevated him to be his second in command.

"What have you brought me?" Ba'al Zebub asked.

"Thirty women, Sir," Apausha said. "And their male escort, sent to ensure their modesty until they are given to their new husbands."

Ba'al Zebub rubbed his sausage-thick claws together. A hiss of pleasure escaped his throat.

"How were they procured?"

"General Hudhafah made arrangements with some local collaborators," Apausha said. "He instructed them to only take a few from each settlement in order to gain the greatest possible genetic diversity."

"What did they take in trade?"

"Gold, Sir," Apausha said. "Sergeant Dahaka said the idiots danced like drunken serpents when he gave them three Sata'anic *darics* for each unmarried female."

"Only three *darics*?" Ba'al Zebub gasped.

It had cost General Hudhafah less money to buy a human female than it would cost *him* to buy a single flower to bring home to his precious new wife.

"Yes, Sir," Apausha said.

A feral glint came into Ba'al Zebub's eyes.

"Thank you, Lieutenant. You and your crew can go down to the nearest planet for a 24-hour shore leave. When you get back, I'll have you transport the cargo directly to the buyer."

"Where are they going, Sir?" Apausha asked.

"To the Alliance Prime Minister," Ba'al Zebub said.

Apausha sputtered. They'd barely made it the *last* time he'd slipped into the Alliance, and now rumor had it the Leonids were hot to shoot them out of the sky.

"B-b-ut, our wives?" he gave a pathetic squeak.

The Sata'anic Emir grinned.

"Don't worry," he said. "When you get shoreside, you'll find your needs get met."

His needs met? He didn't *want* his needs met. He wanted to go home and see his wife. But when duty called, low-ranking men like *them* had no choice but to obey. How would Ba'al Zebub, the highest ranking man in the Empire after only Shay'tan himself, understand his desire to go home to his *one* wife when the Sata'anic high lord possessed thirty-six? Tucking his tail against his side, Apausha made the appropriate gesture of respect and thanked their god for the privilege of performing this duty.

"Shay'tan be praised."

Chapter 111

July – 3,390 BC
Earth: Village of Assur

JAMIN

When his father finally returned, Jamin expected a fight. He expected to be yelled at. What he *didn't* anticipate was his father's look of utter defeat as he plunked down on a cushion and ran his fingers through his hair.

"Your behavior concerns me."

"She disrespected me!" Jamin said angrily. "If you don't demand respect, soon you won't have a village."

His father stared down at his hands, making a tented triangle, and then tapped his lips with the point.

"To be a good leader, you must be tolerant and wise."

"You must be *strong!*" Jamin gripped his lion-tooth necklace.

"If strength is all it takes," his father shook his head, "than you will never be chief, because you are no longer the best warrior this village has."

A sense of vertigo clenched at Jamin's gut. *Never be the chief?*

He exploded.

"You're *replacing* your own son?"

"Not *replace*," his father sighed. "But if you believe *strength* is all it takes to be the chief, then you're no longer the right man for the job."

"I *will* be chief!" Jamin shouted. "I was born to it! I'm your *son*."

"Perhaps...." the chief said, "but you've become arrogant in that assumption. All I can do *now* is teach what I *should* have been teaching you all along. The first lesson is this: you're *entitled* to nothing."

"Nothing?"

"No, nothing," his father said. "If you want to be chief, you must *earn* it, just as I did."

Jamin stormed out of the house and past the gates. Damn it! His father was replacing him with the winged demon. He'd known it all along!

As he stomped past the goat pens, he spotted Shahla, waiting, no doubt to hook up with one of the other warriors. He veered towards her. He was all done mourning his unfaithful former fiancé!

He sidled up to her like a lion taking down a gazelle.

"Shahla!" he greeted. "I haven't seen you in ages."

"You haven't *wanted* to see me," she said warily.

He shot her with his most appealing smile.

"I missed you."

He tucked a piece of her hair behind her ear. As a former lover, he knew how badly Shahla craved to be held.

"I thought you loved Ninsianna?" her voice grew caustic.

"My father wanted to solidify his power by forcing me to marry the shaman's daughter," he said. "He was afraid that Nineveh would lure our apprentice healer away."

It wasn't a lie. It had been the argument he'd used to get his father to order Ninsianna to marry him after she'd balked.

"Well my family is the *third* highest ranking family in the village!" She jabbed a finger in his face. "And my father has even more gold than *your* father does from successful trading. So why should I believe you?"

"Because it's better to be loved—" he caressed her cheek, "than to please my father."

It wasn't a *total* a lie. Shahla *did* love him, or more precisely, she loved his future position of power.

"Oh, Jamin!"

She melted into his arms.

Fire burned through him. The fire of hatred and righteous indignation. It made him hard. It made him want to *spear* something. He dragged her behind the goat shed, eager to remove the *stain* which Ninsianna had left upon his soul. He shoved her into the dirt and took her from the rear so he wouldn't have to see her face. He pictured he fucked Ninsianna, not the village strumpet, and he wanted to hurt her. Oh, gods! He wanted to hurt Ninsianna the same way that she'd hurt him!

He pushed into Shahla, roaring as he found release.

As he collapsed, shuddering, Shahla skittered away from him, clutching her shawl-dress. Her cheek bled where he'd shoved it into the dirt.

"Shahla?" he reached for her.

She cringed from his touch. Every warrior in the village had fucked her, but her tears tugged at his heartstrings.

"Don't you love me, even a little?" she wept.

Jamin opened his mouth, but could not utter the lie.

"It's complicated," he mumbled. "My father—"

"It's Mikhail's fault!" she exclaimed. "You need to strike at your enemy's heart before he ends up ruling this tribe!"

Strike at his enemy's heart...

That was the plan he'd percolated with Roshan, the Halifian chieftain that Mikhail had slain. Shahla might not be the woman he loved, but she was clever, conniving, and had always been unwavering in her support.

Would it be so awful if he formed an alliance of convenience? For the sake of the tribe?

His heart screamed *'no'* as he took her into his arms.

"You're everything I could ask for in a wife," he said. "Someday, when I am chief, we can have many fine sons."

Shahla burst into tears. "You really love me?"

He forced himself not to grimace.

"Why do you think I can't keep my hands off of you?" he said evasively. "But as long as the winged demon controls my father, this is all we can ever have."

"What can I do to help?"

His mind spun, formulating a plan.

"Find out where Pareesa likes to hunt," he said. "I'll take care of the rest."

Shahla reached down to caress his cock. He closed his eyes and pretended it was Ninsianna. This time, it was *her* soft breasts he cupped in his hands, *her* lips whispering sweet nothings into his ears, *her* he slid into as he made Shahla cry out in release. He exhaled her name as his heart reached into the void. Ninsianna. The woman he had lost…

Or maybe not…

If there was one thing he'd learned from Roshan, it was how to set up a merry goose chase so you could hit the *real* target…

Chapter 112

July – 3,390 BC
Earth: Village of Assur

NINSIANNA

Ninsianna ran her fingers through the bucket of kishk; her nose crinkled as Mama added the sour-smelling rennet from the stomach of a sheep. Together they stirred in the salt and worked it through the grain until the kernels absorbed the mixture. Whenever summer rolled around, the goat produced far more milk than they could use. Kishk, curdled, dried milk, was a way to preserve the highly perishable dairy product for times of year when the goat didn't produce enough. Although lately there had been a lot *less* excess!

Ninsianna laughed.

"What's so funny?"

"Oh, nothing," Ninsianna said. "I was just thinking how determined Mikhail looked this morning when he coaxed Little Nemesis into the milking shed."

Mama stirred the half-full bucket.

"If he gets any more 'determined,' I fear we shall have no milk at all."

Ninsianna laughed.

"Never have I seen a man so vexed by a goat!" she said. "He had hoof prints on his *cheek* when he came out with the milk! I swear, if he'd had his sword with him, we'd be eating Little Nemesis for dinner!"

"Hold the cloth?" Mama hoisted the bucket to strain the mixture. "Pull it tight so the frame doesn't collapse into the dirt."

They spread the saturated grain onto a strip of linen mounted on a wooden frame to dry the kishk in the sun. Once it was dry, they would store it in a pottery crock. Whenever they wanted porridge, they could simply add hot water.

"Ninsianna!" Papa called out the open doorway.

"I'm coming, Papa!"

She rinsed the curds off her hands and then went into the house. Papa was on his knees, rummaging through his chest of magic.

"It's time to teach you the *right* way to go into the dreamtime," Papa said, "so you don't keep getting stuck."

She sat down next to him, eager to learn the lesson. She'd been asking, for weeks, in a roundabout way, for ways to interpret her visions without coming right out and saying, *"Papa, I've been having visions of crocodile-men who fly in sky canoes."*

Papa lay out the usual implements: a bowl for water, an eagle's feather, some tinder to light a fire, and a semi-precious stone. He sent her to the water-bucket to fill the bowl and placed each implement in the direction that element was said to reside. He sat cross-legged on the carpet and patted the spot beside him.

"You woke up screaming again last night," he said.

"It was just a nightmare."

"You didn't stop until Mikhail came up to hold you."

She stared at her fingers. How could she explain that, every night, she called out to Mikhail and he did not come?

"I'm just worried about him," she mumbled.

"Balderdash," her father said. "You're worried about the Evil One."

She met the eyes which mirrored her own, or at least they had until the goddess had given her the gift of *sight*.

"I don't know *why* he doesn't save me in the dream," she said. "But when I call for him, Mikhail isn't there."

Tears welled in her eyes. The nightmares felt so *real*.

"Maybe he's supposed to *teach* us something?" Papa said.

"He can't remember his past."

"Which is why, perhaps, the goddess keeps sending you nightmares?"

"How can he teach us something he can't remember?"

"He *knows* things."

"But he can't *remember* them."

"He *knows* things," Papa said. "All you have to do is push him into situations where he *needs* that information, and then get him to teach it to us."

Ninsianna stared at her hands. It felt too much like deceit. But Papa was right. With the Halifians amassing at their border and this *new* threat attacking their allies, it was only a matter of time before those factions united and it was *war*.

"What does this have to do with the dreamtime?" she asked.

"Something is blocking his memories," Papa said. "Maybe it's an evil spirit?"

Ninsianna looked away, rather than explain "the goddess made me bind his memories because they are too painful." She'd *tried* telling Papa what She-Who-Is had made her do, and he'd pooh-poo'd it. He *still* couldn't believe she possessed abilities that even his father had lacked, especially since she had no idea how to undo what she had done.

"So how can I get at those memories through the dreamtime?"

"You travel into it."

"How?" she said. "I keep getting lost."

"The first way is through the *edge* of the dreamtime," Papa said. "Every creature has a spirit-light, an eggshell of energy which spreads out around them. When you pass close to someone, your eggshells touch and exchange information."

"Would those be the colors that I see?" she asked.

"Most people can't see colors," Papa said, "But everybody has this ability to some degree. It's the sensation of knowing someone is sick because, when you talk with them, you can feel their sickness inside your own body. But you must hone that ability so you can tell the difference between your *own* feelings and somebody else's."

"Like Mama does?"

"Yes. Mama can sense what other people are feeling."

"But she cannot see it?"

"Not usually," Papa said. "The ability see is rare."

"But *you* can see."

"I can," Papa said. "I inherited it from my father, Lugalbanda, but I have a hard time doing what your mother does, feeling what other people feel."

"Did Uncle Merariy also inherit the ability to see?" she asked.

Her father scowled.

"The only *gift* my brother has is the ability to steal."

"Is that why you hate him?"

Papa sighed.

"Merariy was the eldest son. He felt *he* should have been shaman, even though he lacked ability. So he *stole* something that belonged to somebody else."

"He's the village drunk," Ninsianna scoffed. "And his daughter hangs around with the village slut."

"Just make sure you keep her away from Mikhail," Papa scowled. "Merariy may try to *use* her to lure him away."

"Gita is *ugly*."

"She was *born* at the Temple of Ki."

A sense of *fear* clenched her gut. Mikhail's overdeveloped sense of duty might compel him to wander out into the desert, on a three-month journey across enemy territory without any water, all to find a temple which no longer existed; all in the vain hope it might give him clues about the last time his people had visited this world. And then where would she be? The so-called "*Chosen One*." Why, just this morning, she'd caught Gita lurking by the well.

"How else can you enter the dreamtime?" she asked.

Papa got up, walked to the door which faced the street, and set the crossbar which bolted the door against entry. He paused at the table, where Mama had assembled her healer's basket, his expression thoughtful, and then kneeled in front of the box which contained his shamanic supplies—the one where she'd pilfered the sacred beverage. Instead of taking out the vial, however, he dug to the very bottom until he found a small, leather pouch. He sat, cross-legged, and patted the carpet next to him, directing her to sit.

He opened the pouch and shook out some dried leaves.

"What is it?" she asked.

"This—" Papa shot her a wry grin "—would cause your mother to cut my testicles off and make me eat them."

He rummaged through the palm-sized leaves, greenish-grey and crumbled, until he found a small, prickly flower which might have once been yellow, but now appeared brown.

He handed it to her.

"What is it?"

"Kratom,"[158] Papa said. "It's similar to blue water lily in that it aids the transition into the dream world. But it's a lot more powerful. You must never blend it with any other herb or it could kill you. Especially if you suspect you may be with child."

He shot her a raised eyebrow. From her disappointed smile, he knew that Mikhail had, thus far, honored his promise to not have sex until they were married.

Ninsianna fondled the tiny, yellow flowers.

"So, how does this work?"

"You follow the threads."

"The connections that bind all living creatures together?"

"Yes. It's easiest when you've formed a connection to another person, but with kratom, you can follow a thread from a person you know well to a person *they* are connected to."

"A friend of a friend?"

"Exactly," Papa said. "Now close your eyes and picture somebody you have a strong connection with."

Ninsianna softened her gaze. After a moment, she became aware of the threads connected into different parts of her body. She found the strongest connection.

"Got it."

"Follow that thread until you bump into the person you're thinking of," Papa said. "You should get a vague sense of what they are doing."

---

[158] *Kratom:* a tropical evergreen tree. The leaves and flowers have a stimulant, and also a mild psychoactive effect.

She closed her eyes.

"I can see Mikhail."

"What is he doing?"

"Working in Yalda and Zhila's field."

"Can you see who else is around him?"

She *tried* to picture it, but only got the vaguest sense of color.

"No."

"That's what the kratom is for."

He counted out several flowers and a handful of leaves and placed them into a cup, and then poured in some of Yalda and Zhila's beer.

"Bottoms up," he said.

The beer masked a bitter taste. After a few minutes, she began to feel delightfully tipsy.

"Now what?" she asked.

"Try again," Papa said. "Only *this* time, picture you are looking through Mikhail's eyes."

She pictured hiding inside of Mikhail's head. After a moment, she got a sense of who he was with.

"I see the Chief's man, Kiaresh," she said. "They're talking about..." she tilted her head. "I know what they're talking about, but I can't *hear* what Kiaresh is saying."

"While they are talking," Papa said, "they'll form a temporary connection. Can you see it?"

"Yes."

"Follow the thread from Mikhail into who he is with," Papa said.

She found the thread and followed it into the other person.

"Oh! Now I can hear both sides of the conversation. Kiaresh wants to learn archery, but he's afraid Jamin will go off the deep end. Mikhail suggested his wife train with Alalah, and then *she* can teach *him*."

"Good," Papa said. "Following threads is easy. As you get better at it, you'll be able to project images into the other person's mind. But if they're untrained, they'll have a hard time differentiating their own thoughts from somebody else's."

"Really?"

"Yes. Why don't you try calling him home for lunch?"

"Mikhail," she pictured. *"Come home, and I'll strip you naked..."*

She *felt*, not the emotion, but rather a *vision* of how *amenable* he was to that suggestion. So? All of his self-control was nothing but a mask? She would have to try it later, to see if she couldn't make his control slip.

"Ninsianna?" her father shook her. "You're supposed to stay *here*, not wander off and get lost."

Her face turned flaming red.

"I wasn't *lost*," she stammered. "I was just wondering—" What was she wondering, that she could say to her father? "I was *wondering* how you might see a place if you've never been there before, and you're not connected to anyone who is there?"

"Like our enemies?"

"Yes."

"That, child," he gave her a wolfish grin, "is what the kratom is for. The third kind of seeing is called remote viewing. It's dangerous because your consciousness leaves your body *completely*, like a kite connected by a thread. Sometimes you fly over the earth to see. Other times you travel through the dreamtime."

"Like my vision of Mikhail?"

"Exactly."

"It's not very practical," Ninsianna sighed. "After the last two times I journeyed, I slept like the dead."

"If you do it often enough, you can train your mind to travel without the aid of hallucinogens," he said. "But it's *still* dangerous. While your mind surfs the dreamtime, your body is vulnerable. Sometimes people get lost. Or become so interested in what is on the other side that they let go of the thread that connects their mind to their body."

"Like grandpapa Lugalbanda did when grandmamma died?" Ninsianna's voice lilted with pride.

Papa didn't meet her gaze.

"Yes," Papa murmured. "A shaman can will himself to pass."

Ninsianna reached for another glass of kratom.

"So how do we remote view."

"First, you take....."

Her father led her through the mother of all acid trips.

Chapter 113

July – 3,390 BC
Earth: desert outside Assur

JAMIN

For several days he reconnoitered the desert, searching for tracks left by the People of the Desert. On the fourth day, he went to "the spot." To his disbelief, he found fresh goat-tracks. He took it as a sign that, maybe, he might be able to reach an accord?

He followed the tracks inland to a place where a hill obscured the Halifian's tents. First he buried his obsidian blade beneath a rock, and then tucked his spear into a ditch so it wouldn't be noticed. He adjusted his cape to make sure the leaf-shaped bone pin was visible, tucked his flint utility knife into his kilt, and then hoisted the pack onto his back.

He climbed the hill's crest and stood there until he was noticed. Within seconds, a dozen men swarmed the hill. While all wore brown robes, none wore the brightly-colored robes which Gimal had described.

Jamin held up his hands.

"I come with an offering," he called out, "to give your shaykh."

One of the Halifians, a man with unusual hazel-green eyes, stopped his kinsmen from slaughtering him outright. He recognized Nusrat from the first time he'd met Roshan, the man Mikhail had slain.

"You have a lot of nerve," Nusrat said in heavily accented Ubaid.

"I owe your tribe a debt," he answered in Halifian.

The man gestured to his brothers.

"Search him."

"We should kill him," one of the brothers said.

"We probably will," Nusrat said, "but not until our father gives the order."

Jamin held out his arms while they deprived him of the cheap blade. One of the men punched him in the stomach, but while he grunted, he did not cry out. He stood in a posture of non-aggression while the men rummaged through his pack.

"What is this?" Nusrat asked.

"An installment," Jamin said, "on what I owe your father."

"You *owe* him eighteen lives," Nusrat said.

"The *Angelic* owes your father eighteen lives," Jamin said. "I owe him word of a son-in-law's love, and his dying wish that his widow and daughter be cared for."

A young boy, just at the cusp of adolescence, came running out from the tents. He bore the same green eyes as his father.

"Grandfather will see him," the boy said.

"You are *lucky*," Nusrat said. "If he'd refused, I'd turn you over to *them*."

He gestured at his brothers who pawed through his pack, fighting over who would get what.

"Bring it!" Nusrat ordered.

His brothers grumbled, but stuffed the items back into the sack. *None* would dare take it without gaining permission from their father.

Jamin adjusted his cape as they strode into the encampment, arranging the folds to appear more *chiefly*. Dark eyes peered out of the tents. Two hostile-looking men stood guard at the largest tent.

"You may enter," one of the guards said.

He allowed Jamin and the green-eyed man to step inside the tent, but stopped the other brothers from entering with them.

"Hey!" they complained.

"Give me the pack," the guard said.

The guard placed the pack just inside the door.

Perched on a cushion sat the man he'd met one summer, seated by the river, giving water to his herd of goats. At first he'd been afraid, but the scarred man – for the scar which ran from his mouth to his ear had then still been fresh – had given him a modest meal and inquired about his mother. Jamin had poured his heart out, for his heart was broken at his mother's death. The man had tussled his hair, given him the pin, and made him a promise – "let me water my goats *here* for ten weeks every summer, and we will not trample your fields or molest your stock."

The armistice, for he hadn't realized that he *had*, as the Chief's only child, bound his tribe to a treaty, had resulted in peace for the last fifteen years. For fifteen years he'd kept his warriors away from that spot on the river, and for fifteen years, this particular tent-group had kept their herds on the narrow path and not allowed them to forage on Assurian fields.

"Peace be upon your herd—" Jamin gave the blessing which Marwan had given that first day.

"There *is* no peace," Marwan said. "You lured my kin into a trap."

"If you believed that," Jamin said, "you wouldn't have kept your herds to the agreed upon spot."

Marwan gave a bitter laugh.

"Let it never be said that Kiyan's son lacks a manhood."

The sheikh gestured for him to sit. Jamin sat on the other side of Nusrat. The past fifteen years had not been kind to the desert shaykh; his face had grown thinner, his skin had become wrinkled and brown, and the knuckles in his knife-hand had grown swollen with use and age. He'd always had a snaggletooth, but now it bore evidence of rot. But he still possessed the same intense dark eyes and hawk-like beak.

The guard carried forward the pack.

"What is this?" Marwan asked.

"It's the other half of what I promised Roshan."

The old man's burned with hatred.

"Roshan is *dead*," he almost spat. "Why didn't you bring it sooner?"

What he said next would either result in his death, or heal their alliance.

"I didn't know where you *were*," he said truthfully. "I only, just yesterday, found evidence of your herds."

Marwan crossed his arms, but nodded for Roshan to rummage through the pack. The green-eyed man laid each carefully wrapped package upon the felted carpet for examination.

"Be careful of that one," Jamin said of a tiny, clay urn. "It's worth more than all of the rest combined."

Roshan passed the jar to his father. Marwan pulled out the stopper and gave it a whiff. His face transformed into a pleased grin.

"Where did you get this?"

"I liberated it from my father," Jamin said.

The desert shaykh fished out an olive and held it out.

"You first," he said.

Jamin didn't take offense at the implication of poison. He chewed the olive, relishing the grassy flavor, and swallowed it. The desert shaykh ate one, his expression stoic. The terrible scar which ran from his lip to his ear curved up into a facsimile of a smile.

"It's been a long time since I've had such a delicacy," the shaykh said.

"I promised it to Roshan," Jamin said. "The best I can do is deliver it to his family."

A look passed between Marwan and his son.

"It won't be that easy," Nusrat said. "Roshan's father cannot be appeased."

"Their tent-group lives far away."

"Their tent-group has allied with powerful enemies."

"The Amorites?" he guessed.

"And others," Marwan practically spat. "Alliances of which I am not permitted to speak."

"So *they* are taking our women?"

"*Your* women?" Marwan said. "*Your* women have remained untouched."

"But I thought…"

"If I *take* your women, I will take them for my sons." Marwan crossed his arms. "I don't sell women as sex-slaves."

Nusrat finished laying out the contents of the pack. A jar of olives, a measure of grain, salt from the Pars Sea, a bag filled with semi-precious stones, and a tiny bracelet, woven with silver beads. Nusrat handed the bracelet to his father.

"What is this?" Marwan asked.

"Roshan spoke fondly of his wife and daughter," Jamin said. "I thought—"

"She will *reject* it," Marwan said.

"How do you know?"

"Because she tore off the necklace Roshan gave her," Marwan said. "The one which *used* to belong to your mother. But maybe she'd like *that* one—" he pointed at Jamin's lion-fang necklace "—so long as it comes with your heart impaled upon the fangs."

Jamin's shoulders slumped with defeat. His father was *furious* he had taken his mother's necklace.

Something niggled at his subconscious…

"How did you know the necklace belonged to my mother?" Jamin asked.

Marwan retreated behind a hooded expression.

"I know things," he said. "Let's just leave it at that."

They sat in silence. Marwan did not offer him something to eat, which was not a good sign.

"So why are you *really* here?" Marwan asked.

"I need a favor," Jamin said.

"A *favor*," Marwan asked. "Your last *favor* got eighteen men killed."

"It's not that kind of favor," Jamin said. "It will benefit *you* as much as it benefits me."

"How?"

"There's a young woman in my village," Jamin said. "She dishonored me. Since *your* people seem to be interested in *gathering* young women—"

"We're not *Amorites!*" Marwan spat. "We don't take slaves."

"Not a slave," Jamin said. "You wouldn't want her as a wife. But give her to a tribe far away, someone you don't *like,* because the girl is trouble.*"*

"Your former fiancé?" Nusrat guessed.

"No," Jamin said. "This one is a friend of the Angelic."

"How old is this woman?"

"She is twelve."

"You want us to kidnap a *child?*"

He realized how absurd it sounded. How could he explain it without looking like a fool?

"The *Angelic* seeks to double our army by training our women," Jamin said.

Nusrat broke into laughter.

"Are we supposed to perceive this as a threat?" Marwan asked.

"He has given them weapons which make them fight like men," Jamin said.

"All the more reason to stay away," Marwan said.

What was *with* the desert shaykh? Why had he maintained their treaty, even after his son-and-law had been killed?

"You're not going to help me?"

"No," Marwan said. "We've given you enough. But I *do* appreciate your bringing Roshan's widow these gifts."

The guard stepped forward and forced him to stand up.

"You may leave us," Marwan said.

"But I came in good faith," Jamin said.

"I *know,*" Marwan said. "Which is why I shall let you live."

The guard shoved him out of the tent and led him back to the hill. Marwan's sons followed him.

"Don't come back," the guard warned. "If you do, Marwan will kill you."

Jamin trudged back to his weapons and retrieved his obsidian blade and spear. Of *course* they hadn't given him back his knife. His father was right about *that* much.

He was headed back to the village when the back of his neck prickled.

"Who's there?" he whirled to face whoever stalked him.

One of Nusrat's brothers stepped out from behind some rocks, followed by threescore men. Some were Halifians, others were Uruk, but most came from tribes he did not recognize. *All* of them, judging by their apparel, were mercenaries; men cast out of some tribe after committing a crime, most often, murder,

The men parted. A cruel-looking man, finely dressed in a colorful, striped robe, stepped through their ranks. He wore a leather bandolier draped across one shoulder, with a half-dozen small, bone-handled knives shoved into the strap.

"I am Rimsin, son of Kudursin, of Amorite tribe of Jebel Bishri," he said. "We hear you're having problems with a woman?"

Chapter 114

Galactic Standard Date: 152,323.07 AE
Neutral Zone: Diplomatic Carrier 'Prince of Tyre'
Lieutenant Apausha

Lt. APAUSHA

Lieutenant Apausha had smuggled many goods into Alliance territory, some onto ships owned by business magnates, but this was the first time he'd ever rendezvoused with the Alliance flagship *itself*. Ba'al Zebub's ornate flagship suffered in comparison to the sleek, white *Prince of Tyre*. She sported organic lines, with a pair of cat-like whiskers on its nose-cone.

"That's one hell of a ship," Apausha's radioman and navigator Hanuud admired her out the viewing window. "Too bad *we* aren't stationed on such a beauty."

"What's wrong with the *Peykaap*?" his pilot Wajid patted the console of the smuggling vessel which had gotten them through more scrapes than they cared to reminisce. "She's the fastest ship in the Empire."

An uneasy feeling rumbled in Apausha's stomach.

"Let's make this drop-off and get the Haven out of here," he said.

"Aye!" his two crewmen agreed.

They guided the *Peykaap* in to dock alongside the Alliance flagship. A disembodied sense of dread made his dorsal ridge stand on end. He'd just transported something from the Sata'an-flagship to the Alliance-flagship. Why in Haven was Lucifer even allowing them this close to his ship? The entire thing stank.

"*Prince of Tyre*," his radioman, Specialist Hanuud called into the transceiver. "This is the *Peykaap*. Where would you like us to dock?"

"*Peykaap*, this is the *Prince of Tyre*. You may dock on the port[159] side of the primary launch bay."

Apausha guided them in *carefully*, cautious not to do anything which might be perceived as a threat. His co-pilot, Wajid, exhaled a sigh of relief as the docking clamps engaged and pulled them in for an airtight seal.

"*Peykaap*, this is the *Prince of Tyre*," the opposing radioman called. "Would you prefer to exit the ship, or do you want *us* to send in a welcome party?"

Apausha's dorsal ridge shot up with surprise.

"You mean they'll let us inside?" Wajid asked incredulously.

---

[159] *Port:* the side of a vessel which is to the left of an observer facing the bow (back); the right-side is called *starboard*.

Apausha glanced back to where the women and single man were sleeping – even the older woman who usually avoided taking her pill. Ba'al Zebub had been quite clear that *all* of them were to be heavily sedated, including the women's escort.

"Could you clarify that," Apausha asked Hanuud.

His radioman clarified that, yes, they were invited to come on board.

"Ain't *no way* I'm going to miss this," Wajid said.

"I don't know…" Apausha had an uneasy feeling.

"C'mon!" Wajid said. "Don't you want to snoop?"

They both looked at Hanuud for the final vote. The spastic lizard nervously tasted the air, but Apausha had never chastised him for speaking his mind.

"I'd really like to see what she looks like," Hanuud said. "It'd make one Haven of a tale to tell my new wife."

Apausha sighed.

"Tell them we promise not to shit on their carpets."

"Yes, Sir!" Hanuud said enthusiastically.

Hanuud relayed the information far more diplomatically than what was actually said. Several minutes later, they traversed the airlock. They expected a formidable military presence, which, of course, they got, but the *last* thing he expected was for the Alliance Prime Minister *himself* to greet them.

"Gentlemen—" Lucifer spread his arms in a universal sign of *welcome*. "I hear you come bearing gifts?"

Apausha glanced at the Angelics who stood, pulse pistols sheathed, but from the way their arms remained bent, they were ready to quick-draw if the delivery should turn south, and then back at the Prime Minister.

Hanuud pinched himself.

"Yes, Sir," Apausha said cautiously. "His great and powerful eminence, Lord Ba'al Zebub, *peace be upon him*—" all three men made the Sata'anic prayer-gesture "—has asked us to deliver thirty future wives."

"Wives, oh yes—" Lucifer gave them a knowing look. "And where did you stick them? In cages? Or did you have to muzzle them?"

"We transported them *humanely*," Apausha said indignantly. "Every effort was made to protect their modesty."

Lucifer laughed, as though he thought that was funny.

"Well herd them out!"

Wajid and Hanuud looked to him for direction.

"You heard the man," Apausha murmured.

His men went back into the ship and led thirty sleepy women and their groggy escort onto the *Prince of Tyre*. Apausha handed Lucifer's Chief of Staff the shipping manifest. Zepar counted off each woman and made them lift their veils. He stopped before the escort, a tall, dark-skinned man who, despite being sedated, was still alert enough to cause trouble if the Angelics tried to pull anything.

"Why a man?" Zepar asked.

"To safeguard their modesty," Apausha said. "He was appointed by their tribal leaders to stand-in for their brothers and fathers."

Zepar harrumphed.

"We don't want men," he said. "Only breeders."

"We intend to take him back on the next shipment," Apausha said.

"Next time," Zepar growled, "only bring goods we can *use*."

He continued his inventory, lifting the women's veils. The heavily sedated women stared vacuously into empty space.

Zepar stopped at the oldest one.

"This one's too old," he touched the slight crows-feet at the edge of Sarvenaz's eyes.

"She's the most valuable one," Apausha said. "General Hudhafah slated her to be a first-wife."

"Is she fertile?"

"Our base doctor certified she'll be good for several children."

"Hmmm...."

The dirty-winged Angelic tapped notes into his flatscreen.

Lucifer walked around the women, pinching their breasts the way one would handle a piece of livestock. Every man in the Empire had heard about the Alliance Prime Minister's appetites and the Chief of Staff who pimped him out like a prize stud stallion.

"How'd you make them so docile," Lucifer asked.

"We've given them a chance to acclimate," Apausha said.

"Acclimate to *what*?"

"Sata'anic mores," Apausha said. "Each woman has been trained to be a future wife."

"Oh, c'mon!" Lucifer poo-pooed him. "You can drop the act."

"What act?"

Lucifer laughed.

"Gentlemen!" he put his arms around Wajid and Hanuud. "You have brought my people a priceless blessing. Please? Let me avail you of the comforts of my ship?"

"We must get back, Sir," Apausha said.

"Right away?" Lucifer scoffed. "C'mon, Lieutenant. Look to your men. They must eat! And rest, after such a long journey."

Wajid and Hanuud both shot him a raised eyebrow-ridge. *They* wanted to explore the enemy's flagship. *He*, on the other hand, didn't like the way that Lucifer smelled. From the way his pheromones fluctuated, it was almost as if, moment to moment, he was two different people.

"We have porridge," Lucifer's eerie silver eyes glittered. "With fresh milk and unlimited dried fruit."

An image of a most luscious porridge, hot and starchy, piled decadently high with freeze-dried fruit, dark tree-syrup, and a buttery-white milk moat, popped into his mind. Apausha's stomach growled.

"I could use a hot shower, Sir," Wajid contradicted him quietly.

"I'd sure like to lie down in a *bed*," Hanuud pleaded.

Apausha sighed. All three men had given up their quarters and slept in the cargo hold to minimize friction with the women.

"We'd appreciate that, Your Eminence," Apausha touched his claws to his forehead and his snout.

"Excellent!" Lucifer clapped. "Eligor will take you to your room."

A burly, white-winged Angelic stepped forward, followed by a slightly smaller, red-speckle-feathered crewman.

"This way, Sirs," Eligor said stoically.

Wajid and Hanuud slipped out of the Prime Minister's embrace. As they followed their escort out of the cargo hold, Lucifer and his Chief of Staff argued about the dark-skinned male escort.

"How was your trip?" the other Angelic, his name-tag said '*Lerajie*', asked with a friendly voice.

"Fine, Sir," Apausha said.

"You're merchant marine, not navy?" Lerajie asked.

"Yes, Sir."

"What's it like?"

He met the *other* Angelic's gaze. With a raised eyebrow, Eligor communicated, "*sorry, my friend doesn't know when to shut the hell up.*" If Lerajie had been sent to pump them for intelligence, he was so blatantly *obvious* about it that it was almost a joke.

"That's classified, Sir," Apausha said.

"Oh, yes, so sorry," Lerajie said. "Didn't mean to pry. It's just, it's not often we get to *talk* to you guys, unless, well…" He trailed off. Usually when they "talked," it was to shoot and kill one another.

"Do you want a shower first," Eligor asked, "or would you rather eat."

"Eat, Sir," Apausha said. "If you don't mind?"

Eligor led them through broad hallways, luxuriously clean and white. Unlike the ornate gold- and jewel-encrusted walls of the *S.R.N. Tsalmaveth*, while the décor was minimalist, the *Prince of Tyre* conveyed a sense of order.

He led them into a cafeteria laid out with a generous stainless-steel commercial food buffet. A chef-hatted and aproned Angelic, heavily scarred, with a missing arm and a partially amputated wing, stood behind the buffet line, guarding an enormous tray of porridge with a stainless-steel spoon.

Apausha forced himself not to gape. Usually, when faced with such horrific war injuries, Sata'anic soldiers were honorably discharged.

"So it's true?" Wajid whispered. "They're really that desperate?"

Apausha shot him a look which said, "*Shut up!*"

"Sir," he said cordially to the cook. "That's a fine looking porridge."

"The Prime Minister said you'd like it," the scarred Angelic said. "He asked me to make it special."

"That was very thoughtful," Apausha said.

"Lucifer, he always *knows* what will best please a man."

The scarred Angelic scooped three generous servings into bowls, and then directed them to the milk and fruit. Wajid decorated his oatmeal with fruit, while Hanuud poured enough tree-syrup on his to turn the milk-moat a deep shade of amber. Apausha selected a table with their backs against the wall. The other Angelics – the room wasn't *full*, but neither was it empty – looked on curiously, but their expressions were devoid of hostility.

Eligor and Lerajie sat down at a table just far away enough to give them privacy, but not so far away that they couldn't react should they try any mischief.

All three lizards dug into their food.

"Pinch me," Hanuud whispered. "I feel like I'm in an episode of *'Behind the Mirror.'*"

"They must *really* be desperate," Wajid said. "I've never seen Angelics act so *friendly.*"

They finished their porridge, went back for seconds, and then they ate dessert. All three lizards patted their bellies and loudly belched – signaling gratitude to the cook. Eligor stood up:

"Are you ready to see your room?"

"Yes, Sir," Apausha said. "That would be nice."

The porridge had made him delightfully lethargic. Between navigating their way out of the uncharted territories, avoiding the Tokoloshe who crawled through the area like the plague, meeting with Ba'al Zebub, and evading Alliance patrols, not to mention the fact they'd all given up their rooms, had all caught up with him.

Maybe Lucifer was right? It was time to sleep in a *real* bed.

Eight hours later, well-rested, showered, and with their uniforms dry-cleaned and pressed, Eligor and Lerajie returned to escort them back to their ship.

"Did you sleep well?" the gregarious Lerajie asked.

"Yes, Sir," all three of them said.

"I've never slept in such a comfortable bed," Hanuud added.

Eligor gave him a raised eyebrow, as if to say, "*dude, you must have things bad.*"

"What about the in-room breakfast?" Lerajie asked.

"It was good," all three of them said.

Eligor said nothing. While not friendly, neither was he hostile. In fact, the man emitted an almost near-total absence of pheromones, making him difficult to read.

As they passed through one of the hallways, they encountered the two cold-eyed "goons" standing like bookends on either side of a door. The door swished open. Out stepped Chief of Staff Zepar, leading one of the human females. Her dress was hopelessly ripped; her face was bruised and bloody. Blood streamed down her thighs, as if she'd been taken, *violently*, against her will. What struck him most, however, was the haunted, *dead* appearance of her eyes.

"Sir?" Eligor and Lerajie both snapped to attention.

Zepar hissed something in a language that was neither Galactic Standard nor one Apausha recognized and shoved the female down the hall.

Apausha flitted his forked tongue out to taste for pheromones. He caught the scent of semen. In the guarded room, another woman screamed as someone began to roar like a ravenous beast. A disembodied sense of horror ran down his spine to the tip of his tail, a roar so deep, so primal, it felt as though the ship itself shuddered with its power.

"Man," his radioman, Hanuud whispered. "That's just—"

"Wrong," his pilot, Wajid finished.

The friendlier of the two Angelics, Lerajie, started towards the door, but his companion, Eligor, muttered something under his breath. The two burly "goons" flexed their muscles, their eyes as ruthless and cold as the worst Tokoloshe pirate.

"We can't—" Lerajie protested.

"Later," Eligor hissed.

"But we shouldn't—"

Eligor grabbed his companion by the arm.

"I said *later!*" His eyes darted over towards Apausha and his men. "We'll discuss this *later*, when we don't have company."

"Shay'tan protect us," both of his crewman gesticulated.

"Let's get the Haven out of here?" Apausha murmured.

Thankfully Wajid knew how to play it cool. He grabbed their high-strung communications officer and dragged the scrawny lizard back to their ship before the well-intentioned do-gooder got them all 'disappeared.'

"I'll file a report with Ba'al Zebub," Apausha promised the moment they got back to the *Peykaap*. The Sata'an were a lot of things, but this struck him as just plain evil.

Chapter 115

July – 3,390 BC
Earth: Village of Assur
Colonel Mikhail Mannuki'ili

MIKHAIL

A small, dark-winged Angelic stares across the chess board. A ticking clock counts out the seconds. He doesn't speak. But then, he never does.

"Tá sé do bhogadh,[160] *Gabriel," I say.*

The boy picks up his black bishop and makes an L-shaped move to capture my white queen.

*

A frantic pounding jarred Mikhail out of his sleep and *kept* on pounding, despite his best effort to block out the noise by covering his head with one wing. With a weary groan, he rolled off his sleeping pallet; his feathers crumpled, and knocked aside the curtain which separated his "bed" from the living quarters.

"I'm coming," he grumbled, swearing to eviscerate whoever dared wake him at this ungodly hour. He yanked the door open. The normally-giggly Gisou stood, filthy and trembling, clutching the remnants of her shawl-dress.

"They took her!" she shrieked.

"Took who?" he asked.

"Pareesa!"

She threw herself into his arms, weeping, and began to blubber out an incomprehensible tale.

Immanu came down the stairs, followed by Ninsianna.

"Trouble?" Immanu guessed.

"Pareesa's been kidnapped," Mikhail said.

"By who?" Immanu asked.

Gisou cried out: "I don't know!"

Immanu grabbed her shoulders and shook her.

"How can you not know who took you?!" Immanu yelled.

"I-I-I...." she stammered.

---

[160] *"Tá sé do bhogadh."* It's your move.

"That's enough!" The order came from Needa, who took in the distraught young woman's condition. She placed herself, firmly, between the women and the men.

Ninsianna hurried to his bed, grabbed his blanket, and placed it gently around Gisou's shoulders.

"They're not angry at *you*—" Ninsianna glared at him. "They're angry at whoever *took* you."

Mikhail realized how he must look, lording over the terrified young woman by at least a cubit. He tucked his wings against his back and, with forced calm, asked:

"Tell us everything you *do* know?"

With halting words, Gisou told her story.

"We were tracking an antelope, when they stepped out from behind some rocks. We tried to fight them but they, oh—" she sobbed "—there were so many! We—we—" her hands flew to her face. "Pareesa shot one of them, but they were so close—we couldn't—they gave me this—" she gestured at an ugly red bruise that had begun to turn purple on her jaw "—and then they tied us up and made us walk."

"Where was this?" Mikhail asked.

"North-west. Maybe a two *kaspu*[161] walk?"

Four hours. Which for a fit girl like Pareesa, could be anywhere from five kilometers, to twenty kilometers away. Though if Gisou was with her, and they were tracking game, she was probably moving slower. He'd never *walked* that direction and, until a few weeks ago, he'd never even *flown* there.

"I'm not familiar with that territory," he said.

"That's no man's land," Immanu said. "Mostly desert. Technically, it's controlled by the Ubaid, but our warriors rarely patrol there."

Damantia! So not only was *he* not familiar with the area, but the warriors would also have a hard time nailing down her position.

"What time, *erm*—" He glanced at his watch. Minutes meant nothing to the Ubaid. "How *long ago* did they take you?"

"Shortly after high noon," Gisou said. "But I'm not sure how far we traveled *after* that. They kept stopping and hiding, probably to avoid being seen by *you*."

Mikhail glanced at his watch and cursed. They hadn't traveled quickly, but it was now three o'clock in the morning.

"How long did you walk?"

"Past nightfall," Gisou said. "They met up with a bigger group. This one had other women."

---

[161] *Kaspu:* an ancient Babylonian measure of distance, around 11.3 Km or 7 miles.

"Concubines?" Immanu asked.

"No. They were captives," Gisou said. "I don't think they were Ubaid."

Immanu hissed: "Slavers!"

He shot his wife a worried look.

"Were they Halifians?" Mikhail asked.

"I don't think so." Gisou shook her head. "At least, *most* of them weren't Halifian. Only two of them—I recognized the language. But some were dressed in multicolored robes."

So were the men who'd jumped Gimal in the desert. A war-party *could* have gotten that far north. But if they had, then *who* was harassing Eshnunna and Gasur to the south? The group he'd seen the day he'd rescued Gimal had disappeared, which meant they'd taken shelter with *somebody*.

"Did you take a head count?" he asked.

"Eight," Gisou said. "I mean, the group who *jumped* us had eight men, two of them Halifians, but when we got to the other tribe's camp?" Her lips moved, silently counting. "Thirty? Maybe thirty-five men?"

Still far less than the hundreds he'd seen crossing the desert, but a sizeable group.

"How did you get away?"

Gisou shivered as she recounted the story.

"We waited until it got dark, then Pareesa chewed through her bindings. She freed *me,* and then we went to free the other women. But the men woke up—" she grabbed my arm. "Mikhail, she *fought* them! Without a weapon. But she wasn't strong enough. She screamed 'Run for help!'"

Gisou began to weep.

"So I ran. The last time I saw her—" she began to weep. "Please! You've got to save her!"

Needa led the distraught girl to sit on a bench. Her teeth chattered, even though the night remained warm from the summer heat. Mikhail went down on one knee so he'd be at eye level.

"Gisou," he said gently. "It's *not* your fault. There were thirty of them, and only two of you. But I need you to think. Can you tell me, *exactly*, the last place you saw Pareesa?"

Her brown eyes met his, red-rimmed with fear. She wiped her nose.

"I will lead you there," she gave a determined nod.

Oh! These Ubaid women! He suppressed a smile.

"No, *laoch beag*."[162] He flared his wings. "I need a *landmark*. One I can see from the air."

---

[162] *Laoch beag:* an endearment, "little brave one."

Gisou stared up at the feathered appendages, deep in thought, and then described, using visible landmarks, the route she'd taken to get home. A thrill shot through him when she described where the enemy had bedded down — a place where two *wadi's* converged into one, the first one dry and grey, the second with reddish soil. He'd found Little Nemesis in such a place after one of her escapes.

"Darned goat," he muttered with a grateful prayer.

"We'd better tell the chief," Immanu said.

"The sentries already went to tell him," Gisou said. "They wanted me to come with them, but the way Jamin's been acting lately…"

"You did the right thing." Ninsianna squeezed her friend's shoulder. "We'll take you to the Chief *now* and you can tell him what he wants to know."

Immanu stared at the girl, his brow furrowed in thought.

"She got away too easy," he said.

"Easy?" Gisou burst out. "You think this was *easy?*"

Needa glared at him.

"I wasn't *accusing* you of anything—" Immanu said defensively. "What I'm saying is we've *seen* this tactic before."

The blood drained out of Ninsianna's mother's face.

"You think it's a trap?" Mikhail asked.

"Maybe," Immanu said. "But it's an *Uruk* tactic, not Amorite or Halifian. Lure the warriors away, and then attack the village while it is weak."

"But they have Pareesa!" Gisou cried out. "We can't just do *nothing!*"

He felt the same way, but he wasn't about to admit how distressed he felt at the fact they'd kidnapped his young protégé.

"You go warn the Chief we have raiders," Mikhail said. "And you—"

"I'll get my bow," Ninsianna said.

"Let me help?" Gisou grabbed his arm. "They took *mine*, but I made one for my younger brother."

The two girls stood together, fearful and eager-eyed. The part of him that loved Ninsianna didn't want to send her into danger. But the soldier in him whispered *"this was what you trained them to do…"*

"Go wake up the other archers," he decided. "Take a position on a roof so the enemy can't take a direct shot. But *do not* place yourself bodily in danger."

He went to his cot and grabbed his sword from underneath his bed, uttering a clicking prayer that the Cherubim had taught him, one so deeply ingrained that not even memory loss had been able to eradicate it from his psyche. A sense of cold detachment settled into his blood.

The raiders had taken one of *his*…

He would get her back…

"Be careful," he pressed his lips against Ninsianna's ear. "If anything were to happen to you…"

Her lip trembled as she nodded.

"You *know* this is a trap," she said.

Chanting a prayer only half-remembered from his Cherubim training, he stepped over the threshold, spread his wings, and leaped upward towards the waxing moon.

Immanu's voice followed him as he raced up into the sky.

"The gods will have no mercy on whoever took Pareesa."

Chapter 116

July – 3,390 BC
Earth: Village of Assur

NINSIANNA

They gathered at Orkedah's house, since she lived closest to the northern gate. The middle-age archer led them up a ladder, onto her roof. Across the street, they could see through the alley to the southern gate.

"Will this do?" Orkedah asked.

"It should," Ninsianna said. "Try to find things that will give us cover."[163]

They crept back downstairs and grabbed anything they could find; two sleeping pallets, a food-prep table, and a wooden chest, all things that could stop an arrow so long as they kept their heads down. Orkedah sent her children, and parents, to safety.

"Maybe we should split up?" Alalah suggested.

"Maybe?" Ninsianna said uncertainly. Pareesa had been the one who paid attention to Mikhail's prattlings about "kill boxes" and "cover." *She'd* just wanted to learn how to shoot ducks. *Darn it!* All this time, she'd been praying for the goddess to explain what she wanted Mikhail to teach her, and it'd been *her* who'd been refusing to learn. He'd been teaching them all along.

Orkedah and Kiana carried up a fire-crock filled with coals.

"What's that for?" Ninsianna asked.

"I overheard Mikhail talking about "tracer arrows," Kiana said. "He showed Pareesa how to wrap an arrow in linen and light it on fire so she could see."

"I remember that," Homa said. "I think you're supposed to use pitch."

"I don't have any pitch," Orkedah said.

"Do you have any grease?" Ninsianna suggested.

Orkedah grew thoughtful.

"I have some leftover duck fat," she said.

"Go and get it," Ninsianna said. "We'll replace it after the raid."

Orkedah disappeared, and then came back up carrying a tiny crock filled with rendered fat. Normally they used it for frying or for flat bread, but

---

[163] *Cover:* a physical barrier that will shield you from a weapon or explosion. Differs from *concealment*, which shields you from view, but not from weapons fire.

tonight, it would have to light their way. Homa tore a piece of cloth into slender ribbons, while Kiana dipped the strips in duck fat and showed the others how to wrap their arrows.

They crouched behind the tables, praying her father was wrong that the Halifians were about to raid. Their hopes were dashed when an arrow whistled.

"Ayiyahh—" a sentry screamed as he was cut down from the wall.

Dozens of arrows flew up over the rooftops.

"Get ready," Ninsianna whispered.

"Should we light the arrows?" Kiana whispered.

"Not yet," Ninsianna said. "We don't want them to know we are here."

Why hadn't she taken Mikhail more seriously when he'd prattled on about tactics? Him and Pareesa, they could go on for hours, until her eyes crossed and it made her head hurt.

A second volley flew over the wall, followed by ropes weighted with rocks. The warriors ran up and down the roof, trying to dislodge the climbing equipment. Several times an enemy fell, but just as often, the whistle of an arrow would be followed by an Assurian scream.

A man dropped into the alley.

"Look!" Alalah said. "Is that one of ours?"

"I can't see!" Ninsianna said.

The man ran to the gate and attempted to lift the bar.

"Not *ours,*" she said. "Light your arrows."

She dipped her arrow into the firepot and nocked it onto her bow.

Her heart pounding, she prayed:

'Great Mother, guide my hand....'

A familiar tingle settled into her body. Her arms, her legs, her fingers filled with warmth. It felt for a moment as if she was *two* people, herself, and somebody *bigger.* Everything began to glow: the man in the alley, her fellow archers, a cat that skittered across the street, even her own hands.

"Don't be frightened," the goddess whispered.

Ninsianna stood up and drew back her bowstring. The flaming arrow blinded her vision, but the sinew hummed reassuringly next to her cheek. She took aim, and then loosened her fingers. The arrow flew, exactly as Mikhail had taught her.

Fire illuminated the man who almost had the gate open. Ninsianna pulled a second arrow and shot him in the back.

"Get down!" Alalah shouted.

Ninsianna flung herself, trembling, down onto the roof as a volley of arrows flew up over the rooftops. Warriors screamed, but no arrow reached *this* side of the street. The enemy didn't know they were here ... *yet.*

"Oh no!" Gisou pointed at a rooftop several houses down.

Men wearing robes fought their way across the rooftops towards the front gate. They battled the warriors defending the wall.

"Who do I shoot?" Homa shouted.

"I can't tell the difference!" Gisou said.

Here and there, her archers shot sporadic fire, but it was difficult to tell in the dark whether they were shooting *their own* men or the enemy. She relied on that sense of *knowing*, the goddess' guiding hand, but what about the other archers? How could an un-*Chosen* know who to shoot?

The mercenaries reached the alley and began to rappel down. Ninsianna shot one. So did Alalah. But it was difficult to see. One of the enemies rushed for the gate. Ninsianna shot an arrow into his back, but she missed a vital organ. The man forced the sturdy bar up that barricaded their front gate.

"They've breached the gate!" she shouted.

The door swung opened...

Mercenaries rushed in.

They were met by second-tier warriors who rushed into the alley carrying spears. Inside the alley, a battle raged for control.

"I'm out of arrows," one of the archers shouted in the dark.

"Me too..."

"So am I..."

"Damn it! We need more arrows!" she prayed.

A noise behind them caused the women to jump.

"It's just me," Behnam whispered.

The old man unwrapped a bundle of freshly fletched arrows, most with brand new arrowheads that glistened with razor sharp edges.

'Thank you, Mother...'

Scrambling like eager gerbils, the women each grabbed a handful.

"Now what?" Yadidatum asked. The unlikely warrior looked worriedly at the alley where her betrothed fought for his life.

"We provide cover for the warriors," Behnam said.

Inside the alley, they couldn't tell who was who. But on the street, a pack of enemies crept, as stealthy as jackals, to cut them off from the other side.

"There's more of them!" Gisou pointed.

"They must have breached the wall someplace else."

"Nock your bows!" Ninsianna shouted.

They crouched behind the tables, bows aimed up towards the sky, bowstrings pulled back to their ears.

"Shoot!"

The women leaped up, took aim, and then dove back down to avoid being hit. The whoosh of arrows sounded like the goddess' breath. Enemies clutched at their chests and screamed.

"Again!"

She pulled another arrow from her quiver and led a second volley, and then a third. On the fourth volley, she sent another tracer. The fiery rags betrayed the attacker's nighttime position. Unfortunately, they were all still *novice* archers. Nervousness made them miss more targets than they hit.

"I wish Pareesa was here," Yadidatum said. "She's our best archer!"

"Pareesa, nothing!" Homa said as she restrung her bow. "I wish Mikhail was here!"

"Just keep shooting!" Ninsianna said, but cover fire could only do so much. With shouts of rage, the enemy drove back the warriors who defended the narrow alley. Men poured through the gap like scarab beetles swarming a carcass in the desert.

"They're inside the village!" Alalah shouted.

The enemy swarmed the wall where they were perched. They *knew* they were here. She didn't need the goddess' whispers to realize they were about to be trapped.

"Fall back!" Ninsianna shouted. "Alalah, Orkedah, that roof over there! Take Kiana with you."

Old Behnam crept up to her, elbow over elbow.

"I suggest three groups," Behnam said. "I'll take that rooftop there. The mud brick crenellation should provide a bit of cover."

Ninsianna gave him a grateful nod. Behnam might be old, but until he'd become too frail to fight hand-to-hand, he'd been a warrior of her grandfather Lugalbanda's generation.

"Yadidatum! Homa. Follow Behnam," Ninsianna shouted. "Gisou, you're with me!"

They ran along the rooftops until they reached a place they could descend safely. One by one, they scurried down the pine log leaning against the side of the house, branch nubs left intact to make a ladder, and ran to the new positions to make a second stand. They scurried up ladders to their new perches and resumed shooting cover fire.

"Ninsianna, we're almost out of arrows!" Gisou shouted.

Ninsianna reached for the next arrow, but her quiver came up empty. She looked around, frantic to find something to shoot. They had nothing.

"Drat!"

She stared, helplessly, as the enemy slew a warrior right in front of her. A clear shot, but she had nothing left to shoot.

A noise behind her caused her to jump. Pareesa's nine-year-old brother Namhu skittered up onto the roof.

"Namhu!" she scolded. "Don't come up behind us!"

"Pareesa would want you to have these."

He held Pareesa's starter-bow, the one she'd handed down to her younger brother, and a bundle of arrows.

"Thank you!" Ninsianna gave silent thanks to She-Who-Is.

"I can help you fight," Namhu said eagerly.

She opened her mouth to say he was too young, but first Mikhail, and then Jamin, had trained the boy, even if he'd only done so to irritate Mikhail.

"You have younger sisters at home, don't you?"

"Two of them," Namhu said. "And a baby sister!"

She handed Namhu two of the arrows.

"Tell them to hide in your grain cellar. If they come after you, kill them, but don't shoot unless they find your hiding place. Do you think you can do that?"

"Yes," Namhu said.

She held her breath as the boy skittered back down the ladder. Words of the Song of the Sword came into her mind. You didn't get much closer to raising armies from dust than recruiting a nine-year-old boy, but the Halifians had a history of taking children for ransom. The children needed protection as much as the women did.

The Chief arrived, surrounded by the older warriors, including her father; every one of them men who had battled the Uruk. They shored up the warriors, who'd begun to falter, despite their advanced age and the fact that many now suffered from infirmities. Her father shot several attackers before they got too close to effectively use a bow. Both sides switched to more traditional methods of fighting, hand-to-hand combat with spears and knives.

Conversations she'd heard between Mikhail and her father about the need to fortify village defenses came into her mind. Through *his* eyes, she could now see all the places he'd warned they were weak, but in their arrogance, they'd bragged that no one had ever breached Assur's walls. Their warriors got beaten back by mercenaries who had constant experience performing raids.

She wondered where Mikhail had gone and if he had found Pareesa.

Chapter 117

July – 3,390 BC
Earth: outside Assur
Colonel Mikhail Mannuki'ili

MIKHAIL

Rather than fly high, he flew low, and from the opposite direction. He could see the fire, and the women tied up around it. What he *couldn't* see were the men who had kidnapped them.

The cry of a small animal, its sleep disturbed by a clumsy foot, finally betrayed where the enemy had set up their ambush. While they knew he'd regained the gift of flight, nobody had ever taught them how to scan the night sky for black-brown wings.

"Ay-iyah!" a man shrieked as an avenging Angelic swooped down, sword drawn, like a terrifying bird of prey.

Mikhail decapitated him before he could finish his scream.

"Mikhail!" somebody shouted. He recognized Pareesa's voice.

The enemy rushed at him, surprised he'd landed *behind* them instead of in the *wadi* to rescue the women. Muttering the Cherubim meditations which separated his ability to think from his ability to feel, Mikhail crouched, wings flared, to take them on from whichever direction they came at him.

Their leader, an Amorite judging by the robe, snapped orders in an unknown language. Two men rushed forward, carrying a net. They attempted to throw it over him, to tangle up his wings, but he'd grown used to this tactic and flapped the net aside.

The subtle glow of the enemy's thoughts preceded their actions like a faint, white echo; a phantasm of intent which had not yet manifested into action. He perceived where their arrows were aimed before the enemy finished drawing their bows and swung his sword up as three came at him simultaneously. He knocked two of the arrows out of the air, but the third slammed into the tender flesh of his wing.

"Unk."

Pain radiated down into his axial muscles, nearly knocking him out of his enhanced state, but thankfully the injury wasn't sufficient to incapacitate him. He forced the pain out of his mind and snapped the arrow off. The only thing which mattered was whether it inhibited his ability to fly.

Mikhail straightened. His heartbeat roared in his ears.

The Amorite rushed at him.

"Look out!" Pareesa cried out.

A fifth man rose up from of the shadows. The *knowing* he accessed during battle felt the attacker's hostile thoughts, as well as the place on his back where the enemy intended to bury his spear. Mikhail spun and cut him down. Warm red blood splattered onto his cheek. An unearthly *hunger*, a terrible bloodlust, the urge to *destroy* rushed into his veins.

The enemy begged for mercy and ran towards Pareesa. She stuck out her foot. The man tripped over her outstretched legs.

The other women screamed as Mikhail cut the man down in front of them.

"Get his knife—" Mikhail kicked it towards Pareesa.

His young prodigy rolled towards the dead man, grabbed the knife, and began to saw at her bindings.

Two more enemies rushed at him with spears. Mikhail snapped one with his blade and kicked the enemy in the chest to knock him back into the second man. He grabbed the second spear and used it to skewer both. He felt no emotion as they writhed in agony, but decapitated the both of them to end their suffering.

The three unknown women who were tied up next to Pareesa sobbed in terror as his Little Fairy struggled to free herself.

More enemies came out of the shadows, but he could *see* their intent before they released their arrows. Swinging his sword to create an arc, he knocked the arrows out of the air. One slipped past his sword and thudded into his shoulder. He whispered the Cherubim prayer for a disciplined mind, for the ability to choose which stimuli he wished to feel. *Work methodically. Take out the biggest threat. Ignore your pain. Attend to your injuries later...*

He leaped after the bowman who he calculated was the best shot, and then cut down a second enemy who rushed to defend the first. They were out of arrows. The rest came at him with spears.

He beckoned to the trio in a universal gesture of '*bring it on...*'

The enemy circled, trying to figure out an angle of attack. He studied them, watched them, observed the flicker of *knowing* as their minds replayed various scenarios and then settled upon a course of action. He could see the forward rush of energy *before* they moved. Their leader shouted, they all rushed at him at once.

He leaped into the air, flapping his wings to gain just enough height that the three stumbled into each other, off balance as their spears met empty air. He dropped back down and grabbed the first one by the neck, twisting the man's head to snap his spine. The second enemy he threw to the ground and pinned his neck beneath one boot, stomping his neck to crush his larynx.

The man gurgled and writhed, unable to catch his breath.

The third enemy came at him with a spear. A 'whoosh' split the air. Pareesa appeared from the shadows, carrying the enemy's bow. She'd shot the last raider with his own arrow.

"That will teach you to kidnap women!" Pareesa hissed at her dying assailant.

She ran towards him, and then stopped. Her brown eyes grew wide with alarm. She drew her bow, not at the enemy, but at *him*.

"Mikhail," her voice warbled. "Your eyes…"

That sense of *knowing*, the one which ruthlessly calculated action, could see no echo of intent in his young mentor's aim. Pareesa was frightened. This was a side of him she had never seen before.

He tilted his head, suddenly unable to speak her language.

"*Osoreru koto wa arimasen,*" he said in the language which filled his mind. Don't be afraid.

He held up his empty hands to show he'd sheathed his sword.

Pareesa trembled, but stood her ground between him and the three unknown women even though, in her spirit-echo, he could see she wanted to throw herself into his arms and weep. She was a natural warrior, but she was also a twelve-summer girl. Reflected in her eyes, he could see his own unearthly blue ones, no longer just irises in a sea of white, but filled with an internal luminescence.

'This is normal,' his mind whispered. This was part of what he became when the gods wielded him as a weapon. Everything was fine as long as he never lost control of his anger.

Pareesa lowered her arrow.

"I overheard these two—" she gestured at two dead Halifians "—tell the others—" she pointed at the dead Amorites "—they were sending a band to attack Assur. They used *me* to lure you into a trap!"

Without a word, he leaped into the air, ignoring the arrow still stuck in his wing as he raced back to Assur.

Chapter 118

July – 3,390 BC
Earth: Village of Assur

NINSIANNA

Ninsianna drew her bowstring and pulled it back to her cheek. In the road which ran between the houses, dark shapes, a formless mass of arms and spears, clashed in the shadows, only marginally lit by the moon.

"Who should I shoot?" her friend, Yadidatum shouted.

"Aim at the enemy," Ninsianna said.

"I can't *see* them," Yadidatum said. "How can I tell friend from foe?"

Ninsianna tracked the movement with the tip of her arrow, focusing her unreliable gift to *see* with something besides her mortal eyes. Was that a Halifian robe? An Amorite? Some other tribe? She jerked the arrow, ready to release the bowstring. No! That was the Chief, his shawl-cape askew as the enemy cut him off from his protector, Varshab, not a colorful robe.

'*Great Mother?*' she prayed. '*Help my aim go true?*'

That familiar *tingle* resonated through her flesh. One of the enemies brightened. '*Here.*' A multi-colored robe!

She released her arrow, whispering a prayer as the feathers left her cheek. A man cried out, and then he fell. Had she hit an enemy? Or had she just killed one of theirs?

Enemies scrambled like ants through Assur's supposedly impenetrable front gate.

'*I did this...*' her subconscious chided her. '*I made this possible when I removed my grandfather's protective spell.*'

Homa released her arrow.

"I think I hit one," she said.

"Make sure you don't hit one of *ours*," Alalah chided her.

"There's Jamin!" Gisou pointed at the elite warriors.

The other archers cheered: "Now they're in for it!"

The elite warriors moved behind him like a pack of lions. Over the years, she'd seen Jamin hunt, watched him train his warriors, and even watched him spar with more-than-serious intent in competitions against other tribes. But unlike the other times, when the *Muhafiz* went in for the kill, this time, Jamin's spirit-light wavered with uncertainty, as though he couldn't *believe* that the men who breached walls were *really* their enemies?

The elite warriors fought helter-skelter, attempting to compensate for the lack of leadership. Several times, one of the warriors got cut off, and it was only their years of watching one another's back which prompted the others to prevent their kinsman from getting cut down. The enemy slipped through their ranks like water through a sieve, out of the alley and into Assur's main street. Within a matter of heartbeats, the elite warriors were surrounded by enemies on both sides.

"Tirdard!" Yadidatum shrieked.

The curvaceous beauty stood up and shot an enemy who'd been about to cut her boyfriend down.

The elite warriors battled, but they were clearly *losing*...

An almost-silent whisper caused Ninsianna to look up.

A night owl...

A black silhouette crossed the crescent moon.

A tingle of excitement rippled down her spine.

'Here is my Champion,' the goddess whispered, 'come to protect you.'

The rustle of feathers was barely audible as her love swooped down from the sky and landed in the attackers midst.

"There's Mikhail!" they cheered.

He cut down the assailants like a scythe harvesting wheat, ensuring with a backstab or quick decapitation that his attackers wouldn't get back up. With his wings unfurled to their full fighting length, not only did they help him levitate, but provided an additional pair of fighting limbs. His arms, his wings, down to the smallest feather, knees and elbows, hands and feet; every part of him was a weapon, wielded with ruthless efficiency. Even without his sword, Mikhail was *deadly*.

The first time she'd seen him fight, she'd mistaken his efficiency for a pitiless dark power, but now that she was *Chosen*, she could see the years of self-discipline, the pattern in his moves, and the smooth choreography of countless hours of training.

He moved in a *killing dance*; his sword singing a deadly song as it made contact with human flesh and splattered blood like rain. Blue light streamed through his entire body. Mikhail had been transformed into an instrument of *HER* will.

The warriors rallied and rushed at their attackers, staying clear of his arcing silver blade. He stood head and shoulders above them, a winged god come to anchor their resolve, urging them to stand together and *fight* as an army instead of every man for himself.

"Keep shooting!" Ninsianna ordered.

She and the archers released arrow after arrow, providing cover as the Assurians turned the tide. The goddess whispered *'this one'* to a man wearing a bandolier and a colorful robe, obviously their leader, but each time she took aim, he scurried behind one of their warriors.

Drat!

The Amorite leader called out to his mercenaries; the attackers ran towards the gate.

"Block them!" Chief Kiyan shouted. "Don't give them any quarter."

Trapped between the Assurians and the avenging Angelic, the enemy regrouped and focused on the man blocking their path...

Mikhail...

The Chief recognized the shift in tactics away from killing *him* to killing Mikhail. The older warriors moved solidly behind the Chief, both following and protecting their leader, but there were too many enemies to come to Mikhail's aid.

The Chief turned to his son who battled their enemies without rhyme, reason, or heart.

"Jamin," he pointed his spear at Mikhail, "back him up!"

Siamek and the younger warriors fell into line, ready to follow Jamin back into the thick of battle. He took one step towards Mikhail and froze...

Ninsianna could almost *see* the flashback that leaped into Jamin's mind.

Mikhail, standing above him, wings flared like a bat. His bloody sword, swinging down for the death-stroke. His soulless eyes, pitiless, inhuman and black...

Chief Kiyan witnessed his son's cowardice.

"Siamek!" he shouted.

Siamek and the warriors formed a semi-circle in front of the Chief.

One of the mercenaries sprung forward to stab the Chief; as he did, he stepped out of the cover provided by a warrior who'd been blocking Ninsianna's shot. She drew her bow and let the arrow fly. It struck the enemy in the chest just as he stabbed the Chief's neck. The Chief danced out of his way, holding a scratch, but otherwise unharmed. He glanced up at Ninsianna, nodding appreciation. He moved forward to engage the next attacker.

"Siamek!" the Chief shouted, "help Mikhail!"

With a hearty shout, Siamek led the elite warriors to fight at Mikhail's side, close enough to protect his back, but smart enough to stay out of his flight path as he hacked and whirled, decapitated and slaughtered. The young men moved with disorganized determination, but with Mikhail moving methodically from the biggest threat to the smallest, their individual skills made up for their lack of coherence. Enemy taunts quickly turned into screams as the tide of battle turned in favor of the Assurians.

A cruel-looking man, dressed in a colorful, striped robe with a leather bandolier, and a handful of similarly-dressed men, made a break for the front gate.

"Stop them!" the Chief shouted.

Jamin lunged at the ringleader, screaming with bloodlust, but while he fought and killed one of the men, the rest escaped through the front gate.

Within a matter of heartbeats, the battle was over. Thirty enemies and eleven Assurians lay dead. As one wounded enemy reached for his bow, Mikhail cut him down without a backwards glance.

"Come, we must tend the wounded!" Ninsianna shouted to the other archers.

They climbed down from the rooftops and moved through the carnage. Some of the dead were Halifian, but most wore clothing from tribes she had never seen. Jamin kneeled in front of one of the enemy who lay moaning, clutching his intestines. He spat in the man's face, and then stabbed him in the throat.

The chief approached Mikhail.

"Wait!" Ninsianna leaped between them. She held her hand up, trembling, praying that her beloved recognized her this time.

Chief Kiyan gave her a puzzled look, still panting from his recent exertions.

"Don't," she warned.

"I was just going to—"

Ninsianna pointed to the bodies piled at Mikhail's feet.

"Not until the blood lust passes."

Her eyes met *his*, beautiful, glowing, radiantly blue; but emotionless and deadly, gazing out of a face stained red with blood and gore. They were *not* the eyes of her beloved, but the *force* which used him as a sword.

"Go," she whispered.

Mikhail took to the air. He circled the village, keeping watch as his shadow passed back and forth across the moon. The villagers came flooding out their houses to help the wounded and to grieve for the Assurians who had died.

Her father came up behind her and put his hand upon her shoulder.

"You described it." Papa shook his head. "But I didn't believe it. Now I understand why the old songs describe his kind as swords of the gods."

With the sight granted to her by the goddess, *HER* purpose for sending Mikhail here was gradually becoming clearer. Mikhail already *knew* everything the goddess needed. Everything else had been stripped away. The fault lay not with *him*, but with *them* for refusing to do what they needed to do.

The words of the Song of the Sword came into her mind, so palpable it felt as though the goddess sang the words.

'A sword of the gods to defend the people, and raise armies from the dust...'

She gave her father a hug.

"I understand now!" she said excitedly. "You must go to the Chief and convince him that *every* villager must train to fight, from the oldest to the youngest, male and female, young and old."

"To be like Mikhail?"

"She-Who-Is sent him to prepare us," she said. "The demons that will come will be a lot worse than these Halifians."

Behnam ran up.

"I sent the archers to help your mother," Behnam said.

"I should go with them," she said.

"No," Papa said. "*You* must help Mikhail. I saw an arrow sticking out of his wing."

Ninsianna's heart leaped into her throat. Mikhail was hurt?

"I will find him and bring him home."

Chapter 119

> *And [Lucifer], who was their leader, said unto them:*
> *'I fear ye won't indeed agree to do this deed,*
> *And I alone shall have to pay the penalty of a great sin'*
> *And they all answered him and said: 'Let us all swear an oath,*
> *And all bind ourselves by mutual imprecations*
> *Not to abandon this plan, but to do this thing.'*
>
> Book of Enoch, Book 1 – Watchers

Galactic Standard Date: 152,323.07 AE
Angelic Air Force carrier 'Jehoshaphat'
General Abaddon 'the Destroyer'

ABADDON

The flight crew moved with frenetic activity as muscular, grey troop carrier settled onto the flight deck. Moisture that had been picked up in the planet's atmosphere and then frozen in space evaporated in wispy clouds as the hull split open.

Abaddon appeared first, for he *always* led his men from the front, burly grey wings spread wide as he lumbered down the ramp, his sword held in front of him like an old-style gunslinger. His crew marched down the ramp behind him, Angelic and Mantoid, although these days, there were precious few Angelics, with their wings held tight against their backs and shoulders slumped.

Abaddon growled as his combat boots slipped on a long, scarlet smear that had crystallized into ice at the bottom of the ramp.

"Clean that up!" he bellowed.

The flight crew scrambled out of the way as he gestured at the blood with his sword, and then reformed, like a flock of pigeons scattering to avoid a hawk.

"Yes, Sir!"

The hanger bay fell silent as Abaddon stepped onto the flight deck and dropped to one knee. The fighting men fell into formation and bowed their heads. He placed his bloody sword in front of him and placed his hand reverently upon the floor.

"It's good to be home, *colún beag*," he murmured.

The *Jehoshaphat's* hyperdrives purred beneath his fingers. Her name meant *"Judgment of God."* She'd been a grateful Parliament's gift for holding Shay'tan at bay after their Emperor had disappeared.

Abaddon stood up to face his men. Not one of them looked him in the eye. They all stared down at their combat boots.

"Praise those who uphold the Emperor's *law*," he shouted hollowly.

"In light there is order, and in order there is life," the men replied a half-hearted refrain.

"At ease," Abaddon said.

The flight crew surged towards the troop carrier armed with torque wrenches to fix their non-existent damage, while two men rolled over a crate filled with power cores to replenish the ones he'd just expended putting on a fireworks display.

His *aide de campe*, a competent Mantoid by the name of Sikurull, handed him a soft, white chamois cloth.

"Another successful mission, Sir?"

"Mission?" Abaddon snarled. "What mission? It was just a bunch of kids who never learned you can't fight a pulse rifle with stones."

Sikurull remained silent as he ran the cloth down the blood-groove of his sword. Stupid, senseless death! The kid who'd leaped into his ship, armed with a suicide vest, hadn't lasted long enough to trip the detonator. He slid the blade, solemnly, back into its sheath.

He was a hard man, forged in the fires of Shay'tan's hammer, the Alliance's oldest serving general. He'd taken his first kill to win back a homeworld so remote that nobody even remembered the planet's name, and come up through the ranks the old-fashioned way, one dead Sata'anic lizard at a time. But lately? He'd begun to question why he was here.

His men broke apart as soon as he dismissed them. Most wandered over to rubberneck the sleek white devil cruiser which sat, parked, in the visitor's section of the hanger.

Abaddon ignored it and headed towards the head.[164]

"Sir?" Lieutenant Sikurull gestured at the ship.

"Let him wait."

"He says it's a matter of utmost importance," Sikurull said.

"Important?" Abaddon snarled. "Like the mission they just sent us on? To terrorize our own people?"

Sikurull's gossamer wings hummed with worry. His *aide-de-camp* knew better than to antagonize him when he was in this kind of *fuck-it-all-to-hell* mood. In a species trained to display cool reserve, Abaddon's temper was feared almost as much as his Sata'anic sword.

---

[164] *Head:* slang for bathroom.

"I'll wait outside, Sir." Sikurull skittered out.

Abaddon unzipped his pants and aimed at the small red dragon some joker had painted at the back of the urinal.

The scrape of feathers, so soft, it sounded like a serpent's hiss, alerted him he wasn't in the bathroom alone. An uncomfortable sensation rippled through his pinfeathers.

"Stupid kids!" he called out. "When is Hashem going to send me to fight a *real* enemy?"

The white-winged figure moved out of the shadows, not his usual playboy *strut*, but the ruthless echo of a rebel leader who'd long lain dead and in the grave. Lucifer's silver eyes glittered like a cat.

"That could be a long time, General," Lucifer said. "My father is determined to *shame* you into retiring."

Retire? Where in Hades would he go? Born into the military, having served his entire life in the military, and already having buried every Angelic he'd ever cared about, the last thing he wanted was to twiddle his thumbs while the Alliance he'd spent his entire life defending ran itself off a cliff. If their entire species was about to journey into that dark night, he intended to go down in a blaze of glory so bright that posterity would forever remember his name.

"Can't a man get a bit of privacy?" Abaddon snapped.

"If you wanted privacy, you'd have gone straight to your quarters."

Abaddon grunted, but the kid knew him. It was an old ritual, one that he'd taught him. To engage the military, a leader had to, quite literally, "win the pissing contest."

Both men stood in silence as they struggled to urinate the longest. Lucifer outlasted him, fortified, no doubt, by an entire bottle of liquor. Both headed, silently, over to the sink to wash their hands. Lucifer leaned casually against the wall, toying with a paper towel, while Abaddon picked the blood out from beneath his fingernails.

"It was a *stupid* insurrection," Abaddon said at last. "Just a bunch of out-of-work factory workers, protesting *your* stupid trade policies. Without jobs, they can't feed their families."

"You, better than anybody, understand why I had to enact them?" Lucifer said softly.

With a disgusted snort, Abaddon whirled and marched out of the bathroom. The flight crew stood at attention, and then fell into chaos when Lucifer sauntered out behind him like some kind of rock star.

"Mister Prime Minister!" they shouted eagerly.

The crewmen swarmed around him like a bunch of baby birds, each vying for a piece of worm as he shook each man's hand and addressed them all by name.

Abaddon broke away and headed deeper into the ship. He didn't have *time* to indulge Lucifer's self-adulation. Crewmen streamed past him, each one giving him a crisp salute, but not a single man would meet his gaze.

Lucifer trotted to catch up.

"Really, General," Lucifer said. "Aren't *you* the one who taught me to *never* take the military for granted?"

Abaddon grunted. Normally Lucifer was able to butter him up, but he was in a rip-roaring piss-foul mood right now. Godsdammit! The Emperor had sent him to disarm *their own people!*

"What do you *want*, Lucifer?"

"Want?" Lucifer's eyes glittered like a pair of silver mirrors. "It's not what I *want*, General, but what I've come to *give* you."

Purely on instinct, he took a sharp left towards the lesser conference room, the one located closest to his personal quarters, and not the "official" room located near the ship's bridge. His hunch paid off when he found Furcas and Pruflas, Lucifer's two enormous "goons," lurking like bookends on either side of the doorway.

The goons gave him a meat-handed salute. While he had no doubt that he could take them, the men had always given him the creeps. It felt like staring into the eyes of a pair of dead men.

"Sir." They lumbered out of the way with flat-footed efficiency and allowed Abaddon to pass.

As he expected, that obsequious ass-kisser, Zepar, waited inside, along with a man who wore the vulgar purple robes of a Hammonite high priest, embroidered with gold fertility symbols. Both men stood up, but the blue-clad figure who sat between them remained in their seat, covered from head to toe in some kind of burqa.

"General," Zepar's oily voice dripped obsequiousness.

Abaddon gave him the minimal courtesy of a salute and then turned to face the priest, a four-limbed species that otherwise bore little resemblance to anything one might deem "humanoid."

"A Hammonite?" he asked.

"We are all children of the One True God," the man made a Sata'anic gesture of respect.

"The Emperor outlawed your religion," Abaddon said.

"And yet we thrive?" The priest fondled the gold phalluses which decorated his stole. "Only Shay'tan's lizards bear offspring faster than Hammonite wives."

Abaddon was old enough to *remember* when Hashem had first issued his "be fruitful and multiply" edict, the one which forbade them to marry, and instead ordered them to flit from partner to partner to promote genetic diversity. He'd been young and handsome back then, a rising star who'd been nicknamed "the Destroyer" by none other than Shay'tan, himself, after he'd handed the old dragon a particularly brutal defeat. Pretty young cadets had fallen into his lap, each eager to bear his offspring.

It hadn't taken long to figure out *why* the Emperor had resorted to such extreme measures. In 635 years of trying, not only had he failed to produce a single offspring, but as word had gotten around that he was infertile, young women had begun to avoid him, reluctant to "waste" their once-every-other-year heat cycle on a scarred old goat that was shooting blanks. Sure, he was high-ranking enough to *order* the "mating appointment clerk" to put him on the list, but who in Hades wanted to fuck a woman who cringed at an old man's touch?

Lucifer wore an expression like a cat that had caught a bird. He gestured at Zepar.

"Unwrap the general's gift."

His chief lackey pulled the woman's veil off.

The women was a dark-haired Angelic with olive skin and a pair of mahogany eyes. Abaddon gaped at the dark-complexioned Seraphim. And then it hit him…

"Where are her wings?"

Lucifer donned a wolf-like grin. "She doesn't have any."

"How."

"I found the root race."

"Where?"

"Right where Hashem left them." Lucifer made a sarcastic gesture. "You know how my father is. Always starting little seed worlds and then forgetting where he put them. And then—" he clasped his hands to his cheeks "—ooopsie! We're dying out, and father forgets that he ceded a thirteenth world to Shay'tan during the last galactic war."

Abaddon's lip curled in a snarl.

"He's known where they were all along?" Amongst a species that prided itself on self-control, *The Destroyer* was infamous for his temper.

"Of course he did," Lucifer said. "It was Shay'tan who brought their existence to my attention. Not that the old dragon is doing it for *our* benefit. You know how Shay'tan is. Everything comes at a price."

Abaddon inhaled the woman's scent. The scent of lutropin, the hormone women emitted whenever they came into heat, was more powerful an aphrodisiac than the most expensive drug.

"What will this cost me?"

Neither Shay'tan, nor Lucifer, ever gave gifts without strings.

"Ahh, the price…" Lucifer rustled his feathers in a familiar sales pitch. "The Emperor has enacted some policies which undermine the stability of the Alliance. All I ask is your *support* when I approach Parliament and ask them to override the Emperor's seed world restrictions."

Abaddon grappled with the legality of Lucifer's proposal. Parliament did, in fact, possess the authority to override the Emperor by a two-thirds vote of both houses. During the Emperor's two-hundred year 'sabbatical', it was the only way they'd been able to get Alliance business done. If Lucifer's demands became unreasonable, he would simply refuse to follow through.

He examined the female that Lucifer had brought him.

"Why is she so quiet," he asked. "What did you do to her?"

"The humans grew up on a primitive planet," Lucifer shrugged. "We've found it necessary to sedate them until they adjust."

"*How* primitive?" Abaddon's feathers prickled.

"Oh, you know how it is?" Lucifer waved one hand. "Shay'tan says one thing. My father says something different. But the old dragon *claims* my father deliberately knocked them back into the Stone Age as a 'control' group for the other twelve colonies. And then he abandoned them."

"Is she sentient?" Abaddon asked. "Will she bear sentient offspring?"

"How shall I put this?" Lucifer gave an exaggerated sigh. "She will bear fine offspring who are every bit as intelligent as you are, but you'll need to find somebody *else* to talk to if you want to discuss troop movements."

"I'm a man of action," Abaddon snorted, "not some intellectual in an ivory tower."

"Which is *why*," Lucifer laughed, "I brought the first gift to *you*."

Abaddon snorted.

"Ass-kissing doesn't work."

"You can't fault me for trying," Lucifer shrugged. "Besides, if I *didn't* try, you'd think I'd had a brain aneurysm or something."

Old dreams, long buried and forgotten, rose to the surface as Abaddon stared at the beautiful, dark-haired female with the mahogany brown eyes. He'd loved a woman once, but before she'd come into her heat-cycle she'd been killed in battle, her last words to whisper his name as she had died in his arms. This woman reminded him of that long-lost love, gone so many centuries that her memory had faded, all except her eyes as the light had gone out of them and left him on the battlefield, grieving.

"I refuse to make a deal with Shay'tan," Abaddon said.

"You won't be making it with Shay'tan," Lucifer said. "You'll be making it with *me*."

"So what are your terms?" Abaddon asked.

"Nothing too opprobrious," Lucifer said glibly. "Impregnate her, and then keep her existence secret until I've match-made enough humans to reach a critical mass."

"Why wait?" Abaddon asked. "If you announce you've found the root race, every hybrid in the galaxy will follow you."

"Humans accept Angelics because we look like them," Lucifer said, "but the other hybrids terrify them. It would be unfair to help ourselves and not our brothers-in-arms, don't you agree?"

He'd had done some heavy fighting alongside the other hybrids. He was *not* about to grab a prize for himself and deny it to the others. They would succeed, or fail, as a single hybrid race.

"So how do we do this?" Abaddon asked.

"It's human custom to get married *before* engaging in sexual relations. Like our species did before the Emperor declared otherwise."

"She will agree?" Abaddon asked.

"Ask her yourself," Lucifer laughed. "She comes to you wearing her wedding dress, and *here*—" he gestured at the Hammonite "—is a priest."

Abaddon could tell the woman had been drugged, but as she made eye contact, butterflies fluttered in his stomach. A creature of legend wanted to marry old blood and guts? He was painfully aware of the battle-scar which ran from temple to chin, the one which had split his eyebrow in half and nearly cost him his eye. No Angelic female would accept a male with such a hideous scar, much less one who was blacklisted for being infertile. But at *his* age, it didn't matter whether or not this female could produce offspring with him or not. His dreams had been reduced to not spending the rest of his life alone.

His heart pounded in his throat as he took her hand and asked the question his god had forbidden him to ever ask.

"My beautiful dear, do you wish to become my wife?"

He kissed her knuckles. The fog cleared as she looked into his eyes, as though he stared into the eyes of that long-lost love, but instead of watching the light go *out* of them, he watched the light pour back *in*. He could tell she was a proud woman by how regally she carried herself, as though she was used to giving orders.

She murmured something in a language he couldn't understand. She traced the scar which had nearly taken out his eye, and then small fingers closed trustingly around his larger ones. Abaddon the Destroyer, the fiercest Air Force general the Alliance had ever produced, thought he might faint.

"It's official!" Lucifer clapped his hands. "She shall be your mate for life."

Abaddon's head hummed as the priest read the nuptials. He couldn't wait until Lucifer got his trade deal so he could show her off.

"Human females are kept in harems." Lucifer handed him the woman's burqa. "She will be most comfortable keeping herself covered except when she is in the safety of your private quarters. It will solve the problem of keeping her identity secret with your crew."

"They will think I have taken a non-hybrid mistress," Abaddon laughed.

"Let the crew imagine what they wish," Lucifer said. "The truth is more preposterous than their wildest dream!"

Abaddon shepherded his bride into his personal quarters. He ordered his crew to keep the matter of the unknown, veiled creature quiet under penalty of court martial and to not disturb him for at least three days.

Chapter 120

July – 3,390 BC
Earth: Village of Assur

NINSIANNA

She found him perched on the roof of her parent's home, crouched in the same leopard-like pose he'd assumed that night at the ship, muttering prayers in the clicking Cherubim language. His eyes glittered with an internal blue light that was every bit as disconcerting as the golden light that burned within her *own* eyes ever since She-Who-Is had chosen to speak through her. It was an emotionless gaze, but neither cruel nor inhuman. Thanks to her gift of tongues, she now understood that he prayed for the lives he'd been forced to reap.

"I'll go inside," she called up to him, "to get supplies to dress your wounds."

They made eye contact.

Mikhail nodded.

Ninsianna forced a smile.

The moment she got inside, her false bravado shattered. How long had it taken him the *last* time he'd killed Halifians? Several hours? Half a day? She shuddered at the memory of his sword at her throat.

Mikhail loves me...

He wouldn't hurt her. She was confident of that. If he tried, She-Who-Is would stop him, again...

...she hoped....

She took a deep breath before going back outside.

"I'm ready," she spoke in Cherubim.

He spread his wings and glided down like a dark, silent shroud. He didn't make eye contact, although she sensed he was more aware of her presence *now* than at any time since he'd known her. Whatever source of power he drew upon, it was definitely *not* She-Who-Is.

"Come under the shade canopy—" she feigned normalcy. "Near the lamp, so I can patch you up."

He sat upon the nearest stool, covered in gore from wingtip to foot. By the eerie blue glint in his eyes, he was not yet fully back from the grip of the killing dance, but she could see the beginnings of emotion by the set of his wings. The blue light her goddess-enhanced eyes had seen stream forth like sunlight during battle began to waiver, no longer necessary in the safety of their home.

She spoke to reassure him before she touched his injuries.

"I must look at your shoulder." She touched a dark stain on his shirt. "I may need to put a few stitches in so it doesn't keep opening up."

She slipped the neckline aside to confirm it was an arrow which he'd broken off. His flesh was as warm, as *inviting* as always, but the cold blue light which radiated out of him was anything but mortal. It felt like touching fire, only the fire was cold.

"You need to take this off so I can get at it," she tugged at his shirt.

His lips moved silently in prayer as she exposed his injuries. The arrowhead was imbedded in his all-too-mortal pectoral muscle. As much as she feared working on him while still possessed by the gods, it would be less painful to remove it *now*, while he was still under a spell, rather than later, when he would feel every awkward poke.

"I need to dig this out." She touched his cheek. "Are you ready?"

Eye contact.

"Yes," he spoke in Cherubim.

Behind the eerie glimmer, she caught a glimpse of her beloved.

The flowing blue spirit-light gradually settled inward, a glimmer of blue still glittering around the edge of his irises. She must work quickly, while the blue light shielded his ability to feel.

She gave him an apologetic smile.

"This will hurt."

She pressed her obsidian blade against his skin and cut into his flesh like a slab of meat. His chest muscles quivered, but other than a quick exhalation, he kept his expression blank. The arrowhead made a sucking sound as she reached into the muscle and pulled it from his flesh. All-too-mortal blood dripped down his inhumanly strong pectoral muscles.

"Souvenir," she placed it on the table. "Now I'll stitch you up."

Mikhail grunted consent.

She doused the wound with a stinging embrocation made of witch hazel, but suppressed the urge to kiss him. Allowing him to linger in that cold mental place would spare him pain. Threading her bone needle with a horse tail thread, she punctured thirty stitches into his pectoral muscle where it spanned his shoulder and chest. His wings twitched, but while his flesh betrayed he was in pain, Mikhail's chiseled features remained distant and stoic.

She counted not one, but *two* arrows in his wings.

"They shot through," she said. "If I strip off the fletching, I can think I can pull the shafts the rest of the way through without cutting you."

This time, as she pulled them out, Mikhail definitely flinched. The more he came back to her, the less he could ignore it. He didn't utter a single syllable of pain, but by the tremble of feathers beneath her fingertips, the killing dance no longer protected him from *feeling* what she was doing.

Plucking out enough feathers to get at the two wounds, she sewed them up. Examining him to see if he had any wounds she'd missed, at last she was satisfied.

She placed the palm of her hand upon his cheek.

"My parents will be bringing wounded here to treat. You will get no sleep in the common area. I want you to sleep in *my* bed tonight."

Mikhail nodded, his eyes filled with pain.

With a sigh, he pulled her into his arms and buried his nose into her neck.

"Ninsianna," he murmured.

Only the tremors beneath his flesh betrayed the emotion he'd been suppressing.

"Come," she led him up to her tiny room. "Up here. You need to sleep."

He stumbled up the stairs, utterly exhausted, and curled up behind her in her narrow bed, holding each other as they fell asleep. There was nothing sexual about their first night together. Just two creatures seeking comfort in the arms of the person they loved. Ninsianna sensed, as she had that first day on the ship, that he needed her to touch him and let him know he was not alone.

Snuggling her head onto his arm and whispering goodnight, she felt him shiver as he wrapped his arms and wings around her and drew her close.

Chapter 121

Galactic Standard Date: 152,323.07 AE
Ascended Realms
Emperor Shay'tan

SHAY'TAN

His adversary drummed his fingers on the three-dimensional chessboard that was also a model of the galaxy, smirking at the sight of his white knight still sitting amongst Shay'tan's black pawns in Zulu sector.

"You look pleased with yourself?" Shay'tan fished for information.

"Oh … it's nothing," Hashem said evasively.

Had She-Who-Is tipped him off? The goddess *swore* she never played favorites, but he knew better than anyone that *HER* definition of "favorites" depended upon her whim.

Shay'tan pondered his next move. His adversary was so focused on the outer reaches of the galaxy that he'd failed to protect his white queen.

He picked up a chess piece.

"Check."

Chapter 122

ΔΥϽΠΔΠϟ

Galactic Standard Date: 152,323.07 AE
Alpha Sector: Command Carrier 'Eternal Light'
Supreme Commander-General Jophiel

JOPHIEL

Her crew knew better than to disturb her when she retreated into her personal quarters to analyze intelligence reports—especially *these* ones—the ones requested by Raphael. They were largely "health and safety checks" from different ends of the galaxy, along with reports from spies. Individually, each report pointed in a different direction, but taken together, they amounted to a *massive* buildup that was about to be aimed ... where?

Her door-chime beeped. Jophiel looked up with surprise.

"You may enter," she spoke through the intercom.

The door slid open. A green, heart-shaped head peered in—Lieutenant Klik'rr. His dual antennae jutted off his head helter-skelter, as though he'd just been roused from a sound sleep.

"Sir?" his gossamer under-wings hummed furiously. "You have an alpha-priority-one message from Haven-4."

A sense of dread settled into her stomach. Only *one* thing mattered on Haven-4.

"Is Uriel okay?"

Klik'rr clasped his prayer-like front legs together.

"He's *sick*. They said you must come right away."

"But they *assured* me he'd be safe!"

Klik'rr bowed his head.

"They said it's the wasting sickness. They don't expect—" His voice modulation box crackled. "Sir?" he gave a mournful chirp. "They don't expect he'll survive."

Jophiel reached for the small wallet of photographs that she kept hidden in the breast-pocket of her uniform of *all* her offspring, even though such sentimentality was discouraged. Klik'rr's words faded. Why hadn't she obeyed the frantic compulsion to go and *see* her own child?

"Sir?" Klik'rr hovered anxiously. "Is there anything I can do?"

Jophiel rose from her seat and braced both hands against the desk.

"Recall Colonel Israfa from Zulu Sector," she choked out. "Send a *'needle'* ship. Tell him to meet me at Haven-4."

Beneath her feet, the *Eternal Light* lurched ominously, or perhaps that was just *her*? She flared her wings, fighting to stay upright. Klik'rr grabbed her arm.

"I told the ATO you'll be leaving immediately—" his words sounded far away. "Your transport shuttle is already prepped for flight."

"Yes, of course," she mumbled.

Klik'rr guided her to the door, where two airmen half-carried her through the labyrinthine hallways in a mindless blur. In her heart, she'd known Uriel needed to stay close to her, and she'd cast him aside! Abandoned him! To pursue her *stupid* career!

The crewmen whispered as she passed; their eyes filled with pity:

"I hear he is dying..."

"MY son died..."

"They're ALL dying..."

"Lucifer is right. The Emperor doesn't care..."

The two airmen led her into the shuttle. Lieutenant Klik'rr buckled her in the way one might an injured child.

"Don't worry, Sir," Klik'rr said. "I'll take care of *everything*. You just worry about your son."

As the shuttle door closed, the flight crew gave a crisp salute. Without being ordered, they all began to pray to countless minor deities in far-flung homeworlds to spare the life of one, tiny baby.

Chapter 123

HD 219134 g. K-type star HR 8832
Cassiopeia System
Colonel Mikhail Mannuki'ili

MIKHAIL

A mortar exploded next to them, spraying them in the face with dirt. A woman screamed. Glicki!

"Fall back! Fall back!" The order came over the radio.

Mikhail rushed to her side, cradling her in his arms. Her green, prayer-like grasping arms were held close to her chest, trembling in pain.

"Glicki," he said. "You're going to be okay."

He touched her green exoskeleton, which had taken the brunt of the shrapnel. Green blood seeped out of the joint of one of the four legs she used to walk.

"Good thing we come with built-in armor?" she chirped out of her voice translator.

Another mortar exploded, even closer. He shielded her with his wings as debris rained down upon them.

"Can you walk?"

"Yes."

She tried to move her leg and screamed in pain. Mikhail examined the wound. She bled profusely; an artery had been hit. If he could tie it off, she would make it. Unfortunately, insectoid physiology was notoriously difficult to tourniquet. He had to get her out of here before she bled out.

"Major Mannuki'ili?" one of the other soldiers asked. "What do we do?"

He looked to the men and women in his special operations group, six of them. One was Angelic, the others were Mantoid. All were fine soldiers. His sensitive ears could hear the Sata'anic lizards creeping through the underbrush on either side of them. Shay'tan wanted this planet, and he would take it from them.

Mikhail looked first to his wounded friend, and then to his special forces team. Although the same height as him and slender, insectoids were heavy. Too heavy for an Angelic to fly out of here, not even with the stronger wings bequeathed to him thanks to his Seraphim blood. Although Mantoids had wings, they were more suited to long flying jumps rather than the true flight Angelics were capable of. With her leg in such condition, Glicki couldn't fly. The Sata'anic lizards blocked their escape. There was only one thing left to do.

His eyes met Glicki's green-gold compound ones. Glicki nodded. She knew what he needed to do, and she agreed.

They clasped hands: "We complete the mission."

Tucking Glicki into a low point in the dirt with a tourniquet around her wounded leg, he covered her with brush, and then signaled his remaining team to fan out through the underbrush. It was time to hunt. Clicking the Cherubim meditations for stalking prey, he pressed his wings against his back and crept up behind a squadron of lizard-people trailing a rumbling tank. His team was vastly outnumbered, but he was about to even those odds. It was not to his pulse-rifle he looked to now, but a silent weapon: his knife. He slipped behind a lagging lizard soldier; the man's tail bobbed from side-to-side with a bayonet strapped to his tail. With sharp claws on their hands and feet, as well as their fangs, Shay'tan had bred them to do their best fighting up close and personal.

Just the way the Cherubim had taught -him- to fight...

Clutching his knife in his hand, Mikhail crept up silently behind him and slit his throat.

*

Mikhail's eyes shot open. He sat up, his wings slamming against the wall as he reached for the knife and came up empty handed. He hyperventilated until he recognized he'd fallen asleep in Ninsianna's bed.

She lay in his arms, his beautiful goddess. His heart and soul.

Soon to be his wife.

'Protect her...' every instinct whispered.

Protect her from what?

From the lizard whose throat he had cut?

He'd barely caught a glimpse of the enemy, but deep in his soul, he *knew* they were already here.

Chapter 124

July – 3,390 BC
Earth: Village of Assur

NINSIANNA

Ninsianna snuggled deeper into her feather "blanket", relishing the warm throb of blood which whirred through the firm bicep she'd been using as a pillow. The sound of voices downstairs dragged her out of her pleasant dream. Suppressing a yawn, she stretched and turned towards Mikhail.

Blue eyes stared into hers, already wide-awake.

"Good morning." She wiggled closer to his warmth.

"Did you sleep okay?" he asked.

"I didn't have any nightmares," she said.

"Good," he replied, his blue eyes serious. "I had a dream last night."

"The battle?" she guessed.

"No," he said. "I *think* it might have been a memory."

"What kind of memory?"

"About a friend."

"Raphael?" she asked.

"No," he said. "She wasn't Angelic. She was some kind of *insect*."

"Like the Cherubim?"

"No." He shook his head. "She was more like *me*. An ordinary soldier. All I know is that she was badly injured, and we had to fight our way out of there to get help before she died."

"Did she survive?"

"I can't remember! All I know is that –I– am still alive!"

His spirit-light no longer flowed towards *her*, but back towards the sky, the way it had when they'd first met. Whoever this female insect was, she meant more to him than simply a colleague.

She ran her fingers across his chest, to the place where she'd pulled the arrow from his pectoral muscle last night. An insect-women? That couldn't be a threat to her, could it? She ran her fingers down to the older injury, the place she'd pulled out an iron spear. Beneath the hole in his broken ribcage, his heart beat steady and strong.

"I'm sure she was alright," Ninsianna said. "With *you* there to protect her…"

"I'm not s—"

Downstairs, someone knocked, loudly, on the door. Her mother answered. A cacophony of voices asked for Mikhail.

Why wouldn't they let the poor man rest?

"Breakfast will be ready soon," she said matter-of-factly. "Would you like me to bring something up?"

He moved to get up.

"We'll eat together—"

She silenced him with a kiss.

"You're covered in blood. Let me fetch some clean clothing so Mama doesn't scold me for leaving you in such a sorry state."

She leaped off her sleeping pallet and grabbed his shirt. It was too bad he'd fallen asleep in his pants – *that* would keep him segregated until she found out what *else* he remembered. Thankfully his overdeveloped sense of modesty would disincline him to wander downstairs before she had a chance to find out what their *guests* wanted.

For good measure, she bent down and grabbed his combat boots.

"I'll be right back!" she lied cheerfully.

She ignored his protest and darted past the antelope-hide which separated her bedroom from the stairs. Voices filtered up, all of them women. Ninsianna rewound her shawl-dress, and ran her fingers through her hair. No doubt she *looked* like she'd spent the night with Mikhail, and not in a platonic way! She clutched his clothing to her chest as she climbed, one-handed, down the slanted ladder.

"Ninsianna!" Pareesa greeted her.

"Good morning, Little Fairy."

Except for a few scratches, the littlest archer appeared surprisingly untraumatized. On the carpet beside her knelt three exotically dressed women with straight black hair and almond-shaped eyes. Their embroidered travel cloaks were dyed glorious shades of color: lapis blue, emerald green, and the most amazing cape of all, a magnificent shade of scarlet-red. The youngest was not much older than Pareesa, while the oldest appeared to be the same age as her Mama. While the Amorites traded in sex-slaves, these women were far too finely dressed to be simple concubines.

"These are the women Mikhail helped Pareesa free," Mama said. "The Chief *insists* we help them get back home."

From the way Mama emphasized the word '*insist*,' she understood Mama meant *"the Chief wishes to interrogate them and discover all he can about our new enemy."*

"How have you been communicating?" she asked Pareesa.

"Only by gesture," Pareesa said.

"It appears," Mama said, "that we have no words in common."

Ninsianna frowned. While her "gift of tongues" enabled her to speak the languages which Mikhail spoke, she had no idea if she could translate anything *other* than a language of heaven? But this wasn't the *first* time she'd had to learn a completely new language on her own.

"Hello?" she gave the three huddled women a friendly smile. "I am—" she pointed to her own chest "—Ninsianna. This—" she pointed to her mother "—is Needa, and this—" she pointed at the youngest archer "—is Pareesa." She then pointed to the youngest stranger. "And who might *you* be?"

Understanding dawned in the woman's dark eyes.

"*Menman* Seyahat," she said.

"Excellent!" Ninsianna clapped her hands together. "*Menman* Ninsianna—" she pointed back at herself "—and *you*—" she pointed to the next-oldest woman, "—are *who?*"

"*Menman* Fatma," the second woman said eagerly. Fatma turned to Seyahat and said something in whatever language they spoke. By the time the third woman gave her name, "*Menman* Norhan", that familiar tingle radiated into her body. The language came to her.

"You are safe here," Ninsianna said fluently.

The oldest woman gasped.

"You speak our language?"

Ninsianna gestured at the small, clay goddess figurine which adorned her father's altar.

"She-Who-Is has given me the ability to speak all languages, so long as I convey her message."

The three women bowed their foreheads down to the felted carpet.

"Truly, we are blessed," the eldest, Norhan spoke. "First a winged man saves us, and then a golden-eyed goddess speaks for the gods."

Mama shot her a look which warned, *"Don't you dare trot out your silly "Chosen One" story."*

"I am simply a woman with a gift," Ninsianna demurred. "I understand because She-Who-Is wishes to help you get home."

The three women put their heads together and murmured in a low-level conversation. Can we trust these people? Or will they take advantage? Was their family alive or dead?

"Our caravan was attacked when we crossed the Zagros Mountains," the eldest, Norhan said. "We come from Margiana,[165] on the other side of the landlocked sea."[166]

---

[165] *Margiana:* a kingdom which spanned the "Silk Road" from eastern Iran, through Afghanistan, and into Turkmenistan.

[166] *Landlocked Sea:* the Caspian Sea.

Ninsianna translated for her mother.

"Margiana?" Mama frowned. "I've heard of the landlocked sea, but never the lands beyond that."

"Perhaps the tribunal would know?"

"Maybe," Mama said. "Until then, all we can do is make our guests comfortable."

Ninsianna translated for the three Margian women. The youngest woman began to weep.

"Maybe Mikhail could *fly* there?" Pareesa suggested.

"Where?" Ninsianna said crossly. "And while he is gone, who will make sure we don't get attacked again?"

Pareesa's face dropped.

"I just thought…"

"He could carry them?" Ninsianna snapped. "Well he *can't*. If you'd *been* here last night, when I patched him back together, you would understand that Mikhail is not a god!"

"He was injured?" Pareesa gasped.

"Of *course* he was injured," Ninsianna said. "After he freed *you*, he defended the front gate. He took three arrows."

"Where is he?"

"Upstairs, in my room."

Pareesa lifted one eyebrow.

"It's not like that!" Ninsianna protested. "I sent him upstairs to rest so *annoying* early morning guests wouldn't disturb him!"

Pareesa's face lit up.

"I've never seen someone take out that many men!"

Ninsianna shivered. She *had* seen him take out more than that, single-handed. The memory of his pitiless black eyes *still* gave her nightmares.

"He was trained by the Cherubim," she said, "the guardians of the Eternal Emperor. But whenever he kills, it weighs heavily upon his soul. So *don't* talk about it as if it delights you!"

Pareesa chewed her lip, deep in thought. She, better than any of them, seemed to grasp her mentor's strict moral code.

"Okay," she sighed. "I will *try* not to annoy him."

"Oh, little fairy!" Ninsianna hugged her. "That's what he *adores* about you! Just try not to do it too much? Okay? At least for the next few days."

A muffled curse came from the head of the stairs. First one large, bare foot, and then another, followed by a blood-darkened combat fatigues encasing long, muscular legs, and a powerful bare abdomen and chest, climbed down the ladder, followed, last, by a pair of black-brown wings.

The three Margian women threw themselves down upon the carpet and screamed.

"Oh, great god!" they cried out.

Mikhail shot her a puzzled look.

"I told you to stay upstairs!" Ninsianna scolded him.

He glanced down at his blood-splattered pants. Almost self-consciously, he curled his wings around his naked chest.

The movement of his wings caused the three terrified women to cry out.

"Sorry," he mumbled. "I'll just, uhm—" He glanced out the door at the courtyard like a trapped falcon, eyeing the door of its cage. "Maybe I'll go get ready to, uh, *train*?"

He sidled past the three prostrated women and grabbed a clean shirt, more nervous about *them* than they were of the winged avenger. Pareesa giggled and tried to get them to sit back up. While she didn't speak their language, she'd gained their trust by freeing them and leading them back here. The three women watched Mikhail get dressed, owl-eyed.

"Will we train today?" Pareesa asked as he yanked on his combat boots.

"I must speak with the Chief," Mikhail said. "Ask Alalah to lead this afternoon's class?"

"From now on," Pareesa said triumphantly, "the entire village will want to train."

Mikhail nodded. This wasn't the victory he had wanted, but it was the one which he had *gotten*.

"You'd better teach *me* to use that fancy weapon, *son*," Mama said, "in case some Halifian decides an old hag like me is nubile enough for the slavers."

Mikhail raised one eyebrow. Ninsianna may have inherited her father's eyes and broad mouth, but thank the goddess she otherwise resembled her mother. At 36 years old, Mama was still young, and beautiful enough, to be a target.

Ninsianna turned to the three exotic women.

"Pareesa will take you to get some breakfast," she translated into the Margian language. "And then she'll take you to meet our Chief. He's a good man. He'll know how to get you home."

The three foreign women thanked her and followed Pareesa. As they passed Mikhail, they bowed and murmured words of gratitude. Mikhail waited until they had exited, and then headed towards the courtyard.

"Don't you want me to check your injuries?" Ninsianna asked.

Mikhail paused; but did not turn to face her.

"I've got to fly patrol—" his voice sounded distant.

His spirit light said something different. He *intended* to fly back to his ship and pry more memories out of its shattered hull. Without waiting for an answer, he flared his wings and was gone.

Chapter 125

July – 3,390 BC
Earth: Crashed ship

MIKHAIL

He circled the valley, taking note of any sign that their enemies had tried to breach his ship, but the People of the Desert had left his ship alone ever since the *last* time he'd tangled with them, the day before he'd met Gimal in the desert. Fortunately, or unfortunately, it depended on whether he looked at it from a perspective of concealment, or eventual escape, the ship remained half-buried.

Fluttering to the ground, he checked the booby traps he'd set out to make sure nobody went into his ship; not just the Halifians, but curious Ubaid. He'd taken to checking his ship weekly, more to mark his territory than any hope that the piddling repairs he made would ever get it flying again. A journey that had taken two days on foot took less than an hour now that he'd regained the gift of flight.

With a groan of exertion, he rolled the enormous boulder away from the crack in his hull – since the door, itself, was buried against the side of the cliff – and stepped inside. It felt like stepping into a cave.

The ship smelled dusty, not damp, for this time of year the oasis dried down, but stale, from lack of use. He went to the computer, which he kept trying to get operational, and tried again. The computer could tell him who he was, why he was here, and everything he needed to know about Major Glicki.

As usual, the computer remained completely dead.

"Didn't think so," he grunted.

He moved to the pilot's station, completely dark thanks to the rocks piled over the windshield. He ran his fingers down a crack. Couldn't go into space with *that* in his windshield. The moment he pressurized, BAM!! Explosive decompression. A painful way to die.

He sat in the pilot's seat and pulled out his flight log. Since he'd been running black ops, the log was encoded in case it fell into enemy hands. While he could read the script, he couldn't remember what it meant.

He scanned the log.

'*HMS Light Emerging...*'

That was Raphael's ship.

The rest of the log listed planets, ships and coordinates, but it didn't *mean* anything. They were all simply numbers and names.

One set of coordinates, however, caught his attention:

HD 219134 g. K-type star HR 8832. Cassiopeia.

That was where he'd killed the lizard. That was where he'd led a Special Forces platoon. That was where the woman in the dream had either met her maker, or survived.

After that mission, the logo he used to log his own name had changed from "Major" to his current rank of "Colonel."

He flipped through his logs and tried to get an estimate of time. Several years ago, perhaps? The log was purposefully vague, more to jog his memory than to recreate where he had been. But he had *been* places, lots of places, all over the galaxy.

And couldn't *remember…*

But whatever he'd been up to, he suspected it had been important.

He set down the log and moved deeper into his ship, into his sleeping quarters, and rummaged through his things, searching for anything which might connect him to Major Glicki. Since this was a scout ship, he suspected he purposefully kept it free of memories in case he was ever captured, so they couldn't use the people he cared about as leverage to make him talk.

But there was *one* personal item he'd dared to keep with him…

He opened his locker and took down a small, carved box. It had been elaborately carved with Seraphim symbols, not the modern version which he spoke, but closer, perhaps, to the archaic language which Immanu used.

On the lid it said:

I will wait for you, just but on the other side…

He opened the lid and fondled the velvet lining. While he couldn't remember doing it, he'd spent a great deal of time carving this box.

Inside sat the smoke-charred ruins of a wooden doll. A sob of grief lodged in his throat. It was the reaction he *always* had every time he looked at the doll, but he couldn't remember who he grieved for.

He took it out and stared at the tiny carved Angelic female. It was by no means the work of a master craftsman. It had been carved by a child, for another child. He suspected, no, *knew*, that he'd been the one to carve it, and had gotten it back because the recipient was now dead.

"Who were you?" he asked.

The doll stared back at him with her too-large eyes.

Was this Major Glicki?

No.

He ran his finger over the doll's broken tail. She was definitely Angelic, but with unusual characteristics. He must have added the tail to amuse her.

Why had he brought it with him, been carrying it in his pocket, when his ship had been shot down?

There were no answers here. Only a sense of loss.

"We will meet each other again," he promised the doll.

He put her back into her elaborately carved grave, put her back on the shelf, and shut the door.

Chapter 126

Galactic Standard Date: 152,323.07
Zulu Sector: H.M.S. Light Emerging
Colonel Raphael Israfa

RAPHAEL

Because her primary function was to gather intelligence, the *Light Emerging* boasted some of the most brilliant engineers in the fleet. Therefore, it was a matter of no small importance when their head engineer summoned Raphael down to weigh in on a problem about a malfunctioning drone.

"See that, right there?" the engineer pointed at a scratch. "It's been jimmied."

"But there's nobody out here!" a second engineer remarked.

"It's a *scratch*," the first engineer said. "Somebody drilled into this and then replaced the screw."

Raphael bent over the malfunctioning drone and examined the maintenance access panel. It had *definitely* been drilled out, and then replaced.

"What systems have been compromised?" he asked.

"She's relaying data," the second engineer said, "but for some reason, she appears "blind" to certain frequencies."

"Are you sure one of *us* didn't do this?" he pointed at the scratch. "Before it was deployed?"

The head engineer shook his furry, antelope-like head. Normally Saori's were assigned to the Centauri cavalry, but at his request, Jophiel had transferred this particular engineer *here* to help him track down Mikhail's last distress call.

"I took this one out of the box, brand new," the first engineer said. "She still had that new spaceship smell. Not a mark on her."

Raphael looked to the second engineer, a competent Mantoid who'd been miffed when he'd transferred in the socially-lacking, but incredibly competent Saori, as a same-rank peer. Ever since, the two had bickered like siblings.

"I *thought* it was brand new," the second engineer grudgingly agreed, "but maybe we failed to notice? The drone manufacturer may have sold us a remanufactured dud?"

"It would explain why the drone keeps malfunctioning?" Raphael suggested.

"It *would*," the first engineer said. "But this is the *second* drone we've lost in a single week. My guess is sabotage."

"There's nobody *out* here, Sir," the second engineer protested. "Why would they sabotage us?"

"Somebody is out here," the first engineer said, "or else *why* would they keep sabotaging our drones."

"Who?" the second engineered laughed. "Trans-dimensional aliens?"

Both engineers laughed nervously. Trans-dimensional alien abductions were a recurring urban legend out here in the uncharted territories.

Raphael pondered the mystery of the scratch-marked drone. The first malfunctioning drone had borne burn marks, as if somebody had hit it with an energy weapon, but it had left no detectable traces of plasma, so more likely it'd been struck by a micro-asteroid. Sabotaging spy drones was an old Sata'anic trick, but usually those drones were deployed over a well-known base. If the lizards spotted one, sometimes they'd hack into it and feed them misinformation.

But thus far, they hadn't seen *any* sign of life.

Before he could contemplate the problem, an anxious hum caused all *three* of them to glance at the doorway. Glicki limped in, favoring the injury which had earned her the rank of '*Major*'. She clasped her prayer-like tibia together in an anxious prayer; her red, compound eyes glistened with tears.

"What is it, Major?" Raphael greeted his second-in-command.

Glicki's under-wings hummed louder.

"Sir? It's your son."

Chapter 127

When the gods created mankind,
Death they dispensed to mankind,
Life they kept for themselves.

— The Epic of Gilgamesh

July – 3,390 BC
Earth: Village of Assur

NINSIANNA

The entire village streamed outside the walls to the place they buried their dead; with graves dug shallowly into the earth, and then piled high with rocks to make a cairn. Atop each grave, a clay figure had been placed representing the deceased, dressed in scraps of fabric and piled high with the family's customary "prayer offering" to the shaman: three urns of beer and eighty loaves of bread.

Sweating beneath her heavy shamanic headdress and itchy bone neckplate, Ninsianna recited the *Atra-hasis*, her people's origin story:

> God and man were mixed together in the clay.
> A god sacrificed, a spirit created from the god's flesh.
> She-Who-Is announced 'life' would be mankind's sign,
> And so he would not be forgotten, a ghost would be created.[167]

It was these ghosts that the Ubaid now placated; for a person, not properly mourned, would linger among the living and wreak havoc in their loved one's lives.

"The water--" her father held out an elaborately decorated clay pitcher. It had been painted with spirals, all-seeing eyes, and a symbol they now recognized was more than a myth: a winged man carrying the deceased up to the heavens.

Ninsianna moved to stand at the head of the first grave; a clay figurine had been shaped to represent a sentry who'd lost his life.

---

[167] *Atra-hasis*: the Sumerian origin story which states the gods sacrificed one of their own and used that god's flesh to imbue humanity with an immortal soul.

> The spirit has entered, the spirit has departed,
> May you enter the eternal realm,
> And never know hunger or thirst again.[168]

She poured a drop of water on the statue. The man's widow wept as the clay figurine turned blood-red, but the warrior had died bravely and passed into the dreamtime. His widow stood surrounded by their children, family and friends. Ninsianna repeated the ritual at the next few cairns, but when she got to the seventh one, chills ran up her spine.

'*Help me…*'

Formless fingers touched her body. Shadows moved around her. She could *feel* the dead woman's mortal wound; her fear, her terror, her last thoughts as she had perished.

Ninsianna dropped the pitcher.

"Papa?"

Her father grabbed it before it shattered.

"It's just Ashusikildigir," he murmured reassuringly. "She's worried about who will take care of her children."

Ninsianna stared down at the only female statue, laid out, in a single grave, side by side with her husband. Both had died when raiders had kicked down their door; a house that had been targeted, she suspected, because they had daughters of "marriageable age." Rather than capitulate, Ashusikildigir and her husband had fought to the death. Their daughters stood alone at the gravesite; one thirteen, the other eleven. Unlike all of the *other* clay statutes which had been shaped to resemble the living and fired by a potter, *their* parents' statues were unfired river-mud; hastily shaped by immature, impoverished hands. Instead of the normal "offering" for prayers by the shaman, the girls had laid out a goat-skin filled with water and two loaves of bread

"What do I do?" Ninsianna squeaked.

"Let her in as far as your throat," Papa said. "Loan her use of your voice to speak to the living."

Mama had warned her to never allow just *any* old spirit into her body, especially not the kind who lingered around the living, but Papa believed it was their job to help the dead speak. It was one thing when She-Who-Is did it; she relished the familiar thread of power which slipped into her body whenever the goddess, or one of her servants, gave her information. But this was only a mortal! There was *no way* she was about to let a *dead* person, and had she mentioned, *DEAD*, take possession of her body!

"No," her voice trembled.

---

[168] Lines from the cuneiform tablet: "*Ningiszida's Journey to the Netherworld.*"

"You must."

"No!" she shook with terror.

"You *must*," her father gripped her arm. "These girls have given *everything* they have."

She stared at the paltry offer of two loaves of bread, but that wasn't the problem. Even as a little girl, she'd been terrified of the dead, but ever since she'd fallen down the well, sometimes she could *feel* the Dark Lord's shadow-cats move around her. But she'd seen her father perform this ritual many times. Maybe there was another way? One more suited to the *Chosen* of She-Who-Is?

She held her hands aloft and said, in her most dramatic voice:

"Ashusikildigir is trapped between the realms. She cannot enter the dreamtime until someone swears to finish raising her children."

She held her breath and prayed…

Please, somebody do the right thing?

In a land that was prone to famine, few families were eager to rear somebody else's child. Sometimes, like now, the extended family needed to be *shamed* into fulfilling their moral responsibilities. She glanced over at her cousin and suppressed a twinge of guilt. Gita wasn't her problem, her father was still alive. Ashusikildigir and her husband, on the other hand, were both *dead*, leaving their daughters without a protector. She waited, hands raised, for the other villagers to grow weary of the family's cowardice.

The villagers began to hiss at a couple hiding at the back of the crowd.

"Shame on you!"

A young mother with three small children, one still on the breast, stepped forward; Ashusikildigir's sister. Her husband stayed behind, his expression furious. It was obvious which one hoped to shirk their family obligations.

"Do you swear upon your sister's grave to raise her two daughters as though they were your own?" Ninsianna asked.

Ashusikildigir's sister gave her husband a fearful glance.

"I do."

Ninsianna could *see* the angry red light which flowed off the husband, issuing invisible threats to his wife. He had no intention of keeping *her* promise. The girls would be turned out at the first opportunity, potentially along with his *own* wife and children.

'*Great Mother,*' she prayed, '*how do I solve this problem?*'

"Wait a moment!" She put her hands across her eyes, a trick she'd seen her father do when he wished to enhance what he was saying. "I sense …"

She walked to stand in front of the dead woman's brother-in-law. Focusing on the *thread* which connected her to the goddess, She-Who-Is sent her an image…

Like a hyena, Ninsianna moved in for the kill.

"You borrowed seed from Ashusikildigir's husband to plant your crops and haven't repaid it. This seed is part of the girl's estate. You must repay this debt immediately."

"But I'm *willing* to help raise them!" the brother-in-law protested.

"See that you do," Ninsianna said. "Or the Chief will demand recompense so two innocents don't go hungry."

"That I will!" Chief Kiyan spoke up. He was a stickler about making people repay their debts. Especially when it left *him* holding the consequences in the form of two parentless children.

"I will take the oath," the brother-in-law grumbled.

Ninsianna made the brother-in-law swear first, and then the sister, aware that the death oath was legally binding. If either of them failed to follow through, the tribunal would treat them the same way they would a parent who abandoned their own child. The sister looked relieved. The problem had never lain with her.

Ninsianna sensed the dead touch her again, but this time it didn't feel ominous. The wind whispered *'thank you'* as Ashusikildigir crossed into the dreamtime.

Resuming the ceremony, she offered water to the remaining graves until all eleven Assurians had been laid to rest. When she reached the final grave, she glanced at Mikhail. Now came the *real* challenge; to convince the reluctant villagers that the goddess had set a great task.

That *thread* which connected her to the goddess welled with power. Her body tingled. All of the villagers radiated colorful spirit-lights. A cloud appeared from nowhere, blotting out the sun. The land grew dark. A frigid wind cooled the summer heat and caused the villagers to clutch at their capes.

With a smile, Ninsianna welcomed the Great Mother into her body. Power surged through her veins as words bubbled to her lips.

"I have sent my *Champion* to teach you how to fight," the air vibrated with power. "The Evil One has seized his mortal vessel. You must unite the tribes, *all* human tribes, to stand against him, or your world will be destroyed."

As the goddess released her, Ninsianna swooned.

Mikhail held her up.

The cloud dissipated as mysteriously as it had appeared.

Chief Kiyan stepped forward.

"You heard her," he said. "Starting tomorrow, every man, woman and child must train to defend this village, using whatever means they can."

Chapter 128

Galactic Standard Date: 152,323.07
Diplomatic Carrier 'Prince of Tyre'
Prime Minister Lucifer

LUCIFER

His eyes bolted open with a startle.

"If we raid the cobalt mining world," a red-maned nightmare wearing the bars of a Tokoloshe general said, "the inhabitants will *beg* Shay'tan to ride in and rescue them."

"But can you get the two emperors to *fight—*" a second bear-shaped Tokoloshe squinted at Lucifer. "We need them to look the other way."

"Hashem laid claim to that world eons ago," Zepar cut in. "He won't let Shay'tan take it away from him. Especially not if his own *Prime Minister—*" all six Tokoloshe laughed "—goes before Parliament and *shames* them into action," Zepar finished.

Lucifer fought through a fog of meaningless conversation.

This *had* to be a dream.

He closed his eyes, and opened them again, but there were still six cannibals seated around his conference table. In the center sat some kind of farm animal, stripped of its flesh and, by the scratch marks on the table, eaten while still alive.

He pinched himself, but the Tokoloshe remained. So did the half-eaten plate of raw meat at *his* place at the table. The entire room *stank* of fear and blood.

Lucifer began to gag.

"Zepar?" his voice warbled.

"Yes, Master," his Chief of Staff said.

"Can I speak to you a moment," he said. "Out in the hallway?"

The cannibals eyed him with a perplexed expression as he leaped up from his seat and, with a gag of revulsion, noted the crimson speckles all over his snow-white feathers. Zepar frowned, and then murmured something in a language he did not understand. He led Lucifer out into the hallway, closely flanked by the goons, Furcas and Pruflas.

"Is something the matter, Sire?" Zepar sounded annoyed.

"Why are we meeting with the *cannibals*?" Lucifer asked.

"Because you ordered it," Zepar said blandly. "Don't you remember?"

No. He *didn't* remember. But he couldn't say that, because then Zepar would send him back to that quack, the one who'd drilled holes into his head and then, two months later, he'd learned he'd been in "recovery" in a sanatorium. Right now, the Emperor was looking for an excuse, *any* excuse, to disband Parliament so he didn't have to deal with a pesky democracy.

"That's not what I *mean*," Lucifer said. "I *mean* this is a waste of time!"

He fluttered down the hallway in a mock-huff, half walking, half flying, to get as far away from the disgusting creatures as he could possibly get. A snow white trail of pinfeathers, all of them stress-molted, floated in his wake.

Zepar ran after him:

"Lucifer! Lucifer!"

Lucifer turned a corner, down a service corridor that he rarely used, and broke into a run. Unfortunately the hallway, while wide enough to flare his wings, wasn't high enough to actually take flight. He spied two men standing guard on either side of a doorway, ordinary crewmen. He vaguely recalled this was where they'd put his so-called "wives."

"Let me in," Lucifer said.

"But Zepar said—"

"Let me *in*," Lucifer demanded. He glanced nervously down the hallway. He could hear Furcas and Pruflas' heavy footsteps.

"Yes, Sir." The guard, named Ruax, opened the door.

Lucifer ducked inside. As soon as he did, he was met with ear-splitting screams.

He clamped his hands over his ears, dumbstruck at the sight. There were not just *three* human females in his so-called "harem," the number of "wives" he'd had the *last* time he'd woken up from a blackout, but now there were fourteen? Every one of them as terrified, stupid and violent as the first one?

The door opened behind him.

"There you are!" Zepar said, the way one might say to a lost toddler.

"Why are these women *here*?" Lucifer asked. "Shouldn't they be in with the ones we are gifting to hybrid generals?"

Zepar said with a patronizing voice.

"Don't you *remember*? All of these women are your *wives*."

A sense of vertigo caused him to grab the edge of one of the bunks.

"I only need to sire *one* heir," he mumbled, trying to figure out what in *Hades* was going on, "and you gave me *three*. What I need now is *leverage*."

"Which is why you asked to meet with the Tokoloshe," Zepar said.

"I'd rather get *leverage* by matchmaking these women to hybrid generals," Lucifer said, "like we did with General Abaddon."

Zepar's laugh took on a cruel edge.

"We can't," he said.

"What do you *mean* we can't?" Lucifer shouted. "I'm the Alliance Prime Minister!"

"We can't, Sire," Zepar said with a patient voice, "because every one of these women is carrying your child."

Chapter 129

July – 3,390 BC
Earth: Village of Assur

JAMIN

He lingered at the back of the funeral, furious at his father's announcement. But he did not dare face Ninsianna and her eerie golden eyes.

Whispers had gone through the village. Someone had passed intelligence to their enemies. A traitor... But so far, no one had traced their suspicions back to *him*. How could they? Attacking Assur had not been part of the plan!

Eleven dead! And thirty-eight mercenaries. They were supposed to kill Mikhail, not double back and attack the village!

Before the Amorites had betrayed him, Rimsin, son of Kudursin, had pulled out a circle of gold, hammered flat, and decorated with a bas-relief lizard he *claimed* was called a "dragon." According to the Amorites, these so-called "lizard-gods" were buying women, not for themselves, but to sell to Mikhail's people.

He'd been right all along!

But now he was in a pickle. If he told his father, he'd have to say how he had come by this information. His father wasn't stupid. He'd know that he'd sold them out.

His cheek twitched; a nervous tic which had grown worse ever since the winged demon had stolen his girl. He could fix this. Mikhail's people were the *real* enemy.

"Jamin?" Shahla asked.

He jumped.

Shahla knew what he had done...

"This wasn't supposed to happen," Shahla wept. "All I did was tell the trader where Pareesa like to hunt."

His fists clenched as he contemplated the best way to kill her. He could lure her away and kill her with a spear. No. Her screams would attract attention. Slit her throat with a knife? Too messy ... someone would find the blood. Perhaps he could strangle her? Strangulation would be silent and not leave a mess. Kind, even... He'd make love to her, and then, right as she orgasmed, place his hands around her throat. But then where would he hide the body? Her father Laum was a wealthy man. He would not let his daughter simply disappear.

Another kidnapping? Perhaps he could sell her to the Amorites?

No…

For all her sleeping around, Shahla had never conceived a child. The slavers insisted the lizards wanted breeding stock, not concubines. Defective merchandise was turned out into the desert to die. Shahla was a resourceful woman, with no qualms about using her body for favors. What would happen if she made her way back to Assur? The villagers would execute him. He *had* to kill her. It was the only way to guarantee her silence.

Shahla leaned into him, her head against her shoulder.

"It's not our fault," Shahla sniffled. "We were only trying to do what is best for the village."

Her arms slid around his waist. So trusting… Shahla was in love with him, or more accurately, the *position* he could afford her.

'You're not a murderer…' the wind whispered.

No, he wasn't a murderer. Which is why he felt so *guilty*…

The "trader" in question was one of her father's compatriots, a man who, not only *traded* with Laum, but also fenced contraband for the mercenaries who'd approached him in the desert. It had been Rimsin's idea, to leave him "blameless." The "trader," while conducting business with her father, had asked Shahla where Pareesa liked to hunt and, no doubt, while he'd been inside their village, reported back every house where he'd noted a marriageable-aged daughter. If she ever accused him, perhaps he could accuse her father of masterminding this attack?

Which made Rimsin's betrayal all that much more *infuriating*….

He slipped his arms around Shahla's shoulders.

"My father is a *fool*."

He pointed to the people who surrounded Mikhail like a saving god. That should be *him*, ordered to train the warriors, but instead of training more elite warriors, his father intended to squander their resources by training a bunch of ineffective men, women, and even children?

It would only *weaken* them! Not make them stronger.

He noted the way Mikhail watched everything, analyzing the weak spots. This latest "training strategy" was just a ploy to weaken their defenses. Only *he* knew that Mikhail was working for their *real* enemy….

The Angelic race…

"Tell me what I can do to help?" Shahla searched his eyes. "That's what the wife of a future chief would do, wouldn't she? Do whatever is necessary to support her husband?

Even if he didn't love her, he wasn't a murderer. But he *had* to keep her silent…

"Let's go," Jamin nuzzled her neck. "I want to make love to my future wife."

Chapter 130

July – 3,390 BC
Earth: Village of Assur
Colonel Mikhail Mannuki'ili

MIKHAIL

They trudged down from the village, singularly, and in groups. The men he'd been charged with training. Young and old, herders and craftsmen. Farmers, with their clothing still stained from the fields. A few stood proud and tall, men who could take down a boar with a single spear, but most clustered together in nervous flocks; they were only here because the Chief had ordered it.

Over two hundred men! What in *Hades* had he gotten himself into?

Next marched the elite warriors, their cadence subdued. Jamin was absent. They positioned themselves to his right; not out of any deference to *him*, he was certain, but from a lifetime of deferring to their *Muhafiz*.

The last person to appear was Kiaresh, the man the Chief had assigned to be his liaison. Heavily muscled, he was younger than the Chief, but older than the rest of the elite warriors; the only remaining "elite" warrior to have served when the Ubaid still waged war against the Uruk. Battle scars and wisdom etched the older man's face.

He gave Mikhail and apologetic grimace.

"He's not coming?" Mikhail guessed.

"No," Kiaresh said. "When I left, he was still arguing with his father."

Mikhail let out a frustrated hiss.

"I can't *train* them if their *Muhafiz* refuses to show up."

"You *claimed* your Army of God can fight regardless of who is leader?" Kiaresh said.

"I need them to *integrate* with the elite warriors!" He swung his palm to gesture at the farmers and goat-herders. "The elite warriors need to *lead*."

"Well, then," Kiaresh gave him a bemused grin, "I guess you'll all get to learn together?" To twist the knife, he added, "Colonel."

According to Immanu, Kiaresh reported directly to the Chief. He was *"Jamin's babysitter, mentor, and the Chief's eyes."* And now, it appeared, the man was tasked with babysitting and mentoring *him*...

Okay. So now *he* was supposed to be the *actual* leader?

"What do you suggest?" he asked.

Kiaresh glanced at Siamek.

"Convince *him*," he said, "and the rest will fall into line."

Mikhail grimaced. "Siamek hates my guts."

"Eh…" Kiaresh shrugged. "You shouldn't make presumptions."

What the heck was *that* supposed to mean? That Siamek *didn't* hate his guts? Or that Siamek didn't hate his guts quite as much as Jamin did? Why couldn't he just train them in small, manageable groups? Like he had the archers? And then let *them* train the rest of the village?

Because you saw how many Amorites crossed the desert that day with Gimal…

And now they were allied with the Halifian tribe and every other mercenary, reject, or psychotic who'd ever had it out for the Ubaid. If the enemy decided to attack Assur for real, prophecy, or no silly prophecy, Assur was screwed.

He made a decision…

"Siamek!" he called out. "Front and center!"

The tall, slender warrior stepped forward.

"Here!" Siamek called out.

"You need to say *'Yes, Sir,'*" Mikhail said.

"We report to Jamin." Siamek stared stiffly forward.

"Jamin isn't *here*," Mikhail said. "Which means that *you* need to be prepared to take over."

The elite warriors grumbled, but the murmured "*Yeah*" from the farmers and goat-herders who'd seen Jamin falter kept the hot-headed warriors from storming off. *That,* and the fact he suspected the Chief had just given them all an ass-chewing.

"Yes, Sir," Siamek said sourly.

He stared straight ahead.

Mikhail turned to face the other men. While he'd been measuring dick-size against Siamek, a dozen young women had slipped into the group, clustered around Pareesa like a flock of brightly colored birds.

Pareesa flashed him a proud grin. These were *her* recruits, not just archers, but women who wanted to learn how to *fight*. By the way they'd come wearing their shawl-dresses girded up like kilts, she must have apprised them they'd be getting thrown to the ground.

Her confidence fortified him in a way that Immanu's silly prophecies did not.

He took a deep breath and flared his wings. Flared? Not-flared? Was that too aggressive? All of Ninsianna's advice to "be approachable" warred with Immanu's admonitions to "put the bastards into their place." He defaulted to a comfortable parade rest, wings loose but erect, not because it felt "leaderish," but because he expected they'd be standing here for the next several hours.

Kiaresh gave a subtle nod.

"Three days ago—" Mikhail began to speak "—our village was *attacked*. They breached our walls, even though I am told that *no one* has breached them in nearly fifteen years."

"I remember!" an older man, a farmer, called out.

"The Chief made us build the walls higher," another said, a craftsman.

"It won't do a lot of good if the enemy has arrows," the old farmer replied. "My nephew was just killed by a man he never saw."

Some of the older men muttered in quiet agreement. *They* were old enough to remember the war against the Uruk.

Siamek nodded.

"They enemy didn't almost win because we are weak—" Mikhail gestured at the elite warriors. "They almost *succeeded* because this village has placed its defense into the hands of a small group of men, and men are *fallible*."

The elite warriors averted their eyes. Jamin's hesitation had only been momentary, but everyone had seen it.

"Some of you are old enough to have fought against the Uruk," Mikhail said. "When the Chief was still your *Muhafiz*, he *knew* which person he could turn to. But then you found peace, and most of you retired. The older warriors went back to their herds and their fields, and gradually he turned our defense over to his *son*—"

Siamek gave a warning growl.

"Nobody is slandering Jamin's bravery," Mikhail added hastily. "That isn't what this is about." He gave Siamek a sidelong glance. "My *point* is that, for the past fifteen years, Assur hasn't *needed* a standing army. The young men who fight for you *now* have never had to fight the kind of enemy who attacked us the other night."

He began to pace.

"After I freed Pareesa," he said, "I returned to a village which, to *my* eyes, was in the process of *losing* to a much smaller force." He looked out at the farmers and goat-herders. "Does anybody disagree with that assessment?"

"No," most of them muttered.

"If the older warriors didn't have so much experience battling the Uruk," he said. "If *Siamek* hadn't had the wherewithal to rally behind the chief—" he didn't add '*after Jamin faltered*' "—not only might we have lost our chief, but we *would* have lost more than the eleven people who died."

"Yeah!" the older men agreed.

The elite warriors all stared down at their feet.

"I wasn't here when Assur was at war with the Uruk," Mikhail said. "But every year that goes by, the older warriors lose practice. Many who fought against the Uruk have already *died*, and when they do, they take their knowledge with them. The young have never had to fight this kind of enemy."

"So what makes *you* qualified to teach?" Dadbeh called out.

Mikhail touched the pin which graced the pocket over his heart. An enormous tree, with deep-seated roots, her crown decorated with stars. Across the top, a banner proclaimed, "*In light, there is order, and in order there is life.*"

The words flowed easily, as though he had heard somebody speak them many times.

"I come from an army who knows how to work together," he said, "so that one soldier's weakness doesn't become the weakness of an entire unit. When you train together, you learn each other's weaknesses and strengths. You learn to shore each other up. You will fight, not just for the man beside you, but for the *ideal,* that every man in that army is your *brother.*"

"But some of us don't know *how* to fight!" a young man said. He gestured at his clique of fellow craftsmen. "Our talents lay elsewhere."

"I will *teach* you," he said.

"How?" the young man asked. "Last I heard, you can't remember your past?"

Kiaresh winced. The elite warriors snickered.

Mikhail folded his wings against his back.

"That's a valid observation." He forced himself to unclench his fist. "If not for the tags Ninsianna found wrapped around my neck—" he tugged the dog tags out of the neckline of his shirt "—I wouldn't even know my own name."

Nervous laughter rippled through the men.

"I may not *remember* who I was before I came to your village," he said. "But as you all witnessed the other night, there are things that I just *know*, like how to pick up a stick and use it as a spear—"

He borrowed Kiaresh's spear and threw it into the side of a far-off goat shed.

"—even if I can't remember my own father's name." He stepped back to stand between his two lieutenants.

"There are some in this tribe who would give a supernatural explanation as to why I am able to do these things, but the truth is simple. What few memories I *do* have all involve some type of training. Long, hard, brutal training amongst men—" he glanced over at Pareesa "—and *women,* who were all much better fighters than *me.*"

A murmur went through the men.

"Believe it or not—" his expression grew sheepish "—what few memories I *do* have all involve getting my tail feathers handed back to me by the Cherubim. Again. And again. And again."

The murmur rippled into laughter.

He began to pace, not only because it afforded him the opportunity to look each man in the eye, but because it gave him someplace to channel the nervous energy rustling through his feathers. Without his memories, he had no idea what type of missions he'd led except for a vague recollection that the designation '*Colonel*' meant he *must* have led men at *some* point in his career.

"Why should we follow you if you can't remember anything?" Firouz asked.

He stopped in front of Firouz and Dadbeh, whose first act upon seeing him for the first time had been to attack him.

"Let me be frank?" he squelched the urge to argue. "The *ladies—*" he gestured at Homa, Gisou and Pareesa "—learned archery because they *wanted* to learn. And I, in turn, did my best to explain. But the truth is, we come from different worlds. We speak different languages, use different weapons, and each of us learned to fight under completely different masters. So the only way this will *work* is if you help me break down what I know so we can *translate* it into skills that will help defend your village. Because what we're doing right now didn't help much when the enemy banged at our front gate. Did it?"

The two men shifted uneasily. Their eyes turned to Siamek. Jamin's second-in-command hesitated, and then gave them a nod. The two young men grumbled agreement. Without Jamin here to stir up discontent, the elite warriors would give him a chance to prove his worth ... or fail miserably.

"Mikhail, uhm, Sir?" an older farmer asked. "I just spent all morning hauling water to my fields. After this, I have to go home and repair my goat fence. And then, after supper, I need to haul even *more* water to my fields because by nightfall every ounce of water will have evaporated. When will I find *time* to do this training?"

Agreement rippled through the ordinary men.

"We were just attacked," Mikhail said. "If we can't hold onto our land, then planting serves no purpose."

"If we don't plant food," the old farmer said, "we shall starve. What good is staying on our lands if our children starve to death come winter?"

"Yeah," another man said. "The Halifians won't *have* to evict us. All they have to do is harass us and we'll starve *ourselves* to death!"

Mikhail scrutinized the clique of farmers. Unlike the elite warriors, who *hated* him because they'd gotten off on the wrong foot, or the arrogant craftsmen, who disdained the thought of attending to the common defense, the farmers, as well as the goat herders, wore expressions of worry and fear.

"I have no recollection of planting my own food," Mikhail said honestly. "The only thing I remember is training to be a soldier."

"Then how can you lead us?" the old farmer asked.

"Because the Emperor's armies aren't the *only* warriors I ever trained with," he said. "Before I defended the Emperor, I trained with the Cherubim. They don't believe in idleness. Everything they do serves two purposes."

His eyes turned inward.

"One day, on the way to class, I encountered a gardener," he said. "She was an ancient woman, too old to be kneeling on the ground. As she weeded, she moved all four of her arms in a different direction—" he mimicked the motion "—carefully pulling out the weeds as though she were deep in a trance. I asked her what she was doing and she said it was the most important lesson a Cherubim could ever learn. She made me kneel down in the dirt beside her and taught me this movement—" he moved both hands in a circular motion, first one, and then the other, and then added the movement of his wings "—even though I only have two hands and she had four of them."

He turned back to the warriors.

"There are no female Cherubim, except for their queen. Empress Jingu."

The men gasped.

Mikhail stared down at his feet. "I never understood *why*, but she *insisted* on teaching me, personally, to defend myself, as small and weak as I was, against my Cherubim mentors."

He turned to Siamek.

"Stab me with your spear."

"Wh-what?"

"I want you to stab me with your spear."

"But ... really?"

Mikhail nodded. Siamek gave him a half-hearted jab. Mikhail knocked it to one side with a fan block which looked remarkably similar to Jingu's weeding motion.

"This time, I want you to stab me for real," he said. "Pretend I'm a Halifian, and you—" he gestured at Firouz "—and you—" he gestured at Dadbeh "—and *you*—" he gestured at Tirdard. "I want you to stab me. *All* of you. At once."

The men hesitated, and then began to poke at him, cautiously, with the butt-end of their spears. It had been a long time since he'd done this exercise, but it felt so *familiar*, as though the Cherubim had instilled it into his muscles. One after another, he effortlessly deflected every single spear. Of course, it helped that these men didn't *really* want to hurt him.

Well, maybe they *did*...

Firouz came at him with a ferocious jab.

More than a little...

The spears grew faster, the men more aggressive. They bared their teeth. Mikhail crouched into a fighting stance, his chest heaved with the exertion. Human and Angelic grew drenched with sweat, but no matter how vigorously they stabbed, not once did a spear make contact with anything more damaging than his feathers.

An appreciative murmur went through the rest of the men.

"You were taught that by an old woman?" Siamek asked.

"No. She taught me to *weed a garden*," he said. "I didn't find out it was a defensive kata until later, when Master Yoritomo threw me into the middle of a group of older students and told them to go at me. Compared to the Cherubim, I am quite a runt. I think Jingu wanted to make sure I didn't get beaten up too badly."

"Weeding?" Firouz laughed. "You want us to learn to weed?"

"Oh, lover boy!" Dadbeh called out in his best, falsetto impersonation of Ninsianna. "I'd like you to *weed—* " he grabbed at his crotch "*—my garden*."

"Yes, my love," Firouz said in a false deep voice. "I shall plant my seed until you scream and sigh."

The warriors laughed. Mikhail turned a deep shade of pink.

"Keep stabbing me," he said. "I can keep this up all day."

The warriors slapped each other on the back, but while they laughed *at* him, for some reason, it lacked the rancor of their earlier jabs and slights.

He turned back to face the old farmer.

"Tell me what chores you need to do," he said, "and I'll see if we can't adapt a training exercise to put that job to use?"

"That sounds brilliant," the old farmer said. "I'm sure we'd *all* love to see *them—* " he pointed at the elite warriors "*—learn a few Cherubim weeding exercises.*"

The farmers began to laugh.

The elite warriors traded insults.

The goat-herders wondered how *they* could adapt training exercises to help *them*.

"Maybe we can *chase* them?" Pareesa pointed at a distant goat. "Goddess knows Mikhail gets lots of exercise chasing after Little Nemesis?"

He suppressed a laugh.

Several of the craftsmen mocked Pareesa, reminding her she was just a little girl.

"This *girl*," she taunted back, "killed one of her attackers. How many did *you* kill?"

"If you hadn't gotten yourself *kidnapped*," the young potter who'd pestered him earlier asked, "maybe Mikhail would have been *here* when the enemy attacked?"

Pareesa flew at him.

Homa and Gisou pulled her back.

If she got hold of the young man's fingers, Mikhail knew she would *snap* them, just like he had taught her.

"All right, line up!" he ordered. It was time to instill some semblance of order.

He unsnapped his pulse rifle from his holster and held it flat in both of his hands.

The men grew quiet. Every eye focused eagerly on *him*...

"I can't explain why She-Who-Is erased all memory of learning to use *this* weapon, even though, if you stick it in my hand, my body knows what to do with it," he said, "and yet I can recall, in intricate detail, my time spent weeding the garden."

He stuck the pulse rifle back in its holster.

"Why don't you use *that* weapon to defend us?" Siamek asked. His expression wasn't disrespectful, but curious. It was the twenty-million credit question which every man in the village wanted to know.

"You have a story about a man who finds a magic tallow lamp?" Mikhail said. "A spirit appears and gives the man three wishes?"

Siamek nodded.

"This weapon is like that," he said. "I used up two of my wishes the day your men attacked Ninsianna because I was too badly wounded to defend myself. I won't use it again unless I am desperate, because I only get so many wishes, and then, the spirit won't grant them anymore."

Shame flushed Siamek's face. Mikhail broke eye contact, not wishing his apprehension about elevating his former adversary to show. Curse Jamin! That first meeting had tainted every experience that had followed like rancid meat.

"I can't tell you why I don't remember how my sky canoe got here," he said. "And yet I can remember marching with a group of men just like you, for hours on end, until it felt as though our legs would fall off. But to fend off our enemies, we need to work together."

The men gave a hearty cheer.

He gestured at the old farmer.

"This man has reminded me that we need to get *creative*." He glanced at the young women, who'd all brought wooden buckets, no doubt at the bequest of Pareesa. He grabbed a bucket and held it up. "The archers use these to help them build up the strength to draw their bows. Since many of you need to haul water to your fields, maybe this would be an appropriate place to start?"

"Why should *we* haul water to *their* fields?" one of the craftsmen asked.

"Because if you *don't*," the old farmer said, "none of you will eat."

"How will *this* help us fight the Halifians?" the craftsman retorted.

"Before you can learn to *fight*," Mikhail said, "you must think as a *unit*. We're not just going to walk down to the river. We're going to *march*, in formation, and then once we fill the buckets, we're going to—" he glanced over "—Pareesa?"

"Yo!" her head popped up like a gerbil.

"Show the men what to do!"

She pranced to the front like a gazelle and gave him a wink. The imp enjoyed the attention. She then stood with one hand on her hip, her attitude cocky as she lifted one of the buckets in a bicep curl."

"If a skinny little girl like *me* can do this," she taunted, "then it should be *easy* for you *boys*, right?"

"We can do it better than *you* can, little girl," Firouz teased.

"Go ahead and try!"

"The winner has to shovel out other person's goat pen."

"It's a deal!" Pareesa laughed.

The men made wagers, farmers against the craftsmen, men against the women, and *all* of the "ordinary folk" against the elite warriors.

"Let's get started!" he barked. "Siamek? Have each of your warriors lead a group down to the river."

Siamek lined up the elite warriors, and then *they* broke up the other men into teams. Their first march was sloppy, but by the time they finished watering the fields, their feet hit the soil in unison.

They broke for the night and went home.

Chapter 131

Late-July - 3,390 BC
Earth: Village of Assur

NINSIANNA

With a sigh of relief, Ninsianna plunked down her basket of vegetables and wiped the sweat off of her brow. With the sun well past its apex, the temperature *should* have begun to cool, but this time of year the heat was reluctant to release its grip. Mikhail used to help her perform the back-breaking labor of weeding the garden, picking rhinoceros beetles off of the plants and dropping them into a bowl of water to drown them before they could devour their crops. But along with his newfound prestige came a deficit of time.

She grabbed a ceramic cup and dipped it into the bucket. The tepid water slid down her throat, already warm even though the temperature was cooler inside the house. She fished a strand of hair out of her mouth that had plastered itself to her cheek and plopped down upon the bench, wishing fervently she had time to take a nap.

Papa hurried in the door behind her, carrying an assortment of trinkets related to his trade. An eagle feather, although Ninsianna preferred to use one of Mikhail's, a small bowl for water, and a tiny clay plate used for burning dried parrotia leaves.

"Why not select a symbol for the Earth from your basket?" Papa asked. He cleared a small space in the center of the room and unrolled a carpet for them to sit upon.

"Which one?" She contemplated the bounty of their labors. Small white eggplants rested upon a bright green bed of broad beans, mustard greens and leeks.

"What does your intuition tell you, child?"

"I think today I shall use a leek."

"And why is that?"

"Because the tastiest part of it grows in the earth," Ninsianna said. "But the stalk reaches towards the sky."

Papa gave a satisfied grunt. He lowered himself to the carpet and began to arrange the items; they were more to aid his *own* focus than a requirement of She-Who-Is. He gestured for Ninsianna to join him. She grabbed the fattest leek and placed it in the north to complete the circle.

"Are we going to spy on the Halifians?" she asked. "I heard Eshnunna was attacked again and three women taken."

"That would necissitate the use of kratom," Papa said. "I don't wish to spend the rest of the day sleeping it off."

"*Must* you use Kratom?"

"I find it helpful," he said. "But not often. It scares your mother."

He lit a fat bundle of parrotia leaves on fire and placed it on the dish to smolder. A pleasant, light smoke wafted gently towards the open door and the beckoning sunlight.

"So what will we be learning today?" she asked.

"To look into anothers' spirit-light to discern the source of illness," Papa said.

"The gift is beautiful," Ninsianna said, "but rather distracting. Sometimes I find myself watching the light somebody casts off when they speak instead listening to their actual words."

"The light always tells the truth," Papa said. "Whereas words can lie."

"So how do I see sickness?"

A shadow fell across the door.

Mama stepped in, supporting an elderly neighbor, Mahtab, who puffed for breath as she walked. A cloud of blackness surrounded her heart; and an angry red line spread down into her arm. Papa helped Mahtab over to the bench. The old woman clutched her chest. Gradually, her breathing settled down and the blackness lessened, but the red line didn't go away.

Mama wore an unreadable expression, the one she wore when the news was bad.

"What do you see?" she asked.

Ninsianna tapped into that sense of *knowing*. Unfamiliar words tripped across her tongue.

"Aterioschlerosis," she said. "Her left anterior descending artery is clogged with plaque."

"Her what?" Papa's eyebrows reared up like bushy caterpillars.

Ninsianna knew she'd just spoken in the language of heaven, but while she understood what she'd just *said*, the words didn't *mean* anything, at least not in the archaic version of the tongue. How could she translate something she *knew*, but had no way to describe? For the first time, she understood how difficult it must be for Mikhail to communicate knowledge for which he possessed no memories, and no way to express that knowing in words.

"Do you know how, after we slaughter a sheep," she said, "we pull out its heart?"

Mama and Papa both nodded.

"You've got that big, red bloodline that goes *in*—" she used her fist and fingers to shape a heart "—and the big blue bloodline that goes *out*. And then, right about *here*—" she patted where her tendons showed on her fist "—there's a bunch of smaller bloodlines, called *arteries*—" she used the Ubaid equivalent for the word, which literally meant *'blood spurter.'* "Mahtab's heart isn't getting enough *blood* because some, uhm—" She stopped, at a total loss of how to describe the substance. "Fat? Do you know how, when it gets cool, the fat rises to the top of a cook-pot and gets stiff?"

She held her breath, praying her parents understood.

"So it's like a reed-straw with mud in it?" Mama said excitedly. "We need to clean it out so Marbeh can get enough blood?"

She stared at Ninsianna eagerly, as though, for the first time, her gift as a shaman had some use other than to spout questionable prophecies. Mama had described, perfectly, what *needed* to happen. But how could they fix it?

Ninsianna cast a desperate plea to the goddess, but all she could *see* was that poor Mahtab's heart was clogged with a nasty yellow substance.

"I don't know how to fix it," she admitted miserably.

Mama began to pace.

"We'd have to reach inside her chest!" Mama ruminated.

"It's impossible!" Ninsianna said.

"You reached inside Mikhail's chest," Mama said, "to stitch his lung."

"That was different," Ninsianna said. "He was *already* injured. And the goddess guided my hands."

Mama went to her healer's basket and pulled out the red box which Mikhail called a "first aid kit." He'd given it to her mother in gratitude for fixing his broken wing.

"Mikhail has spoken of such things," Mama said. "He insists it wasn't divine intervention, but *this*—" she held up the tiny silver sword which Mikhail called a *scalpel*. "He said, where he comes from, it's *common* to treat injuries with a healer's sword."

Ninsianna's hands trembled at the memory of the power she had felt that day, the *feeling* as she'd reached inside his chest and touched his living heart. But to enter that state, to trust so completely that the goddess guided her hands, she needed to consume the belladonna and poppy potion, the one which had brought her to the Dark Lord's attention. Ever since she'd fallen down the well, she'd been too terrified to dare.

"What do *you* see, Papa?" she deflected the question to her father.

"I see *nothing*," he said, "but the first image you described. Mahtab's heart, surrounded by black and red."

"So how do we fix this?" Mama asked.

Ninsianna reached down into the thread of consciousness that connected her to She-Who-Is. It felt like diving into a river. All of the thoughts that had ever existed, and someday *would* exist, washed over her like water.

Overwhelming images flooded into her brain; tiny swords, and a contraption which cracked a man's chest open like a nut.

She dove deeper, searching for information which Mama could use, some kind of embrocation they could make using supplies they could forage or harvest. Information flowed past in an endless current, warm and tingling, so many wonderful things!

"Ninsianna, you must focus..." Papa sounded far away.

"She has gone too deep into the dreamtime," Mama said. "Immanu! Pull her out!"

"I can't!" he cried out. "I can't even *see* her."

"Ninsianna... Ninsianna.... Nin.si.an.na......" the voices drifted further and further away.

The stars sang, welcoming their lost sister. She wanted to stay, not return to the room with the tired old woman. She drifted wherever the goddess' thoughts took her, into a bright white room where two men played chess. One of the men was a big red dragon, while the other reminded her of her father.

A thrill went through her as she recognized the tree-pin affixed to the bearded man's cloak. She understood the game they played, even though the Ubaid didn't have any such game. The dragon tried to take the other player's white queen, but the bearded man moved a white knight to block the move. On the far corner of the board, a second white knight sat surrounded by black chess pieces, forgotten by both of the players.

A thrill went through her as she recognized Mikhail.

The opponents argued, thoroughly engrossed in their game.

As she watched, a white bishop moved of its own volition. A sense of *urgency* clamored in the goddess' stream-of-consciousness, making sure she noticed what the two old gods had missed. The Evil One was on the move!

The players nodded amicably and disappeared.

With the room now empty, Ninsianna remembered why she was here. She *pictured* what she wanted to know; a herb which she could harvest locally that would help poor Mahtab's heart. She swam, this time with purpose, until the goddess showed her how to help her neighbor reduce the pain in her tired old heart.

A voice called out:

"Ninsianna!"

She recognized Mikhail's voice.

"Where are you?" she called out, but the stars sang louder, pleading with her to stay.

A sense of fear clenched in her gut. Hadn't Papa warned her about this? To always stay tethered to her body?

"Papa?" she called out.

But Papa didn't answer.

"Mama?"

Nothing...

"Mikhail!" she screamed.

His voice came to her, not an answer, but a pleading chant:

"Come back. Come back. Come back..." he pleaded.

She followed his voice; it wasn't difficult, nothing stopped her, but she'd traveled so *far* that it took forever before she finally felt his hand caress her cheek. She focused, not just on his voice, but the way his warmth flowed into her.

"Come back to me."

She felt his lips press against her forehead. Ninsianna opened her eyes.

"Mikhail," she smiled breathlessly. "When did you get home?"

He crushed her into his chest, so tight that it almost hurt.

"Oh, thank the gods!" It was almost a cry of grief.

"Why are you trembling?" she asked.

"You were gone so long we were afraid you wouldn't find your way back again." Papa said.

The sky outside had grown dark, and Mama had lit the tallow lanterns.

"Where is Mahtab?" she asked.

"She went home hours ago," Mama said.

Mikhail released her, but continued to hold her hand as though he feared she might run away.

"Immanu sent for me when he couldn't make you respond," Mikhail said.

"What did you see?" Papa asked.

"I saw the Eternal Emperor and Shaytan playing a game of chess," she said. "Shaytan tried to take the white queen, but the Emperor blocked it with a second white knight. And then I saw *you*, my love, way off in the corner with us. But then..." she frowned.

"What did you *see?*" her father shook her.

A cold chill made the hair on her arms raise up.

"I saw a white bishop," she lowered her voice. "He moved on his own. I don't think that either god is *aware* he is moving in their midst."

"Who is he?" Papa asked.

"The Evil One," she whispered. "He's manipulating the chess pieces."

Mikhail's forehead wrinkled.

"I think I've heard this before," he said. "Two old gods divide the galaxy between them in a game of chess."

"But what does this have to do with *us*?" Papa asked.

"I don't know," Ninsianna said. "It seemed so far away."

"Did this bishop have any weapons?" Mikhail asked. "Any troops? Did you see someplace *specific* that he might attack?"

"No." She gave him an apologetic smile. "It was a game piece on a chessboard made of stars."

Mikhail remained silent, his brow creased, deep in thought. She had brought him a prophecy of a threat, a *vague* threat, with no information to help him form a plan.

"You must be *careful* when you enter the dreamtime," Papa scolded her. "If you get lost, you'll be trapped in there forever."

"But I found the information that Mama wanted," she said. "Mahtab should drink tea twice per day with three leaves of the yellow foxglove[169] in it. It won't prolong her life, but it will make her more comfortable while she is here."

"I would have preferred you didn't scare us to get that information," Mama said. "I already knew it."

"Did you learn it in the dreamtime, too?"

"No, child," Mama said. "I learned it the hard way. By apprenticing with Gasur's village healer and memorizing it."

---

[169] *Digitalis lanata* (common name "Foxglove") is used to treat heart disorders. It is fatal at the wrong dose.

Chapter 132

⊗

Galactic Standard Date: 152,323.07 AE
Uncharted Territories:
Diplomatic Carrier 'Prince of Tyre'
Special Agent Eligor

ELIGOR

It wasn't every day that Eligor got summoned to Zepar's office. Lucifer's Chief of Staff liked to "dabble in science", as he called it. It was *here* that they kept the women locked up until they were either "gifted", or Lucifer felt like "marrying" one of the poor, stupid monkeys so he'd have an excuse to rape them. He'd been here before, but Lerajie hadn't. The speckle-winged idiot gaped at the room which was more of a mad scientist's laboratory than any kind of office.

Both he, and Lerajie, saluted the Chief of Staff.

Through a plate glass window behind him, they could see, strapped to a dentist's chair, the dark-skinned man that the lizards had dumped off with the women. The man's head had been immobilized, no, *clamped,* to some kind of metal helmet strung with wires and what appeared to be a drilling device.

"Sir," Eligor said, careful to keep his voice neutral.

"I'm finished with him," Zepar waved his hand. "Bring this human to the Prime Minister's private quarters."

Eligor looked at Lerajie. Lerajie looked like he wanted to throttle the weaselly Chief of Staff. Things had been weird on this ship for a very long time, but the last few months? Well … even with the so-called 'combat pay' and bonuses, if not for the carrot of being first on Lucifer's 'mail order bride' list the minute the Prime Minister pulled off whatever little coup d'état he was cooking up with the females he was 'gifting' all over the Alliance, both of them would have been out of here.

"Well?" Zepar asked. His eyes had that cold, feral stare that always made Eligor shudder.

"Sorry, Sir." Eligor interrupted before Lerajie could tell him to go to hell. "Right away, Sir."

They unstrapped the dark-skinned man and helped him to his feet. The male had been a problem since the day lizards had transported him onto their ship. The women were *'simple'*, to put it kindly. Or at least that was how the fourteen pregnant females Lucifer had ordered them to guard around-the-clock acted. Like monkeys. Big, stupid, very attractive monkeys.

But the male? The male was so combative that even Lucifer's goons couldn't handle him. Eligor had been called in to hold him down while they sedated him. The man had been drugged into a stupor ever since, but as Eligor had looked into the man's eyes, there had been real intelligence. The sounds that had come from his mouth had not been the hisses and guttural yowls of the fourteen females Lucifer had impregnated, but the pattern of a language. A proto-language, perhaps?

The dark-skinned man shuffled down the hall, nearly falling as they led him through the ship. He didn't act like a sentient creature *now*.

"We've got to report this to somebody!" Lerajie exclaimed. "Even if they're not sentient, we can't keep standing by and doing nothing. They're the precursor to our species!"

"Do you really think Lucifer will just let you just waltz off of his ship?"

"I don't care *what* I signed," Lerajie said. "The Emperor would be furious if he found out how Lucifer is treating his root stock!"

"I'm not worried about the non-disclosure agreements." Eligor noted the icy stare of the two guards who perpetually stood outside Lucifer's door like a matched pair of gargoyles. "Shh... Not here."

They handed over the dark-skinned man. They were immediately dismissed. The two goons shoved the heavily-sedated male through the door. Eligor and Lerajie headed towards the mess hall to grab a bite to eat.

"What do you mean, it's not getting tossed in jail that worries you," Lerajie asked as soon as they were out of earshot of the goons.

"Did you ever hear from Pistis again after he threatened to blab about the female Lucifer gifted to Brigadier-General Kasdeja?" Eligor asked.

"He quit," Lerajie said.

"His sire contacted me looking for him," Eligor said. "No one knows where he went."

"So?" Lerajie said.

"What about Decarabia," Eligor asked. "He got drunk on shore leave and bragged that Lucifer had given Lieutenant-General Gusion "a little something sweet" in front of a bar full of mechanics."

"So?" Lerajie said. "Zepar threw him in the brig."

"The brig is *empty*," Eligor said. "Decarabia is no longer on the ship."

"That doesn't mean anything," Lerajie said. "He probably just transferred him to a planet-bound security facility."

"There's no record of it," Eligor said. "In fact, there's no record of *him* ever being on this ship."

"So?" Lerajie said.

Eligor harrumphed.

"What about Tabbris? Have you heard from *him* since he tried to file a report through official channels about the rough treatment of the human females Lucifer raped?"

"No," Lerajie's eyes widened. "You don't think…"

"Open your eyes," Eligor said. "Before you get yourself killed."

Chapter 133

End-July – 3,390 BC
Earth: Village of Assur
Colonel Mikhail Mannuki'ili

MIKHAIL

It was a sorry looking, hang-dog dead group of men who gathered for today's lesson. Even though it was after supper, the lengthening shadows did little to alleviate the mid-summer heat. Mikhail stood, wings flared, each feather fluffed out in the vain hope of catching a non-existent breeze. How was he supposed to motivate these men to give more than they'd already given to their fields, their trades, and their families, when all that he wanted was to crawl under the nearest shade canopy?

"I'm glad to see you all came back for more," he said.

The warriors grumbled a half-hearted response. By the way most leaned on their practice-staffs for support, they wanted to dump a quick bucket of water on their fields and go home for a nap. Had they not gotten fresh reports of villages being raided, he might have indulged that urge, but they couldn't afford to be complacent. Assur must learn to protect *itself*. Not just depend upon *him* for a security blanket.

He tried to get the men psyched up to put more effort into their training. ""I can't hear you!!! What was that again?"

"Yes … Sir!" The response was only slightly more energetic than the first one.

"Good!" He gave them a crisp Alliance salute. Most gave a halfway decent salute in return. Not perfect, but they were getting better.

"When will we get to hit one another?" Firouz grabbed his buddy Dadbeh and pretended to punch him. Dadbeh hit him back, for real, though not hard.

"I think we've got the marching part down," Dadbeh did his best impersonation of a mock march. "One-two-three-four, what I need is a drunken whore!"

"Five-six-seven-eight," Firouz called out the next stanza. "Two for one, at a discount rate!"

"Nine-ten-eleven-twelve," Dadbeh thrust his hips back and forth. "If she's dry, use a bit of salve."

The other warriors began to laugh, which happened a lot when those two got warmed up with their antics. He'd tried separating them, but somehow they always ended up back at one another's side. With the heat sapping their vitality, he'd finally decided to just let the two play off of one another and provide a little comic relief. Although his memories of Raphael were few, he could recall the good-natured Angelic playing pranks to get him to lighten up.

"It has been two weeks of nothing but march, march, march!" Firouz complained. "We want to get to the good part."

"Yeah, the good part!" Numerous other warriors chimed in.

"And which part would that be?" Mikhail rustled his feathers.

"You know," Dadbeh said. "The part where your eyes glow blue and you take on seventeen men at once with your little pinkie finger."

"I'm teaching *you* how to fight the exact same way the Eternal Emperor taught *me.*" Mikhail suppressed his irritability, made worse by the heat.

"These don't *look* like firesticks." Dadbeh held out his spear. "Just stick one of *those* in our hands, and we won't *need* to march back and forth to the river carrying buckets of water!"

Mikhail suppressed a sense of irritation.

"We must work with the tools She-Who-Is had given us—" he faced the larger group. "Before I start pulling men out for specialized training, you must first learn to fight *together.* That way, no matter *who* you end up fighting beside, you know you can rely on them to watch your back."

"But we *already* work well together!" Firouz slapped his arms around Dadbeh's shoulders, still trying to garner attention for himself. "We share everything. Even the same women."

"And what will happen when you don't have your best friend watching your back?" Mikhail pressed his wings tightly against his back. "I notice you two don't fight so well when you're paired with somebody else."

The two young men didn't have an answer to that question. Of course they didn't! Until now, groups of friends had practiced whatever skills sparked their interest, not the more boring, but necessary parts which made the coordination of massive armies possible. He refocused the group's attention back on today's lesson.

"Yesterday we discussed how to incorporate additional strength-training exercises into your daily routine," he said. "Does anybody have any questions?"

"Yes, Sir," one villager asked.

"Ebad, correct?" Mikhail asked. "What is your question?" Ebad was an enthusiastic, if awkward student.

"My family are potters, Sir, not farmers," Ebad said. "What should I be doing instead?"

"Buckets of clay, perhaps?"

While he'd been addressing the men, Homa had jogged up and waited patiently for him to finish. Although archer training had never been as formal as the military skills he was attempting to instill into the larger group, his archers instinctively understood that they were the example to which the newer warriors should aspire to. With much formality, he turned to address her.

"Yes, Homa?"

"Behnam said fourteen more archers showed up for training today," Homa said. "All women with small children. They can only stay until the sitter summons them to go home. Should they be allowed to join the group?"

"What is their reason for the half-lesson?" Mikhail asked. Yalda and Zhila had put out a call to the elderly citizens of the village to offer to watch young children so their mothers could train.

"All of them are nursing mothers," Homa said. "When the baby cries, they need to feed them. Behnam wants to know how *your* people solve this problem?"

There were *some* memories that lurked just beneath the surface, quick glimpses of faces or bits of conversation, but try as he might, nothing could shake free memories of how his own people had reared their young. You would have thought he'd never seen a baby before?

"I can't remember," he said. "Tell him to accommodate them as best he can. That's the age group the kidnappers seem to be targeting the most."

"Yes, sir!" Homa said. With a crisp salute, her eyes darted to the men with a proud *'see ... this is how it's done'* look. Her military protocol would have been perfect had she not stopped to give Pareesa a high-five.

"Yesterday we learned how to do basic blocks and hits," Mikhail said. "Today we'll practice these skills on one another. Did everybody bring rags to wrap around your hands?"

"Yes, Sir!"

"I forgot," a few said.

"In battle, as in life," he said, "if you come unprepared, you will be at a disadvantage. It's important to learn this lesson now, sparring with your neighbors, instead of later, at the end of a Halifian spear. Therefore, those of you who forgot your hand rags will fight one another. When you get hit, it's going to hurt."

Mikhail ignored the grumbles and showed them how to wrap a strip of rag around each hand so that they wouldn't be punching with bare knuckles. Earlier in the week he'd taught them to do basic kicks, punches and blocks against an imaginary opponent. Today would be the first time they fought one another.

"Find a sparring partner and pair off," he ordered. "Do we have anybody who doesn't have a partner?"

"I don't have a partner!" Pareesa called out.

"And why is it, little fairy, that you never seem to be able to find a partner?" He donned a mock-serious expression. Pareesa had always been an enthusiastic learner, but ever since she'd been captured, she pursued combat skills with a vengeance.

"They're all afraid," she bragged, putting her hands on her hips and tossing her head like a prizefighter.

"Afraid?" he asked. "Of who?"

"Actually, you," she leaned in and whispered. "Taking *you* on scares them worse than anything –I– could ever do to them."

"You're not afraid because you know I hold my punches," he said. Then he said louder, "all right everyone, I'll demonstrate with Pareesa ... ready stance!"

She spread her feet to shoulder-width, bending her knees and pulling her arms into her sides so she could move in any direction. They banged fists in a gesture of mutual respect. He was nearly twice her size, but he'd learned not to underestimate his diminutive fairy general. What she lacked in size, she more than made up for in ferocity.

"No cheating," she whispered. "The rest of us don't have wings."

"Go!" He allowed her to make the first move.

He tucked his wings against his back so as not to gain an unfair advantage. This worked against him. Without his wings extended, not only was he deprived of two extra fighting limbs, but he was forced to carry their dead weight. It slowed him down and upset his balance, allowing Pareesa to land a few good kicks and punches.

"You're not using the high block enough." He lightly clubbed her with a hammer fist on top of her head. "You're a woman. Most opponents will be taller than you."

"Blocks are boring!" She aimed a crescent kick straight at his knee. "Kicking is more fun."

"You can't kick," Mikhail blocked her kick and brought down a second, identical fist onto the top of her head, "if you're unconscious."

Pareesa grunted in pain and punched at his abdomen, which he blocked. The others gathered in a circle and cheered Pareesa on, which made the little spitfire increase her kicks and punches. For a creature born without wings, she was quite adept at becoming airborne.

"Hah!" She crowed as she finally landed a round house kick to his hip. She added a clicking Cherubim phrase she'd begged Ninsianna to teach her. "I should kick your tail feathers!"

"You dropped your fists. Always keep your guard up." He gave her a right hook in the area she'd left open during the kick. "And you would say *'I will kick'*, not *'I should kick.'*" He corrected her Cherubim grammar as Pareesa grunted in pain.

"Take that!" she laughed, spinning around to give him a back kick, a move he hadn't yet taught the others.

"That's not part of today's lesson," he said.

"Neither is this..." She grabbed his shoulders and spun her weight around his torso in a dancelike move he'd never seen. Thrown off balance, one wingtip hit the ground to prevent him from falling. He knocked her grip off of his shoulders in a double elbow thrust to both arms. The trainees cheered her bold maneuver.

"What was that?" He landed a left reverse punch to her shoulder as she regained her balance.

"Stag dance move," she smirked. She blocked his jab and returned one of her own. "Hunting season. You weren't here yet."

"You'll have to teach me that sometime." He gave a side kick to her gut and knocked her back. "You could have avoided that kick by doing a low block."

Pareesa grunted and punched repeatedly at his abdomen. "I would much ... rather ... punch ... you!" She became frustrated when she wasn't able to land any blows.

"I have a longer reach than you." He easily blocked her hits and reached in to give a punch to her abdomen. "I hope you didn't have a large supper."

"Oomph!" Pareesa grunted in pain. "No fair."

"Life isn't fair, little fairy." He did the same punch again. "If you're going to fight men, you must overcome our height and weight advantage."

"Why do you think I'm here?" She blocked his third punch by *finally* doing the block he'd been trying to get her to do all along. "I don't feel like getting carried off again by slavers."

"Okay, enough!" He stepped back and offered both fists to bang together. "Very good, Pareesa. Does anyone have any questions?"

Pareesa did a victory dance and rejoined the young men who perpetually hovered around her. She still had the slender figure of an adolescent, but the ferocity of a hardened warrior. The other women slapped her raised palm. Over the past two weeks, their numbers had climbed from twelve to seventeen.

He had the trainees pair off and spar each other, correcting errors and reminding them to remember basic moves such as blocking hits or keeping their hands up so their chest and face weren't vulnerable. As the sun dipped down towards the horizon, he ended the day's lesson with a quick march down to the river for water. The men dove into to the cool water, enjoying relief from the mid-summer heat, before marching in unison to water their fields. They were all in good spirits when he dismissed them for the night.

Chapter 134

义

Galactic Standard Date: 152,323.07 AE
Earth: Sata'an Forward Operating Base
Lieutenant Kasib

LT. KASIB

Lieutenant Kasib tucked his tail up alongside his right side in a crisp salute and knocked on the crude door they'd jury-rigged for privacy.

"Come in," General Hudhafah called.

Kasib's long forked tongue tasted the air the moment he stepped into his commanding officer's office, searching for pheromones which would indicate the general's mood. His mood, thankfully, was relaxed. In his claws, he held a glass of a fermented grain beverage he'd developed a taste for; one Kasib went out of his way to procure for him. The locals called it "beer."

"You have something to report?" the General asked.

"Our *allies*, the Amorites, keep coming up short, Sir," Kasib said. "Some of the tribes are fighting back."

"Find out who their leaders are and kill them. Without a head, the serpent will die."

"Would you like me to send a troop carrier to quash the rebellion?"

"We're spread too thin—" Hudhafah sighed "—and almost out of supplies. Until the armada gets here with reinforcements, let our intermediaries take the loss, not our men."

"How shall I convince them it's worth the trouble, Sir?" Kasib asked.

General Hudhafah stared into his golden glass of beer. He bared his fangs in a grin.

"We've got *plenty* of gold. Offer a bounty; ten *darics* for every ringleader's head."

Chapter 135

July 31st – 3,390 BC
Earth: Village of Assur
Colonel Mikhail Mannuki'ili

MIKHAIL

He fluttered to the ground and set down the heavy rucksack. The door opened before he had a chance to knock. A pair of ancient eyes, nearly blind from cataracts, peered out from the cheerful hearth-light.

"Come in!" Zhila said.

"Yes, do," her sister, Yalda, called from somewhere deep inside the house.

"Thank you, Ma'am," he said. "I appreciate your letting me spend the night."

He carried the rucksack inside their house and set the uniform he'd spent half the day ironing–without the benefit of electricity–onto a work-table so it wouldn't get wrinkled.

A heavenly scent assailed his nostrils.

"Is that bread?" he asked hopefully.

"And roasted lamb," Yalda called out from the beehive hearth.

His stomach rumbled. Since Immanu had ceremonially cast him out of the house three days ago for the "bride's seclusion", he'd been subsisting on porridge and what little meat he had time to hunt.

Zhila gestured for him to sit. He eased himself down onto the cushions so as not to crush his long primary feathers. In the center of a linen tablecloth sat a large, goose-necked urn, surrounded by plates piled high with a simple, but generous feast.

Yalda hobbled in from the courtyard, carrying a woven basket filled with freshly baked bread. Her younger sister handed him the basket and helped her sister sit, and then plopped down on the opposite side of the urn.

"Is everything ready?" Yalda asked him.

"I *think* so," he said. "I hope she'll like the result."

"And the Halifians?" Zhila asked.

"There was no sign of them," Mikhail said. "The nearest tent-group is thirty-eight, uhm—" he translated the distance from Galactic kilometers "—maybe seventeen leagues to our south."

"That's right on the border of Uruk land," Zhila said.

"A two day's walk," Yalda said.

"A *fit* warrior could make it in a single day," Zhila said.

"I doubt they'll bother him," Yalda contradicted her sister. "This time of year, there's no water out there for their herds."

She handed him a plate, and then scooped a serving of lentils, fresh greens, and strips of marinated lamb. The two old women relayed the latest gossip as they filled their bellies, until it felt as though he might burst.

He dragged forward his rucksack.

"I brought something you might like?"

He pulled out a pair of sturdy hinges and a couple of metal brackets which he'd unscrewed from one of his foot-lockers. The widow-sisters turned them over or, in Zhila's case, felt the cold steel and the way it bent in the middle.

"What is it?" they asked simultaneously.

"They're called '*insi*'—" he used the Galactic Standard word for hinges. "I thought, while I was here, I'd repair your front door?"

The two old women's faces both lit up.

"A door from the heavens?" Yalda said.

"At our house?" Zhila said.

"Ninkasi will be honored—" they both invoked the goddess of bread and beer.

Yalda reached beside the urn and held up a handful of hollow river reeds.

"Have you ever drunk beer before?" she asked.

"At the gathering of shamans," he said.

"Those were out of a *cup*," Yalda said scornfully.

"Immanu adds a special ingredient," Zhila chuckled. "To help the shaman's dream-walk."

"I have to wake up *early* tomorrow," he said apprehensively.

"Don't worry!" Zhila slapped the back of his wing. "*This* batch will help a man "perform", if you catch my drift."

Mikhail's face flushed hot. The Ubaid had a habit of speaking their minds, *especially* when it came to "who was laying down with whom."

Yalda passed around the straws and showed him how to sip out of the vat, beneath the unappetizing-looking crud which floated at the top, but above the dirt-like sediment which settled onto the bottom. In between the two layers, however, floated a sweet, golden river of fermented ambrosia.

He sipped the beverage as the widow-sisters related their descent from an ancient line of brewers and fermenters ... all adherents to the cult of Ninkasi. First he grew warm, and then his speech began to slur, but his two elderly hosts remained spry and clear-headed. According to the warriors, Yalda and Zhila could drink any man under the table.

"So, young man," Yalda elbowed him in the ribs, "do you even *know* what you're supposed to do on your wedding night?"

"I can't remember?" he said sheepishly.

"Hah!" Zhila slapped him on the back. "Memory loss! Whether or not you're a virgin, it will be your first time."

Mikhail's cheeks turned a deep shade of scarlet. Zhila gave her sister a conspiratorial wink. They shared a rapport he could only envy. He only hoped he and Ninsianna would grow to share a similar closeness.

"I remember my first time," Yalda poked him with a bony finger.

"There are a few things you need to know—" Zhila waggled her eyebrows "—about pleasing a woman."

They cackled like two old hens, telling him *w-a-y* more graphic information than he wanted to know about how to please Ninsianna on their wedding night. His ears turned pink, and then a deep shade of scarlet. Finally, he grumbled defeat:

"I think I need to lie down."

Laughing *at* him, but not maliciously, they helped him stumble to the corner. Sinking gratefully down upon the cushions, he wrapped himself in his own wings and *prayed* he wouldn't spend his wedding day in a brain-splitting hangover. He was good at many things, but imbibing ungodly amounts of alcohol wasn't one of them.

Or milking goats…

He didn't even want to *think* about his long-running war with Immanu's dairy goat. Trying not to obsess about demonic goats besting him in battle with their evil little horns, he drifted off to the sleep to the sound of the widow-sisters cackling about the sexual prowess of husbands long dead and in the grave.

Chapter 136

Galactic Standard Date: 152,323.08
Haven-4: Galactic Youth Training Academy
Colonel Raphael Israfa

RAPHAEL

Haven-4 wasn't really a planet, but an artificial moon placed in orbit around the seat of the Alliance Parliament, Haven-3. Colonel Raphael Israfa didn't have a chance to marvel at the Emperor's engineering acumen as his ship approached the planet. He simply popped into existence on the base's airfield.

"Oh, thank the gods!" he cried out as the living "needle" ship opened her marsupium. He tumbled out, stripped down to his socks and underclothing because the ship was so small he could barely fit, and yanked off the oxygen mask; resisting the urge to flap his wings.

"Colonel Israfa?" said the Delphinium who'd been sent to meet him.

"Did you expect someone else?" he said more sharply than he meant.

"Sir." The frog-featured matron held out a freshly-pressed uniform.

He yanked on his slacks and boots, and then headed towards the base's infirmary, his wings helter-skelter as he fumbled with his shirt. The matron hopped after him, struggling to keep up with his longer stride.

"How is he?" he asked.

"Not well, Sir," the matron said.

"Why didn't you notify us sooner?"

"Orders, Sir." She looked down. "The Emperor didn't want us distracting his mother."

He buttoned his shirt as they marched past the barracks where *he'd* been raised; building after building of dormitory-style housing. Once upon a time, this entire planet had been filled with hybrid children: Angelics, Centauri, Leonids and Merfolk, but most of the barracks were now closed, the glass boarded up, and the pool completely dry ever since the Merfolk had merged with their sister-species, Leviathans. An army of civil servants tended the grass, but his adult eyes could see the decay.

They cut across the parade field, where the children lined up before going in for lunch. They ranged in age from toddlers to teenagers, all dressed neatly in immaculately-pressed cadet uniforms, lined up by rank, ability and patrol. While the field had been "roomy" back when he'd grown up in the youth academy, now it appeared ridiculously large, with the children spread out to make it appear there were more than there really were. Their eager young faces shone with religious zeal.

"What is our sacred duty?" a Leonid sergeant drilled the kids.

"To bow down to the naturally evolved races," the kids called out, "and defend the Emperor with our dying breath."

Raphael shivered. The vow had always given him a sense of pride—their willingness to fight, and if necessary, die to defend the Alliance—but he wasn't so keen now that the "dying breath" would be given by his infant son.

They passed into the hospital which, despite the contracting nature of the base, now sported a brand new wing. The matron checked him in past a security checkpoint.

"This is the Supreme Commander-General's consort," she announced.

The grim-faced guard scanned his fingerprints, and then bolted the door behind him. The wall next to the doorway bore evidence of recent weapons-fire.

"Why do the locks face in?" Raphael asked.

"Sometimes the parents want to take their kids and leave," the guard said.

The matron led him through a labyrinth of hallways, into a high-tech wing that reeked of death and disinfectant. He stared into the soulless eyes of parents who walked up and down the hallway, each cradling a dying baby. You could tell by the way they walked, out-of-sync, that the parents barely knew one another. They stared at their offspring, baffled, as if they did not recognize the life they had created.

Unlike the rest of the planet, the hospital was full...

"I didn't realize it had gotten this bad," Raphael said.

The matron wiped a tear from her bulbous eyes.

"We do the best we can, Sir," she said. "But we're no closer to finding a cure than when the illness first appeared."

She led him to a private room at the end of the ICU ward.

"My condolences," she said softly.

He opened up the door.

The Alliance's most formidable general sat on the floor, reduced to a crumpled pile of sobbing feathers, rocking their infant son. It was a surreal juxtaposition, the cold, sterile nursery, the sobbing mother, and the IV's, monitors, and wires hooked up to the tiny baby clinging to life.

"Jophie—" he could hardly speak. "I have come."

He sat beside her; pulling her, and the son he had never met, into his embrace. Jophiel shifted one wing so he could move closer. Their wings touched in front, his golden feathers interweaving with her snowy white ones to create a basket weave of protection against whatever force was trying to take their child.

Uriel was thin and blue, far smaller than he'd expect a five-month-old infant should appear, with a smattering of auburn in his hair and pinfeathers. Raphael touched his son's tiny hand.

"Hey, little guy, Daddy is here."

His heart leaped into his throat as Uriel grasped one finger.

"He won't eat!" Jophiel sobbed. "All he does is cry."

"Why didn't they tell us sooner?"

"It's become so common that they no longer notify the parents until the final day," she said. "The Emperor thinks it's *cruel* to make us watch our children die."

"Isn't there is something we can *do?*" he asked. "Bring him to a specialist? Get a second opinion?"

"There's no cure! All our great technology and they don't even know what causes it."

"Shhhh...." He kissed her temple. "It's not your fault."

"It is!" She clutched their son to her breast. "I begged the Emperor to let me retire. Twelve babies I have given the Alliance, but I didn't want to give this one up!"

"Then why did you?" he asked bitterly.

"Because we *must* replenish our race!" she said. "If -I- refuse, every female hybrid will follow suit!"

"Maybe you *should* refuse?" He recited the rebellious talk he'd often heard from Glicki. "We'd fight twice as hard to protect our wives and sons."

"There just aren't *enough* of us to allow half of us to quit." She buried her face into his shoulder. "Damn him! Damn him, and his shortsightedness in creating a race of beings that would breed itself into extinction!"

"But I thought..."

"Contrary to popular belief," she said bitterly, "the Eternal Emperor is neither omniscient nor omnipotent! A great geneticist, yes! But he doesn't have the power to create life."

"I wouldn't know," Raphael sighed. "I've only seen him once, at a distance."

Her irises appeared silver against the bloodshot spiderwebs which marred her eyes. Uriel's chest heaved in hiccups as he fought to inhale each and every breath. His tiny wings twitched as though some great pain wracked his little body. Raphael fought back tears. He'd cut off his own wings, rip out his heart and sell his soul to save the tiny infant who clung to life in his arms.

"Does the Emperor know?" he asked.

Does he even care...?

"I have no idea," she sighed. "Even if he does, there is nothing he can do for him."

Jophiel placed her head upon his shoulder. Drawing her close, Raphael rocked with her. Both parents instinctively breathed each labored breath along with their dying child.

Chapter 137

August 1ˢᵗ – 3,390 BC
Earth: Village of Assur

NINSIANNA

Her friends jammed into her tiny bedroom like dried dates stuffed into a jar for storage. Of the most blessed days to be married, *Arah Ululu*[170], when the earliest grain could be harvested, halfway between the summer solstice and the autumn *Akitu* festival, was especially auspicious.

"It's crooked," Mama said.

"It is not!" Homa said. "She's just *standing* crooked."

"Is too," Gisou agreed with Mama. "You sewed the flower into the seam. See?"

"We need to rip out that fringe and redo it," Mama said.

"Mama!" Ninsianna cried out. "There's no more time!"

For the past week, she'd been so busy training new archers that she hadn't had *time* to finish embroidering her bridal shawl. She'd finally resorted to inviting her archer-sisters over for a sewing party.

"Why not rip out just that one flower?" Yadidatum suggested.

"But then it won't be symmetrical!" Homa said. "I spent all day making sure they were even."

"It's not like the men will notice," Yadidatum laughed.

"Yadidatum is right." Mama said. "Either you can get married in an uneven shawl-dress that everyone will notice, or get married in a straight dress with one less flower."

Ninsianna sighed. *Mikhail* would see it. But he only cared about functionality, never any sort of fashion. Her critics, on the other hand, would ridicule the "Chosen One's" dress. She could almost *hear* that bitch, Shahla, making fun of her during the ceremony.

"Well?" Mama held out the obsidian shard they used to cut thread.

Papa said respect was nine-tenths pageantry and a smidgeon of charisma, words that appeared all-too-true by the way the villagers ooh'd and aah'd his shamanic tricks. But Mikhail insisted respect should be earned through perfection.

She was marrying *him*....

---

[170] *Arah Ululu*: coincides with entry into the constellation of Virgo.

"Rip it out," she sighed. "We can sew it back correctly after the wedding."

Her bridesmaids stripped her down to her loin-cloth. Homa ripped out the flower and Gisou reorganized the wheat-sheath belt she wore to attract fertility. Yadidatum braided her hair, while Pareesa handed her flowers and sheathes of wheatgrass to weave into the braids. Mama took out a vase of crushed calamus-flower blended with oil and dabbed the fragrant perfume behind her ears, on her throat and, with a chuckle, on her inner thighs.

"Mama!" she gasped.

"Trust me," Mama said. "He'll like it."

Her bridesmaids erupted in giggles. Oh, how she missed him! His quiet strength. The sight of his muscles flexing when he fetched water, or the way he took her up into the sky whenever she tried to break his formidable self-control.

Her mind headed down into a naughty and dirty place...

"Why are you smiling?" Pareesa asked with mock-innocence.

"Oh, no reason," she said with a blush.

"I know what she's thinking!" Gisou said.

"She's thinking of all the naughty things she is going to do to that handsome winged stud of hers!" Homa laughed.

"You know what they say about men with big feet," Gisou said.

"What about big feet?" Pareesa asked cluelessly.

"Girls!" Mama shushed them. "We have young ears present!"

"It's not like I don't know what you're talking about!" Pareesa blustered.

"Oh yeah, what?" Gisou taunted.

"We can *hear* Mama and Papa, down in their bedroom," Pareesa said.

Mama gave an indignant gasp.

"Pareesa's mother would have your head on a platter if she overheard you—" she gave the older girls a pointed look. "And *you*, young lady—" she cast a baleful eye at Pareesa "—have a few more years before you speak of such things!"

"Yes, Ma'am!" Pareesa stared down at her feet, but her eyes bore a mischievous twinkle as she glanced sideways at Ninsianna. Since being captured, Pareesa had grown more serious, so this glimpse of the 'old' Pareesa was a welcome sight.

Homa finished her shawl-dress. Yadidatum wrapped it back around her body. With a strategic tie, the fabric with the missing flower disappeared.

Out in the street, a parade of cheerful voices called up to her window.

"Ninsianna!" Papa called up the stairs. "It's time!"

Mama gave her a hug.

"Let's go." All of a sudden, Mama burst into great, big blubbering tears.

"Mama?" Ninsianna gaped at her usually-stoic mother. "Is something the matter?"

"It's nothing!" Mama wiped her tears with her sleeve. "I'm just … so happy."

"Happy?"

"Yes. You get to marry a man who *loves* you!"

They clamored down the stairs in a fit of giggles. Ninsianna clutched her shawl-dress, praying it wouldn't snag in the ladder's rungs. In front of their family altar, Papa stood clad in his finest five-fringed kilt, wearing his shaman's headdress and gold-beaded breastplate. He kissed Ninsianna on the cheek.

"Remember," he gestured at the tiny clay statue above his shaman's box. "She-Who-Is saw fit to pick your husband *herself.*"

"Praise be the Mother," she murmured.

"Praise be the sacred union," her bridesmaids uttered the sacrament.

Mama handed Papa a gossamer linen veil, the one which *she* had worn, and her grandmother before her, to their wedding. Papa draped the veil over her hair.

"This will be the first time I ask the goddess to bless a union of my own flesh and blood." His eyes grew moist.

She kissed Papa on the cheek.

"Don't worry," she said, "I will always be your little girl.

Papa took her arm and led her outside to the street where a throng of well-wishers lingered outside to walk them to the temple. Originally they'd planned a small ceremony because Mikhail *despised* being the center of attention. With them still owing the Chief recompense for her bride-price, he felt those resources should be limited to family and close friends. But ever since the night of the raid, her *intended* had become a security blanket for rattled villagers. Since it was the *Aruh Ululu* festival anyways, the Chief wished to reassure them that his winged champion wasn't about to fly away.

In other words, the old tightwad had offered to host the feast....

A party-like atmosphere followed her as they wound through the streets. Well-wishers thronged behind her, while some of the more gutter-minded citizens made off-color jokes about being transformed from a maiden into a woman. Ninsianna blushed, her cheeks rosy and pink, as they passed through the final alley, into the central square.

Her bridesmaids cast flower petals upon the ground as they approached the Temple. Mikhail stood on the front steps, radiant in his Alliance dress-uniform, with medals which twinkled in the sun. There was something *divine* about the way he stood in front of the carved wooden doorway, with his magnificent black-brown wings framed by the arch.

His face lit up as he spotted her. He flashed a rare smile as she took his hand.

"You look beautiful," he murmured.

She felt so giddy—she broke into a giggle.

Papa entered the temple, and then came back out, carrying a smoldering bundle of *qat*. He circled the perimeter, cleansing the air with incense, and chanting a song to invoke the gods of marriage. At the appropriate moment, he raised his hands and called for the highest secular authority—in this case the Chief—to accept their petition to be married.

Both *she*, and Mikhail, glanced nervously across the square as the Chief appeared, wearing his finest ceremonial dress. There was no sign of Jamin, a terrible insult, but from the way Mikhail let out his breath, *he* wasn't any more anxious to have her former fiancé participate in their wedding ceremony than she was.

"Are we ready to begin?" Chief Kiyan asked.

"Yes," they both said solemnly.

The Chief took their hands and held them apart.

"Has this man sufficiently paid the bride-price?" he addressed her father.

"He has paid with his labor," Papa said, "his good deeds, and his continued promise to settle Ninsianna's debts."

The Chief gave Mikhail a stern look; no doubt a reminder that they *still* owed him a share of whatever crop they eked out of Yalda and Zhila's barley-field. He then looked towards Yalda and Zhila.

"Since he has no family, it's my understanding that *you* have guaranteed final payment of the bride-price?"

"We do," the two elderly women spoke with a single voice.

"Marriage is sacred," the Chief spoke, more to the village than to them. "It is only through the act of procreation, by bearing children, by raising them to contribute to the common good, and teaching them to glorify the gods, that a man can become immortal. Once your hands are joined in marriage, you may only separate for infertility or other egregious offense. A husband may only take one wife, must always provide for her support, and must treat her, and their children, with a measured hand. Mikhail, do you agree?"

Mikhail shot her a bemused expression at the implied "wife beating."

"I do."

"Ninsianna," the Chief said, "a wife must cleve to her husband; never forsake him, and always obey his word. Do you agree?"

She shot Mikhail a look at the word *"obey"* which warned, *"not on your life."*

"I do," she said.

"Then as arbiter of the *law*, I accept this marriage contract." The Chief placed their hands together. "The promise that is made thus shall not be cast asunder without further appeal to *the law*."

The Chief stepped back. Papa stepped forward to invoke the blessings of the goddess. He held out an urn of sacred myrrh-oil and poured a few drops onto a clay plate. Mikhail dipped one finger in the oil, and then rubbed it onto her forehead.

"With this oil, I promise the fruit of my labor," he spoke solemnly.

Ninsianna did the same.

"With this oil," she said, "I promise the fruit of my womb."

The sun caught Mikhail's eyes, causing them to shine a brilliant, unearthly blue. She was barely conscious of Papa wrapping a braided wheat-sheath cord around the both of their arms, symbolizing the binding together of two spirits into one, or the perfume Mikhail used to anoint her forehead as he declared:

"…so shall we be together, until death wrenches us apart."

With her gift of sight, she *saw* the radiant pink light which poured out of his heart to bind them both together as he made his commitment.

Papa poked her in the side.

"*You're* supposed to say it—" he said.

"Oh!" she startled. "I do!"

The villagers laughed.

Mikhail's eyes grew serious. He reached beneath his shirt and pulled out his "dog tags," now *two* silver medallions, one on its original silver chain, the other strung on a braided rawhide. He slid the silver chain off of his neck and held it in front of her.

"Wherever you go—" he spoke in Galactic Standard "—let it be known that you are the *wife* of Colonel Mikhail Mannuki'ili of the Second Galactic Alliance." He clasped the silver necklace around her neck. "Let it be *known* that you are my heart and soul."

A tear slid down her cheek. *This* wasn't part of an Ubaid ceremony.

He then spoke, loudly, in Ubaid:

"You are *mine!*"

The villagers cheered.

Mama wept.

Papa puffed up like a proud spotted *bulbul* bird.

"Mikhail," he said, "you may kiss your bride."

Fire burned through her as Mikhail's lips touched hers. He gathered her into his arms, lifting her up to his far greater height. The villagers cat-called as their kiss lingered and lingered…

Mikhail encircled the both of them in his wings.

His kiss deepened, no longer held back with restraint. Ninsianna gasped. This was a far different man than the disciplined warrior who always maintained his self-control.

"Go find a bed!" some of the villagers cat-called.

...two of the hecklers sounded suspiciously like Yalda and Zhila.

He slid his lips across her cheek to whisper in her ear.

"Do you wish to stay for the feast?"

"Mmm...." she mumbled in a pleasantly fuzzy haze. "No?"

He flared his wings and catapulted them both into the sky. Ninsianna squealed. The wedding guests clapped until they flew out of range.

* * * * *

IMMANU and NEEDA

"In a hurry, aren't they?" Needa squeezed her husband's hand.

"At least they waited." Immanu pinched her bottom. "We didn't..."

"They don't know that." Needa's cheeks grew pink at the memory of their first encounter.

"Nor does Ninsianna know she was already well on the way when we finally got around to performing the nuptials."

"Do you think their children will have wings?" Needa asked.

"Only the goddess knows."

Chapter 138

August 1ˢᵗ – 3,390 BC
Earth: Village of Assur

JAMIN

Jamin clenched his fist as Ninsianna said "I do." He felt angry. He felt sick. Filled with hatred and grief. He wanted to cry. He wanted to scream. He wanted to stab the winged demon in the heart.

He felt like a spear, pulled back, and ready to throw…

Shahla looked back, hoping to see him. She'd pulled a tantrum after he'd refused to announce they were "getting married" and made excuses for not telling his father. She was driving him crazy with talk about *their* wedding, who they'd invite, and the dress she would wear.

How had he gotten himself into this mess? Not only had he gotten eleven people killed, but now he was forced to pretend he was in love with her so she wouldn't tell everyone what he had done.

Some of the villagers glanced back at him, their expressions filled with pity. How would they feel if they found out it was *his* ill-conceived plot which had gotten some of them killed?

He realized he was being watched…

Preternatural black eyes glistened, wet with tears.

"What's the matter?" he sneered. "Jealous, of your cousin?"

Gita stepped from the shadows, a pale, gaunt wraith that looked as though she hadn't had enough to eat since the day she'd been born. A year older than Ninsianna, she appeared no older than Pareesa. Her raggedy brown woolen cloak, a cast-off of Shahla's, was drawn tightly around her as if she was cold even though the temperature was oppressive.

His anger softened as he noticed one eye was nearly swollen shut.

An overwhelming urge to *kill* the father who had beaten her welled to the surface. That was his *job*, to defend this village. What good was he, as *Muhafiz*, if he couldn't protect the *least* of them? Oh, the irony, that Ninsianna had declared herself to be "*Chosen*." Gita was living proof that his unfaithful ex-fiancé and her family were anything but altruistic.

"Why?" he asked softly.

"Your *father*," she said accusingly, "paid him a visit."

"What did he say?"

"I don't know," she said. "I wasn't there. But he said, if Mikhail *leaves*, he shall cast the *both* of us out into the desert to die."

Jamin's cheek twitched. He *knew* who'd put his father up to such a threat. Immanu didn't want his brother luring away his prize. The bastard didn't *care* that his brother would take it out on Gita.

Once upon a time, he'd have waited until Merariy was good and drunk and then rolled him in a back alley, claiming he'd been someplace else when his father tried to call him on it. But no more! He was *done* watching out for the rejects of this village when they were too stupid to watch out for themselves!

His cheek twitched. He was wound so tight he wanted to scream.

"Can't you see what this is doing to you?" She placed her hand on his arm. "Let it go."

She? Was telling. Him? To let things … go? Why? So he could end up just like *her?*

"What do you want, Gita?" Jamin hissed.

She gave him that black stare that reminded him of hunger. The emptiness he'd felt in his heart ever since Ninsianna had broken off their engagement.

"I want you to leave Shahla alone," she said. "You don't love her. She doesn't deserve to be used."

Her words were so quiet; he could barely hear them above the crowd as they dug into the lavish feast his father had laid out for -*his*- betrothed's wedding. Hatred welled in his heart. Betrayed! By his own father!

His cheek twitched, causing a cruel sneer to appear upon his face. He turned to cut Gita down the way *he* was feeling all cut up inside right now.

His words met with empty air. The black-eyed girl had disappeared…

Chapter 139

August 1ˢᵗ – 3,390 BC
Earth: Crash Site
Colonel Mikhail Mannuki'ili

MIKHAIL

Mikhail surveyed his ship as he circled in for a landing. Although he still had no idea how to repair the fractured hull or get the engines back online, the ruined ship made a superb honeymoon getaway.

"My wife," he said the moment their feet hit the ground, "may I present your bower for the next two weeks?"

"My husband," she pulled him down for a kiss, "do we ever have to leave?"

Fire burned down from his lips to his belly, igniting a fire that he wouldn't be able to suppress for much longer.

"If you keep kissing me like that," he growled. "We're not going to *make* it inside the ship."

Ninsianna threw back her head and laughed.

"Does anybody care?"

He scooped her up and ordered "watch your head!" as he carried her over the threshold, inside his ship. Ninsianna gasped when she saw the inside. It was her first time back and he'd been diligently making repairs. If not for the crack in the hull, the interior was restored to the condition it had been in before he'd been shot down. The ship would have appeared ready for duty if not for the flowers he'd gathered to decorate the interior, a suggestion given to him by Yalda and Zhila in one of their tipsy 'advice sessions' before the wedding.

"Well?" he asked, waiting to see her reaction.

"Oh, Mikhail!" She reached up to give him a hug. "It's beautiful. Is this what your ship looked like before you crashed?"

"I can assure you, ma'am, that there were absolutely *no* flowers on my ship before it crashed," he said with a deadpan expression that he might have pulled off had a smirk not snuck past his poker face.

"I mean, all this work," she said, trailing off. "You did this for me?"

"Of course," he said. "I couldn't bring my new wife back to an unshipshape ship."

Ninsianna wrapped her arms around his neck, pulling him down for a hungry kiss. Her fingers trailed through his hair as she pressed up against him. Every instinct clamored to take her right there on the floor and make her his, but he wanted to do this right. He couldn't remember whether or not he'd ever lain down with a woman before, but knew down to the core of his being this would be the first time he'd ever *made love* to one.

"There is more." He reluctantly stepped back from her embrace. "Come…" He tugged her past the galley, decorated with flowers and set for dinner for two, to their sleeping quarters.

"What did you do to the beds?" she asked.

He'd disassembled the four bunks, knocked out the supports that would have prevented the mattresses from touching, and reassembled two frames to make a single large bed. He'd lined the room with flowers and dozens of tiny clay lamps to light up the room in a soft, romantic light. He'd darted back an hour before the ceremony started, his wings enabling him to pull off a feat of romantic engineering no human could have accomplished.

"Does it meet your approval, my love?"

"Oh, yes!" she cried. "Now … kiss me…"

He gave himself permission to do what he'd been wanting to do ever since he'd opened his eyes and found a beautiful young woman on his ship, unable to speak his language, but able to communicate by placing her palm upon his heart.

Wrapping his arms around her waist, he kissed her like a thirsty man drinking water from a sacred spring. Ninsianna fumbled with his buttons as she removed his constricting jacket. His medals *clinked* as it slid to the floor. Slipping his hand down the back of her shawl-dress, he cupped her firm, round buttocks and pulled her closer, gasping with pleasure as she rubbed her abdomen against the most intimate part of his anatomy. He lifted her so her body would align with his.

Two buttons from his shirt *plinked" against the floor as she gave up trying to manipulate the unfamiliar fastenings and simply broke the thread. She pressed her lips to his chest, tugging at his shirt as he kissed her from earlobe to collarbone. His feathers rustled with pent-up desire. He groaned as she slid his shirt off and touched his bare skin.

Fumbling off her shawl-dress, he marveled at her brownish-pink nipples standing erect and ready for his inquisitive tongue. Ninsianna gasped as he bent down to suckle first one, and then the other. Frantically, she worked down his zipper. Kicking off his boots, he nearly fell over as she reached beneath the waistband and touched him.

"Do you like that?" she fondled his erection.

His wings slapped against the wall as he involuntarily convulsed.

"If you keep doing that," he gasped. "This will be over before it's started."

She stood like a fine marble statue, her eyes glittering with desire as he touched the delicate string which held her loincloth to her hips. This was not the rawhide string she used every day, but one braided with flowers and the first stalks of grain from the summer harvest, a prayer to She-Who-Is that their union would be a fertile one. Slipping down her loincloth, he marveled at her furry mound. His flesh trembled as she slid her fingers beneath his modern underpants and slid them down.

It was Ninsianna, as always, who took the lead...

"Are you ready?" she led him towards the bed.

He lay her down as though draping a fine linen scarf upon the covers, supporting his weight on his hands and knees so he wouldn't crush her. With the upper-level bunks now gone, he had room to flare his wings. Urgency burned like wildfire through his veins. He fought to keep control as Ninsianna explored his body.

"Ninsianna ... have you ever...?"

"No," she blushed. "Have you?"

He gave a wistful smile.

"I can't remember," he said. "But I'll try to be careful."

A shadow of fear crossed her face. He was afraid he might hurt her badly enough that she would be afraid of future matings. The widow-sisters had told him he must delay his own satisfaction and pleasure his new wife before breaking the barrier that would transform her from maiden into married woman. Kissing her until the cloud of fear left her eyes; he kissed down her neck, past her breasts, and down to her abdomen, caressing her inner thighs.

"That tickles," she giggled. She squirmed as he awkwardly ventured into uncharted territory.

He nibbled on her belly-button, relishing the tremble of muscle beneath her soft skin. She smelled of flowers and the soap root he would forever associate with her. As his lips moved down towards her furry mound, she grabbed his hair and shrieked. She skittered away from him, laughing.

He grabbed her hips and pulled her towards him. She didn't resist, but her eyes glittered with a blend of fear, anticipation, and something else – a dare? He paused, moving his hands across her thighs, to give her time to grow accustomed to his touch.

She parted her legs with a nervous giggle. He stared at that most secret place, as though he'd never seen such a wonder before.

The urge to *taste* her grew overwhelming as a sweet, musky scent worked its way into his brain.

Ninsianna moaned as he kissed her inner thighs. His testicles sent insistent shudders through his body, but he was *determined* that her first time would be pleasurable. She shifted, opening herself more fully to his inquiring tongue. He kissed the moist folds and spread them apart, relishing her pleasant, musky scent. There. A tiny little button beckoned to him, pulsating in anticipation of his touch. This was where he'd been told a woman liked to be pleasured.

Looking up the length of her abdomen, her beautiful, golden eyes glittered with anticipation. He licked her, watching her expression as shudders wracked her body. Her scent changed. Grew muskier. More earthy. As though she were fertile earth waiting for him to plant his seed. She threw back her head and arched her back, pushing his head down further towards the part of her body screaming for release.

Suckling the tiny mound to increase her level of arousal, he couldn't help but smile at the funny little happy noises she made with each twitch of his tongue. He sent a silent thanks to his two elderly friends who'd suggested such novel lovemaking — at the time he'd thought it obscene. It was their advice he relied upon, not instinct, as he gently slid one finger inside to give her time to adjust to the feel of him. She stiffened, and then relaxed as she realized there was no pain.

She hesitantly arched her hips to give him greater access.

Wait. He must wait until she became acclimated to his touch. He ignored the insistent twanging of his engorged member and focused on what *she* was feeling. She tilted her pelvis to meet his tongue. He gently stretched the thin membrane that partially obstructed the entrance and waited until she began to move against his fingers to satisfy her own desire.

He could sense she was close to release by the way she writhed and made adorable little mewling noises like a kitten seeking out its mother's breast. Removing his fingers, he licked her mound until she began to shudder. Her sweet juices exploded onto his waiting tongue. Panting as though she had just run a marathon, she sighed and stretched out spread-eagle on the bed, grabbing his hair and pulling him back up to taste her own juices off his lips. She shot him a satisfied smile.

"That didn't hurt at all," she said with a husky voice.

"That was just the teaser." He kissed her as his throbbing erection pressed insistently into her abdomen. "Are you ready for the main event?"

The shadow of fear crossed her face as concern about pain made her fret. He caressed her until she became aroused a second time. He suppressed the frantic twang his manhood shrieked throughout his entire body and took her to the edge. He wanted her even *more* aroused when he broke her maiden head. She pleaded for release from the torturous pleasure.

"Please, Mikhail!" She fought to capture his manhood with her hips. Frantic with desire, she bent up and sank her teeth into his neck as she grabbed his buttocks and pulled him closer.

It was time…

Maneuvering to the entrance of her feminine mysteries, he maintained eye contact as he rubbed against her warm, moist entrance until she'd thoroughly bathed him in the juice of her desire. Her warm, slippery wetness made him shudder. The wetter he was, the less he would hurt her.

Memory loss *was* a beautiful thing, because nothing felt familiar as he pushed through the barrier preventing his entrance. She froze as he slid with a single, smooth movement into the place some ancient god had designed so mortal creatures would fit together.

"It hurts," she whispered, pain clouding her eyes.

He forced himself to remain still. Wait. He must wait until *she* took the lead or the mating would be … would be …

A shadow flitted through his memory; an ancient woman, a voice:

"You must bond properly, or the lifemate bond will be incomplete…."

Ninsianna kissed him, causing the errant thought to fly out of his mind. Wait. He must wait or he would hurt her.

He deepened his kiss until he felt her body relax. She began to writhe, adjusting to the feel of him inside of her as she grew bolder and moved along his shaft. Distracting her by nibbling down her neck, he arched his back and slid partway out, and then even more slowly back in until his full length had been absorbed. A rush of emotion, *feeling*, overwhelm, washed through him. He felt her shudder, the pain mixing with pleasure as she moaned.

The sensation did things he was certain he'd never felt before. Wings slapped against the sheets; feathers flew as he instinctively tried to carry the both of them into the air. The feel of her moving against him caused warmth like he'd never experienced before to radiate out from his heart, into his outer extremities and brain.

Ninsianna cried out. She clutched him as she climaxed a second time.

Stars exploded inside his mind. Mikhail cried out, feeling his consciousness slip beyond his mortal body as, just for a moment, he experienced what it must feel like to be a god. In his mind, he shouted his intentions to the universe that come what may, nothing would ever part him from her. Not even death.

Exhausted, he collapsed against her.

"Ohmygods," she panted. "That was….."

"Amazing….." He silenced her with a kiss.

"Tell me that you love me?"

"I love you more than life itself," he pulled her to his chest. "And I shall never be parted from you."

He couldn't remember his past, but he was certain that he'd never felt so happy. Shifting one wing to cover them both, with happy exhaustion, they drifted off to sleep in each other's arms.

Chapter 140

Galactic Standard Date: 152,323.08 AE
Ascended Realms
Asclepius – an old god

ASCLEPIUS

The prayer resonated, not like that of a mortal, but as though it came from a god who was almost as powerful as *SHE* was. Asclepius closed his eyes and focused on *who* could be making such a ruckus.

"Oh, it's you?"

He reached out with the neutrinos which comprised his consciousness to mingle with those of an old friend and fellow god.

The deity, who mortals called the Eternal Emperor, but who he called simply by his given name, Hashem, materialized into the higher ascended realms, carrying with him the baggage of an entire galactic empire.

"Good day, old friend," Asclepius said. "I'm surprised to see you."

"I have a favor to ask," Hashem said.

"You know I can't interfere."

"I do it all the time," Hashem said.

"That's because you *descend* to do it," Asclepius said. "Manually. Through your own efforts, the way a mortal does. If you try to manipulate matter, you'll have to answer to *HIM*."

Both old gods shuddered. She-Who-Is ruled her universe with an iron fist, but the *real* danger was her primordial husband, He-Who's-Not, also known as the Dark Lord. To protect his wife against her evil father, *HE* had ruled that no one could use their power to interfere in *HER* dominion. Sometimes they could get away with a tiny push, or petition *HIM* and make their case, but exercises of power were normally denied. "*Go build your own universe,*" the Dark Lord often said. But few gods had. The moment they tried, the Evil One showed up and devoured it.

"I don't need a miracle," Hashem said. "Just information."

"What kind of information?"

"You used to be a physician; the best that ever existed."

He and Hashem, back before they'd both ascended, had been quite a team, with one scientist treating the symptoms, and the other working diligently to engineer a cure. Hashem had been the *first* to figure out how to transcend time and space, but then, he'd decided to stay behind.

"Do you need a miracle?" Asclepius asked. "Because if you do, you'll have to petition *HER*?"

"Nothing so drastic," Hashem said, "Just a diagnosis."

"Why haven't *you* been able to diagnose it?" Asclepius said. "You're a brilliant geneticist."

"I can modify the building blocks of a species that is weak," Hashem said, "but I'm not good at saving individual lives. Despite my best efforts, the problem continues to elude me."

Asclepius sighed. If Hashem hadn't been able to solve a biological problem, then chances were it couldn't be solved. But the problem intrigued him. Here, in the ascended realms, things got rather boring.

"Who is the patient?" he asked.

"Uriel," Hashem said. "He's the son of my Supreme Commander-General."

Asclepius closed his eyes and followed the threads which connected Hashem to his subjects – so many of them –through the woman he spoke of, until he got to the infant.

"He's dying," Asclepius said. "It's way past the point of engineering a cure."

Tears welled in his colleague's golden eyes. If there was anything worse than an ascended deity's anger, it was when they wept. The heavens shuddered in sympathetic resonance to his grief.

"Is there anything you can do?" Hashem begged. "Anything at all?"

"It's forbidden to interfere unless I descend," Asclepius said, "and when I do, I'll be as blind and cut off from my power as *you* are."

Hashem cried out. "He's just a baby!"

"You were warned when you spliced together your armies that the species were genetically incompatible," Asclepius said. "You should have followed your own dogma and allowed them to evolve those traits naturally."

"The child is innocent," Hashem said. "I don't believe *SHE* would hold an infant responsible for *my* mistakes."

"When you created your armies," Asclepius said. "You created physical shells enticing enough to lure highly evolved spirits out of the upper realms. When you did, you bound yourself, and them, to the rules of the material realm."

Both old gods clasped their hands together and bowed their heads in deference to the *Unknowable One*.

"What does that have to do with the wasting sickness?" Hashem asked.

Asclepius wracked his brains, searching for a *diplomatic* way to point out his colleague's blind spot.

"Why do you refuse to leave your subjects to fend for themselves?"

"Why, I love them," Hashem said. "They are like my own children."

"You *choose* to love," Asclepius scolded him, "but then you deny it to the armies who defend you."

"What do you mean?"

"Their spirits incarnated into mortal form to experience love, but then you turned around and denied it to them so you could perpetuate your military might!"

"But I am their *father*," Hashem said. "Why isn't that enough?"

"Because you refuse to let them grow up," Asclepius said. "As children evolve, they move away from their parents. If you do a good job, eventually they will return."

"I have strict seed world policies," Hashem said indignantly. "Free will is the cornerstone of my empire."

"Which you deny to the creatures that *defend* you," Asclepius said. "Is it any wonder they're refusing to incarnate in to be your *slave* army?"

Hashem looked as though he'd just been slapped.

"They're not slaves," he mumbled.

"They're not considered "real people", so they don't have a right to vote," Asclepius said. "They *have* to serve 500 years in the military; you don't give them a choice. You make them place themselves beneath every other life form in your galaxy, even the pre-sentient ones, and now, not only have you forbidden them to marry, but you take away their children and never let them see them!"

Tears welled in Hashem's eyes.

"It's not like that..."

"No?" Asclepius said. "Well that's what it *looks* like from up here."

Hashem began to pace.

"Jophiel begged me not to give up this child," he said. "She wishes to be with the father and raise him as her ancestors did, before inbreeding became a problem."

"The inbreeding is your own fault," Asclepius scolded. "The hybrid races lived naturally until your constant intrigues with Shay'tan forced them all into the military."

"How can I *fix* this?" Hashem asked.

"If I tell you how to save this child," Asclepius warned, "there will be consequences. What your Supreme Commander-General does, the rest of your armies will follow."

Hashem's shoulders sagged.

"Jophiel is like a daughter to me," he said. "Just tell me how to fix it?"

Asclepius struggled to find *words* that Hashem would understand. For a creature who'd given up all the power in the universe to nurture his creations, sometimes his fellow god was *so* incredibly dense...

"You created the hybrids out of mammals," Asclepius said. "Mammals will choose starvation over the denial of physical comfort. In your effort to maintain genetic diversity, you separated them from each other, into cold, sterile environments, until the most physical among them have begun to waste away."

Hashem ran his fingers through his beard, his expression thoughtful.

"I could never understand this need to be touched," he said. "But I see it in my experiments all the time. I have spliced together countless adaptations, only to have them die when their parents reject them."

Asclepius resisted the urge to chastise Hashem about his cluelessness. The other old gods jokingly called him a trans-dimensional alien. Never been in the material realm before, didn't 'get' it. He spent too much time spinning theories and not enough time in the 'real' world even though he'd given up heaven to linger there. It was rumored that She-Who-Is had paired the brilliant, but not too street-smart Hashem to play against the earthy Shay'tan on a wager against the Dark Lord.

"You can't deny physical beings love," Asclepius said. "That's why they accepted your offer to descend in the first place, and that's why they are now *declining* your offer, no matter *how* tempting the mortal shells you offer them to inhabit."

"Either way, the hybrid races are doomed," Hashem sighed. "Your way just means it will happen sooner."

A tidbit of information niggled at Asclepius' subconscious. Something *SHE* wanted Hashem to know, but didn't want to tell him directly because it would violate a bet she had running with the Dark Lord.

"Shay'tan has the solution to your problem," Asclepius whispered.

"What?" Hashem asked.

"Shhh....!" Asclepius hushed him. "I've already said too much."

Hashem understood the code words 'said too much.' The old gods had developed such code for when they needed to exchange information that She-Who-Is, or He-Who's-Not, might not approve of. Hashem wisely changed the subject.

"And the child?"

"Tell the parents they must care for their son *themselves*," Asclepius said.

"Choose to love?" Hashem's bushy eyebrows knit together with hope. "I don't know how to enact that, but I will give it my best shot."

Hashem gripped Asclepius' forearm.

"Thank you, old friend," he said. "I will take your advice to heart."

The old god released his hold on the ascended realms. It took an enormous act of will to cram a consciousness as big as his across the barriers which separated time and space. *If* he ever decided to abandon his silly quest and take his rightful place among them, he would rival She-Who-Is in his glorious magnificence. The other gods would never admit it, but they admired him.

Asclepius focused his consciousness towards the child. Its parents huddled together, breathing along with their dying son as he struggled to take every breath. Asclepius took pity on them. Just because he'd long ago shed his material form didn't mean he couldn't remember what it had been like to feel pain.

It was just a nudge...

Reaching out with his mind, he directed a tiny tendril of consciousness into that part of the infant's body that struggled to hold onto the lifespark and strengthened it. Small enough that *HE* wouldn't notice.

Let Hashem do the rest ... and pay the price.

Chapter 141

August - 3,390 BC
Earth: Crash Site

NINSIANNA

Yawning and stretching in her downy bed, Ninsianna opened her eyes to find her new husband intently staring at her. A slight smile upticked the corner of his mouth.

"I think my wing fell asleep."

"Huh?"

She caressed the enormous, black-brown wing that covered them both. Blankets were just a hindrance to a species that came equipped with their very own feather comforter! She ran her fingers beneath the quills to tickle his warm, avian skin.

"Not that one." His smirk blossomed into a full-blown smile. "The other wing."

She patted the bed underneath her back. At some point during the night, she'd rolled onto his other wing, completely enclosing herself in his enormous wings. She ran her fingers through the soft, downy feathers.

Mikhail twitched.

"Ow!"

"Pins and needles?" she asked.

"You cut off the circulation," he gently chided her.

"Why didn't you say something?"

"I didn't wish to wake you." He ran his thumb across her lips, his expression tender. "I feared I'd wake up and discover that I dreamed you."

"We're now married," she smiled, "until death do us part."

His dog tags jingled against her chest, a rude reminder of a mission she wished he would *forget*. His brow furrowed in worry. He straightened the twin dogtag which he'd placed upon her neck.

Thankfully the goddess had given her gender a way to distract a man. Running her hand down his rock solid abdomen, she found him standing at attention, rising up to meet her touch. Naked pleasure crossed his usually serious face as she ran her fingers along the shaft and blood rushed to a certain greedy part of his anatomy.

He gave a cry of discomfort, half laughter, and half pain, as pins and needles shot up his numb wing.

"We shall have to do something to wake your wing up." She stroked him. "Can you think of any way to get the blood flowing again?"

"If my blood flows any faster," he said with a growl, "my head will explode." He shifted his weight on top of her, nuzzling down her neck as he pulled the errant wing out from underneath them both and laughed, cried, said "ow", and then laughed again as the blood began circulating back into the limb.

"It's not your head I'm interested in," she teased. She stroked him into a quivering mass of anticipation as she guided him between her legs.

This time there was no discomfort, only pleasure...

Chapter 142

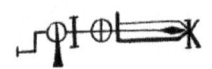

Galactic Standard Date: 152,323.08
Haven-4: Youth Training Academy
Colonel Raphael Israfa

RAPHAEL

A fresh, crisp scent shook Raphael out of his fitful sleep. He glanced down at the tiny baby who slept nestled in his mother's arms. Was it just wishful thinking? Or did Uriel's breathing seem a little easier?

The scent of ozone grew stronger, as though they slept in a forest after a thunderstorm had just passed, scrubbing the air clean and filling it with sunshine. In one corner, the dust sparkled even though he could detect no source of sunlight. It took a moment for his mind to recognize an ascended being coalescing into physical form.

Raphael leaped to his feet and drew his pulse rifle. His hands shaking, he aimed it at the Eternal Emperor.

"I won't let you take him!"

He flared his wings to look intimidating ... to a god?

The golden-eyed deity appeared mildly surprised, but his face crinkled with understanding.

"Put that away, son," he said. "Nobody's come to hurt Uriel."

"But I thought..."

"That I'd come to take your son into the dreamtime?" The Emperor glanced down at the tiny baby, his expression worried. "I've done everything I can to *keep* your son alive. The rest is up to him."

Raphael took in the Emperor's appearance. Instead of the white robe worn in adoration holograms, he wore a perfectly ordinary laboratory coat, buttoned up wrong with the collar sat askew. Spackles of green, some kind of chemical, marred the coat, while his silver-grey hair jutted out, helter-skelter, like a mad scientist who'd spent an all-nighter. If not for the *divinity* shining out of his golden eyes, had Raphael not witnessed his mystical appearance, he might mistake the Emperor for a doctor.

"Please, Colonel," the Emperor gestured, palms-down. "Holster your weapon."

Raphael realized the Emperor could have smote him on the spot. Fumbling like a first-year cadet, he slipped the weapon into its holster, and then threw himself down upon his knees, casting his son's life to the Emperor's mercy.

"Isn't there anything you can do for him? Please? He's just a baby!"

The Eternal Emperor Hashem gave a weary sigh.

"Contrary to popular belief," he said. "I am neither omnipotent, nor omniscient. If I had the power to solve all problems, then problems wouldn't exist."

Jophiel had spoken of the Emperor as though he were a trusted father figure as they had lain together in the afterglow of the mating appointment which had given them Uriel, but this was the first time Raphael had seen this side of the emperor and god. How could one so powerful appear so mortal?

"Then Uriel will die, won't he?" Tears welled into his eyes. He was glad Jophiel was not awake to hear that their son was doomed.

"No, he won't," the Emperor sighed. "I've gone to an old friend and pleaded intervention. Your son will live, but now I must bear the consequences for that choice."

Raphael clapped his hand over his mouth to suppress a sob. His inclination to gush was tempered by how old and weary the Emperor looked, as though he carried not just the weight of the Alliance, but the entire universe upon his shoulders. All this time, while he and his fellow citizens had been praying to the Emperor for help, perhaps, in reality, the Emperor needed help from *them*?

What was it Jophiel had said? *No* creature could coordinate something as vast as this empire alone, not even the Eternal Emperor. He needed *her*, needed *him*, needed all of them, every last citizen, to work together to protect what he had built.

What was it Jophiel had said? *"We are –all– soldiers of God, from the mightiest hero to the meekest old woman, praying for a better future..."*

"How can I help, Your Majesty?"

"Follow your heart," the Emperor said. "That is the choice I have made, to *love*. Even if that choice does not make sense."

"I don't understand?" Raphael's wings perked up in inquiry.

"It *means* that Jophiel must raise her child *herself*." He met Raphael's gaze. "Nor will I discourage her from choosing to be with *you*, if that is what her heart desires. But know this ... what Jophiel does, the others will follow. Do you understand this? Do you understand the terrible price we must *all* pay for following our heart?"

The magnitude of this choice settled onto Raphael's shoulders. The breeding laws had been acted for a *reason*...

"If we marry," Raphael swallowed, "our race will die out, won't it?"

"It will die out either way," the Emperor sighed. "Despite my best efforts, your species continues to wither. But I have heard a rumor. They say that Shay'tan has the solution within his grasp?"

"Shay'tan, Sir? What kind of solution?"

"I don't know!" the Emperor gesticulated with frustration. "The price for choosing to stay *here*, in the material realms, is ignorance!"

"But Your Majesty—" Raphael scrambled back to his feet. "I'm an intelligence officer. A *good* one."

"Then perhaps you can help?" The Emperor gestured at the sleeping infant. "In exchange for your son's life, you must help me find this solution which Shay'tan has found. Whatever it is, the fate of the Alliance rests upon it."

"I won't let you down, Your Majesty," Raphael cried out. "You have my word!"

Whatever cards Shay'tan held up his scaly sleeve, it had something to do with the mysterious buildup in Zulu Sector and his missing best friend! He just *knew* it, in his gut.

Jophiel stirred just as the Eternal Emperor shimmered out of the room.

"Who was that?"

Raphael kissed her forehead and pulled her closer. "Shhhh...."

He offered Uriel his finger so his son could wrap his tiny fingers around his larger one. The baby was *definitely* breathing easier.

"Look, Jophie," he said. "I think our son is going to live."

Chapter 143

August - 3,390 BC
Earth: Village of Assur

JAMIN

The spears were piled up, the bindings waiting to wrap the warriors' hands. At the edge of the field, he'd set the targets at varying paces, freshly painted with goat's blood to mark the bullseye. These were *real* weapons. Men's weapons. Not bundles of sticks and strings. It was time to remind his men *who* was their *Muhafiz*.

Jamin squinted down at his shadow, and then up at the sun, more than an hour past midday. The instructions he'd given the boy had been quite explicit: find all of the elite warriors and order them to convene here at noon. With Mikhail on his honeymoon, *now* was his opportunity to seize back control.

A magpie flew overhead, mocking him with its laughing cry. He threw a rock at the bird, impotent to hit a creature that could fly. Fuming, he grabbed his spear and stormed back into the village. He found the messenger loitering by the well. He grabbed the boy by the hair.

"Where are they?" he demanded.

"T-they couldn't make it," the boy sputtered.

"WHERE ARE THEY?"

"In the date palm orchard—" the boy shielded his face. "Just past the fields."

Snarling like an angry lion, Jamin passed through the north gate, down the embankment, and across the fields to the place where their fields petered out. He found the elite warriors surrounded by women and a handful of pre-adolescent boys.

"Now you are training with children?" he shrieked.

Siamek answered, "Your father *ordered* us to train."

"And *I* ordered you to meet me west of the village!"

Alalah, a middle-aged mother of eight, stepped between him and his warriors.

"-I- told them to come here," she wagged her finger in his face.

"-I- outrank you!"

"And your *father* outranks *you*," Alalah said. "How can we defend this village if the Chief's own son keeps undermining everything he does?"

Jamin raised his hand, but the upstart hag raised one finger at him and said:

"You will answer to your father."

Damn his father! Immanu had cast a spell upon him, singing songs about the sky-people. And now he'd enchanted his *people.*

He whirled to Siamek and gestured at the women and child "archers".

"Don't you see," he hissed, "he does this to *humiliate* you!"

That little snit, Pareesa, inserted herself between the elite warriors.

"Mikhail *does* this so we don't get killed by Halifian arrows!"

Jamin held up his spear. It was carved out of a rare, dark wood, and the finest obsidian spear-point, held over a fire until the wood became strong, and then carved with symbols that proclaimed his rank. He'd won three Solstice Festivals with this spear, killed countless game, and had killed the auroch which had gutted him like a fish, all while holding his intestines in and fighting the urge to faint.

"*This* is a weapon!" he hissed. "Not those foolish sticks!"

Pareesa made a rat-face.

"You're just afraid you'll get outshot by a girl."

The women giggled. Several of the elite warriors clamped their hands over their mouths to avoid laughing in his face.

He reached out to smack her, but Pareesa danced out of the way. He grabbed at her arm, but she snatched his wrist and twisted his thumb back, causing him to yelp.

"Damn you! I'm the *Muhafiz!*"

He slammed his spear into the ground, inches from her foot. The women stopped laughing. The spear quivered with unspent energy.

"I'm not afraid of you!" In a seamless move, Pareesa reached into her quiver, strung her bow—

"Foot!"

—and let an arrow fly.

It landed at the edge of his footwear, so close, it split the hide.

"Goddamn you!" He lurched towards her, *this* time intending to hurt her.

Pareesa reached into her quiver—

"Hand!"

—and let a second arrow fly.

He noted the twang of the bowstring *after* pain stabbed into his upraised hand. He stared at it with disbelief. Pareesa had *shot* him? A drop of blood seeped around the arrow and dripped down his palm.

The children sniggered.

"You bitch!!!"

He yanked his spear out of the ground with his uninjured hand. *This* time, he would *kill* her. He cocked it back…

"Heart!"

Pareesa strung a third arrow and aimed it at his chest. Her eyes took on a pitiless black stare that tore at his testicles.

"Stop!" Siamek jumped between them, knocking the spear out of his hand before he had a chance to strike. His eyes were wild and fearful. "Jamin, please!"

Pareesa hissed something in the Cherubim language.

Jamin froze...

She stood as cold and emotionless as the mentor she now mimicked, bow drawn, so closely resembling the winged demon that it was all he could do to not imagine she possessed a pair of wings. The air did not reverberate with that horrifying deep voice which had spoken to him the day Mikhail had killed the Halifians at his sky canoe, but Pareesa was one of them now. An enemy. She even spoke their language.

"Pareesa is our best archer," Alalah said coldly. "I will not tolerate this behavior, and neither will the Chief! Now go home and take care of that hand!"

Jamin slunk home holding his hand, the arrow sticking through it for the whole village to see. No one dared say a word. Not even that pesky little voice that had taken to whispering to him in the wind.

He didn't care *how* long it took. He was going to kill her...

Chapter 144

August – 3,390 BC
Earth: Village of Assur
Colonel Mikhail Mannuki'ili

MIKHAIL

The temperature dropped perceptibly the closer they got to the river. Dogs barked and children ran through the streets, calling their names as Mikhail circled the village. Ninsianna waved and greeted each child by name, nearly pulling him off balance. He touched down in a flurry of feathers a few feet from the front door. Before she could wriggle out of his grasp, he stepped towards the threshold. Ninsianna giggled as his wings got caught in the doorway, unable to fit both *her*, and his wings, through the narrow entrance. They squeezed through the door at an awkward angle, leaving a trail of feathers.

"My wife," he set her down.

"My husband," she stood on tiptoe to give him a kiss.

They scrutinized the too-small room. Inside was as miserably hot as it was outside.

"Home sweet home..." she said without enthusiasm.

"For now," he said. "At least until I can build our dream house."

The house he pictured was nothing like the ones in this village. The ceilings would be high enough for him to stretch his wings, with lots of windows to catch the breeze. The kitchen would be large enough to fill with family – *lots* of children – and friends, and there would be a real bathroom with running water. But to build it, he needed time. And to get time, he needed to hurry up and finish training her people to take care of *themselves*!

"I see our parents moved your things out of the main living area," Ninsianna said. "I presume they moved them into my room?"

"Where we'll be sleeping really, r-e-a-l-l-y close together!" He pulled her close and nuzzled down her neck until she shrieked with laughter. Ninsianna's room was small and her bed even smaller. He wouldn't have room to flare his wings without knocking them into the wall.

The sound of voices alerted them they were no longer alone. Ninsianna's parents had headed back from the fields the moment they'd seen them glide in for a landing. Both Immanu and Needa carried baskets filled with the bounty they'd planted *together,* as a family, only months before. For some reason, it all felt *right*.

"Welcome home!" her mother hugged them both and kissed both cheeks. "I trust you two had a fruitful honeymoon?"

"Mom!" Ninsianna blushed at the implied meaning.

"Trying my hardest, ma'am," Mikhail grinned as he pulled Ninsianna against him for a hug. For someone who had kept his libido so tightly leashed, he *enjoyed* making love to his wife.

"Mikhail!" Ninsianna exclaimed. "You're worse than *she* is!"

"Supper will be ready in an hour," Needa said. "Mikhail, could you please go milk the goat?"

Mikhail groaned. He, an Angelic Special Forces Colonel, the fiercest warrior this village had ever seen, supposedly a sword of the very gods who ruled this galaxy, consistently lost his daily battle with their recalcitrant dairy goat. No matter what he tried, food bribes, coercion, force, even terror, the goat would not cooperate. He usually ended up spilling as much milk as he was able to extract.

"A wise man must learn to *coax* a reluctant female." Immanu gave him a knowing look. "It's your only weakness…"

"The goat?" he asked.

"No … the gift of persuasion…" Immanu donned his most enigmatic shaman look. "A wise leader must know not only how to defeat his enemies in combat, but also how to persuade them. You must overcome that weakness."

Mikhail puzzled over Immanu's cryptic words, before shooting him a grin. "It sounds like an excuse to get *me* to milk the goat instead of you."

"That too…" Immanu chuckled.

An hour later, with cloven hoof prints all over his pants, they sat down for supper and caught up on what had been happening while they'd been away.

"Alalah and Pareesa gave archery lessons to the elite warriors," Immanu said. "They're looking pretty good."

"What about Jamin?" Ninsianna caught his scowl and shot out her hand to cover his. "Honey … we need him. He's the best warrior we have."

"Jamin won't be shooting a bow, or anything else, anytime soon," Immanu said. "He tried to bully Pareesa. Your little *çok puan ile mızrak* didn't take too kindly to that."

Çok puan ile mızrak … spear of many points. Or as *he* jokingly called her, *"my little weapon of mass destruction."* Ever since Pareesa had escaped capture, she'd devoted all of her time to learning everything she could about the art of warfare.

"Did you take the issue up with the Chief?" Mikhail asked.

"The Chief sided with Pareesa," Immanu said. "Jamin shouldn't be undermining his authority by discouraging the warriors from training."

"Good," Mikhail snorted satisfaction.

"You'd better watch your back with that one—" Needa's eyes filled with worry. "If he ever has the chance to strike at you—"

"I know." He suppressed the urge to go *throttle* their leader's son. "What about the combat recruits?"

"The Chief trained them *himself*," Immanu said proudly. "He showed them we old-timers still have a few good tricks."

They finished dinner over small talk about things that had gone on while they were absent. Eager to turn in for an early night, Mikhail grabbed his blushing bride by the hand, bid her parents goodnight, and dragged her upstairs, trying very hard not to be *too* loud as he thumped his wings against the wall.

Chapter 145

ᐃᕹᑎᐊᑎᏕ

Galactic Standard Date: 152,323.08 AE
Haven-1: Palace of the Eternal Emperor
Supreme Commander-General Jophiel

JOPHIEL

A brown dragon-like snout peered out the door where she stood waiting, flanked by the two Cherubim guards who had been instructed to usher her inside the moment she arrived. The moment he spied her, a pleased grin appeared on Dephar's face.

"Ahh! Jophiel! Come in!" The Mu'aqqibat dragon held open the door as his golden eyes glowed brighter, the mark of a pre-ascended creature. "You'll find him in the usual place."

She thanked the wingless dragon, slender and tall like the serpents that flanked both sides of Asclepius's caduceus, a symbol of knowledge and wisdom. Dephar had always made her feel welcome, even when she showed up unexpectedly to disturb the Emperor's research on a matter of military urgency. She shifted the sleeping Uriel to her hip so she could give the Emperor's top research genius a proper salute, and inquired about Dephar's *own* research before making her way through the labyrinth of cages.

It was a vibrant place, piled helter-skelter, despite the best efforts of an army of laboratory technicians to keep things organized. She found him bent over an experiment with his laboratory coat buttoned up all wrong. She didn't take offense when he didn't acknowledge her right away. The Emperor's work required absolute concentration.

"Shhhh," he said. "It's about to hatch."

The Emperor motioned for her to step close to the incubator so she could see creation in progress. Fist-sized leathery eggs, perhaps belonging to a lizard, turtle, or snake, wiggled as they began to hatch. This is how Jophiel loved him best. In his lab, wearing crumpled clothing that looked as though it had been slept in, up to his elbows creating variations of life.

"What are they?" She watched a claw chip through one of the eggs.

"Gourocks from Gemini-28—" the Emperor focused intently. "Miniature land dragons. Nearly extinct. I've given them a little enhancement. We shall see if that helps them survive?"

"What is the enhancement?"

"Just a tweak," he said. "You tell me?"

The first baby dragon struggled out of its shell and squeaked. Soon, two dozen more followed. All were identical except for the last one, which didn't hatch. The Emperor took the egg and studied it.

"It *should* hatch," he said, perplexed. "My tests showed all of the eggs had developing embryos."

"I don't see what the enhancement is," she said. "I'm not familiar with gourocks."

"Let's see how their mama reacts?" he rolled over a larger cage until the doors lined up, and then lifted them so the dog-sized adult gourock whose eggs had been enhanced could view her offspring. "C'mon, mama...." Hashem coaxed. "Let's see how you like your new babies?"

The mother tasted the air with her forked tongue and walked in, claws splayed for balance upon the ground. She was a creature who had evolved in a dry environment. She recognized her eggs and studied the babies. Giving them a sniff, she gave a reptilian bark to call her babies to her side.

"Oh … I see it now!" Jophiel whispered, amazed at the subtlety of the Emperor's tinkering. "They have webbed feet and their skin is slightly different. These babies can survive a wetter environment!"

"And they're smarter, too. Gemini-28 has been experiencing climate change. The sea levels are rising. Soon, there won't be much dry land left to walk upon. These babies will survive a marshy environment."

As they watched, the last remaining egg began to shudder. A tiny claw pushed through the shell.

Jophiel whispered: "C'mon, little guy…"

The last baby hatched, but its evolution from desert to swamp creature was far more extreme. Whereas the others had slightly webbed feet and smoother skin, the last one's aquatic features were far more pronounced. The feet were larger, fully webbed, like flippers; the skin was soft like a frog, and the tail had a paddle to propel it through the water. The head was streamlined so it could swim with less resistance, but also longer to fit a significantly larger brain. The mother gourock hissed and swatted it with her tail, rejecting it. The baby gourock curled up into a ball and whimpered.

"And those are the consequences of tinkering with the work of She-Who-Is." He picked up the little lizard and put it into a separate cage. Millions of such cages lined the walls of the Emperor's laboratory, a testament to his constant tinkering.

"Poor little guy." Jophiel pulled Uriel closer. "His mama didn't want him."

The Emperor sighed.

"I used to think I could just create life and everything would be good," he said. "But the older I get, the more I realize *everyone* needs a family." He looked Jophiel in the eye. "So what shall we do to rectify this problem?"

"I would like to tender my resignation, Sir," she said. "With the baby taking up so much of my time, I don't see how I can defend your Alliance."

The Emperor gave her a wistful smile.

"I *wish* I could grant your wish—"

"Not a wish," she said. "I want you to *court martial* me!"

"You're my most trusted advisor," he said. "Without *you*, I'm afraid the Alliance would collapse."

"But already hybrids are refusing to give up their babies!" she protested. "They demand to raise their own offspring because –I- am doing it. Please, Sir! Discharge me as a traitor and condemn my actions. Your empire depends upon it!"

"Blaming a scapegoat is something Shay'tan would do," the Emperor sighed. "This is *my* mistake, and I must bear the consequences of it."

"But, Sir!"

"But, nothing," he said. "Resignation denied. I'm assigning a full-time Delphinium nanny to help you care for Uriel on your command carrier. And I'm in the process of assembling a team of experts to figure out how I can let *other* Alliance hybrids have access to their offspring without jeopardizing the stability of the fleet."

"But I'll be—"

"Choosing to love," he said firmly. "It's my new policy. You'll be my first test subject. I hope to enact it, eventually, galaxy-wide."

"Choose to love?" She didn't know what to say. "How will that work?"

His golden eyes twinkled.

"I have no idea," he said. "We'll just have to work things out as we go."

Her mind raced through all of the *difficulties* this policy would cause for her, especially once she began to enact it throughout the rest of the fleet. She'd been forced to defend these difficulties, earlier, when she'd gone to the Emperor to beg for maternity leave, and lost. The problems hadn't gone away, just because Uriel had almost died.

But…

Her heart didn't *care*…

"If you insist, Sir?"

The Emperor grinned.

"I'm also recommending you promote that wonderfully efficient personal assistant of yours, what's his name, Captain Klik'rr, to Major," he said. "If it takes six naturally evolved creatures to replace a single hybrid, than we shall just have to start assigning a half-dozen assistants to take up the slack. It's about time we promoted the newer sentient races into the upper ranks of the military. Don't you agree?"

"Th-thank you, your eminence!" What he'd just handed her was better than her wildest dreams.

"Now let me see that fine son of yours."

Over the next hour, the Emperor played with Uriel and picked Jophiel's brain for ideas about how to allow the hybrid races, who were the legs his empire stood upon, to have more access to their offspring. At some point, one of the Emperor's lab technicians came in to take the Mama and baby lizards back to Gemini-28 and release them into the wild.

The conversation turned back to the Emperor's favorite subject, tinkering with the DNA which made up life. The new genetic traits he'd just instilled in the gourocks would be dominant. Within several generations, most gourocks would inherit the adaptation which would allow them to survive their changing climate. All but the poor little guy who'd been rejected. If his own mother rejected him, it was unlikely any mate would accept him. Sending him back to the homeworld to die was pointless.

As she went to leave, the Emperor gave her a gift.

"Here." He handed her the gourock's cage. "Everybody needs a family. Maybe Uriel will enjoy having a water dragon for a pet?"

Chapter 146

August – 3,390 BC
Earth: Village of Assur

SHAHLA

The people of the river bathed at least once per day, twice when the heat became oppressive, and three times on a day like today. Normally Shahla bathed where the men could admire her figure as she lay supine in the hot Mesopotamian sun with the water glistening off her nipples. Today, however, she'd sought refuge upriver. She put her head down in Gita's lap, weeping.

"Why don't you just break up with him?" Gita asked.

"Mama said I have to make *sacrifices*," Shahla hiccoughed, "to bring *prestige* to our family."

Gita snorted.

"You two are like oil and water," Gita said. "He doesn't *respect* you."

She touched the red mark on Shahla's cheek where Jamin had slapped her.

"You're one to talk! Your father beats you."

"At least I have enough sense to avoid him," Gita said.

"It's not Jamin's fault," Shahla sobbed. "He asked me to help him bandage up his hand and I told him he shouldn't have hit Pareesa."

"That doesn't mean he has a right to hit *you*!"

Gita rummaged through her satchel and pulled out a brush; one of Shahla's old ones, with a broken tine. She'd given it to the reclusive girl shortly after her father had reappeared in the village. The other children, now grown men and women, made fun of her peculiar friend, but they didn't understand the compulsion which had prompted her to take Gita under her wing.

Shahla closed her eyes as Gita pulled the broken comb through her hair.

"Sing for me?" she begged.

Gita began to hum.

A sense of *peace* settled into Shahla's body as Gita sang; a dull-feathered nightingale whose song was both a lament, and also a beacon which could illuminate the darkest night. Images flowed into her mind of a magnificent stone temple, surrounded by white-robed priestesses who carried flowers to an altar. They set the flowers at her feet, and braided them into her hair.

Gita stroked the bruise which Jamin had smote onto her cheek. Her flesh tingled. In the dream, the priestesses wrapped her injuries in linen and gold.

This was what she imagined it would be like once Jamin married her. No more selling her body for favors for her father, no more kowtowing to her mother whom, no matter what she did, it never seemed enough.

Gita finished brushing her hair. With a sigh, Shahla sat up.

"It's Ninsianna's fault," she said. "She put a spell on him."

"She probably *did*," Gita said, "but it doesn't excuse his behavior."

"You'd think you wanted him back with Ninsianna," Shahla said curtly.

"Ninsianna can *handle* him," Gita said. "You never could."

Shahla yanked the comb out of Gita's hand. She did this often, whenever she was angry. She took back her gifts. But never once had Gita complained.

Fathomless black eyes looked straight through her. Shahla shivered. Sometimes Gita reminded her of a spider, waiting for the tremor of a fly caught in the periphery of her web.

"Dadbeh loves you," Gita said softly. "Jamin has nothing but hatred right now."

"Someday Jamin will be Chief," Shahla stuck up her chin. "When he is, he said he will marry me."

"If he really loved you," Gita snapped, "he would have married you as soon as he started sleeping with you again."

"He says his father is against it," Shahla said.

"Chief Kiyan just wants his son to be happy," Gita said. "If Jamin asked, I'm certain the Chief would allow it. Goddess only knows your father has pushed often enough for a union!"

"His father will *disown* him if he finds out what Jamin did," she said.

Gita's head shot up.

"What?"

Shahla clamped her hand over her mouth. *Drat!*

Her best friend studied her intently, those prescient black eyes looking straight through her. She desperately wanted to confide in someone, but she didn't dare. Not only would Jamin be punished, but so would *she*.

Jamin would *kill* her if he found out…

"I mean," she stammered, "I mean if he finds *out* that Jamin wanted to *kill* Pareesa when he hit her."

Gita rolled her eyes.

"Everybody in the village knows that," she laughed. "She emasculated him, right in front of his men."

"And then –I– reminded him of that." Shahla touched her bruised cheek. She handed Gita back the comb.

"Sing for me?" she pleaded. "Again?"

This time Gita sang one of the 'marching songs' the men chanted as they carried buckets from the Hiddekel River, arms outstretched to strengthen their muscles, marching in perfect formation to water the fields.

A smile lightened Shahla's dark mood.

"And you accuse *me* of mooning over a hopeless cause?"

"What do you mean?"

"You think I don't know you've got it *bad* for Ninsianna's husband?"

Gita paused, her eyes focused far away. Shahla could almost *feel* the air around them change as her best friend made a life-altering decision.

"It's not like that," she said. "I'm just *tired* of being a victim. I'd like to take his self-defense class, and I want *you* to take it with me."

Gita clutched her hand as though she wished to *will* her to go with her so she didn't have to do it alone. *Alone.* Never in her life had Shahla seen anyone as abandoned and alone as the black-eyed girl nobody in the village but *her* had ever bothered to see.

Her lip trembled.

"A chief's wife must be supportive," her voice warbled.

From the disappointed twitch of Gita's lip, she understood her friend would go without her.

Shahla lowered her voice to a whisper.

"Besides, if I go, Jamin will kill me."

Chapter 147

August – 3,390 BC
Earth: Village of Assur
Colonel Mikhail Mannuki'ili

MIKHAIL

Normally, when it got this hot, he found relief by riding an air current, but today the air was so hot and dry that it felt like flying inside a blast furnace. Mikhail veered west until he came to the river, and then headed south, riding a current which carried slightly cooler air. It carried him past the place where he usually turned around; to where Assur's land ended and Eshnunna's began. Nobody ever came down here; few ventured far from the fields unless they wished to hunt. But a well-trodden path had been cut through the reeds to the water.

He fluttered to the ground and studied the tracks pressed into the mud. They were a close match for the ones Little Nemesis had left all over his cargo pants this morning, along with the tracks from two humans, one of them a child. Just centimeters from the river, the tracks dried out, indicating they'd baked all day in the sun.

"Maybe somebody from Eshnunna?" he muttered. So close to the border, it could be goats from either village.

He leaped back into the air, expecting the tracks to turn south, but they headed inland. The tracks disappeared when the ground turned rocky and dry.

His watch chimed, reminding him that he was scheduled to train the warriors in half an hour. Drat! He'd have to come back later and track down the mystery-goats.

He raced back to the village, since he was an hour's flight south, and fluttered to the ground all sticky and sweaty. Siamek had already ordered the elite warriors lead the warm-up.

"What took you?" Siamek asked.

"I found some goat tracks," he said, "on the border between Assur and Eshnunna."

Siamek stared south, his expression thoughtful.

"That's an all-day run," he said. "Two days, if you are herding goats."

"Could it be one of *our* herds?" Mikhail asked.

"I doubt it," Siamek said. "They've been staying close ever since the raid."

"So that leaves Eshnunna?"

"It's possible," Siamek said.

"Who *usually* waters their herds their?" Mikhail asked.

Siamek shrugged.

"I have no idea," he said. "Jamin told us not to patrol that area. It's too far from the village to be of concern."

Tirdard, who blissfully led the new recruits through a tortuous series of warm-up exercises, finished up. The recruits moved into a begrudging formation, wilted and sweaty and depleted from a day spent working in the sun.

"Okay, men ... and *ladies*," Mikhail called out. "Did you bring your staffs?"

The new recruits grumbled.

"We did that while you were gone," Ipquidad, a craftsman complained.

"When are we going to do something *interesting*," an inept young potter, Ebad, asked. "It's always the exact same thing. Hit. Throw. And carry buckets of water."

"Yeah," another craftsman named Yaggit said. "When will we do something *meaningful?*"

He started to say, "*repetition means perfection,*" but he'd been around humans long enough to grasp that, in many ways, they were like children. Whenever he trained Pareesa, he had to inject *new* things into the lesson to keep her interested enough to perform the necessary, but more boring, parts; and *she* was a dedicated student. These men were only here because the Chief had ordered it.

"Starting tomorrow," he said, "we'll start teaching you how to conduct patrols so the elite warriors—" he gestured at the men who'd led the warmup "—have more *notice* as to what our enemies are up to."

This pacified some of the recruits, but others complained:

"I have to weed my fields."

"I can't go far, my wife is sick."

"Who's going to milk my herd while I am gone?"

Unfortunately, the inept potter said: "I will go!"

"Alright, alright!" he said, exasperated. "Whoever needs to stay close, we'll pair you with the second-tier warriors, but as for the rest of you, we'll start rotating you through multi-day patrols."

That appeased *everybody*, including the elite warriors who were chafing at being forced to stay close and babysit the new recruits. From now on, he wanted to know *who*, exactly, was traversing their land.

He picked up the lesson from where the Chief had left things off, forming a defensive line with a spear. Only they didn't *have* enough spears for everybody to use. Nor was it likely the farmers would be carrying a spear if they were attacked while out in their fields – *most* Ubaid were farmers by trade. It was time to teach them something *everybody* could use.

He grabbed an ordinary walking stick, shoulder-height, and cut from the branch of an acacia tree.

"The foundation of Cherubim training is the ability to defend yourself using nothing but your empty hands," he said. "Once you've mastered the art of unarmed combat, they add weapons made from things you use in everyday life." He held up his staff. "No matter where you go, chances are you'll always be able to find a stick."

"Why can't we just use our spears?" Firouz scowled.

"What happens once you run out of weapons?" Mikhail flared his wings just enough to watch Firouz flinch. There. Me … alpha male. You … obey. Oh how he hated this game! He tucked his wings against his back as soon as the elite warrior fell back into line.

"Hold out your sticks so that you stand at least a staff-length apart." He demonstrated the correct way to hold the staff. "Place your staff with your hand at the midpoint—" he walked up the line, correcting mistakes. "It shouldn't look much different from the way you might carry a walking stick. But if you get into the *habit* of carrying it like this, you can quickly move it into any position."

With a blur, he swung the staff in a routine of imaginary feints and jabs. A murmur of appreciation went through the trainees. It was a drastically different set of movies than the deadly spear-thrusts the Chief had taught in his absence.

He made them call out "one" and "two", and then randomly assigned them to practice on one another … a trick he'd learned to meld the elite and second-tier warriors in with the newbies without triggering all their useless social customs about "position" and rank. The trainees practiced thwacking one another until the training took on a satisfying percussion.

Kiaresh, his "babysitter," came striding up, a staff in his hand.

"You've gathered quite the harem?" Kiaresh glanced over at the female warriors.

"They merely wish to defend themselves."

"They *wish* to catch a husband—" the older man shot him a wolfish grin. "Word has gotten around that the fastest way a girl can catch a suitor is to take *your* class."

Mikhail gazed across the now-36 females who buzzed around Pareesa like bees. Ever since Ninsianna's cousin Gita had joined, he'd avoided interacting with them individually out of fear he'd set off another jealous fit.

"They seem to care for *each other's* company more than the men."

Kiaresh laughed and slapped him on the back of one wing.

"My friend, for one so brilliant, you are breathtakingly naive."

While pretending to look elsewhere, he scrutinized the way the women kept giving the men that furtive side-glance which Ninsianna used whenever she wished to cause his temperature to rise. The men, in turn, seemed to show off even *more* when the women did that. Maybe Kiaresh was right?

As though summoned from a daydream, Ninsianna walked up from the river, carrying her bow, with a nice fat goose slung over one shoulder. She sat down on a rock levy and shot him an enormous smile. He suppressed the urge to do a hop-flap over to kiss her, but his entire body tingled, aware of her presence.

He spun his staff in a blindingly fast training kata. Now *he* was showing off...

"Pareesa?" he called his diminutive sidekick, "could you please help me demonstrate something?"

Pareesa answered in the Cherubim language"

"*Yorokobi, kyōshi to.*" My pleasure. Ever since she'd noticed he spoke in *Cherubim* while prying training moves out of his recalcitrant memory, she insisted he teach her the names of those maneuvers in the Cherubim tongue.

"Just like we practiced earlier, okay?" he said.

"*Hai, sensei wa,*" she grinned at him. Yes teacher. I am ready.

He swung his pole to make contact with hers in a complicated series of strikes and blocks. He hit carefully at first, but as she adjusted to the strength of his blows, he increased his speed to give her a good workout. Pareesa came at him with a ferocity which no longer surprised him.

"Hey! Hey! Hey!" he laughed. "Don't get too big for your kilt, little fairy."

Pareesa made a surprise lunge that was *not* part of the training routine. She hit him on the shoulder, and then danced out of his way.

"Slowpoke!" she taunted. Judging by the circles underneath her eyes, the little imp had spent the entire night practicing a maneuver he'd only just taught her yesterday.

"Are you sure you want to do this in front of everybody?" he asked.

"Give me your best shot."

He glanced over at Ninsianna's bemused expression.

"Remember that you *asked* for this," he warned.

He swung his staff like a whirligig, and then jerked it up to knock Pareesa's staff out of her hand. At the same time, he hooked one foot behind her knee and brought his arm across her chest to knock her to the ground. She landed with a surprised "Oof!" Mikhail pressed the point of his staff at her throat.

"Do you yield?"

Pareesa lay there, blinking with surprise.

"I guess," she grumbled, "since I am *dead*."

The trainees laughed, most of them pleased to see her get her comeuppance.

"It was a *fine* death."

He reached down to pull her up.

Pareesa laughed as she strutted back to the other women. Half a dozen young men made a beeline for her, slapping her on the back and making crude comments about her fighting abilities.

"Everybody, pair up!" he ordered. "It's time to practice what Pareesa just demonstrated."

As the trainees sparred, Ninsianna sauntered over. Was it his imagination, or did she deliberately sway her hips to taunt him?

"She has a crush on you, you know?" Ninsianna said.

"Who?"

"Pareesa. She has a crush on you," she repeated with a smile. "Why do you think she trains so hard."

"Really?" He frowned. "How can you tell?"

"I can see her spirit light, remember?" She used the cover provided by one wing to reach around and possessively pinch his backside.

"She's a little girl."

"She's a fierce warrior in a young woman's body," Ninsianna said. "And she is *exactly* the same age I was when I developed my first crush on an older man." Her eyes crinkled up in an enigmatic smile.

"Oh," Mikhail raised one eyebrow. "An older man? Who?"

Her smile grew even wider as she lowered her gaze and peeked at him through veiled eyelashes, a look that never failed to make his heart race.

"Why? Are you jealous?" she teased.

"Yes," he admitted.

"It happens to everyone," she laughed. "Young girl. Sexy older man. Lucky you. You get to have Pareesa follow you around like a love-sick puppy!"

His stomach sank.

"How do I discourage her without hurting her feelings?"

"Very delicately," she said. "Or she'll hate your guts."

Mikhail groaned. The *last* thing he needed was his first, and most ardent supporter, to turn on him just when he needed her the most.

"So how should I handle this?"

She gestured at the potter's son, Ebad, who'd been mooning after Pareesa for months.

"Ask Pareesa to help you train the most incompetent young men," she said, "and about a dozen of his worst-performing friends. It will solve two problems at once."

"Pareesa will chew them up for dinner and spit out their bones," he said. "She won't be happy I've saddled her with someone as inept as Ebad."

"He will learn ... for her," Ninsianna said. "And she will be the better for it. Tell her you want her to do it as a special favor because you're afraid he'll get himself killed."

Now *that* wasn't a lie!

"I'll think about it," he said.

"You'll *do* it," she laughed.

"How did I ever get so lucky to get a wife as smart as *you*?" he grinned.

"You fell out of the sky, remember?" she said. "Anyhow ... I have got to go dress this bird so Mama can cook it for supper. I'll see you in a few hours?"

He bent to kiss her, lingering to taste her sweet lips. She nipped his lower lip and pressed into him. Desire tingled through his body and made the outside world fade.

The sound of sticks hitting each other and grunts of pain ceased. Hoots and cat-calls came from the back of the line. Between tending the fields, training new warriors, consulting with the Chief about the village defenses, and helping Alalah and Behnam work the kinks out of the women's archery training program, he could never seem to find enough time to spend with her, even now that they were married and sharing the same bed.

Reluctantly, he pulled away and turned back to his work, watching Ninsianna's pert buttocks jiggle as she went about her business.

"Okay, everybody," he said. "Next we have to learn the *proper* way to form a patrol."

Chapter 148

August - 3,390 BC
Earth: Village of Assur

JAMIN

They'd gotten stuck with the three Margian women after the Amorites had double-crossed him and Pareesa had dragged them back to their village. They were alien in appearance, with far darker hair than even *his* wavy black lion's mane and beard, with an odd manner of dress, pale amber skin, and peculiarly-shaped dark eyes. Since nobody knew *where* this mythological "great, grassy plain" that the women described was, *he'd* been assigned to babysit the unwanted guests until his father could figure out how to send them home.

His father's housekeeper, Urda, a dour old woman with a cantankerous disposition, laid out a simple lunch of flat bread, mashed lentils flavored with garlic and oil, assorted fruits and a pot of cool herbal tea. The women expressed gratitude first to the cook, and then his father, using hand-signals to accentuate what few Ubaid words they had learned. Daintily, the three women tore off a slice of bread and dipped it into the mashed lentils. As much as Jamin hated having them here, he couldn't fault their manners.

"You find ... home?" the oldest sister, Fatma, asked in halting Ubaid.

"Sorry, no." His father shook his head. "Nobody knows." He shook his finger *'no'* and then put his hands over his eyes and ears to indicate that, thus far, none of his connections had ever heard of Margiana.

The middle sister, Seyahat, dabbed at her eyes with her magnificently embroidered red wool cloak. Without Ninsianna here to translate, everything, even sharing a meal with the three women, became a frustrating challenge. The youngest girl, Norhan, their sister-in-law, pointed at various objects and asked *him* to say their names in Ubaid, and then repeated them in awkward sentences. Jamin scowled, but said the names anyways to appease his father.

They were finishing lunch when a knock interrupted. Varshab answered the door, and then stuck his head into the living room.

"It's Mikhail," he said, "and Kiaresh. They'd like to discuss the patrol schedule."

"-*I*- set the patrols," Jamin growled.

"Which were obviously inadequate since the enemy breached our walls," his father said sharply. He ignored Jamin's glower and told Varshab to let them in. Unlike previous visits, Varshab didn't bother disarming them. The three Margian women skittered like frightened birds to the furthest side of the room.

"Sir," the winged demon said. "I'd like permission to take the new recruits to patrol the outer perimeter of our land."

"You mean *our* land," Jamin cut in.

"Jamin...." His father growled.

The Angelic didn't take the bait. Except for a subtle rustle of feathers, the bastard pretended he hadn't heard.

"To patrol the entire perimeter is a journey of several days." The old fool grinned. "At least it is when you don't have wings. With things so unsettled, I don't want to compromise our defenses."

"How about a small patrol to the southern border?" Mikhail asked. "I found some suspicious goat tracks leading into the river. It was a well-traveled path, leading inland, towards the desert, not north or south, like you'd expect if it was an Ubaid herder."

A knife of *fear* wrenched Jamin's gut. That was the place where Marwan watered his herd every summer...

"It's a waste of time!" Jamin sputtered. "That's two day's walk from the village."

"It's only a single day if you run," Kiaresh contradicted him.

The Chief ran his fingers through his beard, deep in thought.

"You think its Halifians?" he asked.

"It's *somebody*," Mikhail said. "I suspect they come at night, since I've never seen them while flying during the day. Judging from their tracks, it's a man and a boy."

"How many goats?"

"A sizeable herd," Mikhail said. "Enough to sustain a tent-group."

"It's probably just herders from Eshnunna," Jamin scoffed.

"I *hope* so," Mikhail said. "But if it's not, I think we should know about it? Don't you?"

What could he say? *I –already- know who it is.*

"Yes," he said weakly.

"How many men do you need?" his father asked Mikhail.

"That's up to *you*, Sir? How many would you like to give me?"

Drat! If Mikhail evicted the Halifians, or *worse*, captured one of them for questioning, they'd *definitely* tell him about the treaty, and *probably* rat him out about the deal he'd made with the Amorites to kidnap Pareesa.

His father looked at Mikhail, then at *him*, and then at Kiaresh. His eyes took on a calculating expression.

"Those decisions are usually made by our *Muhafiz*." He gestured at Jamin, putting him on the spot.

Worst-case scenarios raced through Jamin's mind. Did his father know about the Amorites? Was this all a plan to expose him? He studied the Angelic—cold bastard! You could never tell what he was thinking. But Kiaresh appeared enthusiastic, while his father seemed more curious than anything else.

"Two Halifians?" Jamin said. "You think a man and a boy?"

"Those were the tracks," Mikhail said. "I have no idea what we'll find once we get down there."

A man and a boy? Maybe he could rush down there, before the Angelic got there with his ridiculous "patrol", and bribe them to go away. Which meant he had to pick the slowest, most *incompetent* men. Of course Mikhail always insisted on commandeering his elite warriors to train the incompetent ones. He needed to send men who didn't speak Halifian. Kiaresh spoke a little, as did Siamek, so he'd find an excuse to keep them home, but the rest of the elite warriors only spoke a few curse-words.

What an idiot! He'd give Mikhail his wish....

"Take Dadbeh and Firouz," he said. "They know that area reasonably well. And a handful of the brand new warriors. What do you call your groupings?"

"Units," Mikhail said. "A unit is comprised of six men."

"Take two units of men who are not in the first, or the second tier," Jamin said. "You can leave tomorrow morning. I want the rest of my spearmen close to the village, not chasing imaginary goats."

The bastard gave him one of his ridiculous Alliance "salutes".

"It shall be as you wish," Mikhail said formally, "*Muhafiz*."

"Good!" his father clapped his hands together. "And you shall lead them."

Jamin almost choked.

"What?"

The three owl-eyed Margian women all nodded, as if they understood what he'd just been roped into.

"I can't!"

"Why not?"

He looked for an excuse.

"My hand." He held up his hand which was still bandaged. "His little yippy dog *shot* me, in case you've forgotten."

"Mikhail will be there," his father pooh-poohed. "He'll protect you."

The winged bastard hid a smirk behind that damned unreadable expression.

"It'll be good for everyone," his father beamed. "It's about time you two started working together. You can lead them, and Mikhail will be your right-hand man."

Like hell...

But he couldn't tell his father that, at least not until he dealt with this latest drama. All he needed was to find an excuse to break off, find the goatherders, warn them away, and then get back in time to mock Mikhail for wasting their time.

"And when you get back to the village," his father continued, "I have an idea for *another* morale-building exercise." He put his arm around Jamin's shoulders. "It's something my son does exceedingly well."

"What do you have in mind?" Mikhail asked.

"A herd of gazelles has begun their annual migration," his father said.

"You wish to stage a hunt?"

"Yes," his father said. "The village is low on meat. It's time to replenish our stores."

Jamin fought the urge to rail.

"Pick thirty of your new recruits," his father said. "Jamin will teach you how to creep up on the animals and set a trap, while *you* can teach *him* how to use a bow."

Mikhail didn't appear to be any more pleased with this hare-brained "hunt" than Jamin, but he schooled a neutral expression and said, "It shall be as you wish."

As they were speaking, the youngest Margian woman, Norhan, sidled up to touch the bow which Mikhail had set down on a table. She picked it up and expertly lined it up. According to Ninsianna, the women claimed the Amorites had learned the art of using the bow from *them*. Or more specifically, their people.

Norhan pointed at Mikhail, the bow, and then to a woven tapestry. The *animals* woven into that tapestry depicted an Ubaid hunt. Using her paltry Ubaid, she pointed at Mikhail and said:

"You. Half—" she pointed at a picture of an eagle. "We, half—" she pointed at a larger animal which sometimes they hunted for meat and the valuable tail, which was prized by healers. "Half—" She looked to Jamin.

"Horse," he said.

"We, half *horse*. Shoot bow. On horse."

She drew the bow, which didn't have an arrow, and pretended to shoot it. As she did, she made the whinnying call of a horse.

"You have people who are half-man, half-horse?" his father asked.

Norhan's almond-shaped knit together, attempting to communicate using not enough words.

"No. Half man, half horse, *GODS*," she said. "Like him." She pointed at Mikhail. "We, Margians, we—" she pretended to prance around the room "—not gods. Margians *sit* on horse, ride horse, shoot bow. Be like gods."

She stared at his father, triumphant at what had to be the closest thing they'd had to a conversation since Pareesa had dumped the three women at his house.

His father scrutinized Mikhail.

"Do you *have* half-man, half-horse people where you come from?"

"I don't think so," Mikhail said. "But if we did, I can't remember."

Chapter 149

Galactic Standard Date: 152,323.08 AE
Alliance Territory
Centauri Cavalry General Kunopegos

KUNOPEGOS

The four-star general who commanded the Centauri Cavalry looked *down* on the Alliance Prime Minister … literally. General Kunopegos used that height difference *now* to communicate how displeased he was with whatever stunt Lucifer was trying to pull.

"You want me to reproduce with *that?*" Kunopegos growled. "How will I accomplish *that?* She's one-tenth my size!" Crossing his muscular arms in front of his barrel chest, he glowered down at Lucifer.

"Very carefully," Lucifer waved his hand as though it was merely a trifle. "But human females are capable of being, how shall I put it delicately? Accommodating…" He added hastily, "—or, if you prefer, we have the technology to impregnate her artificially. Either way, your foal will need to be harvested 11 weeks early and spend time in an incubator."

"I don't like the thought of my foal born premature," Kunopegos said.

"Well, if you want to keep trying the Emperor's way…" Lucifer flipped one hand to the side as though to say, '*It's your extinction.*'

As Lucifer spoke, all of the fruitless mating attempts he'd tried over the years replayed in Kunopegos mind. The filly he'd asked to secretly marry him in defiance of the 'be fruitful and multiply' decree. She'd abandoned him after the sixth mating attempt had failed. The humiliation of being blacklisted. The way mares avoided him whenever they came into their heat cycle so they didn't have to tell their commanding officer 'no.'

"I've tried every solution and it's failed!" Sparks flew from Kunopegos hoof as it clanged against the deck. "Ever since I was blacklisted, females won't go for a romp in the pasture! Even when they're *not* in heat!"

His eyes drifted back to the female Lucifer had brought on board with him, clad in a shapeless garment that covered her from the top of her head down to her toes, tiny even by Angelic standards. She looked more like a doll than somebody he should consider begating offspring upon.

"Many foals are naturally born premature—" Lucifer said. "They spend time in an incubator with no ill effect. If you want a foal, you'll have to make a few accommodations."

"Why can't the Emperor just rear them in an incubator from scratch?" Kunopegos lamented. "It works fine for the lesser species?"

Over his five hundred plus years as a Centauri cavalry officer, he had *personally* helped the Emperor seed life onto sterile planets and nurture those worlds towards sentience, from oxygen-generating pond-scum to the most evolved species. The Emperor created life wherever he went, but for some reason, the more sentient the species, the lower his success rate.

"The Emperor hasn't been able to reproduce some critical element of the early gestational period. We can help the little foals along who arrive too early—" a bitter edge came into Lucifer's voice "—but we can't replace their mother."

Kunopegos glanced over at his second in command, deliberating whether to give the signal to manufacture a fake distress call so he could get the heck out of there without ticking off the Emperor's son.

Was he *seriously* considering what Lucifer proposed?

"So, is this one an experienced brood mare?" he asked. "Or a filly?"

"A filly, I'm afraid." Lucifer's eerie silver eyes gleamed as though he found that thought to be exciting. "You'll have to be careful not to damage her."

An untried filly? Would be willing to mate? With *him*?

"I'd feel better if I knew she was experienced," Kunopegos said apprehensively. "I'm afraid I'll hurt her."

"Human females prefer to stay with one stallion and rear their foals in a herd," Lucifer said. "Unless a mare is widowed young. Let's just say there are few mares willing to leave their families. It's a filly. Or nothing at all."

"They rear their own foals?" Kunopegos said incredulously. "They don't just drop them off at the nearest youth training academy like Centauri mares do?"

"Humans are herd animals," Lucifer said.

As he spoke, images of galloping through the ship's pasture with a handsome bay colt with *his* eyes pranced through Kunopegos mind. On his back, the doll-like female sat nursing a newborn filly with a coal-black coat and *her* unusual almond-shaped eyes. They ran off together into the sunset, a stallion and his herd, the way his ancestors had once reared their families.

"So how do I do this?" Kunopegos asked. "Go into a stall with a dirty magazine and hand a vial over to my chief medical officer?"

"No, no!" Lucifer laughed. "But she's been trained to pleasure you. I timed this visit for her peak fertility. You should know whether or not the mating is successful within three days."

"And what do *you* want in return?" The Alliance Prime Minister rarely granted favors without wanting something in return.

"My father has had the solution to our dilemma all along," Lucifer clucked, "but would rather let us die out rather than break his silly prohibition about seed worlds."

As Lucifer spoke, a recurring nightmare Kunopegos had experienced ever since he'd been blacklisted replayed in his mind. He ran through a pasture, chasing a herd that was headed for a cliff. He called out to them, begging them to stop, but the entire herd leaped to their death. In the dream, he looked down at countless broken Centauri bodies, all smashed upon the rocks below. He always woke up in a cold sweat, his heart racing at the terror of finding himself the last of his species.

"The Emperor has known where they were all along?" Kunopegos slammed one hoof against the deck, drawing sparks. "I've been banging my head against the wall for 500 years!"

"Hashem didn't bring them forward," Lucifer said. "Shay'tan did. My father ceded that world to Shay'tan millennia ago. Shay'tan would like to, how shall I put it? Tweak my father's nose by opening up the human homeworld to trade."

"Hashem really intends to let us die out?" Kunopegos felt as though somebody had just shot him out the airlock. No. It *couldn't* be true!

"He ordered you to start promoting the newer sentient races into positions *we* used to hold," Lucifer said. "We are being replaced."

Kunopegos heart sunk down to his hooves. It *was* true. The evidence had been staring him in the face all along and he'd been in denial. He glanced up at the Prime Minister and shivered. Lucifer's cold, silver eyes glittered with emotion? Anger? No. Viscous satisfaction…

"I received the promotion order," Kunopegos said. "I heard Supreme Commander-General Jophiel threatened to quit if he didn't make some concessions with his insane breeding program."

"The Emperor omitted the fact he's been hiding the root race," Lucifer said. "Do you really trust his explanation now?"

"So what do you want--" Kunopegos pointed at the tiny female "--if I accept this gift?"

"Just keep her existence a secret," Lucifer said, "until I have a chance to move the rest of my chess pieces into position."

"We all saw what happened to the *last* hybrid who tried that stunt." He didn't add that the hybrid in question had been none other than Lucifer's biological father.

"I'm only going to petition Parliament to open the human homeworld to trade," Lucifer said, "but it will take time to build support for an override. It's important we hybrids speak in a unified voice to let the Emperor know we will not allow him to marginalize us into extinction."

"You'll be petitioning *Parliament*," Kunopegos clarified. "I won't support an armed uprising."

"Of course not!" Lucifer's mock-indignation didn't meet his eyes. "He is, after all, my father. Now—" he gestured at the two burly Angelics who perpetually followed him around "—would you like to meet your new wife?"

The two Angelics brought the female closer. She stood as docile as an old brood mare as he cantered around her and examined her from every angle. Kunopegos touched her cheek, near her almond-shaped black eyes.

"Her mane is so black, and her hide almost yellow."

"Humans come in a variety of markings," Lucifer said, "just like *your* ancestors did before they became inbred."

One of Kunopegos forebears had possessed pinto-paint markings; another buckskin. Thanks to the breeding program, *all* hybrids knew their lineage, but those markings had been lost for tens of thousands of years. Without realizing he'd done so, Kunopegos enclosed the human filly's hand in his large, brown one.

Unlike *most* races in the galaxy, she didn't flinch.

"Does she have a name?" he asked.

"Aigiarn," Lucifer said. "It means shining moon. She comes from a nomadic tribe of steppe-dwellers who live amongst the race that contributed the other half of your DNA, horses. She will be happiest riding upon your back."

Kunopegos whinnied in surprise.

"You mean Shay'tan's colony also has our equine ancestors?" His hooves clomped with excitement. "Why can't we reproduce with *them*? Like the Mer-Levi?"

"Alas," Lucifer clucked. "Humans were *already* sentient when the Emperor decided to tinker with their DNA, but your equestrian ancestors are no more sentient than my avian ones are."

"But Leviathans—"

"—were already marginally sentient," Lucifer interrupted. "The Emperor transplanted a few of their ancestors to a new homeworld after tinkering with their DNA, and then forgot about them."

This was no secret. Kunopegos was old enough to remember when an Alliance ship had investigated an unusual energy signature in a remote part of the galaxy and discovered a race of sentient aquatic mammals descended from the same creatures that had contributed the aquatic half of Merfolk DNA. In the time since the loss of Nibiru, the original human homeworld, the Levi had evolved into fully sentient creatures and achieved space travel. The news had been both good and bad. Merfolk were no longer going extinct, but they were no longer … well … Merfolk. After several generations of intermarriage with Leviathans, the Mer-Levi children no longer resembled the half-human hybrids they were descended from.

"The Emperor didn't feel horses were important enough to gift with sentience," Lucifer said. "If you reproduce with an animal, your offspring will be mentally defective."

"But human females will breed true?"

"At least as far as sentience is concerned," Lucifer said, "although half your offspring will resemble this human. You'll be making a sacrifice to guarantee the survival of your own species."

"If this is the only way my bloodline will survive, then that's what I must do." Turning to the female, Kunopegos made his choice. "Come, my beautiful filly. Let's get to know one another."

Aigiarn swung up onto the equestrian half of his back and kicked him in the haunches, urging him to run. The thighs that gripped his back were sure of themselves and strong. His apprehensions melted. This was not a frail, exotic flower.

"OOooooh," he pranced like a colt. "Perhaps I'll enjoy this little romp?"

Lucifer's knowing smile did not reach his eyes.

"Gyaah!" Aigiarn slapped his haunches for their pre-mating run in the ship's communal pasture.

Chapter 150

The MAR.TU who know no grain....
The MAR.TU who know no house nor town,
The boors of the mountains....
The MAR.TU who digs up truffles...
Who does not bend his knees (to cultivate the land),
Who eats raw meat,
Who has no house during his lifetime,
Who is not buried after death.

— Sumerian writing about the Amorite tribe

September – 3,390 BC
Earth: Village of Assur
Colonel Mikhail Mannuki'ili

MIKHAIL

It turned out to be *more* than an all-day run, burdened by a dozen of what had to be his most *incompetent* new recruits. They didn't get to the border until well after dark. Mikhail showed them how to camouflage their bivouacs[171] while Jamin, Firouz and Dadbeh knelt over the animal tracks, scrutinizing them in the moonlight.

"Mikhail is right," Dadbeh said. "These tracks appear to be made almost daily."

"It's probably just someone from Eshnunna," Jamin grumbled.

"Then why did you send us here?" Firouz asked.

"Because I want to show my father that Mikhail doesn't know what he is doing," Jamin said.

All three men turned to eye him with a hostile look. Without Siamek here to act as an intermediary, the men had automatically fallen back into their lifelong habit of following their *Muhafiz*.

Mikhail tested the direction of the wind, and then showed his trainees how to build a "blind"[172] downwind of where the goats would drink.

"Place it with the leaves facing *upwards*," he explained. "Like they grow in nature. If you place them upside-down, it will draw your enemy's eye."

"Like this?" Ipquidad asked. The tall, chubby teenager needed several bushes.

---

[171] *Bivouac shelter:* a temporary campsite, usually hidden.
[172] *Hunting blind:* a cover device for hunters to reduce the chance of detection.

"Why didn't Pareesa come?" Ebad asked, the potter's son.

"That's a stupid question." Ipquidad gave Jamin a resentful look and then pointed at his own hand. All twelve recruits hid a smirk.

"The *Muhafiz* picked the patrols," Mikhail said.

"Do you think we'll have to *fight* them?" Ebad asked.

"It's just an adult and a boy," Mikhail said. "We'll find out who they are, and if they don't belong here, we'll order them to leave."

"What if they're Halifian?"

"We're just here to chase them off," Mikhail said.

"The Halifians are our enemies."

"So you want to kill *children?*"

The young men thought on it a moment, and then shook their heads.

"I don't want to kill *anybody*," Ipquidad said. "I just want them to leave us alone."

"Not all of the men who attacked us were Halifians," Mikhail said. "Some were Amorite, some were from other tribes. It's *never* appropriate to target civilians."

The new recruits murmured agreement. They were eager to learn something other than the tedious basic training, but not so anxious to engage in actual combat.

"How many men have you killed?" Ipquidad asked.

"Since I got here?" Mikhail asked.

"No, before? Do you remember any other battles?"

Mikhail stared up at the moon.

"I have *one* memory," he said. "Lizards. They hurt a friend."

"How many did you kill?"

"Just one," he said, "that I can remember. But I think I killed a lot more."

"I can't wait until *I'm* good enough to kill my enemies," said Yaggit, the most competent of the whole incompetent bunch.

"Don't be in such a hurry to take a life," Mikhail said. "It weighs heavily on me. Every single one."

They fell silent. Mikhail helped them get battened down, and then said, "Get some sleep. I'll take the first watch."

Jamin, Dadbeh and Firouz bedded down apart from the others. Mikhail moved a few dozen meters inland, along the trail where the goats would likely come. The seconds ticked by; that "hurry up and wait" feeling that always preceded battle. He whispered a focusing prayer that he remembered learning from the Cherubim. As he did, everything developed a faint, blue glow.

Ninsianna called this "magic." He simply called it the mind's ability to focus on whatever information it needed to survive. Crickets chirped; frogs gave a hearty garrump; bats flew after insects; and in the river, something large – most likely a crocodile – lay in wait at the place where the goats would come to drink.

He stared up at the stars. Which one had he come from? And why, in all these months, had none of his people come looking for him?

A soft sound, so quiet that at first he mistook it for a mouse, crept through the underbrush away from the river. Drawing his sword, he spread his wings and hop-flapped over to the intruder.

Jamin shrieked as he dropped out of the air.

"What are you doing?" Mikhail asked.

"Can't a man take a piss?"

"Isn't this a little far?"

"What are you, my *father* now?" Jamin snarled.

"You're the *Muhafiz*," he said. "Do whatever you like."

Jamin huffed off into the bushes, and then came back, making a great show of rearranging his kilt. He stormed back to his bedroll, far less quiet heading back than when he'd been slithering into the underbrush.

Ebad relieved him for the watch. Mikhail wrapped himself in his wings, curled up, and promptly fell asleep. While he didn't like letting his guard down next to somebody he didn't know all that well, given how quietly Jamin had just stalked through the bush, he wouldn't put it past the bastard to try to stab him in his sleep. Ebad, at least, appeared to look up to him, even if the young man was completely incompetent.

It seemed like only minutes, but then Ebad shook him awake.

"Sir," he whispered. "I think I see something?"

That familiar drug of fear and excitement made his blood race. Ebad pointed at the horizon.

"There."

"I don't see anything."

"Keep watching," Ebad said. "I thought I saw a torch."

They watched for several minutes. And then, he saw it...

"Do you think that's our goat herder?" Ebad asked.

Mikhail studied the flickering light. It was definitely a torch. But what worried him more lay further south; a significant amount of *smoke* which came up from behind a hill, clearly visible in the moonlight.

"There's a campfire—" he pointed at the hill. "A fairly large one, judging by the amount of smoke."

"What smoke?"

Mikhail showed him how to pick a landmark, and then scan the nighttime sky for smoke. It hadn't been visible until the moon had shifted to the west, which is why *he* hadn't spotted it when he'd sat the watch.

He slapped Ebad on the back.

"Good job," he said. "You wake the others. I'll fly out and see who's camped on our border."

He leaped into the air, flying low so the moon wouldn't show his wings against the sky. When he got close to the flickering light, he spotted a man wearing brown Halifian robes, and a boy no more than nine years old, herding the goats towards the river. *That* his recruits could handle. What concerned him more was whoever was bold enough to light such a significant fire to their south.

With a whisper of feathers, he flew to the hill which masked the unknown group's fire and crept up to the summit. In the valley below, a rough-looking group of mercenaries, he counted eight, slept beside the fire. Tied up next to them were five, no six, women.

He resisted the urge to fly right in right away and kill them. This was a *training* mission. More than anything, he wanted to show Jamin that he knew what he was *doing*. Creeping back down the hill, he spread his wings and took to the air.

The men were all awake when he got back to the river. The new recruits milled about aimlessly, while Jamin and his two elite warriors had set up an ambush. He fluttered to the ground.

"I found something," he said. "Eight mercenaries, six women."

"Was it the goat herder?" Jamin asked.

"I found a man and a boy," Mikhail said. "Not part of the same group. The mercenaries are on a different trail."

"How do you—" Jamin glanced at his wings. "Never mind. So how do we *get* to these mercenaries, oh winged one," he added sarcastically, "if we can't simply fly?"

Mikhail glanced at the new recruits. If he had to hazard a guess, Jamin had deliberately chosen the *least* competent men in order to set him up to fail. The newbies were nowhere *near* ready to go up against eight hardened mercenaries.

"I'll fly back to Assur," he said, "and rally the rest of your men. If I leave now, they can be here in ten hours."

"In broad daylight," Jamin snorted. "-*If*- they're still even there."

Dadbeh and Firouz came to listen to the plan.

"Were they Halifian?" the two men's eyes glittered with hatred.

"Amorite, I think," Mikhail said, "judging by their colored robes."

A change came over Jamin.

"Amorite?" he said.

"Yes."

"We can't let them get away!"

Mikhail gestured at the new recruits.

"They're nowhere *near* ready to take on that kind of muscle."

"What are you, *afraid*, oh sword of the gods?" Jamin taunted.

"Afraid, no—"

"How about it?" Jamin addressed the new recruits directly. "We outnumber them two-to-one. These *mercenaries* killed eleven of our people. Are you too *cowardly* to take them on?"

"No!" the new recruits said.

Jamin's dark eyes glittered with victory.

"You have your answer," Jamin said.

"I suggest—"

"*-I-* am the *Muhafiz*," Jamin snarled. "What you suggest is *irrelevant*."

Mikhail suppressed the urge to throttle the pompous piece of goat-dung. This is what the Chief wanted, for *him*, and his son, to work together. Only a lifetime of discipline, to always follow his commander, prevented him from breaking rank and telling Jamin to go to Hades.

"As you wish," he said through gritted teeth, "Sir."

They quickly broke camp and moved downriver to the place where Mikhail had spotted another trail. They humped it inland, his new recruits gasping for breath as they struggled to keep up with Jamin, Dadbeh and Firouz.

The sky began to lighten.

"Hurry up," Mikhail urged his new recruits. "We need to hit them before dawn."

They got to the hill where he'd reconnoitered the area. The Amorites lay around the campfire, fast asleep. Jamin laid out his plan to Firouz and Dadbeh. Mikhail waited for *their* part in the plan, but the elite warriors ignored them.

"Are those Ubaid women?" Ipquidad pointed.

"Three of them are," Ebad whispered back. "I'm not sure about the others. I don't recognize their clothes."

"Are they from Assur?" Yaggit asked.

"I don't recognize them," Ipquidad said.

"I don't either," Ebad said.

"It doesn't matter," Mikhail said. "They are prisoners. We are going to free them."

He laid out a plan for the men to back up the elite warriors and, while the Amorites were distracted, to free the women.

"Kill if you have to," Mikhail said, "but don't risk your life. If we can, I'd like to capture them alive."

"Why?" Ebad asked. "They didn't have any qualms about killing *our* people."

"I want to find out *where* they are taking our women."

The new recruits nodded. Two units. Six men each. Twelve men. Not a single one with *any* combat experience. He gave each group a different task. Dadbeh and Firouz had already begun to creep up to the camp behind Jamin, racing to beat the sunrise.

It was up to *him* to make sure his little "pack of jackals" stayed alive.

"Okay," he whispered. "Let's go."

He crept forward silently, wishing *fervently* he could take to the air, drop into the mercenaries' midst, and start smiting enemies the moment they reached for their weapons. His men breathed heavily, far too fast and anxious. He schooled them on how to breathe so they wouldn't pass out before they began the battle.

It's too bad Pareesa's not here. She'd definitely whip them into shape...

Maybe Ninsianna was right? Maybe he *should* saddle his young protégé with leadership of these hopelessly incompetent young men?

Jamin, Firouz and Dadbeh prepared for their final sprint.

Mikhail slid his sword out of its scabbard. The steel felt warm as he threaded his fingers around the grip.

"Stay with your battle buddy," he whispered. "Always stick together."

He began to chant the prayers that helped him focus during battle. The recruits' clumsy feet, their too-loud breathing, their overwhelming stench of sweat and fear, all receded as he focused on a single task: take down the enemy.

"Ay-iyah!" Jamin shouted.

He rushed forward with his spear. He, Firouz and Dadbeh each stabbed one of the enemies before they could react and immediately leaped towards the next one.

The rest of the mercenaries sprang to their feet.

"Argh!" the Amorites shouted.

One of Mikhail's units ganged up on one of the Amorites, awkwardly jabbing at him the way one might poke at a honey badger, while the second unit ran to free the women. Meanwhile, Jamin made his second kill.

"Yeah!" he shook his bloody spear.

He dove towards the third one. Ninsianna was right. They *would* be stronger if he and Jamin could just get along...

Dadbeh and Firouz closed in on the fifth Amorite. When they worked together, the pair was unstoppable.

One of the Amorites lunged towards Ebad's back...

"Look out!" Mikhail shouted.

Half-flying, he leaped between Ebad and the Amorite. He brought his sword down on the man's spear.

"Ah, we meet again, winged one," the Amorite said in broken Ubaid. Dressed more finely than the other men, he wore a leather bandolier strung across his colorful, striped robe. Tucked into the leather were a half-dozen small, bone-handled knives.

"I don't recall the pleasure," Mikhail circled, his sword held in front to fend off the next feint.

"I am Rimsin, son of Kudursin," the Amorite said. "We met the other night."

The man rushed at him. Mikhail danced out of the way. He remembered the man who'd made a run for the gate; the one Jamin had rushed after, but been unable to stop. At the time, he'd pegged him for the ringleader. He and the Amorite circled, both looking for an opening.

"Why are you taking our women?" Mikhail asked.

"I might ask *you* the same thing?"

"What do you mean?"

The Amorite lunged at him. Almost too fast to be seen, one of the knives in his bandolier found its way into his other hand. He stabbed with the spear, and then back-stabbed with the knife. Mikhail stepped out of the way and deflected the spear with his sword. The Amorite taunted:

"It appears your people have an insatiable appetite for women, because the lizard-gods have declared we're to bring every breeding-age woman we can find for three golden *darics* apiece."

"You lie!"

Mikhail struck at him.

"I tell the truth." The Amorite pointed at someone behind him. "If you don't believe me, just ask the traitor who hired us to *kill* you."

A spear came out of nowhere and lodged in the Amorite's chest. The Amorite fell, clutching his heart. He gasped for breath and tried to speak. With a shaking hand, he pointed at the man who had killed him.

Jamin…

"Why did you do that?" Mikhail shouted. "He was about to tell us what we needed to know!"

"He was our *enemy*," Jamin hissed, "and now he is *dead.*"

Mikhail kneeled beside the Amorite.

"Tell me?" he pressed his hand into the man's wound. "Tell me, please? What do you know about my people?"

The man wheezed. His breath came out as a bloody gurgle. He stared, his eyes panicked, as gradually he bled out. He tried to speak, but nothing came out but bubbles of blood.

He died…

…leaving Mikhail no more enlightened than before they'd begun this fight.

He rose to his feet, oblivious to his men's cheers as they freed the women and gloated over the bodies of eight dead enemies. Dark rage shuddered into his body. His vision narrowed into a dark tunnel, caring only for his quarry. He fought an overwhelming urge to *destroy*.

Mikhail pointed at Jamin.

"We *needed* that information!"

Jamin moved into a fighting stance.

"They attacked my *village*," he hissed.

They circled, two lions, both with murderous intent. The warriors fell silent. With a fearful cry, the women huddled together.

Mikhail flared his wings.

"They could have told us where to find the other women!"

"You *heard* what he said," Jamin hissed. "*Your* people are the ones who are buying them."

In a flash, Jamin held his knife. He rushed at Mikhail.

Mikhail danced out of the way.

Every ounce of his *being* screamed *"KILL HIM!!!"* But if he touched him, not only would *he* no longer have a home, but neither would his *wife*…

He forced his sword hand down, and then *slid* it back into its sheath.

"Out of respect for your *father*," he said through gritted teeth, "I won't lay a hand on you. But don't push me."

"Or what?"

"Or else I'll finish what I *should* have done the first day that I met you."

Jamin lunged straight for his heart. Mikhail knocked the blade aside and yelped as the sharp obsidian knicked his bicep. Jamin circled. Damn, the man was fast. He *had* to make the pompous jerk see reason.

"Stop!" he yelped as Jamin charged at him again.

This time, he saw an opening. As he stepped to one side, he snaked his arm through Jamin's elbow, grabbed the butt-end of the knife, and stepped back, now holding Jamin's weapon.

Jamin stabbed at him, and realized he was now empty-handed.

"Argh!"

He rushed at Mikhail, head first, and slammed into him in a hurricane of kicks and fists. *Damantia!* The man might be shorter than he was, but he was *strong*…

Mikhail grunted as a punch landed on his chin.

Hooking one leg behind Jamin's knee, he wrestled him to the ground, face-first, and twisted his arm up behind his back.

Jamin screamed, "I'll kill you! I'll kill you!"

Mikhail looked up. Both Firouz and Dadbeh had their spears aimed at his chest.

"I didn't hurt him," Mikhail said. "All I did was defend myself."

"Kill him!" Jamin shouted.

The two elite warriors wavered.

The new recruits lined up behind *them*, twelve to one. Ebad, and then Ipquidad, and then the others, all shakily leveled their spears at their so-called "leaders."

"Don't do it," Ebad said. "Jamin attacked *him*."

"Yeah," the other new recruits all said.

A silent understanding passed between Dadbeh and Firouz.

"Let him up," Firouz gestured at Jamin.

"We'll make sure he doesn't do it again," Dadbeh said.

"You have our word," both men said together.

Mikhail released his grip and, like a man releasing a cobra, danced back, one hand on the hilt of his sword. Jamin sat up and rubbed his bruised chin.

"You all *heard* what the Amorite said—" Jamin jabbed an accusing finger at him. "He said Mikhail's people are the ones who are buying our women."

A glance passed between Firouz and Dadbeh.

"I was busy killing *that* one," they both pointed at one of the dead Amorites.

"What about *you*?" Jamin asked Ebad.

"We were freeing the women."

"And you?"

"*We* were busy fighting *that* one," several of the other recruits pointed at a body.

"What about *you*?" he asked Ipquidad. "You were right behind me?"

"I was fighting *that* one," Ipquidad pointed at one of the dead Amorites. "The only thing I heard was myself screaming."

Jamin glared at him with hateful, black eyes.

"Search their bodies. He said they are trading our women for gold. Find it, and we'll have *proof* of who our *real* enemy is."

The warriors searched the bodies and found all manner of contraband: lapis lazuli beads, bits of silver, dozens of arrows, but not a single piece of evidence that these men had come in contact with a technologically advanced society. Furious, Jamin kicked the body of the Amorite who he'd speared in the chest.

"Bastard!"

Tossing his cape around his shoulders in a manner befitting the *Muhafiz*, he ordered the men to gather their things and, without waiting for them, began the long march home.

Chapter 151

Galactic Standard Date: 152,323.09 AE
Tango Sector: Command Carrier 'Jehoshaphat'
General Abaddon aka 'the Destroyer'

ABADDON

Three grey hairs. With the happiest feeling his old heart could remember, Abaddon counted them again. Three grey hairs. Not two. Not four. But three of them graced the chestnut tresses which cascaded from her scalp to the small of her back.

He sank his nose into her neck and inhaled the scent of hCG.[173] After 630 years of failure, her scent was so intoxicating that he couldn't bear to be away from her. He pressed a hand against her abdomen, still flat despite the child he could *smell* growing in her womb.

"Has the sickness passed, *mo grá*?" He touched the bluish shadows which had appeared under her eyes about the same time she'd begun to stumble to the toilet each morning and vomit. Unable to fight this battle *for* her, he did the only thing he could: held her while she suffered dry heaves, pulled back her hair, and wiped her face before carrying her back to the bed to cuddle until the color began to creep back into her complexion.

Mahogany brown eyes smiled back at him. She felt better. Lucifer had insinuated the root race was not very intelligent, but already she'd learned dozens of core phrases. Perhaps she saw him as more than a washed-up old geezer?

"You have made me the happiest man alive," he whispered in her ear.

Her lips turned up in a smile as he nibbled on her earlobe. The Emperor had stolen this from his species, this exquisite feeling of being joined as one heart and soul with your mate.

"Husband," Sarvenaz's forehead furrowed in concentration. "You no … work … late?"

His heart thrilled at the forbidden endearment. It had been the second word he'd taught her, right after he'd taught her to say his name.

"Ahh, *chol beag*," he pulled her closer. "You know I must go. The Alliance is not going to protect itself."

---

[173] hCG: Human chorionic gonadotropin is a hormone produced by the placenta after implantation..

She threw one leg possessively over his. It was a game they played each morning when he had to leave. He *liked* this game even though, for the first time in his 630 yearlong military career it made him late for work. At his rank, who would chastise him?

"I don't know what I did to deserve you? You act as though everything I do is wonderful."

"Husband..." Sarvenaz tried to pull up an adequate word. "Husband is..." She slid her fingers through the grey feathers of his wings.

"Angelic," he said. "Husband is an Angelic."

"No," she said. "Husband is..." She chewed her lip. If he was patient, she usually found a way to communicate. "Husband is ... *énas theós*." She touched his wings again.

Abaddon curled the wing around her. "It's called a wing, *mo grá*. The Eternal Emperor gave them to our species so we could protect him."

"No just wing." The sparkle in her eye indicated she'd come up with a word to describe what she wished to say. "Sarvenaz people..." She made a motion with her hand as though it were a puppet talking.

"Say? Speak? Tell?" Abaddon went through possible words.

"Sarvanez people say-speak-tell," she said. "Your people. Sarvanez people say-speak-tell ... your people."

She repeated it several more times until it dawned upon him what she was trying to say.

"Your people have stories about my people?"

"Yes," Sarvanez said with a triumphant smile. "Sarvenez people say-speak-tell *stories* about husband's people. Angels."

"And what do these stories tell?"

"Husband's people..." Sarvenaz made a gesture with her hands as though they were the rays of the sun. She followed up the sign language with a hand to her forehead, her lips and her heart. It reinforced what Lucifer had said about their homeworld being lodged someplace in the Sata'anic Empire.

"I can't believe Shay'tan let you go."

He pulled her tighter. Sarvenaz's dark eyes shone victoriously. She could sense she'd already won their daily tussle, even before she pulled out the heavy artillery.

Abaddon gave a content sigh, signaling his complete and utter defeat. His subordinates were talented enough to keep things running. He'd already served far beyond his mandatory 500 years in the Alliance military. As soon as Lucifer got his override through Parliament, he intended to tender his resignation and retire. He didn't know how many years he had left, but he intended to spend that time siring as many offspring as his wife would give him.

"Husband ... say-speak-tell ... story?" Her eyes sparkled with curiosity. Although her speech was still limited, she analyzed the pattern of his language, increasing her vocabulary each time he told a tale.

Did she have any idea how lucky she was, to escape the yoke the old dragon imposed upon females in Sata'anic culture? Yes. He would tell her *that* story today.

"Have you ever seen a Sata'anic female?"

Sarvenaz shook her head. Male and female were two of the earliest words she'd mastered, and she'd recognized the Sata'anic lizards when he'd shown her a picture.

"Shay'tan keeps the women confined to the Hades cluster so the males don't get any ideas about defecting."

Sarvenaz watched his mouth form the words, her lips moving silently to repeat each one she recognized. It was how he gauged how much she *really* understood. For all the bribes he'd turned down cold over the years, money, power, even governorship over his own world, the old dragon couldn't have sent him a more tempting bribe than the one hanging off of his every word.

"I'm one of the few Alliance citizens to ever see one," he said. "One day during a border skirmish I captured a Sata'anic destroyer. When I went inside, do you know what I found?"

Sarvenaz smiled, her lips silently repeating the words 'Alliance' and '*found*.'

"I found a Sata'anic general in the launch bay," Abaddon said, "squeezing his three wives and a clutch of unhatched eggs into an escape pod meant for two. Since Shay'tan keeps all females confined in harems on their homeworlds, I knew I had captured a very high ranking general, indeed!"

"Sata'an ... general?" Sarvenaz pointed to the uniform he neatly placed over the back of a chair each night so it wouldn't wrinkle. Although the *names* of Alliance military ranks puzzled her, she'd readily grasped the concept that there was a chain of command on this ship and that *he* was top dog.

"Yes," he said. "A general. Like me. After his pulse rifle was exhausted and he had no more weapons to fire at me, he drew his sword and stood between me and his family. He begged me to kill him, but to allow his wives and offspring to escape. We conversed a few minutes about a man's wish to protect his family, and how he regretted that his reluctance to be parted from them had put their lives in danger."

He traced the line of Sarvenaz's jaw, the way her eyebrows rose in curiosity as he told his tale. Until he'd met the Sata'anic general, he'd always thought of the lizards as monsters. But since that day, he kept comparing

Sata'anic morals to hybrid ones and, honestly, sometimes he found his own people came up short.

"I took pity upon him," Abaddon said. "The general ordered his wives to finish squeezing into the life pod. They were crying as he shut the door and programmed the coordinates to where they could find safety, but they obeyed. As soon as the escape pod cleared the ship, he knelt, dropped his sword, and bowed his head to give me access to his neck so I could decapitate him in a single stroke."

"Husband ... kill ... general?" Sarvenaz frowned.

Aha! She *did* understand!

"Yes," Abaddon said. "I smote him. Not because I hated him, but because I respected him too much to dishonor him by turning him over for interrogation. If I had, Shay'tan would have cast his family out into the street in punishment."

Sarvenaz nodded, the frown line disappearing from her brow. Although he doubted she understood exactly *why* he'd chosen to let the general's family go, she seemed to understand he bore that dead general enormous respect. He pointed to the sword leaning casually against the same chair where he kept his uniform.

"To this day, I honor that Sata'an general's memory by carrying his sword."

Sarvenaz smiled and snuggled closer, rubbing her hand down his hard, flat abdomen and looked at him with a hungry expression.

"I have to go to work now, *mo grá*," he said.

She pulled out the heavy artillary by sliding her hand down to the juncture between his legs. With a satisfied groan, he "stood" at attention. He was putty in her hands, but he wasn't without his *own* weapons in this delightful war they waged each morning.

He nibbled down her neck until she shrieked with laughter. Oh! How he loved to hear her laugh! In a species prone towards seriousness, her laughter was a drug. It filled his heart with joy.

He nuzzled her neck and counted again, just to be sure. Three grey hairs. Whatever Lucifer had cooking up his sleeve paled in comparison to the gift he'd just been given. At last, he had a mate. She didn't want to leave him, and he was *finally* going to be a father.

The old General swore he would *never* let her go…

No matter what the cost.

Chapter 152

Galactic Standard Date: 152,323.09 AE
Sata'an Empire: Hades-6
Lieutenant Apausha

Lt. APAUSHA

Lord Ba'al Zebub's palace was a stone's throw from Shay'tan's in the capital city of Dis. While nobody *dared* out-build their beloved emperor and god (the Sata'anic Bible had scripture about a planetary governor who'd had the audacity to build a tower that rivaled Shay'tan's), there were ways to distinguish oneself without triggering the old dragon's competitive steak. Ba'al Zebub had perfected that competition to an art form, always keeping his height just *slightly* lower than Shay'tan's…

…and then he'd build the rest *below ground*…

Lieutenant Apausha snapped to crisp attention as the guards at Ba'al Zebub's front gate asked for his credentials.

"Apausha, son of Isawi," he said, "here for my debriefing."

The young guard peered at the computer screen.

"It says here you're the son of … Salahadin?"

Apausha clenched his fist, but forced his expression to remain blank. *Of course* Ba'al Zebub had the *unredacted* records, not the one the rest of the military had clearance to see.

"That's a mistake, Sir," Apausha said. "I'm the son of Isawi. A lowly, but *loyal* civil servant."

The guard poked at his computer screen, and then summoned the other guard over, a much older lizard whose wrinkled scales rivaled his battle scars. The old guard donned a pair of bug-eyed spectacles and peered at the screen. His gold-green eyes widened.

"You're Supreme General Salahadin's son?"

"No, Sir," Apausha said. "The Emperor, a thousand praises upon his name—" he made the Sata'anic prayer-gesture "—relieved us of that disgrace by assigning my mother to marry Isawi before our eggs hatched."

The old guard scrutinized him.

"I served under your father," he said. "He was a good man. The bravest I ever met."

"Salahadin is *dead*," Apausha said stiffly. "He died in disgrace."

The old guard turned to the young one.

"Apausha, son of Isawi, has an appointment. Please make a note in his record that he wishes to be recognized by his *step*-father's name the next time he seeks entrance to our Lord's castle. Though if I were him—" the old lizard met his gaze "—I'd look into the *real* story."

"Yes, Sir," the young guard said.

He made up a security pass, and then summoned a page to lead Apausha into the castle. The page led him through the ostentatious palace, out into the courtyard. There Ba'al Zebub was holding court with a pair of shady businessmen, non-lizards, whom he used as fronts to siphon money from the old dragon's coffers. Apausha knew this because *he* was the one who ran questionable supplies from enemy territory out to some recently-annexed planet, and then ran it *into* the Empire as that planet's tribute.

A merchant mariner didn't ask questions if he wanted to stay alive…

"Reporting for my debriefing, Sir!" Apausha tucked his tail up along his left-hand side, flattened his dorsal ridge in submission, and snapped to attention.

Rather than say "*as you were*" like any other military leader, Ba'al Zebub always forced him to maintain that posture until the effort caused his muscles to tremble. The Sata'anic Emir lumbered around him, causing the stench of recently-consumed meat to reek out of his corpulent pores. Apausha resisted the urge to flick the air with his long-forked tongue. It would only make the stench *worse*.

Ba'al Zebub waddled back to the two businessmen without addressing him, sat back down and finished his conversation, leaving Apausha to stand at attention in the blinding sunlight. The three men stabbed knives and forks into some kind of dead, cooked animal and shoved it into their mouths. While the lower-caste lizards sometimes ate fish or insects, only the upper castes ever ate a mammal.

Apausha resisted the urge to wipe at his own sweat. It was a familiar game, to intimidate Ba'al Zebub's inferiors in front of an audience. After twenty minutes or so, the two businessmen shook Ba'al Zebub's hand and were escorted from the palace by one of the pages.

Ba'al Zebub sank back into his cushioned chair.

"I take it you made a successful delivery?" Ba'al Zebub asked.

"Yes, Your Eminence," Apausha said. "The Alliance Prime Minister appeared pleased."

"He accepted delivery *himself?*"

"Yes, Sir."

Ba'al Zebub's fat maw opened up in a fang-laden grin.

"I bet he treated you like *royalty*, didn't he?" Ba'al Zebub chuckled.

"The Angelics were cordial—" Apausha picked his words carefully. "They appeared to appreciate our god's magnimosity."

Ba'al Zebub barked a guttural laugh.

"And did they ask for more?" he asked.

"Yes, Sir," Apausha said. "They said they'd be willing to accept as many as you care to ship them."

"Oh, I bet they would!" Ba'al Zebub laughed. "Only they're going to pay, *dearly*, for the next shipment."

Apausha twisted his tail. He *knew* what Ba'al Zebub would order next, and he did not want to do it. Neither did his men.

He bowed more deeply and respectfully than he had ever bowed to *any* man, except for Emperor Shay'tan *himself*....

"Sir," he said, "my men and I witnessed something that we thought you should know about."

"What?" Ba'al Zebub stabbed another slab of meat.

"It's Lucifer, Sir?" Apausha's voice warbled. "He *raped* those women! Almost in front of us! I can't believe our Emperor, may a thousand rays of sunlight grace his beneficence; would ever allow *any* woman to suffer the cruelty we witnessed on that ship!"

Ba'al Zebub chewed his meat and swallowed it; and then he belched.

"Did he *pay* what I asked?" Ba'al Zebub asked.

"Yes, Sir," Apausha said. "Three hundred million credits, Sir, payable in Sata'anic *darics*."

"And did you *bring* me this gold?" Ba'al Zebub asked.

"Yes, Your Eminence," Apausha said. "They're unloading it from my ship."

"Then I want you to take ten thousand of those *darics*," Apausha growled, "get back on your ship, and go *back* to wherever this "Earth" planet is, deliver it to General Hudhafah, and tell him I want *ten times* that many women as quickly as you can get your scaly tail from one end of the galaxy to the other."

"But, Your Eminence—"

"But nothing!!!" Ba'al Zebub exploded onto his feet in a mass of fat and muscle. Despite his girth, he was an *extremely* dangerous lizard. "I get paid to carry out Shay'tan's will, and *you* get paid to do what I tell you. You do *not* get paid to think!"

Apausha trembled....

"But Sir—"

"—unless you'd rather your *own* wife suffer the fate of your mother?" Ba'al Zebub hissed.

Apausha resisted the urge to leap at the fat bastard and shove his meat-fork down his throat. He had Marina to think of now and, if he was lucky, perhaps he could restore to his *own* children, once she'd conceived them, one-tenth of the good name which his *own* biological father had squandered.

He bowed his head.

"You asked that I relate to you *everything* that we observed," Apausha said. "How you act on that information is your decision."

Ba'al Zebub harrumpfed. The fat bastard didn't *like* him, but nobody besides *him* could pilot the *Peykaap* though the kinds of heat which he did on a daily basis. He sat back down and took a sip of his fermented beverage, and then summoned a page.

"Take Lieutenant Apausha back to his ship," Ba'al Zebub said. "He's got three days shore leave to see his wife, and then he, and his men, must get back to work."

The page bowed deeply and said, "Yes, Your Lordship."

He led Apausha back out to the front gate in silence. As they passed the old guard, the one who'd known his *real* father, he gave Apausha a crisp salute, the kind you'd give to a four-star general.

It was time to go back to Zulu Sector and fetch more human women…

Chapter 153

Galactic Standard Date: 152,323.09
Orbit: Haven-1
Colonel Raphael Israfa

RAPHAEL

Raphael greeted the biomechanical 'needle' using the voice translation device developed to communicate with the strange life form. Although life in the Milky Way tended to clump into one of six basic life forms, occasionally something didn't fit life as they knew it. Needles fit that category. The living remnants of some great civilization that had risen and fallen in a distant galaxy, they were a curious synergy of biology and machine.

Needles were sentient, gentle creatures whose level of intelligence was about that of a 5-year-old humanoid. Obedient and eager to please, they had to be cared for like children. As much as Raphael *wished* they cared for the trusting biomechanoids because it was the right thing to do, the reason needles were pampered was because they were trans-dimensional creatures that could leap instantly from one end of the galaxy to the other. The next-fastest method of transportation, faster than light drives, also called "FTL's", took weeks, even months to make the same journey.

"Hey, buddy! It's time to go play with your friend on Jophiel's ship," Raphael said. "Would you like that?"

The little ship excitedly bumped Raphael's hand with its nose.

"Here's your oxygen mask, Sir." Ensign Zzz'ler handed him the life support gear. Needles only provided transportation and warmth, not life support, so oxygen was a necessity.

"Time to strip."

He removed the outer layers of his uniform and shoes before lowering himself into the slender marsupium.[174] The Mantoid helped him jam his wings into the compartment, crushing a few golden feathers in the process. The confines of the needle were so tight that he didn't even have room for a full accompaniment of clothing! Had he been more muscular, like General Abaddon, or taller, like Mikhail, he wouldn't fit at all!

He patted the inside of the marsupium, signaling the needle to shut the cargo doors, and suppressed the urge to fight his way out. The slender biomechanoids were a claustrophobic ride. Luckily, the creatures could

---

[174] *Marsupium:* pouch.

jump as soon as they exited the cargo bay; landing close enough to the receiving ship that time spent in the coffin-like passenger compartment was mercifully brief.

"Let's go," he said into the voice communicator built into the oxygen mask as he patted the tender insides of the needle, giving the non-auditory signal it had been trained to recognize.

The long, slender creature shifted around him as they guided it out one of the torpedo ports. Needles were like carrier pigeons. They preferred to jump back and forth between familiar locations. Something truly terrifying must have happened to cause an entire herd of them to suddenly jump galaxies twenty-five years ago. He felt the discombobulating juxtaposition of the needle slipping into the subspace between dimensions and out the other side near Jophiel's ship.

"Ohthankthegodsthatsover," he gasped the moment the needle released him. Climbing out onto the flight deck inside Jophiel's command carrier, he ruffled his crushed feathers.

"Here's a change of clothes, Sir," the flight crewman who had been assigned to care for his needle said.

"Thank you, Lieutenant … Hadraniel, correct?"

"Yes, Sir," the crewman grinned.

He pulled on a uniform jacket and shoes before turning back to his trusty little needle. He spoke into the voice translator so it would understand him.

"Thank you, my friend." He tickled one side of its javelin-like nose. If it was a nose. Nobody knew for sure.

The playful ship wriggled and rolled over so he could scratch its tender underbelly. *Nobody* rode a needle by choice, but he and this little ship had been logging in quite a few hours lately. Thanks to the needle, he'd been able to pull off a feat of spatial engineering no mortal could have otherwise accomplished: be at opposite ends of the galaxy in the same day.

"Lieutenant Hadraniel will release you so you can go play with the Supreme Commander-General's needle," he told it. He turned his attention to the crewman assigned to care for his ship. "Where can I find the Supreme Commander-General and my son this fine afternoon?"

"She is in her quarters anxiously awaiting you to relieve her of duty, Sir." A hint of mirth betrayed Hadraniel's amusement at how much extra work the sudden insertion of a five-month-old 'airman' was causing their commanding officer.

As Raphael moved through the ship, he marveled at the diversity of the crewmen: Anglics, Leonids, Centauri and even a Mer-Levi in their hydroponic wheelchair, along with representation from every other species who served in the Alliance military. Most didn't give him a second look, but he noticed the envious glares that some of the hybrids gave him. Their relationship was causing morale problems amongst the fleet. Already, female hybrids were balking at giving up their offspring, while hybrid males were demanding the right to choose a single mate.

Jophiel had been right. As *she* went, so did the entire Alliance fleet.

Raphael gave the lower-ranking crewmen a crisp salute, careful to neither grin, nor to appear too stern. They saluted back. Raphael gave them a respectful nod. Although they all resented his special privilege, he wanted to make damned sure they had no reason to resent him *personally*.

As he wound his way through the labyrinthian hallways of the Alliance flagship, he mused about how he could accomplish his long-term goal of convincing Jophiel to say *yes* to his proposal of marriage. She was worried about adopting a double-standard between what *she* wanted, and the rest of the fleet. She'd not yet given an answer to his request to make their relationship a permanent one.

Raphael chuckled. Actually, she had... She'd told him 'no.' But he wasn't about to take 'no' for an answer. He was every bit as determined to undermine *her* resistance as he'd always been to get Mikhail to smile.

He paused outside her door to straighten his collar and a few errant feathers, and then he pressed the "intercom" button.

"You may enter," Jophiel called out.

As he stepped through the door, he spied the Leonid's top commander, General Re Harakhti, draped casually in a chair in front of Jophiel's desk. The Leonid was enormous, with a golden pelt of fur, and a reddish-brown mane which announced he was *king* of his fleet of space marines. Out of all of the four branches of the military, the Leonids were the most animal-like in their appearance, resembling the Nibiruian lions which the Emperor had grafted onto their DNA. The creature had gone extinct, along with every *other* inhabitant of Nibiru, but Leonids were still here.

Barely...

Stacks of folders sat in disarray, unlike the neat stacks which had greeted him the first time his Supreme Commander-general had summoned him into her office and coldly asked if he'd like to sire offspring number twelve. Angelic and Leonid bent over a flatscreen, musing about the latest intelligence reports. At her feet, Uriel had belly-wiggled over to the wires and was in the process of pulling his mother's computer down upon his head. Curled up fast asleep at his side was the gourock water-dragon.

"Reporting for duty as requested, Sir!" He gave her a crisp salute, and did the same for the Leonid general. "Sir."

Her genuinely relieved smile took his breath away. She brushed a strand of white-blonde hair out of her eyes that had fallen out of her tightly-coiffed regulation bun and, when it refused to stay, simply blew it out of the way with an exaggerated 'puff.'

"I am hereby ordering you to take YOUR son and get him out of my hair!!!" she said. "He's getting into everything!"

"MY son?" Raphael said with mock indignation.

"When he misbehaves, he is YOUR son," Jophiel laughed.

Uriel got hold of the Leonid's tail and shoved it into his mouth. General Re Harakhti roared a bone-rattling laugh. Most people found it terrifying, but Raphael counted many Leonids among his closest friends.

"If you think this is bad," the Leonid said, "wait until he starts to teethe."

He gently tugged his tail out of the infant's mouth.

Uriel cooed.

"Yes, Sir!" Raphael grabbed the wiggly five-month-old and swooshed him around in a circle. "Hey, little guy, Daddy's here."

Uriel reached for Raphael's golden feathers, causing a malodorous air to waft up to his nostrils.

"Whew!!! Little buddy ... you need a diaper change!"

"I told her that twenty minutes ago." The Leonid waved his paw in front of his sensitive nose.

"He's all yours," Jophiel laughed. "Dismissed! Both of you! And oh ... take *that* with you!" She pointed at the dog-sized gourock, which had popped up like a jack-in-the-box the moment he'd come into the room.

"Yes, Sir!" Raphael held up their son's tiny fist to mock salute the two high-ranking generals before grabbing the gourock's collar and heading out the door. "Let's go see about that diaper....."

Jophiel and the Leonid bent back over their intelligence reports, trying to figure out what in *Hades* Shay'tan was up to.

Chapter 154

September – 3,390 BC
Earth: Mesopotamian Plain
Colonel Mikhail Mannuki'ili

MIKHAIL

Every fall, great herds migrated across the alluvial plain in search of the grain which grew wherever the flood waters deposited silt. The herd they stalked now was a creature the Ubaid called *reem*. Sand gazelles. A dainty, goat-like creature that moved in herds, searching for forage. Although hunting gazelles didn't carry the same prestige as taking down a larger animal such as an Auroch, not only would it provide the village with meat, but it was an opportunity to take his most promising warriors, both new and old, on a "morale building" exercise.

After the kerfluffle over the Amorites, Jamin had flat-out *refused* to participate in his father's hunt. So he'd selected thirty warriors to accompany him via the most democratic means possible; a contest. Out of each of the three "tiers," whoever scored highest in a cornucopia of skills had been selected. It was the best way to avoid accusations of favoritism.

As they approached the herd, the animals caught their scent. Dozens of heads shot up, but they were too far away, the animals believed, to be an immediate threat. They went back to eating.

"Do you have such creatures in the kingdom you come from?" asked Varshab, the Chief's personal guard, who'd been sent in place of Jamin.

"Not exactly." He pointed at the dainty creatures. "But I believe I may have seen something like these before."

"Don't be fooled by their diminutive size," Kiaresh joined the conversation. "They are small, but exceptionally fleet of foot."

"And nimble over rough terrain." Varshab pointed off in the distance where the flat river plain rose up to meet the desert, a steep rocky rock face. "If they make it there, by the time we climb up after them, they'll be long gone."

"That shouldn't be a problem for *you*," Kiaresh pointed to Mikhail's wings.

"It's not *about* me." Mikhail glanced over his shoulder at the younger warriors, eager to begin the hunt. "It's about them, working together. If supper gets away from them, I'm not going to fly in and save the day."

Mikhail gestured for Siamek to move towards the front.

"Sir?" Siamek asked.

"Separate into three groups," Mikhail said. "Ten warriors each team leader."

Although Siamek had not yet lost that wary expression, he had no complaints about the way he carried out his duties. He was a solid performing, competent leader, perhaps not the best in each of the individual weapons skills, but the most consistent performer overall. More importantly, he had a modicum of common sense and not a lot of self-ambition beyond what was best for the village, two important traits for a second-in-command.

"Who has to take the three, um, Sir?" Siamek stopped himself from saying 'girls.' Pareesa had qualified on her own, male *or* female, but he'd done a separate contest to make sure two other women qualified for today's hunt.

"I want Pareesa to go with Kiaresh," Mikhail said. "I'll take Azin. You should take Gita."

Siamek blanched. "Why can't I have Azin?"

"I want the teams to be evenly balanced as far as abilities go," Mikhail said. "I know Gita's brand new, but she won her slot fair and square. And she *did* come in second place at the summer Solstice Festival. I want her paired with you and Varshab."

He was trying to walk that fine line between encouraging Pareesa to be the best warrior she could be while *not* encouraging the 'crush' the little fairy purportedly nursed for him. Originally he'd intended to bring the newbie along in *his* group so he could keep an eye on her, but Ninsianna had erupted in a fit of temper, which seemed to be occurring more and more the last two weeks while she fended off a stomach bug. It was important to show the other warriors that women could perform under fire.

"It could be *worse*," Varshab ribbed Siamek. "He could have made you take Ebad."

Siamek snorted, trying not to laugh. Pareesa's prize 'student' had *not* qualified for today's hunt. Nor had any of the other fifteen young men Mikhail had saddled her with for "extra training", including Ipquidad, Yaggit, or any of the other sons of potters, weavers, and tradesmen that Jamin had dragged on their last "adventure."

"You'll survive," Kiaresh slapped Siamek on the back.

The team leaders briefed, Mikhail called the other warriors to gather around and assigned them to teams.

"Two groups will move in a V-formation to herd the gazelles towards that embankment," Mikhail said. "Meanwhile, the third group should circle around that ridge and make sure they don't escape."

"But the river has dropped, Sir," Siamek said. "They'll slip past us on that narrow spit of land."

"That's where the teamwork comes in." Mikhail pointed at the grazing gazelles. "A-team should move ahead so that their end of the V stretches out that way. B-team will block them from coming back this way. C-team will surprise them when they try to climb that embankment. They'll have the high ground, so they should be able to intercept enough gazelles for a respectable hunt."

He'd made them leave their bows behind so they would be forced to work together to get in close to the quarry. Gazelles were swift creatures. It would force the warriors to think quickly on their feet and use the command signals he'd been teaching them to let the other person know what they needed to do.

"Why does C-team get to do all the killing?" Firouz lamented, sans his sidekick Dadbeh, who had not made the cut. Mikhail had assigned him to Kiaresh's group, trying to break up the 'elite' warriors amongst the newer ones who were showing promise in skills such as the ability to follow a chain of command.

"How many gazelles does a hunting group this size usually kill?" Mikhail asked.

"Thirty men?" Siamek said. "We usually get one each. Jamin always got two."

"Let's see how many we get if we do it my way?" Mikhail said. "The worst that can happen is we all go home hungry."

With a 'hoo-rah' and bumped fists, the groups broke up. The sun began to climb in the sky towards its apex as they waited for C-team, headed by Kiaresh, to move into position. After half an hour or so, he spied Pareesa scrambling up the rocks, fleet as a gazelle herself. With a nod to Siamek, the B-team began to circle around the water's edge, cutting the gazelles off from the river. The herd milled about and stomped their feet, sensing predators were moving in for the kill.

"Let's go," Mikhail signaled his group when Siamek gave him the signal to move into position. A-team began to spread out in a line, the fastest members moving their end of the V towards the tail end of Siamek's group. Mikhail anchored the far end, giving his team a series of hand signals to communicate they needed to straighten out their line and move in unison. As expected, when the two lines converged and began to move towards the grazing herd, they began to stampede.

"Hey-yah!" Mikhail gave the signal to rush at the gazelles. The gazelles made a break for it.

The warriors were under orders not to throw their spears until the gazelles approached the rocky embankment. Once the creatures hit the obstacle, experience dictated half would attempt to climb to safety while the other half would try to break back through the line. They were more likely to make a clean kill when an animal ran *at* them, keeping their spears in their hands so they could make another kill right away, than when one was running away, disarming themselves.

"Now!" Siamek shouted, beginning the hunt.

The warriors moved into rough lines, not perfect, but some of the groups gelled to move the way they did during training. The elite warriors tended to cluster together, but as gazelles ran back towards them, they were forced to move with better coordination. The largest buck nipped at the flanks of the female gazelles and began to herd them up towards the cliff, exactly the way that Varshab had said they would. When the gazelles got halfway up the hill, C-team erupted out of the rocky hill and panicked the creatures, turning half of them back as expected. The big buck spied a weakness in Siamek's line and made a break for it.

"Close that line!" Mikhail shouted. His words were drowned out by hundreds of tiny hooves pounding against the rocky soil. As he'd hoped, the gazelles found the places they were weak and dozens escaped, demonstrating better than a month's worth of words *why* they needed to become better coordinated.

Kiaresh signaled one of the C-team warriors close to the failing line left by B-team and scrambled down the rocks. Firouz rushed after the disappearing herd.

"No!" Mikhail shouted in vain. "You're supposed to close the line!"

Firouz chased after the buck, pursuing the status symbol of taking down the largest gazelle *himself* rather than the group goal of capturing the greatest number of gazelles. Meanwhile Siamek regained control over his team and signaled Gita to close the line. With their easiest route of escape now blocked, half began to climb to where C-team waited to ambush them, the other half tried to break through the combined lines of A-team and B-team.

A doe with two kids rushed at him. Mikhail lifted one wing and let them pass. Immanu said that a wise huntsman allows the very young to escape so there will be gazelles to hunt next year. A young male rushed at him, his horns showing he was about a year old. Perfect eating. Mikhail stabbed at the creature with his spear. The poor thing flailed, crying out as the spear missed its heart. Mikhail pulled his knife and finished it off. He had no problems with hunting, but he couldn't bear to watch it suffer.

"Whoo-hoo!" the warriors shouted as fleeing gazelles impaled themselves upon their spears.

"Don't let that line open up!" Mikhail warned one of his own team members, a middle-aged man who showed promise despite claiming he'd never hunted before. The man closed up the line as they tightened around the herd of frantic gazelles like a noose.

He killed a second young buck, and then an aging doe. All around him, his team members did the same. The death-screams of frantic gazelles cried out from the rocky embankment, where C-team was engaged in a bloodbath of animal slaughter. Another doe rushed at him, her belly swollen.

"Let her go!" Azin shouted. "She is with fawn. It's bad luck to kill her."

He lifted his wing and let the creature pass. A second one slipped away, good reflexes allowing it to get the better of him. Immanu had lectured him to not allow the warriors to kill the entire herd. No more than a third or She-Who-Is would punish them for their greed by denying them meat next year. Mikhail gave a rough count and estimated they were almost there. A few more, perhaps.

A blood-curdling scream broke through the air, not a gazelle, but a *human* scream. A bone-rattling roar shook the air. But where? He scanned the warriors. A-team … ten men. B-team … Siamek paused killing gazelles and pointed at the narrow peninsula where Firouz had disappeared. Another scream, and then a roar.

Céilí mór!

The gazelles forgotten, the warriors rushed in the direction Firouz had disappeared. Mikhail spread his wings and leaped into the air, flying above the embankment to see where the screams were coming from. He spied a large predator with a golden pelt leap towards a second predator which dragged the screaming Firouz off by a leg.

The beast was enormous, with a golden pelt of fur.

Mikhail dropped to the ground, his wings trembling with the memory that *wanted* to come to the surface, but wouldn't.

"Just let him go!"

He held out his hand to the creature which had Firouz by the leg, trying to reason with it. A deep rumble growled in its throat. The second creature snarled at him, baring enormous fangs. The larger of the two had a reddish mane. It dropped Firouz's arm and crouched to leap at *him*. Firouz cried out and tried to roll away. The female leaped on the prey animal dropped by her mate. It was a … a … a…

"Please," he told the creature. "We can work this out. Who is your commanding officer?" The overwhelming sensation he should *remember* these creatures muddled his brain.

With an ear-splitting roar, the big male leaped at him. Why was one of his own men attacking him? Disbelief slowed his reaction time. He fell backwards, claws raking at his wings and tearing out clumps of feathers as the creature bit at his head. Standing up, the creature was the same size as *he* was without his wings, but for some reason all he could think about was how *small* this creature was compared to what it *should* be.

"Don't make me kill you," he pleaded. Every fiber of his being screamed that killing this creature would be *wrong!*

Fangs broke through the flesh in one wing, claws dug into his arm. Whatever he *thought* these creatures were didn't matter. He needed to fight back or he would die.

He heard the shout of the other warriors as he pulled his knife and rolled, he and the creature locked in each other's embrace. The big male outweighed him. It came down hard on one wing and knocked him onto the ground, flat on his back. Out of the corner of his eye he saw the other warriors rush towards Firouz, stabbing at the second beast. The female roared as a spear pierced its hide.

"Stop!" Mikhail shouted. Killing these creatures was *wrong!*

The big male snapped at his head; enormous claws ripped out chunks of feathers and clawed at his flesh. It knocked the knife he'd hesitated to use right out of his hands. It was him against the beast.

"Get out of the way!" Varshab shouted at him.

"Don't kill it!" Mikhail pleaded. He rolled so that his wings shielded the creature, preventing them from plunging a spear into its heart. Fangs grazed his cheek, barely missing his eye. Mikhail grabbed the jaws and pulled them apart; the creature's hot breath bellowed in his face. It furiously clawed with front and hind legs; their close proximity was his saving grace, too close for the creature to claw at anything except for his wings. He flailed, no more able to hit the creature with the club-like leading edge of his wings than the creature was able to get at him with its claws.

Mikhail spied his knife and moved his hand, yelping as enormous jaws clamped down around his wrist. He punched it in the head with his other hand and reached for the knife he'd dropped.

The creature snapped at his head, leaving open its chest, a mistake any first-year cadet learned to avoid.

He had no choice. Training took over.

He stabbed the creature in the heart.

The creature's death-cry reverberated through his very soul, making *him* cry out along with it. No! He pushed it off of him, pulling out the knife and pushing his hands over the wound to staunch the bleeding. The other warriors rushed in to finish it off.

"No!" he shouted. He waved them off, his eyes blurry as he pleaded with the creature. "Don't die. Please don't die."

He waited for the creature to explain why it had felt the need to attack, but it didn't speak. There was intelligence in those golden eyes filled with pain. It breathed, and breathed again, and then it was silent. Staring at the blood on his hands, Mikhail raised them up to the sky.

"Why?" he shook his fists into the sky. "Why why why?"

The warriors danced around the dead female like carrion birds, celebrating the noble creature's death. Pareesa helped Firouz to his feet, a little worse for the wear, but he would survive. They slapped Firouz on the back. Tears streamed down Mikhail's cheeks.

They stopped celebrating when they realized he was crying.

"I'm sorry," he told the beast whose name he couldn't remember, but knew he should know.

He stared at the blood on his hands, red against his pale white flesh. He ran his hands through its pelt and put his head down to listen for its heart. It was silent. Even though he couldn't remember this creature's name or where he'd seen one before, in his soul he knew he'd just killed one of his own. He put his forehead down upon his still-warm comrade, sobs wracking his body as he drooped his wings and allowed seven months of mourning lost memories to spill from his shattered psyche.

The warriors gathered around in silence, not understanding why he grieved.

"Mikhail?" Pareesa placed a hand on one wing. "Are you okay?"

"I don't know why," Mikhail hiccoughed, "but I feel as though I just killed my own brother."

"These are lions," Pareesa said. "Big cats. Sometimes we have to hunt them or they'll eat our goats."

Pareesa put her hand on his shoulder and gave it a squeeze, surprisingly strong for such a young woman. He tried to suppress the sobs that kept shuddering in his chest, but he couldn't. They didn't understand.

"Where he comes from," a soft voice said. "There are lions who are people, just as *he* is part eagle."

He looked up to stare into the blackest eyes he'd ever seen, so black it was impossible to tell where the pupil ended and the iris began. The black-eyed girl knelt before the dead creature. He shivered at the sensation of having his soul laid bare before those bottomless black eyes.

—*Mikhail! Come and find me…*

—*Black eyes, peeking through the leaves.*

—*A song…*

—*I search for her, but already she is gone…*

He was trapped in those black eyes, so much like Ninsianna's, only instead of gold, they were black and filled with a terrible hunger.

"They're just animals," Siamek said. "Smart animals, which is why we fear them."

"It's very brave what you did," Varshab said, "killing a lion with nothing but a knife. Only the bravest warriors dare come up against a lion."

The warriors pulled their spears out of the female and pulled out their obsidian blades to skin it.

"You must take its pelt and carry it back to the village," Kiaresh said.

"Only Jamin has ever killed a lion single-handedly," Siamek said.

"We call this beast the king-maker," Varshab said. "Only a great leader dare take on a lion alone."

Mikhail ran his hand through the great beast's pelt. It was not the creature he'd first mistaken it to be. He could see that now. But in the moment … it had seemed like…

"It's just an animal," Pareesa said. "See?"

It wore no uniform, no rank pins. Its claws were dirty and chipped, with no sign of being groomed, and its fur unkempt and not brushed. The fingers on the paws were too short, too paw-like, and it didn't have opposable thumbs. Something about the way its hip and shoulder joints were shaped didn't look right. Whatever his subconscious screamed out at him, this creature was not exact.

Regardless, he reached down and closed its eyes.

"I think Gita is right." He shook his head, frustrated at the memory which refused to come free. "I think where I come from we have *people* who look like this." He glanced up to thank the young woman who'd provided him with a logical explanation for his bizarre emotional reaction, but she'd disappeared.

Two of the warriors helped Firouz hobble over.

"Thank you," Firouz said. He pointed to the big male gazelle he'd taken down for himself, the buck which had been leader of the herd. "I'd killed it and was carrying it back when they came out from behind those tall grasses. I didn't even see them coming."

Mikhail rose to his feet.

"Had you not broken rank," his wings trembled with rage. "This wouldn't have happened. You were supposed to fill the hole in the line! Not go chasing after your own glory! This is why eleven people were killed during the raid!"

Anger filled his body, begging to be let off its leash. He could *feel* it there, a wound so deep, so palpable, so horrible and black that it felt like the chill of death. The warriors backed off. Firouz cowered in fear.

'You must control your anger. Anger opens the door to other things…'

The warning of a Cherubim master he only vaguely recalled replayed over and over again in his mind, words to an incantation to calm his emotions. He stepped back, his mouth moving as he whispered the words to the prayers they'd taught him to control his rage. The emotion seethed beneath the surface like an ancient volcano, trying to get out. The Cherubim had taught him that he must never lose control of his anger.

Calmness poured through his body like water, soothing the angry cauldron simmering beneath the surface, covering the ancient wound he couldn't remember receiving and whispering for it to lie at rest.

'It was nothing but an animal…'

It would be an abomination to kill such a noble creature and not use every part of it as *SHE* intended. He didn't need Immanu to tell him that. He handed his knife to Pareesa.

"I can't do this." He turned so he wouldn't see the warriors, skinning the dead female lion. "This animal is too much like a creature I know to be a friend. Present its hide as a gift to the Chief and make sure they bury the both of their remains side-by-side with honors. When you're done, I'll come back and say the death rituals."

"But it's just an animal," Kiaresh said. "We only pour water over its nose before we skin it to give thanks to the goddess."

"You will bury them with *honor,*" Mikhail said. "While I fly back and get Immanu."

With the blood of his brother still on his hands, he took to the air to fetch his father-in-law.

Chapter 155

Galactic Standard Date: 152,322.11 AE
Alpha Sector: Command Carrier 'Eternal Light'
Colonel Mikhail Mannuki'ili

Three months prior to the crash...

MIKHAIL

"Colonel Mannuki'ili," Supreme Commander-General Jophiel said. "We've received intelligence that the Sata'an Empire is amassing resources in Zulu Sector."

"That's pretty remote, Sir," Mikhail said. "Isn't that area uncharted?"

"There's nothing out there," Jophiel said, "at least not that we know of. Now, all of a sudden, Shay'tan sent a battlecruiser?"

"What are your orders, Sir?" he asked.

"Take a scout ship and start shadowing these so-called traders," Jophiel ordered. "Find out where they're going and what they're up to."

"That's too remote for a scout ship. What's my jumping off point?"

"I'm stationing you with an old friend," she said. "Report to Colonel Israfa on the 'Light Emerging.' I'm positioning his command carrier on the border between Zulu and X-ray so it doesn't arouse too much suspicion. You'll be black-ops on this one, eyes-only, but Colonel Israfa is in the loop."

He noted the unconscious way she caressed her swelling midsection. The corners of her mouth turned downwards in a sad little smile. Mikhail had known her too long to be fooled by her professional demeanor.

"He's a good man, Jophie," Mikhail said softly, using her familiar name. "You shouldn't have sent him so far away."

Her expression softened as a smile tugged at the corner of her lips. Wistful...

"Take good care of him for me, will you?" Jophiel asked.

*

Mikhail shot up, momentarily confused. The room was too small, without light, and smelled of earth rather than the recycled air of his ship. He stared down at the sleeping goddess who lay on the sleeping pallet beside him.

Ninsianna. His wife...

He grabbed at the memory and fought to hang onto it. This time it stayed. Not the context, not the rhyme or reason or why, but the overwhelming sense of *mission* stayed with him.

Along with the Supreme Commander-General's name.

He knew what he had to do.

Chapter 156

ΔΥƆΤΙΔΤΙϚ

Galactic Standard Date: 152,323.09 AE
Alpha Sector: Command Carrier 'Eternal Light'
Supreme Commander-General Jophiel

JOPHIEL

They *tried* to pay attention as she gave her daily briefing, but even the most seasoned eyes kept wandering to the infant strapped to her chest.

"As you were."

Jophiel sighed as the men and women who represented every branch of the military trailed out from the hanger bay. Who would have thought raising her own child would have such an impact on her work? Twelve babies she'd borne the Alliance, but this was the first time she'd actually had to rear one of them.

Major Klik'rr held the usual stack of mission orders to be signed, debriefings to be read, and decisions to be made regarding resource movements and troop rotations; a sharp contrast from her duties as a mother.

"Here's the latest intelligence report from Zulu Sector, Sir."

"Thank you, Klik'rr." She took the report. "I'd also like to see the reports from Romeo, Sierra, and Tango Sectors. Let's see what that old devil Shay'tan is up to?"

"I'll have them on your desk by oh-eight-hundred hours," Klik'rr said.

She knew from experience the reports would be there one hour earlier. Klik'rr was hardworking and efficient, as *most* of the Mantoids were who served under her command. Given that 95% of the military was now comprised of species *other* than hybrids, it was about time the Emperor implemented a more egalitarian promotion system rather than simply promoting hybrids because their name happened to be on the branch of the military in which they served.

"The merit-based promotion order, Sir," Klik'rr said.

She glanced at the general order stating that, from now on, *all* branches of the military would promote within their ranks based on merit, not the seniority-based system which had all-but guaranteed the longer-lived hybrids would always be ahead of the shorter-serving newer sentient races. It had given her people prestige, but also made them so irreplaceable that the Emperor couldn't afford to let them take family leave. If they were to avoid extinction, that system had to end.

She signed it.

"The specs for the newest warships, Sir."

Klik'rr handed her the document ordering that all new warships were to be built to accommodate a *variety* of species, not just the hybrids.

She signed that as well.

Klik'rr silently put the last document onto her smart pad and tilted his antennae in an inquiring look. Her hand trembled.

"I can't do this," she said.

Her feathers rustled. There hadn't been a 'hybrid-anything' for many years, but *she* wouldn't be the one to strike the name of the hybrid race who'd been genetically engineered to *be* that branch of the military from that branch of service's name. For now, they would remain the Angelic Air Force, the Leonid Multi-Purpose Fighting Forces, the Merfolk Navy, and the Centauri Calvary. She glanced down at Uriel sleeping peacefully upon her chest. Maybe the Emperor's concessions would allow them to bring their species back from the brink of extinction?

There was no judgment in Klik'rr's compound eyes as he quietly slipped the document at the bottom of the stack.

"Thank you, dismissed."

She punched the display to scroll through the reports. Most appeared inconsequential, but Raphael was positive that the increase in Sata'anic shipping activity and Mikhail's disappearance were related.

Something was up…

She trusted Raphael's instincts as much as she trusted her own.

The mere thought of the time they spent together made her smile, but even as they relished their happiness, she could sense the fractures reverberating throughout the Alliance.

A pregnant cadet shot her a glare. Jophiel could almost *hear* the woman's thoughts: "*Why do –you– get to have a family, but the rest of us don't?*"

She prayed that Raphael would find this '*solution*' that the Emperor spoke of because, if he didn't, all Hades was about to break loose…

Chapter 157

September – 3,390 BC
Earth: Village of Assur

NINSIANNA

Ninsianna awoke to the rhythmic sound of Mikhail's heartbeat whirring through the brachial artery of the arm she used as a pillow, her cheek resting upon his chest. While she'd been sleeping he'd captured her hand and placed it over his heart, his large, strong hand gently caressing her smaller one. He was already awake, watching her with that unreadable expression he wore whenever he had something on his mind. The village was ecstatic with the bounty they'd brought back and divided amongst the village, fifty-three gazelles and two lion pelts, but for some reason, he refused to speak about it.

"Good morning." He stroked her hair.

"Good morning," she answered, stretching. Today was rest-day. They didn't have to tend the fields, teach any classes, or do anything else except spend time with each. She reached up to touch his cheek. "What's on your mind?"

"I have to go back to my ship," he said. "I think I remember why I was sent here."

A sense of dread fluttered in her stomach. Something significant had happened yesterday during the hunt. She could *see* the way the light streamed from his body and flowed someplace far away, no longer centered on her or her village.

"Why?"

"I dreamed about a woman," he said. "Another Angelic."

"A girlfriend?" she said, more sharply than she meant.

"You'll think this sounds crazy, but I think—" he shook his head. "No. She was some kind of war chief?"

"A *war* chief?" she said incredulously. "Like *Jamin*?"

"Higher," he said. "I called her Supreme Commander-General."

Her gift of tongues translated the unfamiliar title into an image of a radiant white-winged woman, standing fiercely at the right-hand shoulder of a bearded God. A sense of unreality warred with her jealousy.

"A *woman* leads the armies of God?" she sputtered.

"I *think* so." He looked past her, like he did whenever he was trying to remember the past. "She's Angelic, like me, only her wings are white."

White wings... like the Evil One?

"What makes you think it wasn't a dream?" she asked crossly.

A slight hint of bemusement softened his expression.

"She asked me to follow a *spásárthach*.[175] An, uhm—" he struggled for a translation "—what you call a sky canoe. A *big* one."

"Perhaps this *general* sent you to watch over *us?*"

"Perhaps..." He sounded less than certain.

A stab of *jealousy* clenched in her gut. Whoever this general was, a tinge of pink in his spirit-light betrayed she meant far more to him than simply a "war chief."

"Why haven't they just come and gotten you, then?" she asked.

"I was in stealth mode when I was hit," he said. "Black ops. Like a wolf stalking a prey animal through the grass. They have no idea where to look for me. But the fact they shot me down means there *must* be a Sata'an base somewhere on this planet."

"Why would these people be interested in our world?"

"I can't remember!" His voice rose with frustration. "I know I have an enemy, but I can't remember enough about them to piece it all together! All I remember is that it's critically important that I report the existance of this base to Supreme Commander-General Jophiel."

"If you tell them you are *here*—" her voice warbled "—won't they make you leave?"

He stared out the window.

"Every single day, it eats at me, this mission." He lifted her chin so he could stare directly into her eyes. "You fell in love with me because I'm a man of honor, but it was my *duty* to follow that enemy ship and report where it went."

"Your god abandoned you."

"My *god* doesn't know where I am."

"She-Who-Is sent you to protect us."

"I feel no connection to your goddess—" he gestured at the small, clay statue which sat upon her informal altar "—but I *do* feel a connection to the Eternal Emperor. Even though I can't *remember* him, I can feel it in my bones."

The light which flowed out of him, brilliant blue, tinged with white and an edge of gold, flowed away from him, up into a distant star. She could *see* the connection he spoke of, and knew it was real. She had *always* known it

---

[175] *Spásárthach:* space ship.

was real. The only reason he had stayed was because She-Who-Is had broken his wing and stolen his memories.

She glanced up at the clay statue which smiled down at her from her altar.

'Trust me,' the statue seemed to whisper. *'You carry the one thing he wants even more than his duty to his god.'*

"Then we must go back to your ship and send that message," she said. "I've always wanted to see the heavens?"

His expression changed from worry to excitement.

"I think I figured out how to get the communication system running," he said. "Somehow, I must compress a databurst into a beam and hope I've got it aimed in the right direction so I can reach Raphael's ship with what little power I have left. If his ship is still even in this sector. It *has* been seven months..."

Ninsianna propped herself up onto her elbow and stared into her husband's eyes.

"Mikhail ... I don't understand a word you just said."

"The gift of tongues, is it fading?" His brow furrowed in concern.

Ninsianna laughed.

"The gift works just fine. I just don't understand how your tek-no-lo-gee[176] works."

"Oh." Comprehension dawned about the nature of the problem. "Then *you* must come with me so I can bring you into the modern age."

"I'll come because I want some *alone* time—" she lowered her voice to a sultry whisper. She ran her hand down his abdomen. "We never get to spend enough time together anymore."

The troubled expression he'd worn ever since he'd come back from the hunt yesterday faded. In her hands, he was soft, malleable clay! With a growl of pleasure, Mikhail rolled on top of her for a playful morning romp.

It was Ninsianna's squeals of laughter and the sound of wings thumping against the wall that woke Ninsianna's parents up on this fine rest-day.

---

[176] *Tek-no-lo-gee*: technology

Chapter 158

Galactic Standard Date: 152,323.09 AE
Haven-3
Prime Minister Lucifer

LUCIFER

"Sire," Zepar shook Lucifer awake. "Sire! Wake up. You'll be late for your meeting."

A tiny man with a sonic jackhammer pounded into Lucifer's skull. It felt like someone kept sucking his brain out of his head and spitting it back out into his lurching stomach. Not again! Lucifer groaned in agony.

"Couldn't you call in sick?" Lucifer whimpered. It hurt so badly that he didn't dare open his eyes. "I need to go to a *real* doctor so I can get my head examined."

"No!" Zepar said quickly. "You can't, Sire. If you tell an Alliance physician you've been experiencing blackouts, they'll have you removed from office."

"I no longer care." Bile rose in Lucifer's throat, burning the entire way up. "Zepar! Quick! I need a bucket!"

He spent the next 20 minutes heaving curdled chunks of goddess-only-knows what into an ice bucket. He was too shaky to even make it into his bathroom to worship the porcelain god. At some point the vomit-induced fog cleared enough for him to recognize he was back at his penthouse on Haven-3, not on his ship. Finally, he began to regain his equilibrium.

"Tell me about my schedule for the day?"

"You're supposed to meet with the Ministry of Education at eleven o'clock," Zepar said. "You have a prescheduled mating appointment at twelve-thirty, and then we need to hop a three o'clock transport to Haven-1 to make the seven o'clock banquet with the Eternal Emperor."

"When did we get back to Haven?" The last thing he remembered was that *horrible* meeting with the cannibals. "I thought we agreed to keep my ship out in the borderlands so that *bitch* can't bust our chops by running a 'health and safety inspection'?"

"We hopped a needle back last night," Zepar said. "You had quite a bit to drink. Perhaps that's why you feel under the weather?"

"Of course." That old feeling of dread surfaced as Lucifer realized he had no recollection of arriving. "Zepar, what day is it today?"

"Thursday, Sire," Zepar said.

"I mean, the date?" Lucifer asked. "We've been moving around the galaxy so much that I'm planet-lagged. What's the date here on Haven-3?"

"September 17th, Sire," Zepar said. "The Eternal Emperor's birthday. He asked you return to celebrate his 1,178,432nd birthday party tonight."

What?

July ... August ... September ... oh ... fuck...

"Can you leave me alone to get dressed?" His voice betrayed how shaky he felt. "Oh ... and get me the brief for today's meeting with the Ministry of Education. I can't remember why I'm meeting him in the first place."

"Whoever does?" Zepar flipped one hand back in a dismissive gesture. "The brief will be in your hands within 20 minutes." Zepar left him alone to get cleaned up and ready for the day.

Eight weeks? How in Hades had he just lost eight weeks of his life? And worse ... what had he been up to all that time? Holding his head to prevent it from splitting in two, Lucifer frantically spooled up his electronic scheduling device, clicking through his appointments to piece together what he'd been up to.

He noted receipt of that second shipment of human females, and then meeting with various high-placed hybrids that were experiencing fertility problems, some which he vaguely remembered, but a lot which he didn't. Everything fit his plan to stave off extinction. He stopped, however, at the last appointment. His hand trembled as he scrolled back, then forward again, certain his hangover must be causing him to read it wrong.

"Kunopegos is ten times the size of a human," Lucifer said, horrified. He immediately reached for his comms pin. "Zepar ... I need you in half an hour."

He got showered and dressed, playing it as cool as possible. His heart raced. He should step down from office! He *knew* he should step down! It wasn't right that the Alliance's highest elected official lost *months* out of his life! But if he did, all of his efforts to override his father's seed-world policies would go out the window. It was up to *him* to save his species from extinction!

Should he discuss this with Zepar? No. Deep down he'd always known Zepar was only along for the ride. If his Chief of Staff knew how badly he was losing it, he would ditch him in a heartbeat for some other puppet-prince. Lucifer composed his features to play it cool.

"Sire," Zepar said as he came back in. "Are you ready to go?"

"I don't know how to say this," Lucifer said, "but the last thing I remember was we were scheduled to meet General Kunopegos, but then I can't recall what happened afterwards. I need you to fill me in on the details of that meeting."

"You've been pushing yourself too hard." Zepar placed a sympathetic hand upon his shoulder. "Would you like me to cancel your twelve-thirty mating appointment? The only reason I scheduled it was to create a smokescreen. It will look odd if you suddenly lose all interest in females. You *do* have your reputation to maintain, Sire."

"No," Lucifer sighed, his expression wistful. "I'll keep the appointment. It would be nice if I could find a mate who is fully sentient *and* can give my offspring wings."

Zepar started laughing, looking at him as though he were joking.

"What's so funny?" Lucifer asked.

"Sire ...." Zepar said, holding his sides. "You're so *dedicated*. You have fourteen offspring on the way. That's why we left your ship in the uncharted territories. You have an entire harem on board your ship."

"Fourteen?" Lucifer sat down on the edge of his bed in shock. Yes, he remembered something about fourteen women. How could he forget?

Zepar's laughter began to sound further and further away.

"Every single human female you've gifted to an Alliance hybrid is pregnant," Zepar said. "There are over thirty half-human, half-hybrid children waiting to be born. And the Emperor doesn't have a clue!" Zepar shook his shoulder. "Sire! You're a hero!"

"I'm a hero," Lucifer whispered. He rustled his white feathers. "Yes. Of course. Let's get to that Ministry of Education appointment."

The remainder of the day, Lucifer cross-referenced his appointment calendar to figure out what in *Hades* he'd been up to, what legislation he'd introduced, who he'd spoken too, and what they had spoken about. Zepar had invented code words for the back-room deals politicians often did to grease the wheels of government. There were an awful lot of 'fudge records' lately.

Lucifer faked his way through the Ministry of Education meeting. The mating appointment was pleasurable and vacuous. He didn't even have to use his gift. It wasn't until he got to his father's birthday jubilee that a common thread began to dawn on him. He'd never experienced a blackout when he met with his father.

He passed through the extensive security which had been at the Eternal Palace ever since his father had gotten back from the highest ascended realms: the body searches, the eye scanner, the reaction time tests, and the infra-red. What was his father looking for when he ran all those tests? Dignitaries swirled through the palace, all vying for a moment alone with the Eternal Emperor. Lucifer slipped through the line of well-wishers, anxious to throw himself upon his father's mercy. Whatever else was going on, his father was a scientist. He might be able to fix it.

"Father," Lucifer trembled as he stood before the Eternal Emperor and prepared to throw his fate to his mercy. "Can I speak to you please? Alone?"

"Not now." Hashem nodded acknowledgement to the long line of well-wishers who were filing past.

"It's really important," Lucifer begged. He trembled, and then did that thing that was forbidden for mortal creatures to do. He placed his hand upon the Emperor's forearm.

"I told you, Lucifer," Hashem swatted at Lucifer's hand the way one might swat at a fly. "I don't know how to fix you."

"It's not *that* problem." Lucifer kept his voice low so that the well-wishers wouldn't hear. "This is something else. Father ... please ... I really need your help."

He shouldn't be losing time like this. There was something *really* wrong with him, and Zepar was taking advantage of his blackouts for some purpose he couldn't fathom. There was no way he was losing that much time without Zepar being aware of it.

"Your Majesty," a female voice purred.

The Emperor turned, smiling towards the source of the voice. Lucifer's gaze followed that of his father, right into the ice-cold stare of that *bitch*, Jophiel, and her flavor-du-jour, Raphael, father of her latest offspring. It seemed Lucifer wasn't the *only* one yearning for something a little more meaningful?

"Jophie!" Hashem put his arm around her and turned his back on Lucifer. "When will you let this fine young man make an honest woman of you?"

"Shhhhh!!!" Jophiel's cheeks flushed pink. "We're trying to be discreet."

Lucifer's blood began to boil. Here he'd tried for 225 years to fulfill his father's wishes and produce offspring, spending every available minute that he wasn't performing the duties of Parliament attempting to 'perform' his duty to produce a lawful heir, and now Hashem urged Jophiel, the only female Angelic who could consistently produce offspring, to just take herself out of commission?

Memory of how many times he'd pleaded with his father to pay attention to the problems of his empire rankled him. When his mother died, Hashem had skipped town and left Lucifer holding the bag. Then suddenly, after 200 years gone, his father had come back, taken one look at Jophiel, and created a brand-new military position that was the social equivalent of *his* position. Hashem had been lavishing attention on the icy Angelic female ever since. All because of a freak resemblance to his mother! Just like that, he'd been replaced, 200 years of faithful service running the Alliance in his father's absence just pushed aside and forgotten!

Lucifer didn't even bother to say goodbye.

He radioed Zepar:

"Get my needle ready," he said. "I'm coming back."

"But the Emperor—"

"Is a piece of shit. I want you to call Ba'al Zebub. Tell him we'll take every human he can lay his hands on, male or female. I don't care how much it costs."

Chapter 159

September – 3,390 BC
Earth: Crash Site

MIKHAIL

So far as subspace antennae went, it was nothing to brag about, but he *hoped* the contraption he'd built out of salvaged pieces of his ship would be able to conduct enough power to open a micro-wormhole.

Thank the gods! The wormhole generator, itself, had survived when that idiot, Jamin, had thrown a spear into his antenna array!

He heaved himself off his back and shook the dust from his wings.

"What does that spiderweb do?" Ninsianna pointed at the thick bundle of wires which ran through the crack in his roof.

"It carries the lightning," he said.

"The blue lightning?"

"Yes."

"To this little silver sword?"

He grinned. "See, you're getting it."

Ninsianna gave him an uncertain smile.

"I still don't understand how it will throw your message across the heavens."

"It's like a game of catch," he said. "I will throw the message, and *pray* that Raphael is at the other end."

"What if he isn't?" she asked.

"Then he won't get the message," Mikhail said. "It will bounce around the heavens until somebody else picks it up."

"Like this enemy?"

"Maybe," he frowned. "But I have to take the risk."

Her lip trembled. Despite her bravado, he knew she felt apprehensive about what would happen if he *did* make contact. He reached out and took her hand.

"You're going to love the modern world," he reassured her.

"And your Emperor?"

"He will love you. I think…" He *tried* to pull up an image of the man he *knew* he served, and who Immanu's legends said he served, but every time he did, all he could think about was Ninsianna's golden eyes. "Maybe I'm not important enough for him to bother with—" he said with a shrug "—but I know Raphael will love you."

"You can't remember him."

"Much," he admitted. "But from what I remember, he's—" he tried to pull up the word. "Warm?"

"Warm?"

"Yes," he said. "When I think of Raphael, it just feels *right*."

He gave her hand a squeeze, and then let go so he could finish his antenna array. This time the design would work. He knew it. He'd learned how to make this repair somewhere. It had come to him last night, right after he'd dreamed of Jophiel.

Ninsianna grew silent the closer he came to completing his design. With a final twist of his screwdriver, he stood back.

"That should do it."

"What if Raphael isn't there?

"Then I stay," his wings drooped. "But I have to *try.*"

Ninsianna reached up and wiped away a smudge of grease from his cheek. Despite her false bravado, her eyes appeared troubled. He took her into his arms.

"You *know* you are my world?" he asked. "Don't you?"

"I'd like to believe that."

"I will *never* leave you."

"What if this Emperor gives you an order?"

"Then I shall take you with me."

"And if he forbids it?"

"Then I shall complete my mission," he said, "and come back as soon as I am done."

She scrutinized, not his expression, but the thing she called his spirit-light. Whatever she saw, it seemed to reassure her. She stepped towards the tripod.

"Aim the sub-reflector at the Orion belt—" she said.

"But *these* are the last known coordinates of the *Light Emerging*."

"Raphael is in *that* direction," she pointed a different way. "But you must wait or it won't make it. There's an object in the way."

"It's a clear sky," he said.

"Not here," she said. "Up there," she pointed towards the sky. "A rock."

"An asteroid?"

"Yes. It is in the way."

He realized it wasn't just *her* he was speaking to, but the goddess who spoke through her, or one of the many *other* annoying deities that relished the opportunity to use his wife as their private radio receiver. Her eyes glowed golden-white.

"Ninsianna," he grabbed her shoulders. "What do you see?"

"I see the Earth," she said, "three planets from the sun. Just beyond us is another planet, and then, beyond that, there's a ring of rocks. One of those rocks will be in the way until just before sundown, and then you can call Raphael."

He placed both hands on her cheeks.

"Ninsianna," he said. "It scares me when you go too far."

The light in her eyes grew slightly less bright.

"I can *see* Raphael," she said.

"Really?"

"Yes," she smiled. "He has golden wings."

As she spoke, that vague image which had been little more than a feeling began to emerge, as if out of a fog.

"With red streaks on his underfeathers," he said.

"That's him," she laughed. "He's still looking for you. He told his—"

Her expression grew perplexed.

"What is it?" he asked.

"A talking bug?"

"How is this possible?"

Her eyes glowed brighter.

"There's a scientific principal for the dreamtime," some other consciousness spoke through her. "The subatomic particles that make up the universe connect all-that-is in a unified theory of physics. Life is consciousness, solidified into physical form. Consciousness is pure energy, the *Unknowable One,* who birthed all souls. Any two minds can connect across infinite time and space simply by joining their neutrinos inside the time-space continuum…"

Damn! That freaked him out!

"Ninsianna? Are you still here?"

She picked up his screwdriver and began to adjust his antenna as if she'd worked on electronics her entire life.

"You'll only have point zero two three seconds to send your data burst before you run out of power—" whatever old god had decided to gift her with his knowledge spoke through her. "Record your message and compress it into an encoded data stream no larger than one point two three gigabytes of data or it will fail."

"I computed one point seven two gigabytes," Mikhail said.

"Your computations are wrong."

As she finished the antenna, she continued to rattle off facts. Immanu said this was a gift, but *damn it!* It didn't feel like a gift! He wanted his wife back.

"Ninsianna," he grabbed the screwdriver. "Come back, sweetheart. You said you would always come back."

He could *see* the moment whatever old god had seized his wife decided to relinquish her. She swayed and blinked, her expression confused.

"What happened?" she asked.

"You were talking about a unified theory of physics."

Her brows knit together.

"I have no idea what that means."

He gave her a hug.

"According to your friend," he said, "I have to record a much shorter message. Will you stand at my side so Raphael can see you?"

"What friend?" she asked.

"Never mind," he kissed her cheek. "We'll send it out and hope for the best. Either way, at least I can say I *tried* to complete my mission. If they never come for me, I'm perfectly okay with that."

Her face lit up.

"Really?"

"Yes." He kissed the top of her head.

He led her inside his ship to the place he'd jury-rigged the camera. He'd *known* he wouldn't have time to make a full report. But one-point-two-three gigabytes? That was barely enough power to send a single image.

He aimed the camera to show the cracked hull of his ship, and then arranged his bow and arrows, a spear, and other symbols of his current lifestyle.

"Where do I stand?" she asked. She'd never seen a broadcast image before, but she'd heard his recorded distress call.

"Here," he pulled her closer. "At my side, where you belong."

Grinning like a cat that had just swallowed a big, fat robin, he threw his arm possessively thrown around his wife's shoulders and hit the 'record' button.

"Raphael, my ship is toast. The Sata'an have set up a base on an M-class planet at these coordinates ... Zulu three zero one eight five two nine ... meet Ninsianna, my wife ... end transmission."

He clicked off the receiver.

"Now what?" she asked.

"First I have to compress it," he said. "And then, when it's ready, we can send the message to Raphael?"

"What about the space rock?"

"Tell me when it's okay," he said, "and I'll hit this button."

He ran it through a compression sequence, and then, when Ninsianna said "almost," he powered up the microwormhole generator. Static electricity began to fill the air. His feathers stood on end. Little by little, the subspace antenna began to glow blue.

"Are you ready?" he asked.

"Not yet," not-quite-Ninsianna said.

Sparks of electricity arced through the crack in his hull. The equipment which powered his antenna reached a high-pitched screech. A sound like a freight train spun outside his ship. The air around them began to pulsate.

Tell me? Tell me? Tell me....

His pinfeathers rose in their follicles.

"Now!" Ninsianna shouted.

Mikhail hit the "send" button, praying to the Emperor, Ninsianna's goddess, and any other deity that might be of help.

A strange juxtaposition, as if space itself suddenly contracted, reverberated through the ship, but as quickly as it had begun, the power in his entire ship shut off, leaving them in the dark.

"Did it go?" she asked.

He used the light on his watch to check the final reading.

"Well I'll be darned," he said. "One-point-two-three gigabytes."

Would Raphael receive the message? And if he did, would he receive *enough* of it to figure out where they were?

Whatever the result, it felt as though a weight had been lifted from his shoulders. He'd sent a message. So far as he was concerned, his mission was now complete.

"The magic lanterns are gone..." Ninsianna said mournfully.

"I guess that means we'll have to think of *other* things to do in the dark."

He pulled her close, signaling a desire to engage in his *new* favorite activity.

"Do you think we could feel our way back to the sleeping quarters?" she asked. "Suddenly I feel very tired."

One of the side effects of traveling into the dreamtime was how *exhausted* his wife usually felt once she came back. What *he* wanted to do could wait. Cradling her like a precious gift, he picked her up and carried her back to the bed.

Chapter 160

Galactic Standard Date: 152,323.09 AE
Earth: Sata'an Forward Operating Base
Lieutenant Kasib

Lt. KASIB

Lieutenant Kasib's claws trembled as he knocked on the door to his commanding officer's office. General Hudhafah stood, poking pins into a map of the planet. Each day they logged new territory, new resources, and new tribes that either needed to be wooed with promises of the *good* things Sata'anic rule would bring, or troublemakers roughed up so the rest of their populace could be brought under Sata'anic control.

"Sir—" Kasib's tail twitched with worry "—the *Jamaran* just registered a data burst emanating from the planet."

"Where did it originate?" Hudhafah's dorsal ridge reared in anger.

"The area called Mesopotamia. It didn't last long enough to isolate the source."

"Was it long enough to convey significant data?" Hudhafah asked. His gold-green serpentine eyes narrowed into slits.

"No, sir," Kasib said. "It cut off before complete coordinates could be relayed. The signal was extremely weak. It's unlikely the message got through."

"Good," Hudhafah exhaled. "The last thing we need is a command carrier full of hybrids showing up to investigate." The general pointed to a cluster of pins on the map. "Isn't that one of the areas where we've been getting rumors of someone organizing tribes to fight our allies?"

"Yes, Sir," Kasib said. "We've been unable to locate the remains of the Angelic ship. Do you think he survived the crash?"

General Hudhafah picked up another pin, a red one signaling potential enemy forces, and absent-mindedly jabbed himself in the finger, not hard enough to draw blood.

"When dealing with hybrids," Hudhafah said, "It's necessary to imagine the unimaginable."

"Should we send in our forces to hunt him down?"

Hudhafah stared at the tiny black pins clustered around the Sata'an Forward Operating Base and the even smaller cluster that shuttled back and forth between the *SRN Jamaran* in orbit and the planet. Kasib knew what he worried about. Their resources were stretched far too thin.

"What was the bounty we put on the ringleader's life of that tribe near where the data-burst emanated from?" Hudhafah asked.

"Ten gold *darics*, Sir," Kasib said.

"Quadruple that reward." Hudhafah's fangs showed. "An entire bag of gold. If it *is* an Angelic, let's watch the humans kill the only creature who can prevent us from annexing their planet."

"Shay'tan be praised." Kasib gestured to his head, his snout and his heart in a universal gesture of worship of their benevolent Emperor and god.

Chapter 161

September – 3,390 BC
Earth: Crash Site

NINSIANNA

So comfy…

Ninsianna resisted waking up, languishing in the dreamy warmth of her husband's firm torso and soft wings.

"Good morning, sleepyhead." He gave her a full-blown smile. "At the rate you're going, we'll be late getting back."

"But it's so nice and warm!" she whimpered, luxuriating in his warm feathers. "I don't want to leave!"

"We could always stay another day." He nuzzled her cheek. "Who would have thought life in an agrarian society could be so hectic?"

Ninsianna groaned. Last night's dream, while not a nightmare, had been an urgent reminder not to impede her husband's *real* mission, to help her people stand against the Evil One. Thankfully, since sending his message, Mikhail's spirit-light had centered back here on *her* world. Or more precisely, onto *her*. She must not indulge the temptation to make him cater to her every whim, as he seemed perfectly happy to spend the rest of his life doing.

Ninsianna gave him a regretful smile. "You must train our people. And I promised Mama I would help her bleed sap from a myrrh bush to make the paste that defeats evil spirits in an infected wound."

With a kiss, Mikhail released his hold, allowing her to slip from the warmth of his downy wings. As soon as she sat up, her stomach lurched. With a cry of dismay, she ran into the bath room.

"Are you okay?" he followed her.

"Yes," she choked out between dry heaves.

He gathered her hair and pulled it out of the way until she finished, and then he wet a cloth and tenderly wiped her face. She leaned back into his warmth, both of them splayed upon the bathroom floor.

She had asked for a sign, and She-Who-Is had given it to her.

"Was it something you ate?" he asked.

"This is perfectly normal."

"Normal?" he said. "Every morning you've been dizzy, and now you're throwing up. I'm flying back to fetch your mother."

"There's nothing Mama can do about it."

"Maybe she could give you a tea?"

She wasn't sure how he'd take it, though she *suspected* he wanted it as much as *she* did. She turned to face him so she could see his reaction.

"It's morning sickness."

"Morning sickness? What is making you sick in the morning?"

It took a moment to realize that he didn't have a clue.

"*You* made me sick," she said.

"*Me?*" A look of horrified confusion crossed his beautiful, chiseled features. "What did I do wrong?"

She clamped a hand over her mouth to suppress a giggle. Here he was, a creature of the heavens, and he didn't understand basic biology.

"What's so funny?"

"Haven't you noticed that I've been feeling unwell for weeks?"

"You said it was nothing," he said. "Are you ill?"

"Mikhail ... I'm pregnant."

"What?"

"We're having a baby."

"A baby? How did this happen?"

He looked so perplexed, she couldn't help it. She began to laugh.

"I distinctly remember there was lots of passionate lovemaking," she said. "Did you somehow miss it?"

"No ... but..."

"And then there was moaning and thumping your wings against the walls. And that funny little sound you make when you orgasm..."

"But..."

"And then there is that really funny face you make when you're trying to control your passion, just ... like ... this." She did her best impersonation of the face he made whenever he reached ecstasy.

"I *don't* make a face like that," he said. "Do I?"

"Yes, you do," Ninsianna said. "And I love it. And I love you. And now we'll have a baby to love, too."

"But..." Her words finally registered. An ecstatic smile lit up his face. He reached out and pulled her into an embrace. "Really?"

"Really." She nestled her cheek into his chest.

"I had hoped, but ... wow! So fast?"

He picked her up and carried her back to their sleeping quarters. Laying her down gently like the most precious thing in the world, he crawled in next to her and covered her with one wing. He gazed into her eyes, his expression one of utter contentment.

She curled into his side, relishing the sensation of being loved by an angel.

"Mikhail?" she asked.
"Hmmmm.....?"
  "Do you think our baby will have wings?"

Chapter 162

Galactic Standard Date: 152,323.09 AE
Zulu Sector: Command Carrier 'Light Emerging'
Colonel Raphael Israfa

RAPHAEL

"Colonel Israfa," Major Glicki said, "I picked up a weak transmission from Zulu sector. I'm running it through a decompression sequencer now."

"Put it on screen right away!"

Raphael jumped out of his seat as an image of his best friend came upon their central viewing screen. It had been seven months. Mikhail was still alive!

His hair had grown long, and his uniform appeared disheveled, but other than that, he appeared no worse for the wear.

<< *Raphael, my ship is toast. The Sata'an Empire has set up a large base on an M-class planet at these coordinates ... Zulu three zero one eight crackle crackle...* >>

"Boost it again!" Raphael ordered. "I need those coordinates!"

"I'm sorry, Sir," Glicki said, "That was all he was able to send. With a signal so weak and our position different than when we lost him, it's a miracle he got a message through to us at all."

"Sir?" Sergeant Sachiel, another Angelic, pointed to the petite, dark-haired woman standing at Mikhail's side. "I thought Colonel Mannuki'ili went on this mission alone?"

Raphael took a closer look at the image frozen on the screen. Mikhail had his arm around a pretty, dark-haired Angelic, her features even darker than the unusual coloring possessed by his friend. He was also smiling, something Mikhail almost never did. Had he crash-landed on a planet with a surviving colony of the dark-featured Seraphim? He'd thought they had all been wiped out?

"Magnify the image and run the female through a facial recognition scanner of all known Angelics," Raphael ordered. "Maybe we can isolate his position that way."

"Sir?" The quaver in Glicki's voice was perceptible even through the mechanical aid of the voice-booster. She broadcast the magnified image onto the screen. "You'd better take a look at this."

She blew the image up to focus on the female. It took a moment for the reality of what they were looking to register.

"Is that...?" Ensign Zzz'lrr asked.

"Holy crap," Sergeant Sachiel said.

"It can't be!" another Mantoid said.

They all stared in stunned disbelief at the magnified 12-foot high image of a wingless human female standing at the Colonel's side.

"Glicki!" Raphael shouted. "Get Supreme Commander-General Jophiel on the horn. Alpha-priority-one! I don't care *what* she's doing. Tell her I need to speak to her yesterday!"

"Sir ... she is scheduled to meet with the Eternal Emperor," Glicki said. "What do I say to get her out of that meeting?"

"Tell Hashem I found his solution!" Raphael whooped with glee. "Colonel Mannuki'ili found the Holy Grail!"

Epilogue

Galactic Standard Date: 152,323.09 AE
Ascended realms
Eternal Emperor Hashem

The ETERNAL EMPEROR HASHEM

"You devil!!!" Hashem shouted as soon as enough of his consciousness had phased into existence to form a mouth. "How long have you been keeping the human root stock up your sleeve?"

"That's for *me* to know," Shay'tan said congenially, as he sat in front of the galactic chess board. "And for *you* to find out."

"Goddess!!!" Hashem shouted.

When *SHE* didn't make an appearance, he called her again.

The normally even-tempered Hashem let out a rare stream of curse-words that would have made a Marid pirate colony blush. He'd been around the block enough times to recognize when *he* was the chess piece being played in the eternal game between She-Who-Is and He-Who's-Not. The 'room' where he and Shay'tan met wasn't really a room at all, but an artificial construct comprised of the consciousness of She-Who-Is. There was no way she didn't know what was going on!

"If you're looking for someone to chastise me," Shay'tan nonchalantly sharpened his claws. "Then you're whining to the wrong deity. Everybody knows She-Who-Is is the biggest cheater going. How do you think she's kept He-Who's-Not from destroying the universe all these years?"

Hashem looked at the chess pieces splayed across the board. In a heartbeat, the game had just been turned upon its head. Whoever gained control over the human homeworld would get complete dominion over this galaxy. Without a fresh infusion of genetic matter, his hybrid armies would die out. On the other hand, with unfettered access to the root race, Hashem could breed a *new* generation of super-soldiers and kick Shay'tan out of this galaxy once and for all.

Noticing the black chess pieces surrounding his missing White Knight One, Hashem suddenly smiled. The human homeworld was *not* within the bounds of either empire. It was completely up for grabs! Whoever's armies got dominion over that world first would win. The only problem was, Shay'tan knew *exactly* where the planet was and had a base there, while

Hashem didn't. He must *find* the confounded planet and prevent Shay'tan from sending in reinforcements.

"White Knight Two to Zulu-Sector-Three." Hashem picked up his second white knight and made the L-shaped leap into Zulu Sector where the first white knight had gone missing.

Hashem phased out of the ascended realms before Shay'tan could protest. He needed to mobilize his forces for what was likely to become the largest battle over a critical resource planet since the Second Galactic War.

Begin Book 2 – 'Prince of Tyre'

PREVIEW: Prince of Tyre

Galactic Standard Date: 152,183.02 AE
Haven 1: Eternal Palace
Eternal Emperor Hashem

240 Years Ago....

HASHEM

The dark-winged Angelic screamed as her labor pains intensified. "He has a right to know!"

"She-Who-Is forbids it." The Eternal Emperor Hashem paced the secret back room of his genetics laboratory as though –he- were the expectant father. "You must keep this child's existence a secret."

"You and your stupid game of chess!" Asherah spat in an uncustomary bout of cussing. "Shemijaza is my husband!"

"He should have thought of that before he launched a rebellion!"

For millennia Hashem and Shay'tan had played chess to resolve their differences, and if that didn't work, then they gathered their armies and went to war. Neither old god had gained dominion over the galaxy until one day Hashem's greatest general rebelled. Declaring himself to be the leader of a 'Third Empire,' Shemijaza seized a string of planets too close to the old dragon's border to quash without igniting an intergalactic war. With the Sata'an Empire nipping at his Galactic Alliance, the last thing Hashem needed was a civil war!

Dark-haired, dark-winged, with eyes so blue they were the color of the Haven sky, Hashem had thought it a stroke of genius to send the beautiful, soft-spoken Asherah as an ambassador to entice the rebel leader into rejoining the Alliance.

"You were sent to negotiate a treaty!" Hashem jutted his finger at the foolish woman. "Not to marry him! I can't let the Third Empire gain legitimacy by allowing Shemijaza to produce an heir!"

"I'm half-Seraphim." Asherah panted to control her pain as her contraction intensified. "When we consummated our marriage, my life became tied to his. I should be dead already!"

"You're half shipboard Angelic," Hashem said. "You can survive if you so choose, as you have already demonstrated by coming here!"

"We're not farm animals to be bred and used as cannon fodder in your endless war against Shay'tan!" Asherah clutched her belly. "Our species is going extinct and you do *nothing* to help us! It's the only reason Shemijaza rebelled!"

Hashem's wild, white hair jutted outwards as though he were a mad scientist. What had once been a symbol of his brilliance as a geneticist, his ability to splice together disparate life forms to create new ones, had become an embarrassing monument to his own incompetence. The genes which carried his army's animal features were recessive. To maintain them, he'd been forced to inbreed them until they had lost the ability to reproduce. Nothing, not his ascended powers, nor the best in vitro fertilization methods his teams of scientists could dream up, had been able to fix it.

"Moloch is using your husband to gain a foothold in this universe," Hashem warned. "Shemijaza's child will be even more genetically evolved than he is! You must keep the child's existence a secret!"

"I saw no sign of this Moloch." Asherah gripped the bed rails as her contraction built to its crescendo. "Shemijaza had blackouts. Times he seemed a bit callous. Headaches. He is sick! Not evil. The only evil I see is a selfish old god who would deprive a child of his father!"

Dark feathers flew everywhere as Asherah's instinct to take flight warred with her need to remain Haven-bound because a newborn couldn't fly. The child was coming, whether or not he wished for it to exist.

"The child's head is crowning, your Majesty" Dephar interrupted, his chief geneticist who was acting as midwife. He grabbed a scalpel and clamps with the same practiced ease he used whenever he delivered any other genetics experiment Hashem had cooked up.

"Shemijaza!!!" Asherah threw back her head and screamed her husband's name.

Her cries awoke something Hashem had never felt before, perhaps it was pity? Yes. He wished to alleviate her suffering so he wouldn't have to feel it himself. With no words to convince her this was the right thing to do, he resorted to something he hadn't done since he'd ceased being mortal.

"Take my hand, Asherah--" he moderated his power so he could safely touch her "--and let me help you bear this pain." His hand grew warm where it brushed her skin, the sensation igniting some mortal need he'd long forgotten existed.

"He has a right to know!" Asherah slapped away his hand. Tears streamed down her cheeks as she focused her attention inwards, seeking to make contact through the bond purebred Seraphim formed with their mate.

Asherah was only half-Seraphim, but he'd reason to worry she'd formed the bond which granted her kind telepathy, no matter how far apart they were in the universe. He'd gone through great lengths to make the rebel leader believe she'd committed suicide. If Shemijaza found out Asherah had just borne him a son, he would raze the Alliance into dust to get her back.

With Shay'tan sapping his resources, there was no way he could withstand war on a second front.

"Goddess!!!" Hashem shouted. "I don't know how to prevent this!"

The scent of ozone and fresh flowers supplanted the sterile, medicinal scent of the genetics laboratory. A buzz that felt like tiny jolts of electricity filled the air as golden light descended from the ethers and coalesced into a tall, slender female with pointed ears and gossamer wings. SHE rarely descended into material form because it made her vulnerable, but keeping this child a secret was paramount. With a rustle of wings which sounded like crinkling cellophane, She-Who-Is plastered a sympathetic expression upon her chiseled features and stepped forward to console the grieving mother.

"I wouldn't ask you to make this sacrifice if the fate of the universe didn't depend upon it," She-Who-Is' tone was hypnotically reassuring. "Ki warned you of this when you sang her Song to conceive your son, didn't she?"

"Yes," Asherah sobbed.

Hashem felt a twinge of envy. Why had a mortal been given access to the Song of Creation and not him? By Ki, no less? She-Who-Is' mother?

"Your Eminence," Dephar bowed with awe. "The child is stuck in the birth canal."

"I shall deliver him myself." SHE lilted a perfectly shaped eyebrow in Hashem's direction. "He is that important." SHE placed her hand upon Asherah's swollen abdomen to eliminate the Seraphim's physical pain. "Push, my daughter. I wish to meet this prince of Tyre."

The child slid into HER waiting arms. He didn't cry as others did upon being cast out of their mother's womb, but looked at HER as though he could already understand what she said. He reached for her face as Dephar cut the umbilical cord and gurgled a sound which sounded like *'Inanna.'*

The goddess' lips turned up in a smile, genuine this time as she recognized something in the newborn which pleased her immensely.

"You're Lucifer, Bringer of Light." SHE glanced over to the sobbing Seraphim, too grief-stricken to hold the son whose conception had forced her to abandon her husband. "Be grateful, young prince, that this mortal loves you enough to keep you hidden from your -*real*- father. All-That-Is depends upon you not falling into Moloch's hands."

Asherah wept. She-Who-Is reached towards her temple to grant her the mercy of wiping Shemijaza from her mind, but Asherah slapped away HER hand. Even Dephar gasped at the Seraphim's audacity.

"Don't you play your memory games on me!" Asherah hissed. She sat up in her childbed as regal as a queen. "I shall do as you ask, but the soul doesn't forget! Someday Shemijaza and I will reunite!"

Hashem cringed. She-Who-Is might be all-powerful, but Asherah understood the rules of the larger game which bound even old gods such as himself. Not quite genetically evolved enough to achieve immortality on her own, the Seraphim was too close to perfection to manipulate against her will.

"So be it." She-Who-Is wrapped the infant in a blanket and handed him to Hashem. "You must protect this child with your immortal life."

"Yes, your Eminence." Hashem bowed. "I'll raise him as though he were my own son."

The goddess' eyes burned gold with power. With a disdainful flick of her gossamer wings, She-Who-Is shimmered out of the material plain.

Hashem looked down at the child who had just been placed into his care. The infant didn't cry. Not even a squeak. He had his mother's delicate facial features, but the snow-white wings and white-blonde hair of his father. Instead of blue, the child had inherited Shemijaza's eyes, silver like the moon, a genetic throwback to a bloodline they had all believed to be extinct.

Morning Star…

Would this child also inherit his father's intellect?

Hashem shivered even though he'd long evolved past the ability to feel the cold. Shemijaza had outsmarted him. Outsmarted Shay'tan. Outsmarted every creature in the galaxy including She-Who-Is. Asherah had brought warning of a new threat snuffling around the rebel leader, one terrifying enough to cause the half-Seraphim to abandon her mate and flee.

Morning Star…

A bloodline that was even older than She-Who-Is. Heaven help them if Moloch got his hands on Shemijaza's offspring!

"Asherah?" Hashem presented the infant to the grieving Seraphim. "Your son…"

"Go away!" Asherah curled up in a fetal position and refused to look at her child. "You wanted him, now you've got him!"

The infant stared up at him, his eerie silver eyes filled with trust. It couldn't be good for the child to be rejected by his own mother. Hashem knew from his work as a geneticist that most rejected offspring simply withered and died.

Morning Star …

The most genetically advanced bloodline in existence!

Hashem glanced around at the cold, sterile artifices of his genetics laboratory. She-Who-Is had given -him- the prize, and neither Shay'tan nor the child's own father even knew it! All he'd to do was make sure Moloch didn't find out, either.

He took the infant and gave Asherah the space to grieve.

Join my readers group....

THANK YOU for supporting an independent author! If you sign up for my NEWSLETTER, I will give you Book 2 of this series, *Sword of the Gods: Prince of Tyre,* absolutely *FREE*. This is a full-length epic fantasy novel which I otherwise never discount, not a teaser trailer or novella. I promise to keep your email address confidential and never spam you! Only send word of new releases, special discounts, fun contests, and tidbits about my research into whatever book I am writing, including the real-life history behind the myth of fallen angels!

Click HERE to get started: https://wp.me/P2k4dY-OR

YOUR FREE eBOOK

Confirm your subscription to receive Book 2 of the Sword of the Gods saga, *'Prince of Tyre,'* for FREE.

Just click 'SUBSCRIBE'

★★★★★

Learn more >>

★★★★★ "This was such a rollercoaster emotionally, I could not put it down!"

★★★★★ "This series is SUCH a good twist on modern religions and really gives something to think about, if one is open-minded..." --Reader review

★★★★★ "This author's work is very addictive. I want to read them all..."

Or you can support my work by returning to wherever you purchased Book 1 and purchasing it there (or both!). Here are the worldwide purchase links for *Prince of Tyre.*

Be epic!
Anna Erishkigal

P.S. - Here's the book description for *Prince of Tyre:*

At the dawn of time, two ancient adversaries battled for control of Earth. One man rose to stand at humanity's side. A man whose name we still remember today...

The legend about the greatest superhero to ever walk the Earth continues in Prince of Tyre. Mikhail has a new mission: train the warriors to fight back against the mysterious kidnappings so his adopted village will be safe for Ninsianna and their expected child. But the journey from soldier to general is never easy, especially when the Chief's son undermines his authority. Challenges compound when they learn 'lizard demons' have put a bounty on Mikhail's head.

In Haven, rumors of a cure to stave off extinction winds its way through the Emperor's armies. Raphael is charged with finding this 'Holy Grail,' unaware the solution lies closer to home. The Eternal Emperor and Shay'tan are so busy outwitting one another that neither notices Lucifer is a little 'off' … or that a much more ancient Evil One outmaneuvers them. A tragic death forces the Alliance to choose which leader they will follow in an epic showdown. The Emperor … or Lucifer?

Note: this book is NOT Christian fiction.

Available at:
https://wp.me/P2k4dY-15

A Moment of your Time, Please...

Did you enjoy reading this book? If so, I would be most grateful if you would do me the honor of leaving a written review. It doesn't need to be much. Just a heartfelt sentence letting others know what you think. I would be oh-so-grateful...

Thank you!

About the Author

Anna Erishkigal is an attorney who writes fantasy fiction as a pleasurable alternative to coming home from court and cross-examining her children. She writes under a pen-name so her colleagues don't question whether her legal pleadings are fantasy fiction as well. Much of law, it turns out, -is- fantasy fiction. Lawyers just prefer to call it 'zealously representing your client.'

Seeing the dark underbelly of life makes for some interesting fictional characters, the kind you either want to incarcerate, or run home and write about. In fiction, you can fudge facts without worrying too much about the truth. In legal pleadings, if your client lies to you, you look stupid in front of the judge.

At least in fiction, if a character becomes troublesome, you can always kill them off.

P.S. - I have a love-hate relationship with social media, but you can always write to me at: anna_erishkigal@yahoo.com

PREVIEW: The Caliphate: A Post-Apocalyptic Suspense Novel

Eisa McCarthy lives in Caliphate City under the control of the radical Islamic group, the Ghuraba. Seven years ago General Mohammad bin-Rasulullah defeated the United States in a ruthless betrayal and set up their worldwide Caliphate in the ruins of Washington, D.C. The Ghuraba's supreme holy leader, the Abu al-Ghuraba, claims Eisa's father gave him control of the U.S. nuclear arsenal, a claim bolstered by the smoldering ashes of many cities and her Syrian-born mother's testimony. But after her mother is accused of apostasy, she learns her father may not be the 'martyr' the Ghuraba claim.

Do the Ghuraba *really* possess the launch codes for the ICBM missiles? Or did her father 'lock them out' as Colonel Everhart, the rebel commander, wants her to tell the world? If she fights, the Ghuraba will kill her little sister, but if she doesn't, eventually the Ghuraba will hack in and nuke them all. All Eisa has are a string of Muslim prayer beads and a pre-Islamic myth her father told her the night he disappeared.

The fate of the world, and her little sister's life, hang in the balance as Eisa sorts through ancient myth, her Muslim faith, and what really happened the night the Ghuraba seized control.

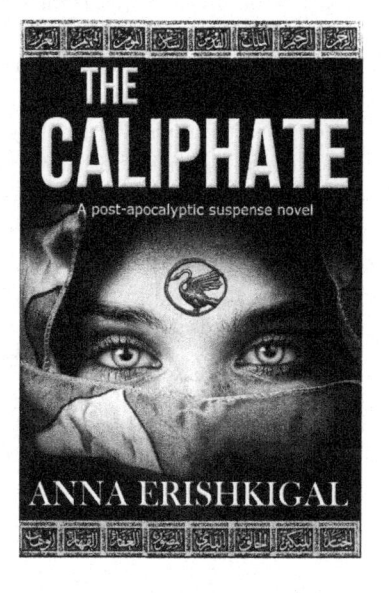

"The parallels the author draws between the current landscape in Syria and Iraq and a future United States are unsettling, as they portray present-day atrocities with unflinching accuracy..." —Dale Amidei, Jon's Trilogy

"This story is intense, extremely interesting and is a page turner. The reality of its depth will leave the reader rather shaken, realizing that these battles are going on today in some countries. I recommend this book..." –Reader review

"The story of Eisa McCarthy is one of survival ... When she swears that she will make a widow out of her sister, you can feel her anguish and her determination not to be helpless anymore ... Reading the book made me glad that this was just a novel, that it was not my reality. Then it struck me, it may not be my reality, but hundreds of women live through such time each day in the world today..." –Candy Laine, the Pune Diaries

"Beautifully written, thought provoking, and scarily germane to today's current political climate. This book gives readers a real taste of what life would be like if ISIS ever rose to power on American soil. Highly recommended..." –Reader review

Available at: https://wp.me/P5T1EY-kB

PREVIEW: The Auction Trilogy
(A Modern-Day Jane Eyre)

Dumped at the altar and left without a home, Rosie Xalbadora takes a job as a governess at the edge of the Australian outback. There she meets Pippa Bristow, a sensitive child who copes with her parent's bitter divorce by escaping into a magical world of fairy queens and unicorns. Pippa's enigmatic father, Adam Bristow, will endure whatever it takes to shield his daughter from his selfish, oil heiress ex-wife.

Struggling to shield Pippa from her mother's games, Rosie must face her own painful past while fighting a growing attraction to her handsome, emotionally unavailable employer. But help comes in the form of a quirky neighbor, a friendly Outback town, and two ghost riders who visit Rosie each night in her dreams. When Rosie and Pippa save a small, white pony from slaughter, their ill-timed compassion puts Adam's custody dispute, Pippa's fantasies, and Rosie's worst fears all up for bid in an epic showdown.

The Auction Trilogy is a contemporary romantic family saga styled with the heart-wrenching, Gothic undertones of *Jane Eyre* and just a hint of the supernatural.

The Auction Trilogy contains:
— If Wishes Were Horses
— Well of Dreams
— Behold a Pale Horse

"A mystical, magical landscape, and old legends take on a new life..." —Romancing History Blog

"I was instantly drawn into the characters' lives, and felt like I was right alongside Rosie as she struggled to keep her life from falling apart..." –N.Y. Times Best Selling Author Stacey Joy Netzel

"This modern-day rendition [of Jane Eyre] ... is spot on with the Bronte storyline, but with a refreshingly modern twist. You'll want to cry with the heroine as she struggles to protect the little girl from her crazy and manipulative mother, and you'll cheer for Adam & Rosie as they take baby steps toward trusting one another and believing in true love..." — Dark Lilith Book Blogs

"The mental imagery of this story is incredible. I fell in love alongside Rosie with the Station and its dream walks. A beautifully written tale!" —Reader review

Available at: http://wp.me/P5T1EY-A

PREVIEW: Angel of Death: A Love Story

Azrael Thanatos wants nothing more than to follow in the footsteps of his scientist mother. Sent to study humans on a wager between the Eternal Emperor and Shay'tan, he has no idea that Earth is gateway to a fiery prison. Far from home, he is befriended by Elissar, a precocious child with silver eyes. When Moloch instigates the invasion of Carthage to escape, Azrael sacrifices his life to snatch his friend from the Devourer of Children's maw.

Saved by a mysterious goddess, Azrael is given a new mission. *Watchman*. Roaming the Earth without shape or form, he reaps those who would help Moloch escape and drags them to Gehenna, a prison to which only Lucifer holds the key. It's a hellish immortality, for who wants to serve alongside the Fallen or exist when no living creature can survive your touch. Haunted by Elissar's death, he despairs of never finding love or friendship as time grinds civilizations into dust. For who would love Death?

Then one day a child takes his hand and lives...

Life for Elisabeth is not easy. The Angel of Death took her entire family the night a drunk driver plowed through a stop sign and left her in a wheel chair. Azrael is forbidden to interfere as she bounces through foster homes, hardship and grueling rehabilitation. Then one day he is forced to reveal he is not a figment of her imagination.

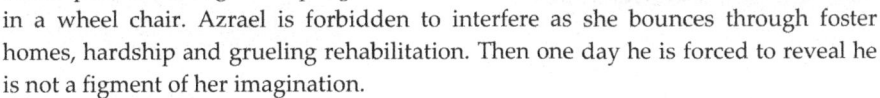

Oh, how she hates this angel who has taken everyone she has ever loved! The invasion of Iraq inspires her to join the Army as a trauma nurse, unaware that Death has fallen in love with the woman who can defeat him.

Will she take his hand a second time?

"This book provides a sympathetic portrayal of the angel of death and Lucifer. It does for the Bible what 'Wicked' does for 'The Wizard of Oz'..." –Reader review

"A love story so epic the passage of time cannot dim it. Or keep them apart! True soulmates transcending lifetimes of pain. Ingenious!!" –Reader review

"This is the best book I have read in a long time ... Fresh outlook and great characters make this a satisfying, hard to set down read..." –Reader review

"Probably the best mix of science fiction, history and romance I have ever read. This book will make you think about what you know and believe..." –Reader review

Available at: https://wp.me/P5T1EY-u

PREVIEW: A Gothic Christmas Angel

Winner of the eFestival of Words Best of the Independent eBook Awards - Best Novella of 2014

The Ghosts of Old Miseries are never far behind...

Dumped by her boyfriend on Christmas Eve, Cassie Baruch thought her pain would end when she aimed her car at an ancient beech tree. But when a gorgeous black-winged angel appears and tells her *"this ain't no stinking paranormal romance, kid,"* she realizes death hasn't solved her problems. Can Jeremiel help her exorcise the ghosts of problems past and find a little closure?

This modern paranormal spin on the myth of guardian angels blends *'A Christmas Carol'* with *'It's A Wonderful Life'* to give people hope they can come to grips with the past and overcome.

"Very few books move me to tears but this one did in the most glorious fashion. There is a message here, told with humor and grace. Wonderful!" —Reader review

"She made me care. And she made me cry. And I'm very, very thankful for the ending." —Reader review

"A book that touched me like no other book has!" —Reader review

"Once again Anna spins words into gold. The gothic twist to this modern Christmas Carol is terrific..." —Reader review

"If I could, I'd give this story an infinity amount of stars! This book/story gave me chills." —Reader review

Available at: http://wp.me/P5T1EY-w

The Chess Pieces

Apausha: a Lieutenant in the Sata'an Merchant Marine

Baal Zebub: Sata'anic political equivalent of Prime Minister

Behnam: an elderly man of Assur and one of the members of the Tribunal.

Bishamonten: the Cherubim god of war.

Dadbeh: a warrior of Assur. A prankster.

Dahaka: a sergeant in Shay'tan's army, General Hudhafah's right-hand man.

Dephar: the Eternal Emperor's chief geneticist. He is a Mu'aqqibat 'dragon' which is not a true dragon, but might be described as something similar to a 'Chinese dragon.'

Ebad: son of a potter, an incompetent warrior-recruit.

Eligor: an Angelic stationed upon the *'Prince of Tyre.'*

Eternal Emperor Hashem: an ascended being.

Firouz: a warrior of Assur, a bit of a prankster.

Furcas: one of Lucifer's two personal bodyguards. A 'goon.'

Gimal: a trader from Gasur.

Gita: the black-eyed girl, Ninsianna's cousin.

Glicki: a Mantoid Major stationed on the *'Light Emerging.'* Raphael's second-in-command.

Harrood: a teenage warrior from Gasur.

He-Who's-Not: primordial chaos, aka Dark Lord, guardian of She-Who-Is

Hudhafah: a general in the Sata'an infantry responsible for overseeing the Sata'anic annexation of Earth.

Immanu: Ninsianna's father, a shaman.

Ipquidad: a young man of Assur.

Jamin: Ninsianna's jealous ex-fiancé, Chief Kiyan's son.

Jiljab: Chief of a nearby village, Gasur.

Jophiel: Supreme Commander-General of the Alliance fleet.

Kasib: a lieutenant in the Sata'an infantry, Chief Acquisitions Officer for General Hudhafah.

Ki: mother goddess of She-Who-Is.

Kiaresh: a warrior of Assur from the Chief's generation.

Kiyan: Chief of Assur, Jamin's father.

Klik'rr: Jophiel's second in command on the 'Eternal Light.' A Mantoid.

Larajie: a crewman on the *'Prince of Tyre.'*

Little Nemesis: the goat.

Lucifer: Alliance Prime Minister, Hashem's adopted son.

Lugalbanda: deceased warrior-shaman who had the ability to stop an enemy's heart. Immanu's father. Ninsianna and Gita's grandfather.

Marbas: Commander of the Alliance flagship, the 'Prince of Tyre.'

Marwan: shaykh of the rival Halifian tribe.

Merariy: Immanu's bitter, drunken brother and also Gita's father. He and Immanu do not speak.

Mikhail: Colonel Mikhail Mannuki'ili, Angelic Special Forces. Trained by the Cherubim.

Moloch: Evil One, the Devourer of Children.

Namhu: a boy of Assur, one of Pareesa's brothers.

Needa: a healer of Assur. Ninsianna's mother.

Ninsianna: a young woman of Assur, has a special relationship with She-Who-Is.

Nusrat: one of Marwan's sons, a Halifian. The 'green-eyed man.'

Pravuil: one of Lucifer's legislative aides. She is 'as plain as dirt.'

Pruflas: one of Lucifer's two personal bodyguards. A 'goon.'

Qishtea: son of Chief Sinalshu of Nineveh, an allied village.

Raphael: commander of the *Light Emerging*, Mikhail's best friend.

Re Harakhti: General Re Harakhti is in charge of the Leonid Multi-Purpose Forces, which in modern human terms might be considered a similar branch of military as the Marines.

Rimsin: an Amorite slave-trader.

Roshan: a Halifian, Marwan's son-in-law. Was heir to the powerful Baranuman River tent-group until Mikhail killed him in battle.

Sagal-Zimu: a young shaman from Gasur.

Shahla: Jamin's former girlfriend. A harlot.

Shay'tan: emperor of the Sata'an Empire. A 'real' dragon and an old god.

She-Who-Is: architect of the universe, the Goddess.

Siamek: a warrior of Assur. Jamin's second-in-command.

Sinalshu: Chief of Nineveh, an allied village.

Tinashe: the ebony skinned woman.

Tirdard: an elite warrior of Assur.

Ugazum: a warrior of Assur.

Valepor: a Lieutenant-General for the Leonids.

Varshab: Chief Kiyan's 'enforcer.'

Yadiditum: Ninsianna's best friend.

Yaggitt: an incompetent warrior-recruit.

Yalda: the eldest woman in Assur and the chief legislate of the Tribunal. Her younger sister is Zhila.

Yazan: shaykh of the distant 'western' Halifian tribe. His now-deceased son Nusrat was married to Aturdokht, Marwan's daughter.

Yoritomo: the highest-ranking Cherubim master, second only to Queen Jingu. The Eternal Emperor's most trusted personal guardian.

Zahid: eldest son of Marwan, a Halifian. The 'cruel-faced man.'

Zartosht: an elderly shaman from Nineveh.

Zhila: the second-eldest woman in Assur and sister to Yalda.

Zepar: Lucifer's chief of staff.

List of Species

Humans: a species that went extinct after an asteroid hit their homeworld, Nibiru, approximately 74,000 years ago. All attempts to reseed humans onto other planets failed and they died out. It's rumored this is the species which spawned the Eternal Emperor, but the Eternal Palace has refused to comment.

Angelics: genetically engineered super-soldiers spliced together from a genetic base of humans and the keen eyesight and wings of eagles. They carry the highest percentage of human DNA. They act as the Alliance's air force. Due to inbreeding to maintain their animal features, fewer than 7,500 Angelics remain in existence today.

Leonids: genetically engineered super-soldiers spliced together from a genetic base of lions and humans. They are the most animalistic of the four branches of the Alliance military. They act as multi-purpose situational forces. When the going gets tough, the Emperor says, 'Send in the Leonids!' Due to inbreeding to maintain their animal features, fewer than 3,500 Leonids remain in existence today.

Centauri: genetically engineered super-soldiers spliced together from a genetic base of horses and humans. They act as the Alliance's cavalry. Due to inbreeding to maintain their animal features, fewer than 4,000 remain in existence today.

Merfolk: genetically engineered super-soldiers spliced together from a genetic base of humans and aquatic mammals. They were engineered to act as the Alliance's navy. Five hundred years ago their species merged with a sister-species, Leviathans. Only a handful of purebred Merfolk still exist today. The hybrids are known as Mer-Levi.

Leviathans: a genetically enhanced species of sentient aquatic mammals originating from the same homeworld that humans came from, Nibiru. They evolved separately after being successfully reseeded on a remote planet. Many of their species merged with Merfolk into the Mer-Levi.

Mantoids: a naturally evolved species of sentient six-legged insects. They have supplemented Angelics in the Alliance Air Force.

Spiderids: a naturally evolved species of sentient eight-legged insects. They have supplemented Leonids in the Alliance Air Force.

Delphiniums: a naturally evolved species of sentient frog-like amphibians. They have almost totally replaced Merfolk as the Alliance's Navy.

Saori: a naturally evolved species of gazelle-sized sentient mammals. They supplement and support the Centauri Cavalry, but due to their small size, haven't been able to replace them.

Mu'aqqibat: a naturally evolved species of sentient serpent-like creatures with short arms and legs and a head that resembles a dragon. They are an 'ancient species' and many of their number teeter at the threshold of becoming ascended beings.

Cherubim: a naturally evolved species of fierce, ant-like creatures which dwell in hive-like colonies of Monks ruled by a single queen. They are the personal guard of the Eternal Emperor and teeter at the threshold of becoming ascended beings. Their population has remained stable at exactly 1,000 for the past 15,000 years.

- **Seraphim:** a sub-species of dark-winged Angelic which was wiped out 25 years ago by unknown aggressors. Only one member of this species survives, Colonel Mikhail Mannuki'ili. The Colonel went missing 7 months ago and is presumed dead.
- **Grigori:** a species of fire-breathing dragon which disappeared from the galaxy approximately 150,000 years ago. It's rumored Emperor Shay'tan was once a Grigori, a true dragon, a question which always elicits a toothy, enigmatic smirk.
- **Sata'anic Lizards:** a species of sentient lizard which make up the largest portion of Shay'tan's armies. They suddenly appeared 74,000 years ago to replace Shay'tan's predecessor species of soldier, the Nephilim, a species which is now extinct.
- **Marid:** a naturally evolved species of blue-skinned humanoids which had begun to spread out in the uncharted territories until the Sata'an Empire annexed part of their territory three generations ago. They are now divided into two sub-species: the Sata'anic Marid, who serve in Shay'tan's armies, and the Free Marid Confederation, whose homeworlds still remain free.
- **Catoplebas:** a naturally evolved, boar-like species that makes up part of Shay'tan's armies. They are known for their pugnacious disposition.
- **Tokoloshe:** a sentient, bear-like species infamous for its aggressive nature and their disgusting habit of cannibalizing their enemies. The Tokoloshe have spread across the uncharted territories like a plague and all species fear them. Rumor has it they are a science experiment gone terribly wrong, but whenever asked, Emperor Shay'tan and Emperor Hashem point their fingers at each other and say 'he did it.' It's rumored this is the motivation behind the Eternal Emperor's strict 'seed world' policies prohibiting interference with emerging pre-sentient species.
- **Ascended Beings:** aka 'old gods.' Most are creatures which were born mortal but, after countless lifetimes, genetically evolved enough to figure out how to make themselves immortal. They possess various levels of ability, ranging from demi-gods who can merely heal themselves to 'elemental' gods who have learned to harness the laws of physics. A few such as She-Who-Is were born full-fledged gods by virtue of the fact they have gods for parents.
- **Needles:** biomechanical space dwelling creatures the size of a large porpoise with a marsupium (pouch) that can transport cargo or, if small enough, a humanoid, through space. They can instantaneously 'leap' across subspace the way an ascended being can, but are only marginally sentient. Nobody knows where needles came from. A small herd of them just appeared one day and the Alliance put them to use.
- **Daarda'ail:** a sentient life form made up of billions of non-sentient bacteria which form a 'hive mind.' It's frequently used to supplement computer systems to make them self-thinking.
- **Nephilim:** a race of giants who once formed the backbone of Shay'tan's armies, until they rebelled. Shay'tan retaliated by wiping them out.

Other Books

Sword of the Gods Saga
The Chosen One
Prince of Tyre
Agents of Ki
The Dark Lord's Vessel
Archangel (coming soon)

Children of the Fallen:
Angel of Death: A Love Story
A Gothic Christmas Angel

Song of the River series:
The Auction Trilogy: A Modern Day Jane Eyre

Standalone Fiction
The Watchmaker: a novellette
The Caliphate: A Post-Apocalyptic Suspense Novel

Find my latest books at:
http://www.anna-erishkigal.com

Made in United States
North Haven, CT
09 May 2022